WESTERN COLORS

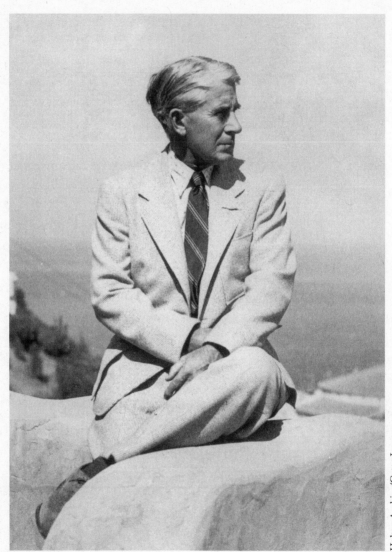

WESTERN COLORS

Riders of the Purple Sage

The Rainbow Trail

Desert Gold

ZANE GREY

A Tom Doherty Associates Book
New York

WESTERN COLORS

Riders of the Purple Sage was first published in 1912; *The Rainbow Trail* was first published in 1915; *Desert Gold* was first published in 1913.

A Forge Book
Published by Tom Doherty Associates, LLC
175 Fifth Avenue
New York, NY 10010

www.tor-forge.com

Forge® is a registered trademark of Tom Doherty Associates, LLC.

ISBN 978-0-7653-7419-6 (hardcover)

Forge books may be purchased for educational, business, or promotional use. For information on bulk purchases, please contact Macmillan Corporate and Premium Sales Department at 1-800-221-7945, extension 5442, or write specialmarkets@macmillan.com.

First Edition: April 2014

Printed in the United States of America

0 9 8 7 6 5 4 3 2 1

CONTENTS

Riders of the Purple Sage   9

The Rainbow Trail   289

Desert Gold   555

WESTERN COLORS

RIDERS
OF THE
PURPLE SAGE

CHAPTER 1

LASSITER

A sharp clip-clop of iron-shod hoofs deadened and died away, and clouds of yellow dust drifted from under the cottonwoods out over the sage.

Jane Withersteen gazed down the wide purple slope with dreamy and troubled eyes. A rider had just left her and it was his message that held her thoughtful and almost sad, awaiting the churchmen who were coming to resent and attack her right to befriend a Gentile.

She wondered if the unrest and strife that had lately come to the little village of Cottonwoods was to involve her. And then she sighed, remembering that her father had founded this remotest border settlement of southern Utah and that he had left it to her. She owned all the ground and many of the cottages. Withersteen House was hers, and the great ranch, with its thousands of cattle, and the swiftest horses of the sage. To her belonged Amber Spring, the water which gave verdure and beauty to the village and made living possible on that wild purple upland waste. She could not escape being involved by whatever befell Cottonwoods.

That year, 1871, had marked a change which had been gradually coming in the lives of the peace-loving Mormons of the border. Glaze—Stone Bridge—Sterling, villages to the north, had risen against the invasion of

Gentile settlers and the forays of rustlers. There had been opposition to the one and fighting with the other. And now Cottonwoods had begun to wake and bestir itself and grow hard.

Jane prayed that the tranquillity and sweetness of her life would not be permanently disrupted. She meant to do so much more for her people than she had done. She wanted the sleepy quiet pastoral days to last always. Trouble between the Mormons and the Gentiles of the community would make her unhappy. She was Mormon-born, and she was a friend to poor and unfortunate Gentiles. She wished only to go on doing good and being happy. And she thought of what that great ranch meant to her. She loved it all—the grove of cottonwoods, the old stone house, the amber-tinted water, and the droves of shaggy, dusty horses and mustangs, the sleek, clean-limbed, blooded racers, and the browsing herds of cattle and the lean, sun-browned riders of the sage.

While she waited there she forgot the prospect of untoward change. The bray of a lazy burro broke the afternoon quiet, and it was comfortingly suggestive of the drowsy farmyard, and the open corrals, and the green alfalfa fields. Her clear sight intensified the purple sage-slope as it rolled before her. Low swells of prairie-like ground sloped up to the west. Dark, lonely cedar-trees, few and far between, stood out strikingly, and at long distances ruins of red rocks. Farther on, up the gradual slope, rose a broken wall, a huge monument, looming dark purple and stretching its solitary, mystic way, a wavering line that faded in the north. Here to the westward was the light and color and beauty. Northward the slope descended to a dim line of cañons from which rose an up-flinging of the earth, not mountainous, but a vast heave of purple uplands, with ribbed and fan-shaped walls, castle-crowned cliffs, and gray escarpments. Over it all crept the lengthening, waning afternoon shadows.

The rapid beat of hoofs recalled Jane Withersteen to the question at hand. A group of riders cantered up the lane, dismounted, and threw their bridles. They were seven in number, and Tull, the leader, a tall, dark man, was an elder of Jane's church.

"Did you get my message?" he asked, curtly.

"Yes," replied Jane.

"I sent word I'd give that rider Venters half an hour to come down to the village. He didn't come."

"He knows nothing of it," said Jane. "I didn't tell him. I've been waiting here for you."

"Where is Venters?"

"I left him in the courtyard."

"Here, Jerry," called Tull, turning to his men, "take the gang and fetch Venters out here if you have to rope him."

The dusty-booted and long-spurred riders clanked noisily into the grove of cottonwoods and disappeared in the shade.

"Elder Tull, what do you mean by this?" demanded Jane. "If you must arrest Venters you might have the courtesy to wait till he leaves my home. And if you do arrest him it will be adding insult to injury. It's absurd to accuse Venters of being mixed up in that shooting fray in the village last night. He was with me at the time. Besides, he let me take charge of his guns. You're only using this as a pretext. What do you mean to do to Venters?"

"I'll tell you presently," replied Tull. "But first tell me why you defend this worthless rider?"

"Worthless!" exclaimed Jane, indignantly. "He's nothing of the kind. He was the best rider I ever had. There's not a reason why I shouldn't champion him and every reason why I should. It's no little shame to me, Elder Tull, that through my friendship he has roused the enmity of my people and become an outcast. Besides, I owe him eternal gratitude for saving the life of little Fay."

"I've heard of your love for Fay Larkin and that you intend to adopt her. But—Jane Withersteen, the child is a Gentile!"

"Yes. But, Elder, I don't love the Mormon children any less because I love a Gentile child. I shall adopt Fay if her mother will give her to me."

"I'm not so much against that. You can give the child Mormon teaching," said Tull. "But I'm sick of seeing this fellow Venters hang around you. I'm going to put a stop to it. You've so much love to throw away on these beggars of Gentiles that I've an idea you might love Venters."

Tull spoke with the arrogance of a Mormon whose power could not be brooked and with the passion of a man in whom jealousy had kindled a consuming fire.

"Maybe I do love him," said Jane. She felt both fear and anger stir her heart. "I'd never thought of that. Poor fellow! He certainly needs someone to love him."

"This'll be a bad day for Venters unless you deny that," returned Tull, grimly.

Tull's men appeared under the cottonwoods and led a young man out into the lane. His ragged clothes were those of an outcast. But he stood tall and straight, his wide shoulders flung back, with the muscles of his bound arms rippling and a blue flame of defiance in the gaze he bent on Tull.

For the first time Jane Withersteen felt Venters's real spirit. She wondered if she would love this splendid youth. Then her emotion cooled to the sobering sense of the issue at stake.

"Venters, will you leave Cottonwoods at once and forever?" asked Tull, tensely.

"Why?" rejoined the rider.

"Because I order it."

Venters laughed in cool disdain.

The red leaped to Tull's dark cheek.

"If you don't go it means your ruin," he said, sharply.

"Ruin!" exclaimed Venters, passionately. "Haven't you already ruined me? What do you call ruin? A year ago I was a rider. I had horses and cattle of my own. I had a good name in Cottonwoods. And now when I come into the village to see this woman you set your men on me. You hound me. You trail me as if I were a rustler. I've no more to lose—except my life."

"Will you leave Utah?"

"Oh! I know," went on Venters, tauntingly, "it galls you, the idea of beautiful Jane Withersteen being friendly to a poor Gentile. You want her all yourself. You're a wiving Mormon. You have use for her—and Withersteen House and Amber Spring and seven thousand head of cattle!"

Tull's hard jaw protruded, and rioting blood corded the veins of his neck.

"Once more. Will you go?"

"*No!*"

"Then I'll have you whipped within an inch of your life," replied Tull, harshly. "I'll turn you out in the sage. And if you ever come back you'll get worse."

Venters's agitated face grew coldly set and the bronze changed to gray.

Jane impulsively stepped forward. "Oh! Elder Tull!" she cried. "You won't do that!"

Tull lifted a shaking finger toward her.

"That'll do from you. Understand, you'll not be allowed to hold this boy to a friendship that's offensive to your Bishop. Jane Withersteen, your father left you wealth and power. It has turned your head. You haven't yet come to see the place of Mormon women. We've reasoned with you, borne with you. We've patiently waited. We've let you have your fling, which is more than I ever saw granted to a Mormon woman. But you haven't come to your senses. Now, once for all, you can't have any further friendship with Venters. He's going to be whipped, and he's got to leave Utah!"

"Oh! Don't whip him! It would be dastardly!" implored Jane, with slow certainty of her failing courage.

Tull always blunted her spirit, and she grew conscious that she had feigned a boldness which she did not possess. He loomed up now in different guise, not as a jealous suitor, but embodying the mysterious despotism she had known from childhood—the power of her creed.

"Venters, will you take your whipping here or would you rather go out in the sage?" asked Tull. He smiled a flinty smile that was more than inhuman, yet seemed to give out of its dark aloofness a gleam of righteousness.

"I'll take it here—if I must," said Venters. "But by God!—Tull, you'd better kill me outright. That'll be a dear whipping for you and your praying Mormons. You'll make me another Lassiter!"

The strange glow, the austere light which radiated from Tull's face, might have been a holy joy at the spiritual conception of exalted duty. But there was something more in him, barely hidden, a something personal and sinister, a deep of himself, an engulfing abyss. As his religious mood was fanatical and inexorable, so would his physical hate be merciless.

"Elder, I—I repent my words," Jane faltered. The religion in her, the long habit of obedience, of humility, as well as agony of fear, spoke in her voice. "Spare the boy!" she whispered.

"You can't save him now," replied Tull, stridently.

Her head was bowing to the inevitable. She was grasping the truth, when suddenly there came, in inward constriction, a hardening of gentle forces within her breast. Like a steel bar it was, stiffening all that had been soft and weak in her. She felt a birth in her of something new and unintelligible. Once more her strained gaze sought the sage-slopes. Jane Withersteen loved that wild and purple wilderness. In times of sorrow it had been her strength, in happiness its beauty was her continual delight. In her extremity she found herself murmuring, "Whence cometh my help!" It was a prayer, as if forth from those lonely purple reaches and walls of red and clefts of blue might ride a fearless man, neither creed-bound nor creed-mad, who would hold up a restraining hand in the faces of her ruthless people.

The restless movements of Tull's men suddenly quieted down. Then followed a low whisper, a rustle, a sharp exclamation.

"Look!" said one, pointing to the west.

"A rider!"

Jane Withersteen wheeled and saw a horseman, silhouetted against the western sky, come riding out of the sage. He had ridden down from the left, in the golden glare of the sun, and had been unobserved till close at hand. An answer to her prayer!

"Do you know him? Does any one know him?" questioned Tull, hurriedly.

His men looked and looked, and one by one shook their heads.

"He's come from far," said one.

"Thet's a fine hoss," said another.

"A strange rider."

"Huh! He wears black leather," added a fourth.

With a wave of his hand, enjoining silence, Tull stepped forward in such a way that he concealed Venters.

The rider reined in his mount, and with a lithe forward-slipping action appeared to reach the ground in one long step. It was a peculiar movement in its quickness and inasmuch that while performing it the rider did not swerve in the slightest from a square front to the group before him.

"Look!" hoarsely whispered one of Tull's companions. "He packs two black-butted guns—low down—they're hard to see—black agin them black chaps."

"A gunman!" whispered another. "Fellers, careful now about movin' your hands."

The stranger's slow approach might have been a mere leisurely manner of gait or the cramped short steps of a rider unused to walking; yet, as well, it could have been the guarded advance of one who took no chances with men.

"Hello, stranger!" called Tull. No welcome was in this greeting, only a gruff curiosity.

The rider responded with a curt nod. The wide brim of a black sombrero cast a dark shade over his face. For a moment he closely regarded Tull and his comrades, and then, halting in his slow walk, he seemed to relax.

"Evenin', ma'am," he said to Jane, and removed his sombrero with quaint grace.

Jane, greeting him, looked up into a face that she trusted instinctively and which riveted her attention. It had all the characteristics of the range rider's—the leanness, the red burn of the sun, and the set changelessness that came from years of silence and solitude. But it was not these which held her; rather the intensity of his gaze, a strained weariness, a piercing wistfulness of keen, gray sight, as if the man was forever looking for that which he never found. Jane's subtle woman's intuition, even in that brief instant, felt a sadness, a hungering, a secret.

"Jane Withersteen, ma'am?" he inquired.

"Yes," she replied.

"The water here is yours?"

"Yes."

"May I water my horse?"

"Certainly. There's the trough."

"But mebbe if you knew who I was—" He hesitated, with his glance on the listening men. "Mebbe you wouldn't let me water him—though I ain't askin' none for myself."

"Stranger, it doesn't matter who you are. Water your horse. And if you are thirsty and hungry come into my house."

"Thanks, ma'am. I can't accept for myself—but for my tired horse—"

Trampling of hoofs interrupted the rider. More restless movements on the part of Tull's men broke up the little circle, exposing the prisoner Venters.

"Mebbe I've kind of hindered somethin'—for a few moments, perhaps?" inquired the rider.

"Yes," replied Jane Withersteen, with a throb in her voice.

She felt the drawing power of his eyes; and then she saw him look at the bound Venters, and at the men who held him, and their leader.

"In this here country all the rustlers an' thieves an' cutthroats an' gun-throwers an' all-round no-good men jest happen to be Gentiles. Ma'am, which of the no-good class does that young feller belong to?"

"He belongs to none of them. He's an honest boy."

"You *know* that, ma'am?"

"Yes—yes."

"Then what has he done to get tied up that way?"

His clear and distinct question, meant for Tull as well as for Jane Withersteen, stilled the restlessness and brought a momentary silence.

"Ask him," replied Jane, her voice rising high.

The rider stepped away from her, moving out with the same slow, measured stride in which he had approached; and the fact that his action placed her wholly to one side, and him no nearer to Tull and his men, had a penetrating significance.

"Young feller, speak up," he said to Venters.

"Here, stranger, this's none of your mix," began Tull. "Don't try any interference. You've been asked to drink and eat. That's more than you'd have got in any other village on the Utah border. Water your horse and be on your way."

"Easy—easy—I ain't interferin' yet," replied the rider. The tone of his voice had undergone a change. A different man had spoken. Where, in addressing Jane, he had been mild and gentle, now, with his first speech to Tull, he was dry, cool, biting. "I've jest stumbled onto a queer deal. Seven Mormons all packin' guns, an' a Gentile tied with a rope, an' a woman who swears by his honesty! Queer, ain't that?"

"Queer or not, it's none of your business," retorted Tull.

"Where I was raised a woman's word was law. I ain't quite outgrowed that yet."

Tull fumed between amaze and anger.

"Meddler, we have a law here something different from woman's whim—Mormon law! . . . Take care you don't transgress it."

"To hell with your Mormon law!"

The deliberate speech marked the rider's further change, this time from kindly interest to an awakening menace. It produced a transformation in Tull and his companions. The leader gasped and staggered backward at a blasphemous affront to an institution he held most sacred. The man Jerry, holding the horses, dropped the bridles and froze in his tracks. Like posts the other men stood, watchful-eyes, arms hanging rigid, all waiting.

"Speak up now, young man. What have you done to be roped that way?"

"It's a damned outrage!" burst out Venters. "I've done no wrong. I've offended this Mormon Elder by being a friend to that woman."

"Ma'am, is it true—what he says?" asked the rider of Jane; but his quiveringly alert eyes never left the little knot of quiet men.

"True? Yes, perfectly true," she answered.

"Well, young man, it seems to me that bein' a friend to such a woman would be what you wouldn't want to help an' couldn't help. . . . What's to be done to you for it?"

"They intend to whip me. You know what that means—in Utah!"

"I reckon," replied the rider, slowly.

With his gray glance cold on the Mormons, with the restive bit-champing of the horses, with Jane failing to repress her mounting agitation, with Venters standing pale and still, the tension of the moment tightened. Tull broke the spell with a laugh, a laugh without mirth, a laugh that was only a sound betraying fear.

"Come on, men!" he called.

Jane Withersteen turned again to the rider.

"Stranger, can you do nothing to save Venters?"

"Ma'am, you ask me to save him—from your own people?"

"Ask you? I beg of you!"

"But you don't dream who you're askin'."

"Oh sir, I pray you—save him!"

"These are Mormons, an' I . . ."

"At—at any cost—save him. For I—I care for him!"

Tull snarled. "You love-sick fool! Tell your secrets. There'll be a way to teach you what you've never learned. . . . Come men, out of here!"

"Mormon, the young man stays," said the rider.

Like a shot his voice halted Tull.

"What!"

"He stays."

"Who'll keep him? He's my prisoner!" cried Tull, hotly. "Stranger, again I tell you—don't mix here. You've meddled enough. Go your way now or—"

"Listen! . . . He stays."

Absolute certainty, beyond any shadow of doubt, breathed in the rider's low voice.

"Who are you? We are seven here."

The rider dropped his sombrero and made a rapid movement, singular in that it left him somewhat crouched, arms bent and stiff, with the big black gun-sheaths swung round to the fore.

"*Lassiter!*"

It was Venters's wondering, thrilling cry that bridged the fateful connection between the rider's singular position and the dreaded name.

Tull put out a groping hand. The life of his eyes dulled to the gloom with which men of his fear saw the approach of death. But death, while it hovered over him, did not descend, for the rider waited for the twitching fingers, the downward flash of hand that did not come. Tull, gathering himself together, turned to the horses, attended by his pale comrades.

CHAPTER 2

COTTONWOODS

Venters appeared too deeply moved to speak the gratitude his face expressed. And Jane turned upon the rescuer and gripped his hands. Her smiles and tears seemingly dazed him. Presently, as something like calmness returned, she went to Lassiter's weary horse.

"I will water him myself," she said, and she led the horse to a trough under a huge old cottonwood. With nimble fingers she loosened the bridle and removed the bit. The horse snorted and bent his head. The trough was of solid stone, hollowed out, moss-covered and green and wet and cool, and the clear brown water that fed it spouted and splashed from a wooden pipe.

"He has brought you far to-day?"

"Yes, ma'am, a matter of over sixty miles, mebbe seventy."

"A long ride—a ride that— Ah, he is blind!"

"Yes, ma'am," replied Lassiter.

"What blinded him?"

"Some men once roped an' tied him, an' then held white-hot iron close to his eyes."

"Oh! Men? You mean devils. . . . Were they your enemies— Mormons?"

"Yes, ma'am."

"To take revenge on a horse! Lassiter, the men of my creed are unnaturally cruel. To my everlasting sorrow I confess it. They have been driven, hated, scourged till their hearts have hardened. But we women hope and pray for the time when our men will soften."

"Beggin' your pardon, ma'am—that time will never come."

"Oh, it will! . . . Lassiter, do you think Mormon women wicked? Has your hand been against them, too?"

"No. I believe Mormon women are the best an' noblest, the most long-sufferin', and the blindest, unhappiest women on earth."

"Ah!" She gave him a grave, thoughtful look. "Then you will break bread with me?"

Lassiter had no ready response, and he uneasily shifted his weight from one leg to another, and turned his sombrero round and round in his hands. "Ma'am," he began, presently, "I reckon your kindness of heart makes you overlook things. Perhaps I ain't well known hereabouts, but back up North there's Mormons who'd rest oneasy in their graves at the idea of me sittin' to table with you."

"I dare say. But—will you do it anyway?" she asked.

"Mebbe you have a brother or relative who might drop in an' be offended, an' I wouldn't want to—"

"I've not a relative in Utah that I know of. There's no one with a right to question my actions." She turned smilingly to Venters. "You will come in, Bern, and Lassiter will come in. We'll eat and be merry while we may."

"I'm only wonderin' if Tull an' his men'll raise a storm down in the village," said Lassiter, in his last weakening stand.

"Yes, he'll raise the storm—after he has prayed," replied Jane. "Come."

She led the way, with the bridle of Lassiter's horse over her arm. They entered a grove and walked down a wide path shaded by great low-branching cottonwoods. The last rays of the setting sun sent golden bars through the leaves. The grass was deep and rich, welcome contrast to sage-tired eyes. Twittering quail darted across the path, and from a tree-top somewhere a robin sang its evening song, and on the still air floated the freshness and murmur of flowing water.

The home of Jane Withersteen stood in a circle of cottonwoods, and was a flat, long, red-stone structure, with a covered court in the center through which flowed a lively stream of amber-colored water. In the massive blocks of stone and heavy timbers and solid doors and shutters showed the hand of a man who had builded against pillage and time; and in the flowers and mosses lining the stone-bedded stream, in the bright colors of rugs and blankets on the court floor, and the cozy corner with hammock and books, and the clean-linened table, showed the grace of a daughter who lived for happiness and the day at hand.

Jane turned Lassiter's horse loose in the thick grass. "You will want him to be near you," she said, "or I'd have him taken to the alfalfa fields." At her call appeared women who began at once to bustle about, hurrying to and fro, setting the table. Then Jane, excusing herself, went within.

She passed through a huge low-ceiled chamber, like the inside of a fort, and into a smaller one where a bright wood-fire blazed in an old open fireplace, and from this into her own room. It had the same comfort as was manifested in the home-like outer court; moreover, it was warm and rich in soft hues.

Seldom did Jane Withersteen enter her room without looking into her mirror. She knew she loved the reflection of that beauty which since early childhood she had never been allowed to forget. Her relatives and friends, and later a horde of Mormon and Gentile suitors, had fanned the flame of natural vanity in her. So that at twenty-eight she scarcely thought at all of her wonderful influence or good in the little community where her father had left her practically its beneficent landlord; but cared most for the dream and the assurance and the allurement of her beauty. This time, however, she gazed into her glass with more than the usual happy motive, without the usual slight conscious smile. For she was thinking of more than the desire to be fair in her own eyes, in those of her friend; she wondered if she were to seem fair in the eyes of this Lassiter, this man whose name had crossed the long, wild brakes of stone and plains of sage, this gentle-voiced, sad-faced man who was a hater and a killer of Mormons. It was not now her usual half-conscious vain obsession that actuated her as she hurriedly changed her riding-dress to one of white, and then looked long at the stately form with its gracious contours, at the fair face with its strong chin and full firm lips, at the dark-blue, proud, and passionate eyes.

"If by some means I can keep him here a few days, a week—he will never kill another Mormon," she mused. "Lassiter! . . . I shudder when I think of that name, of him. But when I look at the man I forget who he is—I almost like him. I remember only that he saved Bern. He has suffered. I wonder what it was—did he love a Mormon woman once? How splendidly he championed us poor misunderstood souls! Somehow he knows—much."

Jane Withersteen joined her guests and bade them to her board. Dismissing her woman, she waited upon them with her own hands. It was a bountiful supper and a strange company. On her right sat the ragged and half-starved Venters; and though blind eyes could have seen what he counted for in the sum of her happiness, yet he looked the gloomy outcast his allegiance had made him, and about him there was the shadow of the ruin presaged by Tull. On her left sat the black-leather-garbed Lassiter looking like a man in a dream. Hunger was not with him, nor composure, nor speech, and when he twisted in frequent unquiet movements the heavy guns that he had not removed knocked against the table-legs. If it had been otherwise possible to forget the presence of Lassiter those telling little jars would have rendered it unlikely. And Jane Withersteen talked and smiled and laughed with all the dazzling play of lips and eyes that a beautiful, daring woman could summon to her purpose.

When the meal ended, and the men pushed back their chairs, she leaned closer to Lassiter and looked square into his eyes.

"Why did you come to Cottonwoods?"

Her question seemed to break a spell. The rider arose as if he had just remembered himself and had tarried longer than his wont.

"Ma'am, I have hunted all over southern Utah and Nevada for—somethin'. An' through your name I learned where to find it—here in Cottonwoods."

"My name! Oh, I remember. You did know my name when you spoke first. Well, tell me where you heard it and from whom?"

"At the little village—Glaze, I think it's called—some fifty miles or more west of here. An' I heard it from a Gentile, a rider who said you'd know where to tell me to find—"

"What?" she demanded, imperiously, as Lassiter broke off.

"Milly Erne's grave," he answered low, and the words came with a wrench.

Venters wheeled in his chair to regard Lassiter in amazement, and Jane slowly raised herself in white, still wonder.

"Milly Erne's grave?" she echoed, in a whisper. "What do you know of Milly Erne, my best-beloved friend—who died in my arms? What were you to her?"

"Did I claim to be any thin'?" he inquired. "I know people—relatives—who have long wanted to know where she's buried. That's all."

"Relatives? She never spoke of relatives, except a brother who was shot in Texas. Lassiter, Milly Erne's grave is in a secret burying-ground on my property."

"Will you take me there? . . . You'll be offendin' Mormons worse than by breakin' bread with me."

"Indeed yes, but I'll do it. Only we must go unseen. To-morrow, perhaps."

"Thank you, Jane Withersteen," replied the rider, and he bowed to her and stepped backward out of the court.

"Will you not stay—sleep under my roof?" she asked.

"No, ma'am, an' thanks again. I never sleep indoors. An' even if I did there's that gatherin' storm in the village below. No, no. I'll go to the sage. I hope you won't suffer none for your kindness to me."

"Lassiter," said Venters, with a half-bitter laugh, "my bed, too, is the sage. Perhaps we may meet out there."

"Mebbe so. But the sage is wide an' I won't be near. Good night."

At Lassiter's low whistle the black horse whinnied, and carefully picked his blind way out of the grove. The rider did not bridle him, but walked beside him, leading him by touch of hand, and together they passed slowly into the shade of the cottonwoods.

"Jane, I must be off soon," said Venters. "Give me my guns. If I'd had my guns—"

"Either my friend or the Elder of my church would be lying dead," she interposed.

"Tull would be—surely."

"Oh, you fierce-blooded, savage youth! Can't I teach you forbearance, mercy? Bern, it's divine to forgive your enemies. 'Let not the sun go down upon thy wrath.'"

"Hush! Talk to me no more of mercy or religion—after to-day. To-day this strange coming of Lassiter left me still a man, and now I'll die a man! . . . Give me my guns."

Silently she went into the house to return with a heavy cartridge-belt and gun-filled sheath and a long rifle; these she handed to him, and as he buckled on the belt she stood before him in silent eloquence.

"Jane," he said, in gentler voice, "don't look so. I'm not going out to murder your churchman. I'll try to avoid him and all his men. But can't you see I've reached the end of my rope? Jane, you're a wonderful woman. Never was there a woman so unselfish and good. Only you're blind in one way. . . . Listen!"

From behind the grove came the clicking sound of horses in a rapid trot.

"Some of your riders," he continued. "It's getting time for the night shift. Let us go out to the bench in the grove and talk there."

It was still daylight in the open, but under the spreading cottonwoods shadows were obscuring the lanes. Venters drew Jane off from one of these into a shrub-lined trail, just wide enough for the two to walk abreast, and in a roundabout way led her far from the house to a knoll on the edge of the grove. Here in a secluded nook was a bench from which, through an opening in the tree-tops, could be seen the sage-slope and the wall of rock and the dim lines of cañons. Jane had not spoken since Venters had shocked her with his first harsh speech; but all the way she had clung to his arm, and now, as he stopped and laid his rifle against the bench, she still clung to him.

"Jane, I'm afraid I must leave you."

"Bern!" she cried.

"Yes, it looks that way. My position is not a happy one—I can't feel right—I've lost all—"

"I'll give you anything you—"

"Listen, please. When I say loss I don't mean what you think. I mean loss of good-will, good name—that which would have enabled me to stand up in this village without bitterness. Well, it's too late. . . . Now, as to the future, I think you'd do best to give me up. Tull is implacable. You ought to see from his intention to-day that—but you can't see. Your blindness— your damned religion! . . . Jane, forgive me—I'm sore within and something rankles. Well, I fear that invisible hand will turn its hidden work to your ruin."

"Invisible hand? Bern!"

"I mean your Bishop." Venters said it deliberately and would not release her as she started back. "He's the law. The edict went forth to ruin me. Well, look at me! It'll now go forth to compel you to the will of the Church."

"You wrong Bishop Dyer. Tull is hard, I know. But then he has been in love with me for years."

"Oh, your faith and your excuses! You can't see what I know—and if you did see it you'd not admit it to save your life. That's the Mormon of you. These elders and bishops will do absolutely any deed to go on building up the power and wealth of their church, their empire. Think of what they've done to the Gentiles here, to me—think of Milly Erne's fate!"

"What do you know of her story?"

"I know enough—all, perhaps, except the name of the Mormon who brought her here. But I must stop this kind of talk."

She pressed his hand in response. He helped her to a seat beside him on the bench. And he respected a silence that he divined was full of woman's deep emotion, beyond his understanding.

It was the moment when the last ruddy rays of the sunset brightened momentarily before yielding to twilight. And for Venters the outlook before him was in some sense similar to a feeling of his future, and with searching eyes he studied the beautiful purple, barren waste of sage. Here was the unknown and the perilous. The whole scene impressed Venters as a wild, austere, and mighty manifestation of nature. And as it somehow reminded him of his prospect in life, so it suddenly resembled the woman near him; only in her there were greater beauty and peril, a mystery more unsolvable, and something nameless that numbed his heart and dimmed his eye.

"Look! A rider!" exclaimed Jane, breaking the silence. "Can that be Lassiter?"

Venters moved his glance once more to the west. A horseman showed dark on the sky-line, then merged into the color of the sage.

"It might be. But I think not—that fellow was coming in. One of your riders, more likely. Yes, I see him clearly now. And there's another."

"I see them, too."

"Jane, your riders seem as many as the bunches of sage. I ran into five yesterday way down near the trail to Deception Pass. They were with the white herd."

"You still go to that cañon? Bern, I wish you wouldn't. Oldring and his rustlers live somewhere down there."

"Well, what of that?"

"Tull has already hinted of your frequent trips into Deception Pass."

"I know." Venters uttered a short laugh. "He'll make a rustler of me next. But, Jane, there's no water for fifty miles after I leave here, and that nearest is in the cañon. I must drink and water my horse. There! I see more riders. They are going out."

"The red herd is on the slope, toward the Pass."

Twilight was fast falling. A group of horsemen crossed the dark line of low ground to become more distinct as they climbed the slope. The silence broke to a clear call from an incoming rider, and, almost like the peal of a hunting-horn, floated back the answer. The outgoing riders moved swiftly, came sharply into sight as they topped a ridge to show wild and black above the horizon, and then passed down, dimming into the purple of the sage.

"I hope they don't meet Lassiter," said Jane.

"So do I," replied Venters. "By this time the riders of the night shift know what happened to-day. But Lassiter will likely keep out of their way."

"Bern, who is Lassiter? He's only a name to me—a terrible name."

"Who is he? I don't know, Jane. Nobody I ever met knows him. He talks a little like a Texan, like Milly Erne. Did you note that?"

"Yes. How strange of him to know of her! And she lived here ten years and has been dead two. Bern, what do you know of Lassiter? Tell me what he has done—why you spoke of him to Tull—threatening to become another Lassiter yourself?"

"Jane, I only heard things, rumors, stories, most of which I disbelieved. At Glaze his name was known, but none of the riders or ranchers I knew there ever met him. At Stone Bridge I never heard him mentioned. But at Sterling and villages north of there he was spoken of often. I've never been in a village which he had been known to visit. There were many conflicting stories about him and his doings. Some said he had shot up this and that Mormon village, and others denied it. I'm inclined to believe he has, and you know how Mormons hide the truth. But there was one feature about Lassiter upon which all agree—that he was what riders in this country call a gunman. He's a man with marvelous quickness and accuracy in the use of a Colt. And now that I've seen him I know more. Lassiter was born without fear. I watched him with eyes which saw him my friend. I'll never forget the moment I recognized him from what had been told me of his crouch before the draw. It was then I yelled his name. I believe that yell saved Tull's life. At any rate, I know this, between Tull and death then there was not the breadth of the littlest hair. If he or any of his men had moved a finger downward . . ."

Venters left his meaning unspoken, but at the suggestion Jane shuddered.

The pale afterglow in the west darkened with the merging of twilight into night. The sage now spread out black and gloomy. One dim star glimmered in the southwest sky. The sound of trotting horses had ceased, and there was silence broken only by a faint, dry pattering of cottonwood leaves in the soft night wind.

Into this peace and calm suddenly broke the high-keyed yelp of a coyote, and from far off in the darkness came the faint answering note of a trailing mate.

"Hello, the sage-dogs are barking," said Venters.

"I don't like to hear them," replied Jane. "At night, sometimes, when I lie awake, listening to the long mourn or breaking bark or wild howl, I think of you asleep somewhere in the sage, and my heart aches."

"Jane, you couldn't listen to sweeter music, nor could I have a better bed."

"Just think! Men like Lassiter and you have no home, no comfort, no rest, no place to lay your weary heads. Well! . . . Let us be patient. Tull's anger may cool, and time may help us. You might do some service to the village—who can tell? Suppose you discovered the long-unknown hiding place of Oldring and his band, and told it to my riders? That would disarm Tull's ugly hints and put you in favor. For years my riders have trailed the tracks of stolen cattle. You know as well as I how dearly we've paid for our ranges in this wild country. Oldring drives our cattle down into that network of deceiving cañons, and somewhere far to the north or east he drives them up and out to Utah markets. If you will spend time in Deception Pass try to find the trails."

"Jane, I've thought of that. I'll try."

"I must go now. And it hurts, for now I'll never be sure of seeing you again. But to-morrow, Bern?"

"To-morrow surely. I'll watch for Lassiter and ride in with him."

"Good night."

Then she left him and moved away, a white, gliding shape that soon vanished in the shadows.

Venters waited until the faint slam of a door assured him she had reached the house; and then, taking up his rifle, he noiselessly slipped through the bushes, down the knoll, and on under the dark trees to the edge of the grove. The sky was now turning from gray to blue; stars had begun to lighten the earlier blackness; and from the wide flat sweep before him blew a cool wind, fragrant with the breath of sage. Keeping close to the edge of the cottonwoods, he went swiftly and silently westward. The grove was long, and he had not reached the end when he heard something that brought him to a halt. Low-padded thuds told him horses were coming his way. He sank down in the gloom, waiting, listening. Much before he had expected, judging from sound, to his amazement he descried horsemen near at hand. They were riding along the border of the sage, and instantly he knew the hoofs of the horses were muffled. Then the pale starlight afforded him indistinct sight of the riders. But his eyes were keen and used to the dark, and by peering closely he recognized the huge bulk and black-bearded visage of Oldring and the lithe, supple form of the rustler's lieutenant, a masked rider. They passed on; the darkness swallowed them. Then, farther out on the sage, a dark, compact body of horsemen went by, almost without sound, almost like specters, and they, too, melted into the night.

CHAPTER 3

AMBER SPRING

No unusual circumstance was it for Oldring and some of his men to visit Cottonwoods in the broad light of day; but for him to prowl about in the dark with the hoofs of his horses muffled meant that mischief was brewing. Moreover, to Venters the presence of the masked rider with Oldring seemed especially ominous. For about this man there was mystery; he seldom rode through the village; and when he did ride through it was swiftly; riders seldom met him by day on the sage; but wherever he rode there always followed deeds as dark and mysterious as the mask he wore. Oldring's band did not confine themselves to the rustling of cattle.

Venters lay low in the shade of the cottonwoods, pondering this chance meeting, and not for many moments did he consider it safe to move on. Then, with sudden impulse, he turned the other way and went back along the grove. When he reached the path leading to Jane's home he decided to go down to the village. So he hurried onward, with quick, soft steps. Once beyond the grove he entered the one and only street. It was wide, lined with tall poplars, and under each row of trees, inside the footpath, were ditches where ran the water from Jane Withersteen's spring.

Between the trees twinkled lights of cottage candles, and far down flared bright windows of the village stores. When Venters got closer to these he saw knots of men standing together in earnest conversation. The usual lounging on the corners and benches and steps was not in evidence. Keeping in the shadow, Venters went closer and closer until he could hear voices. But he could not distinguish what was said. He recognized many Mormons, and looked hard for Tull and his men, but looked in vain. Venters concluded that the rustlers had not passed along the village street. No doubt these earnest men were discussing Lassiter's coming. But Venters felt positive that Tull's intention toward himself that day had not been and would not be revealed.

So Venters, seeing there was little for him to learn, began retracing his steps. The church was dark, Bishop Dyer's home next to it was also dark, and likewise Tull's cottage. Upon almost any night at this hour there would be lights here, and Venters marked the unusual omission.

As he was about to pass out of the street to skirt the grove, he once more slunk down at the sound of trotting horses. Presently he descried two mounted men riding toward him. He hugged the shadow of a tree. Again the starlight, brighter now, aided him, and he made out Tull's stalwart figure, and beside him the short, froglike shape of the rider Jerry. They were silent, and they rode on to disappear.

Venters went his way with busy, gloomy mind, revolving events of the day, trying to reckon those brooding in the night. His thoughts overwhelmed him. Up in that dark grove dwelt a woman who had been his friend. And he skulked about her home, gripping a gun stealthily as an Indian, a man without place or people or purpose. Above her hovered the shadow of grim, hidden, secret power. No queen could have given more royally out of a bounteous store than Jane Withersteen gave her people, and likewise to those unfortunates whom her people hated. She asked only the divine right of all women—freedom; to love and to live as her heart willed. And her prayer and her hope were vain.

"For years I've seen a storm clouding over her and the village of Cottonwoods," muttered Venters, as he strode on. "Soon it'll burst. I don't like the prospect." That night the villagers whispered in the street—and nightriding rustlers muffled horses—and Tull was at work in secret—and out there in the sage hid a man who meant something terrible—Lassiter!

Venters passed the black cottonwoods, and, entering the sage, climbed the gradual slope. He kept his direction in line with a western star. From time to time he stopped to listen and heard only the usual familiar bark of coyote and sweep of wind and rustle of sage. Presently a low jumble of rocks loomed up darkly somewhat to his right, and, turning that way, he whistled softly. Out of the rocks glided a dog that leaped and whined about him. He climbed over rough, broken rock, picking his way carefully, and then went down. Here it was darker, and sheltered from the wind. A white object guided him. It was another dog, and this one was asleep, curled up between a saddle and a pack. The animal awoke and thumped his tail in greeting. Venters placed the saddle for a pillow, rolled in his blankets, with his face upward to the stars. The white dog snuggled close to him. The other whined and pattered a few yards to the rise of ground and there crouched on guard. And in that wild covert Venters shut his eyes under the great white stars and intense vaulted blue, bitterly comparing their loneliness to his own, and fell asleep.

When he awoke, day had dawned, and all about him was bright steelgray. The air had a cold tang. Arising, he greeted the fawning dogs and stretched his cramped body, and then, gathering together bunches of dead sage sticks, he lighted a fire. Strips of dried beef held to the blaze for a moment served him and the dogs. He drank from a canteen. There was nothing else in his outfit; he had grown used to a scant fare. Then he sat over the fire, palms outspread, and waited. Waiting had been his chief occupation for months, and he scarcely knew what he waited for, unless it was the passing of the hours. But now he sensed action in the immediate present; the day promised another meeting with Lassiter and Jane, perhaps news of the rustlers; on the morrow he meant to take the trail to Deception Pass.

And while he waited he talked to his dogs. He called them Ring and Whitie; they were sheep-dogs, half collie, half deer-hound, superb in build, perfectly trained. It seemed that in his fallen fortunes these dogs understood the nature of their value to him, and governed their affection and faithfulness accordingly. Whitie watched him with somber eyes of love, and Ring, crouched on the little rise of ground above, kept tireless guard. When the sun rose, the white dog took the place of the other, and Ring went to sleep at his master's feet.

By-and-by Venters rolled up his blankets and tied them and his meager pack together, then climbed out to look for his horse. He saw him, presently, a little way off in the sage, and went to fetch him. In that country, where every rider boasted of a fine mount and was eager for a race, where thoroughbreds dotted the wonderful grazing ranges, Venters rode a horse that was sad proof of his misfortunes.

Then, with his back against a stone, Venters faced the east, and, stick in hand and idle blade, he waited. The glorious sunlight filled the valley with purple fire. Before him, to left, to right, waving, rolling, sinking, rising, like low swells of a purple sea, stretched the sage. Out of the grove of cottonwoods, a green patch on the purple, gleamed the dull red of Jane Withersteen's old stone house. And from there extended the wide green of the village gardens and orchards marked by the graceful poplars; and farther down shone the deep, dark richness of the alfalfa fields. Numberless red and black and white dots speckled the sage, and these were cattle and horses.

So, watching and waiting, Venters let the time wear away. At length he saw a horse rise above a ridge, and he knew it to be Lassiter's black. Climbing to the highest rock, so that he would show against the sky-line, he stood and waved his hat. The almost instant turning of Lassiter's horse attested to the quickness of that rider's eye. Then Venters climbed down, saddled his horse, tied on his pack, and, with a word to his dogs, was about to ride out to meet Lassiter, when he concluded to wait for him there, on higher ground, where the outlook was commanding.

It had been long since Venters had experienced friendly greeting from a man. Lassiter's warmed in him something that had grown cold from neglect. And when he had returned it, with a strong grip of the iron hand that held his, and met the gray eyes, he knew that Lassiter and he were to be friends.

"Venters, let's talk awhile before we go down there," said Lassiter, slipping his bridle. "I ain't in no hurry. Them's sure fine dogs you've got." With a rider's eye he took in the points of Venters' horse, but did not speak his thought. "Well, did anythin' come off after I left you last night?"

Venters told him about the rustlers.

"I was snug hid in the sage," replied Lassiter, "an' didn't see or hear no one. Oldrin's got a high hand here, I reckon. It's no news up in Utah how he holes in cañons an' leaves no track." Lassiter was silent a moment.

"Me an' Oldrin' wasn't exactly strangers some years back when he drove cattle into Bostil's Ford, at the head of the Rio Virgin. But he got harassed there an' now he drives some place else."

"Lassiter, you knew him? Tell me, is he Mormon or Gentile?"

"I can't say. I've knowed Mormons who pretended to be Gentiles."

"No Mormon ever pretended that unless he was a rustler," declared Venters.

"Mebbe so."

"It's a hard country for any one, but hardest for Gentiles. Did you ever know or hear of a Gentile prospering in a Mormon community?"

"I never did."

"Well, I want to get out of Utah. I've a mother living in Illinois. I want to go home. It's eight years now."

The older man's sympathy moved Venters to tell his story. He had left Quincy, run off to seek his fortune in the gold fields, had never gotten any farther than Salt Lake City, wandered here and there as helper, teamster, shepherd, and drifted southward over the divide and across the barrens and up the rugged plateau through the passes to the last border settlements. Here he became a rider of the sage, had stock of his own, and for a time prospered, until chance threw him in the employ of Jane Withersteen.

"Lassiter, I needn't tell you the rest."

"Well, it'd be no news to me. I know Mormons. I've seen their women's strange love an' patience an' sacrifice an' silence an' what I call madness for their idea of God. An' over against that I've seen the tricks of the men. They work hand in hand, all together, an' in the dark. No man can hold out against them, unless he takes to packin' guns. For Mormons are slow to kill. That's the only good I ever seen in their religion. Venters, take this from me, these Mormons ain't just right in their minds. Else could a Mormon marry one woman when he already had a wife, an' call it duty?"

"Lassiter, you think as I think," returned Venters.

"How'd it come then that you never throwed a gun on Tull or some of them?" inquired the rider, curiously.

"Jane pleaded with me, begged me to be patient, to overlook. She even took my guns from me. I lost all before I knew it," replied Venters, with the red color in his face. "But, Lassiter, listen. Out of the wreck I saved a Winchester, two Colts, and plenty of shells. I packed these down into Deception Pass. There, almost every day for six months, I have practiced with my rifle till the barrel burned my hands. Practiced the draw—the firing of a Colt, hour after hour!"

"Now that's interestin' to me," said Lassiter, with a quick uplift of his head and a concentration of his gray gaze on Venters. "Could you throw a gun before you began that practicin'?"

"Yes. And now. . . ." Venters made a lightning-swift movement.

Lassiter smiled, and then his bronzed eyelids narrowed till his eyes seemed mere gray slits. "You'll kill Tull!" He did not question; he affirmed.

"I promised Jane Withersteen I'd try to avoid Tull. I'll keep my word. But sooner or later Tull and I will meet. As I feel now, if he even looks at me I'll draw!"

"I reckon so. There'll be hell down there, presently." He paused a moment and flicked a sage-brush with his quirt. "Venters, seein' as you're considerable worked up, tell me Milly Erne's story."

Venters's agitation stilled to the trace of suppressed eagerness in Lassiter's query.

"Milly Erne's story? Well, Lassiter, I'll tell you what I know. Milly Erne had been in Cottonwoods years when I first arrived there, and most of what I tell you happened before my arrival. I got to know her pretty well. She was a slip of a woman, and crazy on religion. I conceived an idea that I never mentioned—I thought she was at heart more Gentile than Mormon. But she passed as a Mormon, and certainly she had the Mormon woman's locked lips. You know, in every Mormon village there are women who seem mysterious to us, but about Milly there was more than the ordinary mystery. When she came to Cottonwoods she had a beautiful little girl whom she loved passionately. Milly was not known openly in Cottonwoods as a Mormon wife. That she really was a Mormon wife I have no doubt. Perhaps the Mormon's other wife or wives would not acknowledge Milly. Such things happen in these villages. Mormon wives wear yokes, but they get jealous. Well, whatever had brought Milly to this country—love or madness of religion—she repented of it. She gave up teaching the village school. She quit the church. And she began to fight Mormon upbringing for her baby girl. Then the Mormons put on the screws—slowly as is their way. At last the child disappeared. Lost, was the report. The child was stolen, I know that. So do you. That wrecked Milly Erne. But she lived on in hope. She became a slave. She worked her heart and soul and life out to get back her child. She never heard of it again. Then she sank. . . . I can see her now, a frail thing, so transparent you could almost look through her—white like ashes—and her eyes! . . . Her eyes have always haunted me. She had one real friend—Jane Withersteen. But Jane couldn't mend a broken heart, and Milly died."

For moments Lassiter did not speak, or turn his head.

"The man!" he exclaimed, presently, in husky accents.

"I haven't the slightest idea who the Mormon was," replied Venters; "nor has any Gentile in Cottonwoods."

"Does Jane Withersteen know?"

"Yes. But a red-hot running-iron couldn't burn that name out of her!"

Without further speech Lassiter started off, walking his horse, and Venters followed with his dogs. Half a mile down the slope they entered a luxuriant growth of willows, and soon came into an open space carpeted with grass like deep green velvet. The rushing of water and singing of birds filled their ears. Venters led his comrade to a shady bower and showed him Amber Spring. It was a magnificent outburst of clear, amber water pouring from a dark, stone-lined hole. Lassiter knelt and drank, lingered there to drink again. He made no comment, but Venters did not need words. Next to his horse a rider of the sage loved a spring. And this spring was the most beautiful and remarkable known to the upland riders of Southern Utah. It was the spring that made old Withersteen a feudal lord and now enabled his daughter to return the toll which her father had exacted from the toilers of the sage.

The spring gushed forth in a swirling torrent, and leaped down joyously to make its swift way along a willow-skirted channel. Moss and ferns and lilies overhung its green banks. Except for the rough-hewn stones that held and directed the water, this willow thicket and glade had been left as nature had made it.

Below were artificial lakes, three in number, one above the other in banks of raised earth; and round about them rose the lofty green-foliaged shafts of poplar trees. Ducks dotted the glassy surface of the lakes; a blue heron stood motionless on a water-gate; kingfishers darted with shrieking flight along the shady banks; a white hawk sailed above; and from the trees and shrubs came the song of robins and cat-birds. It was all in strange contrast to the endless slopes of lonely sage and the wild rock environs beyond. Venters thought of the woman who loved the birds and the green of the leaves and the murmur of water.

Next on the slope, just below the third and largest lake, were corrals and a wide stone barn and open sheds and coops and pens. Here were clouds of dust, and cracking sounds of hoofs, and romping colts and hee-hawing burros. Neighing horses trampled to the corral fences. And from the little windows of the barn projected bobbing heads of bays and blacks and sorrels. When the two men entered the immense barnyard, from all around the din increased. This welcome, however, was not seconded by the several men and boys who vanished on sight.

Venters and Lassiter were turning toward the house when Jane appeared in the lane leading a horse. In riding-skirt and blouse she seemed to have lost some of her statuesque proportions, and looked more like a girl-rider than the mistress of Withersteen. She was bright, smiling, and her greeting was warmly cordial.

"Good news," she announced. "I've been to the village. All is quiet. I expected—I don't know what. But there's no excitement. And Tull has ridden out on his way to Glaze."

"Tull gone?" inquired Venters, with surprise. He was wondering what could have taken Tull away. Was it to avoid another meeting with Lassiter that he went? Could it have any connection with the probable nearness of Oldring and his gang?

"Gone, yes, thank goodness," replied Jane. "Now I'll have peace for a while. Lassiter, I want you to see my horses. You are a rider, and you must be a judge of horseflesh. Some of mine have Arabian blood. My father got his best strain in Nevada from Indians who claimed their horses were bred down from the original stock left by the Spaniards."

"Well, ma'am, the one you've been ridin' takes my eye," said Lassiter, as he walked round the racy, clean-limbed, and fine-pointed roan.

"Where are the boys?" she asked, looking about. "Jerd, Paul, where are you? Here, bring out the horses."

The sound of dropping bars inside the barn was the signal for the horses to jerk their heads in the windows, to snort and stamp. Then they came pounding out of the door, a file of thoroughbreds, to plunge about the barnyard, heads and tails up, manes flying. They halted afar off, squared away to look, came slowly forward with whinnies for their mistress, and doubtful snorts for the strangers and their horses.

"Come—come—come," called Jane, holding out her hands. "Why Bells—Wrangle, where are your manners? Come, Black Star—come, Night. Ah, you beauties! My racers of the sage!"

Only two came up to her; those she called Night and Black Star. Venters never looked at them without delight. The first was soft dead black, the other glittering black, and they were perfectly matched in size, both being high and long-bodied, wide through the shoulders, with lithe, powerful legs. That they were a woman's pets showed in the gloss of skin, the fineness of mane. It showed, too, in the light of big eyes and the gentle reach of eagerness.

"I never seen their like," was Lassiter's encomium; "an' in my day I've seen a sight of horses. Now, ma'am, if you was wantin' to make a long an' fast ride across the sage—say to elope—"

Lassiter ended there with dry humor, yet behind that was meaning. Jane blushed and made arch eyes at him.

"Take care, Lassiter, I might think that a proposal," she replied, gaily. "It's dangerous to propose elopement to a Mormon woman. Well, I was expecting you. Now will be a good hour to show you Milly Erne's grave. The day-riders have gone, and the night-riders haven't come in. Bern, what do you make of that? Need I worry? You know I have to be made worry."

"Well, it's not usual for the night shift to ride in so late," replied Venters, slowly, and his glance sought Lassiter's. "Cattle are usually quiet after dark. Still I've known even a coyote to stampede your white herd."

"I refuse to borrow trouble. Come," said Jane.

They mounted, and, with Jane in the lead, rode down the lane, and, turning off into a cattle trail, proceeded westward. Venters's dogs trotted behind them. On this side of the ranch the outlook was different from that on the other; the immediate foreground was rough and the sage more rugged and less colorful; there were no dark-blue lines of cañons to hold the eye, nor any uprearing rock walls. It was a long roll and slope into gray obscurity. Soon Jane left the trail and rode into the sage, and presently she dismounted and threw her bridle. The men did likewise. Then, on foot, they followed her, coming out at length on the rim of a low escarpment. She passed by several little ridges of earth to halt before a faintly defined mound. It lay in the shade of a sweeping sage-brush close to the edge of the promontory; and a rider could have jumped his horse over it without recognizing a grave.

"Here!"

She looked sad as she spoke, but she offered no explanation for the neglect of an unmarked, uncared-for grave. There was a little bunch of pale, sweet lavender daisies, doubtless planted there by Jane.

"I only come here to remember and to pray," she said. "But I leave no trail!"

A grave in the sage! How lonely this resting place of Milly Erne! The cottonwoods or the alfalfa fields were not in sight, nor was there any rock or ridge or cedar to lend contrast to the monotony. Gray slopes, tinging the purple, barren and wild, with the wind waving the sage, swept away to the dim horizon.

Lassiter looked at the grave and then out into space. At that moment he seemed a figure of bronze.

Jane touched Venters's arm and led him back to the horses.

"Bern!" cried Jane, when they were out of hearing. "Suppose Lassiter were Milly's husband—the father of that little girl lost so long ago!"

"It might be, Jane. Let us ride on. If he wants to see us again he'll come."

So they mounted and rode out to the cattle trail and began to climb. From the height of the ridge, where they had started down, Venters looked back. He did not see Lassiter, but his glance, drawn irresistibly farther out on the gradual slope, caught sight of a moving cloud of dust.

"Hello, a rider!"

"Yes, I see," said Jane.

"That fellow's riding hard. Jane, there's something wrong."

"Oh, yes, there must be . . . How he rides!"

The horse disappeared in the sage, and then puffs of dust marked his course.

"He's short-cut on us—he's making straight for the corrals."

Venters and Jane galloped their steeds and reined in at the turning of the lane. This lane led down to the right of the grove. Suddenly into its lower entrance flashed a bay horse. Then Venters caught the fast rhythmic beat of pounding hoofs. Soon his keen eye recognized the swing of the rider in his saddle.

"It's Judkins, your Gentile rider!" he cried. "Jane, when Judkins rides like that it means hell!"

CHAPTER 4

DECEPTION PASS

The rider thundered up and almost threw his foam-flecked horse in the sudden stop. He was of giant form, and with fearless eyes.

"Judkins, you're all bloody!" cried Jane, in affright. "Oh, you've been shot!"

"Nothin' much, Miss Withersteen. I got a nick in the shoulder. I'm some wet an' the hoss's been throwin' lather, so all this ain't blood."

"What's up?" queried Venters, sharply.

"Rustlers sloped off with the red herd."

"Where are my riders?" demanded Jane.

"Miss Withersteen, I was alone all night with the herd. At daylight this mornin' the rustlers rode down. They began to shoot at me on sight. They chased me hard an' far, burnin' powder all the time, but I got away."

"Jud, they meant to kill you," declared Venters.

"Now I wonder," returned Judkins. "They wanted me bad. An' it ain't regular for rustlers to waste time chasin' one rider."

"Thank Heaven you got away," said Jane. "But my riders—where are they?"

"I don't know. The night-riders weren't there last night when I rode down, an' this mornin' I met no day-riders."

"Judkins! Bern, they've been set upon—killed by Oldring's men!"

"I don't think so," replied Venters, decidedly. "Jane, your riders haven't gone out in the sage."

"Bern, what do you mean?" Jane Withersteen turned deathly pale.

"You remember what I said about the unseen hand?"

"Oh! . . . Impossible!"

"I hope so. But I fear—" Venters finished, with a shake of his head.

"Bern, you're bitter; but that's only natural. We'll wait to see what's happened to my riders. Judkins, come to the house with me. Your wound must be attended to."

"Jane, I'll find out where Oldring drives the herd," vowed Venters.

"No, no! Bern, don't risk it now—when the rustlers are in such shooting mood."

"I'm going. Jud, how many cattle in that red herd?"

"Twenty-five hundred head."

"Whew! What on earth can Oldring do with so many cattle? Why, a hundred head is a big steal. I've got to find out."

"Don't go," implored Jane.

"Bern, you want a hoss thet can run. Miss Withersteen, if it's not too bold of me to advise, make him take a fast hoss or don't let him go."

"Yes, yes, Judkins. He must ride a horse that can't be caught. Which one—Black Star—Night?"

"Jane, I won't take either," said Venters, emphatically. "I wouldn't risk losing one of your favorites."

"Wrangle, then?"

"Thet's the hoss," replied Judkins. "Wrangle can outrun Black Star an' Night. You'd never believe it, Miss Withersteen, but I know. Wrangle's the biggest an' fastest hoss on the sage."

"Oh, no, Wrangle can't beat Black Star. But, Bern, take Wrangle, if you will go. Ask Jerd for anything you need. Oh, be watchful, careful . . . God speed you!"

She clasped his hand, turned quickly away, and went down the lane with the rider.

Venters rode to the barn, and, leaping off, shouted for Jerd. The boy came running. Venters sent him for meat, bread, and dried fruits, to be packed in saddlebags. His own horse he turned loose into the nearest corral. Then he went for Wrangle. The giant sorrel had earned his name for a trait the opposite of amiability. He came readily out of the barn, but once in the yard he broke from Venters, and plunged about with ears laid back. Venters had to rope him, and then he kicked down a section of fence, stood on his hind legs, crashed down and fought the rope. Jerd returned to lend a hand.

"Wrangle don't git enough work," said Jerd, as the big saddle went on. "He's únruly when he's corraled, an' wants to run. Wait till he smells the sage!"

"Jerd, this horse is an iron-jawed devil. I never straddled him but once. Run? Say, he's swift as wind!"

When Venters's boot touched the stirrup the sorrel bolted, giving him the rider's flying mount. The swing of this fiery horse recalled to Venters days that were not really long past, when he rode into the sage as the leader of Jane Withersteen's riders. Wrangle pulled hard on a tight rein. He galloped out of the lane, down the shady border of the grove, and hauled up at the watering-trough, where he pranced and champed his bit. Venters got off and filled his canteen while the horse drank. The dogs, Ring and Whitie, came trotting up from their drink. Then Venters remounted and turned Wrangle toward the sage.

A wide, white trail wound away down the slope. One keen, sweeping glance told Venters that there was neither man nor horse nor steer within the limit of his vision, unless they were lying down in the sage. Ring loped in the lead and Whitie loped in the rear. Wrangle settled gradually into an easy swinging canter, and Venter's thoughts, now that the rush and flurry of the start were past, and the long miles stretched before him, reverted to a calm reckoning of late singular coincidences.

There was the night ride of Tull's, which, viewed in the light of subsequent events, had a look of his covert machinations; Oldring and his Masked Rider and his rustlers riding muffled horses; the report that Tull had ridden out that morning with his man Jerry on the trail to Glaze; the strange disappearance of Jane Withersteen's riders; the unusually determined attempt to kill the one Gentile still in her employ, an intention frustrated, no doubt, only by Judkins's magnificent riding of her racer; and lastly the driving of the red herd. These events, to Venters's color of mind, had a dark relationship. Remembering Jane's accusation of bitterness, he tried hard to put aside his rancor in judging Tull. But it was bitter knowledge that made him see the truth. He had felt the shadow of an unseen hand; he had watched till he saw its dim outline, and then he had traced it to a man's hate, to the rivalry of a Mormon Elder, to the power of a Bishop, to the long, far-reaching arm of a terrible creed. That unseen hand had made its first move against Jane Withersteen. Her riders had been called in, leaving her without help to drive seven thousand head of cattle. But to Venters it seemed extraordinary that the power which had called in these riders had left so many cattle to be driven by rustlers and harried by wolves. For hand in glove with that power was an insatiate greed; they were one and the same.

"What can Oldring do with twenty-five hundred head of cattle?" muttered Venters. "Is he a Mormon? Did he meet Tull last night? It looks like a black plot to me. But Tull and his churchmen wouldn't ruin Jane Withersteen unless the Church was to profit by that ruin. Where does Oldring come in? I'm going to find out about these things."

Wrangle did twenty-five miles in three hours and walked little of the way. When he had gotten warmed up he had been allowed to choose his own gait. The afternoon had well advanced when Venters struck the trail of the red herd and found where it had grazed the night before. Then Venters rested the horse and used his eyes. Near at hand were a cow and a calf and several yearlings and farther out in the sage some straggling steers. He caught a glimpse of coyotes skulking near the cattle. The slow, sweeping gaze of the rider failed to find other living things within the field of sight. The sage about him was breast-high to his horse, oversweet with its warm, fragrant breath, gray where it waved to the light, darker where the wind left it still, and beyond the wonderful haze-purple lent by distance. Far across that wide waste began the slow lift of uplands through which Deception Pass cut its tortuous many-cañoned way.

Venters raised the bridle of his horse and followed the broad cattle trail. The crushed sage resembled the path of a monster snake. In a few miles of travel he passed several cows and calves that had escaped the drive. Then he stood on the last high bench of the slope with the floor of the valley beneath. The opening of the cañon showed in a break of the sage, and the cattle trail paralleled it as far as he could see. That trail led to an undiscovered point where Oldring drove cattle into the pass, and many a rider who had followed it had never returned. Venters satisfied himself that the rustlers had not deviated from their usual course, and then he turned at right angles off the cattle trail and made for the head of the pass.

The sun lost its heat and wore down to the western horizon, where it changed from white to gold and rested like a huge ball about to roll on its golden shadows down the slope. Venters watched the lengthening of the rays and bars, and marveled at his own league-long shadow. The sun sank. There was instant shading of brightness about him, and he saw a kind of cold purple bloom creep ahead of him to cross the cañon, to mount the opposite slope and chase and darken and bury the last golden flare of sunlight.

Venters rode into a trail that he always took to get down into the cañon. He dismounted and found no tracks but his own made several days previous. Nevertheless he sent the dog Ring ahead and waited. In a little while Ring returned. Whereupon Venters led his horse on to the break in the ground.

The opening into Deception Pass was one of the remarkable natural phenomena in a country remarkable for vast slopes of sage, uplands insulated by gigantic red walls, and deep cañons of mysterious source and outlet. Here the valley floor was level, and here opened a narrow chasm, a ragged vent in yellow walls of stone. The trail down the five hundred feet of sheer depth always tested Venters's nerve. It was bad going for even a burro. But Wrangle, as Venters led him, snorted defiance or disgust rather than fear, and, like a hobbled horse on the jump, lifted his ponderous iron-shod fore hoofs and crashed down over the first rough step. Venters warmed to greater admiration of the sorrel; and, giving him a loose bridle, he stepped down foot by foot. Oftentimes the stones and shale started by Wrangle buried Venters to his knees; again he was hard put to it to dodge a rolling boulder; there were times when he could not see Wrangle for dust, and once he and the horse rode a sliding shelf of yellow, weathered cliff. It was a trail on which there could be no stops, and, therefore, if perilous, it was at least one that did not take long in the descent.

Venters breathed lighter when that was over, and felt a sudden assurance in the success of his enterprise. For at first it had been a reckless determination to achieve something at any cost, and now it resolved it-self into an adventure worthy of all his reason and cunning, and keenness of eye and ear.

Piñon pines clustered in little clumps along the level floor of the pass. Venters rode into the trail and up the cañon. Gradually the trees and caves and objects low down turned black, and this blackness moved up the walls till night enfolded the pass, while day still lingered above. The sky darkened; and stars began to show, at first pale and then bright. Sharp notches of the rim-wall, biting like teeth into the blue, were landmarks by which Venters knew where his camping site lay. He had to feel his way through a thicket of slender oaks to a spring where he watered Wrangle and drank himself. Here he unsaddled and turned Wrangle loose, having no fear that the horse would leave the thick, cool grass adjacent to the spring. Next he satisfied his own hunger, fed Ring and Whitie, and, with them curled beside him, composed himself to await sleep.

There had been a time when night in the high altitude of these Utah uplands had been satisfying to Venters. But that was before the oppression of enemies had made the change in his mind. As a rider guarding the herd he had never thought of the night's wildness and loneliness, as an outcast, now when the full silence set in and the deep darkness, and trains of radiant stars shone cold and calm, he lay with an ache in his heart. For a year he had lived as a black fox, driven from his kind. He longed for the sound of a voice, the touch of a hand. In the daytime there was riding from place to place, and the grim gun practice to which something drove him, and other tasks that at least necessitated action; at night, before he won sleep there was strife in his soul. He yearned to leave the endless sage-slopes, the wilderness of cañons; and it was in the lonely night that this yearning grew unbearable. It was then that he reached forth to feel Ring or Whitie, immeasurably grateful for the love and companion-ship of two dogs.

On this night the same old loneliness beset Venters, the old habit of sad thought and burning unquiet had its way. But from it evolved a con-viction that his useless life had undergone a subtle change. He had sensed it first when Wrangle swung him up to the high saddle; he knew it now when he lay in the gateway of Deception Pass. He had no thrill of ad-venture, rather a gloomy perception of great hazard, perhaps death. He meant to find Oldring's retreat. The rustlers had fast horses, but none that could catch Wrangle. Venters knew no rustler could creep upon him at night when Ring and Whitie guarded his hiding place. For the rest he had eyes and ears, and a long rifle and an unerring aim, which he meant to use. Strangely his foreshadowing of change did not hold a thought of the killing of Tull. It related only to what was to happen to him in Deception Pass; and he could no more lift the veil of that mystery than tell where the trails led to in that unexplored cañon. Moreover, he did not care. And at length, tired out by stress of thought, he fell asleep.

When his eyes unclosed, day had come again, and he saw the rim of the opposite wall tipped with the gold of sunrise. A few moments sufficed for the morning's simple camp duties. Near at hand he found Wrangle, and to his surprise the horse came to him. Wrangle was one of the horses that left his viciousness in the home corral. What he wanted was to be free of mules and burros and steers, to roll in dust-patches, and then to run down the wide, open, windy sage-plains, and at night browse and sleep in the cool wet grass of a springhole. Jerd knew the sorrel when he said of him: "Wait till he smells the sage!"

Venters saddled and led him out of the oak thicket, and, leaping astride, rode up the cañon with Ring and Whitie trotting behind. An old grass-grown trail followed the course of a shallow wash where flowed a thin stream of water. The cañon was a hundred rods wide; its yellow walls were perpendicular; it had abundant sage and a scant growth of oak and piñon. For five miles it held to a comparatively straight bearing, and then began a heightening of rugged walls and a deepening of the floor. Beyond this point of sudden change in the character of the cañon Venters had never explored, and here was the real door to the intricacies of Deception Pass.

He reined Wrangle to a walk, halted now and then to listen, and then proceeded cautiously with shifting and alert gaze. The cañon assumed proportions that dwarfed those of its first ten miles. Venters rode on and on, not losing in the interest of his wild surroundings any of his caution or keen search for tracks or sight of living thing. If there ever had been a trail here, he could not find it. He rode through sage and clumps of piñon trees and grassy plots where long-petaled purple lilies bloomed. He rode through a dark constriction of the pass no wider than the lane in the grove at Cottonwoods. And he came out into a great amphitheater into which jutted huge towering corners of a confluence of intersecting cañons.

Venters sat his horse, and, with a rider's eye, studied this wild cross-cut of huge stone gullies. Then he went on, guided by the course of running water. If it had not been for the main stream of water flowing north he would never have been able to tell which of those many openings was a continuation of the pass. In crossing this amphitheater he went by the mouths of five cañons, fording little streams that flowed into the larger one. Gaining the outlet which he took to be the pass, he rode on again under overhanging walls. One side was dark in shade, the other light in sun. This narrow passageway turned and twisted and opened into a valley that amazed Venters.

Here again was a sweep of purple sage, richer than upon the higher levels. The valley was miles long and several wide and inclosed by unscalable walls. But it was the background of this valley that so forcibly struck him. Across the sage-flat rose a strange up-flinging of yellow rocks. He could not tell which were close and which were distant. Scrawled mounds of stone, like mountain waves, seemed to roll up to steep bare slopes and towers.

In this plain of sage Venters flushed birds and rabbits, and when he had proceeded about a mile he caught sight of the bobbing white tails of a herd of running antelope. He rode along the edge of the stream which wound toward the western end of the slowly-looming mounds of stone. The high slope retreated out of sight behind the nearer projection. To Venters the valley appeared to have been filled in by a mountain of melted stone that had hardened in strange shapes of rounded outline. He followed the stream till he lost it in a deep cut. Therefore Venters quit the dark slit which baffled further search in that direction, and rode out along the curved edge of stone where it met the sage. It was not long before he came to a low place, and here Wrangle readily climbed up.

All about him was a ridgy roll of wind-smoothed, rain-washed rock. Not a tuft of grass or a bunch of sage colored the dull rust-yellow. He saw where, to the right, this uneven flow of stone ended in a blunt wall.

Leftward, from the hollow that lay at his feet, mounted a gradual slow-swelling slope to a great height topped by leaning, cracked, and ruined crags. Not for some time did he grasp the wonder of that acclivity. It was no less than a mountain-side, glistening in the sun like polished granite, with cedar-trees springing as if by magic out of the denuded surface. Winds had swept it clear of weathered shale, and rains had washed it free of dust. Far up the curved slope its beautiful lines broke to meet the vertical rim-wall, to lose its grace in a different order and color of rock, a stained yellow cliff of cracks and caves and seamed crags. And straight before Venters was a scene less striking but more significant to his keen survey. For beyond a mile of the bare, hummocky rock began the valley of sage, and the mouths of cañons, one of which surely was another gateway into the pass.

He got off his horse, and, giving the bridle to Ring to hold, he commenced a search for the cleft where the stream ran. He was not successful and concluded the water dropped into an underground passage. Then he returned to where he had left Wrangle, and led him down off the stone to the sage. It was a short ride to the opening cañons. There was no reason for a choice of which one to enter. The one he rode into was a clear, sharp shaft in yellow stone a thousand feet deep, with wonderful wind-worn caves low down and high above buttressed and turreted ramparts. Farther on Venters came into a region where deep indentations marked the line of cañon walls. These were huge, cove-like blind pockets extending back to a sharp corner with a dense growth of underbrush and trees.

Venters penetrated into one of these offshoots, and, as he had hoped, he found abundant grass. He had to bend the oak saplings to get his horse through. Deciding to make this a hiding place if he could find water, he worked back to the limit of the shelving walls. In a little cluster of silver spruces he found a spring. This inclosed nook seemed an ideal place to leave his horse and to camp at night, and from which to make stealthy trips on foot. The thick grass hid his trail; the dense growth of oaks in the opening would serve as a barrier to keep Wrangle in, if, indeed, the luxuriant browse would not suffice for that. So Venters, leaving Whitie with the horse, called Ring to his side, and, rifle in hand, worked his way out to the open. A careful photographing in mind of the formation of the bold outlines of rimrock assured him he would be able to return to his retreat, even in the dark.

Bunches of scattered sage covered the center of the cañon, and among these Venters threaded his way with the step of an Indian. At intervals he put his hand on the dog and stopped to listen. There was a drowsy hum of insects, but no other sound disturbed the warm midday stillness. Venters saw ahead a turn, more abrupt than any yet. Warily he rounded this corner, once again to halt bewildered.

The cañon opened fan-shaped into a great oval of green and gray growths. It was the hub of an oblong wheel, and from it, at regular distances, like spokes, ran the outgoing cañons. Here a dull red color predominated over the fading yellow. The corners of wall bluntly rose, scarred and scrawled, to taper into towers and serrated peaks and pinnacled domes.

Venters pushed on more heedfully than ever. Toward the center of this circle the sage-brush grew smaller and farther apart. He was about to sheer off to the right, where thickets and jumbles of fallen rock would afford him cover, when he ran right upon a broad cattle trail. Like a road it was, more than a trail; and the cattle tracks were fresh. What surprised him more, they were wet! He pondered over this feature. It had not rained. The only solution to this puzzle was that the cattle had been driven through water, and water deep enough to wet their legs.

Suddenly Ring growled low. Venters rose cautiously and looked over the sage. A band of straggling horsemen were riding across the oval. He sank down startled and trembling. "Rustlers!" he muttered. Hurriedly he glanced about for a place to hide. Near at hand there was nothing but sage-brush. He dared not risk crossing the open patches to reach the rocks. Again he peeped over the sage. The rustlers—four—five—seven—eight in all, were approaching, but not directly in line with him. That was relief for a cold deadness which seemed to be creeping inward along his veins. He crouched down with bated breath and held the bristling dog.

He heard the click of iron-shod hoofs on stone, the coarse laughter of men, and then voices gradually dying away. Long moments passed. Then he rose. The rustlers were riding into a cañon. Their horses were tired, and they had several pack animals; evidently they had traveled far. Venters doubted that they were the rustlers who had driven the red herd. Old-ring's band had split. Venters watched these horsemen disappear under a bold cañon wall.

The rustlers had come from the northwest side of the oval. Venters kept a steady gaze in that direction, hoping, if there were more, to see from what cañon they rode. A quarter of an hour went by. Reward for his vigilance came when he descried three more mounted men, far over to the north. But out of what cañon they had ridden it was too late to tell. He watched the three ride across the oval and round the jutting red corner where the others had gone.

"Up that cañon!" exclaimed Venters. "Oldring's den! I've found it!"

A knotty point for Venters was the fact that the cattle tracks all pointed west. The broad trail came from the direction of the cañon into which the rustlers had ridden, and undoubtedly the cattle had been driven out of it across the oval. There were no tracks pointing the other way. It had been in his mind that Oldring had driven the red herd toward the rendezvous, and not from it. Where did that broad trail come down into the pass, and where did it lead? Venters knew he wasted time in pondering the question, but it held a fascination not easily dispelled. For many years Oldring's mysterious entrance and exit to Deception Pass had been all-absorbing topics to sage-riders.

All at once the dog put an end to Venters's pondering. Ring sniffed the air, turned slowly in his tracks with a whine, and then growled. Venters wheeled. Two horsemen were within a hundred yards, coming straight at him. One, lagging behind the other, was Oldring's Masked Rider.

Venters cunningly sank, slowly trying to merge into sage-brush. But, guarded as his action was, the first horse detected it. He stopped short, snorted, and shot up his ears. The rustler bent forward, as if keenly peering ahead. Then, with a swift sweep, he jerked a gun from its sheath and fired.

The bullet zipped through the sage-brush. Flying bits of wood struck Venters, and the hot, stinging pain seemed to lift him in one leap. Like a flash the blue barrel of his rifle gleamed level and he shot once—twice.

The foremost rustler dropped his weapon, and toppled from his saddle, to fall with his foot catching in a stirrup. The horse snorted wildly and plunged away, dragging the rustler through the sage.

The Masked Rider huddled over his pommel, slowly swaying to one side, and then, with a faint, strange cry, slipped out of the saddle.

CHAPTER 5

THE MASKED RIDER

Venters looked quickly from the fallen rustlers to the cañon where the others had disappeared. He calculated on the time needed for running horses to return to the open, if their riders heard shots. He waited breathlessly. But the estimated time dragged by and no riders appeared. Venters began presently to believe that the rifle reports had not penetrated into the recesses of the cañon, and felt safe for the immediate present.

He hurried to the spot where the first rustler had been dragged by his horse. The man lay in deep grass, dead, jaw fallen, eyes protruding—a sight that sickened Venters. The first man at whom he had ever aimed a weapon he had shot through the heart. With the clammy sweat oozing from every pore Venters dragged the rustler in among some boulders and covered him with slabs of rock. Then he smoothed out the crushed trail in grass and sage. The rustler's horse had stopped a quarter of a mile off and was grazing.

When Venters rapidly strode toward the Masked Rider not even the cold nausea that gripped him could wholly banish curiosity. For he had shot Oldring's infamous lieutenant, whose face had never been seen.

Venters experienced a grim pride in the feat. What would Tull say to this achievement of the outcast who rode too often to Deception Pass?

Venters's curious eagerness and expectation had not prepared him for the shock he received when he stood over a slight, dark figure. The rustler wore the black mask that had given him his name, but he had no weapons. Venters glanced at the drooping horse; there were no gunsheaths on the saddle.

"A rustler who didn't pack guns!" muttered Venters. "He wears no belt. He couldn't pack guns in that rig . . . Strange!"

A low, gasping intake of breath and a sudden twitching of body told Venters the rider still lived.

"He's alive! . . . I've got to stand here and watch him die. And I shot an unarmed man."

Shrinkingly Venters removed the rider's wide sombrero and the black cloth mask. This action disclosed bright chestnut hair, inclined to curl, and a white youthful face. Along the lower line of cheek and jaw was a clear demarcation, where the brown of tanned skin met the white that had been hidden from the sun.

"Oh, he's only a boy! . . . What! Can he be Oldring's Masked Rider?"

The boy showed signs of returning consciousness. He stirred; his lips moved; a small brown hand clenched in his blouse.

Venters knelt with a gathering horror of his deed. His bullet had entered the rider's right breast, high up to the shoulder. With hands that shook, Venters untied a black scarf and ripped open the blood-wet blouse.

First he saw a gaping hole, dark red against a whiteness of skin, from which welled a slender red stream. Then, the graceful, beautiful swell of a woman's breast!

"A woman!" he cried. "A girl! . . . I've killed a girl!"

She suddenly opened eyes that transfixed Venters. They were fathomless blue. Consciousness of death was there, a blended terror and pain, but no consciousness of sight. She did not see Venters. She stared into the unknown.

Then came a spasm of vitality. She writhed in a torture of reviving strength, and in her convulsions she almost tore from Venters's grasp.

Slowly she relaxed and sank partly back. The ungloved hand sought the wound, and pressed so hard that her wrist half buried itself in her bosom. Blood trickled between her spread fingers. And she looked at Venters with eyes that saw him.

He cursed himself and the unerring aim of which he had been so proud. He had seen that look in the eyes of a crippled antelope which he was about to finish with his knife. But in her it had infinitely more— a revelation of mortal spirit. The instinctive clinging to life was there, and the divining helplessness and the terrible accusation of the stricken.

"Forgive me! I didn't know!" burst out Venters.

"You shot me—you've killed me!" she whispered, in panting gasps. Upon her lips appeared a fluttering, bloody froth. By that Venters knew the air in her lungs was mixing with blood. "Oh, I knew—it would— come—some day! . . . Oh, the burn! . . . Hold me—I'm sinking—it's all dark. . . . Ah, God! . . . Mercy—"

Her rigidity loosened in one long quiver and she lay back limp, still, white as snow, with closed eyes.

Venters thought then that she died. But the faint pulsation of her breast assured him that life yet lingered. Death seemed only a matter of moments, for the bullet had gone clear through her. Nevertheless, he tore sage-leaves from a bush, and, pressing them tightly over her wounds, he bound the black scarf round her shoulder, tying it securely under her arm. Then he closed the blouse, hiding from his sight that blood-stained, accusing breast.

"What—now?" he questioned, with flying mind. "I must get out of here. She's dying—but I can't leave her."

He rapidly surveyed the sage to the north and made out no animate object. Then he picked up the girl's sombrero and the mask. This time the mask gave him as great a shock as when he first removed it from her face. For in the woman he had forgotten the rustler, and this black strip of felt-cloth established the identity of Oldring's Masked Rider. Venters had solved the mystery. He slipped his rifle under her, and, lifting her carefully upon it, he began to retrace his steps. The dog trailed in his shadow. And the horse, that had stood drooping by, followed without a call. Venters chose the deepest tufts of grass and clumps of sage on his return. From time to time he glanced over his shoulder. He did not rest. His concern was to avoid jarring the girl and to hide his trail. Gaining the narrow cañon, he turned and held close to the wall till he reached his hiding place. When he entered the dense thicket of oaks he was hard put to it to force a way through. But he held his burden almost upright, and by slipping sidewise and bending the saplings he got in. Through sage and grass he hurried to the grove of silver spruces.

He laid the girl down, almost fearing to look at her. Though marble pale and cold, she was living. Venters then appreciated the tax that long carry had been to his strength. He sat down to rest. Whitie sniffed at the pale girl and whined and crept to Venters's feet. Ring lapped the water in the runway of the spring.

Presently Venters went out to the opening, caught the horse, and, leading him through the thicket, unsaddled him and tied him with a long halter. Wrangle left his browsing long enough to whinny and toss his head. Venters felt that he could not rest easily till he had secured the other rustler's horse; so, taking his rifle and calling for Ring, he set out. Swiftly yet watchfully he made his way through the cañon to the oval and out to the cattle trail. What few tracks might have betrayed him he obliterated, so only an expert tracker could have trailed him. Then, with many a wary backward glance across the sage, he started to round up the rustler's horse. This was unexpectedly easy. He led the horse to lower ground, out of sight from the opposite side of the oval, along the shadowy western wall, and so on into his cañon and secluded camp.

The girl's eyes were open; a feverish spot burned in her cheeks; she moaned something unintelligible to Venters, but he took the movement of her lips to mean that she wanted water. Lifting her head, he tipped the canteen to her lips. After that she again lapsed into unconsciousness or a weakness which was its counterpart. Venters noted, however, that the burning flush had faded into the former pallor.

The sun set behind the high cañon rim, and a cool shade darkened the walls. Venters fed the dogs and put a halter on the dead rustler's horse. He allowed Wrangle to browse free. This done, he cut spruce boughs and made a lean-to for the girl. Then, gently lifting her upon a blanket, he folded the sides over her. The other blanket he wrapped about his

shoulders and found a comfortable seat against a spruce tree that upheld the little shack. Ring and Whitie lay near at hand, one asleep, the
other watchful.

Venters dreaded the night's vigil. At night his mind was active, and
this time he had to watch and think and feel beside a dying girl whom he
had all but murdered. A thousand excuses he invented for himself, yet
not one made any difference in his act or his self-reproach.

It seemed to him that when night fell black he could see her white
face so much more plainly.

"She'll go, presently," he said, "and be out of agony—thank God!"

Every little while certainty of her death came to him with a shock,
and then he would bend over and lay his ear on her breast. Her heart still
beat.

The early night blackness cleared to the cold starlight. The horses
were not moving, and no sound disturbed the deathly silence of the cañon.

"I'll bury her here," thought Venters, "and let her grave be as much a
mystery as her life was."

For the girl's few words, the look of her eyes, the prayer, had
strangely touched Venters.

"She was only a girl," he soliloquized. "What was she to Oldring?
Rustlers don't have wives nor sisters nor daughters. She was bad—that's all.
But somehow. . . . Well, she may not have willingly become the companion of rustlers. That prayer of hers to God for mercy! . . . Life is strange
and cruel. I wonder if other members of Oldring's gang are women? Likely
enough. But what was his game? Oldring's Masked Rider! A name to make
villagers hide and lock their doors. A name credited with a dozen murders,
a hundred forays, and a thousand stealings of cattle. What part did the girl
have in this? It may have served Oldring to create mystery."

Hours passed. The white stars moved across the narrow strip of
dark-blue sky above. The silence awoke to the low hum of insects. Venters watched the immovable white face, and as he watched, hour by hour
waiting for death, the infamy of her passed from his mind. He thought
only of the sadness, the truth of the moment. Whoever she was—whatever
she had done—she was young and she was dying.

The after-part of the night wore on interminably. The starlight failed and the gloom blackened to the darkest hour. "She'll die at the gray of dawn," muttered Venters, remembering some old woman's fancy. The blackness paled to gray, and the gray lightened and day peeped over the eastern rim. Venters listened at the breast of the girl. She still lived. Did he only imagine that her heart beat stronger, ever so slightly, but stronger? He pressed his ear closer to her breast. And he rose with his own pulse quickening.

"If she doesn't die soon—she's got a chance—the barest chance—to live," he said.

He wondered if the internal bleeding had ceased. There was no more film of blood upon her lips. But no corpse could have been whiter. Opening her blouse he untied the scarf, and carefully picked away the sage-leaves from the wound in her shoulder. It had closed. Lifting her lightly, he ascertained that the same was true of the hole where the bullet had come out. He reflected on the fact that clean wounds closed quickly in the healing upland air. He recalled instances of riders who had been cut and shot, apparently to fatal issues; yet the blood had clotted, the wounds closed, and they had recovered. He had no way to tell if internal hemorrhage still went on, but he believed that it had stopped. Otherwise she would surely not have lived so long. He marked the entrance of the bullet, and concluded that it had just touched the upper lobe of her lung. Perhaps the wound in the lung had also closed. As he began to wash the blood stains from her breast and carefully rebandage the wound, he was vaguely conscious of a strange, grave happiness in the thought that she might live.

Broad daylight and a hint of sunshine high on the cliff-rim to the west brought him to consideration of what he had better do. And while busy with his few camp tasks he revolved the thing in his mind. It would not be wise for him to remain long in his present hiding place. And if he intended to follow the cattle trail and try to find the rustlers he had better make a move at once. For he knew that rustlers, being riders, would not make much of a day's or night's absence from camp for one or two of their number; but when the missing ones failed to show up in reasonable time there would be a search. And Venters was afraid of that.

"A good tracker could trail me," he muttered. "And I'd be cornered here. Let's see. Rustlers are a lazy set when they're not on the ride. I'll risk it. Then I'll change my hiding place."

He carefully cleaned and reloaded his guns. When he rose to go he bent a long glance down upon the unconscious girl. Then, ordering Whitie and Ring to keep guard, he left the camp.

The safest cover lay close under the wall of the cañon, and here through the dense thickets Venters made his slow, listening advance toward the oval. Upon gaining the wide opening he decided to cross it and follow the left wall till he came to the cattle trail. He scanned the oval as keenly as if hunting for antelope. Then, stooping, he stole from one cover to another, taking advantage of rocks and bunches of sage, until he had reached the thickets under the opposite wall. Once there, he exercised extreme caution in his surveys of the ground ahead, but increased his speed when moving. Dodging from bush to bush he passed the mouths of two cañons, and in the entrance of a third cañon he crossed a wash of swift, clear water, to come abruptly upon the cattle trail.

It followed the low bank of the wash, and, keeping it in sight, Venters hugged the line of sage and thicket. Like the curves of a serpent the cañon wound for a mile or more and then opened into a valley. Patches of red showed clear against the purple of sage, and farther out on the level dotted strings of red led away to the wall of rock.

"Ha, the red herd!" exclaimed Venters.

Then dots of white and black told him there were cattle of other colors in this inclosed valley. Oldring, the rustler, was also a rancher. Venters's calculating eye took count of stock that outnumbered the red herd.

"What a range!" went on Venters. "Water and grass enough for fifty thousand head, and no riders needed!"

After his first burst of surprise and rapid calculation Venters lost no time there, but slunk again into the sage on his back trail. With the discovery of Oldring's hidden cattle-range had come enlightenment on several problems. Here the rustler kept his stock; here was Jane Withersteen's red herd; here were the few cattle that had disappeared from the Cottonwoods slopes during the last two years. Until Oldring had driven the red herd his thefts of cattle for that time had not been more than enough to supply meat for his men. Of late no drives had been reported from Sterling or the villages north. And Venters knew that the riders had wondered at Oldring's inactivity in that particular field. He and his band had been active enough in their visits to Glaze and Cottonwoods; they always had gold; but of late the amount gambled away and drunk and thrown away in the villages had given rise to much conjecture. Oldring's more frequent visits had resulted in new saloons, and where there had formerly been one raid or shooting fray in the little hamlets there were now many. Perhaps Oldring had another range farther on up the pass, and from there drove the cattle to distant Utah towns where he was little known. But Venters came finally to doubt this. And, from what he had learned in the last few days, a belief began to form in Venters's mind that Oldring's intimidations of the villages and the mystery of the Masked Rider, with his alleged evil deeds, and the fierce resistance offered any trailing riders, and the rustling of cattle—these things were only the craft of the rustler-chief to conceal his real life and purpose and work in Deception Pass.

And like a scouting Indian Venters crawled through the sage of the oval valley, crossed trail after trail on the north side, and at last entered the cañon out of which headed the cattle trail, and into which he had watched the rustlers disappear.

If he had used caution before, now he strained every nerve to force himself to creeping stealth and to sensitiveness of ear. He crawled along so hidden that he could not use his eyes except to aid himself in the toilsome progress through the brakes and ruins of cliff-wall. Yet from time to time, as he rested, he saw the massive red walls growing higher and wilder, more looming and broken. He made note of the fact that he was turning and climbing. The sage and thickets of oak and brakes of alder gave place to piñon pine growing out of rocky soil. Suddenly a low, dull murmur assailed his ears. At first he thought it was thunder, then the slipping of a weathered slope of rock. But it was incessant, and as he progressed it filled out deeper and from a murmur changed into a soft roar.

"Falling water," he said. "There's volume to that. I wonder if it's the stream I lost."

The roar bothered him, for he could hear nothing else. Likewise, however, no rustlers could hear him. Emboldened by this, and sure that nothing but a bird could see him, he arose from his hands and knees to hurry on. An opening in the piñons warned him that he was nearing the height of slope.

He gained it, and dropped low with a burst of astonishment. Before him stretched a short cañon with rounded stone floor bare of grass or sage or tree, and with curved, shelving walls. A broad rippling stream flowed toward him, and at the back of the cañon a waterfall burst from a wide rent in the cliff, and, bounding down in two green steps, spread into a long white sheet.

If Venters had not been indubitably certain that he had entered the right cañon his astonishment would not have been so great. There had been no breaks in the walls, no side cañons entering this one where the rustlers' tracks and the cattle trail had guided him, and, therefore, he could not be wrong. But here the cañon ended, and presumably the trails also.

"That cattle trail headed out of here," Venters kept saying to himself. "It headed out. Now what I want to know is how on earth did cattle ever get in here?"

If he could be sure of anything it was of the careful scrutiny he had given that cattle track, every hoof-mark of which headed straight west. He was now looking east at an immense round boxed corner of cañon down which tumbled a thin, white veil of water, scarcely twenty yards wide. Somehow, somewhere, his calculations had gone wrong. For the first time in years he found himself doubting his rider's skill in finding tracks, and his memory of what he had actually seen. In his anxiety to keep under cover he must have lost himself in this offshoot of Deception Pass, and thereby, in some unaccountable manner, missed the cañon with the trails. There was nothing else for him to think. Rustlers could not fly, nor cattle jump down thousand-foot precipices. He was only proving what the sage-riders had long said of this labyrinthine system of deceitful cañons and valleys—trails led down into Deception Pass, but no rider had ever followed them.

On a sudden he heard above the soft roar of the waterfall an unusual sound that he could not define. He dropped flat behind a stone and listened. From the direction he had come swelled something that resembled a strange muffled pounding and splashing and ringing. Despite his nerve the chill sweat began to dampen his forehead. What might not be possible in this stone-walled maze of mystery? The unnatural sound passed beyond him as he lay gripping his rifle and fighting for coolness. Then from the open came the sound, now distinct and different. Venters

recognized a hobble-bell of a horse, and the cracking of iron on sub-
merged stones, and the hollow splash of hoofs in water.

Relief surged over him. His mind caught again at realities, and curiosity prompted him to peep from behind the rock.

In the middle of the stream waded a long string of packed burros
driven by three superbly mounted men. Had Venters met these dark-
clothed, dark-visaged, heavily armed men anywhere in Utah, let alone in
this robbers' retreat, he would have recognized them as rustlers. The
discerning eye of a rider saw the signs of a long, arduous trip. These men
were packing in supplies from one of the northern villages. They were
tired, and their horses were almost played out, and the burros plodded
on, after the manner of their kind when exhausted, faithful and patient,
but as if every weary, splashing, slipping step would be their last.

All this Venters noted in one glance. After that he watched with a
thrilling eagerness. Straight at the waterfall the rustlers drove the burros, and straight through the middle, where the water spread into a fleecy,
thin film like dissolving smoke. Following closely, the rustlers rode into
this white mist, showing in bold black relief for an instant, and then they
vanished.

Venters drew a full breath that rushed out in brief and sudden utterance.

"Good heaven! Of all the holes for a rustler! . . . There's a cavern
under that waterfall, and a passageway leading out to a cañon beyond.
Oldring hides in there. He needs only to guard a trail leading down from
the sage-flat above. Little danger of this outlet to the pass being discovered. I stumbled on it by luck, after I had given up. And now I know the
truth of what puzzled me most—why that cattle trail was wet!"

He wheeled and ran down the slope, and out to the level of the sage-
brush. Returning he had no time to spare, only now and then, between
dashes, a moment when he stopped to cast sharp eyes ahead. The abundant grass left no trace of his trail. Short work he made of the distance to
the circle of cañons. He doubted that he would ever see it again; he knew
he never wanted to; yet he looked at the red corners and towers with the
eyes of a rider picturing landmarks never to be forgotten.

Here he spent a panting moment in a slow-circling gaze of the sage-
oval and the gaps between the bluffs. Nothing stirred except the gentle

wave of the tips of the brush. Then he pressed on past the mouths of several cañons and over ground new to him, now close under the eastern wall. This latter part proved to be easy traveling, well screened from possible observation from the north and west, and he soon covered it and felt safer in the deepening shade of his own cañon. Then the huge, notched bulge of red rim loomed over him, a mark by which he knew again the deep cove where his camp lay hidden. As he penetrated the thicket, safe again for the present, his thoughts reverted to the girl he had left there. The afternoon had far advanced. How would he find her? He ran into camp, frightening the dogs.

The girl lay with wide open, dark eyes, and they dilated when he knelt beside her. The flush of fever shone in her cheeks. He lifted her and held water to her dry lips, and felt an inexplicable sense of lightness as he saw her swallow in a slow, choking gulp. Gently he laid her back.

"Who—are—you?" she whispered, haltingly.

"I'm the man who shot you," he replied.

"You'll—not—kill me—now?"

"No, no."

"What—will—you—do—with me?"

"When you get better—strong enough—I'll take you back to the cañon where the rustlers ride through the waterfall."

As with a faint shadow from a flitting wing overhead, the marble whiteness of her face seemed to change.

"Don't—take—me—back—there!"

CHAPTER 6

THE MILL-WHEEL OF STEERS

Meantime, at the ranch, when Judkins's news had sent Venters on the trail of the rustlers, Jane Withersteen led the injured man to her house and with skilled fingers dressed the gunshot wound in his arm.

"Judkins, what do you think happened to my riders?"

"I—I'd rather not say," he replied.

"Tell me. Whatever you'll tell me I'll keep to myself. I'm beginning to worry about more than the loss of a herd of cattle. Venters hinted of— but tell me, Judkins."

"Well, Miss Withersteen, I think as Venters thinks—your riders have been called in."

"Judkins! . . . By whom?"

"You know who handles the reins of your Mormon riders."

"Do you dare insinuate that my churchmen have ordered in my riders?"

"I ain't insinuatin' nothin', Miss Withersteen," answered Judkins, with spirit. "I know what I'm talking about. I didn't want to tell you."

"Oh, I can't believe that! I'll not believe it! Would Tull leave my herds at the mercy of rustlers and wolves just because—because—? No, no! It's unbelievable."

"Yes, thet particular thing's onheard of around Cottonwoods. But, beggin' pardon, Miss Withersteen, there never was any other rich Mormon woman here on the border, let alone one thet's taken the bit between her teeth."

That was a bold thing for the reserved Judkins to say, but it did not anger her. This rider's crude hint of her spirit gave her a glimpse of what others might think. Humility and obedience had been hers always. But had she taken the bit between her teeth? Still she wavered. And then, with a quick spurt of warm blood along her veins, she thought of Black Star when he got the bit fast between his iron jaws and ran wild in the sage. If she ever started to run! Jane smothered the glow and burn within her, ashamed of a passion for freedom that opposed her duty.

"Judkins, go to the village," she said, "and when you have learned anything definite about my riders please come to me at once."

When he had gone Jane resolutely applied her mind to a number of tasks that of late had been neglected. Her father had trained her in the management of a hundred employees and the working of gardens and fields; and to keep record of the movements of cattle and riders. And beside the many other duties she had added to this work was one of extreme delicacy, such as required all her tact and ingenuity. It was an unobtrusive, almost secret aid which she rendered to the Gentile families of the village. Though Jane Withersteen never admitted so to herself, it amounted to no less than a system of charity. But for her invention of numberless kinds of employment, for which there was no actual need, these families of Gentiles, who had failed in a Mormon community, would have starved.

In aiding these poor people Jane thought she deceived her keen churchmen, but it was a kind of deceit for which she did not pray to be forgiven. Equally as difficult was the task of deceiving the Gentiles, for they were as proud as they were poor. It had been a great grief to her to discover how these people hated her people; and it had been a source of great joy that through her they had come to soften in hatred. At any time this work called for a clearness of mind that precluded anxiety and worry; but under the present circumstances it required all her vigor and obstinate tenacity to pin her attention upon her task.

Sunset came, bringing with the end of her labor a patient calmness and power to wait that had not been hers earlier in the day. She expected

Judkins, but he did not appear. Her house was always quiet; tonight, however, it seemed unusually so. At supper her women served her with a silent assiduity; it spoke what their sealed lips could not utter—the sympathy of Mormon women. Jerd came to her with the key of the great door of the stone stable, and to make his daily report about the horses. One of his daily duties was to give Black Star and Night and the other racers a ten-mile run. This day it had been omitted, and the boy grew confused in explanations that she had not asked for. She did inquire if he would return on the morrow, and Jerd, in mingled surprise and relief, assured her he would always work for her. Jane missed the rattle and trot, canter and gallop of the incoming riders on the hard trails. Dusk shaded the grove where she walked; the birds ceased singing; the wind sighed through the leaves of the cottonwoods, and the running water murmured down its stone-bedded channel. The glimmering of the first star was like the peace and beauty of the night. Her faith welled up in her heart and said that all would soon be right in her little world. She pictured Venters about his lonely campfire sitting between his faithful dogs. She prayed for his safety, for the success of his undertaking.

Early the next morning one of Jane's women brought in word that Judkins wished to speak to her. She hurried out, and in her surprise to see him armed with rifle and revolver, she forgot her intention to inquire about his wound.

"Judkins! Those guns? You never carried guns."

"It's high time, Miss Withersteen," he replied. "Will you come into the grove? It ain't jest exactly safe for me to be seen here."

She walked with him into the shade of the cottonwoods.

"What do you mean?"

"Miss Withersteen, I went to my mother's house last night. While there, some one knocked, an' a man asked for me. I went to the door. He wore a mask. He said I'd better not ride any more for Jane Withersteen. His voice was hoarse an' strange, disguised I reckon, like his face. He said no more, an' ran off in the dark."

"Did you know who he was?" asked Jane, in a low voice.

"Yes."

Jane did not ask to know; she did not want to know, she feared to know. All her calmness fled at a single thought.

"Thet's why I'm packin' guns," went on Judkins. "For I'll never quit ridin' for you, Miss Withersteen, till you let me go."

"Judkins, do you want to leave me?"

"Do I look thet way? Give me a hoss—a fast hoss, an' send me out on the sage."

"Oh, thank you, Judkins! You're more faithful than my own people. I ought not accept your loyalty—you might suffer more through it. But what in the world can I do? My head whirls. The wrong to Venters—the stolen herd—these masks, threats, this coil in the dark! I can't understand! But I feel something dark and terrible closing in around me."

"Miss Withersteen, it's all simple enough," said Judkins, earnestly. "Now please listen—an' beggin' your pardon—jest turn thet deaf Mormon ear aside, an' let me talk clear an' plain in the other. I went around to the saloons an' the stores an' the loafin' places yesterday. All your riders are in. There's talk of a vigilance band organized to hunt down rustlers. They call themselves 'The Riders.' Thet's the report—thet's the reason given for your riders leavin' you. Strange thet only a few riders of other ranchers joined the band! An' Tull's man, Jerry Card—he's the leader. I seen him an' his hoss. He ain't been to Glaze. I'm not easy to fool on the looks of a hoss thet's traveled the sage. Tull an' Jerry didn't ride to Glaze! . . . Well, I met Blake an' Dorn, both good friends of mine, usually, as far as their Mormon lights will let 'em go. But these fellers couldn't fool me, an' they didn't try very hard. I asked them, straight out like a man, why they left you like thet. I didn't forget to mention how you nursed Blake's poor old mother when she was sick, an' how good you was to Dorn's kids. They looked ashamed, Miss Withersteen. An' they jest froze up—thet dark set look thet makes them strange an' different to me. But I could tell the difference between thet first natural twinge of conscience, an' the later look of some secret thing. An' the difference I caught was thet they couldn't help themselves. They hadn't no say in the matter. They looked as if their bein' unfaithful to you was bein' faithful to a higher duty. An' there's the secret. Why, it's as plain as—as sight of my gun here."

"Plain! . . . My herds to wander in the sage—to be stolen! Jane Withersteen a poor woman! Her head to be brought low and her spirit broken! . . . Aye, Judkins, it's plain enough."

"Miss Withersteen, let me get what boys I can gather, an' hold the white herd. It's on the slope now, not ten miles out—three thousand head, an' all steers. They're wild, an' likely to stampede at the pop of a jack-rabbit's ears. We'll camp right with them, an' try to hold them."

"Judkins, I'll reward you some day for your service, unless all is taken from me. Get the boys and tell Jerd to give you pick of my horses, except Black Star and Night. But—do not shed blood for my cattle nor heedlessly risk your lives."

Jane Withersteen rushed to the silence and seclusion of her room, and there could not longer hold back the bursting of her wrath. She went stone-blind in the fury of a passion that had never before showed its power. Lying upon her bed, sightless, voiceless, she was a writhing, living flame. And she tossed there while her fury burned and burned, and finally burned itself out.

Then, weak and spent, she lay thinking, not of the oppression that would break her, but of this new revelation of self. Until the last few days there had been little in her life to rouse passions. Her forefathers had been Vikings, savage chieftains who bore no cross and brooked no hindrance to their will. Her father had inherited that temper; and at times, like antelope fleeing before fire on the slope, his people fled from his red rages. Jane Withersteen realized that the spirit of wrath and war had lain dormant in her. She shrank from black depths hitherto unsuspected. The one thing in man or woman that she scorned above all scorn, and which she could not forgive, was hate. Hate headed a flaming pathway straight to hell. All in a flash, beyond her control there had been in her a birth of fiery hate. And the man who had dragged her peaceful and loving spirit to this degradation was a minister of God's word, an Elder of her church, the counselor of her beloved Bishop.

The loss of herds and ranges, even of Amber Spring and the Old Stone House, no longer concerned Jane Withersteen; she faced the foremost thought of her life, what she now considered the mightiest problem—the salvation of her soul.

She knelt by her bedside and prayed; she prayed as she had never prayed in all her life—prayed to be forgiven for her sin; to be immune from that dark, hot hate; to love Tull as her minister, though she could not love him as a man; to do her duty by her church and people and those dependent upon her bounty; to hold reverence of God and womanhood inviolate.

When Jane Withersteen rose from that storm of wrath and prayer for help she was serene, calm, sure—a changed woman. She would do her duty as she saw it, live her life as her own truth guided her. She might never be able to marry a man of her choice, but she certainly never would become the wife of Tull. Her churchmen might take her cattle and horses, ranges and fields, her corrals and stables, the house of Withersteen and the water that nourished the village of Cottonwoods; but they could not force her to marry Tull, they could not change her decision or break her spirit. Once resigned to further loss, and sure of herself, Jane Withersteen attained a peace of mind that had not been hers for a year. She forgave Tull, and felt a melancholy regret over what she knew he considered duty, irrespective of his personal feeling for her. First of all, Tull, as he was a man, wanted her for himself; and secondly, he hoped to save her and her riches for his church. She did not believe that Tull had been actuated solely by his minister's zeal to save her soul. She doubted her interpretation of one of his dark sayings—that if she were lost to him she might as well be lost to heaven. Jane Withersteen's common sense took arms against the binding limits of her religion; and she doubted that her Bishop, whom she had been taught had direct communication with God—would damn her soul for refusing to marry a Mormon. As for Tull and his churchmen, when they had harassed her, perhaps made her poor, they would find her unchangeable, and then she would get back most of what she had lost. So she reasoned, true at last to her faith in all men, and in their ultimate goodness.

The clank of iron hoofs upon the stone courtyard drew her hurriedly from her retirement. There, beside his horse, stood Lassiter, his dark apparel and the great black gun-sheaths contrasting singularly with his gentle smile. Jane's active mind took up her interest in him and her half-determined desire to use what charm she had to foil his evident design in visiting Cottonwoods. If she could mitigate his hatred of Mormons, or at least keep him from killing more of them, not only would she be saving her people, but also be leading back this blood-spiller to some semblance of the human.

"Mornin', ma'am," he said, black sombrero in hand.

"Lassiter, I'm not an old woman, or even a madam," she replied, with her bright smile. "If you can't say Miss Withersteen—call me Jane."

"I reckon Jane would be easier. First names are always handy for me."

"Well, use mine, then. Lassiter, I'm glad to see you. I'm in trouble."

Then she told him of Judkins's return, of the driving of the red herd, of Venters's departure on Wrangle, and the calling-in of her riders.

"'Pears to me you're some smilin' an' pretty for a woman with so much trouble," he remarked.

"Lassiter! Are you paying me compliments? But, seriously, I've made up my mind not to be miserable. I've lost much, and I'll lose more. Nevertheless, I won't be sour, and I hope I'll never be unhappy—again."

Lassiter twisted his hat round and round, as was his way, and took his time in replying.

"Women are strange to me. I got to back-trailin' myself from them long ago. But I'd like a game woman. Might I ask, seein' as how you take this trouble, if you're goin' to fight?"

"Fight! How? Even if I would, I haven't a friend except that boy who doesn't dare stay in the village."

"I make bold to say, ma'am—Jane—that there's another, if you want him."

"Lassiter! . . . Thank you. But how can I accept you as a friend? Think! Why, you'd ride down into the village with those terrible guns and kill my enemies—who are also my churchmen."

"I reckon I might be riled up to jest about that," he replied, dryly.

She held out both hands to him.

"Lassiter! I'll accept your friendship—be proud of it—return it—if I may keep you from killing another Mormon."

"I'll tell you one thing," he said, bluntly, as the gray lightning formed in his eyes. "You're too good a woman to be sacrificed as you're goin' to be . . . No, I reckon you an' me can't be friends on such terms."

In her earnestness she stepped closer to him, repelled yet fascinated by the sudden transition of his moods. That he would fight for her was at once horrible and wonderful.

"You came here to kill a man—the man whom Milly Erne—"

"The man who dragged Milly Erne to hell—put it that way! . . . Jane Withersteen, yes, that's why I came here. I'd tell so much to no other livin' soul. . . . There're things such a woman as you'd never dream of—so don't mention her again. Not till you tell me the name of the man!"

"Tell you! I? Never!"

"I reckon you will. An' I'll never ask you. I'm a man of strange beliefs an' ways of thinkin', an' I seem to see into the future an' feel things hard to explain. The trail I've been followin' for so many years was twisted an' tangled, but it's straightenin' out now. An', Jane Withersteen, you crossed it long ago to ease poor Milly's agony. That, whether you want or not, makes Lassiter your friend. But you cross it now strangely to mean somethin' to me—God knows what!—unless by your noble blindness to incite me to greater hatred of Mormon men."

Jane felt swayed by a strength that far exceeded her own. In a clash of wills with this man she would go to the wall. If she were to influence him it must be wholly through womanly allurement. There was that about Lassiter which commanded her respect, she had abhorred his name; face to face with him, she found she feared only his deeds. His mystic suggestion, his foreshadowing of something that she was to mean to him, pierced deep into her mind. She believed fate had thrown in her way the lover or husband of Milly Erne. She believed that through her an evil man might be reclaimed. His allusion to what he called her blindness terrified her. Such a mistaken idea of his might unleash the bitter, fatal mood she sensed in him. At any cost she must placate this man; she knew the die was cast, and that if Lassiter did not soften to a woman's grace and beauty and wiles, then it would be because she could not make him.

"I reckon you'll hear no more such talk from me," Lassiter went on, presently. "Now, Miss Jane, I rode in to tell you that your herd of white steers is down on the slope behind them big ridges. An' I seen somethin' goin' on that'd be mighty interestin' to you, if you could see it. Have you a field glass?"

"Yes, I have two glasses. I'll get them and ride out with you. Wait, Lassiter, please," she said, and hurried within. Sending word to Jerd to saddle Black Star and fetch him to the court, she then went to her room and changed to the riding-clothes she always donned when going into the sage. In this male attire her mirror showed her a jaunty, handsome rider. If she expected some little meed of admiration from Lassiter, she had no cause for disappointment. The gentle smile that she liked, which made of him another person, slowly overspread his face.

"If I didn't take you for a boy!" he exclaimed. "It's powerful queer what difference clothes make. Now I've been some scared of your dignity, like when the other night you was all in white, but in this rig—"

Black Star came pounding into the court, dragging Jerd half off his feet, and he whistled at Lassiter's black. But at sight of Jane all his defiant lines seemed to soften, and with tosses of his beautiful head he whipped his bridle.

"Down, Black Star, down," said Jane.

He dropped his head, and, slowly lengthening, he bent one fore leg, then the other, and sank to his knees. Jane slipped her left foot in the stirrup, swung lightly into the saddle, and Black Star rose with a ringing stamp. It was not easy for Jane to hold him to a canter through the grove, and like the wind he broke when he saw the sage. Jane let him have a couple of miles of free running on the open trail, and then she coaxed him in and waited for her companion. Lassiter was not long in catching up, and presently they were riding side by side. It reminded her how she used to ride with Venters. Where was he now? She gazed far down the slope to the curved purple lines of Deception Pass, and involuntarily shut her eyes with a trembling stir of nameless fear.

"We'll turn off here," Lassiter said, "an' take to the sage a mile or so. The white herd is behind them big ridges."

"What are you going to show me?" asked Jane. "I'm prepared—don't be afraid."

He smiled as if he meant that bad news came swiftly enough without being presaged by speech.

When they reached the lee of a rolling ridge Lassiter dismounted, motioning to her to do likewise. They left the horses standing, bridles down. Then Lassiter, carrying the field glasses, began to lead the way up the slow rise of ground. Upon nearing the summit he halted her with a gesture.

"I reckon we'd see more if we didn't show ourselves against the sky," he said. "I was here less than a hour ago. Then the herd was seven or eight miles south, an' if they ain't bolted yet—"

"Lassiter! . . . Bolted?"

"That's what I said. Now let's see."

Jane climbed a few more paces behind him and then peeped over the ridge. Just beyond began a shallow swale that deepened and widened into a valley, and then swung to the left. Following the undulating sweep of sage, Jane saw the straggling lines and then the great body of the white herd. She knew enough about steers, even at a distance of four or five miles, to realize that something was in the wind. Bringing her field glass into use she moved it slowly from left to right, which action swept the whole herd into range. The stragglers were restless; the more compactly massed steers were browsing. Jane brought the glass back to the big sentinels of the herd, and she saw them trot with quick steps, stop short and toss wide horns, look everywhere, and then trot in another direction.

"Judkins hasn't been able to get his boys together yet," said Jane. "But he'll be there soon. I hope not too late. Lassiter, what's frightening those big leaders?"

"Nothin' jest on the minute," replied Lassiter. "Them steers are quietin' down. They've been scared, but not bad yet. I reckon the whole herd has moved a few miles this way since I was here."

"They didn't browse that distance—not in less than an hour. Cattle aren't sheep."

"No, they jest run it, an' that looks bad."

"Lassiter, what frightened them?" repeated Jane, impatiently.

"Put down your glass. You'll see at first better with a naked eye. Now look along them ridges on the other side of the herd, the ridges where the sun shines bright on the sage. . . . That's right. Now look an' look hard, an' wait."

Long-drawn moments of straining sight rewarded Jane with nothing save the low, purple rim of ridge and the shimmering sage.

"It's begun again!" whispered Lassiter, and he gripped her arm. "Watch. . . . There, did you see that?"

"No, no. Tell me what to look for?"

"A white flash—a kind of pin-point of quick light—a gleam as from sun shinin' on somethin' white."

Suddenly Jane's concentrated gaze caught a fleeting glint. Quickly she brought her glass to bear on the spot. Again the purple sage, magnified in color and size and wave, for long moments irritated her with its monotony. Then from out of the sage on the ridge flew up a broad, white object, flashed in the sunlight, and vanished. Like magic it was, and bewildered Jane.

"What on earth is that?"

"I reckon there's some one behind that ridge throwin' up a sheet or a white blanket to reflect the sunshine."

"Why?" queried Jane, more bewildered than ever.

"To stampede the herd," replied Lassiter, and his teeth clicked.

"Ah!" She made a fierce, passionate movement, clutched the glass tightly, shook as with the passing of a spasm, and then dropped her head. Presently she raised it to greet Lassiter with something like a smile.

"My righteous brethren are at work again," she said, in scorn. She had stifled the leap of her wrath, but for perhaps the first time in her life a bitter derision curled her lips. Lassiter's cool gray eyes seemed to pierce her. "I said I was prepared for anything; but that was hardly true. But why would they—anybody stampede my cattle?"

"That's a Mormon's godly way of bringin' a woman to her knees."

"Lassiter, I'll die before I ever bend my knees. I might be led; I won't be driven. Do you expect the herd to bolt?"

"I don't like the looks of them big steers. But you can never tell. Cattle sometimes stampede as easily as buffalo. Any little flash or move will start them. A rider gettin' down an' walkin' toward them sometimes will make them jump an' fly. Then again nothin' seems to scare them. But I reckon that white flare will do the biz. It's a new one on me, an' I've seen some ridin' an' rustlin'. It jest takes one of them God-fearin' Mormons to think of devilish tricks."

"Lassiter, might not this trick be done by Oldring's men?" asked Jane, ever grasping at straws.

"It might be, but it ain't," replied Lassiter. "Oldrin's an honest thief. He don't skulk behind ridges to scatter your cattle to the four winds. He rides down on you, an' if you don't like it you can throw a gun."

Jane bit her tongue to refrain from championing men who at the very moment were proving to her that they were little and mean compared even with rustlers.

"Look! . . . Jane, them leadin' steers have bolted! They're drawin' the stragglers, an' that'll pull the whole herd."

Jane was not quick enough to catch the details called out by Lassiter, but she saw the line of cattle lengthening. Then, like a stream of white bees pouring from a huge swarm, the steers stretched out from the main body. In a few moments, with astonishing rapidity, the whole herd got into motion. A faint roar of trampling hoofs came to Jane's ears, and gradually swelled: low, rolling clouds of dust began to rise above the sage.

"It's a stampede, an' a hummer," said Lassiter.

"Oh, Lassiter! The herd's running with the valley! It leads into the cañon! There's a straight jump-off!"

"I reckon they'll run into it, too. But that's a good many miles yet. An' Jane, this valley swings round almost north before it goes east. That stampede will pass within a mile of us."

The long, white, bobbing line of steers streaked swiftly through the sage, and a funnel-shaped dust-cloud arose at a low angle. A dull rumbling filled Jane's ears.

"I'm thinkin' of millin' that herd," said Lassiter. His gray glance swept up the slope to the west. "There's some specks an' dust way off toward the village. Mebbe that's Judkins an' his boys. It ain't likely he'll get here in time to help. You'd better hold Black Star here on this high ridge."

He ran to his horse, and, throwing off saddle-bags and tightening the cinches, he leaped astride and galloped straight down across the valley.

Jane went for Black Star, and, leading him to the summit of the ridge, she mounted and faced the valley with excitement and expectancy. She had heard of milling stampeded cattle, and knew it was a feat accomplished by only the most daring riders.

The white herd was now strung out in a line two miles long. The dull rumble of thousands of hoofs deepened into continuous low thunder, and as the steers swept swiftly closer the thunder became a heavy roll. Lassiter crossed in a few moments the level of the valley to the eastern rise of ground and there waited the coming of the herd. Presently, as the head of the white line reached a point opposite to where Jane stood, Lassiter spurred his black into a run.

Jane saw him take a position on the off side of the leaders of the stampede, and there he rode. It was like a race. They swept on down the valley, and when the end of the white line neared Lassiter's first stand the head had begun to swing round to the west. It swung slowly and stubbornly, yet surely, and gradually assumed a long, beautiful curve of moving white. To Jane's amaze she saw the leaders swinging, turning till they headed back toward her and up the valley. Out to the right of these wild, plunging steers ran Lassiter's black, and Jane's keen eye appreciated the fleet stride and sure-footedness of the blind horse. Then it seemed that the herd moved in a great curve, a huge half-moon, with the points of head and tail almost opposite, and a mile apart. But Lassiter relentlessly crowded the leaders, sheering them to the left, turning them little by little. And the dust-blinded wild followers plunged on madly in the tracks of their leaders. This ever-moving, ever-changing curve of steers rolled toward Jane, and when below her, scarce half a mile, it began to narrow and close into a circle. Lassiter had ridden parallel with her position, turned toward her, then aside, and now he was riding directly away from her, all the time pushing the head of that bobbing line inward.

It was then that Jane, suddenly understanding Lassiter's feat, stared and gasped at the riding of this intrepid man. His horse was fleet and tireless, but blind. He had pushed the leaders around and around till they were about to turn in on the inner side of the end of that line of steers. The leaders were already running in a circle; the end of the herd was still running almost straight. But soon they would be wheeling. Then, when Lassiter had the circle formed, how would he escape? With Jane Withersteen prayer was as ready as praise; and she prayed for this man's safety. A circle of dust began to collect. Dimly, as through a yellow veil, Jane saw Lassiter press the leaders inward to close the gap in the sage. She lost sight of him in the dust; again she thought she saw the black, riderless now, rear and drag himself and fall. Lassiter had been thrown—lost! Then he reappeared running out of the dust into the sage. He had escaped, and she breathed again.

Spellbound, Jane Withersteen watched this stupendous mill-wheel of steers. Here was the milling of the herd. The white running circle closed in upon the open space of sage. And the dust circles closed above into a pall. The ground quaked and the incessant thunder of pounding hoofs rolled on. Jane felt deafened, yet she thrilled to a new sound. As the circle of sage lessened the steers began to bawl, and when it closed entirely there came a great upheaval in the center, and a terrible thumping of heads and clicking of horns. Bawling, climbing, goring, the great mass of steers on the inside wrestled in a crashing din, heaved and groaned under the pressure. Then came a dead-lock. The inner strife ceased, and the hideous roar and crash. Movement went on in the outer circle, and that, too, gradually stilled. The white herd had come to a stop, and the pall of yellow dust began to drift away on the wind.

Jane Withersteen waited on the ridge with full and grateful heart. Lassiter appeared, making his weary way toward her through the sage. And up on the slope Judkins rode into sight with his troop of boys. For the present, at least, the white herd would be looked after.

When Lassiter reached her and laid his hand on Black Star's mane, Jane could not find speech.

"Killed—my—hoss," he panted.

"Oh! I'm sorry," cried Jane. "Lassiter! I know you can't replace him, but I'll give you any one of my racers—Bells, or Night, even Black Star."

"I'll take a fast hoss, Jane, but not one of your favorites," he replied. "Only—will you let me have Black Star now an' ride him over there an' head off them fellers who stampeded the herd?"

He pointed to several moving specks of black and puffs of dust in the purple sage.

"I can head them off with this hoss, an' then—"

"Then, Lassiter?"

"They'll never stampede no more cattle."

"Oh! No! No! . . . Lassiter, I won't let you go!"

But a flush of fire flamed in her cheeks, and her trembling hands shook Black Star's bridle, and her eyes fell before Lassiter's.

CHAPTER 7

THE DAUGHTER OF WITHERSTEEN

Lassiter, will you be my rider?" Jane had asked him.

"I reckon so," he had replied.

Few as the words were, Jane knew how infinitely much they implied. She wanted him to take charge of her cattle and horses and ranges, and save them if that were possible. Yet, though she could not have spoken aloud all she meant, she was perfectly honest with herself. Whatever the price to be paid, she must keep Lassiter close to her; she must shield from him the man who had lured Milly Erne to Cottonwoods. In her fear she so controlled her mind that she did not whisper this Mormon's name to her own soul, she did not even think it. Besides, beyond this thing she regarded as a sacred obligation thrust upon her, was the need of a helper, of a friend, of a champion in this critical time. If she could rule this gunman, as Venters had called him, if she could even keep him from shedding blood, what strategy to play his name and his presence against the game of oppression her churchmen were waging against her? Never would she forget the effect upon Tull and his men when Venters shouted Lassiter's name. If she could not wholly control Lassiter, then what she could do might put off the fatal day.

One of her sage racers was a dark bay, and she called him Bells because of the way he struck his iron shoes on the stones. When Jerd led out this slender, beautifully built horse Lassiter suddenly became all eyes. A rider's love of a thoroughbred shone in them. Round and round Bells he walked, plainly weakening all the time in his determination not to take one of Jane's favorite racers.

"Lassiter, you're half horse, and Bells sees it already," said Jane, laughing. "Look at his eyes. He likes you. He'll love you, too. How can you resist him? Oh, Lassiter, but Bells can run! It's nip and tuck between him and Wrangle, and only Black Star can beat him. He's too spirited a horse for a woman. Take him. He's yours."

"I jest am weak where a hoss's concerned," said Lassiter. "I'll take him, an' I'll take your orders, ma'am."

"Well, I'm glad, but never mind the ma'am. Let it still be Jane."

From that hour, it seemed, Lassiter was always in the saddle, riding early and late; and coincident with his part in Jane's affairs the days assumed their old tranquillity. Her intelligence told her this was only the lull before the storm, but her faith would not have it so.

She resumed her visits to the village, and upon one of these she encountered Tull. He greeted her as he had before any trouble came between them, and she, responsive to peace if not quick to forget, met him halfway with manner almost cheerful. He regretted the loss of her cattle; he assured her that the vigilantes which had been organized would soon rout the rustlers; when that had been accomplished her riders would likely return to her.

"You've done a headstrong thing to hire this man Lassiter," Tull went on, severely. "He came to Cottonwoods with evil intent."

"I had to have somebody. And perhaps making him my rider may turn out best in the end for the Mormons of Cottonwoods."

"You mean to stay his hand?"

"I do—if I can."

"A woman like you can do anything with a man. That would be well, and would atone in some measure for the errors you have made."

He bowed and passed on. Jane resumed her walk with conflicting thoughts. She resented Elder Tull's cold, impassive manner that looked down upon her as one who had incurred his just displeasure. Otherwise he would have been the same calm, dark-browed, impenetrable man she

had known for ten years. In fact, except when he had revealed his passion
in the matter of the seizing of Venters, she had never dreamed he could
be other than the grave, reproving preacher. He stood out now a strange,
secretive man. She would have thought better of him if he had picked up
the threads of their quarrel where they had parted. Was Tull what he appeared to be? The question flung itself involuntarily over Jane Withersteen's inhibitive habit of faith without question. And she refused to
answer it. Tull could not fight in the open. Venters had said, Lassiter had
said, that her Elder shirked fight and worked in the dark. Just now in this
meeting Tull had ignored the fact that he had sued, exhorted, demanded
that she marry him. He made no mention of Venters. His manner was
that of the minister who had been outraged, but who overlooked the
frailties of a woman. Beyond question he seemed unutterably aloof from
all knowledge of pressure being brought to bear upon her, absolutely guilt-
less of any connection with secret power over riders, with night journeys,
with rustlers and stampedes of cattle. And that convinced her again of
unjust suspicions. But it was convincement through an obstinate faith.
She shuddered as she accepted it; and that shudder was the nucleus of a
terrible revolt.

Jane turned into one of the wide lanes leading from the main street
and entered a huge, shady yard. Here were sweet-smelling clover, alfalfa,
flowers, and vegetables, all growing in happy confusion. And like these
fresh green things were the dozens of babies, tots, toddlers, noisy urchins,
laughing girls, a whole multitude of children of one family. For Collier
Brandt, the father of all this numerous progeny, was a Mormon with four
wives.

The big house where they lived was old, solid, picturesque, the lower
part built of logs, the upper of rough clapboards, with vines growing up
the outside stone chimneys. There were many wooden-shuttered windows, and one pretentious window of glass, proudly curtained in white.
As this house had four mistresses, it likewise had four separate sections,
not one of which communicated with another, and all had to be entered
from the outside.

In the shade of a wide, low, vine-roofed porch Jane found Brandt's
wives entertaining Bishop Dyer. They were motherly women, of comparatively similar ages, and plain-featured, and just at this moment anything

but grave. The Bishop was rather tall, of stout build, with iron-gray hair and beard, and eyes of light blue. They were merry now; but Jane had seen them when they were not, and then she feared him as she had feared her father.

The women flocked around her in welcome.

"Daughter of Withersteen," said the Bishop, gaily, as he took her hand, "you have not been prodigal of your gracious self of late. A Sabbath without you at service! I shall reprove Elder Tull."

"Bishop, the guilt is mine. I'll come to you and confess," Jane replied, lightly; but she felt the undercurrent of her words.

"Mormon love-making!" exclaimed the Bishop, rubbing his hands. "Tull keeps you all to himself."

"No. He is not courting me."

"What? The laggard! If he does not make haste I'll go a-courting myself up to Withersteen House."

There was laughter and further bantering by the Bishop, and then mild talk of village affairs, after which he took his leave, and Jane was left with her friend Mary Brandt.

"Jane, you're not yourself. Are you sad about the rustling of the cattle? But you have so many; you are so rich."

Then Jane confided in her, telling much, yet holding back her doubts and fears.

"Oh, why don't you marry Tull and be one of us?"

"But, Mary, I don't love Tull," said Jane, stubbornly.

"I don't blame you for that. But, Jane Withersteen, you've got to choose between the love of man and love of God. Often we Mormon women have to do that. It's not easy. The kind of happiness you want I wanted once. I never got it, nor will you, unless you throw away your soul. We've all watched your affair with Venters in fear and trembling. Some dreadful thing will come of it. You don't want him hanged or shot—or treated worse, as that Gentile boy was treated in Glaze for fooling round a Mormon woman. Marry Tull. It's your duty as a Mormon. You'll feel no rapture as his wife—but think of Heaven! Mormon women don't marry for what they expect on earth. Take up the cross, Jane. Remember your father found Amber Spring, built these old houses, brought Mormons here, and fathered them. You are the daughter of Withersteen!"

Jane left Mary Brandt and went to call upon other friends. They received her with the same glad welcome as had Mary, lavished upon her the pent-up affection of Mormon women, and let her go with her ears ringing of Tull, Venters, Lassiter, of duty to God and glory in Heaven.

"Verily," murmured Jane, "I don't know myself when, through all this, I remain unchanged—nay, more fixed of purpose."

She returned to the main street and bent her thoughtful steps toward the center of the village. A string of wagons drawn by oxen was lumbering along. These "sage-freighters," as they were called, hauled grain and flour and merchandise from Sterling; and Jane laughed suddenly in the midst of her humility at the thought that they were her property, as was one of the three stores for which they freighted goods. The water that flowed along the path at her feet, and turned into each cottage-yard to nourish garden and orchard, also was hers, no less her private property because she chose to give it free. Yet in this village of Cottonwoods, which her father had founded and which she maintained, she was not her own mistress; she was not to abide by her own choice of a husband. She was the daughter of Withersteen. Suppose she proved it, imperiously! But she quelled that proud temptation at its birth.

Nothing could have replaced the affection which the village people had for her; no power could have made her happy as the pleasure her presence gave. As she went on down the street, past the stores with their rude platform entrances, and the saloons, where tired horses stood with bridles dragging, she was again assured of what was the bread and wine of life to her—that she was loved. Dirty boys playing in the ditch, clerks, teamsters, riders, loungers on the corners, ranchers on dusty horses, little girls running errands, and women hurrying to the stores all looked up at her coming with glad eyes.

Jane's various calls and wandering steps at length led her to the Gentile quarter of the village. This was at the extreme southern end, and here some thirty Gentile families lived in huts and shacks and log-cabins and several dilapidated cottages. The fortunes of these inhabitants of Cottonwoods could be read in their abodes. Water they had in abundance, and therefore grass and fruit-trees and patches of alfalfa and vegetable gardens. Some of the men and boys had a few stray cattle, others obtained such intermittent employment as the Mormons reluctantly tendered them. But none of the families was prosperous, many were very poor, and some lived only by Jane Withersteen's beneficence.

As it made Jane happy to go among her own people, so it saddened her to come in contact with these Gentiles. Yet that was not because she was unwelcome; here she was gratefully received by the women, passionately by the children. But poverty and idleness, with their attendant wretchedness and sorrow, always hurt her. That she could alleviate this distress more now than ever before proved the adage that it was an ill wind that blew nobody good. While her Mormon riders were in her employ she had found few Gentiles who could stay with her, and now she was able to find employment for all the men and boys. No little shock was it to have man after man tell her that he dare not accept her kind offer.

"It won't do," said one Carson, an intelligent man who had seen better days. "We've had our warning. Plain and to the point! Now there's Judkins, he packs guns, and he can use them, and so can the daredevil boys he's hired. But they've little responsibility. Can we risk having our homes burned in our absence?"

Jane felt the stretching and chilling of the skin of her face as the blood left it.

"Carson, you and the others rent these houses?" she asked.

"You ought to know, Miss Withersteen. Some of them are yours."

"I know? . . . Carson, I never in my life took a day's labor for rent or a yearling calf or a bunch of grass, let alone gold."

"Bivens, your store-keeper, sees to that."

"Look here, Carson," went on Jane, hurriedly, and now her cheeks were burning. "You and Black and Willet pack your goods and move your families up to my cabins in the grove. They're far more comfortable than these. Then go to work for me. And if aught happens to you there I'll give you money—gold enough to leave Utah!"

The man choked and stammered, and then, as tears welled into his eyes, he found the use of his tongue and cursed. No gentle speech could ever have equaled that curse in eloquent expression of what he felt for Jane Withersteen. How strangely his look and tone reminded her of Lassiter!

"No, it won't do," he said, when he had somewhat recovered himself. "Miss Withersteen, there are things that you don't know, and there's not a soul among us who can tell you."

"I seem to be learning many things, Carson. Well, then, will you let me aid you—say till better times?"

"Yes, I will," he replied, with his face lighting up. "I see what it means to you, and you know what it means to me. Thank you! And if better times ever come I'll be only too happy to work for you."

"Better times will come. I trust God and have faith in man. Good day, Carson."

The lane opened out upon the sage-inclosed alfalfa fields, and the last habitation, at the end of that lane of hovels, was the meanest. Formerly it had been a shed; now it was a home. The broad leaves of a wide-spreading cottonwood sheltered the sunken roof of weathered boards. Like an Indian hut, it had one door. Round about it were a few scanty rows of vegetables, such as the hand of a weak woman had time and strength to cultivate. This little dwelling-place was just outside the village limits, and the widow who lived there had to carry her water from the nearest irrigation ditch. As Jane Withersteen entered the unfenced yard a child saw her, shrieked with joy, and came tearing toward her with curls flying. This child was a little girl of four called Fay. Her name suited her, for she was an elf, a sprite, a creature so fairy-like and beautiful that she seemed unearthly.

"Muvver sended for oo," cried Fay, as Jane kissed her, "an' oo never tome."

"I didn't know, Fay; but I've come now."

Fay was a child of outdoors, of the garden and ditch and field, and she was dirty and ragged. But rags and dirt did not hide her beauty. The one thin little bedraggled garment she wore half covered her fine, slim body. Red as cherries were her cheeks and lips; her eyes were violet blue, and the crown of her childish loveliness was the curling golden hair. All the children of Cottonwoods were Jane Withersteen's friends; she loved them all. But Fay was dearest to her. Fay had few playmates, for among the Gentile children there were none near her age, and the Mormon children were forbidden to play with her. So she was a shy, wild, lonely child.

"Muvver's sick," said Fay, leading Jane toward the door of the hut.

Jane went in. There was only one room, rather dark and bare, but it was clean and neat. A woman lay upon a bed.

"Mrs. Larkin, how are you?" asked Jane, anxiously.

"I've been pretty bad for a week, but I'm better now."

"You haven't been here all alone—with no one to wait on you?"

"Oh, no! My women neighbors are kind. They take turns coming in."

"Did you send for me?"

"Yes, several times."

"But I had no word—no messages ever got to me."

"I sent the boys, and they left word with your women that I was ill and would you please come."

A sudden deadly sickness seized Jane. She fought the weakness, as she fought to be above suspicious thoughts, and it passed, leaving her conscious of her utter impotence. That, too, passed as her spirit rebounded. But she had again caught a glimpse of dark underhand domination, running its secret lines this time into her own household. Like a spider in the blackness of night an unseen hand had begun to run these dark lines, to turn and twist them about her life, to plait and weave a web. Jane Withersteen knew it now, and in the realization further coolness and sureness came to her, and the fighting courage of her ancestors.

"Mrs. Larkin, you're better, and I'm so glad," said Jane. "But may I not do something for you—a turn at nursing, or send you things, or take care of Fay?"

"You're so good. Since my husband's been gone what would have become of Fay and me but for you? It was about Fay that I wanted to speak to you. This time I thought surely I'd die, and I was worried about Fay. Well, I'll be around all right shortly, but my strength's gone and I won't live long. So I may as well speak now. You remember you've been asking me to let you take Fay and bring her up as your daughter?"

"Indeed yes, I remember. I'll be happy to have her. But I hope the day—"

"Never mind that. The day'll come—sooner or later. I refused your offer, and now I'll tell you why."

"I know why," interposed Jane. "It's because you don't want her brought up as a Mormon."

"No, it wasn't altogether that." Mrs. Larkin raised her thin hand and laid it appealingly on Jane's. "I don't like to tell you. But—it's this: I told all my friends what you wanted. They know you, care for you, and they said for me to trust Fay to you. Women will talk, you know. It got to the ears of Mormons—gossip of your love for Fay and your wanting her. And it came straight back to me, in jealousy perhaps, that you wouldn't take Fay as much for love of her as because of your religious duty to bring up another girl for some Mormon to marry."

"That's a damnable lie!" cried Jane Withersteen.

"It was what made me hesitate," went on Mrs. Larkin, "but I never believed it at heart. And now I guess I'll let you—"

"Wait! Mrs. Larkin, I may have told little white lies in my life, but never a lie that mattered, that hurt any one. Now believe me. I love little Fay. If I had her near me I'd grow to worship her. When I asked for her I thought only of that love. . . . Let me prove this. You and Fay come to live with me. I've such a big house, and I'm so lonely. I'll help nurse you, take care of you. When you're better you can work for me. I'll keep little Fay and bring her up—without Mormon teaching. When she's grown, if she should want to leave me, I'll send her, and not empty-handed, back to Illinois where you came from. I promise you."

"I knew it was a lie," replied the mother, and she sank back upon her pillow with something of peace in her white, worn face. "Jane Withersteen, may Heaven bless you! I've been deeply grateful to you. But because you're a Mormon I never felt close to you till now. I don't know much about religion as religion, but your God and my God are the same."

CHAPTER 8

SURPRISE VALLEY

Back in that strange cañon, which Venters had found indeed a valley of surprises, the wounded girl's whispered appeal, almost a prayer, not to take her back to the rustlers crowned the events of the last few days with a confounding climax. That she should not want to return to them staggered Venters. Presently, as logical thought returned, her appeal confirmed his first impression—that she was more unfortunate than bad—and he experienced a sensation of gladness. If he had known before that Oldring's Masked Rider was a woman his opinion would have been formed and he would have considered her abandoned. But his first knowledge had come when he lifted a white face quivering in a convulsion of agony; he had heard God's name whispered by blood-stained lips; through her solemn and awful eyes he had caught a glimpse of her soul. And just now had come the entreaty to him: "Don't—take—me—back—there!"

Once for all Venters's quick mind formed a permanent conception of this poor girl. He based it, not upon what the chances of life had made her, but upon the revelation of dark eyes that pierced the infinite, upon a few pitiful, halting words that betrayed failure and wrong and misery, yet breathed the truth of a tragic fate rather than a natural leaning to evil.

"What's your name?" he inquired.

"Bess," she answered.

"Bess what?"

"That's enough—just Bess."

The red that deepened in her cheeks was not all the flush of fever. Venters marveled anew, and this time at the tint of shame in her face, at the momentary drooping of long lashes. She might be a rustler's girl, but she was still capable of shame; she might be dying, but she still clung to some little remnant of honor.

"Very well, Bess. It doesn't matter," he said. "But this matters—what shall I do with you?"

"Are—you—a rider?" she whispered.

"Not now. I was once. I drove the Withersteen herds. But I lost my place—lost all I owned—and now I'm—I'm a sort of outcast. My name's Bern Venters."

"You won't—take me—to Cottonwoods—or Glaze? I'd be—hanged."

"No, indeed. But I must do something with you. For it's not safe for me here. I shot that rustler who was with you. Sooner or later he'll be found, and then my tracks. I must find a safer hiding place where I can't be trailed."

"Leave me—here."

"Alone—to die!"

"Yes."

"I will not." Venters spoke shortly with a kind of ring in his voice.

"What—do you want—to do—with me?" Her whispering grew difficult, so low and faint that Venters had to stoop to hear her.

"Why, let's see," he replied, slowly. "I'd like to take you some place where I could watch by you, nurse you, till you're all right again."

"And—then?"

"Well, it'll be time to think of that when you're cured of your wound. It's a bad one. And—Bess, if you don't want to live—if you don't fight for life—you'll never—"

"Oh! I want—to live! I'm afraid—to die. But I'd rather—die—than go back—to—to—"

"To Oldring?" asked Venters, interrupting her in turn.

Her lips moved in an affirmative.

"I promise not to take you back to him or to Cottonwoods or to Glaze."

The mournful earnestness of her gaze suddenly shone with unutterable gratitude and wonder. And as suddenly Venters found her eyes beautiful as he had never seen or felt beauty. They were as dark-blue as the sky at night. Then the flashing changed to a long, thoughtful look, in which there was wistful, unconscious searching of his face, a look that trembled on the verge of hope and trust.

"I'll try—to live," she said. The broken whisper just reached his ears. "Do what—you want—with me."

"Rest then—don't worry—sleep," he replied.

Abruptly he arose, as if her words had been decision for him, and with a sharp command to the dogs he strode from the camp. Venters was conscious of an indefinite conflict of change within him. It seemed to be a vague passing of old moods, a dim coalescing of new forces, a moment of inexplicable transition. He was both cast down and uplifted. He wanted to think and think of the meaning, but he resolutely dispelled emotion. His imperative need at present was to find a safe retreat, and this called for action.

So he set out. It still wanted several hours before dark. This trip he turned to the left and wended his skulking way southward a mile or more to the opening of the valley, where lay the strange scrawled rocks. He did not, however, venture boldly out into the open sage, but clung to the right-hand wall and went along that till its perpendicular line broke into the long incline of bare stone.

Before proceeding farther he halted, studying the strange character of this slope and realizing that a moving black object could be seen far against such background. Before him ascended a gradual swell of smooth stone. It was hard, polished, and full of pockets worn by centuries of eddying rain-water. A hundred yards up began a line of grotesque cedar-trees, and they extended along the slope clear to its most southerly end. Beyond that end Venters wanted to get, and he concluded the cedars, few as they were, would afford some cover.

Therefore he climbed swiftly. The trees were farther up than he had estimated, though he had from long habit made allowance for the deceiving nature of distances in that country. When he gained the cover of cedars he paused to rest and look, and it was then he saw how the trees sprang from holes in the bare rock. Ages of rain had run down the slope, circling, eddying in depressions, wearing deep round holes. There had been dry seasons, accumulations of dust, wind-blown seeds, and cedars rose wonderfully out of solid rock. But these were not beautiful cedars. They were gnarled, twisted into weird contortions, as if growth were torture, dead at the tops, shrunken, gray, and old. Theirs had been a bitter fight, and Venters felt a strange sympathy for them. This country was hard on trees—and men.

He slipped from cedar to cedar, keeping them between him and the open valley. As he progressed, the belt of trees widened, and he kept to its upper margin. He passed shady pockets half full of water, and, as he marked the location for possible future need, he reflected that there had been no rain since the winter snows. From one of these shady holes a rabbit hopped out and squatted down, laying its ears flat.

Venters wanted fresh meat now more than when he had only himself to think of. But it would not do to fire his rifle there. So he broke off a cedar branch and threw it. He crippled the rabbit, which started to flounder up the slope. Venters did not wish to lose the meat, and he never allowed crippled game to escape, to die lingeringly in some covert. So after a careful glance below, and back toward the cañon, he began to chase the rabbit.

The fact that rabbits generally ran uphill was not new to him. But it presently seemed singular why this rabbit, that might have escaped downward, chose to ascend the slope. Venters knew then that it had a burrow higher up. More than once he jerked over to seize it, only in vain, for the rabbit by renewed effort eluded his grasp. Thus the chase continued on up the bare slope. The farther Venters climbed the more determined he grew to catch his quarry. At last, panting and sweating, he captured the rabbit at the foot of a steeper grade. Laying his rifle on the bulge of rising stone, he killed the animal and slung it from his belt.

Before starting down he waited to catch his breath. He had climbed far up that wonderful smooth slope, and had almost reached the base of yellow cliff, that rose skyward, a huge scarred and cracked bulk. It frowned down upon him as if to forbid further ascent. Venters bent over for his rifle, and, as he picked it up from where it leaned against the steeper grade, he saw several little nicks cut in the solid stone.

They were only a few inches deep and about a foot apart. Venters began to count them—one—two—three—four—on up to sixteen. That number carried his glance to the top of this first bulging bench of cliff-base. Above, after a more level offset, was still steeper slope, and the line of nicks kept on, to wind round a projecting corner of wall.

A casual glance would have passed by these little dents; if Venters had not known what they signified he would never have bestowed upon them the second glance. But he knew they had been cut there by hand, and, though age-worn, he recognized them as steps cut in the rock by the cliff-dwellers. With a pulse beginning to beat and hammer away his calmness, he eyed that indistinct line of steps, up to where the buttress of wall hid further sight of them. He knew that behind the corner of stone would be a cave or a crack which could never be suspected from below. Chance, that had sported with him of late, now directed him to a probable hiding place. Again he laid aside his rifle, and, removing boots and belt, he began to walk up the steps. Like a mountain goat, he was agile, sure-footed, and he mounted the first bench without bending to use his hands. The next ascent took grip of fingers as well as toes, but he climbed steadily, swiftly, to reach the projecting corner, and slipped around it. Here he faced a notch in the cliff. At the apex he turned abruptly into a ragged vent that split the ponderous wall clear to the top, showing a narrow streak of blue sky.

At the base this vent was dark, cool, and smelled of dry, musty dust. It zigzagged so that he could not see ahead more than a few yards at a time. He noticed tracks of wildcats and rabbits in the dusty floor. At every turn he expected to come upon a huge cavern full of little square stone houses, each with a small aperture like a staring dark eye. The passage lightened and widened, and opened at the foot of a narrow, steep, ascending chute.

Venters had a moment's notice of the rock, which was of the same smoothness and hardness as the slope below, before his gaze went irresistibly upward to the precipitous walls of this wide ladder of granite. These were ruined walls of yellow sandstone, and so split and splintered, so overhanging with great sections of balancing rim, so impending with tremendous crumbling crags, that Venters caught his breath sharply, and, appalled, he instinctively recoiled as if a step upward might jar the ponderous cliffs from their foundation. Indeed, it seemed that these ruined cliffs were but awaiting a breath of wind to collapse and come tumbling down. Venters hesitated. It would be a foolhardy man who risked his life under the leaning, waiting avalanches of rock in that gigantic split. Yet how many years had they leaned there without falling! At the bottom of the incline was an immense heap of weathered sandstone all crumbling to dust, but there were no huge rocks as large as houses, such as rested so lightly and frightfully above, waiting patiently and inevitably to crash down. Slowly split from the parent rock by the weathering process, and carved and sculptured by ages of wind and rain, they waited their moment. Venters felt how foolish it was for him to fear these broken walls; to fear that, after they had endured for thousands of years, the moment of his passing should be the one for them to slip. Yet he feared it.

"What a place to hide!" muttered Venters. "I'll climb—I'll see where this thing goes. If only I can find water!"

With teeth tight shut he essayed the incline. And as he climbed he bent his eyes downward. This, however, after a little grew impossible; he had to look to obey his eager, curious mind. He raised his glance and saw light between row on row of shafts and pinnacles and crags that stood out from the main wall. Some leaned against the cliff, others against each other; many stood sheer and alone; all were crumbling, cracked, rotten. It was a place of yellow, ragged ruin. The passage narrowed as he went up; it became a slant, hard for him to stick on; it was smooth as marble. Finally he surmounted it, surprised to find the walls still several hundred feet high, and a narrow gorge leading down on the other side. This was a divide between two inclines, about twenty yards wide. At one side stood an enormous rock. Venters gave it a second glance, because it rested on a pedestal. It attracted closer attention. It was like a colossal pear of stone standing on its stem. Around the bottom were thousands of little nicks just distinguishable to the eye. They were marks of stone hatchets. The cliff-dwellers had chipped and chipped away at this boulder till it rested its tremendous bulk upon a mere pin-point of its surface. Venters pondered. Why had the little stone-men hacked away at that big boulder? It bore no semblance to a statue or an idol or a godhead or a sphinx. Instinctively he put his hands on it and pushed; then his shoulder and heaved. The stone seemed to groan, to stir, to grate, and then to move. It tipped a little downward and hung balancing for a long instant, slowly returned, rocked slightly, groaned, and settled back to its former position.

Venters divined its significance. It had been meant for defense. The cliff-dwellers, driven by dreaded enemies to this last stand, had cunningly cut the rock until it balanced perfectly, ready to be dislodged by strong hands. Just below it leaned a tottering crag that would have toppled, starting an avalanche on an acclivity where no sliding mass could stop. Crags and pinnacles, splintered cliffs, and leaning shafts and monuments, would have thundered down to block forever the outlet to Deception Pass.

"That was a narrow shave for me," said Venters, soberly. "A balancing rock! The cliff-dwellers never had to roll it. They died, vanished, and here the rock stands, probably little changed. . . . But it might serve another lonely dweller of the cliffs. I'll hide up here somewhere, if I can only find water."

He descended the gorge on the other side. The slope was gradual, the space narrow, the course straight for many rods. A gloom hung between the up-sweeping walls. In a turn the passage narrowed to scarce a dozen feet, and here was darkness of night. But light shone ahead; another abrupt turn brought day again, and then wide open space.

Above Venters loomed a wonderful arch of stone bridging the cañon rims, and through the enormous round portal gleamed and glistened a beautiful valley shining under sunset gold reflected by surrounding cliffs. He gave a start of surprise. The valley was a cove a mile long, half that wide, and its enclosing walls were smooth and stained, and curved inward, forming great caves. He decided that its floor was far higher than the level of Deception Pass and the intersecting cañons. No purple sage colored this valley floor. Instead there were the white of aspens, streaks of branch and slender trunk glistening from the green of leaves, and the darker green of oaks, and through the middle of this forest, from wall to wall, ran a winding line of brilliant green which marked the course of cottonwoods and willows.

"There's water here—and this is the place for me," said Venters. "Only birds can peep over those walls. I've gone Oldring one better."

Venters waited no longer, and turned swiftly to retrace his steps. He named the cañon Surprise Valley and the huge boulder that guarded the outlet Balancing Rock. Going down he did not find himself attended by such fears as had beset him in the climb; still, he was not easy in mind and could not occupy himself with plans of moving the girl and his outfit until he had descended to the notch. There he rested a moment and looked about him. The pass was darkening with the approach of night. At the corner of the wall, where the stone steps turned, he saw a spur of rock that would serve to hold the noose of a lasso. He needed no more aid to scale that place. As he intended to make the move under cover of darkness, he wanted most to be able to tell where to climb up. So, taking several small stones with him, he stepped and slid down to the edge of the slope where he had left his rifle and boots. Here he placed the stones some yards apart. He left the rabbit lying upon the bench where the steps began. Then he addressed a keen-sighted, remembering gaze to the rim-wall above. It was serrated, and between two spears of rock, directly in line with his position, showed a zigzag crack that at night would let through the gleam of sky. This settled, he put on his belt and boots and prepared to descend. Some consideration was necessary to decide whether or not to leave his rifle there. On the return, carrying the girl and a pack, it would be added encumbrance; and after debating the matter he left the rifle leaning against the bench. As he went straight down the slope he halted every few rods to look up at his mark on the rim. It changed, but he fixed each change in his memory. When he reached the first cedar-tree, he tied his scarf upon a dead branch, and then hurried toward camp, having no more concern about finding his trail upon the return trip.

Darkness soon emboldened and lent him greater speed. It occurred to him, as he glided into the grassy glade near camp and heard the whinny of a horse, that he had forgotten Wrangle. The big sorrel could not be gotten into Surprise Valley. He would have to be left here.

Venters determined at once to lead the other horses out through the thicket and turn them loose. The farther they wandered from this cañon the better it would suit him. He easily descried Wrangle through the gloom, but the others were not in sight. Venters whistled low for the dogs, and when they came trotting to him he sent them out to search for the horses, and followed. It soon developed that they were not in the glade nor the thicket. Venters grew cold and rigid at the thought of rustlers having entered his retreat. But the thought passed, for the demeanor of Ring and Whitie reassured him. The horses had wandered away.

Under the clump of silver spruces hung a denser mantle of darkness, yet not so thick that Venters's night-practiced eyes could not catch the white oval of a still face. He bent over it with a slight suspension of breath that was both caution lest he frighten her and chill uncertainty of feeling lest he find her dead. But she slept, and he arose to renewed activity.

He packed his saddle-bags. The dogs were hungry, they whined about him and nosed his busy hands; but he took no time to feed them nor to satisfy his own hunger. He slung the saddle-bags over his shoulders and made them secure with his lasso. Then he wrapped the blankets closer about the girl and lifted her in his arms. Wrangle whinnied and thumped the ground as Venters passed him with the dogs. The sorrel knew he was being left behind, and was not sure whether he liked it or not. Venters went on and entered the thicket. Here he had to feel his way in pitch blackness and to wedge his progress between the close saplings. Time meant little to him now that he had started, and he edged along with slow side movement till he got clear of the thicket. Ring and Whitie stood waiting for him. Taking to the open aisles and patches of the sage, he walked guardedly, careful not to stumble or step in dust or strike against spreading sage-branches.

If he were burdened he did not feel it. From time to time, when he passed out of the black lines of shade into the wan starlight, he glanced at the white face of the girl lying in his arms. She had not awakened from her sleep or stupor. He did not rest until he cleared the black gate of the cañon. Then he leaned against a stone breast-high to him and gently released the girl from his hold. His brow and hair and the palms of his hands were wet, and there was a kind of nervous contraction of his muscles. They seemed to ripple and string tense. He had a desire to hurry and no sense of fatigue. A wind blew the scent of sage in his face. The first early blackness of night passed with the brightening of the stars. Somewhere back on his trail a coyote yelped, splitting the dead silence. Venters's faculties seemed singularly acute.

He lifted the girl again and pressed on. The valley afforded better traveling than the cañon. It was lighter, freer of sage, and there were no rocks. Soon, out of the pale gloom shone a still paler thing, and that was the low swell of slope. Venters mounted it, and his dogs walked beside him. Once upon the stone he slowed to snail pace, straining his sight to avoid the pockets and holes. Foot by foot he went up. The weird cedars, like great demons and witches chained to the rock and writhing in silent anguish, loomed up with wide and twisting naked arms. Venters crossed this belt of cedars, skirted the upper border, and recognized the tree he had marked, even before he saw his waving scarf.

Here he knelt and deposited the girl gently feet first, and slowly laid her out full length. What he feared was to reopen one of her wounds. If he gave her a violent jar, or slipped and fell! But the supreme confidence so strangely felt that night admitted of no such blunders.

The slope before him seemed to swell into obscurity, to lose its definite outline in a misty, opaque cloud that shaded into the over-shadowing wall. He scanned the rim where the serrated points speared the sky, and he found the zigzag crack. It was dim, only a shade lighter than the dark ramparts; but he distinguished it, and that served.

Lifting the girl, he stepped upward, closely attending to the nature of the path under his feet. After a few steps he stopped to mark his line with the crack in the rim. The dogs clung closer to him. While chasing the rabbit this slope had appeared interminable to him; now, burdened as he was, he did not think of length or height or toil. He remembered only to avoid a misstep and to keep his direction. He climbed on, with frequent stops to watch the rim, and before he dreamed of gaining the bench he bumped his knees into it, and saw, in the dim gray light, his rifle and the rabbit. He had come straight up without mishap or swerving off his course, and his shut teeth unlocked.

As he laid the girl down in the shallow hollow of the little ridge, with her white face upturned, she opened her eyes. Wide, staring, black, at once like both the night and the stars, they made her face seem still whiter.

"Is—it—you?" she asked, faintly.

"Yes," replied Venters.

"Oh! Where—are we?"

"I'm taking you to a safe place where no one will ever find you. I must climb a little here and call the dogs. Don't be afraid. I'll soon come for you."

She said no more. Her eyes watched him steadily for a moment and then closed. Venters pulled off his boots and then felt for the little steps in the rock. The shade of the cliff above obscured the point he wanted to gain, but he could see dimly a few feet before him. What he had attempted with care he now went at with surpassing lightness. Buoyant, rapid, sure, he attained the corner of wall and slipped around it. Here he could not see a hand before his face, so he groped along, found a little flat space, and there removed the saddle-bags. The lasso he took back with him to the corner and looped the noose over the spur of rock.

"Ring—Whitie—come," he called softly.

Low whines came up from below.

"Here! Come, Whitie—Ring," he repeated, this time sharply.

Then followed scraping of claws and pattering of feet; and out of the gray gloom below him swiftly climbed the dogs to reach his side and pass beyond.

Venters descended, holding to the lasso. He tested its strength by throwing all his weight upon it. Then he gathered the girl up, and holding her securely in his left arm, he began to climb, at every few steps jerking his right hand upward along the lasso. It sagged at each forward movement he made, but he balanced himself lightly during the interval when he lacked the support of a taut rope. He climbed as if he had wings, the strength of a giant, and knew not the sense of fear. The sharp corner of cliff seemed to cut out of the darkness. He reached it and the protruding shelf, and then, entering the black shade of the notch, he moved blindly but surely to the place where he had left the saddle-bags. He heard the dogs, though he could not see them. Once more he carefully placed the girl at his feet. Then, on hands and knees, he went over the little flat space feeling for stones. He removed a number, and, scraping the deep dust into a heap, he unfolded the outer blanket from around the girl and laid her upon this bed. Then he went down the slope again for his boots, rifle, and the rabbit, and, bringing also his lasso with him, he made short work of that trip.

"Are—you—there?" The girl's voice came low from the blackness.

"Yes," he replied, and was conscious that his laboring breast made speech difficult.

"Are we—in a cave?"

"Yes."

"Oh, listen! . . . The waterfall! . . . I hear it! You've brought me back!"

Venters heard a murmuring moan that one moment swelled to a pitch almost softly shrill and the next lulled to a low, almost inaudible sigh.

"That's—wind blowing—in the—cliffs," he panted. "You're far—from Oldring's—cañon."

The effort it cost him to speak made him conscious of extreme lassitude following upon great exertion. It seemed that when he lay down and drew his blanket over him the action was the last before utter prostration. He stretched inert, wet, hot, his body one great strife of throbbing, stinging nerves and bursting veins. And there he lay for a long while before he felt that he had begun to rest.

Rest came to him that night, but no sleep. Sleep he did not want. The hours of strained effort were now as if they had never been, and he wanted to think. Earlier in the day he had dismissed an inexplicable feeling of change; but now, when there was no longer demand on his cunning and strength and he had time to think, he could not catch the illusive thing that had sadly perplexed as well as elevated his spirit.

Above him, through a V-shaped cleft in the dark rim of the cliff, shone the lustrous stars that had been his lonely accusers for a long, long year. Tonight they were different. He studied them. Larger, whiter, more radiant they seemed; but that was not the difference he meant. Gradually it came to him that the distinction was not one he saw, but one he felt. In this he divined as much of the baffling change as he thought would be revealed to him then. And as he lay there, with the singing of the cliff-winds in his ears, the white stars above the dark, bold vent, the difference which he felt was that he was no longer alone.

CHAPTER 9

SILVER SPRUCE AND ASPENS

The rest of that night seemed to Venters only a few moments of starlight, a dark overcasting of sky, an hour or so of gray gloom, and then the lighting of dawn.

When he had bestirred himself, feeding the hungry dogs and breaking his long fast, and had repacked his saddle-bags, it was clear daylight, though the sun had not tipped the yellow wall in the east. He concluded to make the climb and descent into Surprise Valley in one trip. To that end he tied his blanket upon Ring and gave Whitie the extra lasso and the rabbit to carry. Then, with the rifle and saddle-bags slung upon his back, he took up the girl. She did not awaken from heavy slumber.

That climb up under the rugged, menacing brows of the broken cliffs, in the face of a grim, leaning boulder that seemed to be weary of its age-long wavering, was a tax on strength and nerve that Venters felt equally with something sweet and strangely exulting in its accomplishment. He did not pause until he gained the narrow divide and there he rested. Balancing Rock loomed huge, cold in the gray light of dawn, a thing without life, yet it spoke silently to Venters: "I am waiting to plunge down, to shatter and crash, roar and boom, to bury your trail, and close forever the outlet to Deception Pass!"

On the descent of the other side Venters had easy going, but was somewhat concerned because Whitie appeared to have succumbed to temptation, and while carrying the rabbit was also chewing on it. And Ring evidently regarded this as an injury to himself, especially as he had carried the heavier load. Presently he snapped at one end of the rabbit and refused to let go. But his action prevented Whitie from further misdoing, and then the two dogs pattered down, carrying the rabbit between them.

Venters turned out of the gorge, and suddenly paused stock-still, astounded at the scene before him. The curve of the great Stone Bridge had caught the sunrise, and through the magnificent arch burst a glorious stream of gold that shone with a long slant down into the center of Surprise Valley. Only through the arch did any sunlight pass, so that all the rest of the valley lay still asleep, dark-green, mysterious, shadowy, merging its level into walls as misty and soft as morning clouds.

Venters then descended, passing through the arch, looking up at its tremendous height and sweep. It spanned the opening to Surprise Valley, stretching in almost perfect curve from rim to rim. Even in his hurry and concern Venters could not but feel its majesty, and the thought came to him that the cliff-dwellers must have regarded it as an object of worship.

Down, down, down Venters strode, more and more feeling the weight of his burden as he descended, and still the valley lay below him. As all other cañons and coves and valleys had deceived him, so had this deep-nestling oval. At length he passed beyond the slope of weathered stone that spread fan-shape from the arch; and encountered a grassy terrace running to the right and about on a level with the tips of the oaks and cottonwoods below. Scattered here and there upon this shelf were clumps of aspens, and he walked through them into a glade that surpassed, in beauty and adaptability for a wild home, any place he had ever seen. Silver spruces bordered the base of a precipitous wall that rose loftily. Caves indented its surface, and there were no detached ledges or weathered sections that might dislodge a stone. The level ground, beyond the spruces, dropped down into a little ravine. This was one dense line of slender aspens from which came the low splashing of water. And the terrace, lying open to the west, afforded unobstructed view of the valley of green tree-tops.

For his camp Venters chose a shady, grassy plot between the silver spruces and the cliff. Here, in the stone wall, had been wonderfully carved by wind or washed by water several deep caves above the level of the terrace. They were clean, dry, roomy. He cut spruce boughs and made a bed in the largest cave and laid the girl there. The first intimation that he had of her being aroused from sleep or lethargy was a low call for water.

He hurried down into the ravine with his canteen. It was a shallow, grass-green place with aspens growing up everywhere. To his delight he found a tiny brook of swift-running water. Its faint tinge of amber reminded him of the spring at Cottonwoods, and the thought gave him a little shock. The water was so cold it made his fingers tingle as he dipped the canteen. Having returned to the cave, he was glad to see the girl drink thirstily. This time he noted that she could raise her head slightly without his help.

"You were thirsty," he said. "It's good water. I've found a fine place. Tell me—how do you feel?"

"There's pain—here," she replied, and moved her hand to her left side.

"Why, that's strange. Your wounds are on your right side. I believe you're hungry. Is the pain a kind of dull ache—a gnawing?"

"It's like—that."

"Then it's hunger." Venters laughed, and suddenly caught himself with a quick breath and felt again the little shock. When had he laughed? "It's hunger," he went on. "I've had that gnaw many a time. I've got it now. But you mustn't eat. You can have all the water you want, but no food just yet."

"Won't I—starve?"

"No, people don't starve easily. I've discovered that. You must lie perfectly still and rest and sleep—for days."

"My hands—are dirty—my face feels—so hot and sticky—my boots hurt." It was her longest speech as yet, and it trailed off in a whisper.

"Well, I'm a fine nurse!"

It annoyed him that he had never thought of these things. But then, awaiting her death and thinking of her comfort were vastly different matters. He unwrapped the blanket which covered her. What a slender girl she was! No wonder he had been able to carry her miles and pack her up that slippery ladder of stone. Her boots were of soft, fine leather, reaching clear to her knees. He recognized the make as one of a bootmaker in Sterling. Her spurs, that he had stupidly neglected to remove, consisted of silver frames and gold chains, and the rowels, large as silver dollars, were fancifully engraved. The boots slipped off rather hard. She wore heavy woollen rider's stockings, half length, and these were pulled up over the ends of her short trousers. Venters took off the stockings to note her little feet were red and swollen. He bathed them. Then he removed his scarf and bathed her face and hands.

"I must see your wounds now," he said, gently.

She made no reply, but watched him steadily as he opened her blouse and untied the bandage. His strong fingers trembled a little as he removed it. If the wounds had reopened! A chill struck him as he saw the angry red bullet-mark, and a tiny stream of blood winding from it down her white breast. Very carefully he lifted her to see that the wound in her back had closed perfectly. Then he washed the blood from her breast, bathed the wound, and left it unbandaged, open to the air.

Her eyes thanked him.

"Listen," he said, earnestly, "I've had some wounds, and I've seen many. I know a little about them. The hole in your back has closed. If you lie still three days the one in your breast will close, and you'll be safe. The danger from hemorrhage will be over."

He had spoken with earnest sincerity, almost eagerness.

"Why—do you—want me—to get well?" she asked, wonderingly.

The simple question seemed unanswerable except on grounds of humanity. But the circumstances under which he had shot this strange girl, the shock and realization, the waiting for death, the hope, had resulted in a condition of mind wherein Venters wanted her to live more than he had ever wanted anything. Yet he could not tell why. He believed the killing of the rustler and the subsequent excitement had disturbed him. For how else could he explain the throbbing of his brain, the heat of his blood, the undefined sense of full hours, charged, vibrant with pulsating mystery where once they had dragged in loneliness?

"I shot you," he said, slowly, "and I want you to get well so I shall not have killed a woman. But—for your own sake, too—"

A terrible bitterness darkened her eyes, and her lips quivered.

"Hush," said Venters. "You've talked too much already."

In her unutterable bitterness he saw a darkness of mood that could not have been caused by her present weak and feverish state. She hated the life she had led, that she probably had been compelled to lead. She had suffered some unforgivable wrong at the hands of Oldring. With that conviction Venters felt a flame throughout his body, and it marked the rekindling of fierce anger and ruthlessness. In the past long year he had nursed resentment. He had hated the wilderness—the loneliness of the uplands. He had waited for something to come to pass. It had come. Like an Indian stealing horses he had skulked into the recesses of the cañons. He had found Oldring's retreat; he had killed a rustler; he had shot an unfortunate girl, then had saved her from this unwitting act, and he meant to save her from the consequent wasting of blood, from fever and weakness. Starvation he had to fight for her and for himself. Where he had been sick at the letting of blood, now he remembered it in grim, cold calm. And as he lost that softness of nature so he lost his fear of men. He would watch for Oldring, biding his time, and he would kill this great black-bearded rustler who had held a girl in bondage, who had used her to his infamous ends.

Venters surmised this much of the change in him—idleness had passed; keen, fierce vigor flooded his mind and body; all that had happened to him at Cottonwoods seemed remote and hard to recall; the difficulties and perils of the present absorbed him, held him in a kind of spell.

First, then, he fitted up the little cave adjoining the girl's room for his own comfort and use. His next work was to build a fireplace of stones and to gather a store of wood. That done, he spilled the contents of his saddle-bags upon the grass and took stock. His outfit consisted of a small-handled axe, a hunting knife, a large number of cartridges for rifle or revolver, a tin plate, a cup, and a fork and spoon, a quantity of dried beef and dried fruits, and small canvas bags containing tea, sugar, salt, and pepper. For him alone this supply would have been bountiful to begin a sojourn in the wilderness, but he was no longer alone. Starvation in the uplands was not an unheard-of thing; he did not, however, worry at all on that score, and feared only his possible inability to supply the needs of a woman in a weakened and extremely delicate condition.

If there was no game in the valley—a contingency he doubted—it would not be a great task for him to go by night to Oldring's herd and pack out a calf. The exigency of the moment was to ascertain if there were game in Surprise Valley. Whitie still guarded the dilapidated rabbit, and Ring slept near by under a spruce. Venters called Ring and went to the edge of the terrace, and there halted to survey the valley.

He was prepared to find it larger than his unstudied glances had made it appear; for more than a casual idea of dimensions and a hasty conception of oval shape and singular beauty he had not had time. Again the felicity of the name he had given the valley struck him forcibly. Around the red perpendicular walls, except under the great arc of stone, ran a terrace fringed at the cliff-base by silver spruces; below that first terrace sloped another wider one densely overgrown with aspens; and the center of the valley was a level circle of oaks and alders, with the glittering green line of willows and cottonwoods dividing it in half. Venters saw a number and variety of birds flitting among the trees. To his left, facing the Stone Bridge, an enormous cavern opened in the wall; and low down, just above the tree-tops, he made out a long shelf of cliff-dwellings, with little black, staring windows or doors. Like eyes they were, and seemed to watch him. The few cliff-dwellings he had seen—all ruins—had left him with haunting memory of age and solitude and of something past. He had come, in a way, to be a cliff-dweller himself, and those silent eyes would look down upon him, as if in surprise that after thousands of years a man had invaded the valley. Venters felt sure that he was the only white man who had ever walked under the shadow of the wonderful Stone Bridge, down into that wonderful valley with its circle of caves and its terraced rings of silver spruces and aspens.

The dog growled below and rushed into the forest. Venters ran down the declivity to enter a zone of light shade streaked with sunshine. The oak-trees were slender, none more than half a foot thick, and they grew close together, intermingling their branches. Ring came running back with a rabbit in his mouth. Venters took the rabbit and holding the dog near him, stole softly on. There were fluttering of wings among the branches and quick bird-notes, and rustling of dead leaves and rapid patterings. Venters crossed well-worn trails marked with fresh tracks; and when he had stolen on a little farther he saw many birds and running quail, and more rabbits than he could count. He had not penetrated the forest of oaks for a hundred yards, had not approached anywhere near the line of willows and cottonwoods which he knew grew along a stream. But he had seen enough to know that Surprise Valley was the home of many wild creatures.

Venters returned to camp. He skinned the rabbits, and gave the dogs the one they had quarreled over, and the skin of this he dressed and hung up to dry, feeling that he would like to keep it. It was a particularly rich, furry pelt with a beautiful white tail. Venters remembered that but for the bobbing of that white tail catching his eye he would not have espied the rabbit, and he would never have discovered Surprise Valley. Little incidents of chance like this had turned him here and there in Deception Pass; and now they had assumed to him the significance and direction of destiny.

His good fortune in the matter of game at hand brought to his mind the necessity of keeping it in the valley. Therefore he took the ax and cut bundles of aspens and willows, and packed them up under the bridge to the narrow outlet of the gorge. Here he began fashioning a fence, by driving aspens into the ground and lacing them fast with willows. Trip after trip he made down for more building material, and the afternoon had passed when he finished the work to his satisfaction. Wildcats might scale the fence, but no coyote could come in to search for prey, and no rabbits or other small game could escape from the valley.

Upon returning to camp he set about getting his supper at ease, around a fine fire, without hurry or fear of discovery. After hard work that had definite purpose, this freedom and comfort gave him peculiar satisfaction. He caught himself often, as he kept busy round the campfire, stopping to glance at the quiet form in the cave, and at the dogs stretched cozily near him, and then out across the beautiful valley. The present was not yet real to him.

While he ate, the sun set beyond a dip in the rim of the curved wall. As the morning sun burst wondrously through a grand arch into this valley, in a golden, slanting shaft, so the evening sun, at the moment of setting, shone through a gap of cliffs, sending down a broad red burst to brighten the oval with a blaze of fire. To Venters both sunrise and sunset were unreal.

A cool wind blew across the oval, waving the tips of oaks, and, while the light lasted, fluttering the aspen leaves into millions of facets of red, and sweeping the graceful spruces. Then with the wind soon came a shade and a darkening, and suddenly the valley was gray. Night came there quickly after the sinking of the sun. Venters went softly to look at the girl. She slept, and her breathing was quiet and slow. He lifted Ring into the cave, with stern whisper for him to stay there on guard. Then he drew the blanket carefully over her and returned to the campfire.

Though exceedingly tired, he was yet loath to yield to lassitude, but this night it was not from listening, watchful vigilance; it was from a desire to realize his position. The details of his wild environment seemed the only substance of a strange dream. He saw the darkening rims, the gray oval turning black, the undulating surface of forest, like a rippling lake, and the spear-pointed spruces. He heard the flutter of aspen leaves and the soft, continuous splash of falling water. The melancholy note of a cañon bird broke clear and lonely from the high cliffs. Venters had no name for this night singer, and he had never seen one; but the few notes, always pealing out just at darkness, were as familiar to him as the cañon silence. Then they ceased, and the rustle of leaves and the murmur of water hushed in a growing sound that Venters fancied was not of earth. Neither had he a name for this, only it was inexpressibly wild and sweet. The thought came that it might be a moan of the girl in her last outcry of life, and he felt a tremor shake him. But no! This sound was not human, though it was like despair. He began to doubt his sensitive perceptions, to believe that he half-dreamed what he thought he heard. Then the sound swelled with the strengthening of the breeze, and he realized it was the singing of the wind in the cliffs.

By and by a drowsiness overcame him, and Venters began to nod, half asleep, with his back against a spruce. Rousing himself and calling Whitie, he went to the cave. The girl lay barely visible in the dimness. Ring crouched beside her, and the patting of his tail on the stone assured Venters that the dog was awake and faithful to his duty. Venters sought his own bed of fragrant boughs; and as he lay back, somehow grateful for the comfort and safety, the night seemed to steal away from him, and he sank softly into intangible space and rest and slumber.

Venters awakened to the sound of melody that he imagined was only the haunting echo of dream music. He opened his eyes to another surprise of this valley of beautiful surprises. Out of his cave he saw the exquisitely fine foliage of the silver spruces crossing a round space of blue morning sky; and in this lacy leafage fluttered a number of gray birds with black and white stripes and long tails. They were mocking-birds, and they were singing as if they wanted to burst their throats. Venters listened. One long, silver-tipped branch drooped almost to his cave, and upon it, within a few yards of him, sat one of the graceful birds. Venters saw the swelling and quivering of its throat in song. He arose, and when he slid down out of his cave the birds fluttered and flew farther away.

Venters stepped before the opening of the other cave and looked in. The girl was awake, with wide eyes and listening look, and she had a hand on Ring's neck.

"Mocking-birds!" she said.

"Yes," replied Venters, "and I believe they like our company."

"Where are we?"

"Never mind now. After a little I'll tell you."

"The birds woke me. When I heard them—and saw the shiny trees—and the blue sky—and then a blaze of gold dropping down—I wondered—"

She did not complete her fancy, but Venters imagined he understood her meaning. She appeared to be wandering in mind. Venters felt her face and hands and found them burning with fever. He went for water, and was glad to find it almost as cold as if flowing from ice. That water was the only medicine he had, and he put faith in it. She did not want to drink, but he made her swallow, and then he bathed her face and head and cooled her wrists.

The day began with a heightening of the fever. Venters spent the time reducing her temperature, cooling her hot cheeks and temples. He kept close watch over her, and at the least indication of restlessness, that he knew led to tossing and rolling of the body, he held her tightly, so no violent move could reopen her wounds. Hour after hour she babbled and laughed and cried and moaned in delirium; but whatever her secret was she did not reveal it. Attended by something somber for Venters, the day passed. At night in the cool winds the fever abated and she slept.

The second day was a repetition of the first. On the third he seemed to see her wither and waste away before his eyes. That day he scarcely went from her side for a moment, except to run for fresh, cool water; and he did not eat. The fever broke on the fourth day and left her spent and shrunken, a slip of a girl with life only in her eyes. They hung upon Venters with a mute observance, and he found hope in that.

To rekindle the spark that had nearly flickered out, to nourish the little life and vitality that remained in her, was Venters's problem. But he had little resource other than the meat of the rabbits and quail; and from these he made broths and soups as best he could, and fed her with a spoon. It came to him that the human body, like the human soul, was a strange thing and capable of recovering from terrible shocks. For almost immediately she showed faint signs of gathering strength. There was one more waiting day, in which he doubted, and spent long hours by her side as she slept, and watched the gentle swell of her breast rise and fall in breathing and the wind stir the tangled chestnut curls. On the next day he knew that she would live.

Upon realizing it he abruptly left the cave and sought his accustomed seat against the trunk of a big spruce, where once more he let his glance stray along the sloping terraces. She would live, and the somber gloom lifted out of the valley, and he felt relief that was pain. Then he roused to the call of action, to the many things he needed to do in the way of making camp fixtures and utensils, to the necessity of hunting food, and the desire to explore the valley.

But he decided to wait a few more days before going far from camp, because he fancied that the girl rested easier when she could see him near at hand. And on the first day her languor appeared to leave her in a renewed grip of life. She awoke stronger from each short slumber; she ate greedily, and she moved about in her bed of boughs; and always, it seemed to Venters, her eyes followed him. He knew now that her recovery would be rapid. She talked about the dogs, about the caves, the valley, about how hungry she was, till Venters silenced her, asking her to put off further talk till another time. She obeyed, but she sat up in her bed, and her eyes roved to and fro, and always back to him.

Upon the second morning she sat up when he awakened her, and would not permit him to bathe her face and feed her, which actions she performed for herself. She spoke little, however, and Venters was quick to catch in her the first intimations of thoughtfulness and curiosity and appreciation of her situation. He left camp and took Whitie out to hunt for rabbits. Upon his return he was amazed and somewhat anxiously concerned to see his invalid sitting with her back to a corner of the cave and her bare feet swinging out. Hurriedly he approached, intending to advise her to lie down again, to tell her that perhaps she might overtax her strength. The sun shone upon her, glinting on the little head with its tangle of bright hair and the small, oval face with its pallor, and dark-blue eyes underlined by dark-blue circles. She looked at him, and he looked at her. In that exchange of glances he imagined each saw the other in some different guise. It seemed impossible to Venters that this frail girl could be Oldring's Masked Rider. It flashed over him that he had made a mistake which presently she would explain.

"Help me down," she said.

"But—are you well enough?" he protested. "Wait—a little longer."

"I'm weak—dizzy. But I want to get down."

He lifted her—what a light burden now!—and stood her upright beside him, and supported her as she essayed to walk with halting steps. She was like a stripling of a boy; the bright, small head scarcely reached his shoulder. But now, as she clung to his arm, the rider's costume she wore did not contradict, as it had done at first, his feeling of her femininity. She might be the famous Masked Rider of the uplands, she might resemble a boy; but her outline, her little hands and feet, her hair, her big eyes and tremulous lips, and especially a something that Venters felt as a subtle essence rather than what he saw, proclaimed her sex.

She soon tired. He arranged a comfortable seat for her under the spruce that overspread the campfire.

"Now tell me—everything," she said.

He recounted all that had happened from the time of his discovery of the rustlers in the cañon up to the present moment.

"You shot me—and now you've saved my life?"

"Yes. After almost killing you I've pulled you through."

"Are you glad?"

"I should say so!"

Her eyes were unusually expressive, and they regarded him steadily; she was unconscious of that mirroring of her emotions, and they shone with gratefulness and interest and wonder and sadness.

"Tell me—about yourself?" she asked.

He made this a briefer story, telling of his coming to Utah, his various occupations till he became a rider, and then how the Mormons had practically driven him out of Cottonwoods, an outcast.

Then, no longer able to withstand his own burning curiosity, he questioned her in turn.

"Are you Oldring's Masked Rider?"

"Yes," she replied, and dropped her eyes.

"I knew it—I recognized your figure—and mask, for I saw you once. Yet I can't believe it! . . . But you never *were* really that rustler, as we riders knew him? A thief—a marauder—a kidnapper of women—a murderer of sleeping riders!"

"No! I never stole—or harmed any one—in all my life. I only rode and rode—"

"But why—why?" he burst out. "Why the name? I understand Oldring made you ride. But the black mask—the mystery—the things laid to your hands—the threats in your infamous name—the night-riding credited to you—the evil deeds deliberately blamed on you and acknowledged by rustlers—even Oldring himself! Why? Tell me why?"

"I never knew that," she answered low. Her drooping head straightened, and the large eyes, larger now and darker, met Venters's with a clear, steadfast gaze in which he read truth. It verified his own conviction.

"Never knew? That's strange! Are you a Mormon?"

"No."

"Is Oldring a Mormon?"

"No."

"Do you—care for him?"

"Yes. I hate his men—his life—sometimes I almost hate him!"

Venters paused in his rapid-fire questioning, as if to brace himself to ask for a truth that would be abhorrent for him to confirm, but which he seemed driven to hear.

"What are—what *were* you to Oldring?"

Like some delicate thing suddenly exposed to blasting heat, the girl wilted; her head dropped, and into her white, wasted cheeks crept the red of shame.

Venters would have given anything to recall that question. It seemed so different—his thought when spoken. Yet her shame established in his mind something akin to the respect he had strangely been hungering to feel for her.

"D—n that question!—forget it!" he cried, in a passion of pain for her and anger at himself. "But once and for all—tell me—I know it, yet I want to hear you say so—you couldn't help yourself?"

"Oh no."

"Well, that makes it all right with me," he went on, honestly. "I—I want you to feel that . . . you see—we've been thrown together—and—and I want to help you—not hurt you. I thought life had been cruel to me, but when I think of yours I feel mean and little for my complaining. Anyway, I was a lonely outcast. And now! . . . I don't see very clearly what it all means. Only we are here—together. We've got to stay here, for long, surely till you are well. But you'll never go back to Oldring. And I'm sure helping you will help me, for I was sick in mind. There's something now for me to do. And if I can win back your strength—then get you away, out of this wild country—help you somehow to a happier life—just think how good that'll be for me!"

CHAPTER 10

LOVE

During all these waiting days Venters, with the exception of the afternoon when he had built the gate in the gorge, had scarcely gone out of sight of camp, and never out of hearing. His desire to explore Surprise Valley was keen, and on the morning after his long talk with the girl he took his rifle and, calling Ring, made a move to start. The girl lay back in a rude chair of boughs he had put together for her. She had been watching him, and when he picked up the gun and called the dog Venters thought she gave a nervous start.

"I'm only going to look over the valley," he said.

"Will you be gone long?"

"No," he replied, and started off. The incident set him thinking of his former impression that, after her recovery from fever, she did not seem at ease unless he was close at hand. It was fear of being alone, due, he concluded, most likely to her weakened condition. He must not leave her much alone.

As he strode down the sloping terrace, rabbits scampered before him, and the beautiful valley quail, as purple in color as the sage on the uplands, ran fleetly along the ground into the forest. It was pleasant under the trees, in the gold-flecked shade, with the whistle of quail and twittering of birds everywhere. Soon he had passed the limit of his former excursions and entered new territory. Here the woods began to show open glades and brooks running down from the slope, and presently he emerged from shade into the sunshine of a meadow. The shaking of the high grass told him of the running of animals, what species he could not tell; but from Ring's manifest desire to have a chase they were evidently some kind wilder than rabbits. Venters approached the willow and cottonwood belt that he had observed from the height of slope. He penetrated it to find a considerable stream of water and great half-submerged mounds of brush and sticks, and all about him were old and new gnawed circles at the base of the cottonwoods.

"Beaver!" he exclaimed. "By all that's lucky! The meadow's full of beaver! How did they ever get here?"

Beaver had not found a way into the valley by the trail of the cliff-dwellers, of that he was certain; and he began to have more than curiosity as to the outlet or inlet of the stream. When he passed some dead water, which he noted was held by a beaver-dam, there was a current in the stream, and it flowed west. Following its course, he soon entered the oak forest again, and passed through to find himself before massed and jumbled ruins of cliff-wall. There were tangled thickets of wild plum-trees and other thorny growths that made passage extremely laborsome. He found innumerable tracks of wildcats and foxes. Rustlings in the thick undergrowth told him of stealthy movements of these animals. At length his further advance appeared futile, for the reason that the stream disappeared in a split at the base of immense rocks over which he could not climb. To his relief he concluded that though beaver might work their way up the narrow chasm where the water rushed, it would be impossible for men to enter the valley there.

This western curve was the only part of the valley where the walls had been split asunder, and it was a wildly rough and inaccessible corner. Going back a little way, he leaped the stream and headed toward the southern wall. Once out of the oaks he found again the low terrace of aspens, and above that the wide, open terrace fringed by silver spruces. This side of the valley contained the wind or water worn caves. As he pressed on, keeping to the upper terrace, cave after cave opened out of the cliff; now a large one, now a small one. Then yawned, quite suddenly and wonderfully above him, the great cavern of the cliff-dwellers.

It was still a goodly distance, and he tried to imagine, if it appeared so huge from where he stood, what it would be when he got there. He climbed the terrace and then faced a long, gradual ascent of weathered rock and dust, which made climbing too difficult for attention to anything else. At length he entered a zone of shade, and looked up. He stood just within the hollow of a cavern so immense that he had no conception of its real dimensions. The curved roof, stained by ages of leakage, with buff and black and rust-colored streaks, swept up and loomed higher and seemed to soar to the rim of the cliff. Here again was a magnificent arch, such as formed the grand gateway to the valley, only in this instance it formed the dome of a cave instead of the span of a bridge.

Venters passed onward and upward. The stones he dislodged rolled down with strange, hollow crack and roar. He had climbed a hundred rods inward, and yet he had not reached the base of the shelf where the cliff-dwellings rested, a long half-circle of connected stone houses, with little dark holes that he had fancied were eyes. At length he gained the base of the shelf, and here found steps cut in the rock. These facilitated climbing, and as he went up he thought how easily this vanished race of men might once have held that stronghold against an army. There was only one possible place to ascend, and this was narrow and steep.

Venters had visited cliff-dwellings before, and they had been in ruins, and of no great character or size, but this place was of proportions that stunned him, and it had not been desecrated by the hand of man, nor had it been crumbled by the hand of time. It was a stupendous tomb. It had been a city. It was just as it had been left by its builders. The little houses were there, the smoke-blackened stains of fires, the pieces of pottery scattered about cold hearths, the stone-hatchets; and stone pestles and mealing-stones lay beside round holes polished by years of grinding maize—lay there as if they had been carelessly dropped yesterday. But the cliff-dwellers were gone!

Dust! They were dust on the floor or at the foot of the shelf, and their habitations and utensils endured. Venters felt the sublimity of that marvelous vaulted arch, and it seemed to gleam with a glory of something that was gone. How many years had passed since the cliff-dwellers gazed out across the beautiful valley as he was gazing now? How long had it been since women ground grain in those polished holes? What time had rolled by since men of an unknown race lived, loved, fought, and died there? Had an enemy destroyed them? Had disease destroyed them, or only that greatest destroyer—time? Venters saw a long line of blood-red hands painted low down upon the yellow roof of stone. Here was strange portent, if not an answer to his queries. The place oppressed him. It was light, but full of a transparent gloom. It smelled of dust and musty stone, of age and disuse. It was sad. It was solemn. It had the look of a place where silence had become master and was now irrevocable and terrible, and could not be broken. Yet, at the moment, from high up in the carved crevices of the arch, floated down the low, strange wail of wind—a knell indeed for all that had gone.

Venters, sighing, gathered up an armful of pottery, such pieces as he thought strong enough and suitable for his own use, and bent his steps toward camp. He mounted the terrace at an opposite point to which he had left. He saw the girl looking in the direction he had gone. His footsteps made no sound in the deep grass, and he approached close without her being aware of his presence. Whitie lay on the ground near where she sat, and he manifested the usual actions of welcome, but the girl did not notice them. She seemed to be oblivious to everything near at hand. She made a pathetic figure drooping there, with her sunny hair contrasting so markedly with her white, wasted cheeks and her hands listlessly clasped and her little bare feet propped in the frame-work of the rude seat. Venters could have sworn and laughed in one breath at the idea of the connection between this girl and Oldring's Masked Rider. She was the victim of more than accident of fate—a victim to some deep plot the mystery of which burned him. As he stepped forward with a half-formed thought that she was absorbed in watching for his return, she turned her head and saw him. A swift start, a change rather than rush of blood under her white cheeks, a flashing of big eyes that fixed their glance upon him, transformed her face in that single instant of turning; and he knew she had been watching for him, that his return was the one thing in her mind. She did not smile; she did not flush; she did not look glad. All these would have meant little compared to her indefinite expression. Venters grasped the peculiar, vivid, vital something that leaped from her face. It was as if she had been in a dead, hopeless clamp of inaction and feeling, and had been suddenly shot through and through with quivering animation. Almost it was as if she had returned to life.

And Venters thought with lightning swiftness, "I've saved her—I've unlinked her from that old life—she was watching as if I were all she had left on earth—she belongs to me!" The thought was startlingly new. Like a blow it was in an unprepared moment. The cheery salutation he had ready for her died unborn, and he tumbled the pieces of pottery awkwardly on the grass, while some unfamiliar, deep-seated emotion, mixed with pity and glad assurance of his power to succor her, held him dumb.

"What a load you had," she said. "Why, they're pots and crocks! Where did you get them?"

Venters laid down his rifle, and, filling one of the pots from his canteen, he placed it on the smoldering camp-fire.

"Hope it'll hold water," he said, presently. "Why, there's an enormous cliff-dwelling just across here. I got the pottery there. Don't you think we needed something? That tin cup of mine has served to make tea, broth, soup—everything."

"I noticed we hadn't a great deal to cook in."

She laughed. It was the first time. He liked that laugh, and though he was tempted to look at her, he did not want to show his surprise or his pleasure.

"Will you take me over there, and all around in the valley—pretty soon when I'm well?" she added.

"Indeed I shall. It's a wonderful place. Rabbits so thick you can't step without kicking one out. And quail, beaver, foxes, wildcats. We're in a regular den. But—haven't you ever seen a cliff-dwelling?"

"No. I've heard about them, though. The—the men say the Pass is full of old houses and ruins."

"Why, I should think you'd have run across one in all your riding around," said Venters. He spoke slowly, choosing his words carefully, and he essayed a perfectly casual manner, and pretended to be busy assorting pieces of pottery. She must have no cause again to suffer shame for curiosity of his. Yet never in all his days had he been so eager to hear the details of any one's life.

"When I rode—I rode like the wind," she replied, "and never had time to stop for anything."

"I remember that day I—I met you in the Pass—how dusty you were, how tired your horse looked. Were you always riding?"

"Oh, no. Sometimes not for months, when I was shut up in the cabin."

Venters tried to subdue a hot tingling.

"You were shut up, then?" he asked, carelessly.

"When Oldring went away on his long trips—he was gone for months sometimes—he shut me up in the cabin."

"What for?"

"Perhaps to keep me from running away. I always threatened that. Mostly, though, because the men got drunk at the villages. But they were always good to me. I wasn't afraid."

"A prisoner! That must have been hard on you?"

"I liked that. As long as I can remember I've been locked up there at times, and those times were the only happy ones I ever had. It's a big cabin high up a cliff, and I could look out. Then I had dogs and pets I had tamed, and books. There was a spring inside, and food stored, and the men brought me fresh meat. Once I was there one whole winter."

It now required deliberation on Venters's part to persist in his unconcern and to keep at work. He wanted to look at her, to volley questions at her.

"As long as you can remember—you've lived in Deception Pass?" he went on.

"I've a dim memory of some other place, and women and children; but I can't make anything of it. Sometimes I think till I'm weary."

"Then you can read—you have books?"

"Oh yes, I can read, and write, too, pretty well, Oldring is educated. He taught me, and years ago an old rustler lived with us, and he had been something different once. He was always teaching me."

"So Oldring takes long trips," mused Venters. "Do you know where he goes?"

"No. Every year he drives cattle north of Sterling—then does not return for months. I heard him accused once of living two lives—and he killed the man. That was at Stone Bridge."

Venters dropped his apparent task and looked up with an eagerness he no longer strove to hide.

"Bess," he said, using her name for the first time, "I suspected Oldring was something besides a rustler. Tell me, what's his purpose here in the Pass? I believe much that he has done was to hide his real work here."

"You're right. He's more than a rustler. In fact, as the men say, his rustling cattle is now only a bluff. There's gold in the cañons!"

"Ah!"

"Yes, there's gold, not in great quantities, but gold enough for him and his men. They wash for gold week in and week out. Then they drive a few cattle and go into the villages to drink and shoot and kill—to bluff the riders."

"Drive a few cattle! But, Bess, the Withersteen herd, the red herd—twenty-five hundred head! That's not a few. And I tracked them into a valley near here."

"Oldring never stole the red herd. He made a deal with Mormons. The riders were to be called in, and Oldring was to drive the herd and keep it till a certain time—I don't know when—then drive it back to the range. What his share was I didn't hear."

"Did you hear *why* that deal was made?" queried Venters.

"No. But it was a trick of Mormons. They're full of tricks. I've heard Oldring's men tell about Mormons. Maybe the Withersteen woman wasn't minding her halter! I saw the man who made the deal. He was a little, queer-shaped man, all humped up. He sat his horse well. I heard one of our men say afterward there was no better rider on the sage than this fellow. What was the name? I forget."

"Jerry Card?" suggested Venters.

"That's it. I remember—it's a name easy to remember—and Jerry Card appeared to be on fair terms with Oldring's men."

"I shouldn't wonder," replied Venters, thoughtfully. Verification of his suspicions in regard to Tull's underhand work—for the deal with Oldring made by Jerry Card assuredly had its inception in the Mormon Elder's brain, and had been accomplished through his orders—revived in Venters a memory of hatred that had been smothered by press of other emotions. Only a few days had elapsed since the hour of his encounter with Tull, yet they had been forgotten and now seemed far off, and the interval one that now appeared large and profound with incalculable change in his feelings. Hatred of Tull still existed in his heart; but it had lost its white heat. His affection for Jane Withersteen had not changed in the least; nevertheless he seemed to view it from another angle and see it as another thing—what, he could not exactly define. The recalling of these two feelings was to Venters like getting glimpses into a self that was gone; and the wonder of them—perhaps the change which was too illusive for him—was the fact that a strange irritation accompanied the memory and a desire to dismiss it from mind. And straightway he did dismiss it, to return to thoughts of his significant present.

"Bess, tell me one more thing," he said. "Haven't you known any women—any young people?"

"Sometimes there were women with the men; but Oldring never let me know them. And all the young people I ever saw in my life was when I rode fast through the villages."

Perhaps that was the most puzzling and thought-provoking thing she had yet said to Venters. He pondered, more curious the more he learned, but he curbed his inquisitive desires, for he saw her shrinking on the verge of that shame, the causing of which had occasioned him such self-reproach. He would ask no more. Still he had to think, and he found it difficult to think clearly. This sad-eyed girl was so utterly different from what it would have been reason to believe such a remarkable life would have made her. On this day he had found her simple and frank, as natural as any girl he had ever known. About her there was something sweet. Her voice was low and well-modulated. He could not look into her face, meet her steady, unabashed, yet wistful eyes and think of her as the woman she had confessed herself. Oldring's Masked Rider sat before him, a girl dressed as a man. She had been made to ride at the head of infamous forays and drives. She had been imprisoned for many months of her life in an obscure cabin. At times the most vicious of men had been her companions; and the vilest of women, if they had not been permitted to approach her, had, at least, cast their shadows over her. But—but in spite of all this— there thundered at Venters some truth that lifted its voice higher than the clamoring facts of dishonor, some truth that was the very life of her beautiful eyes; and it was innocence.

In the days that followed, Venters balanced perpetually in mind this haunting conception of innocence over against the cold and sickening fact of an unintentional yet actual guilt. How could it be possible for the two things to be true? He believed the latter to be true, and he would not relinquish his conviction of the former; and these conflicting thoughts augmented the mystery that appeared to be a part of Bess. In those ensuing days, however, it became clear as clearest light that Bess was rapidly regaining strength; that, unless reminded of her long association with Oldring, she seemed to have forgotten it; that, like an Indian who lives solely from moment to moment, she was utterly absorbed in the present.

Day by day Venters watched the white of her face slowly change to brown, and the wasted cheeks fill out by imperceptible degrees. There came a time when he could just trace the line of demarcation between the part of her face once hidden by a mask and that left exposed to wind and sun. When that line disappeared in clear bronze tan it was as if she had been washed clean of the stigma of Oldring's Masked Rider. The suggestion of the mask always made Venters remember; now that it was gone he seldom thought of her past. Occasionally he tried to piece together the several stages of strange experience and to make a whole. He had shot a masked outlaw, the very sight of whom had been ill omen to riders; he had carried off a wounded woman whose bloody lips quivered in prayer; he had nursed what seemed a frail, shrunken boy; and now he watched a girl whose face had become strangely sweet, whose dark-blue eyes were ever upon him without boldness, without shyness, but with a steady, grave, and growing light. Many times Venters found the clear gaze embarrassing to him, yet, like wine, it had an exhilarating effect. What did she think when she looked at him so? Almost he believed she had no thought at all. All about her and the present there in Surprise Valley, and the dim yet subtly impending future, fascinated Venters and made him thoughtful as all his lonely vigils in the sage had not.

Chiefly it was the present that he wished to dwell upon; but it was the call of the future which stirred him to action. No idea had he of what that future had in store for Bess and him. He began to think of improving Surprise Valley as a place to live in, for there was no telling how long they would be compelled to stay there. Venters stubbornly resisted the entering into his mind of an insistent thought that, clearly realized, might have made it plain to him that he did not want to leave Surprise Valley at all. But it was imperative that he consider practical matters; and whether or not he was destined to stay long there, he felt the immediate need of a change of diet. It would be necessary for him to go farther afield for a variety of meat, and also that he soon visit Cottonwoods for a supply of food.

It occurred again to Venters that he could go to the cañon where Oldring kept his cattle, and at little risk he could pack out some beef. He wished to do this, however, without letting Bess know of it till after he had made the trip. Presently he hit upon the plan of going while she was asleep.

That very night he stole out of camp, climbed up under the Stone Bridge, and entered the outlet to the pass. The gorge was full of luminous gloom. Balancing Rock loomed dark and leaned over the pale descent. Transformed in the shadowy light, it took shape and dimensions of a spectral god waiting—waiting for the moment to hurl himself down upon the tottering walls and close forever the outlet to Deception Pass. At night more than by day Venters felt something fearful and fateful in that rock, and that it had leaned and waited through a thousand years to have somehow to deal with his destiny.

"Old man, if you must roll, wait till I get back to the girl, and then roll!" he said, aloud, as if the stone were indeed a god.

And those spoken words, in their grim note to his ear as well as content to his mind, told Venters that he was all but drifting on a current which he had not power nor wish to stem.

Venters exercised his usual care in the matter of hiding tracks from the outlet, yet it took him scarcely an hour to reach Oldring's cattle. Here sight of many calves changed his original intention, and instead of packing out meat he decided to take a calf out alive. He roped one, securely tied its feet, and swung it up over his shoulder. Here was an exceedingly heavy burden, but Venters was powerful—he could take up a sack of grain and with ease pitch it over a pack-saddle—and he made long distance without resting. The hardest work came in the climb up to the outlet and on through to the valley. When he had accomplished it, he became fired with another idea that again changed his intention. He would not kill the calf, but keep it alive. He would go back to Oldring's herd and pack out more calves. Thereupon he secured the calf in the best available spot for the moment and turned to make a second trip.

When Venters got back to the valley with another calf, it was close upon daybreak. He crawled into his cave and slept late. Bess had no inkling that he had been absent from camp nearly all night, and only remarked solicitously that he appeared to be more tired than usual, and more in the need of sleep. In the afternoon Venters built a gate across a small ravine near camp, and here corralled the calves; and he succeeded in completing his task without Bess being any the wiser.

That night he made two more trips to Oldring's range, and again on the following night, and yet another on the next. With eight calves in his corral, he concluded that he had enough; but it dawned upon him then that he did not want to kill one. "I've rustled Oldring's cattle," he said, and laughed. He noted then that all the calves were red. "Red!" he exclaimed. "From the red herd. I've stolen Jane Withersteen's cattle! . . . That's about the strangest thing yet."

One more trip he undertook to Oldring's valley, and this time he roped a yearling steer and killed it and cut out a small quarter of beef. The howling of coyotes told him he need have no apprehension that the work of his knife would be discovered. He packed the beef back to camp and hung it upon a spruce-tree. Then he sought his bed.

On the morrow he was up bright and early, glad that he had a surprise for Bess. He could hardly wait for her to come out. Presently she appeared and walked under the spruce. Then she approached the campfire. There was a tinge of healthy red in the bronze of her cheeks, and her slender form had begun to round out in graceful lines.

"Bess, didn't you say you were tired of rabbit?" inquired Venters. "And quail and beaver?"

"Indeed I did."

"What would you like?"

"I'm tired of meat, but if we have to live on it I'd like some beef."

"Well, how does that strike you?" Venters pointed to the quarter hanging from the spruce-tree. "We'll have fresh beef for a few days, then we'll cut the rest into strips and dry it."

"Where did you get that?" asked Bess, slowly.

"I stole that from Oldring."

"You went back to the cañon—you risked—" While she hesitated, the tinge of bloom faded out of her cheeks.

"It wasn't any risk, but it was hard work."

"I'm sorry I said I was tired of rabbit. Why! How—when did you get that beef?"

"Last night."

"While I was asleep?"

"Yes."

"I woke last night sometime—but I didn't know."

Her eyes were widening, darkening with thought, and whenever they did so the steady, watchful, seeing gaze gave place to the wistful light. In the former she saw as the primitive woman without thought; in the latter she looked inward, and her gaze was the reflection of a troubled mind. For long Venters had not seen that dark change, that deepening of blue, which he thought was beautiful and sad. But now he wanted to make her think.

"I've done more than pack in that beef," he said. "For five nights I've been working while you slept. I've got eight calves corralled near a ravine. Eight calves, all alive and doing fine!"

"You went five nights!"

All that Venters could make of the dilation of her eyes, her slow pallor, and her exclamation, was fear—fear for herself or for him.

"Yes. I didn't tell you, because I knew you were afraid to be left alone."

"Alone?" She echoed his word, but the meaning of it was nothing to her. She had not even thought of being left alone. It was not, then, fear for herself, but for him. This girl, always slow of speech and action, now seemed almost stupid. She put forth a hand that might have indicated the groping of her mind. Suddenly she stepped swiftly to him, with a look and touch that drove from him any doubt of her quick intelligence or feeling.

"Oldring has men watch the herds—they would kill you—you must never go again!"

When she had spoken, the strength and the blaze of her died, and she swayed toward Venters.

"*Bess, I'll not go again,*" he said, catching her.

She leaned against him, and her body was limp, and vibrated to a long, wavering tremble. Her face was upturned to his. Woman's face, woman's eyes, woman's lips—all acutely and blindly and sweetly and ter-ribly truthful in their betrayal! But as her fear was instinctive, so was her clinging to this one and only friend.

Venters gently put her from him and steadied her upon her feet; and all the while his blood raced wild, and a thrilling tingle unsteadied his nerve, and something—that he had seen and felt in her—that he could not understand—seemed very close to him, warm and rich as a fragrant breath, sweet as nothing had ever before been sweet to him.

With all his will Venters strove for calmness and thought and judg-ment unbiased by pity, and reality unswayed by sentiment. Bess's eyes were still fixed upon him with all her soul bright in that wistful light. Swiftly, resolutely he put out of mind all of her life except what had been spent with him. He scorned himself for the intelligence that made him still doubt. He meant to judge her as she had judged him. He was face to face with the inevitableness of life itself. He saw destiny in the dark, straight path of her wonderful eyes. Here was the simplicity, the sweet-ness of a girl contending with new and strange and enthralling emotions; here the living truth of innocence; here the blind terror of a woman confronted with the thought of death to her savior and protector. All this Venters saw, but, besides, there was in Bess's eyes a slow-dawning con-sciousness that seemed about to break out in glorious radiance.

"Bess, are you thinking?" he asked.

"Yes—oh yes!"

"Do you realize we are here alone—man and woman?"

"Yes."

"Have you thought that we may make our way out to civilization, or we may have to stay here—alone—hidden from the world all our lives?"

"I never thought—till now."

"Well, what's your choice—to go—or to stay here—alone with me?"

"Stay!" New-born thought of self, ringing vibrantly in her voice, gave her answer singular power.

Venters trembled, and then swiftly turned his gaze from her face—from her eyes. He knew what she had only half divined—that she loved him.

CHAPTER 11

FAITH AND UNFAITH

At Jane Withersteen's home the promise made to Mrs. Larkin to care for little Fay had begun to be fulfilled. Like a gleam of sunlight through the cottonwoods was the coming of the child to the gloomy house of Withersteen. The big, silent halls echoed with childish laughter. In the shady court, where Jane spent many of the July days, Fay's tiny feet pattered over the stone flags and splashed in the amber stream. She prattled incessantly. What difference, Jane thought, a child made in her home! It had never been a real home, she discovered. Even the tidiness and neatness she had so observed, and upon which she had insisted to her women, became, in the light of Fay's smile, habits that now lost their importance. Fay littered the court with Jane's books and papers, and other toys her fancy improvised, and many a strange craft went floating down the little brook.

And it was owing to Fay's presence that Jane Withersteen came to see more of Lassiter. The rider had for the most part kept to the sage. He rode for her, but he did not seek her except on business; and Jane had to acknowledge in pique that her overtures had been made in vain. Fay, however, captured Lassiter the moment he first laid eyes on her.

Jane was present at the meeting, and there was something about it which dimmed her sight and softened her toward this foe of her people. The rider had clanked into the court, a tired yet wary man, always looking for the attack upon him that was inevitable and might come from any quarter; and he had walked right upon little Fay. The child had been beautiful even in her rags and amid the surroundings of the hovel in the sage; but now, in a pretty white dress, with her shining curls brushed and her face clean and rosy, she was lovely. She left her play and looked up at Lassiter.

If there was not an instinct for all three of them in that meeting, an unreasoning tendency toward a closer intimacy, then Jane Withersteen believed she had been subject to a queer fancy. She imagined any child would have feared Lassiter. And Fay Larkin had been a lonely, a solitary elf of the sage, not at all an ordinary child, and exquisitely shy with strangers. She watched Lassiter with great, round, grave eyes, but showed no fear. The rider gave Jane a favorable report of cattle and horses; and as he took the seat to which she invited him, little Fay edged as much as half an inch nearer. Jane replied to his look of inquiry and told Fay's story. The rider's gray, earnest gaze troubled her. Then he turned to Fay and smiled in a way that made Jane doubt her sense of the true relation of things. How could Lassiter smile so at a child when he had made so many children fatherless? But he did smile, and to the gentleness she had seen a few times, he added something that was infinitely sad and sweet. Jane's intuition told her that Lassiter had never been a father; but if life ever so blessed him he would be a good one. Fay, also, must have found that smile singularly winning. For she edged closer and closer, and then by way of feminine capitulation, went to Jane, from whose side she bent a beautiful glance upon the rider.

Lassiter only smiled at her.

Jane watched them, and realized that now was the moment she should seize, if she was ever to win this man from his hatred. But the step was not easy to take. The more she saw of Lassiter the more she respected him, and the greater her respect the harder it became to lend herself to mere coquetry. Yet as she thought of her great motive, of Tull, and of that other whose name she had schooled herself never to think of in connection with

Milly Erne's avenger, she suddenly found she had no choice. And her creed gave her boldness far beyond the limit to which vanity would have led her.

"Lassiter, I see so little of you now," she said, and was conscious of heat in her cheeks.

"I've been ridin' hard," he replied.

"But you can't live in the saddle. You come in sometimes. Won't you come here to see me—oftener?"

"Is that an order?"

"Nonsense! I simply ask you to come to see me when you find time."

"Why?"

The query once heard was not so embarrassing to Jane as she might have imagined. Moreover, it established in her mind a fact that there existed actually other than selfish reasons for her wanting to see him. And as she had been bold, so she determined to be both honest and brave.

"I've reasons—only one of which I need mention," she answered. "If it's possible I want to change you toward my people. And on the moment I can conceive of little I wouldn't do to gain that end."

How much better and freer Jane felt after that confession! She meant to show him that there was one Mormon who could play a game or wage a fight in the open.

"I reckon," said Lassiter, and he laughed.

It was the best in her, if the most irritating, that Lassiter always aroused.

"Will you come?" She looked into his eyes, and for the life of her could not quite subdue an imperiousness that rose with her spirit. "I never asked so much of any man—except Bern Venters."

"'Pears to me that you'd run no risk, or Venters either. But mebbe that doesn't hold good for me."

"You mean it wouldn't be safe for you to be often here? You look for ambush in the cottonwoods?"

"Not that so much."

At this juncture little Fay sidled over to Lassiter.

"Has oo a little dirl?" she inquired.

"No, lassie," replied the rider.

Whatever Fay seemed to be searching for in Lassiter's sun-reddened face and quiet eyes she evidently found. "Oo tan turn to see me," she added, and with that, shyness gave place to friendly curiosity. First his sombrero with its leather band and silver ornaments commanded her attention; next his quirt, and then the clinking, silver spurs. These held her for some time, but presently, true to childish fickleness, she left off playing with them to look for something else. She laughed in glee as she ran her little hands down the slippery, shiny surface of Lassiter's leather chaps. Soon she discovered one of the hanging gun-sheaths, and she dragged it up and began tugging at the huge black handle of the gun. Jane Withersteen repressed an exclamation. What significance there was to her in the little girl's efforts to dislodge that heavy weapon! Jane Withersteen saw Fay's play and her beauty and her love as most powerful allies to her own woman's part in a game that suddenly had acquired a strange zest and a hint of danger. And as for the rider, he appeared to have forgotten Jane in the wonder of this lovely child playing about him. At first he was much the shyer of the two. Gradually her confidence overcame his backwardness, and he had the temerity to stroke her golden curls with a great hand. Fay rewarded his boldness with a smile, and when he had gone to the extreme of closing that great hand over her little brown one, she said, simply: "I like oo!"

Sight of his face then made Jane oblivious for the time to his character as a hater of Mormons. Out of the mother longing that swelled her breast she divined the child hunger in Lassiter.

He returned the next day, and the next; and upon the following he came both at morning and at night. Upon the evening of this fourth day Jane seemed to feel the breaking of a brooding struggle in Lassiter. During all these visits he had scarcely a word to say, though he watched her and played absent-mindedly with Fay. Jane had contented herself with silence. Soon little Fay substituted for the expression of regard "I like oo," a warmer and more generous one, "I love oo."

Thereafter Lassiter came oftener to see Jane and her little protégée. Daily he grew more gentle and kind, and gradually developed a quaintly merry mood. In the morning he lifted Fay upon his horse and let her ride as he walked beside her to the edge of the sage. In the evening he played with the child at an infinite variety of games she invented, and then, oftener than not, he accepted Jane's invitation to supper. No other visitor came to Withersteen House during those days. So that in spite of watch-fulness he never forgot, Lassiter began to show he felt at home there. After the meal they walked into the grove of cottonwoods or up by the lakes, and little Fay held Lassiter's hand as much as she held Jane's. Thus a strange relationship was established, and Jane liked it. At twilight they always returned to the house, where Fay kissed them and went in to her mother. Lassiter and Jane were left alone.

Then, if there were anything that a good woman could do to win a man and still preserve her self-respect, it was something which escaped the natural subtlety of a woman determined to allure. Jane's vanity, that after all was not great, was soon satisfied with Lassiter's silent admira-tion. And her honest desire to lead him from his dark, bloodstained path would never have blinded her to what she owed herself. But the driving passion of her religion, and its call to save Mormons' lives, one life in particular, bore Jane Withersteen close to an infringement of her wom-anhood. In the beginning she had reasoned that her appeal to Lassiter must be through the senses. With whatever means she possessed in the way of adornment she enhanced her beauty. And she stooped to artifices that she knew were unworthy of her, but which she deliberately chose to employ. She made of herself a girl in every variable mood wherein a girl might be desirable. In those moods she was not above the methods of an inexperienced though natural flirt. She kept close to him whenever op-portunity afforded; and she was forever playfully, yet passionately under-neath the surface, fighting him for possession of the great black guns. These he would never yield to her. And so in that manner their hands were often and long in contact. The more of simplicity that she sensed in him the greater the advantage she took.

She had a trick of changing—and it was not altogether voluntary—from this gay, thoughtless, girlish coquetishness to the silence and the brooding, burning mystery of a woman's mood. The strength and pas-sion and fire of her were in her eyes, and she so used them that Lassiter had to see this depth in her, this haunting promise more fitted to her years than to the flaunting guise of a wilful girl.

The July days flew by. Jane reasoned that if it were possible for her to be happy during such a time, then she was happy. Little Fay completely filled a long aching void in her heart. In fettering the hands of this Lassiter she was accomplishing the greatest good of her life, and to do good even in a small way rendered happiness to Jane Withersteen. She had attended the regular Sunday services of her church; otherwise she had not gone to the village for weeks. It was unusual that none of her churchmen or friends had called upon her of late; but it was neglect for which she was glad. Judkins and his boy riders had experienced no difficulty in driving the white herd. So these warm July days were free of worry, and soon Jane hoped she had passed the crisis; and for her to hope was presently to trust, and then to believe. She thought often of Venters, but in a dreamy, abstract way. She spent hours teaching and playing with little Fay. And the activity of her mind centered around Lassiter. The direction she had given her will seemed to blunt any branching off of thought from that straight line. The mood came to obsess her.

In the end, when her awakening came, she learned that she had builded better than she knew. Lassiter, though kinder and gentler than ever, had parted with his quaint humor and his coldness and his tranquillity to become a restless and unhappy man. Whatever the power of his deadly intent toward Mormons, that passion now had a rival, and one equally burning and consuming. Jane Withersteen had one moment of exultation before the dawn of a strange uneasiness. What if she had made of herself a lure, at tremendous cost to him and to her, and all in vain!

That night in the moonlit grove she summoned all her courage, and, turning suddenly in the path, she faced Lassiter and leaned close to him, so that she touched him and her eyes looked up to his.

"Lassiter! . . . Will you do anything for me?"

In the moonlight she saw his dark, worn face change, and by that change she seemed to feel him immovable as a wall of stone.

Jane slipped her hands down to the swinging gun-sheaths, and, when she had locked her fingers around the huge, cold handles of the guns, she trembled as with a chilling ripple over all her body.

"May I take your guns?"

"Why?" he asked, and for the first time to her his voice carried a harsh note. Jane felt his hard, strong hands close round her wrists. It was not wholly with intent that she leaned toward him, for the look of his eyes and the feel of his hands made her weak.

"It's no trifle—no woman's whim—it's deep—as my heart. Let me take them?"

"Why?"

"I want to keep you from killing more men—Mormons. You must let me save you from more wickedness—more wanton bloodshed—" Then the truth forced itself falteringly from her lips. "You must—let—me—help me to keep my vow to Milly Erne. I swore to her—as she lay dying—that if ever any one came here to avenge her—I swore I would stay his hand. Perhaps I—I alone can save the—the man who—who—oh, Lassiter! . . . I feel that if I can't change you—then soon you'll go out to kill—and you'll kill by instinct—and among the Mormons you kill will be the one—who . . . Lassiter, if you care a little for me—let me—for my sake—let me take your guns!"

As if her hands had been those of a child, he unclasped their clinging grip from the handles of his guns, and, pushing her away, he turned his gray face to her in one look of terrible realization, and then strode off into the shadows of the cottonwoods.

When the first shock of her futile appeal to Lassiter had passed, Jane took his cold, silent condemnation and abrupt departure not so much as a refusal to her entreaty as a hurt and stunned bitterness for her attempt at his betrayal. Upon further thought and slow consideration of Lassiter's past actions, she believed he would return and forgive her. The man could not be hard to a woman, and she doubted that he could stay away from her. But at the point where she had hoped to find him vulnerable she now began to fear he was proof against all persuasion. The iron and stone quality that she had early suspected in him had actually cropped out as an impregnable barrier. Nevertheless, if Lassiter remained in Cottonwoods, she would never give up her hope and desire to change him. She would change him if she had to sacrifice everything dear to her except hope of heaven. Passionately devoted as she was to her religion, she had yet refused to marry a Mormon. But a situation had developed wherein self paled in the great white light of religious duty of the highest order. That was the leading motive, the divinely spiritual one; but there were other motives, which, like tentacles, aided in drawing her will to the acceptance of a possible abnegation. And through the watches of that sleepless night Jane Withersteen, in fear and sorrow and doubt, came finally to believe

that if she must throw herself into Lassiter's arms to make him abide by
"Thou shalt not kill!" she would yet do well.

In the morning she expected Lassiter at the usual hour, but she was
not able to go at once to the court, so she sent little Fay. Mrs. Larkin was
ill and required attention. It appeared that the mother, from the time of
her arrival at Withersteen House, had relaxed and was slowly losing her
hold on life. Jane had believed that absence of worry and responsibility
coupled with good nursing and comfort would mend Mrs. Larkin's broken health. Such, however, was not the case.

When Jane did get out to the court, Fay was there alone, and at the
moment embarking on a dubious voyage down the stone-lined amber
stream upon a craft of two brooms and a pillow. Fay was as delightfully
wet as she could possibly wish to get.

Clatter of hoofs distracted Fay and interrupted the scolding she was
gleefully receiving from Jane. The sound was not the light-spirited trot
that Bells made when Lassiter rode him into the outer court. This was
slower and heavier, and Jane did not recognize in it any of her other horses.
The appearance of Bishop Dyer startled Jane. He dismounted with his
rapid, jerky motion, flung the bridle, and, as he turned toward the inner
court and stalked up on the stone flags, his boots rang. In his authoritative
front, and in the red anger unmistakably flaming in his face, he reminded
Jane of her father.

"Is that the Larkin pauper?" he asked, bruskly, without any greeting
to Jane.

"It's Mrs. Larkin's little girl," replied Jane, slowly.

"I hear you intend to raise the child?"

"Yes."

"Of course you mean to give her Mormon bringing up?"

"No!"

His questions had been swift. She was amazed at a feeling that someone else was replying for her.

"I've come to say a few things to you." He stopped to measure her
with stern, speculative eye.

Jane Withersteen loved this man. From earliest childhood she had
been taught to revere and love bishops of her church. And for ten years
Bishop Dyer had been the closest friend and counselor of her father, and

for the greater part of that period her own friend and Scriptural teacher. Her interpretation of her creed and her religious activity in fidelity to it, her acceptance of mysterious and holy Mormon truths, were all invested in this Bishop. Bishop Dyer as an entity was next to God. He was God's mouthpiece to the little Mormon community at Cottonwoods. God revealed himself in secret to this mortal.

And Jane Withersteen suddenly suffered a paralyzing affront to her consciousness of reverence by some strange irresistible twist of thought wherein she saw this Bishop as a man. And the train of thought hurdled the rising, crying protests of that other self whose poise she had lost. It was not her Bishop who eyed her in curious measurement. It was a man who tramped into her presence without removing his hat, who had no greeting for her, who had no semblance of courtesy. In looks, as in action, he made her think of a bull stamping cross-grained into a corral. She had heard of Bishop Dyer forgetting the minister in the fury of a common man, and now she was to feel it. The glance by which she measured him in turn momentarily veiled the divine in the ordinary. He looked a rancher; he was booted, spurred, and covered with dust; he carried a gun at his hip, and she remembered that he had been known to use it. But during the long moment while he watched her there was nothing commonplace in the slow-gathering might of his wrath.

"Brother Tull has talked to me," he began. "It was your father's wish that you marry Tull, and my order. You refused him?"

"Yes."

"You would not give up your friendship with that tramp Venters?"

"No."

"But you'll do as *I* order!" he thundered. "Why, Jane Withersteen, you are in danger of becoming a heretic! You can thank your Gentile friends for that. You face the damning of your soul to perdition."

In the flux and reflux of the whirling torture of Jane's mind, that new, daring spirit of hers vanished in the old habitual order of her life. She was a Mormon, and the Bishop regained ascendance.

"It's well I got you in time, Jane Withersteen. What would your father have said to these goings-on of yours? He would have put you in a stone cage on bread and water. He would have taught you something about Mormonism. Remember, you're a *born* Mormon. There have been

Mormons who turned heretic—damn their souls!—but no born Mormon ever left us yet. Ah, I see your shame. Your faith is not shaken. You are only a wild girl." The Bishop's tone softened. "Well, it's enough that I got to you in time. . . . Now tell me about this Lassiter. I hear strange things."

"What do you wish to know?" queried Jane.

"About this man. You hired him?"

"Yes, he's riding for me. When my riders left me I had to have any one I could get."

"Is it true what I hear—that he's a gunman, a Mormon-hater, steeped in blood?"

"True—terribly true, I fear."

"But what's he doing here in Cottonwoods? This place isn't notorious enough for such a man. Sterling and the villages north, where there's universal gun-packing and fights every day—where there are more men like him, it seems to me they would attract him most. We're only a wild, lonely border settlement. It's only recently that the rustlers have made killings here. Nor have there been saloons till lately, nor the drifting in of outcasts. Has not this gunman some special mission here?"

Jane maintained silence.

"Tell me," ordered Bishop Dyer, sharply.

"Yes," she replied.

"Do you know what it is?"

"Yes."

"Tell me that."

"Bishop Dyer, I don't want to tell."

He waved his hand in an imperative gesture of command. The red once more leaped to his face, and in his steel-blue eyes glinted a pin-point of curiosity.

"That first day," whispered Jane, "Lassiter said he came here to find— Milly Erne's grave!"

With downcast eyes Jane watched the swift flow of the amber water. She saw it and tried to think of it, of the stones, of the ferns; but, like her body, her mind was in a leaden vise. Only the Bishop's voice could release her. Seemingly there was silence of longer duration than all her former life.

"For what—else?" When Bishop Dyer's voice did cleave the silence it was high, curiously shrill, and on the point of breaking. It released Jane's tongue, but she could not lift her eyes.

"To kill the man who persuaded Milly Erne to abandon her home and her husband—and her God!"

With wonderful distinctness Jane Withersteen heard her own clear voice. She heard the water murmur at her feet and flow on to the sea; she heard the rushing of all the waters in the world. They filled her ears with low, unreal murmurings—these sounds that deadened her brain and yet could not break the long and terrible silence. Then, from somewhere— from an immeasurable distance—came a slow, guarded, clinking, clanking step. Into her it shot electrifying life. It released the weight upon her numbed eyelids. Lifting her eyes she saw—ashen, shaken, stricken—not the Bishop but the man! And beyond him from round the corner came that soft, silvery step. A long black boot with a gleaming spur swept into sight—and then Lassiter! Bishop Dyer did not see, did not hear: he stared at Jane in the throes of sudden revelation.

"Ah, I understand!" he cried, in hoarse accents. "That's why you made love to this Lassiter—to bind his hands!"

It was Jane's gaze riveted upon the rider that made Bishop Dyer turn. Then clear sight failed her. Dizzily, in a blur, she saw the Bishop's hand jerk to his hip. She saw gleam of blue and spout of red. In her ears burst a thundering report. The court floated in darkening circles around her, and she fell into utter blackness.

The darkness lightened, turned to slow-drifting haze, and lifted. Through a thin film of blue smoke she saw the rough-hewn timbers of the court roof. A cool, damp touch moved across her brow. She smelled powder, and it was that which galvanized her suspended thought. She moved, to see that she lay prone upon the stone flags with her head on Lassiter's knee, and he was bathing her brow with water from the stream. The same swift glance, shifting low, brought into range of her sight a smoking gun and splashes of blood.

"*Ah-h!*" she moaned, and was drifting, sinking again into darkness, when Lassiter's voice arrested her.

"It's all right, Jane. It's all right."

"Did—you—kill—him?" she whispered.

"Who? That fat party who was here? No. I didn't kill him."

"Oh! . . . Lassiter!"

"Say! It was queer for you to faint. I thought you were such a strong woman, not faintish like that. You're all right now—only some pale. I thought you'd never come to. But I'm awkward round womenfolks. I couldn't think of anythin'."

"Lassiter! . . . the gun there! . . . the blood!"

"So that's troublin' you. I reckon it needn't. You see it was this way. I come round the house an' seen that fat party an' heard him talkin' loud. Then he seen me, an' very impolite goes straight for his gun. He oughtn't have tried to throw a gun on me—whatever his reason was. For that's meetin' me on my own grounds. I've seen runnin' molasses that was quicker'n him. Now I didn't know who he was, visitor or friend or relation of yours, though I seen he was a Mormon all over, an' I couldn't get serious about shootin'. So I winged him—put a bullet through his arm as he was pullin' at his gun. An' he dropped the gun there, an' a little blood. I told him he'd introduced himself sufficient, an' to please move out of my vicinity. An' he went."

Lassiter spoke with slow, cool, soothing voice, in which there was a hint of levity, and his touch, as he continued to bathe her brow, was gentle and steady. His impassive face, and the kind, gray eyes, further stilled her agitation.

"He drew on you first, and you deliberately shot to cripple him—you wouldn't kill him—you—*Lassiter?*"

"That's about the size of it."

Jane kissed his hand.

All that was calm and cool about Lassiter instantly vanished.

"Don't do that! I won't stand it! An' I don't care a d—n who that fat party was."

He helped Jane to her feet and to a chair. Then with the wet scarf he had used to bathe her face he wiped the blood from the stone flags, and, picking up the gun, he threw it upon a couch. With that he began to pace the court, and his silver spurs jangled musically, and the great gun-sheaths softly brushed against his leather chaps.

"So—it's true—what I heard him say?" Lassiter asked, presently halting before her. "You made love to me—to bind my hands?"

"Yes," confessed Jane. It took all her woman's courage to meet the gray storm of his glance.

"All these days that you've been so friendly an' like a pardner—all these evenin's that have been so bewilderin' to me—your beauty—an'—an' the way you looked an' came close to me—they were woman's tricks to bind my hands?"

"Yes."

"An' your sweetness that seemed so natural, an' your throwin' little Fay an' me so much together—to make me love the child—all that was for the same reason?"

"Yes."

Lassiter flung his arms—a strange gesture for him.

"Mebbe it wasn't much in your Mormon thinkin', for you to play that game. But to ring the child in—that was hellish!"

Jane's passionate, unheeding zeal began to loom darkly.

"Lassiter, whatever my intention in the beginning, Fay loves you dearly—and I—I've—grown to—to like you."

"That's powerful kind of you, now," he said. Sarcasm and scorn made his voice that of a stranger. "An' you sit there an' look me straight in the eyes! You're a wonderful strange woman, Jane Withersteen."

"I'm not ashamed, Lassiter. I told you I'd try to change you."

"Would you mind tellin' me just what you tried?"

"I tried to make you see beauty in me and be softened by it. I wanted you to care for me so that I could influence you. It wasn't easy. At first you were stone-blind. Then I hoped you'd love little Fay, and through that come to feel the horror of making children fatherless."

"Jane Withersteen, either you're a fool or noble beyond my understandin'. Mebbe you're both. I know you're blind. What you meant is one thing—what you *did* was to make me love you."

"Lassiter!"

"I reckon I'm a human bein', though I never loved any one but my sister, Milly Erne. That was long—"

"Oh, are you Milly's brother?"

"Yes, I was, an' I loved her. There never was any one but her in my life till now. Didn't I tell you that long ago I back-trailed myself from women? I was a Texas ranger till—till Milly left home, an' then I became somethin' else—Lassiter! For years I've been a lonely man set on one thing. I came here an' met you. An' now I'm not the man I was. The change was gradual, an' I took no notice of it. I understand now that never-satisfied longin' to see you, listen to you, watch you, feel you near me. It's plain now why you were never out of my thoughts. I've had no thoughts but of you. I've lived an' breathed for you. An' now when I know what it means—what you've done—I'm burnin' up with hell's fire!"

"Oh, Lassiter—no—no—you don't love me that way!" Jane cried.

"If that's what love is, then I do."

"Forgive me! I didn't mean to make you love me like that. Oh, what a tangle of our lives! You—Milly Erne's brother! And I—heedless, mad to melt your heart toward Mormons. Lassiter, I may be wicked, but not wicked enough to hate. If I couldn't hate Tull, could I hate you?"

"After all, Jane, mebbe you're only blind—Mormon blind. That only can explain what's close to selfishness—"

"I'm not selfish. I despise the very word. If I were free—"

"But you're not free. Not free of Mormonism. An' in playin' this game with me you've been unfaithful."

"Unfaithful!" faltered Jane.

"Yes, I said unfaithful. You're faithful to your Bishop an' unfaithful to yourself. You're false to your womanhood, an' true to your religion. But for a savin' innocence you'd have made yourself low an' vile—betrayin' yourself, betrayin' me—all to bind my hands an' keep me from snuffin' out Mormon life. It's your damned Mormon blindness."

"Is it vile—is it blind—is it only Mormonism to save human life? No, Lassiter, that's God's law, divine, universal for all Christians."

"The blindness I mean is blindness that keeps you from seein' the truth. I've known many good Mormons. But some are blacker than hell. You won't see that even when you know it. Else, why all this blind passion to save the life of that—that . . ."

Jane shut out the light, and the hands she held over her eyes trembled and quivered against her face.

"Blind—yes, an' let me make it clear an' simple to you," Lassiter went on, his voice losing its tone of anger. "Take for instance that idea of yours last night when you wanted my guns. It was good an' beautiful, an' showed your heart—but—why, Jane, it was crazy. Mind I'm assumin' that life to me is as sweet as to any other man. An' to preserve that life is each man's first an' closest thought. Where would any man be on this border without guns? Where, especially, would Lassiter be? Well, I'd be under the sage with thousands of other men now livin', an' sure better men than me. Gun-packin' in the West since the Civil War has growed into a kind of moral law. An' out here on this border it's the difference between a man an' somethin' not a man. Look what your takin' Venters's guns from him all but made him! Why, your churchmen carry guns. Tull has killed a man an' drawed on others. Your Bishop has shot a half dozen men, an' it wasn't through prayers of his that they recovered. An' to-day he'd have shot me if he'd been quick enough on the draw. Could I walk or ride down into Cottonwoods without my guns? This is a wild time, Jane Withersteen, this year of our Lord 1871."

"No time—for a woman!" exclaimed Jane, brokenly. "Oh, Lassiter, I feel helpless—lost—and don't know where to turn. If I *am* blind—then—I need some one—a friend—you, Lassiter—more than ever!"

"Well, I didn't say nothin' about goin' back on you, did I?"

CHAPTER 12

THE INVISIBLE HAND

Jane received a letter from Bishop Dyer, not in his own handwriting, which stated that the abrupt termination of their interview had left him in some doubt as to her future conduct. A slight injury had incapacitated him from seeking another meeting at present, the letter went on to say, and ended with a request which was virtually a command, that she call upon him at once.

The reading of the letter acquainted Jane Withersteen with the fact that something within her had all but changed. She sent no reply to Bishop Dyer; nor did she go to see him. On Sunday she remained absent from the service—for the second time in years—and though she did not actually suffer there was a dead-lock of feelings deep within her, and the waiting for a balance to fall on either side was almost as bad as suffering. She had a gloomy expectancy of untoward circumstances, and with it a keen-edged curiosity to watch developments. She had a half-formed conviction that her future conduct—as related to her churchmen—was beyond her control and would be governed by their attitude toward her. Something was changing in her, forming, waiting for decision to make it a real and fixed thing. She had told Lassiter that she felt helpless and lost in the fateful tangle of their lives; and now she feared that she was approaching the same chaotic condition of mind in regard to her religion. It appalled her to find that she questioned phases of that religion. Absolute faith had been her serenity. Though leaving her faith unshaken, her serenity had been disturbed, and now it was broken by open war between her and her ministers. That something within her—a whisper—which she had tried in vain to hush had become a ringing voice, and it called to her to wait. She had transgressed no laws of God. Her churchmen, however invested with the power and the glory of a wonderful creed, however they sat in inexorable judgment of her, must now practice toward her the simple, common, Christian virtue they professed to preach, "Do unto others as you would have others do unto you!"

Jane Withersteen, waiting in darkness of mind, remained faithful still. But it was darkness that must soon be pierced by light. If her faith were justified, if her churchmen were trying only to intimidate her, the fact would soon be manifest, as would their failure, and then she would redouble her zeal toward them and toward what had been the best work of her life—work for the welfare and happiness of those among whom she lived, Mormon and Gentile alike. If that secret, intangible power closed its coils round her again, if that great invisible hand moved here and there and everywhere, slowly paralyzing her with its mystery and its inconceivable sway over her affairs, then she would know beyond doubt that it was not chance, nor jealousy, nor intimidation, nor ministerial wrath at her revolt, but a cold and calculating policy thought out long before she was born, a dark, immutable will of whose empire she and all that was hers were but an atom.

Then might come her ruin. Then might come her fall into black storm. Yet she would rise again, and to the light. God would be merciful to a driven woman who had lost her way.

A week passed. Little Fay played and prattled and pulled at Lassiter's big black guns. The rider came to Withersteen House oftener than ever. Jane saw a change in him, though it did not relate to his kindness and gentleness. He was quieter and more thoughtful. While playing with Fay or conversing with Jane he seemed to be possessed of another self that watched with cool, roving eyes, that listened, listened always as if the murmuring amber stream brought messages, and the moving leaves whispered something. Lassiter never rode Bells into the court any more, nor did he come by the lane or the paths. When he appeared it was suddenly and noiselessly out of the dark shadow of the grove.

"I left Bells out in the sage," he said, one day at the end of that week. "I must carry water to him."

"Why not let him drink at the trough or here?" asked Jane, quickly.

"I reckon it'll be safer for me to slip through the grove. I've been watched when I rode in from the sage."

"Watched? By whom?"

"By a man who thought he was well hid. But my eyes are pretty sharp. An', Jane," he went on, almost in a whisper, "I reckon it'd be a good idea for us to talk low. You're spied on here by your women."

"Lassiter!" she whispered in turn. "That's hard to believe. My women love me."

"What of that?" he asked. "Of course they love you. But they're Mormon women."

Jane's old, rebellious loyalty clashed with her doubt.

"I won't believe it," she replied, stubbornly.

"Well then, just act natural an' talk natural, an' pretty soon—give them time to hear us—pretend to go over there to the table, an' then quick-like make a move for the door an' open it."

"I will," said Jane, with heightened color. Lassiter was right; he never made mistakes; he would not have told her unless he positively knew. Yet Jane was so tenacious of faith that she had to see with her own eyes, and so constituted that to employ even such small deceit toward her women made her ashamed, and angry for her shame as well as theirs. Then a singular thought confronted her that made her hold up this simple ruse—which hurt her, though it was well justified—against the deceit she had wittingly and eagerly used toward Lassiter. The difference was staggering in its suggestion of that blindness of which he had accused her. Fairness and justice and mercy, that she had imagined were anchor-cables to hold fast her soul to righteousness, had not been hers in the strange, biased duty that had so exalted and confounded her.

Presently Jane began to act her little part, to laugh and play with Fay, to talk of horses and cattle to Lassiter. Then she made deliberate mention of a book in which she kept records of all pertaining to her stock, and she walked slowly toward the table, and when near the door she suddenly whirled and thrust it open. Her sharp action nearly knocked down a woman who had undoubtedly been listening.

"Hester," said Jane, sternly, "you may go home, and you need not come back."

Jane shut the door and returned to Lassiter. Standing unsteadily, she put her hand on his arm. She let him see that doubt had gone, and how this stab of disloyalty pained her.

"Spies! My own women! . . . Oh, miserable!" she cried, with flashing, tearful eyes.

"I hate to tell you," he replied. By that she knew he had long spared her. "It's begun again—that work in the dark."

"Nay, Lassiter—it never stopped!"

So bitter certainty claimed her at last, and trust fled Withersteen House and fled forever. The women who owed much to Jane Withersteen changed not in love for her, nor in devotion to their household work, but they poisoned both by a thousand acts of stealth and cunning and duplicity. Jane broke out once and caught them in strange, stone-faced, unhesitating falsehood. Thereafter she broke out no more. She forgave them because they were driven. Poor, fettered, and sealed Hagars, how she pitied them! What terrible thing bound them and locked their lips, when they showed neither consciousness of guilt toward their benefactress nor distress at the slow wearing apart of long established and dear ties?

"The blindness again!" cried Jane Withersteen. "In my sisters as in me! . . . O God!"

There came a time when no words passed between Jane and her women. Silently they went about their household duties, and secretly they went about the underhand work to which they had been bidden. The gloom of the house and the gloom of its mistress, which darkened even the bright spirit of little Fay, did not pervade these women. Happiness was not among them, but they were aloof from gloom. They spied and listened; they received and sent secret messengers; and they stole Jane's books and records, and finally the papers that were deeds of her possessions. Through it all they were silent, rapt in a kind of trance. Then one by one, without leave or explanation or farewell, they left Withersteen House, and never returned.

Coincident with this disappearance Jane's gardeners and workers in the alfalfa fields and stable men quit her, not even asking for their wages. Of all her Mormon employees about the great ranch only Jerd remained. He went on with his duty, but talked no more of the change than if it had never occurred.

"Jerd," said Jane, "what stock you can't take care of turn out in the sage. Let your first thought be for Black Star and Night. Keep them in perfect condition. Run them every day and watch them always."

Though Jane Withersteen gave with such liberality, she loved her possessions. She loved the rich, green stretches of alfalfa, and the farms, and the grove, and the old stone house, and the beautiful, ever-faithful amber spring, and every one of a myriad of horses and colts and burros and fowls down to the smallest rabbit that nipped her vegetables; but she loved best her noble Arabian steeds. In common with all riders of the upland sage Jane cherished two material things—the cold, sweet, brown water that made life possible in the Wilderness and the horses which were a part of that life. When Lassiter asked her what Lassiter would be without his guns he was assuming that his horse was part of himself. So Jane loved Black Star and Night because it was her nature to love all beautiful creatures—perhaps all living things; and then she loved them because she herself was of the sage and in her had been born and bred the rider's instinct to rely on his four-footed brother. And when Jane gave Jerd the order to keep her favorites trained down to the day it was a half-unconscious admission that presaged a time when she would need her fleet horses.

Jane had now, however, no leisure to brood over the coils that were closing round her. Mrs. Larkin grew weaker as the August days began; she required constant care; there was little Fay to look after; and such household work as was imperative. Lassiter put Bells in the stable with the other racers, and directed his efforts to a closer attendance upon Jane. She welcomed the change. He was always at hand to help, and it was her fortune to learn that his boast of being awkward around women had its root in humility and was not true.

His great, brown hands were skilled in a multiplicity of ways which a woman might have envied. He shared Jane's work, and was of especial help to her in nursing Mrs. Larkin. The woman suffered most at night, and this often broke Jane's rest. So it came about that Lassiter would stay by Mrs. Larkin during the day, when she needed care, and Jane would make up the sleep she lost in night-watches. Mrs. Larkin at once took kindly to the gentle Lassiter, and, without ever asking who or what he was, praised him to Jane. "He's a good man and loves children," she said. How sad to hear this truth spoken of a man whom Jane thought lost beyond all redemption! Yet ever and ever Lassiter towered above her, and behind or through his black, sinister figure shone something luminous that strangely affected Jane. Good and evil began to seem incomprehensibly blended in her judgment. It was her belief that evil could not come forth from good; yet here was a murderer who dwarfed in gentleness, patience, and love any man she had ever known.

She had almost lost track of her more outside concerns when early one morning Judkins presented himself before her in the courtyard.

Thin, hard, burnt, bearded, with the dust and sage thick on him, with his leather wrist-bands shining from use, and his boots worn through on the stirrup side, he looked the rider of riders. He wore two guns and carried a Winchester.

Jane greeted him with surprise and warmth, set meat and bread and drink before him; and called Lassiter out to see him. The men exchanged glances, and the meaning of Lassiter's keen inquiry and Judkins's bold reply, both unspoken, was not lost upon Jane.

"Where's your hoss?" asked Lassiter, aloud.

"Left him down the slope," answered Judkins. "I footed it in a ways, an' slept last night in the sage. I went to the place you told me you 'most always slept, but didn't strike you."

"I moved up some, near the spring, an' now I go there nights."

"Judkins—the white herd?" queried Jane, hurriedly.

"Miss Withersteen, I make proud to say I've not lost a steer. Fer a good while after thet stampede Lassiter milled we hed no trouble. Why, even the sage dogs left us. But it's begun agin—thet flashin' of lights over ridge tips, an' queer puffin' of smoke, an' then at night strange whistles an' noises. But the herd's acted magnificent. An' my boys, say, Miss Withersteen, they're only kids, but I ask no better riders. I got the laugh in the village fer takin' them out. They're a wild lot an' you know boys hev more nerve than grown men, because they don't know what danger is. I'm not denyin' there's danger. But they glory in it, an' mebbe I like it myself—anyway, we'll stick. We're goin' to drive the herd on the far side of the first break of Deception Pass. There's a great round valley over there, an' no ridges or piles of rocks to aid these stampeders. The rains are due. We'll hev plenty of water fer a while. An' we can hold thet herd from anybody except Oldrin'. I come in fer supplies. I'll pack a couple of burros an' drive out after dark to-night."

"Judkins, take what you want from the store-room. Lassiter will help you. I—I can't thank you enough . . . but—wait."

Jane went to the room that had once been her father's, and from a secret chamber in the thick stone wall she took a bag of gold, and, carrying it back to the court, she gave it to the rider.

"There, Judkins, and understand that I regard it as little for your loyalty. Give what is fair to your boys, and keep the rest. Hide it. Perhaps that would be wisest."

"Oh . . . Miss Withersteen!" ejaculated the rider. "I couldn't earn so much in—in ten years. It's not right—I oughtn't take it."

"Judkins, you know I'm a rich woman. I tell you I've few faithful friends. I've fallen upon evil days. God only knows what will become of me and mine! So take the gold."

She smiled in understanding of his speechless gratitude, and left him with Lassiter. Presently she heard him speaking low at first, then in louder accents emphasized by the thumping of his rifle on the stones. "As infernal a job as even you, Lassiter, ever heerd of."

"Why, son," was Lassiter's reply, "this breakin' of Miss Withersteen may seem bad to you, but it ain't bad—yet. Some of these wall-eyed fellers who look jest as if they was walkin' in the shadow of Christ himself, right down the sunny road, now they can think of things an' do things that are really hell-bent."

Jane covered her ears and ran to her own room, and there like a caged lioness she paced to and fro till the coming of little Fay reversed her dark thoughts.

The following day, a warm and muggy one threatening rain, while Jane was resting in the court, a horseman clattered through the grove and up to the hitching-rack. He leaped off and approached Jane with the manner of a man determined to execute a difficult mission, yet fearful of its reception. In the gaunt, wiry figure and the lean, brown face Jane recognized one of her Mormon riders, Blake. It was he of whom Judkins had long since spoken. Of all the riders ever in her employ Blake owed her the most, and as he stepped before her, removing his hat and making manly efforts to subdue his emotion, he showed that he remembered.

"Miss Withersteen, mother's dead," he said.

"Oh—Blake!" exclaimed Jane, and she could say no more.

"She died free from pain in the end, and she's buried—resting at last, thank God! . . . I've come to ride for you again, if you'll have me. Don't think I mentioned mother to get your sympathy. When she was living and your riders quit, I had to also. I was afraid of what might be done— said to her. . . . Miss Withersteen, we can't talk of—of what's going on now—"

"Blake, do you know?"

"I know a great deal. You understand, my lips are shut. But without explanation or excuse I offer my services. I'm a Mormon—I hope a good one. But—there are some things! . . . It's no use, Miss Withersteen, I can't say any more—what I'd like to. But will you take me back?"

"Blake! . . . You know what it means?"

"I don't care. I'm sick of—of—I'll show you a Mormon who'll be true to you!"

"But Blake—how terribly you might suffer for that!"

"Maybe. Aren't you suffering now?"

"God knows indeed I am!"

"Miss Withersteen, it's a liberty on my part to speak so, but I know you pretty well—know you'll never give in. I wouldn't if I were you. And I—I must—something makes me tell you the worst is yet to come. That's all. I absolutely can't say more. Will you take me back—let me ride for you—show everybody what I mean?"

"Blake, it makes me happy to hear you. How my riders hurt me when they quit!" Jane felt the hot tears well to her eyes and splash down upon her hands. "I thought so much of them—tried so hard to be good to them. And not one was true. You've made it easy to forgive. Perhaps many of them really feel as you do, but dare not return to me. Still, Blake, I hesitate to take you back. Yet I want you so much."

"Do it then. If you're going to make your life a lesson to Mormon women, let me make mine a lesson to the men. Right is right. I believe in you, and here's my life to prove it."

"You hint it may mean your life!" said Jane, breathless and low.

"We won't speak of that. I want to come back. I want to do what every rider aches in his secret heart to do for you. . . . Miss Withersteen, I hoped it'd not be necessary to tell you that my mother on her death-bed told me to have courage. She knew how the thing galled me—she told me to come back. . . . Will you take me?"

"God bless you, Blake! Yes, I'll take you back. And will you—will you accept gold from me?"

"Miss Withersteen!"

"I just gave Judkins a bag of gold. I'll give you one. If you will not take it you must not come back. You might ride for me a few months—weeks—days till the storm breaks. Then you'd have nothing, and be in disgrace with your people. We'll forearm you against poverty, and me against endless regret. I'll give you gold which you can hide—till some future time."

"Well, if it pleases you," replied Blake. "But you know I never thought of pay. Now, Miss Withersteen, one thing more. I want to see this man Lassiter. Is he here?"

"Yes, but Blake—what—Need you see him? Why?" asked Jane, instantly worried. "I can speak to him—tell him about you."

"That won't do. I want to—I've got to tell him myself. Where is he?"

"Lassiter is with Mrs. Larkin. She is ill. I'll call him," answered Jane, and going to the door she softly called for the rider. A faint, musical jingle preceded his step—then his tall form crossed the threshold.

"Lassiter, here's Blake, an old rider of mine. He has come back to me, and he wishes to speak to you."

Blake's brown face turned exceedingly pale.

"Yes, I had to speak to you," he said swiftly, "My name's Blake. I'm a Mormon and a rider. Lately I quit Miss Withersteen. I've come to beg her to take me back. Now I don't know you, but I know—what you are. So I've this to say to your face. It would never occur to this woman to imagine—let alone suspect me to be a spy. She couldn't think it might just be a low plot to come here and shoot you in the back. Jane Withersteen hasn't that kind of a mind. . . . Well, I've not come for that. I want to help her—to pull a bridle along with Judkins and—and you. The thing is—do you believe me?"

"I reckon I do," replied Lassiter. How this slow, cool speech contrasted with Blake's hot, impulsive words! "You might have saved some of your breath. See here, Blake, cinch this in your mind. Lassiter has met some square Mormons! An' mebbe—"

"Blake," interrupted Jane, nervously anxious to terminate a colloquy that she perceived was an ordeal for him. "Go at once and fetch me a report of my horses."

"Miss Withersteen! . . . You mean the big drove—down in the sage-cleared fields?"

"Of course," replied Jane. "My horses are all there, except the blooded stock I keep here."

"Haven't you heard—then?"

"Heard? No! What's happened to them?"

"They're gone, Miss Withersteen, gone these ten days past. Dorn told me, and I rode down to see for myself."

"Lassiter—did you know?" asked Jane, whirling to him.

"I reckon so. . . . But what was the use to tell you?"

It was Lassiter turning away his face and Blake studying the stone flags at his feet that brought Jane to the understanding of what she betrayed. She strove desperately, but she could not rise immediately from such a blow.

"My horses! My horses! What's become of them?"

"Dorn said the riders report another drive by Oldring. . . . And I trailed the horses miles down the slope toward Deception Pass."

"My red herd's gone! My horses gone! The white herd will go next. I can stand that. But, if I lost Black Star and Night, it would be like parting with my own flesh and blood. Lassiter—Blake—am I in danger of losing my racers?"

"A rustler—or—or anybody stealin' hosses of yours would most of all want the blacks," said Lassiter. His evasive reply was affirmative enough. The other rider nodded gloomy acquiescence.

"Oh! Oh!" Jane Withersteen choked, with violent utterance.

"Let me take charge of the blacks?" asked Blake. "One more rider won't be any great help to Judkins. But I might hold Black Star and Night, if you put such store on their value."

"Value! Blake, I love my racers. Besides, there's another reason why I mustn't lose them. You go to the stables. Go with Jerd every day when he runs the horses, and don't let them out of your sight. If you would please me—win my gratitude, guard my black racers."

When Blake had mounted and ridden out of the court Lassiter regarded Jane with the smile that was becoming rarer as the days sped by.

"'Pears to me, as Blake says, you do put some store on them hosses. Now, I ain't gainsayin' that the Arabians are the handsomest hosses I ever seen. But Bells can beat Night, an' run neck an' neck with Black Star."

"Lassiter, don't tease me now, I'm miserable—sick. Bells is fast, but he can't stay with the blacks, and you know it. Only Wrangle can do that."

"I'll bet that big raw-boned brute can more'n show his heels to your black racers. Jane, out there in the sage, on a long chase, Wrangle could kill your favorites."

"No, no," replied Jane, impatiently. "Lassiter, why do you say that so often? I know you've teased me at times, and I believe it's only kindness. You're always trying to keep my mind off worry. But you mean more by this repeated mention of my racers?"

"I reckon so." Lassiter paused, and for the thousandth time in her presence moved his black sombrero round and round, as if counting the silver pieces on the band. "Well, Jane, I've sort of read a little that's passin' in your mind."

"You think I might fly from my home—from Cottonwoods—from the Utah border?"

"I reckon. An' if you ever do an' get away with the blacks I wouldn't like to see Wrangle left here on the sage. Wrangle could catch you. I know Venters had him. But you can never tell. Mebbe he hasn't got him now. . . . Besides—things are happenin', an' somethin' of the same queer nature might have happened to Venters."

"God knows you're right! . . . Poor Bern, how long he's gone! In my trouble I've been forgetting him. But, Lassiter, I've little fear for him. I've heard my riders say he's as keen as a wolf. . . . As to your reading my thoughts—well, your suggestion makes an actual thought of what was only one of my dreams. I believe I dreamed of flying from this wild borderland, Lassiter. I've strange dreams. I'm not always practical, and thinking of my many duties, as you said once. For instance—if I dared—if I dared I'd ask you to saddle the blacks and ride away with me—and hide me."

"Jane!"

The rider's sunburned face turned white. A few times Jane had seen Lassiter's cool calm broken—when he had met little Fay, when he had learned how and why he had come to love both child and mistress, when he had stood beside Milly Erne's grave. But one and all they could not be considered in the light of his present agitation. Not only did Lassiter turn white—not only did he grow tense, not only did he lose his coolness, but also he suddenly, violently, hungrily took her into his arms and crushed her to his breast.

"Lassiter!" cried Jane, trembling. It was an action for which she took sole blame. Instantly, as if dazed, weakened, he released her. "Forgive me!" went on Jane. "I'm always forgetting your—your feelings. I thought of you as my faithful friend. I'm always making you out more than human . . . only, let me say—I meant that—about riding away. I'm wretched, sick of this—this—oh, something bitter and black grows on my heart!"

"Jane, the hell—of it," he replied, with deep intake of breath, "is you *can't* ride away. Mebbe realizin' it accounts for my grabbin' you—that way, as much as the crazy boy's rapture your words gave me. I don't understand myself. . . . But the hell of this game is—you *can't* ride away."

"Lassiter! . . . What on earth do you mean? I'm an absolutely free woman."

"You ain't absolutely anythin' of the kind. . . . I reckon I've got to tell you!"

"Tell me all. It's uncertainty that makes me a coward. It's faith and hope—blind love, if you will, that makes me miserable. Every day I awake believing—still believing. The day grows, and with it doubts, fears, and that black bat hate that bites hotter and hotter into my heart. Then comes night—I pray—I pray for all, and, for myself—I sleep—and I awake free once more, trustful, faithful, to believe—to hope! Then, Oh my God! I grow and live a thousand years till night again! . . . But, if you want to see me a woman, tell me why I can't ride away—tell me what more I'm to lose—tell me the worst."

"Jane, you're watched. There's no single move of yours, except when you're hid in your house, that ain't seen by sharp eyes. The cottonwood grove's full of creepin', crawlin' men. Like Indians in the grass! When you rode, which wasn't often lately, the sage was full of sneakin' men. At night they crawl under your windows, into the court, an' I reckon into the house. Jane Withersteen, you know, never locked a door! This here grove's a hummin' bee-hive of mysterious happenin's. Jane, it ain't so much that these spies keep out of my way as me keepin' out of theirs. They're goin' to try to kill me. That's plain. But mebbe I'm as hard to shoot in the back as in the face. So far I've seen fit to watch only. This all means, Jane, that you're a marked woman. You can't get away—not now. Mebbe later, when you're broken, you might. But that's sure doubtful. Jane, you're to lose the cattle that's left—your home an' ranch—an' Amber Spring. You can't even hide a sack of gold! For it couldn't be slipped out of the house, day or night, an' hid or buried, let alone be rid off with. You may lose all. I'm tellin' you, Jane, hopin' to prepare you, if the worst does come. I told you once before about that strange power I've got to feel things."

"Lassiter, what can I do?"

"Nothin', I reckon, except know what's comin' an wait an' be game. If you'd let me make a call on Tull, an' a long deferred call on—"

"Hush! . . . Hush!" she whispered.

"Well, even that wouldn't help you any in the end."

"What does it mean? Oh, what does it mean? I am my father's daughter—a Mormon, yet I can't see! I've not failed in religion—in duty. For years I've given with a free and full heart. When my father died I was rich. If I'm still rich it's because I couldn't find enough ways to become poor. What am I, what are my possessions to set in motion such intensity of secret oppression?"

"Jane, the mind behind it all is an empire builder."

"But Lassiter, I would give freely—all I own to avert this—this wretched thing. If I gave—that would leave me with faith still. Surely my—my churchmen think of my soul? If I lose my trust in them—"

"Child, be still!" said Lassiter, with a dark dignity that had in it something of pity. "You are a woman, fine an' big an' strong, an' your heart matches your size. But in mind you're a child. I'll say a little more—then I'm done. I'll never mention this again. Among many thousands of women you're one who has bucked against your churchmen. They tried you out, an' failed of persuasion, an' finally of threats. You meet now the cold steel of a will as far from Christlike as the universe is wide. You're to be broken. Your body's to be held given to some man, made, if possible, to bring children into the world. But your soul? . . . What do they care for your soul?"

CHAPTER 13

SOLITUDE AND STORM

In his hidden valley Venters awakened from sleep, and his ears rang with innumerable melodies from full-throated mocking-birds, and his eyes opened wide upon the glorious golden shaft of sunlight shining through the great Stone Bridge. The circle of cliffs surrounding Surprise Valley lay shrouded in morning mist, a dim blue low down along the terraces, a creamy, moving cloud along the ramparts. The oak forest in the center was a plumed and tufted oval of gold.

He saw Bess under the spruces. Upon her complete recovery of strength she always rose with the dawn. At the moment she was feeding the quail she had tamed. And she had begun to tame the mocking-birds. They fluttered among the branches overhead, and some left off their songs to flit down and shyly hop near the twittering quail. Little gray and white rabbits crouched in the grass, now nibbling, now laying long ears flat and watching the dogs.

Venters's swift glance took in the brightening valley, and Bess and her pets, and Ring and Whitie. It swept over all to return again and rest upon the girl. She had changed. To the dark trousers and blouse she had added moccasins of her own make, but she no longer resembled a boy. No eye could have failed to mark the rounded contours of a woman. The change had been to grace and beauty. A glint of warm gold gleamed from her hair, and a tint of red shone in the clear dark-brown of cheeks. The haunting sweetness of her lips and eyes, that earlier had been illusive, a promise, had become a living fact. She fitted harmoniously into that wonderful setting; she was like Surprise Valley—wild and beautiful.

Venters leaped out of his cave to begin the day.

He had postponed his journey to Cottonwoods until after the passing of the summer rains. The rains were due soon. But until their arrival and the necessity for his trip to the village, he sequestered in a far corner of mind all thought of peril, of his past life, and almost that of the present. It was enough to live. He did not want to know what lay hidden in the dim and distant future. Surprise Valley had enchanted him. In this home of the cliff-dwellers there was peace and quiet and solitude, and another thing, wondrous as the golden morning shaft of sunlight, that he dared not ponder over long enough to understand.

The solitude he had hated when alone he had now come to love. He was assimilating something from this valley of gleams and shadows. From this strange girl he was assimilating more.

The day at hand resembled many days gone before. As Venters had no tools with which to build, or to till the terraces, he remained idle. Beyond the cooking of the simple fare there were no tasks. And as there were no tasks, there was no system. He and Bess began one thing, to leave it; to begin another, to leave that; and then do nothing but lie under the spruces and watch the great cloud-sails majestically move along the ramparts, and dream and dream. The valley was a golden, sunlit world. It was silent. The sighing wind and the twittering quail and the singing birds, even the rare and seldom-occurring hollow crack of a sliding weathered stone, only thickened and deepened that insulated silence.

Venters and Bess had vagrant minds.

"Bess, did I tell you about my horse Wrangle?" inquired Venters.

"A hundred times," she replied.

"Oh, have I? I'd forgotten. I want you to see him. He'll carry us both."

"I'd like to ride him. Can he run?"

"Run? He's a demon. Swiftest horse on the sage! I hope he'll stay in that cañon."

"He'll stay."

They left camp to wander along the terraces, into the aspen ravines, under the gleaming walls. Ring and Whitie wandered in the fore, often turning, often trotting back, open-mouthed and solemn-eyed and happy. Venters lifted his gaze to the grand archway over the entrance to the valley, and Bess lifted hers to follow his, and both were silent. Sometimes the bridge held their attention for a long time. Today a soaring eagle attracted them.

"How he sails!" exclaimed Bess. "I wonder where his mate is?"

"She's at the nest. It's on the bridge in a crack near the top. I see her often. She's almost white."

They wandered on down the terrace, into the shady, sun-flecked forest. A brown bird fluttered crying from a bush. Bess peeped into the leaves.

"Look! A nest and four little birds. They're not afraid of us. See how they open their mouths. They're hungry."

Rabbits rustled the dead brush and pattered away. The forest was full of a drowsy hum of insects. Little darts of purple, that were running quail, crossed the glades. And a plaintive, sweet peeping came from the coverts. Bess's soft step disturbed a sleeping lizard that scampered away over the leaves. She gave chase and caught it, a slim creature of nameless color, but of exquisite beauty.

"Jewel eyes," she said. "It's like a rabbit—afraid. We won't eat you. There—go."

Murmuring water drew their steps down into a shallow, shaded ravine where a brown brook brawled softly over mossy stones. Multitudes of strange, gray frogs with white spots and black eyes lined the rocky bank and leaped only at close approach. Then Venters's eye descried a very thin, very long green snake coiled round a sapling. They drew closer and closer till they could have touched it. The snake had no fear and watched them with scintillating eyes.

"It's pretty," said Bess. "How tame! I thought snakes always ran."

"No. Even the rabbits didn't run here till the dogs chased them."

On and on they wandered to the wild jumble of massed and broken fragments of cliff at the west end of the valley. The roar of the disappearing stream dinned in their ears. Into this maze of rocks they threaded a tortuous way, climbing, descending, halting to gather wild plums and great lavender lilies, and going on at the will of fancy. Idle and keen perceptions guided them equally.

"Oh, let us climb there!" cried Bess, pointing upward to a small space of terrace left green and shady between huge abutments of broken cliff. And they climbed to the nook and rested and looked out across the valley to the curling column of blue smoke from their campfire. But the cool shade and the rich grass and the fine view were not what they had climbed for. They could not have told, although whatever had drawn them was all-satisfying. Light, sure-footed as a mountain goat, Bess pattered down at Venters's heels; and they went on, calling the dogs, eyes dreamy and wide, listening to the wind and the bees and the crickets and the birds.

Part of the time Ring and Whitie led the way, then Venters, then Bess; and the direction was not an object. They left the sun-streaked shade of the oaks, brushed the long grass of the meadows, entered the green and fragrant swaying willows, to stop, at length, under the huge old cottonwoods, where the beavers were busy.

Here they rested and watched. A dam of brush and logs and mud and stones backed the stream into a little lake. The round, rough beaver houses projected from the water. Like the rabbits the beaver had become shy. Gradually, however, as Venters and Bess knelt low, holding the dogs, the beaver emerged to swim with logs and gnaw at cottonwoods and pat mud walls with their paddle-like tails, and, glossy and shiny in the sun, to go on with their strange, persistent industry. They were the builders. The lake was a mud-hole, and the immediate environment a scarred and dead region, but it was a wonderful home of wonderful animals.

"Look at that one—he puddles in the mud," said Bess. "And there! See him dive! Hear them gnawing! I'd think they'd break their teeth. How's it they can stay out of the water and under the water?"

And she laughed.

Then Venters and Bess wandered farther, and, perhaps not all unconsciously this time, wended their slow steps to the cave of the cliff-dwellers, where she liked best to go.

The tangled thicket and the long slant of dust and little chips of weathered rock and the steep bench of stone and the worn steps all were arduous work for Bess in the climbing. But she gained the shelf, gasping, hot of cheek, glad of eye, with her hand in Venters's. Here they rested. The beautiful valley glittered below with its millions of wind-turned leaves bright-faced in the sun, and the mighty bridge towered heavenward, crowned with blue sky. Bess, however, never rested for long. Soon she was exploring, and Venters followed; she dragged forth from corners and shelves a multitude of crudely fashioned and painted pieces of pottery, and he carried them. They peeped down into the dark holes of the kivas, and Bess gleefully dropped a stone and waited for the long-coming hollow sound to rise. They peeped into the little globular houses, like mud-wasp nests, and wondered if these had been store-places for grain or baby cribs, or what; and they crawled into the larger houses and laughed when they bumped their heads on the low roofs, and they dug in the dust of the floors. And they brought from dust and darkness armloads of treasure which they carried to the light. Flints and stones and strange curved sticks and pottery they found; and twisted grass rope that crumbled in their hands, and bits of whitish stone which crushed to powder at a touch and seemed to vanish in the air.

"That white stuff was bone," said Venters, slowly. "Bones of a cliff-dweller."

"No!" exclaimed Bess.

"Here's another piece. Look! . . . Whew! Dry, powdery smoke! That's bone."

Then it was that Venters's primitive, childlike mood, like a savage's, seeing yet unthinking, gave way to the encroachment of civilized thought. The world had not been made for a single day's play or fancy or idle watching. The world was old. Nowhere could be gotten a better idea of its age than in this gigantic silent tomb. The gray ashes in Venters's hand had once been bone of a human being like himself. The pale gloom of the cave had shadowed people long ago. He saw that Bess had received the same shock—could not in moments such as this escape her feeling, living, thinking destiny.

"Bern, people have *lived* here," she said, with wide, thoughtful eyes.

"Yes," he replied.

"How long ago?"

"A thousand years and more."

"What were they?"

"Cliff-dwellers. Men who had enemies and made their homes high out of reach."

"They had to fight?"

"Yes."

"They fought for—what?"

"For life. For their homes, food, children, parents—for their women!"

"Has the world changed any in a thousand years?"

"I don't know—perhaps very little."

"Have men?"

"I hope so—I think so."

"Things crowd into my mind," she went on, and the wistful light in her eyes told Venters the truth of her thoughts. "I've ridden the border of Utah. I've seen people—know how they live—but they must be few of all who are living. I had my books and I studied them. But all that doesn't help me any more. I want to go out into the big world and see it. Yet I want to stay here more. What's to become of us? Are we cliff-dwellers? We're alone here. I'm happy when I don't think. These—these bones that fly into dust—they make me sick, and a little afraid. Did the people who lived here once have the same feelings as we have? What was the good of their living at all? They're gone! What's the meaning of it all—of us?"

"Bess, you ask more than I can tell. It's beyond me. Only there was laughter here once—and now there's silence. There was life—and now there's death. Men cut these little steps, made these arrow-heads and mealing-stones, plaited the ropes we found, and left their bones to crumble in our fingers. As far as time is concerned it might all have been yester-day. We're here to-day. Maybe we're higher in the scale of human be-ings—in intelligence. But who knows? We can't be any higher in the things for which life is lived at all."

"What are they?"

"Why—I suppose relationship, friendship—love."

"Love!"

"Yes. Love of man for woman—love of woman for man. That's the nature, the meaning, the best of life itself."

She said no more. Wistfulness of glance deepened into sadness.

"Come, let us go," said Venters.

Action brightened her. Beside him, holding his hand, she slipped down the shelf, ran down the long, steep slant of sliding stones, out of the cloud of dust, and likewise out of the pale gloom.

"We beat the slide," she cried.

The miniature avalanche cracked and roared, and rattled itself into an inert mass at the base of the incline. Yellow dust like the gloom of the cave, but not so changeless, drifted away on the wind; the roar clapped in echo from the cliff, returned, went back, and came again to die in the hollowness. Down on the sunny terrace there was a different atmosphere. Ring and Whitie leaped around Bess. Once more she was smiling, gay, and thoughtless, with the dream-mood in the shadow of her eyes.

"Bess, I haven't seen that since last summer. Look!" said Venters, pointing to the scalloped edge of rolling purple clouds that peeped over the western wall. "We're in for a storm."

"Oh, I hope not. I'm afraid of storms."

"Are you? Why?"

"Have you ever been down in one of these walled-up pockets in a bad storm?"

"No, now I think of it, I haven't."

"Well, it's terrible. Every summer I get scared to death, and hide somewhere in the dark. Storms up on the sage are bad, but nothing to what they are down here in the cañons. And in this little valley—why echoes can rap back and forth so quick they'll split our ears."

"We're perfectly safe here, Bess."

"I know. But that hasn't anything to do with it. The truth is I'm afraid of lightning and thunder, and thunder-claps hurt my head. If we have a bad storm, will you stay close by me?"

"Yes."

When they got back to camp the afternoon was closing, and it was exceedingly sultry. Not a breath of air stirred the aspen leaves, and when these did not quiver the air was indeed still. The dark purple clouds moved almost imperceptibly out of the west.

"What have we for supper?" asked Bess.

"Rabbit."

"Bern, can't you think of another new way to cook rabbit?" went on Bess, with earnestness.

"What do you think I am—a magician?" retorted Venters.

"I wouldn't dare tell you. But, Bern, do you want me to turn into a rabbit?"

There was a dark-blue, merry flashing of eyes, and a parting of lips; then she laughed. In that moment she was naïve and wholesome.

"Rabbit seems to agree with you," replied Venters. "You are well and strong—and growing very pretty."

Anything in the nature of compliment he had never before said to her, and just now he responded to a sudden curiosity to see its effect. Bess stared as if she had not heard aright, slowly blushed, and completely lost her poise in happy confusion.

"I'd better go right away," he continued, "and fetch supplies from Cottonwoods."

A startlingly swift change in the nature of her agitation made him reproach himself for his abruptness.

"No, no, don't go!" she said. "I didn't mean—that about the rabbit. I—I was only trying to be—funny. Don't leave me all alone!"

"Bess, I must go sometime."

"Wait then. Wait till after the storms."

The purple cloud-bank darkened the lower edge of the setting sun, crept up and up, obscuring its fiery red heart, and finally passed over the last ruddy crescent of its upper rim.

The intense dead silence awakened to a long, low, rumbling roll of thunder.

"Oh!" cried Bess, nervously.

"We've had big black clouds before this without rain," said Venters. "But there's no doubt about that thunder. The storms are coming. I'm glad. Every rider on the sage will hear that thunder with glad ears."

Venters and Bess finished their simple meal and the few tasks around the camp, then faced the open terrace, the valley, and the west, to watch and await the approaching storm.

It required keen vision to see any movement whatever in the purple clouds. By infinitesimal degrees the dark cloud-line merged upward into the golden red haze of the afterglow of sunset. A shadow lengthened from under the western wall across the valley. As straight and rigid as steel rose the delicate spear-pointed silver spruces; the aspen leaves, by nature pen-dant and quivering, hung limp and heavy; no slender blade of grass moved. A gentle plashing of water came from the ravine. Then again from out of the west sounded the low, dull, and rumbling roll of thunder.

A wave, a ripple of light, a trembling and turning of the aspen leaves, like the approach of a breeze on the water, crossed the valley from the west; and the lull and the deadly stillness and the sultry air passed away on a cool wind.

The night bird of the cañon, with his clear and melancholy notes, announced the twilight. And from all along the cliffs rose the faint murmur and moan and mourn of the wind singing in the caves. The bank of clouds now swept hugely out of the western sky. Its front was purple and black with gray between, a bulging, mushrooming, vast thing instinct with storm. It had a dark, angry, threatening aspect. As if all the power of the winds were pushing and piling behind, it rolled ponderously across the sky. A red flare burned out instantaneously, flashed from west to east, and died. Then from the deepest black of the purple cloud burst a boom. It was like the bowling of a huge boulder along the crags and ramparts, and seemed to roll on and fall into the valley to bound and bang and boom from cliff to cliff.

"Oh!" cried Bess, with her hands over her ears. "What did I tell you?"

"Why, Bess, be reasonable," said Venters.

"I'm a coward."

"Not quite that, I hope. It's strange you're afraid. I love a storm."

"I tell you a storm down in these cañons is an awful thing. I know Oldring hated storms. His men were afraid of them. There was one who went deaf in a bad storm, and never could hear again."

"Maybe I've lots to learn, Bess. I'll lose my guess if this storm isn't bad enough. We're going to have heavy wind first, then lightning and thunder, then the rain. Let's stay out as long as we can."

The tips of the cottonwoods and the oaks waved to the east, and the rings of aspens along the terraces twinkled their myriad of bright faces in fleet and glancing gleam. A low roar rose from the leaves of the forest, and the spruces swished in the rising wind. It came in gusts, with light breezes between. As it increased in strength the lulls shortened in length till there was a strong and steady blow all the time, and violent puffs at intervals, and sudden whirling currents. The clouds spread over the valley, rolling swiftly and low, and twilight faded into a sweeping darkness. Then the singing of the wind in the caves drowned the swift roar of rustling leaves; then the song swelled to a mourning, moaning wail; then with the gathering power of the wind the wail changed to a shriek. Steadily the wind strengthened and constantly the strange sound changed.

The last bit of blue sky yielded to the onsweep of clouds. Like angry surf the pale gleams of gray, amid the purple of that scudding front, swept beyond the eastern rampart of the valley. The purple deepened to black. Broad sheets of lightning flared over the western wall. There were not yet any ropes or zigzag streaks darting down through the gathering darkness. The storm center was still beyond Surprise Valley.

"Listen! . . . Listen!" cried Bess, with her lips close to Venters's ear. "You'll hear Oldring's knell!"

"What's that?"

"Oldring's knell. When the wind blows a gale in the caves it makes what the rustlers call Oldring's knell. They believe it bodes his death. I think he believes so too. It's not like any sound on earth. . . . It's beginning. Listen!"

The gale swooped down with a hollow, unearthly howl. It yelled and pealed and shrilled and shrieked. It was made up of a thousand piercing cries. It was a rising and a moving sound. Beginning at the western break of the valley it rushed along each gigantic cliff, whistling into the caves and cracks, to mount in power, to bellow a blast through the great Stone Bridge. Gone, as into an engulfing roar of surging waters, it seemed to shoot back and begin all over again.

It was only wind, thought Venters. Here sped and shrieked the sculptor that carved out the wonderful caves in the cliffs. It was only a gale, but as Venters listened, as his ears became accustomed to the fury and strife, out of it all or through it or above it, pealed low and perfectly clear and persistently uniform a strange sound that had no counterpart in all the sounds of the elements. It was not of earth or of life. It was the grief and agony of the gale. A knell of all upon which it blew!

Black night enfolded the valley. Venters could not see his companion, and knew of her presence only through the tightening hold of her hand on his arm. He felt the dogs huddle closer to him. Suddenly the dense, black vault overhead split asunder to a blue-white, dazzling streak of lightning. The whole valley lay vividly clear and luminously bright in his sight. Upreared, vast and magnificent, the Stone Bridge glimmered like some grand god of storm in the lightning's fire. Then all flashed black again—blacker than pitch—a thick, impenetrable coal-blackness. And there came a ripping, crashing report. Instantly an echo resounded with clapping crash. The initial report was nothing to the echo. It was a terrible, living, reverberating, detonating crash. The wall threw the sound across, and could have made no greater roar if it had slipped in avalanche. From cliff to cliff the echo went in crashing retort and banged in lessening power, and boomed in thinner volume, and clapped weaker and weaker till a final clap could not reach across to waiting cliff.

In the pitchy darkness Venters led Bess, and, groping his way, by feel of hand found the entrance to her cave and lifted her up. On the instant a blinding flash of lightning illumined the cave and all about him. He saw Bess's face white now with dark, frightened eyes. He saw the dogs leap up, and he followed suit. The golden glare vanished; all was black; then came the splitting crack and the infernal din of echoes.

Bess shrank closer to him and closer, found his hands, and pressed them tightly over her ears, and dropped her face upon his shoulder, and hid her eyes.

Then the storm burst with a succession of ropes and streaks and shafts of lightning, playing continuously, filling the valley with a broken radiance; and the cracking shots followed each other swiftly till the echoes blended in one fearful, deafening crash.

Venters looked out upon the beautiful valley—beautiful now as never before—mystic in its transparent, luminous gloom, weird in the quivering, golden haze of lightning. The dark spruces were tipped with glimmering lights; the aspens bent low in the winds, as waves in a tempest at sea; the forest of oaks tossed wildly and shone with gleams of fire. Across the valley the huge cavern of cliff-dwellers yawned in the glare, every little black window as clear as at noonday; but the night and the storm added to their tragedy. Flung arching to the black clouds, the great Stone Bridge seemed to bear the brunt of the storm. It caught the full fury of the rushing wind. It lifted its noble crown to meet the lightnings. Venters thought of the eagles and their lofty nest in a niche under the arch. A driving pall of rain, black as the clouds, came sweeping on to obscure the bridge and the gleaming walls and the shining valley. The lightning played incessantly, streaking down through opaque darkness of rain. The roar of the wind, with its strange knell and the recrashing echoes, mingled with the roar of the flooding rain, and all seemingly were deadened and drowned in a world of sound.

In the dimming pale light Venters looked down upon the girl. She had sunk into his arms, upon his breast, burying her face. She clung to him. He felt the softness of her, and the warmth, and the quick heave of her breast. He saw the dark, slender, graceful outline of her form. A woman lay in his arms! And he held her closer. He who had been alone in the sad, silent watches of the night was not now and never must be again alone. He who had yearned for the touch of a hand felt the long tremble and the heart-beat of a woman. By what strange chance had she come to love him! By what change—by what marvel had she grown into a treasure!

No more did he listen to the rush and roar of the thunderstorm. For with the touch of clinging hands and the throbbing bosom he grew conscious of an inward storm—the tingling of new chords of thought, strange music of unheard, joyous bells, sad dreams dawning to wakeful delight, dissolving doubt, resurging hope, force, fire, and freedom, unutterable sweetness of desire. A storm in his breast—a storm of real love.

CHAPTER 14

WEST WIND

When the storm abated Venters sought his own cave, and late in the night, as his blood cooled and the stir and throb and thrill subsided, he fell asleep.

With the breaking of dawn his eyes unclosed. The valley lay drenched and bathed, a burnished oval of glittering green. The rain-washed walls glistened in the morning light. Waterfalls of many forms poured over the rims. One, a broad, lacy sheet, thin as smoke, slid over the western notch and struck a ledge in its downward fall, to bound into broader leap, to burst far below into white and gold and rosy mist.

Venters prepared for the day, knowing himself a different man.

"It's a glorious morning," said Bess, in greeting.

"Yes. After the storm the west wind," he replied.

"Last night was I—very much of a baby?" she asked, watching him.

"Pretty much."

"Oh, I couldn't help it!"

"I'm glad you were afraid."

"Why?" she asked, in slow surprise.

"I'll tell you some day," he answered, soberly. Then around the camp-fire and through the morning meal he was silent; afterward he strolled thoughtfully off alone along the terrace. He climbed a great yellow rock raising its crest among the spruces, and there he sat down to face the valley and the west.

"I love her!"

Aloud he spoke—unburdened his heart—confessed his secret. For an instant the golden valley swam before his eyes, and the walls waved, and all about him whirled with tumult within.

"I love her! . . . I understand now."

Reviving memory of Jane Withersteen and thought of the complications of the present amazed him with proof of how far he had drifted from his old life. He discovered that he hated to take up the broken threads, to delve into dark problems and difficulties. In this beautiful valley he had been living a beautiful dream. Tranquillity had come to him, and the joy of solitude, and interest in all the wild creatures and crannies of this incomparable valley—and love. Under the shadow of the great Stone Bridge God had revealed Himself to Venters.

"The world seems very far away," he muttered, "but it's there—and I'm not yet done with it. Perhaps I never shall be. . . . Only—how glorious it would be to live here always and never think again!"

Whereupon the resurging reality of the present, as if in irony of his wish, steeped him instantly in contending thought. Out of it all he presently evolved these things: he must go to Cottonwoods; he must bring supplies back to Surprise Valley; he must cultivate the soil and raise corn and stock, and, most imperative of all, he must decide the future of the girl who loved him and whom he loved. The first of these things required tremendous effort; the last one, concerning Bess, seemed simply and naturally easy of accomplishment. He would marry her. Suddenly, as from roots of poisonous fire, flamed up the forgotten truth concerning her. It seemed to wither and shrivel up all his joy on its hot, tearing way to his heart. She had been Oldring's Masked Rider. To Venters's question, "What were you to Oldring?" she had answered with scarlet shame and drooping head.

"What do I care who she is or what she was!" he cried, passionately. And he knew it was not his old self speaking. It was this softer, gentler man who had awakened to new thoughts in the quiet valley. Tenderness, masterful in him now, matched the absence of joy and blunted the knife-edge of entering jealousy. Strong and passionate effort of will, surprising to him, held back the poison from piercing his soul.

"Wait! . . . Wait!" he cried, as if calling. His hand pressed against his breast, and he might have called to the pang there. "Wait! It's all so strange—so wonderful. Anything can happen. Who am I to judge her? I'll glory in my love for her. But I can't tell it—can't give up to it."

Certainly he could not then decide her future. Marrying her was impossible in Surprise Valley and in any village south of Sterling. Even without the mask she had once worn she would easily have been recognized as Oldring's Rider. No man who had ever seen her would forget her, regardless of his ignorance as to her sex. Then more poignant than all other argument was the fact that he did not want to take her away from Surprise Valley. He resisted all thought of that. He had brought her to the most beautiful and wildest place of the uplands; he had saved her, nursed her back to strength, watched her bloom as one of the valley lilies; he knew her life there to be pure and sweet—she belonged to him, and he loved her. Still these were not all the reasons why he did not want to take her away. Where could they go? He feared the rustlers—he feared the riders—he feared the Mormons. And if he should ever succeed in getting Bess safely away from these immediate perils he feared the sharp eyes of women and their tongues, the big outside world with its problems of existence. He must wait to decide her future, which, after all, was deciding his own. But between her future and his something hung impending. Like Balancing Rock, which waited darkly over the steep gorge ready to close forever the outlet to Deception Pass, that nameless thing, as certain yet intangible as fate, must fall and close forever all doubts and fears of the future.

"I've dreamed," muttered Venters, as he rose. "Well, why not? . . . To dream is happiness! But let me just once see this clearly, wholly; then I can go on dreaming till the thing falls. I've got to tell Jane Withersteen. I've dangerous trips to take. I've work here to make comfort for this girl. She's mine. I'll fight to keep her safe from that old life. I've already seen her forget it. I love her. And if a beast ever rises in me, I'll burn my hand off before I lay it on her with shameful intent. And, by God! sooner or later I'll kill the man who hid her and kept her in Deception Pass!"

As he spoke the west wind softly blew in his face. It seemed to soothe his passion. That west wind was fresh, cool, fragrant, and it carried a sweet, strange burden of far-off things—tidings of life in other climes, of sunshine asleep on other walls—of other places where reigned peace. It carried, too, sad truth of human hearts and mystery—of promise and hope unquenchable. Surprise Valley was only a little niche in the wide world whence blew that burdened wind. Bess was only one of the millions at the mercy of unknown motive in nature and life. Content had come to Venters in the valley; happiness had breathed in the slow, warm air; love as bright as light had hovered over the walls and descended to him; and now on the west wind came a whisper of the eternal triumph of faith over doubt.

"How much better I am for what has come to me!" he exclaimed. "I'll let the future take care of itself. Whatever falls I'll be ready."

Venters retraced his steps along the terrace back to camp, and found Bess in the old familiar seat, waiting and watching for his return.

"I went off by myself to think a little," he explained.

"You never looked that way before. What—what is it? Won't you tell me?"

"Well, Bess, the fact is I've been dreaming a lot. This valley makes a fellow dream. So I forced myself to think. We can't live this way much longer. Soon I'll simply have to go to Cottonwoods. We need a whole pack train of supplies. I can get—"

"Can you go safely?" she interrupted.

"Why, I'm sure of it. I'll ride through the Pass at night. I haven't any fear that Wrangle isn't where I left him. And once on him—Bess, just wait till you see that horse!"

"Oh! I want to see him—to ride him. But—but, Bern, this is what troubles me," she said. "Will—will you come back?"

"Give me four days. If I'm not back in four days you'll know I'm dead. For that only shall keep me."

"Oh!"

"Bess, I'll come back. There's danger—I wouldn't lie to you—but I can take care of myself."

"Bern, I'm sure—oh, I'm sure of it! All my life I've watched hunted men. I can tell what's in them. And I believe you can ride and shoot and see with any rider of the sage. It's not—not that I—fear."

"Well, what is it, then?"

"Why—why—why should you come back at all?"

"I couldn't leave you here alone."

"You might change your mind when you get to the village—among old friends—"

"I won't change my mind. As for old friends—" He uttered a short, expressive laugh.

"Then—there—there must be a—a woman!" Dark red mantled the clear tan of temple and cheek and neck. Her eyes were eyes of shame, upheld a long moment by intense, straining search for the verification of her fear. Suddenly they drooped, her head fell to her knees, her hands flew to her hot cheeks.

"Bess—look here," said Venters, with a sharpness due to the violence with which he checked his quick, surging emotion.

As if compelled against her will—answering to an irresistible voice— Bess raised her head, looked at him with sad, dark eyes, and tried to whisper with tremulous lips.

"There's no woman," went on Venters, deliberately holding her glance with his. "Nothing on earth, barring the chances of life, can keep me away."

Her face flashed and flushed with the glow of a leaping joy; but like the vanishing of a gleam it disappeared to leave her as he had never beheld her.

"I am nothing—I am lost—I am nameless!"

"Do you *want* me to come back?" he asked, with sudden stern coldness. "Maybe *you* want to go back to Oldring!"

That brought her erect, trembling and ashy pale, with dark, proud eyes and mute lips refuting his insinuation.

"Bess, I beg your pardon. I shouldn't have said that. But you angered me. I intend to work—to make a home for you here—to be a—a brother to you as long as ever you need me. And you must forget what you are— were—I mean, and be happy. When you remember that old life you are bitter, and it hurts me."

"I was happy—I shall be very happy. Oh, you're so good that—that it kills me! If I think, I can't believe it. I grow sick with wondering *why*. I'm only a—*let me say it*—only a lost, nameless—girl of the rustlers. *Oldring's*

Girl, they called me. That you should save me—be so good and kind—want to make me happy—why, it's beyond belief. No wonder I'm wretched at the thought of your leaving me. But I'll be wretched and bitter no more. I promise you. If only I could repay you even a little—"

"You've repaid me a hundredfold. Will you believe me?"

"Believe you! I couldn't do else."

"Then listen! . . . Saving you, I saved myself. Living here in this valley with you, I've found myself. I've learned to think while I was dreaming. I never troubled myself about God. But God, or some wonderful spirit, has whispered to me here. I absolutely deny the truth of what you say about yourself. I can't explain it. There are things too deep to tell. Whatever the terrible wrongs you've suffered, God holds you blameless. I see that—feel that in you every moment you are near me. I've a mother and a sister 'way back in Illinois. If I could I'd take you to them—to-morrow."

"*If it were true!* Oh, I might—I might lift my head!" she cried.

"Lift it then—you child. For I swear it's true."

She did lift her head with the singular wild grace always a part of her actions, with that old unconscious intimation of innocence which always tortured Venters; but now with something more—a spirit rising from the depths that linked itself to his brave words.

"I've been thinking—too," she cried, with quivering smile and swelling breast. "I've discovered myself—too. I'm young—I'm alive—I'm so full—oh! I'm a woman!"

"Bess, I believe I can claim credit of that last discovery—before you," Venters said, and laughed.

"Oh, there's more—there's something I must tell you."

"Tell it then."

"When will you go to Cottonwoods?"

"As soon as the storms are past, or the worst of them."

"I'll tell you before you go. I can't now. I don't know how I shall then. But it must be told. I'd never let you leave me without knowing. For in spite of what you say there's a chance you mightn't come back."

Day after day the west wind blew across the valley. Day after day the clouds clustered gray and purple and black. The cliffs sang and the caves rang with Oldring's knell, and the lightning flashed, the thunder rolled, the echoes crashed and crashed, and the rains flooded the valley. Wild flowers sprang up everywhere, swaying with the lengthening grass on the terraces, smiling wanly from shady nooks, peeping wondrously from year-dry crevices of the walls. The valley bloomed into a paradise. Every single moment, from the breaking of the gold bar through the bridge at dawn on to the reddening of rays over the western wall, was one of the colorful change. The valley swam in thick, transparent haze, golden at dawn, warm and white at noon, purple in the twilight. At the end of every storm a rainbow curved down into the leaf-bright forest to shine and fade and leave lingeringly some faint essence of its rosy iris in the air.

Venters walked with Bess, once more in a dream, and watched the lights change on the walls, and faced the wind from out of the west.

Always it brought softly to him strange, sweet tidings of far-off things. It blew from a place that was old and whispered of youth. It blew down the grooves of time. It brought a story of the passing hours. It breathed low of fighting men and praying women. It sang clearly the song of love. That ever was the burden of its tidings—youth in the shady woods, waders through the wet meadows, boy and girl at the hedgerow stile, bathers in the booming surf, sweet, idle hours on grassy, windy hills, long strolls down moonlit lanes—everywhere in far-off lands, fingers locked and bursting hearts and longing lips—from all the world tidings of unquenchable love.

Often, in these hours of dreams, he watched the girl, and asked himself of what was she dreaming? For the changing light of the valley reflected its gleam and its color and its meaning in the changing light of her eyes. He saw in them infinitely more than he saw in his dreams. He saw thought and soul and nature—strong vision of life. All tidings the west wind blew from distance and age he found deep in those dark-blue depths, and found them mysteries solved. Under their wistful shadow he softened, and in the softening felt himself grow a sadder, a wiser, and a better man.

While the west wind blew its tidings, filling his heart full, teaching him a man's part, the days passed, the purple clouds changed to white, and the storms were over for that summer.

"I must go now," he said.

"When?" she asked.

"At once—to-night."

"I'm glad the time has come. It dragged at me. Go—for you'll come back the sooner."

Late in the afternoon, as the ruddy sun split its last flame in the ragged notch of the western wall, Bess walked with Venters along the eastern terrace, up the long, weathered slope, under the great Stone Bridge. They entered the narrow gorge to climb around the fence long before built there by Venters. Farther than this she had never been. Twilight had already fallen in the gorge. It brightened to waning shadow in the wider ascent. He showed her Balancing Rock, of which he had often told her, and explained its sinister leaning over the outlet. Shuddering, she looked down the long, pale incline with its closed-in, toppling walls.

"What an awful trail! Did you carry me up here?"

"I did, surely," replied he.

"It frightens me, somehow. Yet I never was afraid of trails. I'd ride anywhere a horse could go, and climb where he couldn't. But there's something fearful here. I feel as—as if the place was watching me."

"Look at this rock. It's balanced here—balanced perfectly. You know I told you the cliff-dwellers cut the rock, and why. But they're gone and the rock waits. Can't you see—feel how it waits here? I moved it once, and I'll never dare again. A strong heave would start it. Then it would fall and bang, and smash that crag, and jar the walls, and close forever the outlet to Deception Pass!"

"Ah! . . . When you come back I'll steal up here, and push and push with all my might to roll the rock and close forever the outlet to the Pass!" She said it lightly, but in the undercurrent of her voice was a heavier note, a ring deeper than any ever given mere play of words.

"Bess! . . . You can't dare me! Wait till I come back with supplies—then roll the stone."

"I—was—in—fun." Her voice now throbbed low. "Always you must be free to go when you will. Go now . . . this place presses on me—stifles me."

"I'm going—but you had something to tell me?"

"Yes. . . . Will you—come back?"

"I'll come if I live."

"But—but you mightn't come?"

"That's possible, of course. It'll take a good deal to kill me. A man couldn't have a faster horse or keener dog. And, Bess, I've guns, and I'll use them if I'm pushed. But don't worry."

"I've faith in you. I'll not worry until after four days. Only—because you mightn't come—I *must* tell you—"

She lost her voice. Her pale face, her great, glowing, earnest eyes, seemed to stand alone out of the gloom of the gorge. The dog whined, breaking the silence.

"I *must* tell you—because you mightn't come back," she whispered. "You *must* know what—what I think of your goodness—of you. Always I've been tongue-tied. I seemed not to be grateful. It was deep in my heart. Even now—if I were other than I am—I couldn't tell you. But I'm nothing— only a rustler's girl—nameless—infamous. You've saved me—and I'm— I'm yours to do with as you like . . . with all my heart and soul—I love you!"

CHAPTER 15

SHADOWS ON THE SAGE-SLOPE

In the cloudy, threatening, waning summer days shadows lengthened down the sage-slope, and Jane Withersteen likened them to the shadows gathering and closing in around her life.

Mrs. Larkin died, and little Fay was left an orphan with no known relative. Jane's love redoubled. It was the saving brightness of a darkening hour. Fay turned now to Jane in childish worship. And Jane at last found full expression for the mother-longing in her heart. Upon Lassiter, too, Mrs. Larkin's death had some subtle reaction. Before, he had often, without explanation, advised Jane to send Fay back to any Gentile family that would take her in. Passionately and reproachfully and wonderingly Jane had refused even to entertain such an idea. And now Lassiter never advised it again, grew sadder and quieter in his contemplation of the child, and infinitely more gentle and loving. Sometimes Jane had a cold, inexplicable sensation of dread when she saw Lassiter watching Fay. What did the rider see in the future? Why did he, day by day, grow more silent, calmer, cooler, yet sadder in prophetic assurance of something to be?

No doubt, Jane thought, the rider, in his almost superhuman power of foresight, saw behind the horizon the dark, lengthening shadows that were soon to crowd and gloom over him and her and little Fay. Jane

Withersteen awaited the long-deferred breaking of the storm with a courage and embittered calm that had come to her in her extremity. Hope had not died. Doubt and fear, subservient to her will, no longer gave her sleepless nights and tortured days. Love remained. All that she had loved she now loved the more. She seemed to feel that she was defiantly flinging the wealth of her love in the face of misfortune and of hate. No day passed but she prayed for all—and most fervently for her enemies. It troubled her that she had lost, or had never gained, the whole control of her mind. In some measure reason and wisdom and decision were locked in a chamber of her brain, awaiting a key. Power to think of some things was taken from her. Meanwhile, abiding a day of judgment, she fought ceaselessly to deny the bitter drops in her cup, to tear back the slow, the intangibly slow growth of a hot, corrosive lichen eating into her heart.

On the morning of August 10th, Jane, while waiting in the court for Lassiter, heard a clear, ringing report of a rifle. It came from the grove, somewhere toward the corrals. Jane glanced out in alarm. The day was dull, windless, soundless. The leaves of the cottonwoods drooped, as if they had foretold the doom of Withersteen House, and were now ready to die and drop and decay. Never had Jane seen such shade. She pondered on the meaning of the report. Revolver shots had of late cracked from different parts of the grove—spies taking snap shots at Lassiter from a cowardly distance! But a rifle report meant more. Riders seldom used rifles. Judkins and Venters were the exceptions she called to mind. Had the men who hounded her hidden in her grove, taken to the rifle to rid her of Lassiter, her last friend? It was probable—it was likely. And she did not share his cool assumption that his death would never come at the hands of a Mormon. Long had she expected it. His constancy to her, his singular reluctance to use the fatal skill for which he was famed—both now plain to all Mormons—laid him open to inevitable assassination. Yet what charm against ambush and aim and enemy he seemed to bear about him! No, Jane reflected, it was not charm; only a wonderful training of eye and ear, and sense of impending peril. Nevertheless that could not forever avail against secret attack.

That moment a rustling of leaves attracted her attention; then the familiar clinking accompaniment of a slow, soft, measured step, and Lassiter walked into the court.

"Jane, there's a fellow out there with a long gun," he said, and removing his sombrero showed his head bound in a bloody scarf.

"I heard the shot; I knew it was meant for you. Let me see—you can't be badly injured?"

"I reckon not. But mebbe it wasn't a close call! . . . I'll sit here in this corner where nobody can see me from the grove." He untied the scarf and removed it to show a long, bleeding furrow above his left temple.

"It's only a cut," said Jane. "But how it bleeds! Hold your scarf over it just a moment till I come back."

She ran into the house and returned with bandages; and while she bathed and dressed the wound Lassiter talked.

"That fellow had a good chance to get me. But he must have flinched when he pulled the trigger. As I dodged down I saw him run through the trees. He had a rifle. I've been expectin' that kind of gun play. I reckon now I'll have to keep a little closer hid myself. These fellers all seem to get chilly or shaky when they draw a bead on me, but one of them might jest happen to hit me."

"Won't you go away—leave Cottonwoods as I've begged you to—before some one does happen to hit you?" she appealed to him.

"I reckon I'll stay."

"But, oh, Lassiter—your blood will be on my hands!"

"See here, lady, look at your hands now, right now. Aren't they fine, firm, white hands? Aren't they bloody now? Lassiter's blood! That's a queer thing to stain your beautiful hands. But if you could only see deeper you'd find a redder color of blood. Heart color, Jane!"

"Oh! . . . My friend!"

"No, Jane, I'm not one to quit when the game grows hot, no more than you. This game, though, is new to me, an' I don't know the moves yet, else I wouldn't have stepped in front of that bullet."

"Have you no desire to hunt the man who fired at you—to find him—and—and kill him?"

"Well, I reckon I haven't any great hankerin' for that."

"Oh, the wonder of it! . . . I knew—I prayed—I trusted. Lassiter, I almost gave—all myself to soften you to Mormons. Thank God, and thank you, my friend . . . But, selfish woman that I am, this is no great test. What's the life of one of those sneaking cowards to such a man as you? I think of your great hate toward him who—I think of your life's implacable purpose. Can it be—"

"Wait! . . . Listen!" he whispered. "I hear a hoss."

He rose noiselessly, with his ear to the breeze. Suddenly he pulled his sombrero down over his bandaged head, and swinging his gun-sheaths round in front, he stepped into the alcove.

"It's a hoss—comin' fast," he added.

Jane's listening ear soon caught a faint, rapid, rhythmic beat of hoofs. It came from the sage. It gave her a thrill that she was at a loss to understand. The sound rose stronger, louder. Then came a clear, sharp difference when the horse passed from the sage trail to the hard-packed ground of the grove. It became a ringing run—swift in its bell-like clatterings, yet singular in longer pause than usual between the hoofbeats of a horse.

"It's Wrangle! . . . It's Wrangle!" cried Jane Withersteen. "I'd know him from a million horses!"

Excitement and thrilling expectancy flooded out all Jane Withersteen's calm. A tight band closed round her breast as she saw the giant sorrel flit in reddish-brown flashes across the openings in the green. Then he was pounding down the lane—thundering into the court—crashing his great iron-shod hoofs on the stone flags. Wrangle it was surely, but shaggy and wild-eyed, and sage-streaked, with dust-caked lather staining his flanks. He reared and crashed down and plunged. The rider leaped off, threw the bridle, and held hard on a lasso looped round Wrangle's head and neck. Jane's heart sank as she tried to recognize Venters in the rider. Something familiar struck her in the lofty stature, in the sweep of powerful shoulders. But this bearded, long-haired, unkempt man, who wore ragged clothes patched with pieces of skin and boots that showed bare legs and feet—this dusty, dark, and wild rider could not possibly be Venters.

"Whoa, Wrangle, old boy. Come down. Easy now. So—so—so. You're home, old boy, and presently you can have a drink of water you'll remember."

In the voice Jane knew the rider to be Venters. He tied Wrangle to the hitching-rack and turned to the court.

"Oh, Bern! . . . You wild man!" she exclaimed.

"Jane—Jane, it's good to see you! Hello, Lassiter! Yes, it's Venters."

Like rough iron his hard hand crushed Jane's. In it she felt the difference she saw in him. Wild, rugged, unshorn—yet how splendid! He had gone away a boy—he had returned a man. He appeared taller, wider of shoulder, deeper-chested, more powerfully built. But was that only her fancy—he had always been a young giant—was the change one of spirit? He might have been absent for years, proven by fire and steel, grown like Lassiter, strong and cool and sure. His eyes—were they keener, more flashing than before?—met hers with clear, frank, warm regard, in which perplexity was not, nor discontent, nor pain.

"Look at me long as you like," he said, with a laugh. "I'm not much to look at. And Jane, neither you nor Lassiter can brag. You're paler than I ever saw you. Lassiter, here, he wears a bloody bandage under his hat. That reminds me. Some one took a flying shot at me down in the sage. It made Wrangle run some. . . . Well, perhaps you've more to tell me than I've got to tell you."

Briefly, in few words, Jane outlined the circumstances of her undoing in the weeks of his absence.

Under his beard and bronze she saw his face whiten in terrible wrath.

"Lassiter—what held you back?"

No time in the long period of fiery moments and sudden shocks had Jane Withersteen ever beheld Lassiter as calm and serene and cool as then.

"Jane had gloom enough without my addin' to it by shootin' up the village," he said.

As strange as Lassiter's coolness was Venters's curious, intent scrutiny of them both, and under it Jane felt a flaming tide wave from bosom to temples.

"Well—you're right," he said, with slow pause. "It surprises me a little, that's all."

Jane sensed then a slight alteration in Venters, and what it was, in her own confusion, she could not tell. It had always been her intention to acquaint him with the deceit she had fallen to in her zeal to move Lassiter. She did not mean to spare herself. Yet now, at the moment, before these riders it was an impossibility to explain.

Venters was speaking somewhat haltingly, without his former frankness. "I found Oldring's hiding place and your red herd. I learned—

I know—I'm sure there was a deal between Tull and Oldring." He paused and shifted his position and his gaze. He looked as if he wanted to say something that he found beyond him. Sorrow and pity and shame seemed to contend for mastery over him. Then he raised himself and spoke with effort. "Jane, I've cost you too much. You've almost ruined yourself for me. It was wrong, for I'm not worth it. I never deserved such friendship. Well, maybe it's not too late. You must give me up. Mind, I haven't changed. I am just the same as ever. I'll see Tull while I'm here, and tell him to his face."

"Bern, it's too late," said Jane.

"I'll *make* him believe!" cried Venters, violently.

"You ask me to break our friendship?"

"Yes. If you don't, I shall!"

"Forever?"

"Forever!"

Jane sighed. Another shadow had lengthened down the sage-slope to cast further darkness upon her. A melancholy sweetness pervaded her resignation. The boy who had left her had returned a man, nobler, stronger, one in whom she divined something unbending as steel. There might come a moment later when she would wonder why she had not fought against his will, but just now she yielded to it. She liked him as well—nay, more, she thought, only her emotions were deadened by the long, menacing wait for the bursting storm.

Once before she had held out her hand to him—when she gave it; now she stretched it tremblingly forth in acceptance of the decree circumstance had laid upon them. Venters bowed over it, kissed it, pressed it hard, and half-stifled a sound very like a sob. Certain it was that when he raised his head tears glistened in his eyes.

"Some—women—have a hard lot," he said, huskily. Then he shook his powerful form, and his rags lashed about him. "I'll say a few things to Tull—when I meet him."

"Bern—you'll not draw on Tull? Oh, that must not be! Promise me—"

"I promise you this," he interrupted, in stern passion that thrilled while it terrorized her. "If you say one more word for that plotter I'll kill him as I would a mad coyote!"

Jane clasped her hands. Was this fire-eyed man the one whom she had once made as wax to her touch? Had Venters become Lassiter and Lassiter Venters?

"I'll—say no more," she faltered.

"Jane, Lassiter once called you blind," said Venters. "It must be true. But I won't upbraid you. Only don't rouse the devil in me by praying for Tull! I'll try to keep cool when I meet him. That's all. Now there's one more thing I want to ask of you—the last. I've found a valley down in the Pass. It's a wonderful place. I intend to stay there. It's so hidden I believe no one can find it. There's good water, and browse, and game. I want to raise corn and stock. I need to take in supplies—will you give them to me?"

"Assuredly. The more you take the better you'll please me—and perhaps the less my—my enemies will get."

"Venters, I reckon you'll have trouble packin' anythin' away," put in Lassiter.

"I'll go at night."

"Mebbe that wouldn't be best. You'd sure be stopped. You'd better go early in the mornin'—say, just after dawn. That's the safest time to move round here."

"Lassiter, I'll be hard to stop," returned Venters darkly.

"I reckon so."

"Bern," said Jane, "go first to the riders' quarters and get yourself a complete outfit. You're a—a sight. Then help yourself to whatever else you need—burros, packs, grain, dried fruits, and meat. You must take coffee and sugar and flour—all kinds of supplies. Don't forget corn and seeds. I remember how you used to starve. Please—please take all you can pack away from here. I'll make a bundle for you, which you mustn't open till you're in your valley. How I'd like to see it! To judge by you and Wrangle how wild it must be!"

Jane walked down into the outer court and approached the sorrel. Upstarting, he laid back his ears and eyed her.

"Wrangle—dear old Wrangle," she said, and put a caressing hand on his matted mane. "Oh, he's wild, but he knows me! Bern, can he run as fast as ever?"

"Run? Jane, he's done sixty miles since last night at dark, and I could make him kill Black Star right now in a ten-mile race."

"He never could," protested Jane. "He couldn't even if he was fresh."

"I reckon mebbe the best hoss'll prove himself yet," said Lassiter, "an', Jane, if it ever comes to that race I'd like you to be on Wrangle."

"I'd like that, too," rejoined Venters. "But, Jane, maybe Lassiter's hint is extreme. Bad as your prospects are you'll surely never come to the running point."

"Who knows!" she replied, with mournful smile.

"No, no, Jane, it can't be so bad as all that. Soon as I see Tull there'll be a change in your fortunes. I'll hurry down to the village. . . . Now don't worry."

Jane retired to the seclusion of her room. Lassiter's subtle forecasting of disaster, Venters's forced optimism, neither remained in mind. Material loss weighed nothing in the balance with other losses she was sustaining. She wondered dully at her sitting there, hands folded listlessly, with a kind of numb deadness to the passing of time and the passing of her riches. She thought of Venters's friendship. She had not lost that, but she had lost him. Lassiter's friendship—that was more than love—it would endure, but soon he, too, would be gone. Little Fay slept dreamlessly upon the bed, her golden curls streaming over the pillow. Jane had the child's worship. Would she lose that, too; and if she did, what then would be left? Conscience thundered at her that there was left her religion. Conscience thundered that she should be grateful on her knees for this baptism of fire; that through misfortune, sacrifice, and suffering her soul might be fused pure gold. But the old spontaneous, rapturous spirit no more exalted her. She wanted to be a woman—not a martyr. Like the saint of old who mortified his flesh, Jane Withersteen had in her the temper for heroic martyrdom, if by sacrificing herself she could save the souls of others. But here the damnable verdict blistered her that the more she sacrificed herself, the blacker grew the souls of her churchmen. There was something terribly wrong with her soul, something terribly wrong with her churchmen and her religion. In the whirling gulf of her thought there was yet one shining light to guide her, to sustain her in her hope; and it was that, despite her errors and her frailties and her blindness, she had one absolute and unfaltering hold on ultimate and supreme justice. That was love. "Love your enemies as yourself!" was a divine word, entirely free from any church or creed.

Jane's meditations were disturbed by Lassiter's soft, tinkling step in the court. Always he wore the clinking spurs. Always he was in readiness to ride. She passed out, and called him into the huge, dim hall.

"I think you'll be safer here. The court is too open," she said.

"I reckon," replied Lassiter. "An' it's cooler here. The day's sure muggy. Well, I went down to the village with Venters."

"Already! Where is he?" queried Jane, in quick amaze.

"He's at the corrals. Blake's helpin' him get the burros an' packs ready. That Blake is a good fellow."

"Did—did Bern meet Tull?"

"I guess he did," answered Lassiter, and he laughed dryly.

"Tell me! Oh, you exasperate me! You're so cool, so calm! For Heaven's sake, tell me what happened!"

"First time I've been in the village for weeks," went on Lassiter, mildly. "I reckon there ain't been more of a show for a long time. Me an' Venters walkin' down the road! It was funny. I ain't sayin' anybody was particular glad to see us. I'm not much thought of hereabouts, an' Venters he sure looks like what you called him, a wild man. Well, there was some runnin' of folks before we got to the stores. Then everybody vamoosed except some surprised rustlers in front of a saloon. Venters went right in the stores an' saloons, an' of course I went along. I don't know which tickled me the most—the actions of many fellers we met, or Venters's nerve. Jane, I was downright glad to be along. You see *that* sort of thing is my element, an' I've been away from it for a spell. But we didn't find Tull in none of them places. Some Gentile feller at last told Venters he'd find Tull in that long buildin' next to Parsons's store. It's a kind of meetin'-room; and sure enough, when we peeped in, it was half full of men.

"Venters yelled: 'Don't anybody pull guns! We ain't come for that!' Then he tramped in, an' I was some put to keep alongside him. There was a hard, scrapin' sound of feet, a loud cry, an' then some whisperin', an' after that stillness you could cut with a knife. Tull was there, an' that fat party who once tried to throw a gun on me, an' other important-lookin' men, an' that little frog-legged feller who was with Tull the day I rode in here. I wish you could have seen their faces, 'specially Tull's an' the fat party's. But there ain't no use of me tryin' to tell you how they looked.

"Well, Venters an' I stood there in the middle of the room, with that batch of men all in front of us, an' not a blamed one of them winked an eyelash or moved a finger. It was natural, of course, for me to notice many of them packed guns. That's a way of mine, first noticin' them things. Venters spoke up, an' his voice sort of chilled an' cut, an' he told Tull he had a few things to say."

Here Lassiter paused while he turned his sombrero round and round, in his familiar habit, and his eyes had the look of a man seeing over again some thrilling spectacle, and under his red bronze there was strange animation.

"Like a shot, then, Venters told Tull that the friendship between you an' him was all over, an' he was leaving your place. He said you'd both of you broken off in the hope of propitiatin' your people, but you hadn't changed your mind otherwise, an' never would.

"Next he spoke up for you. I ain't goin' to tell you what he said. Only—no other woman who ever lived ever had such tribute! You had a champion, Jane, an' never fear that those thick-skulled men don't know you now. It couldn't be otherwise. He spoke the ringin', lightnin' truth. . . . Then he accused Tull of the underhand, miserable robbery of a helpless woman. He told Tull where the red herd was, of a deal made with Old-rin', that Jerry Card had made the deal. I thought Tull was goin' to drop, an' that little frog-legged cuss, he looked some limp an' white. But Venters's voice would have kept anybody's legs from bucklin'. I was stiff myself. He went on an' called Tull—called him every bad name ever known to a rider, an' then some. He cursed Tull. I never hear a man get such a cursin'. He laughed in scorn at the idea of Tull bein' a minister. He said Tull an' a few more dogs of hell builded their empire out of the hearts of such innocent an' God-fearin' women as Jane Withersteen. He called Tull a blinder of women, a callous beast who hid behind a mock mantle of righteousness—an' the last an' lowest coward on the face of the earth. To prey on weak women through their religion—that was the last unspeakable crime!

"Then he finished, an' by this time he'd almost lost his voice. But his whisper was enough. 'Tull,' he said, '*she* begged me not to draw on you to-day. *She* would pray for you if you burned her at the stake. . . . But, listen! . . . I swear if you and I ever come face to face again, I'll kill you!'

"We backed out of the door then, an' up the road. But nobody follered us."

Jane found herself weeping passionately. She had not been conscious of it till Lassiter ended his story, and she experienced exquisite pain and relief in shedding tears. Long had her eyes been dry, her grief deep; long had her emotions been dumb. Lassiter's story put her on the rack; the appalling nature of Venters's act and speech had no parallel as an outrage; it was worse than bloodshed. Men like Tull had been shot, but had one ever been so terribly denounced in public? Over-mounting her horror, an uncontrollable, quivering passion shook her very soul. It was sheer human glory in the deed of a fearless man. It was hot, primitive instinct to live—to fight. It was a kind of mad joy in Venters's chivalry. It was close to the wrath that had first shaken her in the beginning of this war waged upon her.

"Well, well, Jane, don't take it that way," said Lassiter, in evident distress. "I had to tell you. There's some things a feller jest can't keep. It's strange you give up on hearin' that, when all this long time you've been the gamest woman I ever seen. But I don't know women. Mebbe there's reason for you to cry. I know this—nothin' ever rang in my soul an' so filled it as what Venters did. I'd like to have done it, but—I'm only good for throwin' a gun, an' it seems you hate that. . . . Well, I'll be goin' now."

"Where?"

"Venters took Wrangle to the stable. The sorrel's shy a shoe, an' I've got to help hold the big devil an' put on another."

"Tell Bern to come for the pack I want to give him—and—and to say good-by," called Jane, as Lassiter went out.

Jane passed the rest of that day in a vain endeavor to decide what and what not to put in the pack for Venters. This task was the last she would ever perform for him, and the gifts were the last she would ever make him. So she picked and chose and rejected, and chose again, and often paused in sad revery, and began again, till at length she filled the pack.

It was about sunset, and she and Fay had finished supper and were sitting in the court, when Venters's quick steps rang on the stones. She scarcely knew him, for he had changed the tattered garments, and she missed the dark beard and long hair. Still he was not the Venters of old. As he came up the steps she felt herself pointing to the pack, and heard herself speaking words that were meaningless to her. He said good-by; he kissed her, released her, and turned away. His tall figure blurred in her sight, grew dim through dark, streaked vision, and then he vanished.

Twilight fell around Withersteen House, and dusk and night. Little Fay slept; but Jane lay with strained, aching eyes. She heard the wind moaning in the cottonwoods and mice squeaking in the walls. The night was interminably long, yet she prayed to hold back the dawn. What would another day bring forth? The blackness of her room seemed blacker for the sad, entering gray of morning light. She heard the chirp of awakening birds, and fancied she caught a faint clatter of hoofs. Then low, dull, distant, throbbed a heavy gunshot. She had expected it, was waiting for it; nevertheless, an electric shock checked her heart, froze the very living fiber of her bones. That vise-like hold on her faculties apparently did not relax for a long time, and it was a voice under her window that released her.

"Jane! . . . Jane!" softly called Lassiter.

She answered somehow.

"It's all right. Venters got away. I thought mebbe you'd heard that shot, an' I was worried some."

"What was it—who fired?"

"Well—some fool feller tried to stop Venters out there in the sage—an' he only stopped lead! . . . I think it'll be all right. I haven't seen or heard of any other fellers round. Venters'll go through safe. An', Jane, I've got Bells saddled, an' I'm goin' to trail Venters. Mind, I won't show myself unless he falls foul of somebody an' needs me. I want to see if this place where he's goin' is safe for him. He says nobody can track him there. I never seen the place yet I couldn't track a man to. Now Jane, you stay indoors while I'm gone, an' keep close watch on Fay. Will you?"

"Yes! Oh yes!"

"An' another thing, Jane," he continued, then paused for long— "another thing—if you ain't here when I come back—if you're *gone*— don't fear, I'll trail you—I'll find you."

"My dear Lassiter, where could I be gone—as you put it?" asked Jane, in curious surprise.

"I reckon you might be somewhere. Mebbe tied in an old barn—or corralled in some gulch—or chained in a cave! *Milly Erne was*—till she give in! Mebbe that's news to you. . . . Well, if you're gone I'll hunt for you."

"No, Lassiter," she replied, sadly and low. "If I'm gone just forget the unhappy woman whose blinded, selfish deceit you repaid with kindness and love."

She heard a deep, muttering curse, under his breath, and then the silvery tinkling of his spurs as he moved away.

Jane entered upon the duties of that day with a settled, gloomy calm. Disaster hung in the dark clouds, in the shade, in the humid west wind. Blake, when he reported, appeared without his usual cheer; and Jerd wore a harassed look of a worn and worried man. And when Judkins put in appearance, riding a lame horse, and dismounted with the cramp of a rider, his dust-covered figure and his darkly grim, almost dazed expression told Jane of dire calamity. She had no need of words.

"Miss Withersteen, I have to report—loss of the—white herd," said Judkins, hoarsely.

"Come, sit down; you look played out," replied Jane, solicitously. She brought him brandy and food, and while he partook of refreshments, of which he appeared badly in need, she asked no questions.

"No one rider—could hev done more—Miss Withersteen," he went on, presently.

"Judkins, don't be distressed. You've done more than any other rider. I've long expected to lose the white herd. It's no surprise. It's in line with other things that are happening. I'm grateful for your service."

"Miss Withersteen, I knew how you'd take it. But, if anythin', that makes it harder to tell. You see, a feller wants to do so much fer you, an' I'd got fond of my job. We hed the herd a ways off to the north of the break in the valley. There was a big level an' pools of water an' tip-top browse. But the cattle was in a high nervous condition. Wild—as wild as antelope! You see, they'd been so scared they never slept. I ain't a-goin' to tell you of the many tricks that were pulled off out there in the sage. But there wasn't a day fer weeks that the herd didn't get started to run. We allus managed to ride 'em close an' drive 'em back an' keep 'em bunched. Honest, Miss Withersteen, them steers was *thin*. They was *thin* when water and grass was everywhere. *Thin* at this season—thet'll tell you how your steers was pestered. Fer instance, one night a strange runnin' streak of fire run right through the herd. That streak was a coyote—*with an oiled an' blazin' tail!* Fer I shot it an' found out. We hed hell with the herd that night, an' if the sage an' grass hedn't been wet—we, hosses, steers, an' all would hev burned up. But I said I wasn't goin' to tell you any of the tricks.... Strange now, Miss Withersteen, when the stampede did come it was from natural cause—jest a whirlin' devil of dust. You've seen the like often. An' this wasn't no big whirl, fer the dust was mostly settled. It had dried out in a little swale, an' ordinarily no steer would ever hev run fer it. But the herd was nervous an' wild. An', jest as Lassiter said, when that bunch of white steers got to movin' they was as bad as buffalo. I've seen some buffalo stampedes back in Nebraska, an' this bolt of the steers was the same kind.

"I tried to mill the herd jest as Lassiter did. But I wasn't equal to it, Miss Withersteen. I don't believe the rider lives who could hev turned that herd. We kept along of the herd fer miles, an' more'n one of my boys tried to get the steers a-millin'. It wasn't no use. We got off level ground, goin' down, an' then the steers ran somethin' fierce. We left the little gullies an' washes level-full of dead steers. Finally I saw the herd was makin' to pass a kind of low pocket between ridges. There was a hog-back—as we used to call 'em—a pile of rocks stickin' up, an' I saw the herd was goin' to split round it, or swing out to the left. An' I wanted 'em to go to the right so mebbe we'd be able to drive 'em into the pocket. So with all my boys except three, I rode hard to turn the herd a little to the right. We couldn't budge 'em. They went on an' split around the rocks, an' the most of 'em was turned sharp to the left by a deep wash we hedn't seen—hed no chance to see.

"The other three boys—Jimmy Vail, Joe Wills, an' that little Cairns boy—a nervy kid!—they, with Cairns leadin', tried to buck thet herd round to the pocket. It was a wild, fool idea. I couldn't do nothin'. The boys got hemmed in between the steers an' the wash—thet they hedn't no chance to see, either. Vail an' Wills was run down right before our eyes. An' Cairns, who rode a fine hoss, he did some ridin' I never seen equaled, an' would hev beat the steers if there'd been any room to run in. I was high up an' could see how the steers kept spillin' by twos an' threes over into the wash. Cairns put his hoss to a place thet was too wide for any hoss, an' broke his neck an' the hoss's too. We found thet out after, an' as fer Vail an' Wills—two thousand steers ran over the poor boys. There wasn't much left to pack home fer burying! . . . An' Miss Withersteen, thet all happened yesterday, an' I believe, if the white herd didn't run over the wall of the Pass, it's runnin' yet!"

On the morning of the second day after Judkins's recital, during which time Jane remained indoors a prey to regret and sorrow for the boy riders, and a new and now strangely insistent fear for her own person, she again heard what she had missed more than she dared honestly confess—the soft, jingling step of Lassiter. Almost overwhelming relief surged through her, a feeling as akin to joy as any she could have been capable of in those gloomy hours of shadow, and one that suddenly stunned her with the significance of what Lassiter had come to mean to her. She had begged him, for his own sake, to leave Cottonwoods. She might yet beg that, if her weakening courage permitted her to dare absolute loneliness and helplessness, but she realized now that if she were left alone her life would become one long hideous nightmare.

When his soft steps clinked into the hall, in answer to her greeting, and his tall, black-garbed form filled the door, she felt an inexpressible sense of immediate safety. In his presence she lost her fear of the dim passageways of Withersteen House, and of every sound. Always it had been that, when he entered the court or the hall, she had experienced a distinctly sickening but gradually lessening shock at sight of the huge black guns swinging at his sides. This time the sickening shock again visited her; it was, however, because a revealing flash of thought told her that it was not alone Lassiter who was thrillingly welcome, but also his fatal weapons. They meant so much. How she had fallen—how broken and spiritless must she be—to have still the same old horror of Lassiter's guns and his name, yet feel somehow a cold, shrinking protection in their law and might and use.

"Did you trail Venters—find his wonderful valley?" she asked eagerly.

"Yes, an' I reckon it's sure a wonderful place."

"Is he safe there?"

"That's been botherin' me some. I tracked him, an' part of the trail was the hardest I ever tracked. Mebbe there's a rustler or somebody in this country who's as good at trackin' as I am. If that's so Venters ain't safe."

"Well—tell me all about Bern and his valley."

To Jane's surprise Lassiter showed disinclination for further talk about his trip. He appeared to be extremely fatigued. Jane reflected that one hundred and twenty miles, with probably a great deal of climbing on foot, all in three days, was enough to tire any rider. Moreover, it presently developed that Lassiter had returned in a mood of singular sadness and preoccupation. She put it down to a moodiness over the loss of her white herd, and the now precarious condition of her fortune.

Several days passed, and, as nothing happened, Jane's spirits began to brighten. Once in her musings she thought that this tendency of hers to rebound was as sad as it was futile. Meanwhile, she had resumed her walks through the grove with little Fay.

One morning she went as far as the sage. She had not seen the slope since the beginning of the rains, and now it bloomed a rich deep purple. There was a high wind blowing, and the sage tossed and waved, and colored beautifully from light to dark. Clouds scudded across the sky, and their shadows sailed darkly down the sunny slope.

Upon her return toward the house she went by the lane to the stables, and she had scarcely entered the great open space with its corrals and sheds, when she saw Lassiter hurriedly approaching. Fay broke from her, and, running to a corral fence, began to pat and pull the long, hanging ears of a drowsy burro.

One look at Lassiter armed her for a blow.

Without a word he led her across the wide yard to the rise of the ground upon which the stable stood.

"Jane—look!" he said, and pointed to the ground.

Jane glanced down, and again, and upon steadier vision made out splotches of blood on the stones, and broad, smooth marks in the dust, leading out toward the sage.

"What made these?" she asked.

"I reckon somebody has dragged dead or wounded men out to where there was hosses in the sage."

"Dead—or—wounded—men!"

"I reckon—Jane, are you strong? Can you bear up?"

His hands were gently holding hers, and his eyes—suddenly she could no longer look into them. "Strong?" she echoed, trembling. "I—I will be."

Up the stone-flag drive, nicked with the marks made by the iron-shod hoofs of her racers, Lassiter led her, his grasp ever growing firmer.

"Where's Blake—and—and Jerd?" she asked, haltingly.

"I don't know where Jerd is. Bolted, most likely," replied Lassiter, as he took her through the stone door. "But Blake—poor Blake! He's gone forever! . . . Be prepared, Jane."

With a cold prickling of her skin, with a queer thrumming in her ears, with fixed and staring eyes, Jane saw a gun lying at her feet with chamber swung and empty, and discharged shells scattered near.

Outstretched upon the stable floor lay Blake, ghastly white—dead—one hand clutching a gun, and the other twisted in his bloody blouse.

"Whoever the thieves were, whether your people or rustlers—Blake killed some of them!" said Lassiter.

"Thieves?" whispered Jane.

"I reckon. Hoss-thieves! . . . Look!" Lassiter waved his hand toward the stalls.

The first stall—Bell's stall—was empty. All the stalls were empty. No racer whinnied and stamped greeting to her. Night was gone! Black Star was gone!

CHAPTER 16

GOLD

As Lassiter had reported to Jane, Venters "went through" safely, and after a toilsome journey reached the peaceful shelter of Surprise Valley. When finally he laid wearily down under the silver spruces, resting from the strain of dragging packs and burros up the slope and through the entrance to Surprise Valley, he had leisure to think, and a great deal of the time went in regretting that he had not been frank with his loyal friend, Jane Withersteen.

But, he kept continually recalling, when he had stood once more face to face with her and had been shocked at the change in her and had heard the details of her adversity, he had not had the heart to tell her of the closer interest which had entered his life. He had not lied; yet he had kept silence.

Bess was in transports over the stores of supplies and the outfit he had packed from Cottonwoods. He had certainly brought a hundred times more than he had gone for; enough, surely, for years, perhaps to make permanent home in the valley. He saw no reason why he need ever leave there again.

After a day of rest he recovered his strength, and shared Bess's pleasure in rummaging over the endless packs, and began to plan for the future. And in this planning, his trip to Cottonwoods, with its revived hate of Tull and consequent unleashing of fierce passions, soon faded out of mind. By slower degrees his friendship for Jane Withersteen and his contrition drifted from the active preoccupation of his present thought to a place in memory, with more and more infrequent recalls.

And as far as the state of his mind was concerned, upon the second day after his return, the valley, with its golden hues and purple shades, the speaking west wind and the cool, silent night, and Bess's watching eyes with their wonderful light, so wrought upon Venters that he might never have left them at all.

That very afternoon he set to work. Only one thing hindered him upon beginning, though it in no wise checked his delight, and that was that in the multiplicity of tasks planned to make a paradise out of the valley he could not choose the one with which to begin. He had to grow into the habit of passing from one dreamy pleasure to another, like a bee going from flower to flower in the valley, and he found this wandering habit likely to extend to his labors. Nevertheless, he made a start.

At the outset he discovered Bess to be both a considerable help in some ways and a very great hindrance in others. Her excitement and joy were spurs, inspirations; but she was utterly impracticable in her ideas, and she flitted from one plan to another with bewildering vacillation. Moreover, he fancied that she grew more eager, youthful, and sweet; and he marked that it was far easier to watch her and listen to her than it was to work. Therefore he gave her tasks that necessitated her going often to the cave where he had stored his packs.

Upon the last of these trips, when he was some distance down the terrace and out of sight of camp, he heard a scream, and then the sharp barking of the dogs.

For an instant he straightened up, amazed. Danger for her had been absolutely out of his mind. She had seen a rattlesnake—or a wildcat. Still she would not have been likely to scream at sight of either; and the barking of the dogs was ominous. Dropping his work, he dashed back along the terrace. Upon breaking through a clump of aspens he saw the dark form of a man in the camp. Cold, then hot, Venters burst into frenzied speed to reach his guns. He was cursing himself for a thoughtless fool when the man's tall form became familiar, and he recognized Lassiter. Then the reversal of emotions changed his run to a walk; he tried to call out, but his voice refused to carry; when he reached camp there was Lassiter staring at the white-faced girl. By that time Ring and Whitie had recognized him.

"Hello, Venters, I'm makin' you a visit," said Lassiter, slowly. "An' I'm some surprised to see you've a—a young feller for company."

One glance had sufficed for the keen rider to read Bess's real sex, and for once his cool calm had deserted him. He stared till the white of Bess's cheeks flared into crimson. That, if it were needed, was the concluding evidence of her femininity; for it went fittingly with her sun-tinted hair and darkened, dilated eyes, the sweetness of her mouth and the striking symmetry of her slender shape.

"Heavens! Lassiter!" panted Venters, when he caught his breath. "What relief—it's only you! How—in the name of all—that's wonderful—did you ever get here?"

"I trailed you. We—I wanted to know where you was, if you had a safe place. So I trailed you."

"Trailed me!" cried Venters, bluntly.

"I reckon. It was some of a job after I got to them smooth rocks. I was all day trackin' you up to them little cut steps in the rock. The rest was easy."

"Where's your hoss? I hope you hid him."

"I tied him in them queer cedars down on the slope. He can't be seen from the valley."

"That's good. Well, well! I'm completely dumbfounded. It was my idea that no man could track me in here."

"I reckon. But if there's a tracker in these uplands as good as me he can find you."

"That's bad. That'll worry me. But, Lassiter, now you're here I'm glad to see you. And—and my companion here is not a young fellow! . . . Bess, this is a friend of mine. He saved my life once."

The embarrassment of the moment did not extend to Lassiter. Almost at once his manner, as he shook hands with Bess, relieved Venters and put the girl at ease. After Venters's words and one quick look at

Lassiter, her agitation stilled, and, though she was shy, if she were conscious of anything out of the ordinary in the situation, certainly she did not show it.

"I reckon I'll only stay a little while," Lassiter was saying. "An' if you don't mind troublin', I'm hungry. I fetched some biscuits along, but they're gone. Venters, this place is sure the wonderfullest ever seen. Them cut steps on the slope! That outlet into the gorge! An' it's like climbin' up through hell into heaven to climb through that gorge into this valley! There's a queer-lookin' rock at the top of the passage. I didn't have time to stop. I'm wonderin' how you ever found this place. It's sure interestin'."

During the preparation and eating of dinner Lassiter listened mostly, as was his wont, and occasionally he spoke in his quaint and dry way. Venters noted, however, that the rider showed an increasing interest in Bess. He asked her no questions, and only directed his attention to her while she was occupied and had no opportunity to observe his scrutiny. It seemed to Venters that Lassiter grew more and more absorbed in his study of Bess, and that he lost his coolness in some strange, softening sympathy. Then, quite abruptly, he arose, and announced the necessity for his early departure. He said good-by to Bess in a voice gentle and somewhat broken, and turned hurriedly away. Venters accompanied him, and they had traversed the terrace, climbed the weathered slope, and passed under the Stone Bridge before either spoke again.

Then Lassiter put a great hand on Venters's shoulder and wheeled him to meet a smoldering fire of gray eyes.

"Lassiter, I couldn't tell Jane! I couldn't!" burst out Venters, reading his friend's mind. "I tried. But I couldn't. She wouldn't understand, and she has troubles enough. And I love the girl!"

"Venters, I reckon this beats me. I've seen some queer things in my time, too. This girl—who is she?"

"I don't know."

"Don't know! What is she, then?"

"I don't know that, either. Oh, it's the strangest story you ever heard. I must tell you. But you'll never believe."

"Venters, women were always puzzles to me. But for all that, if this girl ain't a child, an' as innocent, I'm no fit person to think of virtue an' goodness in anybody. Are you goin' to be square with her?"

"I am—so help me God!"

"I reckoned so. Mebbe my temper oughtn't led me to make sure. But, man, she's a woman in all but years. She's sweeter'n the sage."

"Lassiter, I know, I know. And the *hell* of it is that in spite of her innocence and charm she's—she's not what she seems!"

"I wouldn't want to—of course, I couldn't call you a liar, Venters," said the older man.

"What's more, she was Oldring's Masked Rider!"

Venters expected to floor his friend with that statement, but he was not in any way prepared for the shock his words gave. For an instant he was astounded to see Lassiter stunned; then his own passionate eagerness to unbosom himself, to tell the wonderful story, precluded any other thought.

"Son, tell me all about this," presently said Lassiter as he seated himself on a stone and wiped his moist brow.

Thereupon Venters began his narrative at the point where he had shot the rustler and Oldring's Masked Rider, and he rushed through it, telling all, not holding back even Bess's unreserved avowal of her love or his deepest emotions.

"That's the story," he said, concluding. "I love her, though I've never told her. If I did tell her I'd be ready to marry her, and that seems impossible in this country. I'd be afraid to risk taking her anywhere. So I intend to do the best I can for her here."

"The longer I live the stranger life is," mused Lassiter, with downcast eyes. "I'm reminded of somethin' you once said to Jane about hands in her game of life. There's that unseen hand of power, an' Tull's black hand, an' my red one, an' your indifferent one, an' the girl's little brown, helpless one. An', Venters, there's another one that's all-wise an' all-wonderful. *That's* the hand guidin' Jane Withersteen's game of life! . . . Your story's one to daze a far clearer head than mine. I can't offer no advice, even if you asked for it. Mebbe I can help you. Anyway, I'll hold Oldrin' up when he comes to the village, an' find out about this girl. I knew the rustler years ago. He'll remember me."

"Lassiter, if I ever meet Oldring I'll kill him!" cried Venters, with sudden intensity.

"I reckon that'd be perfectly natural," replied the rider.

"Make him think Bess is dead—as she is to him, and that old life."

"Sure, sure, son. Cool down now. If you're goin' to begin pullin' guns on Tull an' Oldrin' you want to be cool. I reckon, though, you'd better keep hid here. Well, I must be leavin'."

"One thing, Lassiter. You'll not tell Jane about Bess? Please don't!"

"I reckon not. But I wouldn't be afraid to bet that after she'd got over anger at your secrecy—Venters, she'd be furious once in her life!—she'd think more of you. I don't mind sayin' for myself that I think you're a good deal of a man."

In the further ascent Venters halted several times with the intention of saying good-by, yet he changed his mind and kept on climbing till they reached Balancing Rock. Lassiter examined the huge rock, listened to Venters's idea of its position and suggestion, and curiously placed a strong hand upon it.

"Hold on!" cried Venters. "I heaved at it once and have never gotten over my scare."

"Well, you do seem oncommon nervous," replied Lassiter, much amused. "Now, as for me, why I always had the funniest notion to roll stones! When I was a kid I did it, an' the bigger I got the bigger stones I'd roll. Ain't that funny? Honest—even now I often get off my hoss jest to tumble a big stone over a precipice, an' watch it drop, an' listen to it bang an' boom. I've started some slides in my time, an' don't you forget it. I never seen a rock I wanted to roll as bad as this one! Wouldn't there jest be roarin', crashin' hell down that trail?"

"You'd close the outlet forever!" exclaimed Venters. "Well, good-by, Lassiter. Keep my secret and don't forget me. And be mighty careful how you get out of the valley below. The rustlers' cañon isn't more than three miles up the Pass. Now you've tracked me here I'll never feel safe again."

In his descent to the valley, Venters's emotion, roused to stirring pitch by the recital of his love story, quieted gradually, and in its place came a sober, thoughtful mood. All at once he saw that he was serious, because he would never more regain his sense of security while in the valley. What Lassiter could do another skillful tracker might duplicate. Among the many riders with whom Venters had ridden he recalled no one who could have taken his trail at Cottonwoods and have followed it to the edge of the bare slope in the pass, let alone up that glistening smooth stone.

Lassiter, however, was not an ordinary rider. Instead of hunting cattle tracks he had likely spent a goodly portion of his life tracking men. It was not improbable that among Oldring's rustlers there was one who shared Lassiter's gift for trailing. And the more Venters dwelt on this possibility the more perturbed he grew.

Lassiter's visit, moreover, had a disquieting effect upon Bess; and Venters fancied that she entertained the same thought as to future seclusion. The breaking of their solitude, though by a well-meaning friend, had not only dispelled all its dream and much of its charm, but had instilled a canker of fear. Both had seen the footprint in the sand.

Venters did no more work that day. Sunset and twilight gave way to night, and the cañon bird whistled its melancholy notes, and the wind sang softly in the cliffs, and the campfire blazed and burned down to red embers. To Venters a subtle difference was apparent in all of these, or else the shadowy change had been in him. He hoped that on the morrow this slight depression would have passed away.

In that measure, however, he was doomed to disappointment. Furthermore, Bess reverted to a wistful sadness that he had not observed in her since her recovery. His attempt to cheer her out of it resulted in dismal failure, and consequently in a darkening of his own mood. Hard work relieved him; still, when the day had passed, his unrest returned. Then he set to deliberate thinking, and there came to him the startling conviction that he must leave Surprise Valley and take Bess with him. As a rider he had taken many chances, and as an adventurer in Deception Pass he had unhesitatingly risked his life; but now he would run no preventable hazard of Bess's safety and happiness, and he was too keen not to see that hazard. It gave him a pang to think of leaving the beautiful valley, just when he had the means to establish a permanent and delightful home there. One flashing thought tore in hot temptation through his mind—why not climb up into the gorge, roll Balancing Rock down the trail, and close forever the outlet to Deception Pass? "That was the beast in me—showing his teeth!" muttered Venters, scornfully. "I'll just kill him good and quick! I'll be fair to this girl, if it's the last thing I do on earth!"

Another day went by, in which he worked less and pondered more and all the time covertly watched Bess. Her wistfulness had deepened into downright unhappiness, and that made his task to tell her all the harder. He kept the secret another day, hoping by some chance she might grow less moody, and to his exceeding anxiety she fell into far deeper gloom. Out of his own secret and the torment of it he divined that she, too, had a secret, and the keeping of it was torturing her. As yet he had no plan thought out in regard to how or when to leave the valley, but he decided to tell her the necessity of it and to persuade her to go. Furthermore, he hoped his speaking out would induce her to unburden her own mind.

"Bess, what's wrong with you?" he asked.

"Nothing," she answered, with averted face.

Venters took hold of her, and gently though masterfully forced her to meet his eyes.

"You can't look at me and lie," he said. "Now—what's wrong with you? You're keeping something from me. Well, I've got a secret, too, and I intend to tell it presently."

"Oh—I *have* a secret. I was crazy to tell you when you came back. That's why I was so silly about everything. I kept holding my secret back—gloating over it. But when Lassiter came I got an idea—that changed my mind. Then I hated to tell you."

"Are you going to now?"

"Yes—yes. I was coming to it. I tried yesterday, but you were so cold. I was afraid. I couldn't keep it much longer."

"Very well, most mysterious lady, tell your wonderful secret."

"You needn't laugh," she retorted, with a first glimpse of reviving spirit. "I can take the laugh out of you in one second."

"It's a go."

She ran through the spruces to the cave, and returned carrying something which was manifestly heavy. Upon nearer view he saw that whatever she held with such evident importance had been bound up in a black scarf he well remembered. That alone was sufficient to make him tingle with curiosity.

"Have you any idea what I did in your absence?" she asked.

"I imagine you lounged about waiting and watching for me," he replied, smiling. "I've my share of conceit, you know."

"You're wrong. I worked. Look at my hands." She dropped on her knees close to where he sat, and, carefully depositing the black bundle, she held out her hands. The palms and inside of her fingers were white, puckered, and worn.

"Why, Bess, you've been fooling in the water," he said.

"Fooling? Look here!" With deft fingers she spread open the black scarf, and the bright sun shone upon a dull, glittering heap of gold.

"Gold!" he ejaculated.

"Yes, gold! See, pounds of gold! I found it—washed it out of the stream—picked it out grain by grain, nugget by nugget!"

"Gold!" he cried.

"Yes. Now—now laugh at my secret!"

For a long minute Venters gazed. Then he stretched forth a hand to feel if the gold was real.

"*Gold!*" he almost shouted. "Bess, there are hundreds—thousands of dollars' worth here!"

He leaned over to her, and put his hand, strong and clenching now, on hers.

"Is there more where this came from?" he whispered.

"Plenty of it, all the way up the stream to the cliff. You know I've often washed for gold. Then I've heard the men talk. I think there's no great quantity of gold here, but enough for—for a fortune for *you*."

"That—was—your—secret!"

"Yes. I hate gold. For it makes men mad. I've seen them drunk with joy and dance and fling themselves around. I've seen them curse and rave. I've seen them fight like dogs and roll in the dust. I've seen them kill each other for gold."

"Is that why you hated to tell me?"

"Not—not altogether." Bess lowered her head. "It was because I knew you'd never stay here long after you found gold."

"You were afraid I'd leave you?"

"Yes."

"Listen! . . . You great, simple child! Listen! . . . You sweet, wonderful, wild, blue-eyed girl! I was tortured by my secret. It was that I knew we—*we* must leave the valley. We can't stay here much longer. I couldn't think how we'd get away—out of the country—or how we'd live, if we ever got out. I'm a beggar. That's why I kept my secret. I'm poor. It takes money to make way beyond Sterling. We couldn't ride horses or burros or walk forever. So while I knew we must go, I was distracted over how to go and what to do. *Now!* We've gold! Once beyond Sterling we'll be safe from rustlers. We've no others to fear."

"Oh! Listen! Bess!" Venters now heard his voice ringing high and sweet, and he felt Bess's cold hands in his crushing grasp as she leaned toward him, pale, breathless. "This is how much I'd leave you! You made me live again! I'll take you away—far away from this wild country. You'll begin a new life. You'll be happy. You shall see cities, ships, people. You shall have anything your heart craves. All the shame and sorrow of your life shall be forgotten—as if they had never been. This is how much I'd leave you here alone—you sad-eyed girl. I love you! Didn't you know it? How could you fail to know it? I love you! I'm free! I'm a man—a man you've made—no more a beggar! . . . Kiss me! This is how much I'd leave you here alone—you beautiful, strange, unhappy girl. But I'll make you happy. What—what do I care for—your past! I love you! I'll take you home to Illinois—to my mother. Then I'll take you to far places. I'll make up all you've lost. Oh, I know you love me—knew it before you told me. And it changed my life. And you'll go with me, not as my companion as you are here, nor my sister, but, Bess, darling! . . . *As my wife!*"

CHAPTER 17

WRANGLE'S RACE RUN

The plan eventually decided upon by the lovers was for Venters to go to the village, secure a horse and some kind of a disguise for Bess, or at least less striking apparel than her present garb, and to return post-haste to the valley. Meanwhile, she would add to their store of gold. Then they would strike the long and perilous trail to ride out of Utah. In the event of his inability to fetch back a horse for her, they intended to make the giant sorrel carry double. The gold, a little food, saddle blankets, and Venters's guns were to compose the light outfit with which they would make the start.

"I love this beautiful place," said Bess. "It's hard to think of leaving it."

"Hard! Well, I should think so," replied Venters. "Maybe—in years—" But he did not complete in words his thought that it might be possible to return after many years of absence and change.

Once again Bess bade Venters farewell under the shadow of Balancing Rock, and this time it was with whispered hope and tenderness and passionate trust. Long after he had left her, all down through the outlet to the Pass, the clinging clasp of her arms, the sweetness of her lips, and the sense of a new and exquisite birth of character in her remained hauntingly and thrillingly in his mind. The girl who had sadly called herself nameless and nothing had been marvelously transformed in the moment of his avowal of love. It was something to think over, something to warm his heart, but for the present it had absolutely to be forgotten so that all his mind could be addressed to the trip so fraught with danger.

He carried only his rifle, revolver, and a small quantity of bread and meat; and thus lightly burdened he made swift progress down the slope and out into the valley. Darkness was coming on, and he welcomed it. Stars were blinking when he reached his old hiding place in the split of cañon wall, and by their aid he slipped through the dense thickets to the grassy enclosure. Wrangle stood in the center of it with his head up, and he appeared black and of gigantic proportions in the dim light. Venters whistled softly, began a slow approach, and then called. The horse snorted and, plunging away with dull, heavy sound of hoofs, he disappeared in the gloom. "Wilder than ever!" muttered Venters. He followed the sorrel into the narrowing split between the walls, and presently had to desist because he could not see a foot in advance. As he went back toward the open Wrangle jumped out of an ebony shadow of cliff, and like a thunderbolt shot huge and black past him down into the starlit glade. Deciding that all attempts to catch Wrangle at night would be useless, Venters repaired to the shelving rock where he had hidden saddle and blanket, and there went to sleep.

The first peep of day found him stirring, and as soon as it was light enough to distinguish objects, he took his lasso off his saddle and went out to rope the sorrel. He espied Wrangle at the lower end of the cove, and approached him in a perfectly natural manner. When he got near enough, Wrangle evidently recognized him, but was too wild to stand. He ran up the glade, and on into the narrow lane between the walls. This favored Venters's speedy capture of the horse, so, coiling his noose ready to throw, he hurried on. Wrangle let Venters get to within a hundred feet, and then he broke. But as he plunged by, rapidly getting into his stride, Venters made a perfect throw with the rope. He had time to brace himself for the shock; nevertheless, Wrangle threw him and dragged him several yards before halting.

"You wild devil," said Venters, as he slowly pulled Wrangle up. "Don't you know me? Come now—old fellow—so—so—"

Wrangle yielded to the lasso and then to Venters's strong hand. He was as straggly and wild-looking as a horse left to roam free in the sage. He dropped his long ears, and stood readily to be saddled and bridled. But he was exceedingly sensitive, and quivered at every touch and sound. Venters led him to the thicket, and, bending the close saplings to let him squeeze through, at length reached the open. Sharp survey in each direction assured him of the usual lonely nature of the cañon; then he was in the saddle riding south.

Wrangle's long, swinging canter was a wonderful ground gainer. His stride was almost twice that of an ordinary horse, and his endurance was equally remarkable. Venters pulled him in occasionally, and walked him up the stretches of rising ground, and along the soft washes. Wrangle had never yet shown any indication of distress while Venters rode him. Nevertheless, there was now reason to save the horse; therefore, Venters did not resort to the hurry that had characterized his former trip. He camped at the last water in the Pass. What distance that was to Cottonwoods he did not know; he calculated, however, that it was in the neighborhood of fifty miles.

Early in the morning he proceeded on his way, and about the middle of the forenoon reached the constricted gap that marked the southerly end of the Pass, and through which led the trail up to the sage-level. He spied out Lassiter's tracks in the dust, but no others, and, dismounting, he straightened out Wrangle's bridle and began to lead him up the trail. The short climb, more severe on beast than on man, necessitated a rest on the level above, and during this he scanned the wide purple reaches of slope.

Wrangle whistled his pleasure at the smell of the sage. Remounting, Venters headed up the white trail with the fragrant wind in his face. He had proceeded for perhaps a couple of miles when Wrangle stopped with a suddenness that threw Venters heavily against the pommel.

"What's wrong, old boy?" called Venters, looking down for a loose shoe or a snake or a foot lamed by a picked-up stone. Unrewarded, he raised himself from his scrutiny. Wrangle stood stiff, head high, with his long ears erect. Thus guided, Venters swiftly gazed ahead to make out a dust-clouded, dark group of horsemen riding down the slope. If they had seen him, it apparently made no difference in their speed or direction.

"Wonder who they are!" exclaimed Venters. He was not disposed to run. His cool mood tightened under grip of excitement, as he reflected that whoever the approaching riders were they could not be friends. He slipped out of the saddle and led Wrangle behind the tallest sage-brush. It might serve to conceal them until the riders were close enough for him to see who they were; after that he would be indifferent to how soon they discovered him.

After looking to his rifle, and ascertaining that it was in working order, he watched, and as he watched, slowly the force of a bitter fierceness, long dormant, gathered ready to flame into life. If those riders were not rustlers he had forgotten how rustlers looked and rode. On they came, a small group, so compact and dark that he could not tell their number. How unusual that their horses did not see Wrangle! But such failure, Venters decided, was owing to the speed with which they were traveling. They moved at a swift canter affected more by rustlers than by riders. Venters grew concerned over the possibility that these horsemen would actually ride down on him before he had a chance to tell what to expect. When they were within three hundred yards, he deliberately led Wrangle out into the trail.

Then he heard shouts, and the hard scrape of sliding hoofs, and saw horses rear and plunge back with up-flung heads and flying manes. Several little white puffs of smoke appeared sharply against the black background of riders and horses, and shots rang out. Bullets struck far in front of Venters, and whipped up the dust and then hummed low into the sage. The range was great for revolvers, but whether the shots were meant to kill or merely to check advance, they were enough to fire that waiting ferocity in Venters. Slipping his arm through the bridle, so that Wrangle could not get away, Venters lifted his rifle and pulled the trigger twice.

He saw the first horseman lean sideways and fall. He saw another lurch in his saddle and heard a cry of pain. Then Wrangle, plunging in fright, lifted Venters, and nearly threw him. He jerked the horse down with a powerful hand, and leaped into the saddle. Wrangle plunged again, dragging his bridle, that Venters had not had time to throw in place. Bending over with a swift movement, he secured it and dropped the loop over the pommel. Then, with grinding teeth, he looked to see what the issue would be.

The band had scattered so as not to afford such a broad mark for bullets. The riders faced Venters, some with red-belching guns. He heard a sharper report, and just as Wrangle plunged again he caught the whizz of a leaden missile that would have hit him but for Wrangle's sudden jump. A swift, hot wave, turning cold, passed over Venters. Deliberately he picked out the one rider with a carbine, and killed him. Wrangle snorted shrilly and bolted into the sage. Venters let him run a few rods, then with iron arm checked him.

Five riders, surely rustlers, were left. One leaped out of the saddle to secure his fallen comrade's carbine. A shot from Venters, which missed the man but sent the dust flying over him, made him run back to his horse. Then they separated. The crippled rider went one way; the one frustrated in his attempt to get the carbine rode another: Venters thought he made out a third rider, carrying a strange-appearing bundle and disappearing in the sage. But in the rapidity of action and vision he could not discern what it was. Two riders with three horses swung out to the right. Afraid of the long rifle—a burdensome weapon seldom carried by rustlers or riders—they had been put to rout.

Suddenly Venters discovered that one of the two men last noted was riding Jane Withersteen's horse Bells—the beautiful bay racer she had given to Lassiter. Venters uttered a savage outcry. Then the small, wiry, frog-like shape of the second rider, and the ease and grace of his seat in the saddle—things so strikingly incongruous—grew more and more familiar in Venters's sight.

"*Jerry Card!*" cried Venters.

It was indeed Tull's right-hand man. Such a white-hot wrath inflamed Venters that he fought himself to see with clearer gaze.

"It's Jerry Card!" he exclaimed, instantly. "*And he's riding Black Star and leading Night!*"

The long-kindling, stormy fire in Venters's heart burst into flame. He spurred Wrangle, and as the horse lengthened his stride Venters slipped cartridges into the magazine of his rifle till it was once again full. Card and his companion were now half a mile or more in advance, riding easily down the slope. Venters marked the smooth gait, and understood it when Wrangle galloped out of the sage into the broad cattle trail, down which Venters had once tracked Jane Withersteen's red herd. This hard-packed trail, from years of use, was as clean and smooth as a road.

Venters saw Jerry Card look back over his shoulder; the other rider did likewise. Then the three racers lengthened their stride to the point where the swinging canter was ready to break into a gallop.

"Wrangle, the race's on," said Venters, grimly. "We'll canter with them and gallop with them and run with them. We'll let them set the pace."

Venters knew he bestrode the strongest, swiftest, most tireless horse ever ridden by any rider across the Utah uplands. Recalling Jane Withersteen's devoted assurance that Night could run neck and neck with Wrangle, and Black Star could show his heels to him, Venters wished that Jane were there to see the race to recover her blacks end in the unqualified superiority of the giant sorrel. Then Venters found himself thankful that she was absent, for he meant that race to end in Jerry Card's death. The first flush, the raging of Venters's wrath, passed, to leave him in sullen, almost cold possession of his will. It was a deadly mood, utterly foreign to his nature, engendered, fostered, and released by the wild passions of wild men in a wild country. The strength in him then—the thing rife in him that was not hate, but something as remorseless—might have been the fiery fruition of a whole lifetime of vengeful quest. Nothing could have stopped him.

Venters thought out the race shrewdly. The rider on Bells would probably drop behind and take to the sage. What he did was of little moment to Venters. To stop Jerry Card, his evil, hidden career as well as his present flight, and then to catch the blacks—that was all that concerned Venters. The cattle trail wound for miles and miles down the slope. Venters saw with a rider's keen vision ten, fifteen, twenty miles of clear purple sage. There were no on-coming riders or rustlers to aid Card. His only chance to escape lay in abandoning the stolen horses and creeping away in the sage to hide. In ten miles Wrangle could run Black Star and Night off their feet, and in fifteen he could kill them outright. So Venters held the sorrel in, letting Card make the running. It was a long race that would save the blacks.

In a few miles of that swinging canter Wrangle had crept appreciably closer to the three horses. Jerry Card turned again, and when he saw how the sorrel had gained, he put Black Star to a gallop. Night and Bells, on either side of him, swept into his stride.

Venters loosened the rein on Wrangle and let him break into a gallop. The sorrel saw the horses ahead and wanted to run. But Venters restrained him. And in the gallop he gained more than in the canter. Bells was fast in that gait, but Black Star and Night had been trained to run. Slowly Wrangle closed the gap down to a quarter of a mile, and crept closer and closer.

Jerry Card wheeled once more. Venters distinctly saw the red flash of his red face. This time he looked long. Venters laughed. He knew what passed in Card's mind. The rider was trying to make out what horse it happened to be that thus gained on Jane Withersteen's peerless racers. Wrangle had so long been away from the village that not improbably Jerry had forgotten. Besides, whatever Jerry's qualifications for his fame as the greatest rider of the sage, certain it was that his best point was not far-sightedness. He had not recognized Wrangle. After what must have been a searching gaze he got his comrade to face about. This action gave Venters amusement. It spoke so surely of the fact that neither Card nor the rustler actually knew their danger. Yet if they kept to the trail—and the last thing such men would do would be to leave it—they were both doomed.

This comrade of Card's whirled far around in his saddle, and he even shaded his eyes from the sun. He, too, looked long. Then, all at once, he faced ahead again and, bending lower in the saddle, began to fling his right arm up and down. That flinging Venters knew to be the lashing of Bells. Jerry also became active. And the three racers lengthened out into a run.

"Now, Wrangle!" cried Venters. "Run, you big devil! Run!"

Venters laid the reins on Wrangle's neck and dropped the loop over the pommel. The sorrel needed no guiding on that smooth trail. He was surer-footed in a run than at any other fast gait, and his running gave the impression of something devilish. He might now have been actuated by Venters's spirit; undoubtedly his savage running fitted the mood of his rider. Venters bent forward, swinging with the horse, and gripped his rifle. His eye measured the distance between him and Jerry Card.

In less than two miles of running Bells began to drop behind the blacks, and Wrangle began to overhaul him. Venters anticipated that the rustler would soon take to the sage. Yet he did not. Not improbably he reasoned that the powerful sorrel could more easily overtake Bells in the heavier going outside of the trail. Soon only a few hundred yards lay between Bells and Wrangle. Turning in his saddle the rustler began to shoot, and the bullets beat up little whiffs of dust. Venters raised his rifle, ready to take snap shots, and waited for favorable opportunity when Bells was out of line with the forward horses. Venters had it in him to kill these men as if they were skunk-bitten coyotes, but also he had restraint enough to keep from shooting one of Jane's beloved Arabians.

No great distance was covered, however, before Bells swerved to the left, out of line with Black Star and Night. Then Venters, aiming high and waiting for the pause between Wrangle's great strides, began to take snap shots at the rustler. The fleeing rider presented a broad target for a rifle, but he was moving swiftly forward and bobbing up and down. Moreover, shooting from Wrangle's back was shooting from a thunderbolt. And added to that was the danger of a low-placed bullet taking effect on Bells. Yet, despite these considerations, making the shot exceedingly difficult, Venters's confidence, like his implacability, saw a speedy and fatal termination of that rustler's race. On the sixth shot the rustler threw up his arms and took a flying tumble off his horse. He rolled over and over, hunched himself to a half-erect position, fell, and then dragged himself into the sage. As Venters went thundering by he peered keenly into the sage, but caught no sign of the man. Bells ran a few hundred yards, slowed up, and had stopped when Wrangle passed him.

Again Venters began slipping fresh cartridges into the magazine of his rifle, and his hand was so sure and steady that he did not drop a single cartridge. With the eye of a rider and the judgment of a marksman he once more measured the distance between him and Jerry Card. Wrangle had gained, bringing him into rifle range. Venters was hard put to it now not to shoot, but thought it better to withhold his fire. Jerry, who, in anticipation of a running fusillade, had huddled himself into a little twisted ball on Black Star's neck, now surmising that his pursuer would make sure of not wounding one of the blacks, rose to his natural seat in the saddle.

In his mind perhaps, as certainly as in Venters's, this moment was the beginning of the real race.

Venters leaned forward to put his hand on Wrangle's neck; then backward to put it on his flank. Under the shaggy, dusty hair trembled and vibrated and rippled a wonderful muscular activity. But Wrangle's flesh was still cold. What a cold-blooded brute, thought Venters, and felt in him a love for the horse he had never given to any other. It would not have been humanly possible for any rider, even though clutched by hate or revenge or a passion to save a loved one or fear of his own life, to be astride the sorrel, to swing with his swing, to see his magnificent stride and hear the rapid thunder of his hoofs, to ride him in that race and not glory in the ride.

So, with his passion to kill still keen and unabated, Venters lived out that ride, and drank a rider's sage-sweet cup of wildness to the dregs.

When Wrangle's long mane, lashing in the wind, stung Venters in the cheek, the sting added a beat to his flying pulse. He bent a downward glance to try to see Wrangle's actual stride, and saw only twinkling, darting streaks and the white rush of the trail. He watched the sorrel's savage head, pointed level, his mouth still closed and dry, but his nostrils distended as if he were snorting unseen fire. Wrangle was the horse for a race with death. Upon each side Venters saw the sage merged into a sailing, colorless wall. In front sloped the lay of ground with its purple breadth split by the white trail. The wind, blowing with heavy, steady blast into his face, sickened him with enduring, sweet odor, and filled his ears with a hollow, rushing roar.

Then for the hundredth time he measured the width of space separating him from Jerry Card. Wrangle had ceased to gain. The blacks were proving their fleetness. Venters watched Jerry Card, admiring the little rider's horsemanship. He had the incomparable seat of the upland rider, born in the saddle. It struck Venters that Card had changed his position, or the position of the horses. Presently Venters remembered positively that Jerry had been leading Night on the right-hand side of the trail. The racer was now on the side to the left. No—it was Black Star. But, Venters argued in amaze, Jerry had been mounted on Black Star. Another clearer, keener gaze assured Venters that Black Star was really riderless. Night now carried Jerry Card.

"He's changed from one to the other!" ejaculated Venters, realizing the astounding feat with unstinted admiration. "Changed at full speed! Jerry Card, that's what you've done unless I'm drunk on the smell of sage. But I've got to see the trick before I believe it."

Thenceforth, while Wrangle sped on, Venters glued his eyes to the little rider. Jerry Card rode as only he could ride. Of all the daring horsemen of the uplands Jerry was the one rider fitted to bring out the greatness of the blacks in that long race. He had them on a dead run, but not yet at the last strained and killing pace. From time to time he glanced backward, as a wise general in retreat calculating his chances and the power and speed of pursuers, and the moment for the last desperate burst. No doubt, Card, with his life at stake, gloried in that race, perhaps more wildly than Venters. For he had been born to the sage and the saddle and the wild. He was more than half horse. Not until the last call—the sudden up-flashing instinct of self-preservation—would he lose his skill and judgment and nerve and the spirit of that race. Venters seemed to read Jerry's mind. That little crime-stained rider was actually thinking of his horses, husbanding their speed, handling them with knowledge of years, glorying in their beautiful, swift, racing stride, and wanting them to win the race when his own life hung suspended in quivering balance. Again Jerry whirled in his saddle and the sun flashed red on his face. Turning, he drew Black Star closer and closer toward Night, till they ran side by side, as one horse. Then Card raised himself in the saddle, slipped out of the stirrups, and, somehow twisting himself, leaped upon Black Star. He did not even lose the swing of the horse. Like a leech he was there in the other saddle, and as the horses separated, his right foot, that had been apparently doubled under him, shot down to catch the stirrup. The grace and dexterity and daring of that rider's act won something more than admiration from Venters.

For the distance of a mile Jerry rode Black Star and then changed back to Night. But all Jerry's skill and the running of the blacks could avail little more against the sorrel.

Venters peered far ahead, studying the lay of the land. Straightaway for five miles the trail stretched, and then it disappeared in hummocky ground. To the right, some few rods, Venters saw a break in the sage, and this was the rim of Deception Pass. Across the dark cleft gleamed the red of the opposite wall. Venters imagined that the trail went down into the Pass somewhere north of those ridges. And he realized that he must and would overtake Jerry Card in this straight course of five miles.

Cruelly he struck his spurs into Wrangle's flanks. A light touch of spur was sufficient to make Wrangle plunge. And now, with a ringing, wild snort, he seemed to double up in muscular convulsions and to shoot forward with an impetus that almost unseated Venters. The sage blurred by, the trail flashed by, and the wind robbed him of breath and hearing. Jerry Card turned once more. And the way he shifted to Black Star showed he had to make his last desperate running. Venters aimed to the side of the trail and sent a bullet puffing the dust beyond Jerry. Venters hoped to frighten the rider and get him to take to the sage. But Jerry returned the shot, and his ball struck dangerously close in the dust at Wrangle's flying feet. Venters held his fire then, while the rider emptied his revolver. For a mile, with Black Star leaving Night behind and doing his utmost, Wrangle did not gain; for another mile he gained little, if at all. In the third he caught up with the now galloping Night and began to gain rapidly on the other black.

Only a hundred yards now stretched between Black Star and Wrangle. The giant sorrel thundered on—and on—and on. In every yard he gained a foot. He was whistling through his nostrils, wringing wet, flying lather, and as hot as fire. Savage as ever; strong as ever, fast as ever, but each tremendous stride jarred Venters out of the saddle! Wrangle's power and spirit and momentum had begun to run him off his legs. Wrangle's great race was nearly won—and run. Venters seemed to see the expanse before him as a vast, sheeted, purple plain sliding under him. Black Star moved in it as a blur. The rider, Jerry Card, appeared a mere dot bobbing dimly. Wrangle thundered on—on—on! Venters felt the increase in quivering, straining shock after every leap. Flecks of foam flew into Venters's eyes, burning him, making him see all the sage as red. But in that red haze he saw, or seemed to see, Black Star suddenly riderless and with broken gait. Wrangle thundered on to change his pace with a violent break. Then Venters pulled him hard. From run to gallop, gallop to canter, canter to trot, trot to walk, and walk to stop, the great sorrel ended his race.

Venters looked back. Black Star stood riderless in the trail. Jerry Card had taken to the sage. Far up the white trail Night came trotting faithfully down. Venters leaped off, still half blind, reeling dizzily. In a moment he had recovered sufficiently to have a care for Wrangle. Rapidly he took off the saddle and bridle. The sorrel was reeking, heaving, whistling, shaking. But he had still the strength to stand, and for him Venters had no fears.

As Venters ran back to Black Star he saw the horse stagger on shaking legs into the sage and go down in a heap. Upon reaching him Venters removed the saddle and bridle. Black Star had been killed on his legs, Venters thought. He had no hope for the stricken horse. Black Star lay flat, covered with bloody froth, mouth wide, tongue hanging, eyes glaring, and all his beautiful body in convulsions.

Unable to stay there to see Jane's favorite racer die, Venters hurried up the trail to meet the other black. On the way he kept a sharp lookout for Jerry Card. Venters imagined the rider would keep well out of range of the rifle, but, as he would be lost on the sage without a horse, not improbably he would linger in the vicinity on the chance of getting back one of the blacks. Night soon came trotting up, hot and wet and run out. Venters led him down near the others, and, unsaddling him, let him loose to rest. Night wearily lay down in the dust and rolled, proving himself not yet spent.

Then Venters sat down to rest and think. Whatever the risk, he was compelled to stay where he was, or comparatively near, for the night. The horses must rest and drink. He must find water. He was now seventy miles from Cottonwoods, and, he believed, close to the cañon where the cattle trail must surely turn off and go down into the Pass. After a while he rose to survey the valley.

He was very near to the ragged edge of a deep cañon into which the trail turned. The ground lay in uneven ridges divided by washes, and these sloped into the cañon. Following the cañon line, he saw where its rim was broken by other intersecting cañons, and farther down red walls and yellow cliffs leading toward a deep, blue cleft that he made sure was Deception Pass. Walking out a few rods to a promontory, he found where the trail went down. The descent was gradual, along a stone-walled trail, and Venters felt sure that this was the place where Oldring drove cattle into the Pass. There was, however, no indication at all that he ever had driven cattle out at this point. Oldring had many holes to his burrow.

In searching round in the little hollows Venters, much to his relief, found water. He composed himself to rest and eat some bread and meat, while he waited for a sufficient time to elapse so that he could safely give the horses a drink. He judged the hour to be somewhere around noon. Wrangle lay down to rest and Night followed suit. So long as they were down Venters intended to make no move. The longer they rested the better, and the safer it would be to give them water. By and by he forced himself to go over to where Black Star lay, expecting to find him dead. Instead he found the racer partially if not wholly recovered. There was recognition, even fire, in his big black eyes. Venters was overjoyed. He sat by the black for a long time. Black Star presently labored to his feet with a heave and a groan, shook himself, and snorted for water. Venters repaired to the little pool he had found, filled his sombrero, and gave the racer a drink. Black Star gulped it at one draught, as if it were but a drop, and pushed his nose into the hat and snorted for more. Venters now led Night down to drink, and after a further time Black Star also. Then the blacks began to graze.

The sorrel had wandered off down the sage between the trail and the cañon. Once or twice he disappeared in little swales. Finally Venters concluded Wrangle had grazed far enough, and, taking his lasso, he went to fetch him back. In crossing from one ridge to another he saw where the horse had made muddy a pool of water. It occurred to Venters then that Wrangle had drunk his fill, and did not seem the worse for it, and might be anything but easy to catch. And, true enough, he could not come within roping reach of the sorrel. He tried for an hour, and gave up in disgust. Wrangle did not seem so wild as simply perverse. In a quandary Venters returned to the other horses, hoping much, yet doubting more, that when Wrangle had grazed to suit himself he might be caught.

As the afternoon wore away Venters's concern diminished, yet he kept close watch on the blacks and the trail and the sage. There was no telling of what Jerry Card might be capable. Venters sullenly acquiesced to the idea that the rider had been too quick and too shrewd for him. Strangely and doggedly, however, Venters clung to his foreboding of Card's downfall.

The wind died away; the red sun topped the far distant western rise of slope; and the long, creeping purple shadows lengthened. The rims of the cañons gleamed crimson, and the deep clefts appeared to belch forth blue smoke. Silence enfolded the scene.

It was broken by a horrid, long-drawn scream of a horse and the thudding of heavy hoofs. Venters sprang erect and wheeled south. Along the cañon rim, near the edge, came Wrangle once more in thundering flight.

Venters gasped in amazement. Had the wild sorrel gone mad? His head was high and twisted, in a most singular position for a running horse. Suddenly Venters decried a frog-like shape clinging to Wrangle's neck. Jerry Card! Somehow he had straddled Wrangle and now stuck like a huge burr. But it was his strange position and the sorrel's wild scream that shook Venters's nerves. Wrangle was pounding toward the turn where the trail went down. He plunged onward like a blind horse. More than one of his leaps took him to the very edge of the precipice.

Jerry Card was bent forward with his teeth fast in the front of Wrangle's nose! Venters saw it, and there flashed over him a memory of this trick of a few desperate riders. He even thought of one rider who had worn off his teeth in this terrible hold to break or control desperate horses. Wrangle had indeed gone mad. The marvel was what guided him. Was it the half-brute, the more than half-horse instinct of Jerry Card? Whatever the mystery, it was true. And in a few more rods Jerry would have the sorrel turning into the trail leading down into the cañon.

"No—Jerry!" whispered Venters, stepping forward and throwing up the rifle. He tried to catch the little humped, frog-like shape over the sights. It was moving too fast; it was too small. Yet Venters shot once . . . twice . . . the third time . . . four times . . . five! All wasted shots and precious seconds!

With a deep-muttered curse Venters caught Wrangle through the sights and pulled the trigger. Plainly he heard the bullet thud. Wrangle uttered a horrible strangling sound. In swift death action he whirled, and with one last splendid leap he cleared the cañon rim. And he whirled downward with the little frog-like shape clinging to his neck!

There was a pause which seemed never ending, a shock, and an instant's silence.

Then up rolled a heavy crash, a long roar of sliding rocks dying away in distant echo, then silence unbroken.

Wrangle's race was run.

CHAPTER 18

OLDRING'S KNELL

Some forty hours or more later Venters created a commotion in Cottonwoods by riding down the main street on Black Star and leading Bells and Night. He had come upon Bells grazing near the body of a dead rustler, the only incident of his quick ride into the village.

Nothing was farther from Venters's mind than bravado. No thought came to him of the defiance and boldness of riding Jane Withersteen's racers straight into the arch-plotter's stronghold. He wanted men to see the famous Arabians; he wanted men to see them dirty and dusty, bearing all the signs of having been driven to their limit; he wanted men to see and to know that the thieves who had ridden them out into the sage had not ridden them back. Venters had come for that and for more—he wanted to meet Tull face to face; if not Tull, then Dyer; if not Dyer, then any one in the secret of these master conspirators. Such was Venters's passion. The meeting with the rustlers, the unprovoked attack upon him, the spilling of blood, the recognition of Jerry Card and the horses, the race, and that last plunge of mad Wrangle—all these things, fuel on fuel to the smoldering fire, had kindled and swelled and leaped into living flame. He could have shot Dyer in the midst of his religious services at the altar; he could have killed Tull in front of wives and babes.

He walked the three racers down the broad, green-bordered village road. He heard the murmur of running water from Amber Spring. Bitter waters for Jane Withersteen! Men and women stopped to gaze at him and the horses. All knew him; all knew the blacks and the bay. As well as if it had been spoken, Venters read in the faces of men the intelligence that Jane Withersteen's Arabians had been known to have been stolen. Venters reined in and halted before Dyer's residence. It was a low, long, stone structure resembling Withersteen House. The spacious front yard was green and luxuriant with grass and flowers; gravel walks led to the huge porch; a well-trimmed hedge of purple sage separated the yard from the church grounds; birds sang in the trees; water flowed musically along the walks; and there were glad, careless shouts of children. For Venters the beauty of this home, and the serenity and its apparent happiness, all turned red and black. For Venters a shade overspread the lawn, the flowers, the old vine-clad stone house. In the music of the singing birds, in the murmur of the running water, he heard an ominous sound. Quiet beauty—sweet music—innocent laughter! By what monstrous abortion of fate did these abide in the shadow of Dyer?

Venters rode on and stopped before Tull's cottage. Women stared at him with white faces and then flew from the porch. Tull himself appeared at the door, bent low, craning his neck. His dark face flashed out of sight; the door banged; a heavy bar dropped with a hollow sound.

Then Venters shook Black Star's bridle, and, sharply trotting, led the other horses to the center of the village. Here at the intersecting streets and in front of the stores he halted once more. The usual lounging atmosphere of that prominent corner was not now in evidence. Riders and ranchers and villagers broke up what must have been absorbing conversation. There was a rush of many feet, and then the walk was lined with faces.

Venters's glance swept down the line of silent stone-faced men. He recognized many riders and villagers, but none of those he had hoped to meet. There was no expression in the faces turned toward him. All of them knew him, most were inimical, but there were few who were not burning with curiosity and wonder in regard to the return of Jane Withersteen's racers. Yet all were silent. Here were the familiar characteristics—masked feeling—strange secretiveness—expressionless expression of mystery and hidden power.

"Has anybody here seen Jerry Card?" queried Venters, in a loud voice.

In reply there came not a word, not a nod or shake of head, not so much as dropping eye or twitching lip—nothing but a quiet, stony stare.

"Been under the knife? You've a fine knife-wielder here—one Tull, I believe! . . . Maybe you've all had your tongues cut out?"

This passionate sarcasm of Venters brought no response; and the stony calm was as oil on the fire within him.

"I see some of you pack guns, too!" he added, in biting scorn. In the long, tense pause, strung keenly as a tight wire, he sat motionless on Black Star. "All right," he went on. "Then let some of you take this message to Tull. Tell him I've seen Jerry Card! . . . Tell him Jerry Card *will never return!*"

Thereupon, in the same dead calm, Venters backed Black Star away from the curb, into the street, and out of range. He was ready now to ride up to Withersteen House and turn the racers over to Jane.

"Hello, Venters," a familiar voice cried hoarsely, and he saw a man running toward him. It was the rider Judkins who came up and gripped Venters' hand. "Venters, I could hev dropped when I seen them hosses. But thet sight ain't a marker to the looks of you. What's wrong? Hev you gone crazy? You must be crazy to ride in here this way—with them hosses—talkin' thet way about Tull an' Jerry Card."

"Jud, I'm not crazy—only mad clean through," replied Venters.

"Wal, now, Bern, I'm glad to hear some of your old self in your voice. Fer when you come up you looked like the corpse of a dead rider with fire fer eyes. You hed thet crowd too stiff fer throwin' guns. Come, we've got to hev a talk. Let's go up the lane. We ain't much safe here."

Judkins mounted Bells and rode with Venters up to the cottonwood grove. Here they dismounted and went among the trees.

"Let's hear from you first," said Judkins. "You fetched back them hosses. Thet *is* the trick. An', of course, you got Jerry the same as you got Horne."

"Horne!"

"Sure. He was found dead yesterday all chewed by coyotes, an' he'd been shot plumb center."

"Where was he found?"

"At the split down the trail—you know where Oldrin's cattle trail runs off north from the trail to the pass."

"That's where I met Jerry and the rustlers. What was Horne doing with them? I thought Horne was an honest cattle-man."

"Lord—Bern, don't ask me thet! I'm all muddled now tryin' to figure things."

Venters told of the fight and the race with Jerry Card and its tragic conclusion.

"I knowed it! I knowed all along that Wrangle was the best hoss!" exclaimed Judkins, with his lean face working and his eyes lighting. "Thet was a race! Lord, I'd like to hev seen Wrangle jump the cliff with Jerry. An' thet was good-by to the grandest hoss an' rider ever on the sage! . . . But, Bern, after you got the hosses why'd you want to bolt right in Tull's face?"

"I want him to know. An' if I can get to him I'll—"

"You can't get near Tull," interrupted Judkins. "Thet vigilante bunch hev takin' to bein' bodyguard for Tull an' Dyer, too."

"Hasn't Lassiter made a break yet?" inquired Venters, curiously.

"Naw!" replied Judkins, scornfully. "Jane turned his head. He's mad in love over her—follers her like a dog. He ain't no more Lassiter! He's lost his nerve; he doesn't look like the same feller. It's village talk. Everybody knows it. He hasn't thrown a gun, an' he won't—"

"Jud, I'll bet he does," replied Venters, earnestly. "Remember what I say. This Lassiter is something more than a gunman. Jud, he's big—he's great! . . . I feel that in him. God help Tull and Dyer when Lassiter does go after them. For horses and riders and stone walls won't save them."

"Wal, hev it your way, Bern. I hope you're right. Nat'rully I've been some sore on Lassiter fer gitten soft. But I ain't denyin' his nerve, or whatever's great in him thet sort of paralyzes people. No later 'n this mornin' I seen him saunterin' down the lane, quiet an' slow. An' like his guns he comes black—*black*, thet's Lassiter. Wal, the crowd on the corner never batted an eye, an' I'll gamble my hoss thet there wasn't one who hed a heart-beat till Lassiter got by. He went in Snell's saloon, an' as there wasn't no gun play I had to go in, too. An' there, darn my pictures, if Lassiter wasn't standin' to the bar, drinkin' an' talkin' with Oldrin'."

"*Oldring!*" whispered Venters. His voice, as all fire and pulse within him, seemed to freeze.

"Let go my arm!" exclaimed Judkins. "Thet's my bad arm. Sure it was Oldrin'. What the hell's wrong with you, anyway? Venters, I tell you somethin's wrong. You're whiter 'n a sheet. You can't be *scared* of the rustler. I don't believe you've got a scare in you. Wal, now, jest let me talk. You know I like to talk, an' if I'm slow I allus git there sometime. As I said, Lassiter was talkin' chummy with Oldrin'. There wasn't no hard feelin's. An' the gang wasn't payin' no pertic'lar attention. But like a cat watchin' a mouse I hed my eyes on them two fellers. It was strange to me, thet confab. I'm gittin' to think a lot fer a feller who doesn't know much. There'd been some queer deals lately an' this seemed to me the queerest. These men stood to the bar alone, an' so close their big gun-hilts butted together. I seen Oldrin' was some surprised at first, an' Lassiter was cool as ice. They talked, an' presently at somethin' Lassiter said the rustler bawled out a curse, an' then he jest fell up against the bar, an' sagged there. The gang in the saloon looked around an' laughed, an' thet's about all. Finally Oldrin' turned, and it was easy to see somethin' hed shook him. Yes sir, thet big rustler—you know he's as broad as he is long, an' the powerfullest build of a man—yes, sir, the nerve had been taken out of him. Then, after a little, he began to talk, an' said a lot to Lassiter, an' by an' by it didn't take much of an eye to see thet Lassiter was gittin' hit hard. I never seen him anyway but cooler'n ice—till then. He seemed to be hit harder 'n Oldrin', only he didn't roar out thet way. He jest kind of sunk in, an' looked an' looked, an' he didn't see a livin' soul in thet saloon. Then he sort of come to, an' shakin' hands—mind you, *shakin' hands* with Oldrin'—he went out. I couldn't help thinkin' how easy even a boy could hev dropped the great gunman then! . . . Wal, the rustler stood at the bar fer a long time, an' he was seein' things far off, too; then he come to an' roared fer whisky, an' gulped a drink thet was big enough to drown me."

"Is Oldring here now?" whispered Venters. He could not speak above a whisper. Judkins' story had been meaningless to him.

"He's at Snell's yet. Bern, I hevn't told you yet thet the rustlers hev been raisin' hell. They shot up Stone Bridge an' Glaze, an' fer three days they've been here drinkin' an' gamblin' an' throwin' of gold. These rustlers hev a pile of gold. If it was gold dust or nugget gold I'd hev reason to think, but it's new coin gold, as if it had jest come from the United States treasury. An' the coin's genuine. Thet's all been proved. The truth is Oldrin's on a rampage. A while back he lost his Masked Rider, an' they say he's wild about thet. I'm wonderin' if Lassiter could hev told the rustler anythin' about thet little masked, hard-ridin' devil. Ride! He was most as good as Jerry Card. An', Bern, I've been wonderin' if you know—"

"Judkins, you're a good fellow," interrupted Venters. "Some day I'll tell you a story. I've no time now. Take the horses to Jane."

Judkins stared, and then, muttering to himself, he mounted Bells, and stared again at Venters, and then, leading the other horses, he rode into the grove and disappeared.

Once, long before, on the night Venters had carried Bess through the cañon and up into Surprise Valley, he had experienced the strangeness of faculties singularly, tinglingly acute. And now the same sensation recurred. But it was different in that he felt cold, frozen, mechanical, incapable of free thought, and all about him seemed unreal, aloof, remote. He hid his rifle in the sage, marking its exact location with extreme care. Then he faced down the lane and strode toward the center of the village. Perceptions flashed upon him, the faint, cold touch of the breeze, a cold, silvery tinkle of flowing water, a cold sun shining out of a cold sky, song of birds and laugh of children, coldly distant. Cold and intangible were all things in earth and heaven. Colder and tighter stretched the skin over his face; colder and harder grew the polished butts of his guns; colder and steadier became his hands, as he wiped the clammy sweat from his face or reached low to his gun-sheaths. Men meeting him in the walk gave him wide berth. In front of Bevin's store a crowd melted apart for his passage, and their faces and whispers were faces and whispers of a dream. He turned a corner to meet Tull face to face, eye to eye. As once before he had seen this man pale to a ghastly livid white, so again he saw the change. Tull stopped in his tracks, with right hand raised and shaking. Suddenly it dropped, and he seemed to glide aside, to pass out of Venters's sight. Next he saw many horses with bridles down—all clean-limbed, dark bays or blacks—rustlers' horses! Loud voices and boisterous laughter, rattle of dice and scrape of chair and clink of gold, burst in mingled din from an open doorway. He stepped inside.

With the sight of smoke-hazed room and drinking, cursing, gambling, dark-visaged men, reality once more dawned upon Venters.

His entrance had been unnoticed, and he bent his gaze upon the drinkers at the bar. Dark-clothed, dark-faced men they all were, burned by the sun, bow-legged as were most riders of the sage, but neither lean nor gaunt. Then Venters's gaze passed to the tables, and swiftly it swept over the hard-featured gamesters, to alight upon the huge, shaggy, black head of the rustler-chief.

"*Oldring!*" he cried, and to him his voice seemed to split a bell in his ears.

It stilled the din.

That silence suddenly broke to the scrape and crash of Oldring's chair as he rose; and then, while he passed, a great gloomy figure, again the thronged room stilled in silence yet deeper.

"Oldring, a word with you!" continued Venters.

"Ho! What's this?" boomed Oldring, in frowning scrutiny.

"Come outside, alone. A word for you—*from your Masked Rider!*"

Oldring kicked a chair out of his way and lunged forward with a stamp of heavy boot that jarred the floor. He waved down his muttering, rising men.

Venters backed out of the door and waited, hearing, as no sound had ever before struck into his soul, the rapid, heavy steps of the rustler.

Oldring appeared, and Venters had one glimpse of his great breadth and bulk, his gold-buckled belt with hanging guns, his high-top boots with gold spurs. In that moment Venters had a strange, unintelligible curiosity to see Oldring alive. The rustler's broad brow, his large black eyes, his sweeping beard, as dark as the wing of a raven, his enormous width of shoulder and depth of chest, his whole splendid presence so wonderfully charged with vitality and force and strength, seemed to afford Venters an unutterable fiendish joy because for that magnificent manhood and life he meant cold and sudden death.

"*Oldring, Bess is alive! But she's dead to you—dead to the life you made her lead—dead as you will be in one second!*"

Swift as lightning Venters's glance dropped from Oldring's rolling eyes to his hands. One of them, the right, swept out, then toward his gun—and Venters shot him through the heart.

Slowly Oldring sank to his knees, and the hand, dragging at the gun, fell away. Venters's strangely acute faculties grasped the meaning of that limp arm, of the swaying hulk, of the gasp and heave, of the quivering beard. But was that awful spirit in the black eyes only one of vitality?

"Man—why—didn't—you—wait! Bess—was—" Oldring's whisper died under his beard, and, with a heavy lurch, he fell forward.

Bounding swiftly away, Venters fled around the corner, across the street, and, leaping a hedge, he ran through yard, orchard, and garden to the sage. Here, under cover of the tall brush, he turned west and ran on to the place where he had hidden his rifle. Securing that, he again set out into a run, and, circling through the sage, came up behind Jane Withersteen's stable and corrals. With laboring, dripping chest and pain as of a knife thrust in his side, he stopped to regain his breath, and while resting, his eyes roved around in search of a horse. Doors and windows of the stable were open wide and had a deserted look. One dejected, lonely burro stood in the near corral. Strange indeed was the silence brooding over the once happy, noisy home of Jane Withersteen's pets.

He went into the corral, exercising care to leave no tracks, and led the burro to the watering trough. Venters, though not thirsty, drank till he could drink no more. Then, leading the burro over hard ground, he struck into the sage and down the slope.

He strode swiftly, turning from time to time to scan the slope for riders. His head just topped the level of sagebrush, and the burro could not have been seen at all. Slowly the green of Cottonwoods sank behind the slope, and at last a wavering line of purple sage met the blue of sky.

To avoid being seen, to get away, to hide his trail—these were the sole ideas in his mind as he headed for Deception Pass; and he directed all his acuteness of eye and ear, and the keenness of a rider's judgment for distance and ground, to stern accomplishment of the task. He kept to the sage far to the left of the trail leading into the Pass. He walked ten miles and looked back a thousand times. Always the graceful, purple wave of sage remained wide and lonely, a clear, undotted waste. Coming to a stretch of rocky ground, he took advantage of it to cross the trail and then continued down on the right. At length he persuaded himself that he would be able to see riders mounted on horses before they could see him on the little burro, and he rode bareback.

Hour by hour the tireless burro kept to his faithful, steady trot. The sun sank, and the long shadows lengthened down the slope. Moving veils of purple twilight crept out of the hollows and, mustering and forming on the levels, soon merged and shaded into night. Venters guided the burro nearer to the trail, so that he could see its white line from the ridges, and rode on through the hours.

Once down in the Pass without leaving a trail, he would hold himself safe for the time being. When late in the night he reached the break in the sage, he sent the burro down ahead of him, and started an avalanche that all but buried the animal at the bottom of the trail. Bruised and battered as he was, he had a moment's elation, for he had hidden his tracks. Once more he mounted the burro and rode on. The hour was the blackest of the night when he made the thicket which enclosed his old camp. Here he turned the burro loose in the grass near the spring, and then lay down on his old bed of leaves.

He felt only vaguely, as outside things, the ache and burn and throb of the muscles of his body. But a dammed-up torrent of emotion at last burst its bounds, and the hour that saw his release from immediate action was one that confounded him in the reaction of his spirit. He suffered without understanding why. He caught glimpses into himself, into unlit darkness of soul. The fire that had blistered him and the cold which had frozen him now united in one torturing possession of his mind and heart, and like a fiery steed with ice-shod feet, ranged his being, ran rioting through his blood, trampling the resurging good, dragging ever at the evil.

Out of the subsiding chaos came a clear question. What had happened? He had left the valley to go to Cottonwoods. Why? It seemed that he had gone to kill a man—Oldring! The name riveted his consciousness upon the one man of all men upon earth whom he had wanted the meet. He had met the rustler. Venters recalled the smoky haze of the saloon, the dark-visaged men, the huge Oldring. He saw him step out of the door, a splendid specimen of manhood, a handsome giant with purple-black and sweeping beard. He remembered inquisitive gaze of falcon eyes. He heard himself repeating: *"Oldring, Bess is alive! But she's dead to you*," and he felt himself jerk, and his ears throbbed to the thunder of a gun, and he saw the giant sink slowly to his knees. Was that only the vitality of him—that awful light in the eyes—only the hard-dying life of a tremendously powerful brute? A broken whisper, strange as death: *"Man— why—didn't—you—wait! Bess—was—"* And Oldring plunged face forward, dead.

"I killed him," cried Venters, in remembering shock. "But it wasn't *that*. Ah, the look in his eyes and his whisper!"

Herein lay the secret that had clamored to him through all the tumult and stress of his emotions. What a look in the eyes of a man shot through the heart! It had been neither hate nor ferocity nor fear of men nor fear of death. It had been no passionate, glinting spirit of a fearless foe, willing shot for shot, life for life, but lacking physical power. Distinctly recalled now, never to be forgotten, Venters saw in Oldring's magnificent eyes the rolling of great, glad surprise—softness—love! Then came a shadow and the terrible superhuman striving of his spirit to speak. Oldring, shot through the heart, had fought and forced back death, not for a moment in which to shoot or curse, but to whisper strange words.

What words for a dying man to whisper! Why had not Venters waited? For what? That was no plea for life. It was regret that there was not a moment of life left in which to speak. Bess was—Herein lay renewed torture for Venters. What had Bess been to Oldring? The old question, like a specter, stalked from its grave to haunt him. He had overlooked, he had forgiven, he had loved, and he had forgotten; and now, out of the mystery of a dying man's whisper, rose again that perverse, unsatisfied, jealous uncertainty. Bess had loved that splendid, black-crowned giant—by her own confession she had loved him; and in Venters's soul again flamed up the jealous hell. Then into the clamoring hell burst the shot that had killed Oldring, and it rang in a wild, fiendish gladness, a hateful, vengeful joy. That passed to the memory of the love and light in Oldring's eyes and the mystery in his whisper. So the changing, swaying emotions fluctuated in Venters's heart.

This was the climax of his year of suffering and the crucial struggle of his life. And when the gray dawn came he rose, a gloomy, almost heartbroken man, but victor over evil passions. He could not change the past;

and, even if he had not loved Bess with all his soul, he had grown into a man who would not change the future he had planned for her. Only, and once for all, he must know the truth, know the worst, stifle all these insistent doubts and subtle hopes and jealous fancies, and kill the past by knowing truly what Bess had been to Oldring. For that matter he knew—he had always known, but he must hear it spoken. Then, when they had safely gotten out of that wild country to take up a new and an absorbing life, she would forget, she would be happy, and through that, in the years to come, he could not but find life worth living.

All day he rode slowly and cautiously up the Pass, taking time to peer around corners, to pick out hard ground and grassy patches, and to make sure there was no one in pursuit. In the night sometime he came to the smooth, scrawled rocks dividing the valley, and here set the burro at liberty. He walked beyond, climbed the slope and the dim, starlit gorge. Then, weary to the point of exhaustion, he crept into a shallow cave and fell asleep.

In the morning, when he descended the trail, he found the sun was pouring a golden stream of light through the arch of the great Stone Bridge. Surprise Valley, like a valley of dreams, lay mystically soft and beautiful, awakening to the golden flood which was rolling away its slumberous bands of mist, brightening its walled faces.

While yet far off he discerned Bess moving under the silver spruces, and soon the barking of the dogs told him that they had seen him. He heard the mocking-birds singing in the trees, and then the twittering of the quail. Ring and Whitie came bounding toward him, and behind them ran Bess, her hands outstretched.

"Bern! You're back! You're back!" she cried, in a joy that rang of her loneliness.

"Yes, I'm back," he said, as she rushed to meet him.

She had reached out for him when suddenly, as she saw him closely, something checked her, and as quickly all her joy fled and with it her color, leaving her pale and trembling.

"Oh! What's happened?"

"A good deal has happened, Bess. I don't need to tell you what. And I'm played out. Worn out in mind more than body."

"Dear—you look strange to me!" faltered Bess.

"Never mind that. I'm all right. There's nothing for you to be scared about. Things are going to turn out just as we have planned. As soon as I'm rested we'll make a break to get out of the country. Only now, right, now, I must know the truth about you."

"Truth about me?" echoed Bess, shrinkingly. She seemed to be casting back into her mind for a forgotten key. Venters himself, as he saw her, received a pang.

"Yes—the truth. Bess, don't misunderstand. I haven't changed that way. I love you still. I'll love you more afterward. Life will be just as sweet—sweeter to us. We'll be—be married as soon as ever we can. We'll be happy—but there's a devil in me. A perverse, jealous devil! Then I've queer fancies. I forgot for a long time. Now all those fiendish little whispers of doubt and faith and fear and hope come torturing me again. I've got to kill them with the truth."

"I'll tell you anything you want to know," she replied, frankly.

"Then, by Heaven, we'll have it over and done with! . . . Bess—did Oldring love you?"

"Certainly he did."

"Did—did you love him?"

"Of course. I told you so."

"How can you tell it so lightly?" cried Venters, passionately. "Haven't you any sense of—of—" He choked back speech. He felt the rush of pain and passion. He seized her in rude, strong hands and drew her close. He looked straight into her dark-blue eyes. They were shadowing with the old wistful light, but they were as clear as the limpid water of the spring. They were earnest, solemn in unutterable love and faith and abnegation. Venters shivered. He knew he was looking into her soul. He knew she could not lie in that moment; but that she might tell the truth, looking at him with those eyes, almost killed his belief in purity.

"What are—what were you to—to Oldring?" he panted, fiercely.

"I am his daughter," she replied, instantly.

Venters slowly let go of her. There was a violent break in the force of his feeling—then creeping blankness.

"What—was it—you said?" he asked, in a kind of dull wonder.

"I am his daughter."

"Oldring's daughter?" queried Venters, with life gathering in his voice.

"Yes."

With a passionately awakening start he grasped her hands and drew her close.

"All the time—you've been Oldring's daughter?"

"Yes, of course all the time—always."

"But Bess, you told me—you let me think—I made out you were—a—so—so ashamed."

"It is my shame," she said, with voice deep and full, and now the scarlet fired her cheek. "I told you—I'm nothing—nameless—just Bess, Oldring's girl!"

"I know—I remember. But I never thought—" he went on, hurriedly, huskily. "That time—when you lay dying—you prayed—you—somehow I got the idea you were bad."

"Bad?" she asked, with a little laugh.

She looked up with a faint smile of bewilderment and the absolute unconsciousness of a child. Venters gasped in the gathering might of the truth. She did not understand his meaning.

"Bess! Bess!" He clasped her in his arms, hiding her eyes against his breast. She must not see his face in that moment. And he held her while he looked out across the valley. In his dim and blinded sight, in the blur of golden light and moving mist, he saw Oldring. She was the rustler's nameless daughter. Oldring had loved her. He had so guarded her, so kept her from women and men and knowledge of life that her mind was as a child's. That was part of the secret—part of the mystery. That was the wonderful truth. Not only was she not bad, but good, pure, innocent above all innocence in the world—the innocence of lonely girlhood.

He saw Oldring's magnificent eyes, inquisitive, searching—softening. He saw them flare in amaze, in gladness, with love, then suddenly strain in terrible effort of will. He heard Oldring whisper and saw him sway like a log and fall. Then a million bellowing, thundering voices—gunshots of conscience, thunderbolts of remorse—dinned horribly in his ears. He had killed Bess's father. Then a rushing wind filled his ears like the moan of wind in the cliffs, a knell indeed—Oldring's knell.

He dropped to his knees and hid his face against Bess, and grasped her with the hands of a drowning man.

"My God! . . . My God! . . . Oh, Bess! . . . Forgive me! Never mind what I've done—what I've thought. But forgive me. I'll give you my life. I'll live for you. I'll love you. Oh, I do love you as no man ever loved a woman. I want you to know—to remember that I fought a fight for you—however blind I was. I thought—I thought—never mind what I thought—but I loved you—I asked you to marry me. Let that—let me have that to hug to my heart. Oh, Bess, I was driven! And I might have known! I could not rest nor sleep till I had this mystery solved. God, how things work out!"

"Bern, you're weak—trembling—you talk wildly," cried Bess. "You've overdone your strength. There's nothing to forgive. There's no mystery except your love for me. You have come back to me!"

And she clasped his head tenderly in her arms and pressed it closely to her throbbing breast.

CHAPTER 19

FAY

At the home of Jane Withersteen little Fay was climbing Lassiter's knee.

"Does oo love me?" she asked.

Lassiter, who was as serious with Fay as he was gentle and loving, assured her in earnest and elaborate speech that he was her devoted subject. Fay looked thoughtful and appeared to be debating the duplicity of men or searching for a supreme test to prove this cavalier.

"Does oo love my new muvver?" she asked, with bewildering suddenness.

Jane Withersteen laughed, and for the first time in many a day she felt a stir of her pulse and warmth in her cheek.

It was a still drowsy summer of afternoon, and the three were sitting in the shade of the wooded knoll that faced the sage-slope. Little Fay's brief spell of unhappy longing for her mother—the childish, mystic gloom—had passed, and now where Fay was there were prattle and laughter and glee. She had emerged from sorrow to be the incarnation of joy and loveliness. She had grown supernaturally sweet and beautiful. For Jane Withersteen the child was an answer to prayer, a blessing, a possession infinitely more precious than all she had lost. For Lassiter, Jane divined that little Fay had become a religion.

"Does oo love my new muvver?" repeated Fay.

Lassiter's answer to this was a modest and sincere affirmative.

"Why don't oo marry my new muvver an' be my favver?"

Of the thousands of questions put by little Fay to Lassiter that was the first he had been unable to answer.

"Fay—Fay, don't ask questions like that," said Jane.

"Why?"

"Because," replied Jane. And she found it strangely embarrassing to meet the child's gaze. It seemed to her that Fay's violet eyes looked through her with piercing wisdom.

"Oo love him, don't oo?"

"Dear child—run and play," said Jane, "but don't go too far. Don't go from this little hill."

Fay pranced off wildly, joyous over freedom that had not been granted her for weeks.

"Jane, why are children more sincere than grown-up persons?" asked Lassiter.

"Are they?"

"I reckon so. Little Fay there—she sees things as they appear on the face. An Indian does that. So does a dog. An' an Indian an' a dog are most of the time right in what they see. Mebbe a child is always right."

"Well, what does Fay see?" asked Jane.

"I reckon you know. I wonder what goes on in Fay's mind when she sees part of the truth with the wise eyes of a child, an' wantin' to know more, meets with strange falseness from you? Wait! You are false in a way, though you're the best woman I ever knew. What I want to say is this. Fay has taken you pretendin' to—to care for me for the thing it looks on the face. An' her little formin' mind asks questions. An' the answers she gets are different from the looks of things. So she'll grow up, gradually takin' on that falseness, an' be like the rest of women, an' men, too. An' the truth of this falseness to life is proved by your appearin' to love me when you don't. Things aren't what they seem."

"Lassiter, you're right. A child should be told the absolute truth. But—is that possible? I haven't been able to do it, and all my life I've loved the truth, and I've prided myself upon being truthful. Maybe that was only egotism. I'm learning much, my friend. Some of those blinding scales have fallen from my eyes. And—and as to caring for you, I think I care a great deal. How much, how little, I couldn't say. My heart is almost broken, Lassiter. So now is not a good time to judge of affection. I can still play and be merry with Fay. I can still dream. But when I attempt serious thought I'm dazed. I don't think. I don't care any more. I don't pray! . . . Think of that, my friend! But in spite of my numb feeling I believe I'll rise out of all this dark agony a better woman, with greater love of man and God. I'm on the rack now; I'm senseless to all but pain, and growing dead to that. Sooner or later I shall rise out of this stupor. I'm waiting the hour."

"It'll soon come, Jane," replied Lassiter, soberly. "Then I'm afraid for you. Years are terrible things, an' for years you've been bound. Habit of years is strong as life itself. Somehow, though, I believe as you—that you'll come out of it all a finer woman. I'm waitin', too. An' I'm wonderin'— I reckon, Jane, that marriage between us is out of all human reason?"

"Lassiter! . . . My dear friend! . . . It's impossible for us to marry."

"Why—as Fay says?" inquired Lassiter, with gentle persistence.

"Why! I never thought why. But it's not possible. I am Jane, daughter of Withersteen. My father would rise out of his grave. I'm of Mormon birth. I'm being broken. But I'm still a Mormon woman. And you—you are Lassiter!"

"Mebbe I'm not so much Lassiter as I used to be."

"What was it you said? Habit of years is strong as life itself! You can't change the one habit—the purpose of your life. For you still pack those black guns! You still nurse your passion for blood."

A smile, like a shadow, flickered across his face.

"No."

"Lassiter, I lied to you. But I beg of you—don't you lie to me. I've great respect for you. I believe you're softened toward most, perhaps all, my people except—But when I speak of your purpose, your hate, your guns, I have only him in mind. I don't believe you've changed."

For answer he unbuckled the heavy cartridge belt, and laid it with the heavy, swinging gun-sheaths in her lap.

"Lassiter!" Jane whispered, as she gazed from him to the black, cold guns. Without them he appeared shorn of strength, defenseless, a smaller man. Was she Delilah? Swiftly, conscious of only one motive—refusal to see this man called craven by his enemies—she rose, and with blundering fingers buckled the belt round his waist where it belonged.

"Lassiter, *I* am the coward."

"Come with me out of Utah—where I can put away my guns an' be a man," he said. "I reckon I'll prove it to you then! Come! You've got Black Star back, an' Night an' Bells. Let's take the racers an' little Fay, an' ride out of Utah. The hosses an' the child are all you have left. Come!"

"No, no, Lassiter. I'll never leave Utah. What would I do in the world with my broken fortunes and my broken heart? I'll never leave these purple slopes I love so well."

"I reckon I ought to 've knowed that. Presently you'll be livin' down here in a hovel, an' presently Jane Withersteen will be a memory. I only wanted to have a chance to show you how a man—*any* man—can be better 'n he was. If we left Utah I could prove—I reckon I could prove this thing you call love. It's strange, an' hell an' heaven at once, Jane Withersteen. 'Pears to me that you've thrown away your big heart on love—love of religion an' duty an' churchmen, an' riders an' poor families an' poor children! Yet you can't see what love is—how it changes a person! . . . Listen, an' in tellin' you Milly Erne's story I'll show you how love changed her.

"Milly an' me was children when our family moved from Missouri to Texas, an' we growed up in Texas ways same as if we'd been born there. We had been poor, an' there we prospered. In time the little village where we went became a town, an' strangers an' new families kept movin' in. Milly was the belle them days. I can see her now, a little girl no bigger 'n a bird, an' as pretty. She had the finest eyes, dark-blue-black when she was excited, an' beautiful all the time. You remember Milly's eyes! An' she had light-brown hair with streaks of gold, an' a mouth that every feller wanted to kiss.

"An' about the time Milly was the prettiest an' the sweetest, along came a young minister who began to ride some of a race with the other fellers for Milly. An' he won. Milly had always been strong on religion, an' when she met Frank Erne she went in heart an' soul for the salvation of souls. Fact was, Milly, through study of the Bible an' attendin' church an' revivals, went a little out of her head. It didn't worry the old folks none, an' the only worry to me was Milly's everlastin' prayin' an' workin' to save my soul. She never converted me, but we was the best of comrades, an' I reckon no brother an' sister ever loved each other better. Well, Frank Erne an' me hit up a great friendship. He was a strappin' feller, good to look at, an' had the most pleasin' ways. His religion never bothered me, for he could hunt an' fish an' ride, an' be a good feller. After buffalo once he come pretty near to savin' my life. We got to be thick as brothers, an' he was the only man I ever seen who I thought was good enough for Milly. An' the day they were married I got drunk for the only time in my life.

"Soon after that I left home—it seems Milly was the only one who could keep me home—an' I went to the bad, as to prosperin'. I saw some pretty hard life in the Pan Handle, an' then I went North. In them days Kansas an' Nebraska was as bad, come to think of it, as these days right here on the border of Utah. I got to be pretty handy with guns. An' there wasn't many riders as could beat me ridin'. An' I can say all modest-like that I never seen the white man who could track a hoss or a steer or a man with me. Afore I knowed it two years slipped by, an' all at once I got homesick, an' pulled a bridle south.

"Things at home had changed. I never got over that home-comin'. Mother was dead an' in her grave. Father was a silent, broken man, killed already on his feet. Frank Erne was a ghost of his old self, through with workin', through with preachin', almost through with livin', an Milly was gone! . . . It was a long time before I got the story. Father had no mind left, an' Frank Erne was *afraid* to talk. So I had to pick up what'd happened from different people.

"It 'pears that soon after I left home another preacher come to the little town. An' he an' Frank become rivals. This feller was different from Frank. He preached some other kind of religion, and he was quick an' passionate, where Frank was slow an' mild. He went after people, women specially. In looks he couldn't compare to Frank Erne, but he had power over women. He had a voice, an' talked an' talked an' preached an' preached. Milly fell under his influence. She became mightily interested in his religion. Frank had patience with her, as was his way, an' let her be as interested as she liked. All religions were devoted to one God, he said, an' it wouldn't hurt Milly none to study a different point of view. So the new preacher often called on Milly, an' sometimes in Frank's absence. Frank was a cattle-man between Sundays.

"Along about this time an incident come off that I couldn't get much light on. A stranger come to town, an' was seen with the preacher. This stranger was a big man with an eye like blue ice, an' a beard of gold. He had money, an' he 'peared a man of mystery, an' the town went to buzzin' when he disappeared about the same time as a young woman known to be mightily interested in the new preacher's religion. Then, presently, along comes a man from somewheres in Illinois, an' he up an' spots this preacher as a famous Mormon proselyter. That riled Frank Erne as nothin' ever before, an' from rivals they come to be bitter enemies. An' it ended in Frank goin' to the meetin'-house where Milly was listenin', an' before her an' everybody else he called that preacher—called him, well, almost as hard as Venters called Tull here sometime back. An' Frank followed up that call with a hoss-whippin', an' he drove the proselyter out of town.

"People noticed, so 'twas said, that Milly's sweet disposition changed. Some said it was because she would soon become a mother, an' others said she was pinin' after the new religion. An' there was women who said right out that she was pinin' after the Mormon. Anyway, one mornin' Frank rode in from one of his trips, to find Milly gone. He had no real near neighbors—livin' a little out of town—but those who was nearest said a wagon had gone by in the night, an' they thought it stopped at her door. Well, tracks always tell, an' there was the wagon tracks an' hoss tracks an' man tracks. The news spread like wildfire that Milly had run off from her husband. Everybody but Frank believed it, an' wasn't slow in tellin' why she run off. Mother had always hated that strange streak of Milly's takin' up with the new religion as she had, an' she believed Milly ran off with the Mormon. That hastened mother's death, an' she died unforgivin'. Father wasn't the kind to bow down under disgrace or misfortune, but he had surpassin' love for Milly, an' the loss of her broke him.

"From the minute I heard of Milly's disappearance I never believed she went off of her own free will. I knew Milly, an' I knew she *couldn't* have done that. I stayed at home awhile, tryin' to make Frank Erne talk. But if he knowed anythin' then he wouldn't tell it. So I set out to find

Milly. An' I tried to get on the trail of that proselyter. I knew if I ever struck a town he'd visited that I'd get a trail. I knew, too, that nothin' short of hell would stop his proselytin'. An' I rode from town to town. I had a blind faith that somethin' was guidin' me. An' as the weeks an' months went by I growed into a strange sort of a man, I guess. Anyway, people were afraid of me. Two years after that, way over in a corner of Texas, I struck a town where my man had been. He'd just left. People said he came to that town *without* a woman. I back-trailed my man through Arkansas an' Mississippi, an' the old trail got hot again in Texas. I found the town where he first went after leavin' home. An' here I got track of Milly. I found a cabin where she had given birth to her baby. There was no way to tell whether she'd been kept a prisoner or not. The feller who owned the place was a mean, silent sort of a skunk, an' as I was leavin' I jest took a chance an' left my mark on him. Then I went home again.

"It was to find I hadn't any home, no more. Father had been dead a year. Frank Erne still lived in the house where Milly had left him. I stayed with him awhile, an' I grew old watchin' him. His farm had gone to weed, his cattle had strayed or been rustled, his house weathered till it wouldn't keep out rain nor wind. An' Frank set on the porch and whittled sticks, an' day by day wasted away. There was times when he ranted about like a crazy man, but mostly he was always sittin' an' starin' with eyes that made a man curse. I figured Frank had a secret fear that I needed to know. An' when I told him I'd trailed Milly for near three years an' had got trace of her, an' saw where she'd had her baby, I thought he would drop dead at my feet. An' when he'd come round more natural-like he begged me to *give up* the trail. But he wouldn't explain. So I let him alone, an' watched him day an' night.

"An' I found there was one thing still precious to him, an' it was a little drawer where he kept his papers. This was in the room where he slept. An' it 'peared he seldom slept. But after bein' patient I got the contents of that drawer an' found two letters from Milly. One was a long letter written a few months after her disappearance. She had been bound an' gagged an' dragged away from her home by three men, an' she named them—Hurd, Metzger, Slack. They was strangers to her. She was taken to the little town where I found trace of her two years after. But she didn't send the letter from that town. There she was penned in. 'Peared that the proselyter, who had, of course, come on the scene, was not run-nin' any risks of losin' her. She went on to say that for a time she was out of her head, an' when she got right again all that kept her alive was the baby. It was a beautiful baby, she said, an' all she thought an' dreamed of was somehow to get baby back to its father, an' then she'd thankfully lay down and die. An' the letter ended abrupt, in the middle of a sentence, an' it wasn't signed.

"The second letter was written more than two years after the first. It was from Salt Lake City. It simply said that Milly had heard her brother was on her trail. She asked Frank to tell her brother to give up the search because if he didn't she would suffer in a way too horrible to tell. She didn't beg. She just stated a fact an' made the simple request. An' she ended that letter by sayin' she would soon leave Salt Lake City with the man she had come to love, an' would never be heard of again.

"I recognized Milly's handwrittin', an' I recognized her way of put-tin' things. But that second letter told me of some great change in her. Ponderin' over it, I felt at last she'd either come to love that feller an' his religion, or some terrible fear made her lie an' say so. I couldn't be sure which. But, of course, I meant to find out. I'll say here, if I'd known Mor-mons then as I do now I'd left Milly to her fate. For mebbe she was right about what she'd suffer if I kept on her trail. But I was young an' wild them days. First I went to the town where she'd first been taken, an' I went to the place where she'd been kept. I got that skunk who owned the place, an' took him out in the woods, an' made him tell all he knowed. That wasn't much as to length, but it was pure hell's-fire in substance. This time I left him some incapacitated for any more skunk work short of hell. Then I hit the trail for Utah.

"That was fourteen years ago. I saw the incomin' of most of the Mor-mons. It was a wild country an' a wild time. I rode from town to town, village to village, ranch to ranch, camp to camp. I never stayed long in one place. I never had but one idea. I never rested. Four years went by, an' I knowed every trail in northern Utah. I kept on an' as time went by, an' I'd begun to grow old in my search, I had firmer, blinder faith in whatever was guidin' me. Once I read about a feller who sailed the seven seas an' traveled the world, an' he had a story to tell, an' whenever he seen the man to whom he must tell that story he knowed him on sight. I was like that, only I had a question to ask. An' always I knew the man of whom I must ask. So I never really lost the trail, though for years it was the dimmest trail ever followed by any man.

"Then come a change in my luck. Along in Central Utah I rounded up Hurd, an' I whispered somethin' in his ear, an' watched his face, an' then throwed a gun against his bowels. An' he died with his teeth so tight shut I couldn't have pried them open with a knife. Slack an' Metzger that same year both heard me whisper the same question, an' neither would they speak a word when they lay dyin'. Long before I'd learned no man of this breed or class—or God knows what—would give up any secrets! I had to see in a man's fear of death the connections with Milly Erne's fate. An' as the years passed at long intervals I would find such a man.

"So as I drifted on the long trail down into southern Utah my name preceded me, an' I had to meet a people prepared for me, an' ready with guns. They made me a gunman. An' that suited me. In all this time signs of the proselyter an' the giant with the blue-ice eyes an' the gold beard seemed to fade dimmer out of the trail. Only twice in ten years did I find a trace of that mysterious man who had visited the proselyter at my home village. What he had to do with Milly's fate was beyond all hope for me to learn, unless my guidin' spirit led me to him! As for the other man I knew, as sure as I breathed an' the stars shone an' the wind blew, that I'd meet him some day.

"Eighteen years I've been on the trail. An' it led me to the last lonely villages of the Utah border. Eighteen years! . . . I feel pretty old now. I was only twenty when I hit that trail. Well, as I told you, back here a ways a Gentile said Jane Withersteen could tell me about Milly Erne an' show me her grave!"

The low voice ceased, and Lassiter slowly turned his sombrero round and round, and appeared to be counting the silver ornaments on the band. Jane, leaning toward him, sat as if petrified, listening intently, waiting to hear more. She could have shrieked, but power of tongue and lips were denied her. She saw only this sad, gray, passion-worn man, and she heard only the faint rustling of the leaves.

"Well, I came to Cottonwoods," went on Lassiter, "an' you showed me Milly's grave. An' though your teeth have been shut tighter'n them of all the dead men lyin' back along that trail, jest the same you told me the secret I've lived these eighteen years to hear! Jane, I said you'd tell me without ever me askin'. I didn't need to ask my question here. The day, you remember, when that fat party throwed a gun on me in your court, an'—"

"Oh! Hush!" whispered Jane, blindly holding up her hands.

"*I seen in your face that Dyer, now a bishop, was the proselyter who ruined Milly Erne!*"

For an instant Jane Withersteen's brain was a whirling chaos, and she recovered to find herself grasping at Lassiter like one drowning. And as if by a lightning stroke she sprang from her dull apathy into exquisite torture.

"*It's a lie!* Lassiter! No, no!" she moaned. "I swear—you're wrong!"

"Stop! You'd perjure yourself! But I'll spare you that. You poor woman! Still blind! Still faithful! . . . Listen. I *know*. Let that settle it. An' I give up my purpose!"

"What is it—you say?"

"I give up my purpose. I've come to see an' feel differently. I can't help poor Milly. An' I've outgrowed revenge. I've come to see I can be no judge for men. I can't kill a man jest for hate. Hate ain't the same with me since I loved you an' little Fay."

"Lassiter! You mean you won't kill him?" Jane whispered.

"No."

"For my sake?"

"I reckon. I can't understand, but I'll respect your feelin's."

"Because you—oh, because you love me? . . . Eighteen years! You were that terrible Lassiter! And *now*—because you love me?"

"That's it, Jane."

"Oh, you'll make me love you! How can I help but love you? My heart must be stone. But—oh, Lassiter, wait, wait! Give me time. I'm not what I was. Once it was so easy to love. Now it's easy to hate. Wait! My faith in God—*some* God—still lives. By it I see happier times for you, poor passion-swayed wanderer! For me—a miserable, broken woman. I loved your sister Milly. I *will* love you. I can't have fallen so low—I can't be so abandoned by God—that I've no love left to give you. Wait! Let us forget Milly's sad life. Ah, I knew it as no one else on earth! There's one thing I shall tell you—if you are at my death-bed, but I can't speak now."

"I reckon I don't want to hear no more," said Lassiter.

Jane leaned against him, as if some pent-up force had rent its way out, she fell into a paroxysm of weeping. Lassiter held her in silent sympathy. By degrees she regained composure, and she was rising, sensible of being relieved of a weighty burden, when a sudden start on Lassiter's part alarmed her.

"I heard hosses—hosses with muffled hoofs!" he said; and he got up guardedly.

"Where's Fay?" asked Jane, hurriedly glancing round the shady knoll. The bright-haired child, who had appeared to be close all the time, was not in sight.

"Fay!" called Jane.

No answering shout of glee. No patter of flying feet. Jane saw Lassiter stiffen.

"*Fay—oh—Fay!*" Jane almost screamed.

The leaves quivered and rustled; a lonesome cricket chirped in the grass; a bee hummed by. The silence of the waning afternoon breathed hateful portent. It terrified Jane. When had silence been so infernal?

"She's—only—strayed—out—of earshot," faltered Jane, looking at Lassiter.

Pale, rigid as a statue, the rider stood, not in listening, searching posture, but in one of doomed certainty. Suddenly he grasped Jane with an iron hand, and turning his face from her gaze, he strode with her from the knoll.

"See—Fay played here last—a house of stones an' sticks. . . . An' here's a corral of pebbles with leaves for hosses," said Lassiter, stridently, and pointed to the ground. "Back an' forth she trailed here. . . . See, she's buried somethin'—a dead grasshopper—there's a tombstone . . . here she went, chasin' a lizard—see the tiny streaked trail . . . she pulled bark off this cottonwood . . . look in the dust of the path—the letters you taught her—she's drawn pictures of birds an' hosses an' people. . . . Look, a cross! Oh, Jane, *your* cross!"

Lassiter dragged Jane on, and as if from a book, read the meaning of little Fay's trail. All the way down the knoll, through the shrubbery, round and round a cottonwood, Fay's vagrant fancy left records of her sweet musings and innocent play. Long had she lingered round a bird-nest to leave therein the gaudy wing of a butterfly. Long had she played beside the running stream, sending adrift vessels freighted with pebbly cargo. Then she had wandered through the deep grass, her tiny feet scarcely turning a fragile blade, and she had dreamed beside some old faded flowers. Thus her steps led her into the broad lane. The little dimpled imprints of her bare feet showed clean-cut in the dust; they went a little way down the lane; and then, at a point where they stopped, the great tracks of a man led out from the shrubbery and returned.

CHAPTER 20

LASSITER'S WAY

Footprints told the story of little Fay's abduction.

In anguish Jane Withersteen turned speechlessly to Lassiter, and confirming her fears, she saw him gray-faced, aged all in a moment, stricken as if by a mortal blow.

Then all her life seemed to fall about her in wreck and ruin.

"It's all over," she heard her voice whisper. "It's ended. I'm going— I'm going—"

"Where?" demanded Lassiter, suddenly looming darkly over her.

"To—to those cruel men—"

"Speak names!" thundered Lassiter.

"To Bishop Dyer—to Tull," went on Jane, shocked into obedience.

"Well—what for?"

"I want little Fay. I can't live without her. They've stolen her as they stole Milly Erne's child. I must have little Fay—I want only her. I give up. I'll go and tell Bishop Dyer—I'm broken. I'll tell him I'm ready for the yoke—only give me back Fay—and—and I'll marry Tull!"

"*Never!*" hissed Lassiter.

His long arm leaped at her. Almost running, he dragged her under the cottonwoods, across the court, into the huge hall of Withersteen

House, and he shut the door with a force that jarred the heavy walls. Black Star and Night and Bells, since their return, had been locked in this hall, and now they stamped on the stone floor.

Lassiter released Jane, and like a dizzy man swayed from her with a hoarse cry and leaned shaking against a table, where he kept his rider's accoutrements. He began to fumble in his saddle-bags. His action brought a clinking, metallic sound—the rattling of gun-cartridges. His fingers trembled as he slipped cartridges into an extra belt. But as he buckled it over the one he habitually wore his hands became steady. This second belt contained two guns, smaller than the black ones swinging low, and he slipped them round so that his coat hid them. Then he fell to swift action. Jane Withersteen watched him, fascinated but uncomprehending; and she saw him rapidly saddle Black Star and Night. Then he drew her into the light of the huge window, standing over her, gripping her arm with fingers like cold steel.

"Yes, Jane, it's ended—but you're not goin' to Dyer! . . . *I'm goin' instead!*"

Looking at him—he was so terrible of aspect—she could not comprehend his words. Who was this man with the face gray as death, with eyes that would have made her shriek had she the strength, with the strange, ruthlessly bitter lips? Where was the gentle Lassiter? What was this presence in the hall, about him, about her—this cold, invisible presence?

"Yes, it's ended, Jane," he was saying, so awfully quiet and cool and implacable, "an' I'm going to make a little call. I'll lock you in here, an' when I get back have the saddle-bags full of meat an' bread. An' be ready to ride!"

"Lassiter!" cried Jane.

Desperately she tried to meet his gray eyes, in vain; desperately she tried again, fought herself as feeling and thought resurged in torment, and she succeeded; and then she knew.

"No—no—no!" she wailed. "You said you'd foregone your vengeance. You promised not to kill Bishop Dyer."

"If you want to talk to me about him—leave off the Bishop. I don't understand that name, or its use."

"Oh, hadn't you foregone your vengeance on—on Dyer?"

"Yes."

"But—your actions—your words—your guns—your terrible looks! . . . They don't seem foregoing vengeance?"

"Jane, now it's justice."

"You'll—kill him?"

"If God lets me live another hour! If not God—then the devil who drives me!"

"You'll kill him—for yourself—for your vengeful hate?"

"No!"

"For Milly Erne's sake?"

"No."

"For little Fay's?"

"No!"

"Oh—for whose?"

"For yours!"

"His blood on my soul!" whispered Jane, and she fell to her knees. This was the long-pending hour of fruition. And the habit of years—the religious passion of her life—leaped from lethargy, and the long months of gradual drifting to doubt were as if they had never been. "If you spill his blood it'll be on my soul—and on my father's. Listen." And she clasped his knees, and clung there as he tried to raise her. "Listen. Am I nothing to you?"

"Woman—don't trifle at words! I love you! An' I'll soon prove it!"

"I'll give myself to you—I'll ride away with you—marry you, if only you'll spare him?"

His answer was a cold, ringing, terrible laugh.

"Lassiter—I'll love you—spare him!"

"No!"

She sprang up in despairing, breaking spirit, and encircled his neck with her arms, and held him in an embrace that he strove vainly to loosen. "Lassiter, would you kill me? I'm fighting my last fight for the principles of my youth—love of religion, love of father. You don't know—you can't guess the truth, and I can't speak it! I'm losing all. I'm changing. All I've gone through is nothing to this hour. Pity me—help me in my weakness. You're strong again—oh, so cruelly, coldly strong! You're killing me— I see you—feel you as some other Lassiter! My master, be merciful—spare him!"

His answer was a ruthless smile.

She clung the closer to him, and leaned her panting breast on him, and lifted her face to his. "Lassiter, *I do love you!* It's leaped out of my agony. It comes suddenly with a terrible blow of truth. You are a man! I never knew it till now. Some wonderful change came to me when you buckled on these guns and showed that gray, awful face. I loved you then. All my life I've loved, but never as now. No woman can love like a broken woman. If it were not for one thing—just one thing—and yet! I *can't* speak it—I'd glory in your manhood—the lion in you that means to slay for me. Believe me—and spare Dyer. Be merciful—great as it's in you to be great. . . . Oh, listen and believe—I have nothing, but I'm a woman—a beautiful woman, Lassiter—a passionate, loving woman—and I love you! Take me—hide me in some wild place—and love me and mend my broken heart. Spare him, and take me away."

She lifted her face closer and closer to his, until their lips nearly touched, and she hung upon his neck, and with strength almost spent pressed and still pressed her palpitating body to his.

"Kiss me!" she whispered, blindly.

"No—not at your price!" he answered. His voice had changed, or she had lost clearness of hearing.

"Kiss me! . . . Are you a man? Kiss me and save me!"

"Jane, you never played fair with me. But now you're blisterin' your lips—blackenin' your soul with lies!"

"By the memory of my mother—by my Bible—no! No, I *have* no Bible! But by my hope of heaven I swear I love you!"

Lassiter's gray lips formed soundless words that meant even her love could not avail to bend his will. As if the hold of her arms was that of a child's he loosened it and stepped away.

"Wait! Don't go! Oh, hear a last word! . . . May a more just and merciful God than the God I was taught to worship judge me—forgive me—save me! For I can no longer keep silent! . . . Lassiter, in pleading for Dyer I've been pleading more for my father. My father was a Mormon master, close to the leaders of the church. It was my father who sent Dyer out to proselyte. It was my father who had the blue-ice eye and the beard of gold. It was my father you got trace of in the past years. Truly, Dyer ruined Milly Erne—dragged her from her home—to Utah—to Cotton-woods. *But it was for my father!* If Milly Erne was ever wife of a Mormon that Mormon was my father! I never knew—never will know whether or not she was a wife. Blind I may be, Lassiter—fanatically faithful to a false religion I may have been, but I know justice, and my father is beyond hu-man justice. Surely he is meeting just punishment—somewhere. Always it has appalled me—the thought of your killing Dyer for my father's sins. So I have prayed!"

"Jane, the past is dead. In my love for you I forgot the past. This thing I'm about to do ain't for myself, or Milly, or Fay. It's not because of anythin' that ever happened in the past, but for what is happenin' right *now. It's for you!* . . . An' listen. Since I was a boy I've never thanked God for anythin'. If there is a God—an' I've come to believe it—I thank Him now for the years that made me Lassiter! . . . I can reach down an' feel these big guns, an' know what I can do with them. An', Jane, only one of the miracles Dyer professes to believe in can save him!"

Again for Jane Withersteen came the spinning of her brain in dark-ness, and as she whirled in endless chaos she seemed to be falling at the feet of a luminous figure—a man—Lassiter—who had saved her from herself, who could not be changed, who would slay rightfully. Then she slipped into utter blackness.

When she recovered from her faint she became aware that she was lying on a couch near the window in her sitting-room. Her brow felt damp and cold and wet; some one was chafing her hands; she recognized Judkins, and then saw that his lean, hard face wore the hue and look of excessive agitation.

"Judkins!" Her voice broke weakly.

"Aw, Miss Withersteen, you're comin' round fine. Now jest lay still a little. You're all right; everythin's all right."

"Where is—he?"

"Who?"

"Lassiter!"

"You needn't worry none about him."

"Where is he? Tell me—instantly."

"Wal, he's in the other room patchin' up a few triflin' bullet-holes."

"Ah! . . . Bishop Dyer?"

"When I seen him last—a matter of half an hour ago, he was on his knees. He was some busy, *but* he wasn't prayin'!"

"How strangely you talk! I'll sit up. I'm—well, strong again. Tell me. Dyer on—his knees! What was he doing?"

"Wal, beggin' your pardon fer blunt talk, Miss Withersteen, Dyer was on his knees an' *not* prayin'. You remember his big, broad hands? You've seen 'em raised in blessin' over old gray men an' little—curly-headed children like—like Fay Larkin! Come to think of thet, I disremember ever hearin' of his liftin' his big hands in blessin' over a *woman*. Wal, when I seen him last—jest a little while ago—he was on his knees, *not* prayin', as I remarked—an' he was pressin' his big hands over some bigger wounds."

"Man, you drive me mad! Did Lassiter kill Dyer?"

"Yes."

"Did he kill Tull?"

"No. Tull's out of the village with most of his riders. He's expected back before evenin'. Lassiter will hev to git away before Tull an' his riders come in. It's sure death fer him here. An' wuss fer you, too, Miss Withersteen. There'll be some of an uprisin' when Tull gits back."

"I shall ride away with Lassiter. Judkins, tell me all you saw—all you know about this killing." She realized, without wonder or amaze, how Judkins's one word, affirming the death of Dyer—that the catastrophe had fallen—had completed the change whereby she had been molded or beaten or broken into another woman. She felt calm, slightly cold, strong as she had not been strong since the first shadow fell upon her.

"I jest saw about all of it, Miss Withersteen, an' I'll be glad to tell you if you'll only hev patience with me," said Judkins, earnestly. "You see, I've been pecooliarly interested, an' nat'rully I'm some excited. An' I talk a lot thet mebbe ain't necessary, but I can't help thet.

"I was at the meetin'-house where Dyer was holdin' court. You know he allus acts as magistrate an' judge when Tull's away. An' the trial was fer tryin' what's left of my boy riders—thet helped me hold your cattle—fer a lot of hatched-up things the boys never did. We're used to thet, an' the boys wouldn't hev minded bein' locked up fer a while, or hevin' to dig ditches, or whatever the judge laid down. You see, I divided the gold you give me among all my boys, an' they all hid it, an' they all feel rich. Howsomever, court was adjourned before the judge passed sentence. Yes, ma'am, court was adjourned some strange an' quick, much as if lightnin' hed struck the meetin'-house.

"I hed trouble attendin' the trial, but I got in. There was a good many people there, all my boys, an' Judge Dyer with his several clerks. Also he hed with him the five riders who've been guardin' him pretty close of late. They was Carter, Wright, Jengessen, an' two new riders from Stone Bridge. I didn't hear their names, but I heard they was handy men with guns, an' they looked more like rustlers than riders. Anyway, there they was, the five all in a row.

"Judge Dyer was tellin' Willie Kern, one of my best an' steadiest boys—Dyer was tellin' him how there was a ditch opened near Willie's home lettin' water through his lot, where it hadn't ought to go. An' Willie was tryin' to git a word in to prove he wasn't at home all the day it happened—which was true, as I know—but Willie couldn't git a word in, an' then Judge Dyer went on layin' down the law. An' all to onct he happened to look down the long room. An' if ever any man turned to stone he was thet man.

"Nat'rully I looked back to see what hed acted so powerful strange on the Judge. An' there, half-way up the room, in the middle of the wide aisle, stood Lassiter! All white an' black he looked, an' I can't think of anythin' he resembled, onless it's death. Venters made thet same room some still an' chilly when he called Tull; but this was different. I give my word, Miss Withersteen; thet I went cold to my very marrow. I don't know why. But Lassiter has a way about him thet's awful. He spoke a word—a name—I couldn't understand it, though he spoke clear as a bell. I was too excited, mebbe. Judge Dyer must hev understood it, an' a lot more thet was mystery to me, fer he pitched forrard out of his chair right onto the platform.

"Then them five riders, Dyer's body-guards, they jumped up, an' two of them thet I found out afterward were the strangers from Stone Bridge, they piled right out of a winder, so quick you couldn't catch your breath. It was plain they wasn't Mormons.

"Jengessen, Carter, an' Wright eyed Lassiter, for what must hev been a second an' seemed like an hour, an' they went white an' strung. But they didn't weaken nor lose their nerve.

"I hed a good look at Lassiter. He stood sort of stiff, bendin' a little, an' both his arms were crooked, an' his hands looked like a hawk's claws. But there ain't no tellin' how his eyes looked. I know this, though, an' thet is his eyes could read the mind of any man about to throw a gun. An' in watchin' him, of course, I couldn't see the three men go fer their guns. An' though I was lookin' right at Lassiter—lookin' hard—I couldn't see how he drawed. He was quicker'n eyesight—thet's all. But I seen the red spurtin' of his guns, an' heard his shots jest the very littlest instant before I heard the shots of the riders. An' when I turned, Wright an' Carter was down, an' Jengessen, who's tough like a steer, was pullin' the trigger of a wobblin' gun. But it was plain he was shot through, plumb center. An' sudden he fell with a crash, an' his gun clattered on the floor.

"Then there was a hell of a silence. Nobody breathed. Sartin I didn't, anyway. I saw Lassiter slip a smokin' gun back in a belt. But he hadn't throwed either of the big black guns, an' I thought thet strange. An' all this was happenin' quick—you can't imagine how quick.

"There come a scrapin' on the floor an' Dyer got up, his face like lead. I wanted to watch Lassiter, but Dyer's face, onct I seen it like thet, glued my eyes. I seen him go fer his gun—why, I could hev done better, quicker—an' then there was a thunderin' shot from Lassiter, an' it hit Dyer's right arm, an' his gun went off as it dropped. He looked at Lassiter like a cornered sage-wolf, an' sort of howled, an' reached down fer his gun. He'd jest picked it off the floor an' was raisin' it when another thunderin' shot almost tore thet arm off—so it seemed to me. The gun dropped again an' he went down on his knees, kind of flounderin' after it. It was some strange an' terrible to see his awful earnestness. Why would such a man cling so to life? Anyway, he got the gun with left hand an' was raisin' it, pullin' trigger in his madness, when the third thunderin' shot hit his left arm, an' he dropped the gun again. But thet left arm wasn't useless yet, fer he grabbed up the gun, an' with a shakin' aim thet would hev been pitiful to me—in any other man—he began to shoot. One wild bullet struck a man twenty feet from Lassiter. An' it killed thet man, as I seen afterward. Then come a bunch of thunderin' shots—nine

I calkilated after, fer they come so quick I couldn't count them—an' I knew Lassiter hed turned the black guns loose on Dyer.

"I'm tellin' you straight. Miss Withersteen, fer I want you to know. Afterward you'll git over it. I've seen some soul-rackin' scenes on this Utah border, but this was the awfulest. I remember I closed my eyes, an' fer a minute I thought of the strangest things, out of place there, such as you'd never dream would come to mind. I saw the sage, an' runnin' hosses—an' thet's the beautifulest sight to me—an' I saw dim things in the dark, an' there was a kind of hummin' in my ears. An' I remember distinctly—fer it was what made all these things whirl out of my mind an' opened my eyes—I remember distinctly it was the smell of gunpowder.

"The court had about adjourned fer thet judge. He was on his knees, an' he wasn't prayin'. He was gaspin' an' tryin' to press his big, floppin', crippled hands over his body. Lassiter had sent all those last thunderin' shots through his body. Thet was Lassiter's way.

"An' Lassiter spoke, an' if I ever forgit his words I'll never forgit the sound of his voice.

"'*Proselyter*, I reckon you'd better call quick on thet God who reveals Hisself to you on earth, because He won't be visitin' the place you're goin' to!'

"An' then I seen Dyer look at his big, hangin' hands thet wasn't big enough fer the last work he set them to. An' he looked up at Lassiter. An' then he stared horrible at somethin' thet wasn't Lassiter, nor any one there, nor the room, nor the branches of purple sage peepin' into the winder. Whatever he seen, it was with the look of a man who *discovers* somethin' too late. Thet's a terrible look! . . . An' with a horrible *understandin'* cry he slid forrard on his face."

Judkins paused in his narrative, breathing heavily while he wiped his perspiring brow.

"Thet's about all," he concluded. "Lassiter left the meetin'-house an' I hurried to catch up with him. He was bleedin' from three gunshots, none of them much to bother him. An' we come right up here. I found you layin' in the hall, an' I hed to work some over you."

Jane Withersteen offered up no prayer for Dyer's soul.

Lassiter's step sounded in the hall—the familiar soft, silver-clinking step—and she heard it with thrilling new emotions in which was a vague joy in her very fear of him. The door opened, and she saw him, the old Lassiter, slow, easy, gentle, cool, yet not exactly the same Lassiter. She rose, and for a moment her eyes blurred and swam in tears.

"Are you—all—all right?" she asked, tremulously.

"I reckon."

"Lassiter, I'll ride away with you. Hide me till danger is past—till we are forgotten—then take me where you will. Your people shall be my people, and your God my God!"

He kissed her hand with the quaint grace and courtesy that came to him in rare moments.

"Black Star an' Night are ready," he said, simply.

His quiet mention of the black racers spurred Jane to action. Hurrying to her room, she changed to her rider's suit, packed her jewelry, and the gold that was left, and all the woman's apparel for which there was space in the saddle-bags, and then returned to the hall. Black Star stamped his iron-shod hoofs and tossed his beautiful head, and eyed her with knowing eyes.

"Judkins, I give Bells to you," said Jane. "I hope you will always keep him and be good to him."

Judkins mumbled thanks that he could not speak fluently, and his eyes flashed.

Lassiter strapped Jane's saddle-bags upon Black Star, and led the racers out into the court.

"Judkins, you ride with Jane out into the sage. If you see any riders comin' shout quick twice. An', Jane, *don't look back!* I'll catch up soon. We'll get to the break into the Pass before midnight, an' then wait until mornin' to go down."

Black Star bent his graceful neck and bowed his noble head, and his broad shoulders yielded as he knelt for Jane to mount.

She rode out of the court beside Judkins, through the grove, across the wide lane into the sage; and she realized that she was leaving Withersteen House forever, and she did not look back. A strange, dreamy, calm peace pervaded her soul. Her doom had fallen upon her, but, instead of finding life no longer worth living she found it doubly significant, full of sweetness as the western breeze, beautiful and unknown as the sage-slope stretching its purple sunset shadows before her. She became aware of Judkins's hand touching hers; she heard him speak a husky good-by; then into the place of Bells shot the dead-black, keen, racy nose of Night, and she knew Lassiter rode beside her.

"*Don't—look—back!*" he said, and his voice, too, was not clear.

Facing straight ahead, seeing only the waving, shadowy sage, Jane held out her gauntleted hand, to feel it enclosed in strong clasp. So she rode on without a backward glance at the beautiful grove of Cottonwoods. She did not seem to think of the past, of what she left forever, but of the color and mystery and wilderness of the sage-slope leading down to Deception Pass, and of the future. She watched the shadows lengthen down the slope; she felt the cool west wind sweeping by from the rear; and she wondered at low, yellow clouds sailing swiftly over her and beyond.

"*Don't—look—back!*" said Lassiter.

Thick-driving belts of smoke traveled by on the wind, and with it came a strong, pungent odor of burning wood.

Lassiter had fired Withersteen House! But Jane did not look back.

A misty veil obscured the clear, searching gaze she had kept steadfastly upon the purple slope and the dim lines of cañons. It passed, as passed the rolling clouds of smoke, and she saw the valley deepening into the shades of twilight. Night came on, swift as the fleet racers, and stars peeped out to brighten and grow, and the huge, windy, eastern heave of sage-level paled under a rising moon and turned to silver. Blanched in moonlight the sage yet seemed to hold its hue of purple, and was infinitely more wild and lonely. So the night-hours wore on, and Jane Withersteen never once looked back.

CHAPTER 21

BLACK STAR AND NIGHT

The time had come for Venters and Bess to leave their retreat. They were at great pains to choose the few things they would be able to carry with them on the journey out of Utah.

"Bern, whatever kind of a pack's this, anyhow?" questioned Bess, rising from her work with reddened face.

Venters, absorbed in his own task, did not look up at all, and in reply said he had brought so much from Cottonwoods that he did not recollect the half of it.

"A woman packed this!" Bess exclaimed.

He scarcely caught her meaning, but the peculiar tone of her voice caused him instantly to rise, and he saw Bess on her knees before an open pack which he recognized as the one given him by Jane.

"By George!" he ejaculated, guiltily, and then at sight of Bess's face he laughed outright.

"A woman packed this," she repeated, fixing woeful, tragic eyes on him.

"Well, is that a crime?"

"There—there *is* a woman after all!"

"Now Bess—"

"You've lied to me!"

Then and there Venters found it imperative to postpone work for the present. All her life Bess had been isolated, but she had inherited certain elements of the eternal feminine.

"But there *was* a woman and you *did* lie to me," she kept repeating, after he had explained.

"What of that? Bess, I'll get angry at you in a moment. Remember you've been pent up all your life. I venture to say that if you'd been out in the world you'd have had a dozen sweethearts and have told many a lie before this."

"I wouldn't anything of the kind," declared Bess, indignantly.

"Well—perhaps not lie. But you'd have had the sweethearts. You couldn't have helped that—being so pretty."

This remark appeared to be a very clever and fortunate one; and the work of selecting and then of stowing all the packs in the cave, went on without further interruption.

Venters closed up the opening of the cave with a thatch of willows and aspens, so that not even a bird or a rat could get in to the sacks of grain. And this work was in order with the precaution habitually observed by him. He might not be able to get out of Utah, and have to return to the valley. But he owed it to Bess to make the attempt, and in case they were compelled to turn back he wanted to find that fine store of food and grain intact. The outfit of implements and utensils he packed away in another cave.

"Bess, we have enough to live here all our lives," he said once, dreamily.

"Shall I go roll Balancing Rock?" she asked, in light speech, but with deep-blue fire in her eyes.

"No—no."

"Ah, you don't forget the gold and the world," she sighed.

"Child, you forget the beautiful dresses and the travel—and everything."

"Oh, I want to go. But I want to stay!"

"I feel the same way."

They let the eight calves out of the corral, and kept only two of the burros Venters had brought from Cottonwoods. These they intended to ride. Bess freed all her pets—the quail and rabbits and foxes.

The last sunset and twilight and night were both the sweetest and saddest they had ever spent in Surprise Valley. Morning brought keen exhilaration and excitement. When Venters had saddled the two burros, strapped on the light packs and the two canteens, the sunlight was dispersing the lazy shadows from the valley. Taking a last look at the caves and the silver spruces, Venters and Bess made a reluctant start, leading the burros. Ring and Whitie looked keen and knowing. Something seemed to drag at Venters's feet and he noticed Bess lagged behind. Never had the climb from terrace to bridge appeared so long.

Not till they reached the opening of the gorge did they stop to rest and take one last look at the valley. The tremendous arch of stone curved clear and sharp in outline against the morning sky. And through it streaked the golden shaft. The valley seemed an enchanted circle of glorious veils of gold and wraiths of white and silver haze and dim, blue, moving shade—beautiful and wild and unreal as a dream.

"We—we can—th—think of it—always—re—remember," sobbed Bess.

"Hush! Don't cry. Our valley has only fitted us for a better life somewhere. Come!"

They entered the gorge, and he closed the willow gate. From rosy, golden, morning light they passed into cool, dense gloom. The burros pattered up the trail with little hollow-cracking steps. And the gorge widened to narrow outlet and the gloom lightened to gray. At the divide they halted for another rest. Venters's keen, remembering gaze searched Balancing Rock, and the long incline, and the cracked toppling walls, but failed to note the slightest change.

The dogs led the descent; then came Bess leading her burro; then Venters leading his. Bess kept her eyes bent downward. Venters, however, had an irresistible desire to look upward at Balancing Rock. It had always haunted him, and now he wondered if he were really to get through the outlet before the huge stone thundered down. He fancied that would be a miracle. Every few steps he answered to the strange, nervous fear and turned to make sure the rock still stood like a giant statue. And, as he descended, it grew dimmer in his sight. It changed form; it swayed; it nodded darkly; and at last, in his heightened fancy, he saw it heave and roll. As in a dream when he felt himself falling yet knew he would never fall, so he saw this long-standing thunderbolt of the little stone-men plunge down to close forever the outlet to Deception Pass.

And while he was giving way to unaccountable dread imaginations the descent was accomplished without mishap.

"I'm glad that's over," he said, breathing more freely. "I hope I'm by that hanging rock for good and all. Since almost the moment I first saw it I've had an idea that it was waiting for me. Now, when it does fall, if I'm thousands of miles away, I'll hear it."

With the first glimpses of the smooth slope leading down to the grotesque cedars and out to the Pass, Venters's cool nerve returned. One long survey to the left, then one to the right, satisfied his caution. Leading the burros down to the spur of rock, he halted at the steep incline.

"Bess, here's the bad place, the place, I told you about, with the cut steps. You start down, leading your burro. Take your time and hold on to him if you slip. I've got a rope on him and a half-hitch on this point of rock, so I can let him down safely. Coming up here was a killing job. But it'll be easy going down."

Both burros passed down the difficult stairs cut by the cliff-dwellers, and did it without a misstep. After that the descent down the slope and over the mile of scrawled, ribbed, and ridged rock required only careful guidance, and Venters got the burros to level ground in a condition that caused him to congratulate himself.

"Oh, if we only had Wrangle!" exclaimed Venters. "But we're lucky. That's the worst of our trail passed. We've only men to fear now. If we get up in the sage we can hide and slip along like coyotes."

They mounted and rode west through the valley and entered the cañon. From time to time Venters walked, leading his burro. When they got by all the cañons and gullies opening into the Pass they went faster and with fewer halts. Venters did not confide in Bess the alarming fact that he had seen horses and smoke less than a mile up one of the intersecting cañons. He did not talk at all. And long after he had passed this cañon and felt secure once more in the certainty that they had been unobserved he never relaxed his watchfulness. But he did not walk any more, and he kept the burros at a steady trot. Night fell before they reached the last water in the Pass and they made camp by starlight. Venters did not want the burros to stray, so he tied them with long halters in the grass near the spring. Bess, tired out and silent, laid her head in a saddle and went to sleep between the two dogs. Venters did not close his eyes. The cañon silence appeared full of the low, continuous hum of insects. He listened until the hum grew into a roar, and then, breaking the spell, once more he heard it low and clear. He watched the stars and the moving shadows, and always his glance returned to the girl's dimly pale face. And he remembered how white and still it had once looked in the starlight. And again stern thought fought his strange fancies. Would all his labor and his love be for naught? Would he lose her, after all? What did the dark shadow around her portend? Did calamity lurk on that long upland trial through the sage? Why should his heart swell and throb with nameless fear? He listened to the silence and told himself that in the broad light of day he could dispel this leaden-weighted dread.

At the first hint of gray over the eastern rim he awoke Bess, saddled the burros, and began the day's travel. He wanted to get out of the Pass before there was any chance of riders coming down. They gained the break as the first red rays of the rising sun colored the rim.

For once, so eager was he to get up to level ground, he did not send Ring or Whitie in advance. Encouraging Bess to hurry, pulling at his patient, plodding burro, he climbed the soft, steep trail.

Brighter and brighter grew the light. He mounted the last broken edge of rim to have the sun-fired, purple sage-slope burst upon him as a glory. Bess panted up to his side, tugging on the halter of her burro.

"We're up!" he cried, joyously. "There's not a dot on the sage. We're safe. We'll not be seen! Oh, Bess—"

Ring growled and sniffed the keen air and bristled. Venters clutched at his rifle. Whitie sometimes made a mistake, but Ring never. The dull thud of hoofs almost deprived Venters of power to turn and see from where disaster threatened. He felt his eyes dilate as he stared at Lassiter leading Black Star and Night out of the sage, with Jane Withersteen, in rider's costume, close beside them.

For an instant Venters felt himself whirl dizzily in the center of vast circles of sage. He recovered partially, enough to see Lassiter standing with a glad smile and Jane riveted in astonishment.

"Why, Bern!" she exclaimed. "How good it is to see you! We're riding away, you see. The storm burst—and I'm a ruined woman! . . . I thought you were alone."

Venters, unable to speak for consternation, and bewildered out of all sense of what he ought or ought not to do, simply stared at Jane.

"Son, where are you bound for?" asked Lassiter.

"Not safe—where I was—I'm—we're going out of Utah—back East," he found tongue to say.

"I reckon this meetin's the luckiest thing that ever happened to you an' to me—an' to Jane—an' to Bess," said Lassiter, coolly.

"*Bess!*" cried Jane, with a sudden leap of blood to her pale cheek.

It was entirely beyond Venters to see any luck in that meeting,

Jane Withersteen took one flashing, woman's glance at Bess's scarlet face, at her slender, shapely form.

"Venters! is this a girl—a woman?" she questioned, in a voice that stung.

"Yes."

"Did you have her in that wonderful valley?"

"Yes, but Jane—"

"All the time you were gone?"

"Yes, but I couldn't tell—"

"Was it for *her* you asked me to give you supplies? Was it for *her* that you wanted to make your valley a paradise?"

"Oh—Jane—"

"Answer me."

"Yes."

"Oh, you liar!" And with these passionate words Jane Withersteen succumbed to fury. For the second time in her life she fell into the ungovernable rage that had been her father's weakness. And it was worse than his, for she was a jealous woman—jealous even of her friends.

As best he could, he bore the brunt of her anger. It was not only his deceit to her that she visited upon him, but her betrayal by religion, by life itself.

Her passion, like fire at white heat, consumed itself in little time. Her physical strength failed, and still her spirit attempted to go on in magnificent denunciation of those who had wronged her. Like a tree cut deep into its roots she began to quiver and shake, and her anger weakened into despair. And her ringing voice sank into a broken, husky whisper. Then, spent and pitiable, up-held by Lassiter's arm, she turned and hid her face in Black Star's mane.

Numb as Venters was when at length Jane Withersteen lifted her head and looked at him, he yet suffered a pang.

"Jane, the girl is innocent!" he cried.

"Can you expect me to believe that?" she asked, with weary, bitter eyes.

"I'm not that kind of a liar. And you know it. If I lied—if I kept silent when honor should have made me speak, it was to spare you. I came to Cottonwoods to tell you. But I couldn't add to your pain. I intended to tell you I had come to love this girl. But, Jane, I hadn't forgotten how good you were to me. I haven't changed at all toward you. I prize your friendship as I always have. But, however it may look to you—don't be unjust. The girl is innocent. Ask Lassiter."

"Jane, she's jest as sweet an' innocent as little Fay," said Lassiter. There was a faint smile upon his face and a beautiful light.

Venters saw, and knew that Lassiter saw, how Jane Withersteen's tortured soul wrestled with hate and threw it—with scorn, doubt, suspicion, and overcame all.

"Bern, if in my misery I accused you unjustly, I crave forgiveness," she said. "I'm not what I once was. Tell me—who is this girl?"

"Jane, she is Oldring's daughter, and his Masked Rider. Lassiter will tell you how I shot her for a rustler, saved her life—all the story. It's a strange story, Jane, as wild as the sage. But it's true—true as her innocence. That you must believe!"

"Oldring's Masked Rider! Oldring's daughter!" exclaimed Jane. "And she's innocent! You ask me to believe much. If this girl is—is what you say, how could she be going away with the man who killed her father?"

"Why did you tell that?" cried Venters, passionately.

Jane's question had roused Bess out of stupefaction. Her eyes suddenly darkened and dilated. She stepped toward Venters and held up both hands as if to ward off a blow.

"Did—did you kill Oldring?"

"I did, Bess, and I hate myself for it. But you know I never dreamed he was your father. I thought he'd wronged you. I killed him when I was madly jealous."

For a moment Bess was shocked into silence.

"But he was my father!" she broke out, at last. "And now I must go back—I can't go with you. It's all over—that beautiful dream. Oh, I *knew* it couldn't come true. You can't take me now."

"If you forgive me, Bess, it'll all come right in the end!" implored Venters.

"It can't be right. I'll go back. After all, I loved him. He was good to me. I can't forget that."

"If you go back to Oldring's men I'll follow you, and then they'll kill me," said Venters, hoarsely.

"Oh no, Bern, you'll not come. Let me go. It's best for you to forget me. I've brought you only pain and dishonor."

She did not weep. But the sweet bloom and life died out of her face. She looked haggard and sad, all at once stunted; and her hand dropped listlessly; and her head drooped in slow, final acceptance of a hopeless fate.

"Jane, look there!" cried Venters, in despairing grief. "Need you have told her? Where was all your kindness of heart? This girl has had a wretched, lonely life. And I'd found a way to make her happy. You've killed it. You've killed something sweet and pure and hopeful, just as sure as you breathe."

"Oh, Bern! It was a slip. I never thought—I never thought!" replied Jane. "How could I tell she didn't know?"

Lassiter suddenly moved forward, and with the beautiful light on his face now strangely luminous, he looked at Jane and Venters and then let his soft, bright gaze rest on Bess.

"Well, I reckon you've all had your say, an' now it's Lassiter's turn. Why, I was jest prayin' for this meetin'. Bess, jest look here."

Gently he touched her arm and turned her to face the others, and then outspread his great hand to disclose a shiny, battered gold locket.

"Open it," he said, with a singularly rich voice.

Bess complied, but listlessly.

"Jane—Venters—come closer," went on Lassiter. "Take a look at the picture. Don't you know the woman?"

Jane, after one glance, drew back.

"Milly Erne!" she cried, wonderingly.

Venters, with tingling pulse, with something growing on him, recognized in the faded miniature portrait the eyes of Milly Erne.

"Yes, that's Milly," said Lassiter, softly. "Bess, did you ever see her face—look hard—with all your heart an' soul?"

"The eyes seem to haunt me," whispered Bess. "Oh, I can't remember—they're eyes of my dreams—but—but—"

Lassiter's strong arm went round her, and he bent his head.

"Child, I thought you'd remember her eyes. They're the same beautiful eyes you'd see if you looked in a mirror or a clear spring. They're your mother's eyes. You are Milly Erne's child. Your name is Elizabeth Erne. You're not Oldring's daughter. You're the daughter of Frank Erne, a man once my best friend. Look! Here's his picture beside Milly's. He was handsome, an' as fine an' gallant a Southern gentleman as I ever seen. Frank come of an old family. You come of the best of blood, lass, an' blood tells."

Bess slipped through his arm to her knees and hugged the locket to her bosom, and lifted wonderful, yearning eyes.

"It—can't—be—true!"

"Thank God, lass, *it is* true," replied Lassiter. "Jane an' Bern here—they both recognize Milly. They see Milly in you. They're so knocked out they can't tell you, that's all."

"Who are you?" whispered Bess.

"I reckon I'm Milly's brother, an' your uncle! . . . Uncle Jim! Ain't that fine?"

"Oh, I can't believe—Don't raise me! Bern, let me kneel. I see truth in your face—in Miss Withersteen's. But let me hear it all—all on my knees. Tell me *how* it's true!"

"Well, Elizabeth, listen," said Lassiter. "Before you was born your father made a mortal enemy of a Mormon named Dyer. They was both ministers an' come to be rivals. Dyer stole your mother away from her home. She gave birth to you in Texas eighteen years ago. Then she was taken to Utah, from place to place, an' finally to the last border settlement—Cottonwoods. You was about three years old when you was taken away from Milly. She never knew what had become of you. But she lived a good while hopin' and prayin' to have you again. Then she gave up an died. An' I may as well put in here your father died ten years ago. Well, I spent my time tracin' Milly, an' some months back I landed in Cottonwoods. An' jest lately I learned all about you. I had a talk with Oldrin' an' told him you was dead, an' he told me what I had so long been wantin' to know. It was Dyer, of course, who stole you from Milly. Part reason he was sore because Milly refused to give you Mormon teachin', but mostly he still hated Frank Erne so infernally that he made a deal with Oldrin' to take you an' bring you up as an infamous rustler an' rustler's girl. The idea was to break Frank Erne's heart if he ever came to Utah—to show him his daughter with a band of low rustlers. Well—Oldrin' took you, brought you up from childhood, an' then made you his Masked Rider. He made you infamous. He kept that part of the contract, but he learned to love you as a daughter, an' never let any but his own men know you was a girl. I heard him say that with my own ears, an' I saw his big eyes grow dim. He told me how he had guarded you always, kept you locked up in his absence, was always at your side or near you on those rides that made you famous on the sage. He said he an' an old rustler whom he trusted had taught you how to read an' write. They selected the books for you. Dyer had wanted you brought up the vilest of the vile! An' Oldrin' brought you up the innocentest of the innocent. He said you didn't know what vileness was. I can hear his big voice tremble now as he said it. He told me how the men—rustlers an' outlaws—who from time to time tried to approach you familiarly—he told me how he shot them dead. I'm tellin' you this 'specially because you've showed such shame—sayin' you was nameless an' all that. Nothin' on earth can be wronger than that idea of yours. An' the truth of it is here. Oldrin' swore to me that if Dyer died, releasin' the contract, he intended to hunt up your father an give you back to him. It seems Oldrin' wasn't all bad, an' he sure loved you."

Venters leaned forward in passionate remorse.

"Oh, Bess! I know Lassiter speaks the truth. For when I shot Oldring he dropped to his knees and fought with unearthly power to speak. And he said: 'Man—why—didn't—you—wait? Bess—was—' Then he fell dead. And I've been haunted by his look and words. Oh, Bess, what a strange, splendid thing for Oldring to do! It all seems impossible. But, dear, you really are not what you thought."

"Elizabeth Erne!" cried Jane Withersteen, "I loved your mother and I see her in you!"

What had been incredible from the lips of men became, in the tone, look, and gesture of a woman, a wonderful truth for Bess. With little tremblings of all her slender body she rocked to and fro on her knees. The yearning wistfulness of her eyes changed to solemn splendor of joy. She believed. She was realizing happiness. And as the process of thought was slow, so were the variations of her expression. Her eyes reflected the transformation of her soul. Dark, brooding, hopeless belief—clouds of gloom—drifted, paled, vanished in glorious light. An exquisite rose flush— a glow—shone from her face as she slowly began to rise from her knees. A spirit uplifted her. All that she had held as base dropped from her.

Venters watched her in joy too deep for words. By it he divined something of what Lassiter's revelation meant to Bess, but he knew he could only faintly understand. That moment when she seemed to be lifted by some spiritual transfiguration was the most beautiful moment of his life. She stood with parted, quivering lips, with hands tightly clasping the locket to her heaving breast. A new conscious pride of worth dignified the old wild, free grace and poise.

"Uncle Jim!" she said, tremulously, with a different smile from any Venters had ever seen on her face.

Lassiter took her into his arms.

"I reckon. It's powerful fine to hear that," replied Lassiter, unsteadily.

Venters, feeling his eyes grow hot and wet, turned away, and found himself looking at Jane Withersteen. He had almost forgotten her presence. Tenderness and sympathy were fast hiding traces of her agitation. Venters read her mind—felt the reaction of her noble heart—saw the joy she was beginning to feel at the happiness of others. And suddenly blinded, choked by his emotions, he turned from her also. He knew what she would do presently; she would make some magnificent amend for her anger; she would give some manifestation of her love; probably all in a moment, as she had loved Milly Erne, so would she love Elizabeth Erne.

"'Pears to me, folks, that we'd better talk a little serious now," remarked Lassiter, at length. "Time flies."

"You're right," replied Venters, instantly. "I'd forgotten time—place— danger. Lassiter, you're riding away. Jane's leaving Withersteen House?"

"Forever," replied Jane.

"I fired Withersteen House," said Lassiter.

"Dyer?" questioned Venters, sharply.

"I reckon where Dyer's gone there won't be any kidnappin' of girls."

"Ah! I knew it. I told Judkins— And Tull?" went on Venters, passionately.

"Tull wasn't around when I broke loose. By now he's likely on our trail with his riders."

"Lassiter, you're going into the Pass to hide till all this storm blows over?"

"I reckon that's Jane's idea. I'm thinkin' the storm'll be a powerful long time blowin' over. I was comin' to join you in Surprise Valley. You'll go back now with me?"

"No. I want to take Bess out of Utah. Lassiter, Bess found gold in the valley. We've a saddle-bag full of gold. If we can reach Sterling—"

"Man! How're you ever goin' to do that? Sterlin' is a hundred miles."

"My plan is to ride on, keeping sharp lookout. Somewhere up the trail we'll take to the sage and go round Cottonwoods and then hit the trail again."

"It's a bad plan. You'll kill the burros in two days."

"Then we'll walk."

"That's more bad an' worse. Better go back down the Pass with me."

"Lassiter, this girl has been hidden all her life in that lonely place," went on Venters. "Oldring's men are hunting me. We'd not be safe there any longer. Even if we would be I'd take this chance to get her out. I want to marry her. She shall have some of the pleasures of life— see cities and people. We've gold—we'll be rich. Why, life opens sweet for both of us. And, by heaven, I'll get her out or lose my life in the attempt!"

"I reckon if you go on with them burros you'll lose your life all right. Tull will have riders all over this sage. You can't get out on them burros. It's a fool idea. That's not doin' best by the girl. Come with me an' take chances on the rustlers."

Lassiter's cool argument made Venters waver, not in determination to go, but in hope of success.

"Bess, I want you to know. Lassiter says the trip's almost useless now.

I'm afraid he's right. We've got about one chance in a hundred to go through. Shall we take it? Shall we go on?"

"We'll go on," replied Bess.

"That settles it, Lassiter."

Lassiter spread wide his hands, as if to signify he could do no more, and his face clouded.

Venters felt a touch on his elbow. Jane stood beside him with a hand on his arm. She was smiling. Some thing radiated from her, and like an electric current accelerated the motion of his blood.

"Bern, you'd be right to die rather than not take Elizabeth out of Utah—out of this wild country. You must do it. You'll show her the great world, with all its wonders. Think how little she has seen! Think what delight is in store for her! You have gold; you will be free; you will make her happy. What a glorious prospect! I share it with you. I'll think of you—dream of you—pray for you."

"Thank you, Jane," replied Venters, trying to steady his voice. "It does look bright. Oh, if we were only across that wide, open waste of sage!"

"Bern, the trip's as good as made. It'll be safe—easy. It'll be a glorious ride," she said, softly.

Venters stared. Had Jane's troubles made her insane? Lassiter, too, acted queerly, all at once beginning to turn his sombrero round with hands that actually shook.

"You are a rider. She is a rider. This will be the ride of your lives," added Jane, in that same soft undertone, almost as if she were musing to herself.

"Jane!" he cried.

"I give you Black Star and Night!"

"*Black Star and Night!*" he echoed.

"It's done. Lassiter, put our saddle-bags on the burros."

Only when Lassiter moved swiftly to execute her bidding did Venters's clogged brain grasp at literal meanings. He leaped to catch Lassiter's busy hands.

"No, no— What are you doing?" he demanded, in a kind of fury. "I won't take her racers. What do you think I am? It'd be monstrous. Lassiter! stop it, I say! . . . You've got her to save. You've miles and miles to go. Tull is trailing you. There are rustlers in the Pass. Give me back that saddle-bag!"

"Son—cool down," returned Lassiter, in a voice he might have used to a child. But the grip with which he tore away Venters's grasping hands was that of a giant. "Listen—you fool boy! Jane's sized up the situation. The burros'll do for us. We'll sneak along an' hide. I'll take your dogs an' your rifle. Why, it's the trick. The blacks are yours, an' sure as I can throw a gun you're goin' to ride safe out of the sage."

"Jane—stop him—please stop him," gasped Venters. "I've lost my strength. I can't do—anything. This's hell for me! Can't you see that? I've ruined you—it was through me you lost all. You've only Black Star and Night left. You love these horses. Oh! I know how you must love them now! And—you're trying to give them to me. To help me out of Utah! To save the girl I love!"

"That will be my glory."

Then in the white, rapt face, in the unfathomable eyes, Venters saw Jane Withersteen in a supreme moment. This moment was one wherein she reached up to the height for which her noble soul had ever yearned. He, after disrupting the calm tenor of her peace, after bringing down on her head the implacable hostility of her churchmen, after teaching her a bitter lesson of life—he was to be her salvation. And he turned away again, this time shaken to the core of his soul. Jane Withersteen was the incarnation of selflessness. He experienced wonder and terror, exquisite pain and rapture. What were all the shocks life had dealt him compared to the thought of such loyal and generous friendship?

And instantly, as if by some divine insight, he knew himself in the remaking—tried, found wanting; but stronger, better, surer—and he wheeled to Jane Withersteen, eager, joyous, passionate, wild, exalted. He bent to her; he left tears and kisses on her hands.

"Jane, I—I can't find words—now," he said. "I'm beyond words. Only—I understand. And I'll take the blacks."

"Don't be losin' no more time," put in Lassiter. "I ain't certain, but I think I seen a speck up the sage-slope. Mebbe I was mistaken. But, anyway, we must all be movin'. I've shortened the stirrups on Black Star. Put Bess on him."

Jane Withersteen held out her arms.

"Elizabeth Erne!" she cried, and Bess flew to her.

How inconceivably strange and beautiful it was for Venters to see Bess clasped to Jane Withersteen's breast!

Then he leaped astride Night.

"Venters, ride straight on up the slope," Lassiter was saying, "an' if you don't meet any riders keep on till you're a few miles from the village, then cut off in the sage an' go round to the trail. But you'll most likely meet riders with Tull. Jest keep right on till you're jest out of gunshot an' then make your cut-off into the sage. They'll ride after you, but it won't be no use. You can ride, an' Bess can ride. When you're out of reach turn on round to the west, an' hit the trail somewhere. Save the hosses all you can, but don't be afraid. Black Star and Night are good for a hundred miles before sundown, if you have to push them. You can get to Sterlin' by night if you want. But better make it along about to-morrow mornin'. When you get through the notch on the Glaze trail, swing to the right. You'll be able to see both Glaze an' Stone Bridge. Keep away from them villages. You won't run no risk of meetin' any of Oldrin's rustlers from Sterlin' on. You'll find water in them deep hollows north of the Notch. There's an old trail there, not much used, an' it leads to Sterlin'. That's your trail. An' one thing more. If Tull pushes you—or keeps on persistent-like, for a few miles—jest let the blacks out an' lose him an' his riders."

"Lassiter, may we meet again!" said Venters, in a deep voice.

"Son, it ain't likely—it ain't likely. Well, Bess Oldrin'—Masked Rider—Elizabeth Erne—now you climb on Black Star. I've heard you could ride. Well, every rider loves a good hoss. An', lass, there never was but one that could beat Black Star."

"Ah, Lassiter, there never was any horse that could beat Black Star," said Jane, with the old pride.

"I often wondered—mebbe Venters rode out that race when he brought back the blacks. Son, was Wrangle the best hoss?"

"No, Lassiter," replied Venters. For this lie he had his reward in Jane's quick smile.

"Well, well, my hoss-sense ain't always right. An' here I'm talkin' a lot, wastin' time. It ain't so easy to find an' lose a pretty niece all in one hour! Elizabeth—good-by!"

"Oh, Uncle Jim! . . . Good-by!"

"Elizabeth Erne, be happy! Good-by," said Jane.

"Good-by—oh—good-by!"

In lithe, supple action Bess swung up to Black Star's saddle.

"Jane Withersteen! . . . Good-by!" called Venters, hoarsely.

"Bern—Bess—riders of the purple sage—good-by!"

CHAPTER 22

RIDERS OF
THE PURPLE SAGE

Black Star and Night, answering to spur, swept swiftly westward along the white, slow-rising, sage-bordered trail. Venters heard a mournful howl from Ring, but Whitie was silent. The blacks settled into their fleet, long-striding gallop. The wind sweetly fanned Venters's hot face. From the summit of the first low-swelling ridge he looked back. Lassiter waved his hand; Jane waved her scarf. Venters replied by standing in his stirrups and holding high his sombrero. Then the dip of the ridge hid them. From the height of the next he turned once more. Lassiter, Jane, and the burros had disappeared. They had gone down into the Pass. Venters felt a sensation of irreparable loss.

"Bern—look!" called Bess, pointing up the long slope.

A small, dark, moving dot split the line where purple sage met blue sky. That dot was a band of riders.

"Pull the black, Bess."

They slowed from gallop to canter, then to trot. The fresh and eager horses did not like the check.

"Bern, Black Star has great eyesight."

"I wonder if they're Tull's riders. They might be rustlers. But it's all the same to us."

The black dot grew to be a dark patch moving under low dust-clouds. It grew all the time, though very slowly. There were long periods when it was in plain sight, and intervals when it dropped behind the sage. The blacks trotted for half an hour, for another half-hour, and still the moving patch appeared to stay on the horizon line. Gradually, however, as time passed, it began to enlarge, to creep down the slope, to encroach upon the intervening distance.

"Bess, what do you make them out?" asked Venters. "I don't think they're rustlers."

"They're sage-riders," replied Bess. "I see a white horse and several grays. Rustlers seldom ride any horses but bays and blacks."

"That white horse is Tull's. Pull the black, Bess. I'll get down and cinch up. We're in for some riding. Are you afraid?"

"Not now," answered the girl, smiling.

"You needn't be. Bess, you don't weigh enough to make Black Star know you're on him. I won't be able to stay with you. You'll leave Tull and his riders as if they were standing still."

"How about you?"

"Never fear. If I can't stay with you I can still laugh at Tull."

"Look, Bern! They've stopped on that ridge. They see us."

"Yes. But we're too far yet for them to make out who we are. They'll recognize the blacks first. We've passed most of the ridges and the thickest sage. Now, when I give the word, let Black Star go and ride!"

Venters calculated that a mile or more still intervened between them and the riders. They were approaching at a swift canter. Soon Venters recognized Tull's white horse, and concluded that the riders had likewise recognized Black Star and Night. But it would be impossible for Tull yet to see that the blacks were not ridden by Lassiter and Jane. Venters noted that Tull and the line of horsemen, perhaps ten or twelve in number, stopped several times and evidently looked hard down the slope. It must have been a puzzling circumstance for Tull. Venters laughed grimly at the thought of what Tull's rage would be when he finally discovered the trick. Venters meant to sheer out into the sage before Tull could possibly be sure who rode the blacks.

The gap closed to a distance of half a mile. Tull halted. His riders came up and formed a dark group around him. Venters thought he saw him wave his arms, and was certain of it when the riders dashed into the sage, to right and left of the trail. Tull had anticipated just the move held in mind by Venters.

"Now Bess!" shouted Venters. "Strike north. Go round those riders and turn west."

Black Star sailed over the low sage, and in a few leaps got into his stride and was running. Venters spurred Night after him. It was hard going in the sage. The horses could run as well there, but keen eyesight and judgment must constantly be used by the riders in choosing ground. And continuous swerving from aisle to aisle between the brush, and leaping little washes and mounds of the pack-rats, and breaking through sage, made rough riding. When Venters had turned into a long aisle he had time to look up at Tull's riders. They were now strung out into an extended line riding northeast. And, as Venters and Bess were holding due north, this meant, if the horses of Tull and his riders had the speed and the staying power, they would head the blacks and turn them back down the slope. Tull's men were not saving their mounts; they were driving them desperately. Venters feared only an accident to Black Star or Night, and skillful riding would mitigate possibility of that. One glance ahead served to show him that Bess could pick a course through the sage as well as he. She looked neither back nor at the running riders, and bent forward over Black Star's neck and studied the ground ahead.

It struck Venters, presently, after he had glanced up from time to time, that Bess was drawing away from him as he had expected. He had, however, only thought of the light weight Black Star was carrying and of his superior speed; he saw now that the black was being ridden as never before, except when Jerry Card lost the race to Wrangle. How easily, gracefully, naturally Bess sat her saddle! She could ride! Suddenly Venters remembered she had said she could ride. But he had not dreamed she was capable of such superb horsemanship. Then all at once, flashing over him, thrilling him, came the recollection that Bess was Oldring's Masked Rider.

He forgot Tull—the running riders—the race. He let Night have a free rein and felt him lengthen out to suit himself, knowing he would keep to Black Star's course, knowing that he had been chosen by the best rider now on the upland sage. For Jerry Card was dead. And fame had rivaled him with only one rider, and that was the slender girl who now swung so easily with Black Star's stride. Venters had abhorred her notoriety, but now he took passionate pride in her skill, her daring, her power over a horse. And he delved into his memory, recalling famous rides which he had heard related in the villages and round the camp-fires. Oldring's Masked Rider! Many times this strange rider, at once well known and unknown, had escaped pursuers by matchless riding. He had run the gauntlet of vigilantes down the main street of Stone Bridge, leaving dead horses and dead rustlers behind. He had jumped his horse over the Gerber Wash, a deep, wide ravine separating the fields of Glaze from the wild sage. He had been surrounded north of Sterling; and he had broken through the line. How often had been told the story of day stampedes, of night raids, of pursuit, and then how the Masked Rider, swift as the wind, was gone in the sage! A fleet, dark horse—a slender, dark form—a black mask—a driving run down the slope—a dot on the purple sage—a shadowy, muffled steed disappearing in the night!

And this Masked Rider of the uplands had been Elizabeth Erne!

The sweet sage wind rushed in Venters's face and sang a song in his ears. He heard the dull, rapid beat of Night's hoofs; he saw Black Star drawing away, farther and farther. He realized both horses were swinging to the west. Then gunshots in the rear reminded him of Tull. Venters looked back. Far to the side, dropping behind, trooped the riders. They were shooting. Venters saw no puffs of dust, heard no whistling bullets. He was out of range. When he looked back again Tull's riders had given up the pursuit. The best they could do, no doubt, had been to get near enough to recognize who really rode the blacks. Venters saw Tull drooping in his saddle.

Then Venters pulled Night out of his running stride. Those few miles had scarcely warmed the black, but Venters wished to save him. Bess turned, and, though she was far away, Venters caught the white glint of her waving hand. He held Night to a trot and rode on, seeing Bess and Black Star, and the sloping upward stretch of sage, and from time to time the receding black riders behind. Soon they disappeared behind a ridge, and he turned no more. They would go back to Lassiter's trail and follow it, and follow in vain. So Venters rode on, with the wind growing sweeter to taste and smell, and the purple sage richer and the sky bluer in his sight; and the song in his ears ringing. By and by Bess halted to wait for him, and he knew she had come to the trail. When he reached her it was to smile at sight of her standing with arms round Black Star's neck.

"Oh! Bern! I love him!" she cried. "He's beautiful; he knows; and how he can run! I've had fast horses. But Black Star! . . . Wrangle never beat him!"

"I'm wondering if I didn't dream that. Bess, the blacks are grand. What it must have cost Jane—ah!—well, when we get out of this wild country with Star and Night, back to my old home in Illinois, we'll buy a beautiful farm with meadows and springs and cool shade. There we'll turn the horses free—free to roam and browse and drink—never to feel a spur again—never to be ridden!"

"I would like that," said Bess.

They rested. Then, mounting, they rode side by side up the white trail. The sun rose higher behind them. Far to the left a low line of green marked the site of Cottonwoods. Venters looked once and looked no more. Bess gazed only straight ahead. They put the blacks to the long, swinging rider's canter, and at times pulled them to a trot, and occasionally to a walk. The hours passed, the miles slipped behind, and the wall of rock loomed in the fore. The Notch opened wide. It was a rugged, stony pass, but with level and open trail, and Venters and Bess ran the blacks through it. An old trail led off to the right, taking the line of the wall, and this Venters knew to be the trail mentioned by Lassiter.

The little hamlet Glaze, a white and green patch in the vast waste of purple, lay miles down a slope much like the Cottonwoods slope, only this descended to the west. And miles farther west a faint green spot marked the location of Stone Bridge. All the rest of that world was seemingly smooth, undulating sage, with no ragged lines of cañons to accentuate its wildness.

"Bess, we're safe—we're free!" said Venters. "We're alone on the sage. We're half-way to Sterling."

"Ah! I wonder how it is with Lassiter and Miss Withersteen."

"Never fear, Bess. He'll outwit Tull. He'll get away and hide her safely. He might climb into Surprise Valley, but I don't think he'll go so far."

"Bern, will we ever find any place like our beautiful valley?"

"No. But, dear, listen! We'll go back some day, after years—ten years. Then we'll be forgotten. And our valley will be just as we left it."

"What if Balancing Rock falls and closes the outlet to the Pass?"

"I've thought of that. I'll pack in ropes and ropes. And if the outlet's closed we'll climb up the cliffs and over them to the valley and go down on rope ladders. It could be done. I know just where to make the climb, and I'll never forget."

"Oh yes, let us go back!"

"It's something sweet to look forward to. Bess, it's like all the future looks to me."

"Call me—Elizabeth," she said, shyly.

"Elizabeth Erne! It's a beautiful name. But I'll never forget Bess. Do you know—have you thought that very soon—by this time to-morrow—you will be Elizabeth Venters?"

So they rode on down the old trail. And the sun sloped to the west, and a golden sheen lay on the sage. The hours sped now; the afternoon waned. Often they rested the horses. The glisten of a pool of water in a hollow caught Venters's eye, and here he unsaddled the blacks and let them roll and drink and browse. When he and Bess rode up out of the hollow the sun was low, a crimson ball, and the valley seemed veiled in purple fire and smoke. It was that short time when the sun appeared to rest before setting, and silence, like a cloak of invisible life, lay heavy on all that shimmering world of sage.

They watched the sun begin to bury its red curve under the dark horizon.

"We'll ride on till late," he said. "Then you can sleep a little, while I watch and graze the horses. And we'll ride into Sterling early to-morrow. We'll be married! . . . We'll be in time to catch the stage. We'll tie Black Star and Night behind—and then—for a country not wild and terrible like this!"

"Oh! Bern! . . . But look! The sun is setting on the sage—the last time for us till we dare come again to the Utah border. Ten years! Oh, Bern, look, so you will never forget!"

Slumbering, fading purple fire burned over the undulating sage ridges. Long streaks and bars and shafts and spears fringed the far western slope. Drifting, golden veils mingled with low, purple shadows. Colors and shades changed in slow, wondrous transformation.

Suddenly Venters was startled by a low, rumbling roar—so low that it was like the roar in a sea-shell.

"Bess, did you hear anything?" he whispered.

"No."

"Listen! . . . Maybe I only imagined— *Ah!*"

Out of the east or north, from remote distance, breathed an infinitely low, continuously long sound—deep, weird, detonating, thundering, deadening—dying.

CHAPTER 23

THE FALL OF
BALANCING ROCK

Through tear-blurred sight Jane Withersteen watched Venters and Elizabeth Erne and the black racers disappear over the ridge of sage.

"They're gone!" said Lassiter. "An' they're safe now. An' there'll never be a day of their comin' happy lives but what they'll remember Jane Withersteen an'—an' Uncle Jim! . . . I reckon, Jane, we'd better be on our way."

The burros obediently wheeled and started down the break with little, cautious steps, but Lassiter had to leash the whining dogs and lead them. Jane felt herself bound in a feeling that was neither listlessness nor indifference, yet which rendered her incapable of interest. She was still strong in body, but emotionally tired. That hour at the entrance to Deception Pass had been the climax of her suffering—the flood of her wrath—the last of her sacrifice—the supremy of her love—and the attainment of peace. She thought that if she had little Fay she would not ask any more of life.

Like an automaton she followed Lassiter down the steep trail of dust and bits of weathered stone; and when the little slides moved with her or piled around her knees, she experienced no alarm. Vague relief came to her in the sense of being enclosed between dark stone walls, deep hidden from the glare of sun, from the glistening sage. Lassiter lengthened the stirrup straps on one of the burros and bade her mount and ride close to him. She was to keep the burro from cracking his little hard hoofs on stones. Then she was riding on between dark, gleaming walls. There were quiet and rest and coolness in this cañon. She noted indifferently that they passed close under shady, bulging shelves of cliff, through patches of grass and sage and thicket and groves of slender trees, and over white, pebbly washes, and around masses of broken rock. The burros trotted tirelessly; the dogs, once more free, pattered tirelessly; and Lassiter led on with never a stop, and at every open place he looked back. The shade under the walls gave place to sunlight. And presently they came to a dense thicket of slender trees, through which they pressed to rich, green grass and water. Here Lassiter rested the burros for a little while, but he was restless, uneasy, silent, always listening, peering under the trees. She dully reflected that enemies were behind them—before them; still the thought awakened no dread or concern or interest.

At his bidding she mounted and rode on close to the heels of his burro. The cañon narrowed; the walls lifted their rugged rims higher; and the sun shone down hot from the center of the blue stream of sky above. Lassiter traveled slower, with more exceeding care as to the ground he chose, and he kept speaking low to the dogs. They were now hunting dogs—keen, alert, suspicious, sniffing the warm breeze. The monotony of the yellow walls broke in change of color and smooth surface, and the rugged outline of rims grew craggy. Splits appeared in deep breaks, and gorges running at right angles, and then the Pass opened wide at a junction of intersecting cañons.

Lassiter dismounted, led his burro, called the dogs close, and proceeded at snail pace through dark masses of rock and dense thickets under the left wall. Long he watched and listened before venturing to cross the mouths of side cañons. At length he halted, tied his burro, lifted a warning hand to Jane, and then slipped away among the boulders, and, followed by the stealthy dogs, disappeared from sight. The time he remained absent was neither short nor long to Jane Withersteen.

When he reached her side again he was pale, and his lips were set in a hard line, and his gray eyes glittered coldly. Bidding her dismount, he led the burros into a covert of stones and cedars, and tied them.

"Jane, I've run into the fellers I've been lookin' for, an' I'm goin' after them," he said.

"Why?" she asked.

"I reckon I won't take time to tell you."

"Couldn't we slip by without being seen?"

"Likely enough. But that ain't my game. An' I'd like to know, in case I don't come back, what you'll do."

"What can I do?"

"I reckon you can go back to Tull. Or stay in the Pass an' be taken off by rustlers. Which'll you do?"

"I don't know. I can't think very well. But I believe I'd rather be taken off by rustlers."

Lassiter sat down, put his head in his hands, and remained for a few moments in what appeared to be deep and painful thought. When he lifted his face it was haggard, lined, cold as sculptured marble.

"I'll go. I only mentioned that chance of my not comin' back. I'm pretty sure to come."

"Need you risk so much? Must you fight more? Haven't you shed enough blood?"

"I'd like to tell you why I'm goin'," he continued, in coldness he had seldom used to her. She remarked it, but it was the same to her as if he had spoken with his old gentle warmth. "But I reckon I won't. Only, I'll say that mercy an' goodness, such as is in you, though they're the grand things in human nature, can't be lived up to on this Utah border. Life's hell out here. You think—or you used to think—that your religion made this life heaven. Mebbe them scales on your eyes has dropped now. Jane, I wouldn't have you no different, an' that's why I'm goin' to try to hide you somewhere in this Pass. I'd like to hide many more women, for I've come to see there are more like you among your people. An' I'd like you to see jest how hard an' cruel this border life is. It's bloody. You'd think churches an' churchmen would make it better. They make it worse. You give names to things—bishops, elders, ministers, Mormonism, duty, faith, glory. You dream—or you're driven mad. I'm a man, an' I know. I name fanatics, followers, blind women, oppressors, thieves, ranchers, rustlers, riders. An' we have—what you've lived through these last months. It can't be helped. But it can't last always. An' remember this—some day the border'll be better, cleaner, for the ways of men like Lassiter!"

She saw him shake his tall form erect, look at her strangely and steadfastly, and then, noiselessly, stealthily slip away amid the rocks and trees. Ring and Whitie, not being bidden to follow, remained with Jane. She felt extreme weariness, yet somehow it did not seem to be of her body. And she sat down in the shade and tried to think. She saw a creeping lizard, cactus flowers, the drooping burros, the resting dogs, an eagle high over a yellow crag. Once the meanest flower, a color, the flight of a bee, or any living thing had given her deepest joy. Lassiter had gone off, yielding to his incurable blood lust, probably to his own death; and she was sorry, but there was no feeling in her sorrow.

Suddenly from the mouth of the cañon just beyond her rang out a clear, sharp report of a rifle. Echoes clapped. Then followed a piercingly high yell of anguish, quickly breaking. Again echoes clapped, in grim imitation. Dull revolver shots—hoarse yells—pound of hoofs—shrill neighs of horses—commingling of echoes—and again silence! Lassiter must be busily engaged, thought Jane, and no chill trembled over her, no blanching tightened her skin. Yes, the border was a bloody place. But life had always been bloody. Men were blood-spillers. Phases of the history of the world flashed through her mind—Greek and Roman wars, dark, mediæval times, the crimes in the name of religion. On sea, on land, everywhere—shooting, stabbing, cursing, clashing, fighting men! Greed, power, oppression, fanaticism, love, hate, revenge, justice, freedom—for these, men killed one another.

She lay there under the cedars, gazing up through the delicate lace-like foliage at the blue sky, and she thought and wondered and did not care.

More rattling shots disturbed the noonday quiet. She heard a sliding of weathered rock, a hoarse shout of warning, a yell of alarm, again the clear, sharp crack of the rifle, and another cry that was a cry of death. Then rifle reports pierced a dull volley of revolver shots. Bullets whizzed over Jane's hiding place; one struck a stone and whined-away in the air.

After that, for a time, succeeded desultory shots; and then they ceased under long, thundering fire from heavier guns.

Sooner or later, then, Jane heard the cracking of horses' hoofs on the stones, and the sound came nearer and nearer. Silence intervened until Lassiter's soft, jingling step assured her of his approach. When he appeared he was covered with blood.

"All right, Jane," he said. "I come back. An' don't worry."

With water from a canteen he washed the blood from his face and hands.

"Jane, hurry now. Tear my scarf in two, an' tie up these places. That hole through my hand is some inconvenient, worse'n this cut over my ear. There—you're doin' fine! Not a bit nervous—no tremblin'. I reckon I ain't done your courage justice. I'm glad you're brave jest now—you'll need to be. Well, I was hid pretty good, enough to keep them from shootin' me deep, but they was slingin' lead close all the time. I used up all the rifle shells, an' then I went after them. Mebbe you heard. It was then I got hit. I had to use up every shell in my own guns, an' they did, too, as I seen. Rustlers an' Mormons, Jane! An' now I'm packin' five bullet-holes in my carcass, an' guns without shells. Hurry, now."

He unstrapped the saddle-bags from the burros, slipped the saddles and let them lie, turned the burros loose, and, calling the dogs, led the way through stones and cedars to an open where two horses stood.

"Jane, are you strong?" he asked.

"I think so. I'm not tired," Jane replied.

"I don't mean that way. Can you bear up?"

"I think I can bear anything."

"I reckon you look a little cold an' thick. So I'm preparin' you."

"For what?"

"I didn't tell you why I jest had to go after them fellers. I couldn't tell you. I believe you'd have died. But I can tell you now—if you'll bear up under a shock?"

"Go on, my friend."

"*I've got little Fay!* Alive—bad hurt—but she'll live!"

Jane Withersteen's dead-locked feeling, rent by Lassiter's deep, quivering voice, leaped into an agony of sensitive life.

"Here," he added, and showed her where little Fay lay on the grass.

Unable to speak, unable to stand, Jane dropped on her knees. By that long, beautiful golden hair Jane recognized the beloved Fay. But Fay's loveliness was gone. Her face was drawn and looked old with grief. But she was not dead—her heart beat—and Jane Withersteen gathered strength and lived again.

"You see I jest had to go after Fay," Lassiter was saying, as he knelt to bathe her little pale face. "But I reckon I don't want no more choices like the one I had to make. There was a crippled feller in that bunch, Jane. Mebbe Venters crippled him. Anyway, that's why they were holdin' up here. I seen little Fay first thing, an' was hard put to it to figure out a way to get her. An' I wanted hosses, too. I had to take chances. So I crawled close to their camp. One feller jumped a hoss with little Fay, an' when I shot him, of course she dropped. She's stunned an' bruised—she fell right on her head—Jane, she's comin' to! She ain't bad hurt!"

Fay's long lashes fluttered; her eyes opened. At first they seemed glazed over. They looked dazed by pain. Then they quickened, darkened, to shine with intelligence—bewilderment—memory—and sudden wonderful joy.

"Muvver—Jane!" she whispered.

"Oh, little Fay, little Fay!" cried Jane, lifting, clasping the child to her.

"*Now*, we've got to rustle!" said Lassiter, in grin coolness. "Jane, look down the Pass!"

Across the mounds of rock and sage Jane caught sight of a band of riders filing out of the narrow neck of the Pass; and in the lead was a white horse, which, even at a distance of a mile or more, she knew.

"Tull!" she almost screamed.

"I reckon. But Jane, we've still got the game in our hands. They're ridin' tired hosses. Venters likely give them a chase. He wouldn't forget that. An' we've fresh hosses."

Hurriedly he strapped on the saddle-bags, gave quick glance to girths and cinches and stirrups, then leaped astride.

"Lift little Fay up," he said.

With shaking arms Jane complied.

"Get back your nerve, woman! This's life or death now. Mind that. Climb up! Keep your wits. Stick close to me. Watch where your hoss's goin' an' ride!"

Somehow Jane mounted; somehow found strength to hold the reins, to spur, to cling on, to ride. A horrible quaking, craven fear possessed her soul. Lassiter led the swift flight across the wide space, over washes, through sage, into a narrow cañon where the rapid clatter of hoofs rapped sharply from the walls. The wind roared in her ears; the gleaming cliffs swept by; trail and sage and grass moved under her. Lassiter's bandaged, blood-stained face turned to her; he shouted encouragement; he looked back down the Pass; he spurred his horse. Jane clung on, spurring likewise. And the horses settled from hard, furious gallop into a long-striding, driving run. She had never ridden at anything like that pace; desperately she tried to get the swing of the horse, to be of some help to him in that race, to see the best of the ground and guide him into it. But she failed of everything except to keep her seat in the saddle, and to spur and spur. At times she closed her eyes, unable to bear sight of Fay's golden curls stream-ing in the wind. She could not pray; she could not rail; she no longer cared for herself. All of life, of good, of use in the world, of hope in heaven centered in Lassiter's ride with little Fay to safety. She would have tried to turn the iron-jawed brute she rode; she would have given herself to that relentless, dark-browed Tull. But she knew Lassiter would turn with her, so she rode on and on.

Whether that run was of moments or hours Jane Withersteen could not tell. Lassiter's horse covered her with froth that blew back in white streams. Both horses ran their limit, were allowed to slow down in time to save them, and went on dripping, heaving, staggering.

"Oh! Lassiter, we must run—we must run!"

He looked back, saying nothing. The bandage had blown from his head, and blood trickled down his face. He was bowing under the strain of injuries, of the ride, of his burden. Yet how cool and gray he looked—how intrepid!

The horses walked, trotted, galloped, ran, to fall again to walk. Hours sped or dragged. Time was an instant—an eternity. Jane Withersteen felt hell pursuing her, and dared not look back for fear she would fall from her horse.

"Oh, Lassiter! Is he coming?"

The grim rider looked over his shoulder, but said no word. Little Fay's golden hair floated on the breeze. The sun shone; the walls gleamed;

the sage glistened. And then it seemed the sun vanished, the walls shaded, the sage paled. The horses walked—trotted—galloped—ran—to fall again to walk. Shadows gathered under shelving cliffs. The cañon turned, brightened, opened into long, wide, wall-enclosed valley. Again the sun, lowering in the west, reddened the sage. Far ahead round, scrawled stones appeared to block the Pass.

"Bear up, Jane, bear up!" called Lassiter. "It's our game, if you don't weaken."

"Lassiter! Go on—*alone!* Save little Fay!"

"Only with you!"

"Oh!—I'm a coward—a miserable coward! I can't fight or think or hope or pray! I'm lost! Oh, Lassiter, look back! Is he coming? I'll not—hold out—"

"Keep your breath, woman, an' ride not for yourself or for me, but for Fay!"

A last breaking run across the sage brought Lassiter's horse to a walk.

"He's done," said the rider.

"Oh, no—no!" moaned Jane.

"Look back, Jane, look back. Three—four miles we've come across this valley, an' no Tull yet in sight. Only a few miles more!"

Jane looked back over the long stretch of sage, and found the narrow gap in the wall, out of which came a file of dark horses with a white horse in the lead. Sight of the riders acted upon Jane as a stimulant. The weight of cold, horrible terror lessened. And, gazing forward at the dogs, at Lassiter's limping horse, at the blood on his face, at the rocks growing nearer, last at Fay's golden hair, the ice left her veins, and slowly, strangely, she gained hold of strength that she believed would see her to the safety Lassiter promised. And, as she gazed, Lassiter's horse stumbled and fell.

He swung his leg and slipped from the saddle.

"Jane, take the child," he said, and lifted Fay up. Jane clasped her with arms suddenly strong. "They're gainin'," went on Lassiter, as he watched the pursuing riders. "But we'll beat 'em yet."

Turning with Jane's bridle in his hand, he was about to start when he saw the saddle-bag on the fallen horse.

"I've jest about got time," he muttered, and with swift fingers that did not blunder or fumble he loosened the bag and threw it over his shoulder. Then he started to run, leading Jane's horse, and he ran, and trotted, and walked, and ran again. Close ahead now Jane saw a rise of bare rock. Lassiter reached it, searched along the base, and, finding a low place dragged the weary horse up and over round, smooth stone. Looking backward, Jane saw Tull's white horse not a mile distant, with riders strung out in a long line behind him. Looking forward, she saw more valley to the right, and to the left a towering cliff. Lassiter pulled the horse and kept on.

Little Fay lay in her arms with wide open eyes—eyes which were still shadowed by pain, but no longer fixed, glazed in terror. The golden curls blew across Jane's lips; the little hands feebly clasped her arm; a ghost of a troubled, trustful smile hovered round the sweet lips. And Jane Withersteen awoke to the spirit of a lioness.

Lassiter was leading the horse up a smooth slope toward cedar-trees of twisted and bleached appearance. Among these he halted.

"Jane, give me the girl an' get down," he said. As if it wrenched him he unbuckled the empty black guns with a strange air of finality. He then received Fay in his arms and stood a moment looking backward. Tull's white horse mounted the ridge of round stone, and several bays or blacks followed. "I wonder what he'll think when he sees them empty guns. Jane, bring your saddle-bag and climb after me."

A glistening, wonderful bare slope, with little holes, swelled up and up to lose itself in a frowning yellow cliff. Jane closely watched her steps and climbed behind Lassiter. He moved slowly. Perhaps he was only husbanding his strength. But she saw drops of blood on the stone, and then she knew. They climbed and climbed without looking back. Her breast labored; she began to feel as if little points of fiery steel were penetrating her side into her lungs. She heard the panting of Lassiter, and the quicker panting of the dogs.

"Wait—here," he said.

Before her rose a bulge of stone, nicked with little cut steps, and above that a corner of yellow wall, and overhanging that a vast, ponderous cliff.

The dogs pattered up, disappeared round the corner. Lassiter mounted the steps with Fay, and he swayed like a drunken man, and he, too, disappeared. But instantly he returned alone, and half ran, half slipped down to her.

Then from below pealed up hoarse shouts of angry men. Tull and several of his riders had reached the spot where Lassiter had parted with his guns.

"You'll need that breath—mebbe!" said Lassiter, facing downward, with glittering eyes.

"Now, Jane, the last pull," he went on. "Walk up them little steps. I'll follow an' steady you. Don't think. Jest go. Little Fay's above. Her eyes are open. She jest said to me, *'Where's muvver Jane?'*"

Without a fear or a tremor or a slip or a touch of Lassiter's hand Jane Withersteen walked up that ladder of cut steps.

He pushed her round the corner of wall. Fay lay, with wide staring eyes, in the shade of a gloomy wall. The dogs waited. Lassiter picked up the child and turned into a dark cleft. It zigzagged. It widened. It opened. Jane was amazed at a wonderfully smooth and steep incline leading up between ruined, splintered, toppling walls. A red haze from the setting sun filled this passage. Lassiter climbed with slow, measured steps, and blood dripped from him to make splotches on the white stone. Jane tried not to step in his blood, but was compelled, for she found no other footing. The saddle-bag began to drag her down; she gasped for breath; she thought her heart was bursting. Slower, slower yet the rider climbed, whistling as he breathed. The incline widened. Huge pinnacles and monuments of stone stood alone, leaning fearfully. Red sunset haze shone through cracks where the wall had split. Jane did not look high, but she felt the overshadowing of broken rims above. She felt that it was a fearful, menacing place. And she climbed on in heartrending effort. And she fell beside Lassiter and Fay at the top of the incline on a narrow, smooth divide.

He staggered to his feet—staggered to a huge, leaning rock that rested on a small pedestal. He put his hand on it—the hand that had been shot through—and Jane saw blood drip from the ragged hole. Then he fell.

"Jane—I—can't—do—it!" he whispered.

"What?"

"Roll the—stone! . . . All my—life I've loved—to roll stones—an' now I—can't!"

"What of it? You talk strangely. Why roll that stone?"

"I planned to—fetch you here—to roll this stone. See! It'll smash the crags—loosen the walls—close the outlet!"

As Jane Withersteen gazed down that long incline, walled in by crumbling cliffs, awaiting only the slightest jar to make them fall asunder, she saw Tull appear at the bottom and begin to climb. A rider followed him—another—and another.

"See! Tull! The riders!"

"Yes—they'll get us—now."

"Why? Haven't you strength left to roll the stone?"

"Jane—it ain't that—I've lost my nerve!"

"*You!* . . . Lassiter!"

"I wanted to roll it—meant to—but I—can't. Venters's valley is down behind here. We could—live there. But if I roll the stone—we're shut in for always. I don't dare. I'm thinkin' of you!"

"Lassiter! Roll the stone!" she cried.

He arose, tottering, but with set face, and again he placed the bloody hand on the Balancing Rock. Jane Withersteen gazed from him down the passageway. Tull was climbing. Almost, she thought, she saw his dark, relentless face. Behind him more riders climbed. What did they mean for Fay—for Lassiter—for herself?

"*Roll the stone! . . . Lassiter, I love you!*"

Under all his deathly pallor, and the blood, and the iron of seared cheek and lined brow, worked a great change. He placed both hands on the rock and then leaned his shoulder there and braced his powerful body.

"Roll the stone!"

It stirred, it groaned, it grated, it moved; and with a slow grinding, as of wrathful relief, began to lean. It had waited ages to fall, and now was slow in starting. Then, as if suddenly instinct with life, it leaped hurtlingly down to alight on the steep incline, to bound more swiftly into the air, to gather momentum, to plunge into the lofty leaning crag below. The crag thundered into atoms. A wave of air—a splitting shock! Dust shrouded the sunset red of shaking rims; dust shrouded Tull as he fell on his knees with uplifted arms. Shafts and monuments and sections of wall fell majestically.

From the depths there rose a long-drawn rumbling roar. The outlet to Deception Pass closed forever.

THE RAINBOW
TRAIL

FOREWORD

The spell of the desert comes back to me, as it always will come. I see the veils, like purple smoke, in the cañons, and I feel the silence. And it seems that again I must try to pierce both and to get at the strange wild life of the last American wilderness—wild still, almost, as it ever was.

While this romance is an independent story, yet readers of *Riders of the Purple Sage* will find in it an answer to a question often asked.

I wish to say also that this story has appeared serially in a different form in one of the monthly magazines under the title of *The Desert Crucible*.

Zane Grey
June 1915

CHAPTER 1

RED LAKE

S hefford halted his tired horse and gazed with slowly realizing eyes.

A league-long slope of sage rolled and billowed down to Red Lake, a dry red basin, denuded and glistening, a hollow in the desert, a lonely and desolate door to the vast, wild, and broken upland beyond.

All day Shefford had plodded onward with the clear horizon-line a thing unattainable; and for days before that he had ridden the wild bare flats and climbed the rocky desert benches. The great colored reaches and steps had led endlessly onward and upward through dim and deceiving distance.

A hundred miles of desert travel, with its mistakes and lessons and intimations, had not prepared him for what he now saw. He beheld what seemed a world that knew only magnitude. Wonder and awe fixed his gaze, and thought remained aloof. Then that dark and unknown northland flung a menace at him. An irresistible call had drawn him to this seamed and peaked border of Arizona, this broken battlemented wilderness of Utah upland; and at first sight they frowned upon him, as if to warn him not to search for what lay hidden beyond the ranges. But Shefford thrilled with both fear and exultation. That was the country which had been described to him. Far across the red valley, far beyond the ragged line of black mesa and yellow range, lay the wild cañon with its haunting secret.

Red Lake must be his Rubicon. Either he must enter the unknown to seek, to strive, to find, or turn back and fail and never know and be always haunted. A friend's strange story had prompted his singular journey; a beautiful rainbow with its mystery and promise had decided him. Once in his life he had answered a wild call to the kingdom of adventure within him, and once in his life he had been happy. But here in the horizon-wide face of that up-flung and cloven desert he grew cold; he faltered even while he felt more fatally drawn.

As if impelled Shefford started his horse down the sandy trail, but he checked his former far-reaching gaze. It was the month of April, and the waning sun lost heat and brightness. Long shadows crept down the slope ahead of him and the scant sage deepened its gray. He watched the lizards shoot like brown streaks across the sand, leaving their slender tracks; he heard the rustle of pack-rats as they darted into their brushy homes; the whir of a low-sailing hawk startled his horse.

Like ocean waves the slope rose and fell, its hollows choked with sand, its ridge-tops showing scantier growth of sage and grass and weed. The last ridge was a sand-dune, beautifully ribbed and scalloped and lined by the wind, and from its knife-sharp crest a thin wavering sheet of sand blew, almost like smoke. Shefford wondered why the sand looked red at a distance, for here it seemed almost white. It rippled everywhere, clean and glistening, always leading down.

Suddenly Shefford became aware of a house looming out of the bareness of the slope. It dominated that long white incline. Grim, lonely, forbidding, how strangely it harmonized with the surroundings! The structure was octagon-shaped, built of uncut stone, and resembled a fort. There was no door on the sides exposed to Shefford's gaze, but small apertures two-thirds the way up probably served as windows and port-holes. The roof appeared to be made of poles covered with red earth.

Like a huge cold rock on a wide plain this house stood there on the windy slope. It was an outpost of the trader Presbrey, of whom Shefford had heard at Flagstaff and Tuba. No living thing appeared in the limit of Shefford's vision. He gazed shudderingly at the unwelcoming habitation, at the dark eyelike windows, at the sweep of barren slope merging into the vast red valley, at the bold, bleak bluffs. Could any one live here? The nature of that sinister valley forbade a home there, and the spirit of the place hovered in the silence and space. Shefford thought irresistibly of how his enemies would have consigned him to just such a hell. He thought bitterly and mockingly of the narrow congregation that had proved him a failure in the ministry, that had repudiated his ideas of religion and immortality and God, that had driven him, at the age of twenty-four, from the calling forced upon him by his people. As a boy he had yearned to make himself an artist; his family had made him a clergyman; fate had made him a failure. A failure only so far in his life, something urged him to add—for in the lonely days and silent nights of the desert he had experienced a strange birth of hope. Adventure had called him, but it was a vague and spiritual hope, a dream of promise, a nameless attainment that fortified his wilder impulse.

As he rode around a corner of the stone house his horse snorted and stopped. A lean, shaggy pony jumped at sight of him, almost displacing a red long-haired blanket that covered an Indian saddle. Quick thuds of hoofs in sand drew Shefford's attention to a corral made of peeled poles, and here he saw another pony.

Shefford heard subdued voices. He dismounted and walked to an open door. In the dark interior he dimly descried a high counter, a stairway, a pile of bags of flour, blankets, and silver-ornamented objects, but the persons he had heard were not in that part of the house. Around another corner of the octagon-shaped wall he found another open door, and through it saw goat-skins and a mound of dirty sheep-wool, black and brown and white. It was light in this part of the building. When he crossed the threshold he was astounded to see a man struggling with a girl—an Indian girl. She was straining back from him, panting, and uttering low guttural sounds. The man's face was corded and dark with passion. This scene affected Shefford strangely. Primitive emotions were new to him.

Before Shefford could speak the girl broke loose and turned to flee. She was an Indian and this place was the uncivilized desert, but Shefford knew terror when he saw it. Like a dog the man rushed after her. It was instinct that made Shefford strike, and his blow laid the man flat. He lay stunned a moment, then raised himself to a sitting posture, his hand to

his face, and the gaze he fixed upon Shefford seemed to combine astonishment and rage.

"I hope you're not Presbrey," said Shefford, slowly. He felt awkward,
not sure of himself.

The man appeared about to burst into speech, but repressed it. There
was blood on his mouth and his hand. Hastily he scrambled to his feet.
Shefford saw this man's amaze and rage change to shame. He was tall
and rather stout; he had a smooth tanned face, soft of outline, with a
weak chin; his eyes were dark. The look of him and his corduroys and his
soft shoes gave Shefford an impression that he was not a man who
worked hard. By contrast with the few other worn and rugged desert
men Shefford had met this stranger stood out strikingly. He stooped to
pick up a soft felt hat and, jamming it on his head, he hurried out. Shefford followed him and watched him from the door. He went directly to
the corral, mounted the pony, and rode out, to turn down the slope toward the south. When he reached the level of the basin, where evidently
the sand was hard, he put the pony to a lope and gradually drew away.

"Well!" exclaimed Shefford. He did not know what to make of this
adventure. Presently he became aware that the Indian girl was sitting on
a roll of blankets near the wall. With curious interest Shefford studied
her appearance. She had long, raven-black hair, tangled and disheveled,
and she wore a soiled white band of cord above her brow. The color of
her face struck him; it was dark, but not red nor bronzed; it almost had a
tinge of gold. Her profile was clear-cut, bold, almost stern. Long black
eyelashes hid her eyes. She wore a tight-fitting waist garment of material
resembling velveteen. It was ripped along her side, exposing a skin still
more richly gold than that of her face. A string of silver ornaments and
turquoise-and-white beads encircled her neck, and it moved gently up
and down with the heaving of her full bosom. Her skirt was some gaudy
print goods, torn and stained and dusty. She had little feet, incased in
brown moccasins, fitting like gloves and buttoning over the ankles with
silver coins.

"Who was that man? Did he hurt you?" inquired Shefford, turning
to gaze down the valley where a moving black object showed on the bare
sand.

"No savvy," replied the Indian girl.

"Where's the trader Presbrey?" asked Shefford.

She pointed straight down into the red valley.

"Toh," she said.

In the center of the basin lay a small pool of water shining brightly in the sunset glow. Small objects moved around it, so small that Shefford thought he saw several dogs led by a child. But it was the distance that deceived him. There was a man down there watering his horses. That reminded Shefford of the duty owing to his own tired and thirsty beast. Whereupon he untied his pack, took off the saddle, and was about ready to start down when the Indian girl grasped the bridle from his hand.

"Me go," she said.

He saw her eyes then, and they made her look different. They were as black as her hair. He was puzzled to decide whether or not he thought her handsome.

"Thanks, but I'll go," he replied, and, taking the bridle again, he started down the slope. At every step he sank into the deep, soft sand. Down a little way he came upon a pile of tin cans; they were everywhere, buried, half buried, and lying loose; and these gave evidence of how the trader lived. Presently Shefford discovered that the Indian girl was following him with her own pony. Looking upward at her against the light, he thought her slender, lithe, picturesque. At a distance he liked her.

He plodded on, at length glad to get out of the drifts of sand to the hard level floor of the valley. This, too, was sand, but dried and baked hard, and red in color. At some season of the year this immense flat must be covered with water. How wide it was, and empty! Shefford experienced again a feeling that had been novel to him—and it was that he was loose, free, unanchored, ready to veer with the wind. From the foot of the slope the water-hole had appeared to be a few hundred rods out in the valley. But the small size of the figures made Shefford doubt; and he had to travel many times a few hundred rods before those figures began to grow. Then Shefford made out that they were approaching him.

Thereafter they rapidly increased to normal proportions of man and beast. When Shefford met them he saw a powerful, heavily built young man leading two ponies.

"You're Mr. Presbrey, the trader?" inquired Shefford.

"Yes, I'm Presbrey, without the Mister," he replied.

"My name's Shefford. I'm knocking about on the desert. Rode from beyond Tuba to-day."

"Glad to see you," said Presbrey. He offered his hand. He was a stalwart man, clad in gray shirt, overalls, and boots. A shock of tumbled light hair covered his massive head; he was tanned, but not darkly, and there was red in his cheeks; under his shaggy eyebrows were deep, keen eyes; his lips were hard and set, as if occasion for smiles or words was rare; and his big, strong jaw seemed locked.

"Wish more travelers came knocking around Red Lake," he added. "Reckon here's the jumping-off place."

"It's pretty—lonesome," said Shefford, hesitating as if at a loss for words.

Then the Indian girl came up. Presbrey addressed her in her own language, which Shefford did not understand. She seemed shy and would not answer; she stood with downcast face and eyes. Presbrey spoke again, at which she pointed down the valley, and then moved on with her pony toward the water-hole.

Presbrey's keen eyes fixed on the receding black dot far down that oval expanse.

"That fellow left—rather abruptly," said Shefford, constrainedly. "Who was he?"

"His name's Willetts. He's a missionary. He rode in to-day with this Navajo girl. He was taking her to Blue Cañon, where he lives and teaches the Indians. I've met him only a few times. You see, not many white men ride in here. He's the first white man I've seen in six months, and you're the second. Both the same day! . . . Red Lake's getting popular! It's odd, though, his leaving. He expected to stay all night. There's no other place to stay. Blue Cañon is fifty miles away."

"I'm sorry to say—no, I'm not sorry, either—but I must tell you I was the cause of Mr. Willetts leaving," replied Shefford.

"How so?" inquired the other.

Then Shefford related the incident following his arrival.

"Perhaps my action was hasty," he concluded, apologetically. "I didn't think. Indeed, I'm surprised at myself."

Presbrey made no comment and his face was as hard to read as one of the distant bluffs.

"But what did the man mean?" asked Shefford, conscious of a little heat. "I'm a stranger out here. I'm ignorant of Indians—how they're controlled. Still I'm no fool. . . . If Willetts didn't mean evil, at least he was brutal."

"He was teaching her religion," replied Presbrey. His tone held faint scorn and implied a joke, but his face did not change in the slightest.

Without understanding just why, Shefford felt his conviction justified and his action approved. Then he was sensible of a slight shock of wonder and disgust.

"I am—I was a minister of the Gospel," he said to Presbrey. "What you hint seems impossible. I can't believe it."

"I didn't hint," replied Presbrey, bluntly, and it was evident that he was a sincere, but close-mouthed, man. "Shefford, so you're a preacher? . . . Did you come out here to try to convert the Indians?"

"No. I said I *was* a minister. I am no longer. I'm just a—a wanderer."

"I see. Well, the desert's no place for missionaries, but it's good for wanderers. . . . Go water your horse and take him up to the corral. You'll find some hay for him. I'll get grub ready."

Shefford went on with his horse to the pool. The water appeared thick, green, murky, and there was a line of salty crust extending around the margin of the pool. The thirsty horse splashed in and eagerly bent his head. But he did not like the taste. Many times he refused to drink, yet always lowered his nose again. Finally he drank, though not his fill. Shefford saw the Indian girl drink from her hand. He scooped up a handful and found it too sour to swallow. When he turned to retrace his steps she mounted her pony and followed him.

A golden flare lit up the western sky, and silhouetted dark and lonely against it stood the trading-post. Upon his return Shefford found the wind rising, and it chilled him. When he reached the slope thin gray sheets of sand were blowing low, rising, whipping, falling, sweeping along with soft silken rustle. Sometimes the gray veils hid his boots. It was a long, toilsome climb up that yielding, dragging ascent, and he had already been lame and tired. By the time he had put his horse away twilight was everywhere except in the west. The Indian girl left her pony in the corral and came like a shadow toward the house.

Shefford had difficulty in finding the foot of the stairway. He climbed to enter a large loft, lighted by two lamps. Presbrey was there, kneading biscuit dough in a pan.

"Make yourself comfortable," he said.

The huge loft was the shape of a half-octagon. A door opened upon the valley side, and here, too, there were windows. How attractive the place was in comparison with the impressions gained from the outside! The furnishings consisted of Indian blankets on the floor, two beds, a desk and table, several chairs and a couch, a gun-rack full of rifles, innumerable silver-ornamented belts, bridles, and other Indian articles upon the walls, and in one corner a wood-burning stove with teakettle steaming, and a great cupboard with shelves packed full of canned foods.

Shefford leaned in the doorway and looked out. Beneath him on a roll of blankets sat the Indian girl, silent and motionless. He wondered what was in her mind, what she would do, how the trader would treat her. The slope now was a long slant of sheeted moving shadows of sand. Dusk had gathered in the valley. The bluffs loomed black beyond. A pale star twinkled above. Shefford suddenly became aware of the intense nature of the stillness about him. Yet, as he listened to this silence, he heard an intermittent and immeasurably low moan, a fitful, mournful murmur. Assuredly it was only the wind. Nevertheless, it made his blood run cold. It was a different wind from that which had made music under the eaves of his Illinois home. This was a lonely, haunting wind, with desert hunger in it, and more which he could not name. Shefford listened to this spirit-brooding sound while he watched night envelop the valley. How black, how thick the mantle! Yet it brought no comforting sense of close-folded protection, of walls of soft sleep, of a home. Instead there was the feeling of space, of emptiness, of an infinite hall down which a mournful wind swept streams of murmuring sand.

"Well, grub's about ready," said Presbrey.

"Got any water?" asked Shefford.

"Sure. There in the bucket. It's rain-water. I have a tank here."

Shefford's sore and blistered face felt better after he had washed off the sand and alkali dust.

"Better not wash your face often while you're in the desert. Bad plan," went on Presbrey, noting how gingerly his visitor had gone about his ablutions. "Well, come and eat."

Shefford marked that if the trader did live a lonely life he fared well. There was more on the table than twice two men could have eaten. It was the first time in four days that Shefford had sat at a table, and he made up for lost opportunity. His host's actions indicated pleasure, yet the strange, hard face never relaxed, never changed. When the meal was finished Presbrey declined assistance, had a generous thought of the Indian girl, who, he said, could have a place to eat and sleep down-stairs, and then with the skill and despatch of an accomplished housewife cleared the table, after which work he filled a pipe and evidently prepared to listen.

It took only one question for Shefford to find that the trader was starved for news of the outside world; and for an hour Shefford fed that appetite, even as he had been done by. But when he had talked himself out there seemed indication of Presbrey being more than a good listener.

"How'd you come in?" he asked, presently.

"By Flagstaff—across the Little Colorado—and through Moencopie."

"Did you stop at Moen Ave?"

"No. What place is that?"

"A missionary lives there. Did you stop at Tuba?"

"Only long enough to drink and water my horse. That was a wonderful spring for the desert."

"You said you were a wanderer. . . . Do you want a job? I'll give you one."

"No, thank you, Presbrey."

"I saw your pack. That's no pack to travel with in this country. Your horse won't last, either. Have you any money?"

"Yes, plenty of money."

"Well, that's good. Not that a white man out here would ever take a dollar from you. But you can buy from the Indians as you go. Where are you making for, anyhow?"

Shefford hesitated, debating in mind whether to tell his purpose or not. His host did not press the question.

"I see. Just foot-loose and wandering around," went on Presbrey. "I can understand how the desert appeals to you. Preachers lead easy, safe, crowded, bound lives. They're shut up in a church with a Bible and good people. When once in a lifetime they get loose—they break out."

"Yes, I've broken out—beyond all bounds," replied Shefford, sadly.

He seemed retrospective for a moment, unaware of the trader's keen and sympathetic glance, and then he caught himself. "I want to see some wild life. Do you know the country north of here?"

"Only what the Navajos tell me. And they're not much to talk. There's a trail goes north, but I've never traveled it. It's a new trail every time an Indian goes that way, for here the sand blows and covers old tracks. But few Navajos ride in from the north. My trade is mostly with Indians up and down the valley."

"How about water and grass?"

"We've had rain and snow. There's sure to be water. Can't say about grass, though the sheep and ponies from the north are always fat. . . . But, say, Shefford, if you'll excuse me for advising you—don't go north."

"Why?" asked Shefford, and it was certain that he thrilled.

"It's unknown country, terribly broken, as you can see from here, and there are bad Indians hiding in the cañons. I've never met a man who had been over the pass between here and Kayenta. The trip's been made, so there must be a trail. But it's a dangerous trip for any man, let alone a tenderfoot. You're not even packing a gun."

"What's this place Kayenta?" asked Shefford.

"It's a spring. Kayenta means Bottomless Spring. There's a little trading-post, the last and the wildest in northern Arizona. Withers, the trader who keeps it, hauls his supplies in from Colorado and New Mexico. He's never come down this way. I never saw him. Know nothing of him except hearsay. Reckon he's a nervy and strong man to hold that post. If you want to go there, better go by way of Keams Cañon, and then around the foot of Black Mesa. It'll be a long ride—maybe two hundred miles."

"How far straight north over the pass?"

"Can't say. Upward of seventy-five miles over rough trails, if there are trails at all. . . . I've heard rumors of a fine tribe of Navajos living in there, rich in sheep and horses. It may be true and it may not. But I do know there are bad Indians, half-breeds and outcasts, hiding in there. Some of them have visited me here. Bad customers! More than that, you'll be going close to the Utah line, and the Mormons over there are unfriendly these days."

"Why?" queried Shefford, again with that curious thrill.

"They are being persecuted by the government."

Shefford asked no more questions and his host vouchsafed no more information on that score. The conversation lagged. Then Shefford inquired about the Indian girl and learned that she lived up the valley somewhere. Presbrey had never seen her before Willetts came with her to Red Lake. And this query brought out the fact that Presbrey was comparatively new to Red Lake and vicinity. Shefford wondered why a lonely six months there had not made the trader old in experience. Probably the desert did not readily give up its secrets. Moreover, this Red Lake house was only an occasionally used branch of Presbrey's main trading-post, which was situated at Willow Springs, fifty miles westward over the mesa.

"I'm closing up here soon for a spell," said Presbrey, and now his face lost its set hardness and seemed singularly changed. It was a difference of light and softness. "Won't be so lonesome over at Willow Springs. . . . I'm being married soon."

"That's fine," replied Shefford, warmly. He was glad for the sake of this lonely desert man. What good a wife would bring into a trader's life!

Presbrey's naïve admission, however, appeared to detach him from his present surroundings, and with his massive head enveloped by a cloud of smoke he lived in dreams.

Shefford respected his host's serene abstraction. Indeed, he was grateful for silence. Not for many nights had the past impinged so closely upon the present. The wound in his soul had not healed, and to speak of himself made it bleed anew. Memory was too poignant; the past was too close; he wanted to forget until he had toiled into the heart of this forbidding wilderness—until time had gone by and he dared to face his unquiet soul. Then he listened to the steadily rising roar of the wind. How strange and hollow! That wind was freighted with heavy sand, and he heard it sweep, sweep, sweep by in gusts, and then blow with dull, steady blast against the walls. The sound was provocative of thought. This moan and rush of wind was no dream—this presence of his in a night-enshrouded and sand-besieged house of the lonely desert was a reality—this adventure was not one of fancy. True indeed, then, must be the wild, strange story that had led him hither. He was going on to seek, to strive, to find. Somewhere northward in the broken fastnesses lay hidden a valley walled in from the world. Would they be there, those lost fugitives whose story had thrilled him? After twelve years would she be alive, a child grown to womanhood in the solitude of a beautiful cañon? Incredible! Yet he believed his friend's story and he indeed knew how strange and tragic life was. He fancied he heard her voice on the sweeping wind. She called to him, haunted him. He admitted the improbability of her existence, but lost nothing of the persistent intangible hope that drove him. He believed himself a man stricken in soul, unworthy, through doubt of God, to minister to the people who had banished him. Perhaps a labor of Hercules, a mighty and perilous work of rescue, the saving of this lost and imprisoned girl, would help him in his trouble. She might be his salvation. Who could tell? Always as a boy and as a man he had fared forth to find the treasure at the foot of the rainbow.

CHAPTER 2

THE SAGI

Next morning the Indian girl was gone and the tracks of her pony led north. Shefford's first thought was to wonder if he would overtake her on the trail; and this surprised him with the proof of how unconsciously his resolve to go on had formed.

Presbrey made no further attempt to turn Shefford back. But he insisted on replenishing the pack, and that Shefford take weapons. Finally Shefford was persuaded to accept a revolver. The trader bade him good-by and stood in the door while Shefford led his horse down the slope toward the water-hole. Perhaps the trader believed he was watching the departure of a man who would never return. He was still standing at the door of the post when Shefford halted at the pool.

Upon the level floor of the valley lay thin patches of snow which had fallen during the night. The air was biting cold, yet stimulated Shefford while it stung him. His horse drank rather slowly and disgustedly. Then Shefford mounted and reluctantly turned his back upon the trading-post.

As he rode away from the pool he saw a large flock of sheep approaching. They were very closely, even densely, packed, in a solid slow-moving mass, and coming with a precision almost like a march. This fact surprised Shefford, for there was not an Indian in sight. Presently he saw that a dog was leading the flock, and a little later he discovered another dog in the rear of the sheep. They were splendid, long-haired dogs, of a wild-looking shepherd breed. He halted his horse to watch the procession pass by. The flock covered fully an acre of ground and the sheep were black, white, and brown. They passed him, making a little pattering roar on the hard-caked sand. The dogs were taking the sheep in to water.

Shefford went on and was drawing close to the other side of the basin, where the flat red level was broken by rising dunes and ridges, when he espied a bunch of ponies. A shrill whistle told him that they had seen him. They were wild, shaggy, with long manes and tails. They stopped, threw up their heads, and watched him. Shefford certainly returned the attention. There was no Indian with them. Presently, with a snort, the leader, which appeared to be a stallion, trotted behind the others, seemed to be driving them, and went clear round the band to get in the lead again. He was taking them in to water, the same as the dogs had taken the sheep.

These incidents were new and pleasing to Shefford. How ignorant he had been of life in the wilderness! Once more he received subtle intimations of what he might learn out in the open; and it was with a less weighted heart that he faced the gateway between the huge yellow bluffs on his left and the slow rise of ground to the black mesa on his right. He looked back in time to see the trading-post, bleak and lonely on the bare slope, pass out of sight behind the bluffs. Shefford felt no fear—he really had little experience of physical fear—but it was certain that he gritted his teeth and welcomed whatever was to come to him. He had lived a narrow, insulated life with his mind on spiritual things; his family and his congregation and his friends—except that one new friend whose story had enthralled him—were people of quiet religious habit; the man deep down in him had never had a chance. He breathed hard as he tried to imagine the world opening to him, and almost dared to be glad for the doubt that had sent him adrift.

The tracks of the Indian girl's pony were plain in the sand. Also there were other tracks, not so plain, and these Shefford decided had been made by Willetts and the girl the day before. He climbed a ridge, half soft sand and half hard, and saw right before him, rising in striking form, two great yellow buttes, like elephant legs. He rode between them, amazed at their height. Then before him stretched a slowly ascending valley, walled on one side by the black mesa and on the other by low bluffs. For miles a dark-green growth of greasewood covered the valley, and Shefford could see where the green thinned and failed, to give place to sand. He trotted his horse and made good time on this stretch.

The day contrasted greatly with any he had yet experienced. Gray clouds obscured the walls of rock a few miles to the west, and Shefford saw squalls of snow like huge veils dropping down and spreading out. The wind cut with the keenness of a knife. Soon he was chilled to the bone. A squall swooped and roared down upon him, and the wind that bore the driving white pellets of snow, almost like hail, was so freezing bitter cold that the former wind seemed warm in comparison. The squall passed as swiftly as it had come, and it left Shefford so benumbed he could not hold the bridle. He tumbled off his horse and walked. By and by the sun came out and soon warmed him and melted the thin layer of snow on the sand. He was still on the trail of the Indian girl, but hers were now the only tracks he could see.

All morning he gradually climbed, with limited view, until at last he mounted to a point where the country lay open to his sight on all sides except where the endless black mesa ranged on into the north. A rugged yellow peak dominated the landscape to the fore, but it was far away. Red and ragged country extended westward to a huge flat-topped wall of gray rock. Lowering swift clouds swept across the sky, like drooping mantles, and they darkened the sun. Shefford built a little fire out of dead greasewood sticks, and with his blanket round his shoulders he hung over the blaze, scorching his clothes and hands. He had been cold before in his life, but he had never before appreciated fire. This desert blast pierced him. The squall enveloped him, thicker and colder and windier than the other, but, being better fortified, he did not suffer so much. It howled away, hiding the mesa and leaving a white desert behind. Shefford walked on, leading his horse, until the exercise and the sun had once more warmed him.

This last squall had rendered the Indian girl's trail difficult to follow. The snow did not quickly melt, and, besides, sheep tracks and the tracks of horses gave him trouble, until at last he was compelled to admit that he could not follow her any longer. A faint path or trail led north, however, and, following that, he soon forgot the girl. Every surmounted ridge held a surprise for him. The desert seemed never to change in the vast whole that encompassed him, yet near him it was always changing. From

Red Lake he had seen a peaked, walled, and cañoned country, as rough as a stormy sea; but when he rode into that country the sharp and broken features held to the distance.

He was glad to get out of the sand. Long narrow flats, gray with grass and dotted with patches of greasewood, and lined by low bare ridges of yellow rock, stretched away from him, leading toward the yellow peak that seemed never to be gained upon.

Shefford had pictures in his mind, pictures of stone walls and wild valleys and domed buttes, all of which had been painted in colorful and vivid words by his friend Venters. He believed he would recognize the distinctive and remarkable landmarks Venters had portrayed, and he was certain that he had not yet come upon one of them. This was his second lonely day of travel and he had grown more and more susceptible to the influence of horizon and the different prominent points. He attributed a gradual change in his feelings to the loneliness and the increasing wildness. Between Tuba and Flagstaff he had met Indians and an occasional prospector and teamster. Here he was alone, and though he felt some strange gladness, he could not help but see the difference.

He rode on during the gray, lowering, chilly day, and toward evening the clouds broke in the west, and a setting sun shone through the rift, burnishing the desert to red and gold. Shefford's instinctive but deadened love of the beautiful in nature stirred into life, and the moment of its rebirth was a melancholy and sweet one. Too late for the artist's work, but not too late for his soul!

For a place to make camp he halted near a low area of rock that lay like an island in a sea of grass. There was an abundance of dead greasewood for a campfire, and, after searching over the rock, he found little pools of melted snow in the depressions. He took off the saddle and pack, watered his horse, and, hobbling him as well as his inexperience permitted, he turned him loose on the grass.

Then while he built a fire and prepared a meal the night came down upon him. In the lee of the rock he was well sheltered from the wind, but the air was bitter cold. He gathered all the dead greasewood in the vicinity, replenished the fire, and rolled in his blanket, back to the blaze. The loneliness and the coyotes did not bother him this night. He was too tired and cold. He went to sleep at once and did not awaken until the fire died out. Then he rebuilt it and went to sleep again. Every half-hour all night long he repeated this, and was glad indeed when the dawn broke.

The day began with misfortune. His horse was gone; it had been stolen, or had worked out of sight, or had broken the hobbles and made off. From a high stone ridge Shefford searched the grassy flats and slopes, all to no purpose. Then he tried to track the horse, but this was equally futile. He had expected disasters, and the first one did not daunt him. He tied most of his pack in the blanket, threw the canteen across his shoulder, and set forth, sure at least of one thing—that he was a very much better traveler on foot than on horseback.

Walking did not afford him the leisure to study the surrounding country; however, from time to time, when he surmounted a bench he scanned the different landmarks that had grown familiar. It took hours of steady walking to reach and pass the yellow peak that had been a kind of goal. He saw many sheep trails and horse tracks in the vicinity of this mountain, and once he was sure he espied an Indian watching him from a bold ridge-top.

The day was bright and warm, with air so clear it magnified objects he knew to be far away. The ascent was gradual; there were many narrow flats connected by steps; and the grass grew thicker and longer. At noon Shefford halted under the first cedar-tree, a lonely, dwarfed shrub that seemed to have had a hard life. From this point the rise of ground was more perceptible, and straggling cedars led the eye on to a purple slope that merged into green of piñon and pine. Could that purple be the sage Venters had so feelingly described, or was it merely the purple of deceiving distance? Whatever it might be, it gave Shefford a thrill and made him think of the strange, shy, and lovely woman Venters had won out here in this purple-sage country.

He calculated that he had ridden thirty miles the day before and had already traveled ten miles today, and therefore could hope to be in the pass before night. Shefford resumed his journey with too much energy and enthusiasm to think of being tired. And he discovered presently that the straggling cedars and the slope beyond were much closer than he had judged them to be. He reached the sage to find it gray instead of purple. Yet it was always purple a little way ahead, and if he half shut his eyes it was purple near at hand. He was surprised to find that he could not breathe freely, or it seemed so, and soon made the discovery that the sweet, pungent, penetrating fragrance of sage and cedar had this strange effect upon him. This was an exceedingly dry and odorous forest, where every open space between the clumps of cedars was choked with luxuriant sage. The piñons were higher up on the mesa, and the pines still higher. Shefford appeared to lose himself. There were no trails; the black mesa on the right and the wall of stone on the left could not be seen; but he pushed on with what was either singular confidence or rash impulse. And he did not know whether that slope was long or short.

Once at the summit he saw with surprise that it broke abruptly and the descent was very steep and short on that side. Through the trees he once more saw the black mesa, rising to the dignity of a mountain; and he had glimpses of another flat, narrow valley, this time with a red wall running parallel with the mesa. He could not help but hurry down to get an unobstructed view. His eagerness was rewarded by a splendid scene, yet to his regret he could not force himself to believe it had any relation to the pictured scenes in his mind. The valley was half a mile wide, perhaps several miles long, and it extended in a curve between the cedar-sloped mesa and a looming wall of red stone. There was not a bird or a beast in sight. He found a well-defined trail, but it had not been recently used. He passed a low structure made of peeled logs and mud, with a dark opening like a door. It did not take him many minutes to learn that the valley was longer than he had calculated. He walked swiftly and steadily, in spite of the fact that the pack had become burdensome. What lay beyond the jutting corner of the mesa had increasing fascination for him and acted as a spur. At last he turned the corner, only to be disappointed at sight of another cedar slope. He had a glimpse of a single black shaft of rock rising far in the distance, and it disappeared as his striding forward made the crest of the slope rise toward the sky.

Again his view became restricted, and he lost the sense of a slow and gradual uplift of rock and an increase in the scale of proportion. Half way up this ascent he was compelled to rest; and again the sun was slanting low when he entered the cedar forest. Soon he was descending, and he suddenly came into the open to face a scene that made his heart beat thick and fast.

He saw lofty crags and cathedral spires, and a wonderful cañon winding between huge beetling red walls. He heard the murmur of flowing water. The trail led down to the cañon floor, which appeared to be level and green and cut by deep washes in red earth. Could this cañon be the mouth of Deception Pass? It bore no resemblance to any place Shefford had heard described, yet somehow he felt rather than saw that it was the portal to the wild fastness he had traveled so far to enter.

Not till he had descended the trail and had dropped his pack did he realize how weary and footsore he was. Then he rested. But his eyes roved to and fro, and his mind was active. What a wild and lonesome spot! The low murmur of shallow water came up to him from a deep, narrow cleft. Shadows were already making the cañon seem full of blue haze. He saw a bare slope of stone out of which cedar-trees were growing. And as he looked about him he became aware of a singular and very perceptible change in the lights and shades. The sun was setting; the crags were gold-tipped; the shadows crept upward; the sky seemed to darken swiftly; then the gold changed to red, slowly dulled, and the grays and purples stood out. Shefford was entranced with the beautiful changing effects, and watched till the walls turned black and the sky grew steely and a faint star peeped out. Then he set about the necessary camp tasks.

Dead cedars right at hand assured him a comfortable night with steady fire; and when he had satisfied his hunger he arranged an easy seat before the blazing logs, and gave his mind over to thought of his weird, lonely environment.

The murmur of running water mingled in harmonious accompaniment with the moan of the wind in the cedars—wild, sweet sounds that were balm to his wounded spirit! They seemed a part of the silence, rather than a break in it or a hindrance to the feeling of it. But suddenly that silence did break to the rattle of a rock. Shefford listened, thinking some wild animal was prowling around. He felt no alarm. Presently he heard the sound again, and again. Then he recognized the crack of unshod hoofs upon rock. A horse was coming down the trail. Shefford rather resented the interruption, though he still had no alarm. He believed he was perfectly safe. As a matter of fact, he had never in his life been anything but safe and padded around with wool, hence, never having experienced peril, he did not know what fear was.

Presently he saw a horse and rider come into dark prominence on the ridge just above his camp. They were silhouetted against the starry sky.

The horseman stopped and he and his steed made a magnificent black statue, somehow wild and strange, in Shefford's sight. Then he came on, vanished in the darkness under the ridge, presently to emerge into the circle of campfire light.

He rode to within twenty feet of Shefford and the fire. The horse was dark, wild-looking, and seemed ready to run. The rider appeared to be an Indian, and yet had something about him suggesting the cowboy. At once Shefford remembered what Presbrey had said about half-breeds. A little shock, inexplicable to Shefford, rippled over him.

He greeted his visitor, but received no answer. Shefford saw a dark, squat figure bending forward in the saddle. The man was tense. All about him was dark except the glint of a rifle across the saddle. The face under the sombrero was only a shadow. Shefford kicked the fire-logs and a brighter blaze lightened the scene. Then he saw this stranger a little more clearly, and made out an unusually large head, broad dark face, a sinister tight-shut mouth, and gleaming black eyes.

Those eyes were unmistakably hostile. They roved searchingly over Shefford's pack and then over his person. Shefford felt for the gun that Presbrey had given him. But it was gone. He had left it back where he had lost his horse, and had not thought of it since. Then a strange, slow-coming cold agitation possessed Shefford. Something gripped his throat.

Suddenly Shefford was stricken at a menacing movement on the part of the horseman. He had drawn a gun. Shefford saw it shine darkly in the firelight. The Indian meant to murder him. Shefford saw the grim, dark face in a kind of horrible amaze. He felt the meaning of that drawn weapon as he had never felt anything before in his life. And he collapsed back into his seat with an icy, sickening terror. In a second he was dripping wet with cold sweat. Lightning-swift thoughts flashed through his mind. It had been one of his platitudes that he was not afraid of death. Yet here he was a shaking, helpless coward. What had he learned about either life or death? Would this dark savage plunge him into the unknown? It was then that Shefford realized his hollow philosophy and the bitter-sweetness of life. He had a brain and a soul, and between them he might have worked out his salvation. But what were they to this ruthless night-wanderer, this raw and horrible wildness of the desert?

Incapable of voluntary movement, with tongue cleaving to the roof of his mouth, Shefford watched the horseman and the half-poised gun. It was not yet leveled. Then it dawned upon Shefford that the stranger's head was turned a little, his ear to the wind. He was listening. His horse was listening. Suddenly he straightened up, wheeled his horse, and trotted away into the darkness. But he did not climb the ridge down which he had come.

Shefford heard the click of hoofs upon the stony trail. Other horses and riders were descending into the cañon. They had been the cause of his deliverance, and in the relaxation of feeling he almost fainted. Then he sat there, slowly recovering, slowly ceasing to tremble, divining that this situation was somehow to change his attitude toward life.

Three horses, two with riders, moved in dark shapes across the sky-line above the ridge, disappeared as had Shefford's first visitor, and then rode into the light. Shefford saw two Indians—a man and a woman; then with surprise recognized the latter to be the Indian girl he had met at Red Lake. He was still more surprised to recognize in the third horse the one he had lost at the last camp. Shefford rose, a little shaky on his legs, to thank these Indians for a double service. The man slipped from his saddle and his moccasined feet thudded lightly. He was tall, lithe, erect, a singularly graceful figure, and as he advanced Shefford saw a dark face and sharp, dark eyes. The Indian was bareheaded, with his hair bound in a band. He resembled the girl, but appeared to have a finer face.

"How do?" he said, in a voice low and distinct. He extended his hand, and Shefford felt a grip of steel. He returned the greeting. Then the Indian gave Shefford the bridle of the horse, and made signs that appeared to indicate the horse had broken his hobbles and strayed. Shefford thanked him. Thereupon the Indian unsaddled and led the horses away, evidently to water them. The girl remained behind. Shefford addressed her, but she was shy and did not respond. He then set about cooking a meal for his visitors, and was busily engaged at this when the Indian returned without the horses. Presently Shefford resumed his seat by the fire and watched the two eat what he had prepared. They certainly were hungry and soon had the pans and cups empty. Then the girl drew back a little into the shadow, while the man sat with his legs crossed and his feet tucked under him.

His dark face was smooth, yet it seemed to have lines under the sur-face. Shefford was impressed. He had never seen an Indian who interested him as this one. Looked at superficially, he appeared young, wild, silent, locked in his primeval apathy, just a healthy savage; but looked at more attentively, he appeared matured, even old, a strange, sad, brooding figure, with a burden on his shoulders. Shefford found himself growing curious.

"What place?" asked Shefford, waving his hand toward the dark opening between the black cliffs.

"Sagi," replied the Indian.

That did not mean anything to Shefford, and he asked if the Sagi was the pass, but the Indian shook his head.

"Wife?" asked Shefford, pointing to the girl.

The Indian shook his head again. "*Bi-la*," he said.

"What you mean?" asked Shefford. "What *bi-la?*"

"Sister," replied the Indian. He spoke the word reluctantly, as if the white man's language did not please him, but the clearness and correct pronunciation surprised Shefford.

"What name—what call her?" he went on.

"Glen Naspa."

"What your name?" inquired Shefford, indicting the Indian.

"Nas Ta Bega," answered the Indian.

"Navajo?"

The Indian bowed with what seemed pride and stately dignity.

"My name John Shefford. Come far 'way back toward rising sun. Come stay here long."

Nas Ta Bega's dark eyes were fixed steadily upon Shefford. He reflected that he could not remember having felt so penetrating a gaze. But neither the Indian's eyes nor face gave any clue to his thoughts.

"Navajo no savvy Jesus Christ," said the Indian, and his voice rolled out low and deep.

Shefford felt both amaze and pain. The Indian had taken him for a missionary.

"No! . . . Me no missionary," cried Shefford, and he flung up a passionately repudiating hand.

A singular flash shot from the Indian's dark eyes. It struck Shefford even at this stinging moment when the past came back.

"Trade—buy wool—blanket?" queried Nas Ta Bega.

"No," replied Shefford. "Me want ride—walk far." He waved his hand to indicate a wide sweep of territory. "Me sick."

Nas Ta Bega laid a significant finger upon his lungs.

"No," replied Shefford. "Me strong. Sick here." And with motions of his hands he tried to show that his was a trouble of the heart.

Shefford received instant impression of this Indian's intelligent comprehension, but he could not tell just what had given him the feeling. Nas Ta Bega rose then and walked away into the shadow. Shefford heard him working around the dead cedar-tree, where he had probably gone to get fire-wood. Then Shefford heard a splintering crash, which was followed by a crunching, bumping sound. Presently he was astounded to see the Indian enter the lighted circle dragging the whole cedar-tree, trunk first. Shefford would have doubted the ability of two men to drag that tree, and here came Nas Ta Bega, managing it easily. He laid the trunk on the fire, and then proceeded to break off small branches, to place them advantageously where the red coals kindled them into a blaze.

The Indian's next move was to place his saddle, which he evidently meant to use for a pillow. Then he spread a goat-skin on the ground, lay down upon it, with his back to the fire, and, pulling a long-haired saddle-blanket over his shoulders, he relaxed and became motionless. His sister, Glen Naspa, did likewise, except that she stayed farther away from the fire, and she had a larger blanket, which covered her well. It appeared to Shefford that they went to sleep at once.

Shefford felt as tired as he had ever been, but he did not think he could soon drop into slumber, and in fact he did not want to.

There was something in the companionship of these Indians that he had not experienced before. He still had a strange and weak feeling—the aftermath of that fear which had sickened him with its horrible icy grip. Nas Ta Bega's arrival had frightened away that dark and silent prowler of the night; and Shefford was convinced the Indian had saved his life. The measure of his gratitude was a source of wonder to him. Had he cared so much for life? Yes—he had, when face to face with death. That was something to know. It helped him. And he gathered from his strange feelings that the romantic quest which had brought him into the wilderness might turn out to be an antidote for the morbid bitterness of heart.

With new sensations had come new thoughts. Right then it was very pleasant to sit in the warmth and light of the roaring cedar fire. There was a deep-seated ache of fatigue in his bones. What joy it was to rest! He had felt the dry scorch of desert thirst and the pang of hunger. How wonderful to learn the real meaning of water and food! He had just finished the longest, hardest day's work of his life! Had that anything to do with a something almost like peace which seemed to hover near in the shadows, trying to come to him? He had befriended an Indian girl, and now her brother had paid back the service. Both the giving and receiving were somehow sweet to Shefford. They opened up hitherto vague channels of thought. For years he had imagined he was serving people, when he had never lifted a hand. A blow given in the defense of an Indian girl had somehow operated to make a change in John Shefford's existence. It had liberated a spirit in him. Moreover, it had worked its influence outside his mind. The Indian girl and her brother had followed his trail to return his horse, perhaps to guide him safely, but, unknowingly perhaps, they had done infinitely more than that for him. As Shefford's eye wandered over the dark, still figures of the sleepers he had a strange, dreamy premonition, or perhaps only a fancy, that there was to be more come of this fortunate meeting.

For the rest, it was good to be there in the speaking silence, to feel the heat on his outstretched palms and the cold wind on his cheek, to see the black wall lifting its bold outline and the crags reaching for the white stars.

CHAPTER 3

KAYENTA

The stamping of horses awoke Shefford. He saw a towering crag, rosy in the morning light, like a huge red spear splitting the clear blue of sky. He got up, feeling cramped and sore, yet with unfamiliar exhilaration. The whipping air made him stretch his hands to the fire. An odor of coffee and broiled meat mingled with the fragrance of wood smoke. Glen Naspa was on her knees broiling a rabbit on a stick over the red coals. Nas Ta Bega was saddling the ponies. The cañon appeared to be full of purple shadows under one side of dark cliffs and golden streaks of mist on the other where the sun struck high up on the walls.

"Good morning," said Shefford.

Glen Naspa shyly replied in Navajo.

"How," was Nas Ta Bega's greeting.

In daylight the Indian lost some of the dark somberness of face that had impressed Shefford. He had a noble head, in poise like that of an eagle, a bold, clean-cut profile, and stern, close-shut lips. His eyes were the most striking and attractive feature about him; they were coal-black and piercing; the intent look out of them seemed to come from a keen and inquisitive mind.

Shefford ate breakfast with the Indians, and then helped with the few preparations for departure. Before they mounted, Nas Ta Bega pointed to horse tracks in the dust. They were those that had been made by Shefford's threatening visitor of the night before. Shefford explained by word and sign, and succeeded at least in showing that he had been in danger. Nas Ta Bega followed the tracks a little way and presently returned.

"Shadd," he said, with an ominous shake of his head. Shefford did not understand whether he meant the name of his visitor or something else, but the menace connected with the word was clear enough.

Glen Naspa mounted her pony, and it was a graceful action that pleased Shefford. He climbed a little stiffly into his own saddle. Then Nas Ta Bega got up and pointed northward.

"Kayenta?" he inquired.

Shefford nodded and then they were off, with Glen Naspa in the lead. They did not climb the trail which they had descended, but took one leading to the right along the base of the slope. Shefford saw down into the red wash that bisected the cañon floor. It was a sheer wall of red clay or loam, a hundred feet high, and at the bottom ran a swift, shallow stream of reddish water. Then for a time a high growth of greasewood hid the surroundings from Shefford's sight. Presently the trail led out into the open, and Shefford saw that he was at the neck of a wonderful valley that gradually widened with great jagged red peaks on the left and the black mesa, now a mountain, running away to the right. He turned to find that the opening of the Sagi could no longer be seen, and he was conscious of a strong desire to return and explore that cañon.

Soon Glen Naspa put her pony to a long, easy, swinging canter and her followers did likewise. As they got outward into the valley Shefford lost the sense of being overshadowed and crowded by the nearness of the huge walls and crags. The trail appeared level underfoot, but at a distance it was seen to climb. Shefford found where it disappeared over the foot of a slope that formed a graceful rising line up to the cedared flank of the mesa. The valley floor, widening away to the north, remained level and green. Beyond rose the jagged range of red peaks, all strangely cut and slanting. These distant deceiving features of the country held Shefford's gaze until the Indian drew his attention to things near at hand. Then Shefford saw flocks of sheep dotting the gray-green valley, and bands of beautiful long-maned, long-tailed ponies.

For several miles the scene did not change except that Shefford imagined he came to see where the upland plain ended or at least broke its level. He was right, for presently the Indian pointed, and Shefford went on to halt upon the edge of a steep slope leading down into a valley vast in its barren gray reaches.

"Kayenta," said Nas Ta Bega.

Shefford at first saw nothing except the monotonous gray valley reaching far to the strange, grotesque monuments of yellow cliff. Then close under the foot of the slope he espied two squat stone houses with red roofs, and a corral with a pool of water shining in the sun.

The trail leading down was steep and sandy, but it was not long. Shefford's sweeping eyes appeared to take in everything at once—the crude stone structures with their earthen roofs, the piles of dirty wool, the Indians lolling around, the tents, and wagons, and horses, little lazy burros and dogs, and scattered everywhere saddles, blankets, guns, and packs.

Then a white man came out of the door. He waved a hand and shouted. Dust and wool and flour were thick upon him. He was muscular and weather-beaten, and appeared young in activity rather than face. A gun swung at his hip and a row of brass-tipped cartridges showed in his belt. Shefford looked into a face that he thought he had seen before, until he realized the similarity was only the bronze and hard line and rugged cast common to desert men. The gray searching eyes went right through him.

"Glad to see you. Get down and come in. Just heard from an Indian that you were coming. I'm the trader Withers," he said to Shefford. His voice was welcoming and the grip of his hand made Shefford's ache.

Shefford told his name and said he was as glad as he was lucky to arrive at Kayenta.

"Hello! Nas Ta Bega!" exclaimed Withers. His tone expressed a surprise his face did not show. "Did this Indian bring you in?"

Withers shook hands with the Navajo while Shefford briefly related what he owed to him. Then Withers looked at Nas Ta Bega and spoke to him in the Indian tongue.

"Shadd," said Nas Ta Bega.

Withers let out a dry little laugh and his strong hand tugged at his mustache.

"Who's Shadd?" asked Shefford.

"He's a half-breed Ute—bad Indian, outlaw, murderer. He's in with a gang of outlaws who hide in the San Juan country. . . . Reckon you're lucky. How'd you come to be there in the Sagi alone?"

"I traveled from Red Lake. Presbrey, the trader there, advised against it, but I came anyway."

"Well." Withers's gray glance was kind, if it did express the foolhardiness of Shefford's act. "Come into the house. . . . Never mind the horse. My wife will sure be glad to see you."

Withers led Shefford by the first stone house, which evidently was the trading-store, into the second. The room Shefford entered was large, with logs smoldering in a huge open fireplace, blankets covering every foot of floor space, and Indian baskets and silver ornaments everywhere, and strange Indian designs painted upon the whitewashed walls. Withers called his wife, and made her acquainted with Shefford. She was a slight, comely little woman, with keen, earnest, dark eyes. She seemed to be serious and quiet, but she made Shefford feel at home immediately. He refused, however, to accept the room offered him, saying that he meant to sleep out under the open sky. Withers laughed at this and said he understood. Shefford, remembering Presbrey's hunger for news of the outside world, told this trader and his wife all he could think of; and he was listened to with that close attention a traveler always gained in the remote places.

"Sure am glad you rode in," said Withers, for the fourth time. "Now you make yourself at home. Stay here—come over to the store—do what you like. I've got to work. To-night we'll talk."

Shefford went out with his host. The store was as interesting as Presbrey's, though much smaller and more primitive. It was full of everything, and smelled strongly of sheep and goats. There was a narrow aisle between sacks of flour and blankets on one side and a high counter on the other. Behind this counter Withers stood to wait upon the buying Indians. They sold blankets and skins and bags of wool, and in exchange took silver money. Then they lingered and with slow, staid reluctance bought one thing and then another—flour, sugar, canned goods, coffee, tobacco, ammunition. The counter was never without two or three Indians leaning on their dark, silver-braceleted arms. But as they were slow to sell and buy and go, so were others slow to come in. Their voices were soft and low and it seemed to Shefford they were whispering. He liked to hear them and to look at the banded heads, the long, twisted rolls of black hair tied with white cords, the still dark faces and watchful eyes, the silver ear-rings, the slender, shapely brown hands, the lean and sinewy shapes, the corduroys with a belt and gun, and the small, close-fitting buckskin moccasins buttoned with coins. These Indians all appeared young, and under the quiet, slow demeanor there was fierce blood and fire.

By and by two women came in, evidently squaw and daughter. The former was a huge, stout Indian with a face that was certainly pleasant if not jolly. She had the corners of a blanket tied under her chin and in the folds behind on her broad back was a naked Indian baby, round and black of head, brown-skinned, with eyes as bright as beads. When the young-ster caught sight of Shefford he made a startled dive into the sack of the blanket. Manifestly, however, curiosity got the better of fear, for pres-ently Shefford caught a pair of wondering dark eyes peeping at him.

"They're good spenders, but slow," said Withers. "The Navajos are careful and cautious. That's why they're rich. This squaw, Yan As Pa, has flocks of sheep and more mustangs than she knows about."

"Mustangs. So that's what you call the ponies?" replied Shefford.

"Yep. They're mustangs, and mostly wild as jackrabbits."

Shefford strolled outside and made the acquaintance of Withers's helper, a Mormon named Whisner. He was a stockily built man past ma-turity, and his sun-blistered face and watery eyes told of the open desert. He was engaged in weighing sacks of wool brought in by the Indians. Near by stood a framework of poles from which an immense bag was suspended. From the top of this bag protruded the head and shoulders of an Indian who appeared to be stamping and packing wool with his feet. He grinned at the curious Shefford. But Shefford was more interested in the Mormon. So far as he knew, Whisner was the first man of that creed he had ever met, and he could scarcely hide his eagerness. Venters's sto-ries had been of a long-past generation of Mormons, fanatical, ruthless, and unchangeable. Shefford did not expect to meet Mormons of this kind. But any man of that religion would have interested him. Besides this, Whisner seemed to bring him closer to that wild secret cañon he had come West to find. Shefford was somewhat amazed and discomfited to have his polite and friendly overtures repulsed. Whisner might have been an Indian. He was cold, incommunicative, aloof; and there was something about him that made the sensitive Shefford feel his presence was resented.

Presently Shefford strolled on to the corral, which was full of shaggy mustangs. They snorted and kicked at him. He had a half-formed wish that he would never be called upon to ride one of those wild brutes, and then he found himself thinking that he would ride one of them, and after a while any of them. Shefford did not understand himself, but he fought his natural instinctive reluctance to meet obstacles, peril, suffering.

He traced the white-bordered little stream that made the pool in the corral, and when he came to where it oozed out of the sand under the bluff he decided that was not the spring which had made Kayenta famous. Presently down below the trading-post he saw a trough from which burros were drinking. Here he found the spring, a deep well of eddying water walled in by stones, and the overflow made a shallow stream meandering away between its borders of alkali, like a crust of salt. Shefford tasted the water. It bit, but it was good.

Shefford had no trouble in making friends with the lazy sleepy-eyed burros. They let him pull their long ears and rub their noses, but the mustangs standing around were unapproachable. They had wild eyes; they raised long ears and looked vicious. He let them alone.

Evidently this trading-post was a great deal busier than Red Lake. Shefford counted a dozen Indians lounging outside, and there were others riding away. Big wagons told how the bags of wool were transported out of the wilds and how supplies were brought in. A wide, hard-packed road led off to the east, and another, not so clearly defined, wound away to the north. And Indian trails streaked off in all directions.

Shefford discovered, however, when he had walked off a mile or so across the valley to lose sight of the post, that the feeling of wildness and loneliness returned to him. It was a wonderful country. It held something for him besides the possible rescue of an imprisoned girl from a wild cañon.

* * *

That night after supper, when Withers and Shefford sat alone before the blazing logs in the huge fireplace, the trader laid his hand on Shefford's and said, with directness and force:

"I've lived my life in the desert. I've met many men and have been a friend to most. . . . You're no prospector or trader or missionary?"

"No," replied Shefford.

"You've had trouble?"

"Yes."

"Have you come in here to hide? Don't be afraid to tell me. I won't give you away."

"I didn't come to hide."

"Then no one is after you? You've done no wrong?"

"Perhaps I wronged myself, but no one else," replied Shefford, steadily.

"I reckoned so. Well, tell me, or keep your secret—it's all one to me."

Shefford felt a desire to unburden himself. This man was strong, persuasive, kindly. He drew Shefford.

"You're welcome in Kayenta," went on Withers. "Stay as long as you like. I take no pay from a white man. If you want work I have it aplenty."

"Thank you. That is good. I need to work. We'll talk of it later. . . . But just yet I can't tell you why I came to Kayenta, what I want to do, how long I shall stay. My thoughts put in words would seem so like dreams. Maybe they are dreams. Perhaps I'm only chasing a phantom—perhaps I'm only hunting the treasure at the foot of the rainbow."

"Well, this is the country for rainbows," laughed Withers. "In summer from June to August when it storms we have rainbows that'll make you think you're in another world. The Navajos have rainbow mountains, rainbow cañons, rainbow bridges of stone, rainbow trails. It sure is rainbow country."

That deep and mystic chord in Shefford thrilled. Here it was again—something tangible at the bottom of his dream.

Withers did not wait for Shefford to say any more, and almost as if he read his visitor's mind he began to talk about the wild country he called home.

He had lived at Kayenta for several years—hard and profitless years by reason of marauding outlaws. He could not have lived there at all but for the protection of the Indians. His father-in-law had been friendly with the Navajos and Piutes for many years, and his wife had been brought up among them. She was held in peculiar reverence and affection by both tribes in that part of the country. Probably she knew more of the Indians' habits, religion, and life than any white person in the West. Both tribes were friendly and peaceable, but there were bad Indians, half-breeds, and outlaws that made the trading-post a venture Withers had long considered precarious, and he wanted to move and intended to some day. His nearest neighbors in New Mexico and Colorado were a hundred miles distant and at some seasons the roads were impassable. To the north, however, twenty miles or so, was situated a Mormon village named Stone Bridge. It lay across the Utah line. Withers did some business with this village, but scarcely enough to warrant the risks he had to run. During the last year he had lost several pack-trains, one of which he had never heard of after it left Stone Bridge.

"Stone Bridge!" exclaimed Shefford, and he trembled. He had heard that name. In his memory it had a place beside the name of another village Shefford longed to speak of to this trader.

"Yes—Stone Bridge," replied Withers. "Ever heard the name?"

"I think so. Are there other villages in—in that part of the country?"

"A few, but not close. Glaze is now only a water-hole. Bluff and Monticello are far north across the San Juan. . . . There used to be another village—but that wouldn't interest you."

"Maybe it would," replied Shefford, quietly.

But his hint was not taken by the trader. Withers suddenly showed a semblance to the aloofness Shefford had observed in Whisner.

"Withers, pardon an impertinence—I am deeply serious. . . . Are you a Mormon?"

"Indeed I'm not," replied the trader, instantly.

"Are you for the Mormons or against them?"

"Neither. I get along with them. I know them. I believe they are a misunderstood people."

"That's for them."

"No. I'm only fair-minded."

Shefford paused, trying to curb his thrilling impulse, but it was too strong.

"You said there used to be another village. . . . Was the name of it—Cottonwoods?"

Withers gave a start and faced round to stare at Shefford in blank astonishment.

"Say, did you give me a straight story about yourself?" he queried, sharply.

"So far as I went," replied Shefford.

"You're no spy on the lookout for sealed wives?"

"Absolutely not. I don't even know what you mean by sealed wives."

"Well, it's damn strange that you'd know the name Cottonwoods. . . . Yes, that's the name of the village I meant—the one that used to be. It's gone now, all except a few stone walls."

"What became of it?"

"Torn down by Mormons years ago. They destroyed it and moved away. I've heard Indians talk about a grand spring that was there once. It's gone, too. Its name was—let me see—"

"Amber Spring," interrupted Shefford.

"By George, you're right!" rejoined the trader, again amazed. "Shefford, this beats me. I haven't heard that name for ten years. I can't help seeing what a tenderfoot—stranger—you are to the desert. Yet, here you are—speaking of what you should know nothing of. . . . And there's more behind this."

Shefford rose, unable to conceal his agitation.

"Did you ever hear of a rider named Venters?"

"Rider? You mean a cowboy? Venters. No, I never heard that name."

"Did you ever hear of a gunman named Lassiter?" queried Shefford, with increasing emotion.

"No."

"Did you ever hear of a Mormon woman named—Jane Withersteen?"

"No."

Shefford drew his breath sharply. He had followed a gleam—he had caught a fleeting glimpse of it.

"Did you ever hear of a child—a girl—a woman—called Fay Larkin?"

Withers rose slowly with a paling face.

"If you're a spy it'll go hard with you—though I'm no Mormon," he said, grimly.

Shefford lifted a shaking hand.

"I *was* a clergyman. Now I'm nothing—a wanderer—least of all a spy."

Withers leaned closer to see into the other man's eyes; he looked long and then appeared satisfied.

"I've heard the name Fay Larkin," he said, slowly. "I reckon that's all I'll say till you tell your story."

Shefford stood with his back to the fire and he turned the palms of his hands to catch the warmth. He felt cold. Withers had affected him strangely. What was the meaning of the trader's somber gravity? Why was the very mention of Mormons attended by something austere and secret?

"My name is John Shefford. I am twenty-four," began Shefford. "My family—"

Here a knock on the door interrupted Shefford.

"Come in," called Withers.

The door opened and like a shadow Nas Ta Bega slipped in. He said something in Navajo to the trader.

"How," he said to Shefford, and extended his hand. He was stately, but there was no mistaking his friendliness. Then he sat down before the fire, doubled his legs under him after the Indian fashion, and with dark eyes on the blazing logs seemed to lose himself in meditation.

"He likes the fire," explained Withers. "Whenever he comes to Kayenta he always visits me like this. . . . Don't mind him. Go on with your story."

"My family were plain people, well-to-do, and very religious," went on Shefford. "When I was a boy we moved from the country to a town called Beaumont, Illinois. There was a college in Beaumont and eventually I was sent to it to study for the ministry. I wanted to be— But never mind that. . . . By the time I was twenty-two I was ready for my career as a clergyman. I preached for a year around at different places and then got a church in my home town of Beaumont. I became exceedingly good friends with a man named Venters, who had recently come to Beaumont. He was a singular man. His wife was a strange, beautiful woman, very reserved, and she had wonderful dark eyes. They had money and were devoted to each other, and perfectly happy. They owned the finest horses ever seen in Illinois, and their particular enjoyment seemed to be riding. They were always taking long rides. It was something worth going far for to see Mrs. Venters on a horse.

"It was through my own love of horses that I became friendly with Venters. He and his wife attended my church, and as I got to see more of them, gradually we grew intimate. And it was not until I did get intimate with them that I realized that both seemed to be haunted by the past. They were sometimes sad even in their happiness. They drifted off into dreams. They lived back in another world. They seemed to be listening. Indeed, they were a singularly interesting couple, and I grew genuinely fond of them. By and by they had a little girl whom they named Jane. The coming of the baby made a change in my friends. They were happier, and I observed that the haunting shadow did not so often return.

"Venters had spoken of a journey west that he and his wife meant to take some time. But after the baby came he never mentioned his wife in connection with the trip. I gathered that he felt compelled to go to clear up a mystery or to find something—I did not make out just what. But eventually, and it was about a year ago, he told me his story—the strangest, wildest, and most tragic I ever heard.

"I can't tell it all now. It is enough to say that fifteen years before he had been a rider for a rich Mormon woman named Jane Withersteen, of this village Cottonwoods. She had adopted a beautiful Gentile child named Fay Larkin. Her interest in Gentiles earned the displeasure of her churchmen, and as she was proud there came a breach. Venters and a gunman named Lassiter became involved in her quarrel. Finally Venters took to the cañons. Here in the wilds he found the strange girl he eventually married. For a long time they lived in a wonderful hidden valley, the entrance to which was guarded by a huge balancing rock. Venters got away with the girl. But Lassiter and Jane Withersteen and the child Fay

Larkin were driven into the cañon. They escaped to the valley where Venters had lived. Lassiter rolled the balancing rock, and, crashing down the narrow trail, it loosened the weathered walls and closed the narrow outlet for ever."

CHAPTER 4

NEW FRIENDS

Shefford ended his narrative out of breath, pale, and dripping with sweat. Withers sat leaning forward with an expression of intense interest. Nas Ta Bega's easy, graceful pose had succeeded to one of strained rigidity. He seemed a statue of bronze. Could a few intelligible words, Shefford wondered, have created that strange, listening posture?

"Venters got out of Utah, of course, as you know," went on Shefford. "He got out, knowing—as I feel I would have known—that Jane, Lassiter, and little Fay Larkin were shut up, walled up in Surprise Valley. For years Venters considered it would not have been safe for him to venture to rescue them. He had no fears for their lives. They could live in Surprise Valley. But Venters always intended to come back with Bess and find the valley and his friends. No wonder he and Bess were haunted. However, when his wife had the baby that made a difference. It meant he had to go alone. And he was thinking seriously of starting when I—when there were developments that made it desirable for me to leave Beaumont. Venters's story haunted me as he had been haunted. I dreamed of that wild valley—of little Fay Larkin grown to womanhood—such a woman as Bess Venters was. And the longing to come was great. . . . And, Withers—here I am."

The trader reached out and gave Shefford the grip of a man in whom emotion was powerful, but deep and difficult to express.

"Listen to this. . . . I wish I could help you. Life is a strange deal. . . . Shefford, I've got to trust you. Over here in the wild cañon country there's a village of Mormons' sealed wives. It's in Arizona, perhaps twenty miles from here, and near the Utah line. When the United States government began to persecute, or prosecute, the Mormons for polygamy, the Mormons over here in Stone Bridge took their sealed wives and moved them out of Utah, just across the line. They built houses, established a village there. I'm the only Gentile who knows about it. And I pack supplies every few weeks in to these women. There are perhaps fifty women, mostly young—second or third or fourth wives of Mormons—sealed wives. And I want you to understand that sealed means *sealed* in all that religion or loyalty can get out of the word. There are also some old women and old men in the village, but they hardly count. And there's a flock of the finest children you ever saw in your life.

"The idea of the Mormons must have been to escape prosecution. The law of the government is one wife for each man—no more. All over Utah polygamists have been arrested. The Mormons are deeply concerned. I believe they are a good, law-abiding people. But this law is a direct blow at their religion. In my opinion they can't obey both. And therefore they have not altogether given up plural wives. Perhaps they will some day. I have no proof, but I believe the Mormons of Stone Bridge pay secret night visits to their sealed wives across the line in the lonely, hidden village.

"Now once over in Stone Bridge I overheard some Mormons talking about a girl who was named Fay Larkin. I never forgot the name. Later I heard the name in this sealed-wife village. But, as I told you, I never heard of Lassiter or Jane Withersteen. Still, if Mormons had found them I would never have heard of it. And Deception Pass—that might be the Sagi. . . . I'm not surprised at your rainbow-chasing adventure. It's a great story. . . . This Fay Larkin I've heard of *might* be your Fay Larkin—I almost believe so. Shefford, I'll help you find out."

"Yes, yes—I must know," replied Shefford. "Oh, I hope, I pray we can find her! But—I'd rather she was dead—if she's not still hidden in the valley."

"Naturally. You've dreamed yourself into rescuing this lost Fay Larkin. . . . But, Shefford, you're old enough to know life doesn't work out as you want it to. One way or another I fear you're in for a bitter disappointment."

"Withers, take me to the village."

"Shefford, you're liable to get in bad out here," said the trader, gravely.

"I couldn't be any more ruined than I am now," replied Shefford, passionately.

"But there's risk in this—risk such as you never had," persisted Withers.

"I'll risk anything."

"Reckon this's a funny deal for a sheep-trader to have on his hands," continued Withers. "Shefford, I like you. I've a mind to see you through this. It's a damn strange story. . . . I'll tell you what—I will help you. I'll give you a job packing supplies in to the village. I meant to turn that over to a Mormon cowboy—Joe Lake. The job shall be yours, and I'll go with you first trip. Here's my hand on it. . . . Now, Shefford, I'm more curious about you than I was before you told your story. What ruined you? As we're to be partners, you can tell me now. I'll keep your secret. Maybe I can do you good."

Shefford wanted to confess, yet it was hard. Perhaps, had he not been so agitated, he would not have answered to impulse. But this trader was a man—a man of the desert—he would understand.

"I told you I was a clergyman," said Shefford in low voice. "I didn't want to be one, but they made me one. I did my best. I failed. . . . I had doubts of religion—of the Bible—of God, as my Church believed in them. As I grew older thought and study convinced me of the narrowness of religion as my congregation lived it. I preached what I believed. I alienated them. They put me out, took my calling from me, disgraced me, ruined me."

"So that's all!" exclaimed Withers, slowly. "You didn't believe in the God of the Bible. . . . Well, I've been in the desert long enough to know there *is* a God, but probably not the one your Church worships. . . . Shefford, go to the Navajo for a faith!"

Shefford had forgotten the presence of Nas Ta Bega, and perhaps Withers had likewise. At this juncture the Indian rose to his full height, and he folded his arms to stand with the somber pride of a chieftain while his dark, inscrutable eyes were riveted upon Shefford. At that moment he seemed magnificent. How infinitely more he seemed than just a common Indian who had chanced to befriend a white man! The difference was obscure to Shefford. But he felt that it was there in the Navajo's mind. Nas Ta Bega's strange look was not to be interpreted. Presently he turned and passed from the room.

"By George!" cried Withers, suddenly, and he pounded his knee with his fist. "I'd forgotten."

"What?" questioned Shefford.

"Why, that Indian understood every word we said. He knows English. He's educated. Well, if this doesn't beat me. . . . Let me tell you about Nas Ta Bega."

Withers appeared to be recalling something half forgotten.

"Years ago, in fifty-seven, I think, Kit Carson with his soldiers chased the Navajo tribes and rounded them up to be put on reservations. But he failed to catch all the members of one tribe. They escaped up into wild cañons like the Sagi. The descendants of these fugitives live there now and are the finest Indians on earth—the finest because unspoiled by the white man. Well, as I got the story, years after Carson's round-up one of his soldiers guided some interested travelers in here. When they left they took an Indian boy with them to educate. From what I know of Navajos I'm inclined to think the boy was taken against his parents' wish. Anyway, he was taken. That boy was Nas Ta Bega. The story goes that he was educated somewhere. Years afterward, and perhaps not long before I came in here, he returned to his people. There have been missionaries and other interested fools who have given Indians a white man's education. In all the instances I know of, these educated Indians returned to their tribes, repudiating the white man's knowledge, habits, life, and religion. I have heard that Nas Ta Bega came back, laid down the white man's clothes along with the education, and never again showed that he had known either.

"You have just seen how strangely he acted. It's almost certain he heard our conversation. Well, it doesn't matter. He won't tell. He can hardly be made to use an English word. Besides, he's a noble red man, if there ever was one. He has been a friend in need to me. If you stay long out here you'll learn something from the Indians. Nas Ta Bega has be-friended you, too, it seems. I thought he showed unusual interest in you."

"Perhaps that was because I saved his sister—well, to be charitable, from the rather rude advances of a white man," said Shefford, and he proceeded to tell of the incident that occurred at Red Lake.

"Willetts!" exclaimed Withers, with much the same expression that Presbrey had used. "I never met him. But I know about him. He's—well, the Indians don't like him much. Most of the missionaries are good men—good for the Indians, in a way, but sometimes one drifts out here who is bad. A bad missionary teaching religion to savages! Sad, isn't it? The worst part is the white people's blindness—the blindness of those who send the missionaries. Well, I dare say Willetts isn't very good. When Presbrey said that was Willetts's way of teaching religion he meant just what he said. If Willetts drifts over here he'll be risking much. . . . This you told me explains Nas Ta Bega's friendliness toward you, and also his bringing his sister Glen Naspa to live with relatives up in the pass. She had been living near Red Lake."

"Do you mean Nas Ta Bega wants to keep his sister far removed from Willetts?" inquired Shefford.

"I mean that," replied Withers, "and I hope he's not too late."

Later Shefford went outdoors to walk and think. There was no moon, but the stars made light enough to cast his shadow on the ground. The dark, illimitable expanse of blue sky seemed to be glittering with num-berless points of fire. The air was cold and still. A dreaming silence lay over the land. Shefford saw and felt all these things, and their effect was continuous and remained with him and helped calm him. He was con-scious of a burden removed from his mind. Confession of his secret had been like tearing a thorn from his flesh, but, once done, it afforded him relief and a singular realization that out here it did not matter much. In a crowd of men all looking at him and judging him by their standards he had been made to suffer. Here, if he were judged at all, it would be by what he could do, how he sustained himself and helped others.

He walked far across the valley toward the low bluffs, but they did not seem to get any closer. And, finally, he stopped beside a stone and looked around at the strange horizon and up at the heavens. He did not feel utterly aloof from them, nor alone in a waste, nor a useless atom amid incomprehensible forces. Something like a loosened mantle fell from about him, dropping down at his feet; and all at once he was conscious of freedom. He did not understand in the least why abasement left him, but it was so. He had come a long way, in bitterness, in despair, believing himself to be what men had called him. The desert and the stars and the wind, the silence of the night, the loneliness of this vast country where there was room for a thousand cities—these somehow vaguely, yet surely, bade him lift his head. They withheld their secret, but they made a promise. The thing which he had been feeling every day and every night was a strange enveloping comfort. And it was at this moment that Shefford, divining whence his help was to come, embraced all that wild and speaking nature around and above him and surrendered himself utterly.

"I am young. I am free. I have my life to live," he said. "I'll be a man. I'll take what comes. Let me learn here!"

When he had spoken out, settled once and for ever his attitude toward his future, he seemed to be born again, wonderfully alive to the influences around him, ready to trust what yet remained a mystery.

Then his thought reverted to Fay Larkin. Could this girl be known to the Mormons? It was possible. Fay Larkin was an unusual name. Deep into Shefford's heart had sunk the story Venters had told. Shefford found that he had unconsciously created a like romance—he had been loving a wild and strange and lonely girl, like beautiful Bess Venters. It was a shock to learn the truth, but, as it had been only a dream, it could hardly be vital.

Shefford retraced his steps toward the post. Halfway back he espied a tall, dark figure moving toward him, and presently the shape and the step seemed familiar. Then he recognized Nas Ta Bega. Soon they were face to face. Shefford felt that the Indian had been trailing him over the sand, and that this was to be a significant meeting. Remembering Withers's revelation about the Navajo, Shefford scarcely knew how to approach him now. There was no difference to be made out in Nas Ta Bega's dark face and inscrutable eyes, yet there was a difference to be felt in his presence. But the Indian did not speak, and turned to walk by Shefford's side. Shefford could not long be silent.

"Nas Ta Bega, were you looking for me?" he asked.

"You had no gun," replied the Indian.

But for his very low voice, his slow speaking of the words, Shefford would have thought him a white man. For Shefford there was indeed an instinct in this meeting, and he turned to face the Navajo.

"Withers told me you had been educated, that you came back to the desert, that you never showed your training. . . . Nas Ta Bega, did you understand all I told Withers?"

"Yes," replied the Indian.

"You won't betray me?"

"I am a Navajo."

"Nas Ta Bega, you trail me—you say I had no gun." Shefford wanted to ask this Indian if he cared to be the white man's friend, but the question was not easy to put, and, besides, seemed unnecessary. "I am alone and strange in this wild country. I must learn."

"Nas Ta Bega will show you the trails and the water-holes and how to hide from Shadd."

"For money—for silver you will do this?" inquired Shefford.

Shefford felt that the Indian's silence was a rebuke. He remembered Withers's singular praise of this red man. He realized he must change his idea of Indians.

"Nas Ta Bega, I know nothing. I feel like a child in the wilderness. When I speak it is out of the mouths of those who have taught me. I must find a new voice and a new life. . . . You heard my story to Withers. I am an outcast from my own people. If you will be my friend—be so."

The Indian clasped Shefford's hand and held it in a response that was more beautiful for its silence. So they stood for a moment in the starlight.

"Nas Ta Bega, what did Withers mean when he said go to the Navajo for a faith?" asked Shefford.

"He meant the desert is my mother. . . . Will you go with Nas Ta Bega into the cañons and the mountains?"

"Indeed I will."

They unclasped hands and turned toward the trading-post.

"Nas Ta Bega, have you spoken my tongue to any other white man since you returned to your home?" asked Shefford.

"No."

"Why do you—why are you different for me?"

The Indian maintained silence.

"Is it because of—of Glen Naspa?" inquired Shefford.

Nas Ta Bega stalked on, still silent, but Shefford divined that, although his service to Glen Naspa would never be forgotten, still it was not wholly responsible for the Indian's subtle sympathy.

"Bi Nai! The Navajo will call his white friend Bi Nai—brother," said Nas Ta Bega, and he spoke haltingly, not as if words were hard to find, but strange to speak. "I was stolen from my mother's hogan and taken to California. They kept me ten years in a mission at San Bernardino and four years in a school. They said my color and my hair were all that was left of the Indian in me. But they could not see my heart. They took fourteen years of my life. They wanted to make me a missionary among my own people. But the white man's ways and his life and his God are not the Indian's. They never can be."

How strangely productive of thought for Shefford to hear the Indian talk! What fatality in this meeting and friendship! Upon Nas Ta Bega had been forced education, training, religion, that had made him something more and something less than an Indian. It was something assimilated from the white man which made the Indian unhappy and alien in his own home—something meant to be good for him and his kind that had ruined him. For Shefford felt the passion and the tragedy of this Navajo.

"Bi Nai, the Indian is dying!" Nas Ta Bega's low voice was deep and wonderful with its intensity of feeling. "The white man robbed the Indian of lands and homes, drove him into the deserts, made him a gaunt and sleepless spiller of blood. . . . The blood is all spilled now, for the Indian is broken. But the white man sells him rum and seduces his daughters. . . . He will not leave the Indian in peace with his own God! . . . Bi Nai, the Indian is dying!"

That night Shefford lay in his blankets out under the open sky and the stars. The earth had never meant much to him, and now it was a bed. He had preached of the heavens, but until now had never studied them.

An Indian slept beside him. And not until the gray of morning had blotted out the starlight did Shefford close his eyes.

With break of the next day came full, varied, and stirring incidents to Shefford. He was strong, though unskilled at most kinds of outdoor tasks. Withers had work for ten men, if they could have been found. Shefford dug and packed and lifted till he was so sore and tired that rest was a blessing.

He never succeeded in getting on a friendly footing with the Mormon Whisner, though he kept up his agreeable and kindly advances. He listened to the trader's wife as she told him about the Indians, and what he learned he did not forget. And his wonder and respect increased in proportion to his knowledge.

One day there rode into Kayenta the Mormon for whom Withers had been waiting. His name was Joe Lake. He appeared young, and slipped off his superb bay with a grace and activity that were astounding in one of his huge bulk. He had a still, smooth face, with the color of red bronze and the expression of a cherub; big, soft, dark eyes; and a winning smile. He was surprisingly different from Whisner or any Mormon character that Shefford had naturally conceived. His costume was that of the cowboy on active service; and he packed a gun at his hip. The handshake he gave Shefford was an ordeal for that young man and left him with his whole right side momentarily benumbed.

"I sure am glad to meet you," he said in a lazy, mild voice. And he was taking friendly stock of Shefford when the bay mustang reached with vicious muzzle to bite at him. Lake gave a jerk on the bridle that almost brought the mustang to his knees. He reared then, snorted, and came down to plant his forefeet wide apart, and watched his master with defiant eyes. This mustang was the finest horse Shefford had ever seen. He appeared quite large for his species, was almost red in color, had a racy and powerful build, and a fine thoroughbred head with dark, fiery eyes. He did not look mean, but he had spirit.

"Navvy, you've sure got bad manners," said Lake, shaking the mustang's bridle. He spoke as if he were chiding a refractory little boy.

"Didn't I break you better 'n that? What's this gentleman goin' to think of you? Tryin' to bite my ear off!"

Lake had arrived about the middle of the forenoon, and Withers announced his intention of packing at once for the trip. Indians were sent out on the ranges to drive in burros and mustangs. Shefford had his thrilling expectancy somewhat chilled by what he considered must have been Lake's reception of the trader's plan. Lake seemed to oppose him, and evidently it took vehemence and argument on Withers's part to make the Mormon tractable. But Withers won him over, and then he called Shefford to his side.

"You fellows got to be good friends," he said. "You'll have charge of my pack-trains. Nas Ta Bega wants to go with you. I'll feel safer about my supplies and stock than I've ever been. . . . Joe, I'll back this stranger for all I'm worth. He's square. . . . And, Shefford, Joe Lake is a Mormon of the younger generation. I want to start you right. You can trust him as you trust me. He's white clean through. And he's the best horse-wrangler in Utah."

It was Lake who first offered his hand, and Shefford made haste to meet it with his own. Neither of them spoke. Shefford intuitively felt an alteration in Lake's regard, or at least a singular increase of interest. Lake had been told that Shefford had been a clergyman, was now a wanderer, without any religion. Again it seemed to Shefford that he owed a forming of friendship to this singular fact. And it hurt him. But strangely it came to him that he had taken a liking to a Mormon.

About one o'clock the pack-train left Kayenta. Nas Ta Bega led the way up the slope. Following him climbed half a dozen patient, plodding, heavily laden burros. Withers came next, and he turned in his saddle to wave good-by to his wife. Joe Lake appeared to be busy keeping a red mule and a wild gray mustang and a couple of restive blacks in the trail. Shefford brought up in the rear.

His mount was a beautiful black mustang with three white feet, a white spot on his nose, and a mane that swept to his knees. "His name's Nack-yal," Withers had said. "It means two bits, or twenty-five cents. He ain't worth more." To look at Nack-yal had pleased Shefford very much indeed, but, once upon his back, he grew dubious. The mustang acted nervous. He actually looked back at Shefford, and it was a look of speculation and disdain. Shefford took exception to Nack-yal's manner and to his reluctance to go, and especially to a habit the mustang had of turning off the trail to the left. Shefford had managed some rather spirited horses back in Illinois; and though he was willing and eager to learn all over again, he did not enjoy the prospect of Lake and Withers seeing this black mustang make a novice of him. And he guessed that was just what Nack-yal intended to do. However, once up over the hill, with Kayenta out of sight, Nack-yal trotted along fairly well, needing only now and then to be pulled back from his strange swinging to the left off the trail.

The pack-train traveled steadily and soon crossed the upland plain to descend into the valley again. Shefford saw the jagged red peaks with an emotion he could not name. The cañons between them were purple in the shadows, the great walls and slopes brightened to red, and the tips were gold in the sun. Shefford forgot all about his mustang and the trail.

Suddenly with a pound of hoofs Nack-yal seemed to rise. He leaped sidewise out of the trail, came down stiff-legged. Then Shefford shot out of the saddle. He landed so hard that he was stunned for an instant. Sitting up, he saw the mustang bent down, eyes and ears showing fight, and his forefeet spread. He appeared to be looking at something in the trail. Shefford got up and soon saw what had been the trouble. A long, crooked stick, rather thick and black and yellow, lay in the trail, and any mustang looking for an excuse to jump might have mistaken it for a rattlesnake. Nack-yal appeared disposed to be satisfied, and gave Shefford no trouble in mounting. The incident increased Shefford's dubiousness. These Arizona mustangs were unknown quantities.

Thereafter Shefford had an eye for the trail rather than the scenery, and this continued till the pack-train entered the mouth of the Sagi. Then those wonderful lofty cliffs, with their peaks and towers and spires, loomed so close and so beautiful that he did not care if Nack-yal did throw him. Along here, however, the mustang behaved well, and presently Shefford decided that if it had been otherwise he would have walked. The trail suddenly stood on end and led down into the deep wash, where some days before he had seen the stream of reddish water. This day there appeared to be less water and it was not so red. Nack-yal sank deep as he took short and careful steps down. The burros and other mustangs were drinking, and Nack-yal followed suit. The Indian, with a hand clutching his mustang's mane, rode up a steep, sandy slope on the other side that Shefford would not have believed any horse could climb. The burros plodded up and over the rim, with Withers calling to them. Joe Lake swung his rope and cracked the flanks of the gray mare and the red mule; and the way the two kicked was a revelation and a warning to Shefford. When his turn came to climb the trail he got off and walked, an action that Nack-yal appeared fully to appreciate.

From the head of this wash the trail wound away up the widening cañon, through greasewood flats and over greasy levels and across sandy stretches. The looming walls made the valley look narrow, yet it must have been half a mile wide. The slopes under the cliffs were dotted with huge stones and cedar-trees. There were deep indentations in the walls, running back to form box cañons, choked with green of cedar and spruce and piñon. These notches haunted Shefford, and he was ever on the lookout for more of them.

Withers came back to ride just in advance and began to talk.

"Reckon this Sagi Cañon is your Deception Pass," he said. "It's sure a strange hole. I've been lost more than once, hunting mustangs in here. I've an idea Nas Ta Bega knows all this country. He just pointed out a cliff-dwelling to me. See it? . . . There 'way up in that cave of the wall."

Shefford saw a steep, rough slope leading up to a bulge of the cliff, and finally he made out strange little houses with dark, eyelike windows. He wanted to climb up there. Withers called his attention to more caves with what he believed were the ruins of cliff-dwellings. And as they rode along the trader showed him remarkable formations of rock where the elements were slowly hollowing out a bridge. They came presently to a region of intersecting cañons, and here the breaking of the trail up and down the deep washes took Withers back to his task with the burros and gave Shefford more concern than he liked with Nack-yal. The mustang grew unruly and was continually turning to the left. Sometimes he tried to climb the steep slope. He had to be pulled hard away from the opening cañons on the left. It seemed strange to Shefford that the mustang never swerved to the right. This habit of Nack-yal's and the increasing caution needed on the trail took all of Shefford's attention. When he dismounted, however, he had a chance to look around, and more and more he was amazed at the increasing proportions and wildness of the Sagi.

He came at length to a place where a fallen tree blocked the trail. All of the rest of the pack-train had jumped the log. But Nack-yal balked. Shefford dismounted, pulled the bridle over the mustang's head, and tried to lead him. Nack-yal, however, refused to budge. Whereupon Shefford got a stick and, remounting, he gave the balky mustang a cut across the flank. Then something violent happened. Shefford received a sudden propelling jolt, and then he was rising into the air, and then falling. Before he alighted he had a clear image of Nack-yal in the air above him, bent double, and seemingly possessed of devils. Then Shefford hit the ground with no light thud. He was thoroughly angry when he got dizzily upon his feet, but he was not quick enough to catch the mustang. Nack-yal leaped easily over the log and went on ahead, dragging his bridle. Shefford hurried after him, and the faster he went, just by so much the cunning Nack-yal accelerated his gait. As the pack-train was out of sight somewhere ahead, Shefford could not call to his companions to halt his mount, so he gave up trying, and walked on now with free and growing appreciation of his surroundings.

The afternoon had waned. The sun blazed low in the west in a notch of the cañon ramparts, and one wall was darkening into purple shadow while the other shone through a golden haze. It was a weird, wild world to Shefford, and every few strides he caught his breath and tried to realize actuality was not a dream.

Nack-yal kept about a hundred paces to the fore and ever and anon he looked back to see how his new master was progressing. He varied these occasions by reaching down and nipping a tuft of grass. Evidently he was too intelligent to go on fast enough to be caught by Withers. Also he kept continually looking up the slope to the left as if seeking a way to climb out of the valley in that direction. Shefford thought it was well the trail lay at the foot of a steep slope that ran up to unbroken bluffs.

The sun set and the cañon lost its red and its gold and deepened its purple. Shefford calculated he had walked five miles, and though he did not mind the effort, he would rather have ridden Nack-yal into camp. He mounted a cedar ridge, crossed some sandy washes, turned a corner of bold wall to enter a wide, green level. The mustangs were rolling and snorting. He heard the bray of a burro. A bright blaze of campfire greeted him, and the dark figure of the Indian approached to intercept and catch

Nack-yal. When he stalked into camp Withers wore a beaming smile, and Joe Lake, who was on his knees making biscuit dough in a pan, stopped proceedings and drawled:

"Reckon Nack-yal bucked you off."

"Bucked! Was that it? Well, he separated himself from me in a new and somewhat painful manner—to me."

"Sure, I saw that in his eye," replied Lake; and Withers laughed with him.

"Nack-yal never was well broke," he said. "But he's a good mustang, nothing like Joe's Navvy or that gray mare Dynamite. All this Indian stock will buck on a man once in a while."

"I'll take the bucking along with the rest," said Shefford.

Both men liked his reply, and the Indian smiled for the first time.

Soon they all sat round a spread tarpaulin and ate like wolves. After supper came the rest and talk before the campfire. Joe Lake was droll; he said the most serious things in a way to make Shefford wonder if he was not joking. Withers talked about the cañon, the Indians, the mustangs, the scorpions running out of the heated sand; and to Shefford it was all like a fascinating book. Nas Ta Bega smoked in silence, his brooding eyes upon the fire.

CHAPTER 5

ON THE TRAIL

Shefford was awakened next morning by a sound he had never heard before—the plunging of hobbled horses on soft turf. It was clear daylight, with a ruddy color in the sky and a tinge of red along the cañon rim. He saw Withers, Lake, and the Indian driving the mustangs toward camp.

The burros appeared lazy, yet willing. But the mustangs and the mule Withers called Red and the gray mare Dynamite were determined not to be driven into camp. It was astonishing how much action they had, how much ground they could cover with their forefeet hobbled together. They were exceedingly skillful; they lifted both forefeet at once, and then plunged. And they all went in different directions. Nas Ta Bega darted in here and there to head off escape.

Shefford pulled on his boots and went out to help. He got too close to the gray mare and, warned by a yell from Withers, he jumped back just in time to avoid her vicious heels. Then Shefford turned his attention to Nack-yal and chased him all over the flat in a futile effort to catch him. Nas Ta Bega came to Shefford's assistance and put a rope over Nack-yal's head.

"Don't ever get behind one of these mustangs," said Withers, warningly, as Shefford came up. "You might be killed. . . . Eat your bite now. We'll soon be out of here."

Shefford had been late in awakening. The others had breakfasted. He found eating somewhat difficult in the excitement that ensued. Nas Ta Bega held ropes which were round the necks of Red and Dynamite. The mule showed his cunning and always appeared to present his heels to Withers, who tried to approach him with a pack-saddle. The patience of the trader was a revelation to Shefford. And at length Red was cornered by the three men, the pack-saddle was strapped on, and then the packs. Red promptly bucked the packs off, and the work had to be done over again. Then Red dropped his long ears and seemed ready to be tractable.

When Shefford turned his attention to Dynamite he decided that this was his first sight of a wild horse. The gray mare had fiery eyes that rolled and showed the white. She jumped straight up, screamed, pawed, bit, and then plunged down to shoot her hind hoofs into the air as high as her head had been. She was amazingly agile and she seemed mad to kill something. She dragged the Indian about, and when Joe Lake got a rope on her hind foot she dragged them both. They lashed her with the ends of the lassoes, which action only made her kick harder. She plunged into camp, drove Shefford flying for his life, knocked down two of the burros, and played havoc with the unstrapped packs. Withers ran to the assistance of Lake, and the two of them hauled back with all their strength and weight. They were both powerful and heavy men. Dynamite circled round and finally, after kicking the campfire to bits, fell down on her haunches in the hot embers. "Let—her—set—there!" panted Withers. And Joe Lake shouted, "Burn up, you durn coyote!" Both men appeared delighted that she had brought upon herself just punishment. Dynamite sat in the remains of the fire long enough to get burnt, and then she got up and meekly allowed Withers to throw a tarpaulin and a roll of blankets over her and tie them fast.

Lake and Withers were sweating freely when this job was finished.

"Say, is that a usual morning's task with the pack-animals?" asked Shefford.

"They're all pretty decent to-day, except Dynamite," replied Withers. "She's got to be worked out."

Shefford felt both amusement and consternation. The sun was just

rising over the ramparts of the cañon, and he had already seen more difficult and dangerous work accomplished than half a dozen men of his
type could do in a whole day. He liked the outlook of his new duty as
Withers's assistant, but he felt helplessly inefficient. Still, all he needed
was experience. He passed over what he anticipated would be pain and
peril—the cost was of no moment.

Soon the pack-train was on the move, with the Indian leading. This
morning Nack-yal began his strange swinging off to the left, precisely as
he had done the day before. It got to be annoying to Shefford, and he lost
patience with the mustang and jerked him sharply round. This, however,
had no great effect upon Nack-yal.

As the train headed straight up the cañon Joe Lake dropped back to
ride beside Shefford. The Mormon had been amiable and friendly.

"Flock of deer up that draw," he said, pointing up a narrow side
cañon.

Shefford gazed to see a half-dozen small, brown, long-eared objects,
very like burros, watching the pack-train pass.

"Are they deer?" he asked, delightedly.

"Sure are," replied Joe, sincerely. "Get down and shoot one. There's
a rifle in your saddle-sheath."

Shefford had already discovered that he had been armed this morning, a matter which had caused him reflection. These animals certainly
looked like deer; he had seen a few deer, though not in their native wild
haunts; and he experienced the thrill of the hunter. Dismounting, he
drew the rifle out of the sheath and started toward the little cañon.

"Hyar! Where you going with that gun?" yelled Withers. "That's a
bunch of burros. . . . Joe's up to his old tricks. Shefford, look out for Joe!"

Rather sheepishly Shefford returned to his mustang and sheathed
the rifle, and then took a long look at the animals up the draw. They resembled deer, but upon second glance they surely were burros.

"Durn me! Now if I didn't think they sure were deer!" exclaimed Joe.
He appeared absolutely sincere and innocent. Shefford hardly knew how
to take this likable Mormon, but vowed he would be on his guard in the
future.

Nas Ta Bega soon led the pack-train toward the left wall of the cañon, and evidently intended to scale it. Shefford could not see any trail,

and the wall appeared steep and insurmountable. But upon nearing the cliff he saw a narrow broken trail leading zigzag up over smooth rock, weathered slope, and through cracks.

"Spread out, and careful now!" yelled Withers.

The need of both advices soon became manifest to Shefford. The burros started stones rolling, making danger for those below. Shefford dismounted and led Nack-yal and turned aside many a rolling rock. The Indian and the burros, with the red mule leading, climbed steadily. But the mustangs had trouble. Joe's spirited bay had to be coaxed to face the ascent; Nack-yal balked at every difficult step; and Dynamite slipped on a flat slant of rock and slid down forty feet. Withers and Lake with ropes hauled the mare out of the dangerous position. Shefford, who brought up the rear, saw all the action, and it was exciting, but his pleasure in the climb was spoiled by sight of blood and hair on the stones. The ascent was crooked, steep, and long, and when Shefford reached the top of the wall he was glad to rest. It made him gasp to look down and see what he had surmounted. The cañon floor, green and level, lay a thousand feet below; and the wild burros which had followed on the trail looked like rabbits.

Shefford mounted presently, and rode out upon a wide, smooth trail leading into a cedar forest. There were bunches of gray sage in the open places. The air was cool and crisp, laden with a sweet fragrance. He saw Lake and Withers bobbing along, now on one side of the trail, now on the other, and they kept to a steady trot. Occasionally the Indian and his bright-red saddle-blanket showed in an opening of the cedars.

It was level country, and there was nothing for Shefford to see except cedar and sage, an outcropping of red rock in places, and the winding trail. Mocking-birds made melody everywhere. Shefford seemed full of a strange pleasure, and the hours flew by. Nack-yal still wanted to be ever-lastingly turning off the trail, and, moreover, now he wanted to go faster. He was eager, restless, dissatisfied.

At noon the pack-train descended into a deep draw, well covered with cedar and sage. There was plenty of grass and shade, but no water. Shefford was surprised to see that every pack was removed; however, the roll of blankets was left on Dynamite.

The men made a fire and began to cook a noonday meal. Shefford, tired and warm, sat in a shady spot and watched. He had become all eyes. He had almost forgotten Fay Larkin; he had forgotten his trouble; and the present seemed sweet and full. Presently his ears were filled by a pattering roar and, looking up the draw, he saw two streams of sheep and goats coming down. Soon an Indian shepherd appeared, riding a fine mustang. A cream-colored colt bounded along behind, and presently a shaggy dog came in sight. The Indian dismounted at the camp, and his flock spread by in two white and black streams. The dog went with them. Withers and Joe shook hands with the Indian, whom Joe called "Navvy," and Shefford lost no time in doing likewise. Then Nas Ta Bega came in, and he and the Navajo talked. When the meal was ready all of them sat down round the canvas. The shepherd did not tie his horse.

Presently Shefford noticed that Nack-yal had returned to camp and was acting strangely. Evidently he was attracted by the Indian's mustang or the cream-colored colt. At any rate, Nack-yal hung around, tossed his head, whinnied in a low, nervous manner, and looked strangely eager and wild. Shefford was at first amused, then curious. Nack-yal approached too close to the mother of the colt, and she gave him a sounding kick in the ribs. Nack-yal uttered a plaintive snort and backed away, to stand, crestfallen, with all his eagerness and fire vanished.

Nas Ta Bega pointed to the mustang and said something in his own tongue. Then Withers addressed the visiting Indian, and they exchanged some words, whereupon the trader turned to Shefford.

"I bought Nack-yal from this Indian three years ago. This mare is Nack-yal's mother. He was born over here to the south. That's why he always swung left off the trail. He wanted to go home. Just now he recognized his mother and she whaled away and gave him a whack for his pains. She's got a colt now and probably didn't recognize Nack-yal. But he's broken-hearted."

The trader laughed, and Joe said, "You can't tell what these durn mustangs will do." Shefford felt sorry for Nack-yal, and when it came time to saddle him again found him easier to handle than ever before. Nack-yal stood with head down, broken-spirited.

Shefford was the first to ride up out of the draw, and once upon the top of the ridge he halted to gaze, wide-eyed and entranced. A rolling, endless plain sloped down beneath him, and led him on to a distant round-topped mountain. To the right a red cañon opened its jagged jaws, and away to the north rose a whorled and strange sea of curved ridges, crags, and domes.

Nas Ta Bega rode up then, leading the pack-train.

"Bi Nai, that is Na-tsis-an," he said, pointing to the mountain. "Navajo Mountain. And there in the north are the cañons."

Shefford followed the Indian down the trail and soon lost sight of that wide green-and-red wilderness. Nas Ta Bega turned at an intersecting trail, rode down into the cañon, and climbed out on the other side. Shefford got a glimpse now and then of the black dome of the mountain, but for the most part the distant points of the country were hidden. They crossed many trails, and went up and down the sides of many shallow cañons. Troops of wild mustangs whistled at them, stood on ridge-tops to watch, and then dashed away with manes and tails flying.

Withers rode forward presently and halted the pack-train. He had some conversation with Nas Ta Bega, whereupon the Indian turned his horse and trotted back, to disappear in the cedars.

"I'm some worried," explained Withers. "Joe thinks he saw a bunch of horsemen trailing us. My eyes are bad and I can't see far. The Indian will find out. I took a roundabout way to reach the village because I'm always dodging Shadd."

This communication lent an added zest to the journey. Shefford could hardly believe the truth that his eyes and his ears brought to his consciousness. He turned in behind Withers and rode down the rough trail, helping the mustang all in his power. It occurred to him that Nack-yal had been entirely different since that meeting with his mother in the draw. He turned no more off the trail; he answered readily to the rein; he did not look afar from every ridge. Shefford conceived a liking for the mustang.

Withers turned sidewise in his saddle and let his mustang pick the way.

"Another time we'll go up round the base of the mountain, where you can look down on the grandest scene in the world," said he. "Two hundred miles of wind-worn rock, all smooth and bare, without a single straight line—cañons, caves, bridges—the most wonderful country in the world! Even the Indians haven't explored it. It's haunted, for them, and they have strange gods. The Navajos will hunt on this side of the mountain, but not on the other. That north side is consecrated ground. My wife has long been trying to get the Navajos to tell her the secret of Nonnezoshe. Nonnezoshe means Rainbow Bridge. The Indians worship it, but as far as she can find out only a few have ever seen it. I imagine it'd be worth some trouble."

"Maybe that's the bridge Venters talked about—the one overarching the entrance to Surprise Valley," said Shefford.

"It might be," replied the trader. "You've got a good chance of finding out. Nas Ta Bega is the man. You stick to that Indian. . . . Well, we start down here into this cañon, and we go down *some*, I reckon. In half an hour you'll see sago-lilies and Indian paint-brush and vermilion cactus."

About the middle of the afternoon the pack-train and its drivers arrived at the hidden Mormon village. Nas Ta Bega had not returned from his scout back along the trail.

Shefford's sensibilities had all been overstrained, but he had left in him enthusiasm and appreciation that made the situation of this village a fairyland. It was a valley, a cañon floor, so long that he could not see the end, and perhaps a quarter of a mile wide. The air was hot, still, and sweetly odorous of unfamiliar flowers. Piñon and cedar-trees surrounded the little log and stone houses, and along the walls of the cañon stood sharp-pointed, dark-green spruce-trees. These walls were singular of shape and color. They were not imposing in height, but they waved like the long, undulating swell of a sea. Every foot of surface was perfectly smooth, and the long curved lines of darker tinge that streaked the red followed the rounded line of the slope at the top. Far above, yet overhanging, were great yellow crags and peaks, and between these, still higher, showed the pine-fringed slope of Navajo Mountain with snow in the sheltered places, and glistening streams, like silver threads, running down.

All this Shefford noticed as he entered the valley from round a corner of wall. Upon nearer view he saw and heard a host of children, who, looking up to see the intruders, scattered like frightened quail. Long gray grass covered the ground, and here and there wide, smooth paths had been worn. A swift and murmuring brook ran through the middle of the valley, and its banks were bordered with flowers.

Withers led the way to one side near the wall, where a clump of cedar-trees and a dark, swift spring boiling out of the rocks and banks of amber moss with purple blossoms made a beautiful camp site. Here the mustangs were unsaddled and turned loose without hobbles. It was certainly unlikely that they would leave such a spot. Some of the burros were unpacked, and the others Withers drove off into the village.

"Sure's pretty nice," said Joe, wiping his sweaty face. "I'll never want to leave. It suits me to lie on this moss. . . . Take a drink of that spring."

Shefford complied with alacrity and found the water cool and sweet, and he seemed to feel it all through him. Then he returned to the mossy bank. He did not reply to Joe. In fact, all his faculties were absorbed in watching and feeling, and he lay there long after Joe went off to the village. The murmur of water, the hum of bees, the songs of strange birds, the sweet, warm air, the dreamy summer somnolence of the valley—all these added drowsiness to Shefford's weary lassitude, and he fell asleep. When he awoke Nas Ta Bega was sitting near him and Joe was busy near a campfire.

"Hello, Nas Ta Bega!" said Shefford. "Was there any one trailing us?"

The Navajo nodded.

Joe raised his head and with forceful brevity said, "Shadd."

"Shadd!" echoed Shefford, remembering the dark, sinister face of his visitor that night in the Sagi. "Joe, is it serious—his trailing us?"

"Well, I don't know how durn serious it is, but I'm scared to death," replied Lake. "He and his gang will hold us up somewhere on the way home."

Shefford regarded Joe with both concern and doubt. Joe's words were at variance with his looks.

"Say, pard, can you shoot a rifle?" queried Joe.

"Yes. I'm a fair shot at targets."

The Mormon nodded his head as if pleased. "That's good. These outlaws are all poor shots with a rifle. So'm I. But I can handle a six-shooter. I reckon we'll make Shadd sweat if he pushes us."

Withers returned, driving the burros, all of which had been unpacked down to the saddles. Two gray-bearded men accompanied him. One of them appeared to be very old and venerable, and walked with a stick. The other had a sad-lined face and kind, mild blue eyes. Shefford observed that Lake seemed unusually respectful. Withers introduced these Mormons merely as Smith and Henninger. They were very cordial and pleasant in their greetings to Shefford. Presently another, somewhat younger, man joined the group, a stalwart, jovial fellow with ruddy face. There was certainly no mistaking his kindly welcome as he shook Shefford's hand. His name was Beal. The three stood round the campfire for a while, evidently glad of the presence of fellow-men and to hear news from the outside. Finally they went away, taking Joe with them. Withers took up the task of getting supper where Joe had been made to leave it.

"Shefford, listen," he said, presently, as he knelt before the fire. "I told them right out that you'd been a Gentile clergyman—that you'd gone back on your religion. It impressed them and you've been well received. I'll tell the same thing over at Stone Bridge. You'll get in right. Of course I don't expect they'll make a Mormon of you. But they'll try to. Meanwhile you can be square and friendly all the time you're trying to find your Fay Larkin. To-morrow you'll meet some of the women. They're good souls, but, like any women, crazy for news. Think what it is to be shut up in here between these walls!"

"Withers, I'm intensely interested," replied Shefford, "and excited, too. Shall we stay here long?"

"I'll stay a couple of days, then go to Stone Bridge with Joe. He'll come back here, and when you both feel like leaving, and if Nas Ta Bega thinks it safe, you'll take a trail over to some Indian hogans and pack me out a load of skins and blankets. . . . My boy, you've all the time there is, and I wish you luck. This isn't a bad place to loaf. I always get sentimental over here. Maybe it's the women. Some of them are pretty, and one of them—Shefford, they call her the Sago Lily. Her first name is Mary, I'm told. Don't know her last name. She's lovely. And I'll bet you forget Fay Larkin in a flash. Only—be careful. You drop in here with rather peculiar credentials, so to speak—as my helper and as a man with no religion! You'll not only be fully trusted, but you'll be welcome to these lonely women. So be careful. Remember it's my secret belief they are sealed wives and are visited occasionally at night by their husbands. I don't *know* this, but I believe it. And you're not supposed to dream of that."

"How many men in the village?" asked Shefford.

"Three. You met them."

"Have they wives?" asked Shefford, curiously.

"Wives! Well, I guess. But only one each that I know of. Joe Lake is the only unmarried Mormon I've met."

"And no men—strangers, cowboys, outlaws—ever come to this village?"

"Except to Indians, it seems to be a secret so far," replied the trader, earnestly. "But it can't be kept secret. I've said that time after time over in Stone Bridge. With Mormons it's 'sufficient unto the day is the evil thereof.'"

"What'll happen when outsiders do learn and ride in here?"

"There'll be trouble—maybe bloodshed. Mormon women are absolutely good, but they're human, and want and need a little life. And, strange to say, Mormon men are pig-headedly jealous. . . . Why, if some of the cowboys I knew in Durango would ride over here there'd simply be hell. But that's a long way, and probably this village will be deserted before news of it ever reaches Colorado. There's more danger of Shadd and his gang coming in. Shadd's half Piute. He must know of this place. And he's got some white outlaws in his gang. . . . Come on. Grub's ready, and I'm too hungry to talk."

Later, when shadows began to gather in the valley and the lofty peaks above were gold in the sunset glow, Withers left camp to look after the straying mustangs, and Shefford strolled to and fro under the cedars. The lights and shades in the Sagi that first night had moved him to enthusiastic watchfulness, but here they were so weird and beautiful that he was enraptured. He actually saw great shafts of gold and shadows of purple streaming from the peaks down into the valley. It was day on the heights and twilight in the valley. The swiftly changing colors were like rainbows.

While he strolled up and down several women came to the spring and filled their buckets. They wore shawls or hoods and their garments were somber, but, nevertheless, they appeared to have youth and comeliness. They saw him, looked at him curiously, and then, without speaking, went back on the well-trodden path. Presently down the path appeared a woman—a girl in lighter garb. It was almost white. She was shapely and walked with free, graceful step, reminding him of the Indian girl, Glen Naspa. This one wore a hood shaped like a huge sunbonnet and it concealed her face. She carried a bucket. When she reached the spring and went down the few stone steps Shefford saw that she did not have on shoes. As she braced herself to lift the bucket her bare foot clung to the mossy stone. It was a strong, sinewy, beautiful foot, instinct with youth. He was curious enough, he thought, but the awakening artist in him made him more so. She dragged at the full bucket and had difficulty in lifting it out of the hole. Shefford strode forward and took the bucket-handle from her.

"Won't you let me help you?" he said, lifting the bucket. "Indeed—it's very heavy."

"Oh—thank you," she said, without raising her head. Her voice seemed singularly young and sweet. He had not heard a voice like it. She moved down the path and he walked beside her. He felt embarrassed, yet more curious than ever; he wanted to say something, to turn and look at her, but he kept on for a dozen paces without making up his mind.

Finally he said: "Do you really carry this heavy bucket? Why, it makes my arm ache."

"Twice every day—morning and evening," she replied. "I'm very strong."

Then he stole a look out of the corner of his eye, and, seeing that her face was hidden from him by the hood, he turned to observe her at better advantage. A long braid of hair hung down her back. In the twilight it gleamed dull gold. She came up to his shoulder. The sleeve nearest him was rolled up to her elbow, revealing a fine round arm. Her hand, like her foot, was brown, strong, and well shaped. It was a hand that had been developed by labor. She was full-bosomed, yet slender, and she walked with a free stride that made Shefford admire and wonder.

They passed several of the little stone and log houses, and women greeted them as they went by and children peered shyly from the doors. He kept trying to think of something to say, and, failing in that, determined to have one good look under the hood before he left her.

"You walk lame," she said, solicitously. "Let me carry the bucket now—please. My house is near."

"Am I lame? . . . Guess so, a little," he replied. "It was a hard ride for me. But I'll carry the bucket just the same."

They went on under some piñon-trees, down a path to a little house identical with the others, except that it had a stone porch. Shefford smelled fragrant wood-smoke and saw a column curling from the low, flat, stone chimney. Then he set the bucket down on the porch.

"Thank you, Mr. Shefford," she said.

"You know my name?" he asked.

"Yes. Mr. Withers spoke to my nearest neighbor and she told me."

"Oh, I see. And you—"

He did not go on and she did not reply. When she stepped upon the porch and turned he was able to see under the hood. The face there was in shadow, and for that very reason he answered to ungovernable impulse and took a step closer to her. Dark, grave, sad eyes looked down at him, and he felt as if he could never draw his own glance away. He seemed not to see the rest of her face, and yet felt that it was lovely. Then a downward movement of the hood hid from him the strange eyes and the shadowy loveliness.

"I—I beg your pardon," he said, quickly, drawing back. "I'm rude. . . . Withers told me about a girl he called—he said looked like a sago-lily. That's no excuse to stare under your hood. But I—I was curious. I wondered if—"

He hesitated, realizing how foolish his talk was. She stood a moment, probably watching him, but he could not be sure, for her face was hidden.

"They call me that," she said. "But my name is Mary."

"Mary—what?" he asked.

"Just Mary," she said, simply. "Good night."

He did not say good night and could not have told why. She took up the bucket and went into the dark house. Shefford hurried away into the gathering darkness.

CHAPTER 6

IN THE HIDDEN VALLEY

Shefford had hardly seen her face, yet he was more interested in a woman than he had ever been before. Still, he reflected, as he returned to camp, he had been under a long strain, he was unduly excited by this new and adventurous life, and these, with the mystery of this village, were perhaps accountable for a state of mind that could not last.

He rolled in his blankets on the soft bed of moss and he saw the stars through the needle-like fringe of the piñons. It seemed impossible to fall asleep. The two domed peaks split the sky, and back of them, looming dark and shadowy, rose the mountain. There was something cold, austere, and majestic in their lofty presence, and they made him feel alone, yet not alone. He raised himself to see the quiet forms of Withers and Nas Ta Bega prone in the starlight, and their slow, deep breathing was that of tired men. A bell on a mustang rang somewhere off in the valley and gave out a low, strange, reverberating echo from wall to wall. When it ceased a silence set in that was deader than any silence he had ever felt, but gradually he became aware of the low murmur of the brook. For the rest there was no sound of wind, no bark of dog or yelp of coyote, no sound of voice in the village.

He tried to sleep, but instead thought of this girl who was called the

Sago Lily. He recalled everything incident to their meeting and the walk
to her home. Her swift, free step, her graceful poise, her shapely form—
the long braid of hair, dull gold in the twilight, the beautiful bare foot
and the strong round arm—these he thought of and recalled vividly. But
of her face he had no idea except the shadowy, haunting loveliness, and
that grew more and more difficult to remember. The tone of her voice
and what she had said—how the one had thrilled him and the other mystified! It was her voice that had most attracted him. There was something
in it besides music—what, he could not tell—sadness, depth, something
like that in Nas Ta Bega's—a beauty springing from disuse. But this
seemed absurd. Why should he imagine her voice one that had not been
used as freely as any other woman's? She was a Mormon; very likely, almost surely, she was a sealed wife. His interest, too, was absurd, and he
tried to throw it off, or imagine it one he might have felt in any other of
these strange women of the hidden village.

But Shefford's intelligence and his good sense, which became opera-
tive when he was fully roused and set the situation clearly before his eyes,
had no effect upon his deeper, mystic, and primitive feelings. He saw the
truth and he felt something that he could not name. He would not be a
fool, but there was no harm in dreaming. And unquestionably, beyond
all doubt, the dream and the romance that had lured him to the wilderness were here, hanging over him like the shadows of the great peaks.
His heart swelled with emotion when he thought of how the black and
incessant despair of the past was gone. So he embraced any attraction
that made him forget and think and feel; some instinct stronger than
intelligence bade him drift.

Joe's rolling voice awoke him next morning and he rose with a singular zest. When or where in his life had he awakened in such a beautiful place? Almost he understood why Venters and Bess had been haunted
by memories of Surprise Valley. The morning was clear, cool, sweet; the
peaks were dim and soft in rosy cloud; shafts of golden sunlight shot
down into the purple shadows. Mocking-birds were singing. His body
was sore and tired from the unaccustomed travel, but his heart was full,
happy. His spirit wanted to run, and he knew there was something out

there waiting to meet it. The Indian and the trader and the Mormon all meant more to him this morning. He had grown a little overnight. Nas Ta Bega's deep "Bi Nai" rang in his ears, and the smiles of Withers and Joe were greetings. He had friends; he had work; and there was rich, strange, and helpful life to live. There was even a difference in the mustang Nack-yal. He came readily; he did not look wild; he had a friendly eye; and Shefford liked him more.

"What is there to do?" asked Shefford, feeling equal to a hundred tasks.

"No work," replied the trader, with a laugh, and he drew Shefford aside. "I'm in no hurry. I like it here. And Joe never wants to leave. To-day you can meet the women. Make yourself popular. I've already made you that. These women are most all young and lonesome. Talk to them. Make them like you. Then some day you may be safe to ask questions. Last night I wanted to ask old Mother Smith if she ever heard the name Fay Larkin. But I thought better of it. If there's a girl here or at Stone Bridge of that name we'll learn it. If there's mystery we'd better go slow. Mormons are hell on secret and mystery, and to pry into their affairs is to mark yourself. My advice is—just be as nice as you can be, and let things happen."

Fay Larkin! All in a night Shefford had forgotten her. Why? He pondered over the matter, and then the old thrill, the old desire, came back.

"Shefford, what do you think Nas Ta Bega said to me last night?" asked Withers in lower voice.

"Haven't any idea," replied Shefford, curiously.

"We were sitting beside the fire. I saw you walking under the cedars. You seemed thoughtful. That keen Indian watched you, and he said to me in Navajo, 'Bi Nai has lost his God. He has come far to find a wife. Nas Ta Bega is his brother.' . . . He meant he'll find both God and wife for you. I don't know about that, but I say take the Indian as he thinks he is—your brother. Long before I knew Nas Ta Bega well my wife used to tell me about him. He's a sage and a poet—the very spirit of this desert. He's worth cultivating for his own sake. But more—remember, if Fay Larkin is still shut in that valley the Navajo will find her for you."

"I shall take Nas Ta Bega as my brother—and be proud," replied Shefford.

"There's another thing. Do you intend to confide in Joe?"

"I hadn't thought of that."

"Well, it might be a good plan. But wait until you know him better and he knows you. He's ready to fight for you now. He's taken your trouble to heart. You wouldn't think Joe is deeply religious. Yet he is. He may never breathe a word about religion to you. . . . Now, Shefford, go ahead. You've struck a trail. It's rough, but it'll make a man of you. It'll lead somewhere."

"I'm singularly fortunate—I—who had lost all friends. Withers, I am grateful. I'll prove it. I'll show—"

Withers's upheld hand checked further speech, and Shefford realized that beneath the rough exterior of this desert trader there was fine feeling. These men of crude toil and wild surroundings were beginning to loom up large in Shefford's mind.

The day began leisurely. The men were yet at breakfast when the women of the village began to come one by one to the spring. Joe Lake made friendly and joking remarks to each. And as each one passed on down the path he poised a biscuit in one hand and a cup of coffee in the other, and with his head cocked sidewise like an owl he said, "Reckon I've got to get me a woman like her."

Shefford saw and heard, yet he was all the time half unconsciously watching with strange eagerness for a white figure to appear. At last he saw her—the same girl with the hood, the same swift step. A little shock or quiver passed over him, and at the moment all that was explicable about it was something associated with regret.

Joe Lake whistled and stared.

"I haven't met her," he muttered.

"That's the Sago Lily," said Withers.

"Reckon I'm going to carry that bucket," went on Joe.

"And what about all the other women who've been to the spring? Don't do it, Joe," advised the trader.

"But her bucket's bigger," protested Joe, weakly.

"That's true. But you ought to know Mormons. If she'd come first, all right. As she didn't—why, don't single her out."

Joe kept his seat. The girl came to the spring. A low "good morning" came from under the hood. Then she filled her bucket and started home.

Shefford observed that this time she wore moccasins and she carried the heavy bucket with ease. When she disappeared he had again the vague, inexplicable sensation of regret.

Joe Lake breathed heavily. "Reckon I've got to get me a woman like her," he said. But the former jocose tone was lacking and he appeared thoughtful.

Withers first took Shefford to the building used for a school. It was somewhat larger than the other houses, had only one room with two doors and several windows. It was full of children of all sizes and ages, sitting on rude board benches.

There were half a hundred of them, sturdy, healthy, rosy boys and girls, clad in home-made garments. The young woman teacher was as embarrassed as her pupils were shy, and the visitors withdrew without having heard a word of lessons.

Withers then called upon Smith, Henninger, and Beal, and their wives. Shefford found himself cordially received, and what little he did say showed him how he would be listened to when he cared to talk. These folk were plain and kindly, and he found that there was nothing about them to dislike. The men appeared mild and quiet, and when not conversing seemed austere. The repose of the women was only on the surface; underneath he felt their intensity. Especially in many of the younger women, whom he met in the succeeding hour, did he feel this power of restrained emotion. This surprised him, as did also the fact that almost every one of them was attractive and some of them were exceedingly pretty. He became so interested in them all as a whole that he could not individualize one. They were as widely different in appearance and temperament as women of any other class, but it seemed to Shefford that one common trait united them—and it was a strange, checked yearning for something that he could not discover. Was it happiness? They certainly seemed to be happy, far more so than those millions of women who were chasing phantoms. Were they really sealed wives, as Withers believed, and was this unnatural wife-hood responsible for the strange intensity? At any rate he returned to camp with the conviction that he had stumbled upon a remarkable situation.

He had been told the last names of only three women, and their husbands were in the village. The names of the others were Ruth, Rebecca, Joan—he could not recall them all. They were the mothers of these beautiful children. The fathers, as far as he was concerned, were as intangible as myths. Shefford was an educated clergyman, a man of the world, and, as such, knew women in his way. Mormons might be strange and different, yet the fundamental truth was that all over the world mothers of children were wives; there was a relation between wife and mother that did not need to be named to be felt; and he divined from this that, whatever the situation of these lonely and hidden women, they knew themselves to be wives. Shefford absolutely satisfied himself on that score. If they were miserable they certainly did not show it, and the question came to him how just was the criticism of uninformed men? His judgment of Mormons had been established by what he had heard and read, rather than what he knew. He wanted now to have an open mind. He had studied the totemism and exogamy of the primitive races, and here was his opportunity to understand polygamy. One wife for one man—that was the law. Mormons broke it openly; Gentiles broke it secretly. Mormons acknowledged all their wives and protected their children; Gentiles acknowledged one wife only. Unquestionably the Mormons were wrong, but were not the Gentiles still more wrong?

The following day Joe Lake appeared reluctant to start for Stone Bridge with Withers.

"Joe, you'd better come along," said the trader, dryly. "I reckon you've seen a little too much of the Sago Lily."

Lake offered no reply, but it was evident from his sober face that Withers had not hit short of the mark. Withers rode off, with a parting word to Shefford, and finally Joe somberly mounted his bay and trotted down the valley. As Nas Ta Bega had gone off somewhere to visit Indians, Shefford was left alone.

He went into the village and made himself useful and agreeable. He made friends with the children and he talked to the women until he was hoarse. Their ignorance of the world was a spur to him, and never in his life had he had such an attentive audience. And as he showed no curiosity, asked no difficult questions, gradually what reserve he had noted wore away, and the end of the day saw him on a footing with them that Withers had predicted.

By the time several like days had passed it seemed from the interest and friendliness of these women that he might have lived long among them. He was possessed of wit and eloquence and information, which he freely gave, and not with selfish motive. He liked these women; he liked to see the somber shade pass from their faces, to see them brighten. He had met the girl Mary at the spring and along the path, but he had not yet seen her face. He was always looking for her, hoping to meet her, and confessed to himself that the best of the day for him were the morning and evening visits she made to the spring. Nevertheless, for some reason hard to divine, he was reluctant to seek her deliberately. Always while he had listened to her neighbors' talk, he had hoped they might let fall something about her. But they did not. He received an impression that she was not so intimate with the others as he had supposed. They all made one big family. Still, she seemed a little outside. He could bring no proofs to strengthen this idea. He merely felt it, and many of his feelings were independent of intelligent reason. Something had been added to curiosity, that was sure.

It was his habit to call upon Mother Smith in the afternoons. From the first her talk to him hinted of a leaning toward thought of making him a Mormon. Her husband and the other men took up her cue and spoke of their religion, casually at first, but gradually opening their minds to free and simple discussion of their faith. Shefford lent respectful attention. He would rather have been a Mormon than an atheist, and apparently they considered him the latter, and were earnest to save his soul. Shefford knew that he could never be one any more than the other. He was just at sea. But he listened, and he found them simple in faith, blind, perhaps, but loyal and good. It was noteworthy that Mother Smith happened to be the only woman in the village who had ever mentioned religion to him. She was old, of a past generation; the young women belonged to the present. Shefford pondered the significant difference.

Every day made more steadfast his impression of the great mystery that was like a twining shadow round these women, yet in the same time many little ideas shifted and many new characteristics became manifest. This last was of course the result of acquaintance; he was learning more about the villagers. He gathered from keen interpretation of subtle words and looks that here in this lonely village, the same as in all the rest of the world where women were together, there were cliques, quarrels, dislikes, loves, and jealousies. The truth, once known to him, made him feel natural and fortified his confidence to meet the demands of an increasingly interesting position. He discovered, with a somewhat grim amusement, that a clergyman's experience in a church full of women had not been entirely useless.

One afternoon he let fall a careless remark that was a subtle question in regard to the girl Mary, whom Withers called the Sago Lily. In response he received an answer couched in the sweet poisoned honey of woman's jealousy. He said no more. Certain ideas of his were strengthened, and straightway he became thoughtful.

That afternoon late, as he did his camp chores, he watched for her. But she did not come. Then he decided to go to see her. But even the decision and the strange thrill it imparted did not change his reluctance.

Twilight was darkening the valley when he reached her house, and the shadows were thick under the piñons. There was no light in the door or window. He saw a white shape on the porch, and as he came down the path it rose. It was the girl Mary, and she appeared startled.

"Good evening," he said. "It's Shefford. May I stay and talk a little while?"

She was silent for so long that he began to feel awkward.

"I'd be glad to have you," she replied, finally.

There was a bench on the porch, but he preferred to sit upon a blanket on the step.

"I've been getting acquainted with everybody—except you," he went on.

"I have been here," she replied.

That might have been a woman's speech, but it certainly had been made in a girl's voice. She was neither shy nor embarrassed nor self-conscious. As she stood back from him he could not see her face in the dense twilight.

"I've been wanting to call on you."

She made some slight movement. Shefford felt a strange calm, yet he knew the moment was big and potent.

"Won't you sit here?" he asked.

She complied with his wish, and then he saw her face, though dimly, in the twilight. And it struck him mute. But he had no glimpse such as had flashed upon him from under her hood that other night. He thought of a white flower in shadow, and received his first impression of the rare and perfect lily Withers had said graced the wild cañons. She was only a girl. She sat very still, looking straight before her, and seemed to be waiting, listening. Shefford saw the quick rise and fall of her bosom.

"I want to talk," he began, swiftly, hoping to put her at her ease. "Every one here has been good to me and I've talked—oh, for hours and hours. But the thing in my mind I haven't spoken of. I've never asked any questions. That makes my part so strange. I want to tell why I came out here. I need some one who will keep my secret, and perhaps help me. . . . Would you?"

"Yes, if I could," she replied.

"You see I've got to trust you, or one of these other women. You're all Mormons. I don't mean that's anything against you. I believe you're all good and noble. But the fact makes—well, makes a liberty of speech impossible. What can I do?"

Her silence probably meant that she did not know. Shefford sensed less strain in her and more excitement. He believed he was on the right track and did not regret his impulse. Even had he regretted it he would have gone on, for opposed to caution and intelligence was his driving mystic force.

Then he told her the truth about his boyhood, his ambition to be an artist, his renunciation to his father's hope, his career as a clergyman, his failure in religion, and the disgrace that had made him a wanderer.

"Oh—I'm sorry!" she said. The faint starlight shone on her face, in her eyes, and if he ever saw beauty and soul he saw them then. She seemed deeply moved. She had forgotten herself. She betrayed girlhood then— all the quick sympathy, the wonder, the sweetness of a heart innocent and untutored. She looked at him with great, starry, questioning eyes, as if they had just become aware of his presence, as if a man had been strange to her.

"Thank you. It's good of you to be sorry," he said. "My instinct guided me right. Perhaps you'll be my friend."

"I will be—if I can," she said.

"But *can* you be?"

"I don't know. I never had a friend. I . . . But, sir, I mustn't talk of myself. . . . Oh, I'm afraid I can't help you."

How strange the pathos of her voice! Almost he believed she was in need of help or sympathy or love. But he could not wholly trust a judgment formed from observation of a class different from hers.

"Maybe you *can* help me. Let's see," he said. "I don't seek to make you talk of yourself. But—you're a human being—a girl—almost a woman. You're not dumb. But even a nun can talk."

"A nun? What is that?"

"Well—a nun is a sister of mercy—a woman consecrated to God—who has renounced the world. In some ways you Mormon women here resemble nuns. It is sacrifice that nails you in this lonely valley. . . . You see—how I talk! One word, one thought brings another, and I speak what perhaps should be unsaid. And it's hard, because I feel I could unburden myself to you."

"Tell me what you want," she said.

Shefford hesitated, and became aware of the rapid pound of his heart. More than anything he wanted to be fair to this girl. He saw that she was warming to his influence. Her shadowy eyes were fixed upon him. The starlight, growing brighter, shone on her golden hair and white face.

"I'll tell you presently," he said. "I've trusted you. I'll trust you with all. . . . But let me have my own time. This is so strange a thing, my wanting to confide in you. It's selfish, perhaps. I have my own ax to grind. I hope I won't wrong you. That's why I'm going to be perfectly frank. I might wait for days to get better acquainted. But the impulse is on me. I've been so interested in all you Mormon women. The fact—the meaning of this hidden village is so—so terrible to me. But that's none of my business. I have spent my afternoons and evenings with these women at the different cottages. You do not mingle with them. They are lonely, but have not such loneliness as yours. I have passed here every night. No light—no sound. I can't help thinking. Don't censure me or be afraid or draw within yourself just because I must think. I may be all wrong. But I'm curious. I wonder about you. Who are you? Mary—Mary what? Maybe I really don't want to know. I came with selfish motive and now I'd like to—to—what shall I say? Make your life a little less lonely for the while I'm here. That's all. It needn't offend. And if you accept it, how much easier I can tell you my secret. You are a Mormon and I—well, I am only a wanderer in these wilds. But—we might help each other. . . . Have I made a mistake?"

"No—no," she cried, almost wildly.

"We can be friends then. You will trust me, help me?"

"Yes, if I dare."

"Surely you may dare what the other women would?"

She was silent.

And the wistfulness of her silence touched him. He felt contrition. He did not stop to analyze his own emotions, but he had an inkling that once this strange situation was ended he would have food for reflection. What struck him most now was the girl's blanched face, the strong, nervous clasp of her hands, the visible tumult of her bosom. Excitement alone could not be accountable for this. He had not divined the cause for such agitation. He was puzzled, troubled, and drawn irresistibly. He had not said what he had planned to say. The moment had given birth to his speech, and it had flowed. What was guiding him?

"Mary," he said, earnestly, "tell me—have you mother, father, sister, brother? Something prompts me to ask that."

"All dead—gone—years ago," she answered.

"How old are you?"

"Eighteen, I think. I'm not sure."

"You *are* lonely."

His words were gentle and divining.

"O God!" she cried. "Lonely!"

Then as a man in a dream he beheld her weeping. There was in her the unconsciousness of a child and the passion of a woman. He gazed out into the dark shadows and up at the white stars, and then at the bowed head with its mass of glinting hair. But her agitation was no longer strange to him. A few gentle and kind words had proved her undoing. He knew then that whatever her life was, no kindness or sympathy entered it. Presently she recovered, and sat as before, only whiter of face it seemed, and with something tragic in her dark eyes. She was growing cold and still again, aloof, more like those other Mormon women.

"I understand," he said. "I'm not sorry I spoke. I felt your trouble, whatever it is. . . . Do not retreat into your cold shell, I beg of you. . . . Let me trust you with my secret."

He saw her shake out of the cold apathy. She wavered. He felt an inexplicable sweetness in the power his voice seemed to have upon her. She bowed her head in acquiescence. And Shefford began his story. Did she grow still, like stone, or was that only his vivid imagination? He told her of Venters and Bess—of Lassiter and Jane—of little Fay Larkin—of the romance, and then the tragedy of Surprise Valley.

"So, when my Church disowned me," he concluded, "I conceived the idea of wandering into the wilds of Utah to save Fay Larkin from that cañon prison. It grew to be the best and strongest desire of my life. I think if I could save her that it would save me. I never loved any girl. I can't say that I love Fay Larkin. How could I when I've never seen her—when she's only a dream girl? But I believe if she were to become a reality—a flesh-and-blood girl—that I would love her."

That was more than Shefford had ever confessed to any one, and it stirred him to his depths. Mary bent her head on her hands in strange, stonelike rigidity.

"So here I am in the cañon country," he continued. "Withers tells me it is a country of rainbows, both in the evanescent air and in the changeless stone. Always as a boy there had been for me some haunting promise, some treasure at the foot of the rainbow. I shall expect the curve of a rainbow to lead me down into Surprise Valley. A dreamer, you will call me. But I have had strange dreams come true. . . . Mary, do you think *this* dream will come true?"

She was silent so long that he repeated his question.

"Only—in heaven," she whispered.

He took her reply strangely and a chill crept over him.

"You think my plan to seek to strive, to find—you think that idle, vain?"

"I think it noble. . . . Thank God I've met a man like you!"

"Don't praise me!" he exclaimed, hastily. "Only help me. . . . Mary, will you answer a few little questions, if I swear by my honor I'll never reveal what you tell me?"

"I'll try."

He moistened his lips. Why did she seem so strange, so far away? The hovering shadows made him nervous. Always he had been afraid of the dark. His mood now admitted of unreal fancies.

"Have you ever heard of Fay Larkin?" he asked, very low.

"Yes."

"Was there only one Fay Larkin?"

"Only one."

"Did you—ever see her?"

"Yes," came the faint reply.

He was grateful. How she might be breaking faith with creed or duty! He had not dared to hope so much. All his inner being trembled at the portent of his next query. He had not dreamed it would be so hard to put, or would affect him so powerfully. A warmth, a glow, a happiness pervaded his spirit; and the chill, the gloom were as if they had never been.

"Where is Fay Larkin now?" he asked, huskily.

He bent over her, touched her, leaned close to catch her whisper.

"She is—dead!"

Slowly Shefford rose, with a sickening shock, and then in bitter pain he strode away into the starlight.

CHAPTER 7

SAGO-LILIES

The Indian returned to camp that night, and early the next day, which was Sunday, Withers rode in, accompanied by a stout, gray-bearded personage wearing a long black coat.

"Bishop Kane, this is my new man, John Shefford," said the trader.

Shefford acknowledged the introduction with the respectful courtesy evidently in order, and found himself being studied intently by clear blue eyes. The bishop appeared old, dry, and absorbed in thought; he spoke quaintly, using in every speech some Biblical word or phrase; and he had an air of authority. He asked Shefford to hear him preach at the morning service, and then he went off into the village.

"Guess he liked your looks," remarked Withers.

"He certainly sized me up," replied Shefford.

"Well, what could you expect? Sure I never heard of a deal like this—a handsome young fellow left alone with a lot of pretty Mormon women! You'll understand when you learn to know Mormons. Bishop Kane's a square old chap. Crazy on religion, maybe, but otherwise he's a good fellow. I made the best stand I could for you. The Mormons over at Stone Bridge were huffy because I hadn't consulted them before fetching you over here. If I had, of course you'd never have gotten here. It was Joe

Lake who made it all right with them. Joe's well thought of, and he certainly stood up for you."

"I owe him something, then," replied Shefford. "Hope my obligations don't grow beyond me. Did you leave Joe at Stone Bridge?"

"Yes. He wanted to stay, and I had work there that'll keep him awhile. Shefford, we got news of Shadd—bad news. The half-breed's cutting up rough. His gang shot up some Piutes over here across the line. Then he got run out of Durango a few weeks ago for murder. A posse of cowboys trailed him. But he slipped them. He's a fox. You know he was trailing us here. He left the trail, Nas Ta Bega said. I learned at Stone Bridge that Shadd is well disposed toward Mormons. It takes the Mormons to handle Indians. Shadd knows of this village and that's why he shunted off our trail. But he might hang down in the pass and wait for us. I think I'd better go back to Kayenta alone, across country. You stay here till Joe and the Indian think it safe to leave. You'll be going up on the slope of Navajo to load a pack-train, and from there it may be well to go down West Cañon to Red Lake, and home over the divide, the way you came. Joe'll decide what's best. And you might as well buckle on a gun and get used to it. Sooner or later you'll have to shoot your way through."

Shefford did not respond with his usual enthusiasm, and the omission caused the trader to scrutinize him closely.

"What's the matter?" he queried. "There's no light in your eye today. You look a little shady."

"I didn't rest well last night," replied Shefford. "I'm depressed this morning. But I'll cheer up directly."

"Did you get along with the women?"

"Very well indeed. And I've enjoyed myself. It's a strange, beautiful place."

"Do you like the women?"

"Yes."

"Have you seen much of the Sago Lily?"

"No. I carried her bucket one night—and saw her only once again. I've been with the other women most of the time."

"It's just as well you didn't run often into Mary. Joe's sick over her. I never saw a girl with a face and form to equal hers. There's danger here for any man, Shefford. Even for you who think you've turned your back on the world! Any of these Mormon women may fall in love with you. They *can't* love their husbands. That's how I figure it. Religion holds them, not love. And the peculiar thing is this: they're second, third, or fourth wives, all sealed. That means their husbands are old, have picked them out for youth and physical charms, have chosen the very opposite to their first wives, and then have hidden them here in this lonely hole. . . . Did you ever imagine so terrible a thing?"

"No, Withers, I did not."

"Maybe that's what depressed you. Anyway, my hunch is worth taking. Be as nice as you can, Shefford. Lord knows it would be good for these poor women if every last one of them fell in love with you. That won't hurt them so long as you keep your head. Savvy? Perhaps I seem rough and coarse to a man of your class. Well, that may be. But human nature is human nature. And in this strange and beautiful place you might love an Indian girl, let alone the Sago Lily. That's all. I sure feel better with that load off my conscience. Hope I don't offend."

"No indeed. I thank you, Withers," replied Shefford, with his hand on the trader's shoulder. "You are right to caution me. I seem to be wild—thirsting for adventure—chasing a gleam. In these unstable days I can't answer for my heart. But I can for my honor. These unfortunate women are as safe with me as—as they are with you and Joe."

Withers uttered a blunt laugh.

"See here, son, look things square in the eye. Men of violent, lonely, toilsome lives store up hunger for the love of woman. Love of a *strange* woman, if you want to put it that way. It's nature. It seems all the beautiful young women in Utah are corralled in this valley. When I come over here I feel natural, but I'm not happy. I'd like to make love to—to that flower-faced girl. And I'm not ashamed to own it. I've told Molly, my wife, and she understands. As for Joe, it's much harder for him. Joe never has had a wife or sweetheart. I tell you he's sick, and if I'd stay here a month I'd be sick."

Withers had spoken with fire in his eyes, with grim humor on his lips, with uncompromising brutal truth. What he admitted was astounding to Shefford, but, once spoken, not at all strange. The trader was a man who spoke his inmost thought. And what he said suddenly focused Shefford's mental vision clear and whole upon the appalling significance

of the tragedy of those women, especially of the girl whose life was lonelier, sadder, darker than that of the others.

"Withers, trust me," replied Shefford.

"All right. Make the best of a bad job," said the trader, and went off
about his tasks.

S hefford and Withers attended the morning service, which was held in
the school-house. Exclusive of the children every inhabitant of the
village was there. The women, except the few eldest, were dressed in
white and looked exceedingly well. Manifestly they had bestowed care
upon this Sabbath morning's toilet. One thing surely this dress occasion
brought out, and it was evidence that the Mormon women were not poor,
whatever their misfortunes might be. Jewelry was not wanting, nor fine
lace. And they all wore beautiful wild flowers of a kind unknown to Shefford. He received many a bright smile. He looked for Mary, hoping to
see her face for the first time in the daylight, but she sat far forward and
did not turn. He saw her graceful white neck, the fine lines of her throat,
and her colorless cheek. He recognized her, yet in the light she seemed a
stranger.

The service began with a short prayer and was followed by the singing of a hymn. Nowhere had Shefford heard better music or sweeter voices.
How deeply they affected him! Had any man ever fallen into a stranger
adventure than this? He had only to shut his eyes to believe it all a creation of his fancy—the square log cabin with its red mud between the
chinks and a roof like an Indian hogan—the old bishop in his black coat,
standing solemnly, his hand beating time to the tune—the few old
women, dignified and stately—the many young women, fresh and handsome, lifting their voices.

Shefford listened intently to the bishop's sermon. In some respects it
was the best he had ever heard. In others it was impossible for an intelligent man to regard seriously. It was very long, lasting an hour and a half,
and the parts that were helpful to Shefford came from the experience
and wisdom of a man who had grown old in the desert. The physical
things that had molded characters of iron, the obstacles that only strong,
patient men could have overcome, the making of homes in a wilderness,

showed the greatness of this alien band of Mormons. Shefford conceded greatness to them. But the strange religion—the narrowing down of the world to the soil of Utah, the intimations of prophets on earth who had direct converse with God, the austere self-conscious omnipotence of this old bishop—these were matters that Shefford felt he must understand better, and see more favorably, if he were not to consider them impossible.

Immediately after the service, forgetting that his intention had been to get the long-waited-for look at Mary in the light of the sun, Shefford hurried back to camp and to a secluded spot among the cedars. Strikingly it had come to him that the fault he had found in Gentile religion he now found in the Mormon religion. An old question returned to haunt him—were all religions the same in blindness? As far as he could see, religion existed to uphold the founders of a Church, a creed. The Church of his own kind was a place where narrow men and women went to think of their own salvation. They did not go there to think of others. And now Shefford's keen mind saw something of Mormonism and found it wanting. Bishop Kane was a sincere, good, mistaken man. He believed what he preached, but that would not stand logic. He taught blindness and mostly it appeared to be directed at the women. Was there no religion divorced from power, no religion as good for one man as another, no religion in the spirit of brotherly love? Nas Ta Bega's "Bi Nai" (brother)—that was love, if not religion, and perhaps the one and the other were the same. Shefford kept in mind an intention to ask Nas Ta Bega what he thought of the Mormons.

Later, when opportunity afforded, he did speak to the Indian. Nas Ta Bega threw away his cigarette and made an impressive gesture that conveyed as much sorrow as scorn.

"The first Mormon said God spoke to him and told him to go to a certain place and dig. He went there and found the Book of Mormon. It said follow me, marry many wives, go into the desert and multiply, send your sons out into the world and bring us young women, many young women. And when the first Mormon became strong with many followers he said again: Give to me part of your labor—of your cattle and sheep—of your silver—that I may build me great cathedrals for you to worship in. And I will commune with God and make it right and good that you have more wives. That is what the bishop preached. That is Mormonism."

"Nas Ta Bega, you mean the Mormons are a great and good people blindly following a leader?"

"Yes. And the leader builds for himself—not for them."

"That is not religion. He has no God but himself."

"They have no God. They are blind like the Mokis who have the creeping growths on their eyes. They have no God they can see and hear and feel, who is with them day and night."

It was late in the afternoon when Bishop Kane rode through the camp and halted on his way to speak to Shefford. He was kind and fatherly.

"Young man, are you open to faith?" he questioned, gravely.

"I think I am," replied Shefford, thankful he could answer readily.

"Then come into the fold. You are a lost sheep. 'Away on the desert I heard its cry.' . . . God bless you. Visit me when you ride to Stone Bridge."

He flicked his horse with a cedar branch and trotted away beside the trader, and presently the green-choked neck of the valley hid them from view. Shefford could not have said that he was glad to be left behind, and yet neither was he sorry.

That Sabbath evening as he sat quietly with Nas Ta Bega, watching the sunset gilding the peaks, he was visited by three of the young Mormon women—Ruth, Joan, and Hester. They deliberately sought him and merrily led him off to the village and to the evening service of singing and prayer. Afterward he was surrounded and made much of. He had been popular before, but this was different. When he thoughtfully wended his way campward under the quiet stars he realized that the coming of Bishop Kane had made a subtle change in the women. That change was at first hard to define, but from every point by which he approached it he came to the same conclusion—the bishop had not objected to his presence in the village. The women became natural, free, and unrestrained. A dozen or twenty young and attractive women thrown much into companionship with one man. He might become a Mormon. The idea made him laugh. But upon reflection it was not funny; it sobered him. What a situation! He felt instinctively that he ought to fly from this hidden valley. But he could not have done it, even had he not been in the trader's employ. The thing was provokingly seductive. It was like an Arabian Nights' tale. What would these strange, fatally bound women do? Would any one of them become involved in sweet toils such as were possible to him? He was no fool. Already eyes had flashed and lips had smiled.

A thousand like thoughts whirled through his mind. And when he had calmed down somewhat two things were not lost upon him—an intricate and fascinating situation, with no end to its possibilities, threatened and attracted him—and the certainty that, whatever change the bishop had inaugurated, it had made these poor women happier. The latter fact weighed more with Shefford than fears for himself. His word was given to Withers. He would have felt just the same without having bound himself. Still, in the light of the trader's blunt philosophy, and of his own assurance that he was no fool, Shefford felt it incumbent upon him to accept a belief that there were situations no man could resist without an anchor. The ingenuity of man could not have devised a stranger, a more enticing, a more overpoweringly fatal situation. Fatal in that it could not be left untried! Shefford gave in and clicked his teeth as he let himself go. And suddenly he thought of her whom these bitter women called the Sago Lily.

The regret that had been his returned with thought of her. The saddest disillusion of his life, the keenest disappointment, the strangest pain, would always be associated with her. He had meant to see her face once, clear in the sunlight, so that he could always remember it, and then never go near her again. And now it came to him that if he did see much of her these other women would find him like the stone wall in the valley. Folly! Perhaps it was, but she would be safe, maybe happier. When he decided, it was certain that he trembled.

Then he buried the memory of Fay Larkin.

Next day Shefford threw himself with all the boy left in him into the work and play of the village. He helped the women and made games for the children. And he talked or listened. In the early evening he called on Ruth, chatted awhile, and went on to see Joan, and from her to another. When the valley became shrouded in darkness he went unseen down the path to Mary's lonely home.

She was there, a white shadow against the black. When she replied to his greeting her voice seemed full, broken, eager to express something that would not come. She was happier to see him than she should have been, Shefford thought. He talked, swiftly, eloquently, about whatever he believed would interest her. He stayed long, and finally left, not having seen her face except in pale starlight and shadow; and the strong clasp of her hand remained with him as he went away under the piñons.

Days passed swiftly. Joe Lake did not return. The Indian rode in and out of camp, watered and guarded the pack-burros and the mustangs. Shefford grew strong and active. He made a garden for the women; he cut cords of fire-wood; he dammed the brook and made an irrigation ditch; he learned to love these fatherless children, and they loved him.

In the afternoons there was leisure for him and for the women. He had no favorites, and let the occasion decide what he should do and with whom he should be. They had little parties at the cottages and picnics under the cedars. He rode up and down the valley with Ruth, who could ride a horse as no other girl he had ever seen. He climbed with Hester. He walked with Joan. Mostly he contrived to include several at once in the little excursions, though it was not rare for him to be out alone with one.

It was not a game he was playing. More and more, as he learned to know these young women, he liked them better, he pitied them, he was good for them. It shamed him, hurt him, somehow, to see how they tried to forget something when they were with him. Not improbably a little of it was coquetry, as natural as a laugh to any pretty woman. But that was not what hurt him. It was to see Ruth or Rebecca, as the case might be, full of life and fun, thoroughly enjoying some jest or play, all of a sudden be strangely recalled from the wholesome pleasure of a girl to become a deep and somber woman. The crimes in the name of religion! How he thought of the blood and the ruin laid at the door of religion! He wondered if that were so with Nas Ta Bega's religion, and he meant to find out some day. The women he liked best he imagined the least religious, and they made less effort to attract him.

Every night in the dark he went to Mary's home and sat with her on the porch. He never went inside. For all he knew, his visits were unknown to her neighbors. Still, it did not matter to him if they found out. To her he could talk as he had never talked to any one. She liberated all his thought and fancy. He filled her mind.

As there had been a change in the other women, so was there in Mary; however, it had no relation to the bishop's visit. The time came when Shefford could not but see that she lived and dragged through the long day for the sake of those few hours in the shadow of the stars with him. She seldom spoke. She listened. Wonderful to him—sometimes she laughed—and it seemed the sound was a ghost of childhood pleasure. When he stopped to consider that she might fall in love with him he drove the thought from him. When he realized that his folly had become sweet and that the sweetness imperiously drew him, he likewise cast off that thought. The present was enough. And if he had any treasures of mind and heart he gave them to her.

She never asked him to stay, but she showed that she wanted him to. That made it hard to go. Still, he never stayed late. The moment of parting was like a break. Her good-by was sweet, low music; it lingered on his ear; it bade him come to-morrow night; and it sent him away into the valley to walk under the stars, a man fighting against himself.

One night at parting, as he tried to see her face in the wan glow of a clouded moon, he said:

"I've been trying to find a sago-lily."

"Have you never seen one?" she asked.

"No." He meant to say something with a double meaning, in reference to her face and the name of the flower, but her unconsciousness made him hold his tongue. She was wholly unlike the other women.

"I'll show you where the lilies grow," she said.

"When?"

"To-morrow. Early in the afternoon I'll come to the spring. Then I'll take you."

Next morning Joe Lake returned and imparted news that was perturbing to Shefford. Reports of Shadd had come in to Stone Bridge from different Indian villages; Joe was not inclined to linger long at the camp, and favored taking the trail with the pack-train.

Shefford discovered that he did not want to leave the valley, and the knowledge made him reflective. That morning he did not go into the village, and stayed in camp alone. A depression weighed upon him. It was dispelled, however, early in the afternoon by the sight of a slender figure in white swiftly coming down the path to the spring. He had an appointment with Mary to go to see the sago-lilies; everything else slipped his mind.

Mary wore the long black hood that effectually concealed her face. It made of her a woman, a Mormon woman, and strangely belied the lithe form and the braid of gold hair.

"Good day," she said, putting down her bucket. "Do you still want to go—to see the lilies?"

"Yes," replied Shefford, with a short laugh.

"Can you climb?"

"I'll go where you go."

Then she set off under the cedars and Shefford stalked at her side. He was aware that Nas Ta Bega watched them walk away. This day, so far, at least, Shefford did not feel talkative; and Mary had always been one who mostly listened. They came at length to a place where the wall rose in low, smooth swells, not steep, but certainly at an angle Shefford would not of his own accord have attempted to scale.

Light, quick, and sure as a mountain-sheep Mary went up the first swell to an offset above. Shefford, in amaze and admiration, watched the little moccasins as they flashed and held on to the smooth rock.

When he essayed to follow her he slipped and came to grief. A second attempt resulted in like failure. Then he backed away from the wall, to run forward fast and up the slope, only to slip, halfway up, and fall again.

He made light of the incident, but she was solicitous. When he assured her he was unhurt she said he had agreed to go where she went.

"But I'm not a—a bird," he protested.

"Take off your boots. Then you can climb. When we get over the wall it'll be easy," she said.

In his stocking-feet he had no great difficulty walking up the first bulge of the walls. And from there she led him up the strange waves of wind-worn rock. He could not attend to anything save the red, polished rock under him, and so saw little. The ascent was longer than he would have imagined, and steep enough to make him pant, but at last a huge round summit was reached.

From here he saw down into the valley where the village lay. But for the lazy columns of blue smoke curling up from the piñons the place would have seemed uninhabited. The wall on the other side was about level with the one upon which he stood. Beyond rose other walls and cliffs, up and up to the great towering peaks between which the green-and-black mountain loomed. Facing the other way, Shefford had only a restricted view. There were low crags and smooth stone ridges, between which were aisles green with cedar and piñon. Shefford's companion headed toward one of these, and when he had followed her a few steps he could no longer see down into the valley. The Mormon village where she lived was as if it were lost, and when it vanished Shefford felt a difference. Scarcely had the thought passed when Mary removed the dark hood. Her small head glistened like gold in the sunlight.

Shefford caught up with her and walked at her side, but could not bring himself at once deliberately to look at her. They entered a narrow, low-walled lane where cedars and piñons grew thickly, their fragrance heavy in the warm air, and flowers began to show in the grassy patches.

"This is Indian paint-brush," she said, pointing to little, low, scarlet flowers. A gray sage-bush with beautiful purple blossoms she called purple sage; another bush with yellow flowers she named buck-brush, and there were vermilion cacti and low, flat mounds of lavender daisies which she said had no name. A whole mossy bank was covered with lace-like green leaves and tiny blossoms the color of violets, which she called loco.

"Loco? Is this what makes the horses go crazy when they eat it?" he asked.

"It is, indeed," she said, laughing.

When she laughed it was impossible not to look at her. She walked a little in advance. Her white cheek and temple seemed framed in the gold of her hair. How white her skin! But it was like pearl, faintly veined and flushed. The profile, clear-cut and pure, appeared cold, almost stern. He knew now that she was singularly beautiful, though he had yet to see her full face.

They walked on. Quite suddenly the lane opened out between two rounded bluffs, and Shefford looked down upon a grander and more awe-inspiring scene than ever he had viewed in his dreams.

What appeared to be a green mountainside sloped endlessly down to a plain, and that rolled and billowed away to a boundless region of strangely carved rock. The greatness of the scene could not be grasped in a glance. The slope was long; the plain not as level as it seemed to be on first sight; here and there round, red rocks, isolated and strange, like lonely castles, rose out of the green. Beyond the green all the earth seemed naked, showing smooth, glistening bones. It was a formidable wall of rock that flung itself up in the distance, carved into a thousand cañons and walls and domes and peaks, and there was not a straight nor a broken nor a jagged line in all that wildness. The color low down was red, dark blue, and purple in the clefts, yellow upon the heights, and in the distance rainbow-hued. A land of curves and color!

Shefford uttered an exclamation.

"That's Utah," said Mary. "I come often to sit here. You see that winding blue line. There. . . . That's San Juan Cañon. And the other dark line, that's Escalante Cañon. They wind down into this great purple chasm—'way over here to the left—and that's the Grand Cañon. They say not even the Indians have been in there."

Shefford had nothing to say. The moment was one of subtle and vital assimilation. Such places as this to be unknown to men! What strength, what wonder, what help, what glory, just to sit there an hour, slowly and appallingly to realize! Something came to Shefford from the distance, out of the purple cañons and from those dim, wind-worn peaks. He resolved to come here to this promontory again and again, alone and in humble spirit, and learn to know why he had been silenced, why peace pervaded his soul.

It was with this emotion upon him that he turned to find his companion watching him. Then for the first time he saw her face fully, and was thrilled that chance had reserved the privilege for this moment. It was a girl's face he saw, flower-like, lovely and pure as a Madonna's, and strangely, tragically sad. The eyes were large, dark gray, the color of the sage. They were as clear as the air which made distant things close, and yet they seemed full of shadows, like a ruffled pool under midnight stars. They disturbed him. Her mouth had the sweet curves and redness of youth, but it showed bitterness, pain, and repression.

"Where are the sago-lilies?" he asked, suddenly.

"Farther down. It's too cold up here for them. Come," she said.

He followed her down a winding trail—down and down till the

green plain rose to blot out the scrawled wall of rock, down into a verdant cañon where a brook made swift music over stones, where the air was sultry and hot, laden with the fragrant breath of flower and leaf. This was a cañon of summer, and it bloomed.

The girl bent and plucked something from the grass.

"Here's a white lily," she said. "There are three colors. The yellow and pink ones are deeper down in the cañons."

Shefford took the flower and regarded it with great interest. He had never seen such an exquisite thing. It had three large petals, curving cuplike, of a whiteness purer than new-fallen snow, and a heart of rich, warm gold. Its fragrance was so faint as to be almost indistinguishable, yet of a haunting, unforgettable sweetness. And even while he looked at it the petals drooped and their whiteness shaded and the gold paled. In a moment the flower was wilted.

"I don't like to pluck the lilies," said Mary. "They die so swiftly."

Shefford saw the white flowers everywhere in the open, sunny places along the brook. They swayed with stately grace in the slow, warm wind. They seemed like three-pointed stars shining out of the green. He bent over one with a particularly lofty stem, and after a close survey of it he rose to look at her face. His action was plainly one of comparison. She laughed and said it was foolish for the women to call her the Sago Lily. She had no coquetry; she spoke as she would have spoken of the stones at her feet; she did not know that she was beautiful. Shefford imagined there was some resemblance in her to the lily—the same whiteness, the same rich gold, and, more striking than either, a strange, rare quality of beauty, of life, intangible as something fleeting, the spirit that had swiftly faded from the plucked flower. Where had the girl been born—what had her life been? Shefford was intensely curious about her. She seemed as different from any other women he had known as this rare cañon lily was different from the tame flowers at home.

On the return up the slope she outstripped him. She climbed lightly and tirelessly. When he reached her upon the promontory there was a stain of red in her cheeks and her expression had changed.

"Let's go back up over the rocks," she said. "I've not climbed for—for so long."

"I'll go where you go," he replied.

Then she was off, and he followed. She took to the curves of the bare rocks and climbed. He sensed a spirit released in her. It was so strange, so keen, so wonderful to be with her, and when he did catch her he feared to speak lest he break this mood. Her eyes grew dark and daring, and often she stopped to look away across the wavy sea of stones to something beyond the great walls. When they got high the wind blew her hair loose and it flew out, a golden stream, with the sun bright upon it. He saw that she changed her direction, which had been in line with the two peaks, and now she climbed toward the heights. They came to more difficult ascent, where the stone still held to the smooth curves, yet was marked by steep bulges and slants and crevices. Here she became a wild thing. She ran, she leaped, she would have left him far behind had he not called. Then she appeared to remember him and waited.

Her face had now lost its whiteness; it was flushed, rosy, warm.

"Where—did you—ever learn—to run over rocks—this way?" he panted.

"All my life I've climbed," she said. "Ah! it's so good to be up on the walls again—to feel the wind—to see!"

Thereafter he kept close to her, no matter what the effort. He would not miss a moment of her, if he could help it. She was wonderful. He imagined she must be like an Indian girl, or a savage who loved the lofty places and the silence. When she leaped she uttered a strange, low, sweet cry of wildness and exultation. Shefford guessed she was a girl freed from her prison, forgetting herself, living again youthful hours. Still she did not forget him. She waited for him at the bad places, lent him a strong hand, and sometimes let it stay long in his clasp. Tireless and agile, sure-footed as a goat, fleet and wild she leaped and climbed and ran until Shefford marveled at her. This adventure was indeed fulfilment of a dream. Perhaps she might lead him to the treasure at the foot of the rainbow. But that thought, sad with memory daring forth from its grave, was irrevocably linked with a girl who was dead. He could not remember her, in the presence of this wonderful creature who was as strange as she was beautiful. When Shefford reached for the brown hand stretched forth to help him in a leap, when he felt its strong clasp, the youth and vitality and life of it, he had the fear of a man who was running toward a precipice and who could not draw back. This was a climb, a lark, a wild race to the Mormon girl, bound now in the village, and by the very free-dom of it she betrayed her bonds. To Shefford it was also a wild race, but toward one sure goal he dared not name.

They went on, and at length, hand in hand, even where no steep step or wide fissure gave reason for the clasp. But she seemed unconscious. They were nearing the last height, a bare eminence, when she broke from him and ran up the smooth stone. When he surmounted it she was standing on the very summit, her arms wide, her full breast heaving, her slender body straight as an Indian's, her hair flying in the wind and blazing in the sun. She seemed to embrace the west, to reach for some-thing afar, to offer herself to the wind and distance. Her face was scarlet from the exertion of the climb, and her broad brow was moist. Her eyes had the piercing light of an eagle's, though now they were dark. Shef-ford instinctively grasped the essence of this strange spirit, primitive and wild. She was not the woman who had met him at the spring. She had dropped some side of her with that Mormon hood, and now she stood totally strange.

She belonged up here, he divined. She was a part of that wildness. She must have been born and brought up in loneliness, where the wind blew and the peaks loomed and silence held dominion. The sinking sun touched the rim of the distant wall, and as if in parting regret shone with renewed golden fire. And the girl was crowned as with a glory.

Shefford loved her then. Realizing it, he thought he might have loved her before, but that did not matter when he was certain of it now. He trembled a little, fearfully, though without regret. Everything pertain-ing to his desert experience had been strange—this the strangest of all.

The sun sank swiftly, and instantly there was a change in the golden light. Quickly it died out. The girl changed as swiftly. She seemed to remember herself, and sat down as if suddenly weary. Shefford went closer and seated himself beside her.

"The sun has set. We must go," she said. But she made no movement.

"Whenever you are ready," replied he.

Just as the blaze had died out of her eyes, so the flush faded out of her face. The whiteness stole back, and with it the sadness. He had to bite his tongue to keep from telling her what he felt, to keep from pouring out a thousand questions. But the privilege of having seen her, of having been with her when she had forgotten herself—that he believed was enough. It had been wonderful; it had made him love her. But it need not add to the tragedy of her life, whatever that was. He tried to eliminate himself. And he watched her.

Her eyes were fixed upon the gold-rimmed ramparts of the distant wall in the west. Plain it was how she loved that wild upland. And there seemed to be some haunting memory of the past in her gaze—some happy part of life, agonizing to think of now.

"We must go," she said, and rose.

Shefford rose to accompany her. She looked at him, and her haunting eyes seemed to want him to know that he had helped her to forget the present, to remember girlhood, and that somehow she would always associate a wonderful happy afternoon with him. He divined that her silence then was a Mormon seal on her lips.

"Mary, this has been the happiest, the best, the most revealing day of my life," he said, simply.

Swiftly, as if startled, she turned and faced down the slope. At the top of the wall above the village she put on the dark hood, and with it that somber something which was Mormon.

Twilight had descended into the valley, and shadows were so thick Shefford had difficulty in finding Mary's bucket. He filled it at the spring, and made offer to carry it home for her, which she declined.

"You'll come to-night—later?" she asked.

"Yes," he replied, hurriedly promising. Then he watched her white form slowly glide down the path to disappear in the shadows.

Nas Ta Bega and Joe were busy at the campfire. Shefford joined them. This night he was uncommunicative. Joe peered curiously at him in the flare of the blaze. Later, after the meal, when Shefford appeared restless and strode to and fro, Joe spoke up gruffly:

"Better hang round camp to-night."

Shefford heard, but did not heed. Nevertheless, the purport of the remark, which was either jealousy or admonition, haunted him with the possibility of its meaning.

He walked away from the campfire, under the dark piñons, out into the starry open; and every step was hard to take, unless it pointed toward the home of the girl whose beauty and sadness and mystery had bewitched him. After what seemed hours he took the well-known path toward her cabin, and then every step seemed lighter. He divined he was rushing to some fate—he knew not what.

The porch was in shadow. He peered in vain for the white form against the dark background. In the silence he seemed to hear his heart-beats thick and muffled.

Some distance down the path he heard the sound of hoofs. With-drawing into the gloom of a cedar, he watched. Soon he made out moving horses with riders. They filed past him to the number of half a score. Like a flash of fire the truth burned him. Mormons come for one of those mysterious night visits to sealed wives!

Shefford stalked far down the valley, into the lonely silence and the night shadows under the walls.

CHAPTER 8

THE HOGAN OF
NAS TA BEGA

The home of Nas Ta Bega lay far up the cedared slope, with the craggy yellow cliffs and the black cañons and the pine-fringed top of Navajo Mountain behind, and to the fore the vast, rolling descent of cedar groves and sage flats and sandy washes. No dim, dark range made bold outline along the horizon; the stretch of gray and purple and green extended to the blue line of sky.

Down the length of one sage level Shefford saw a long lane where the brush and the grass had been beaten flat. This, the Navajo said, was a track where the young braves had raced their mustangs and had striven for supremacy before the eyes of maidens and the old people of the tribe.

"Nas Ta Bega, did you ever race here?" asked Shefford.

"I am a chief by birth. But I was stolen from my home, and now I cannot ride well enough to race the braves of my tribe," the Indian replied, bitterly.

In another place Joe Lake halted his horse and called Shefford's attention to a big yellow rock lying along the trail. And then he spoke in Navajo to the Indian.

"I've heard of this stone—Isende Aha," said Joe, after Nas Ta Bega had spoken. "Get down, and let's see."

Shefford dismounted, but the Indian kept his seat in the saddle.

Joe placed a big hand on the stone and tried to move it. According to Shefford's eye measurement the stone was nearly oval, perhaps three feet high, by a little over two in width. Joe threw off his sombrero, took a deep breath, and, bending over, clasped the stone in his arms. He was an exceedingly heavy and powerful man, and it was plain to Shefford that he meant to lift the stone if that were possible. Joe's broad shoulders strained, flattened; his arms bulged, his joints cracked, his neck corded, and his face turned black. By gigantic effort he lifted the stone and moved it about six inches. Then as he released his hold he fell, and when he sat up his face was wet with sweat.

"Try it," he said to Shefford, with his lazy smile. "See if you can heave it."

Shefford was strong, and there had been a time when he took pride in his strength. Something in Joe's supreme effort and in the gloom of the Indian's eyes made Shefford curious about this stone. He bent over and grasped it as Joe had done. He braced himself and lifted with all his power, until a red blur obscured his sight and shooting stars seemed to explode in his head. But he could not even stir the stone.

"Shefford, maybe you'll be able to heft it some day," observed Joe. Then he pointed to the stone and addressed Nas Ta Bega.

The Indian shook his head and spoke for a moment.

"This is the Isende Aha of the Navajos," explained Joe. "The young braves are always trying to carry this stone. As soon as one of them can carry it he is a man. He who carries it farthest is the biggest man. And just so soon as any Indian can no longer lift it he is old. Nas Ta Bega says the stone has been carried two miles in his lifetime. His own father carried it the length of six steps."

"Well! It's plain to me that I am not a man," said Shefford, "or else I am old."

Joe Lake drawled his lazy laugh and, mounting, rode up the trail. But Shefford lingered beside the Indian.

"Bi Nai," said Nas Ta Bega, "I am a chief of my tribe, but I have never been a man. I never lifted that stone. See what the pale-face education has done for the Indian!"

The Navajo's bitterness made Shefford thoughtful. Could greater injury be done to man than this—to rob him of his heritage of strength?

Joe drove the bobbing pack-train of burros into the cedars where the smoke of the hogans curled upward, and soon the whistling of mustangs, the barking of dogs, the bleating of sheep, told of his reception. And presently Shefford was in the midst of an animated scene. Great, woolly, fierce dogs, like wolves, ran out to meet the visitors. Sheep and goats were everywhere, and little lambs scarcely able to walk, with others frisky and frolicsome. There were pure-white lambs, and some that appeared to be painted, and some so beautiful with their fleecy white all except black faces or ears or tails or feet. They ran right under Nack-yal's legs and bumped against Shefford, and kept bleating their thin-piped welcome. Under the cedars surrounding the several hogans were mustangs that took Shefford's eye. He saw an iron-gray with white mane and tail sweeping to the ground; and a fiery black, wilder than any other beast he had ever seen; and a pinto as wonderfully painted as the little lambs; and, most striking of all, a pure, cream-colored mustang with grace and fine lines and beautiful mane and tail, and, strange to see, eyes as blue as azure. This albino mustang came right up to Shefford, an action in singular contrast with that of the others, and showed a tame and friendly spirit toward him and Nack-yal. Indeed, Shefford had reason to feel ashamed of Nack-yal's temper or jealousy.

The first Indians to put in an appearance were a flock of children, half naked, with tangled manes of raven-black hair and skin like gold bronze. They appeared bold and shy by turns. Then a little, sinewy man, old and beaten and gray, came out of the principal hogan. He wore a blanket round his bent shoulders. His name was Hosteen Doetin, and it meant gentle man. His fine, old, wrinkled face lighted with a smile of kindly interest. His squaw followed him, and she was as venerable as he. Shefford caught a glimpse of the shy, dark Glen Naspa, Nas Ta Bega's sister, but she did not come out. Other Indians appeared, coming from adjacent hogans.

Nas Ta Bega turned the mustangs loose among those Shefford had noticed, and presently there rose a snorting, whistling, kicking, plunging mêlée. A cloud of dust hid them, and then a thudding of swift hoofs told of a run through the cedars. Joe Lake began picking over stacks of goat-skins and bags of wool that were piled against the hogan.

"Reckon we'll have one grand job packing out this load," he growled. "It's not so heavy, but awkward to pack."

It developed, presently, from talk with the old Navajo, that this pile was only a half of the load to be packed to Kayenta, and the other half was round the corner of the mountain in the camp of Piutes. Hosteen Doetin said he would send to the camp and have the Piutes bring their share over. The suggestion suited Joe, who wanted to save his burros as much as possible. Accordingly, a messenger was despatched to the Piute camp. And Shefford, with time on his hands and poignant memory to combat, decided to recall his keen interest in the Navajo, and learn, if possible, what the Indian's life was like. What would a day of his natural life be?

In the gray of dawn, when the hush of the desert night still lay deep over the land, the Navajo stirred in his blanket and began to chant to the morning light. It began very soft and low, a strange, broken murmur, like the music of a brook, and as it swelled that weird and mournful tone was slowly lost in one of hope and joy. The Indian's soul was coming out of night, blackness, the sleep that resembled death, into the day, the light that was life.

Then he stood in the door of his hogan, his blanket around him, and faced the east.

Night was lifting out of the clefts and ravines; the rolling cedar ridges and the sage flats were softly gray, with thin veils like smoke mysteriously rising and vanishing; the colorless rocks were changing. A long, horizon-wide gleam of light, rosiest in the center, lay low down in the east and momentarily brightened. One by one the stars in the deep-blue sky paled and went out and the blue dome changed and lightened. Night had vanished on invisible wings and silence broke to the music of a mocking-bird. The rose in the east deepened; a wisp of cloud turned gold; dim distant mountains showed dark against the red; and low down in a notch a rim of fire appeared. Over the soft ridges and valleys crept a wondrous transfiguration. It was as if every blade of grass, every leaf of sage, every twig of cedar, the flowers, the trees, the rocks came to life at sight of the sun. The red disk rose, and a golden fire burned over the glowing face of that lonely waste.

The Navajo, dark, stately, inscrutable, faced the sun—his god. This was his Great Spirit. The desert was his mother, but the sun was his life. To the keeper of the winds and rains, to the master of light, to the maker of fire, to the giver of life the Navajo sent up his prayer:

Of all the good things of the Earth
  let me always have plenty.
Of all the beautiful things of the Earth
  let me always have plenty.
Peacefully let my horses go and peacefully
  let my sheep go.
God of the Heavens, give me
  many sheep and horses.
God of the Heavens, help me to talk straight.
Goddess of the Earth, my Mother,
  let me walk straight.
Now all is well, now all is well,
  now all is well, now all is well.

Hope and faith were his.

A chief would be born to save the vanishing tribe of Navajos. A bride would rise from a wind—kiss of the lilies in the moonlight.

He drank from the clear, cold spring bubbling from under mossy rocks. He went into the cedars, and the tracks in the trails told him of the visitors of night. His mustangs whistled to him from the ridge-tops, standing clear with heads up and manes flying, and then trooped down through the sage. The shepherd-dogs, guardians of the flocks, barked him a welcome, and the sheep bleated and the lambs pattered round him.

In the hogan by the warm, red fire his women baked his bread and cooked his meat. And he satisfied his hunger. Then he took choice meat to the hogan of a sick relative, and joined in the song and the dance and the prayer that drove away the evil spirit of illness. Down in the valley, in a sandy, sunny place, was his corn-field, and here he turned in the water from the ditch, and worked awhile, and went his contented way.

He loved his people, his women, and his children. To his son he said: "Be bold and brave. Grow like the pine. Work and ride and play that you may be strong. Talk straight. Love your brother. Give half to your friend. Honor your mother that you may honor your wife. Pray and listen to your gods."

Then with his gun and his mustang he climbed the slope of the mountain. He loved the solitude, but he was never alone. There were voices on the wind and steps on his trail. The lofty pine, the lichened rock, the tiny bluebell, the seared crag—all whispered their secrets. For him their spirits spoke. In the morning light Old Stone Face, the mountain, was a red god calling him to the chase. He was a brother of the eagle, at home on the heights where the winds swept and the earth lay revealed below.

In the golden afternoon, with the warm sun on his back and the blue cañons at his feet, he knew the joy of doing nothing. He did not need rest, for he was never tired. The sage-sweet breath of the open was thick in his nostrils, the silence that had so many whisperings was all about him, the loneliness of the wild was his. His falcon eye saw mustang and sheep, the puff of dust down on the cedar level, the Indian riding on a distant ridge, the gray walls, and the blue clefts. Here was home, still free, still wild, still untainted. He saw with the eyes of his ancestors. He felt them around him. They had gone into the elements from which their voices came on the wind. They were the watchers on his trails.

At sunset he faced the west, and this was his prayer:

Great Spirit, God of my Fathers,
Keep my horses in the night.
Keep my sheep in the night.
Keep my family in the night.
Let me wake to the day.
Let me be worthy of the light.
Now all is well, now all is well,
Now all is well, now all is well.

And he watched the sun go down and the gold sink from the peaks and the red die out of the west and the gray shadows creep out of the cañons to meet the twilight and the slow, silent, mysterious approach of night with its gift of stars.

Night fell. The white stars blinked. The wind sighed in the cedars. The sheep bleated. The shepherd-dogs bayed the mourning coyotes. And the Indian lay down in his blankets with his dark face tranquil in the starlight. All was well in his lonely world. Phantoms hovered, illness lingered, injury and pain and death were there, the shadow of a strange white hand flitted across the face of the moon—but now all was well— the Navajo had prayed to the god of his Fathers. Now all was well!

And this, thought Shefford in revolt, was what the white man had killed in the Indian tribes, was reaching out now to kill in this wild remnant of the Navajos. The padre, the trapper, the trader, the prospector, and the missionary—so the white man had come, some of him good, no doubt, but more of him evil; and the young brave learned a thirst that could never be quenched at the cold, sweet spring of his forefathers, and the young maiden burned with a fever in her blood, and lost the sweet, strange, wild fancies of her tribe.

Joe Lake came to Shefford and said, "Withers told me you had a mix-up with a missionary at Red Lake."

"Yes, I regret to say," replied Shefford.

"About Glen Naspa?"

"Yes, Nas Ta Bega's sister."

"Withers just mentioned it. Who was the missionary?"

"Willetts, so Presbrey, the trader, said."

"What'd he look like?"

Shefford recalled the smooth, brown face, the dark eyes, the weak chin, the mild expression, and the soft, lax figure of the missionary.

"Can't tell by what you said," went on Joe. "But I'll bet a peso to a horse-hair that's the fellow who's been here. Old Hosteen Doetin just told me. First visits he ever had from the priest with the long gown.

That's what he called the missionary. These old fellows will never forget what's come down from father to son about the Spanish padres. Well, anyway, Willetts has been here twice after Glen Naspa. The old chap is impressed, but he doesn't want to let the girl go. I'm inclined to think Glen Naspa would as lief go as stay. She may be a Navajo, but she's a girl. She won't talk much."

"Where's Nas Ta Bega?" asked Shefford.

"He rode off somewhere yesterday. Perhaps to the Piute camp. These Indians are slow. They may take a week to pack that load over here. But if Nas Ta Bega or some one doesn't come with a message to-day I'll ride over there myself."

"Joe, what do you think about this missionary?" queried Shefford, bluntly.

"Reckon there's not much to think, unless you see him or find out something. I heard of Willetts before Withers spoke of him. He's friendly with Mormons. I understand he's worked for Mormon interests, some-way or other. That's on the quiet. Savvy? This matter of him coming after Glen Naspa, reckon that's all right. The missionaries all go after the young people. What'd be the use to try to convert the old Indians? No, the missionary's work is to educate the Indian, and, of course, the younger he is the better."

"You approve of the missionary?"

"Shefford, if you understood a Mormon you wouldn't ask that. Did you ever read or hear of Jacob Hamblin? . . . Well, he was a Mormon missionary among the Navajos. The Navajos were as fierce as Apaches till Hamblin worked among them. He made them friendly to the white man."

"That doesn't prove he made converts of them," replied Shefford, still bluntly.

"No. For the matter of that, Hamblin let religion alone. He made presents, then traded with them, then taught them useful knowledge. Mormon or not, Shefford, I'll admit this: a good man, strong with his body, and learned in ways with his hands, with some knowledge of med-icine, can better the condition of these Indians. But just as soon as he begins to preach his religion, then his influence wanes. That's natural. These heathen have their ideals, their gods."

"Which the white man should leave them!" replied Shefford, feelingly.

"That's a matter of opinion. But don't let's argue. . . . Willetts is after Glen Naspa. And if I know Indian girls he'll persuade her to go to his school."

"Persuade her!" Then Shefford broke off and related the incident that had occurred at Red Lake.

"Reckon any means justifies the end," replied Joe, imperturbably. "Let him talk love to her or rope her or beat her, so long as he makes a Christian of her."

Shefford felt a hot flush and had difficulty in controlling himself. From this single point of view the Mormon was impossible to reason with.

"That, too, is a matter of opinion. We won't discuss it," continued Shefford. "But—if old Hosteen Doetin objects to the girl leaving, and if Nas Ta Bega does the same, won't that end the matter?"

"Reckon not. The end of the matter is Glen Naspa. If she wants to go she'll go."

Shefford thought best to drop the discussion. For the first time he had occasion to be repelled by something in this kind and genial Mormon, and he wanted to forget it. Just as he had never talked about men to the sealed wives in the hidden valley, so he could not talk of women to Joe Lake.

Nas Ta Bega did not return that day, but next morning a messenger came calling Lake to the Piute camp. Shefford spent the morning high on the slope, learning more with every hour in the silence and loneliness that he was stronger of soul than he had dared to hope, and that the added pain which had come to him could be borne.

Upon his return toward camp, in the cedar grove, he caught sight of Glen Naspa with a white man. They did not see him. When Shefford recognized Willetts an embarrassment as well as an instinct made him halt and step into a bushy, low-branched cedar. It was not his intention to spy on them. He merely wanted to avoid a meeting. But the missionary's hand on the girl's arm, and her uplifted head, her pretty face, strange, intent, troubled, struck Shefford with an unusual and irresistible curiosity. Willetts was talking earnestly; Glen Naspa was listening intently.

Shefford watched long enough to see that the girl loved the missionary, and that he reciprocated or was pretending. His manner scarcely savored of pretense, Shefford concluded, as he slipped away under the trees.

He did not go at once into camp. He felt troubled, and wished that he had not encountered the two. His duty in the matter, of course, was to tell Nas Ta Bega what he had seen. Upon reflection Shefford decided to give the missionary the benefit of a doubt; and if he really cared for the Indian girl, and admitted or betrayed it, to think all the better of him for the fact. Glen Naspa was certainly pretty enough, and probably lovable enough, to please any lonely man in this desert. The pain and the yearning in Shefford's heart made him lenient. He had to fight himself—not to forget, for that was impossible—but to keep rational and sane when a white flower-like face haunted him and a voice called.

The cracking of hard hoofs on stones caused him to turn toward camp, and as he emerged from the cedar grove he saw three Indian horsemen ride into the cleared space before the hogans. They were superbly mounted and well armed, and impressed him as being different from Navajos. Perhaps they were Piutes. They dismounted and led the mustangs down to the pool below the spring. Shefford saw another mustang, standing bridle down and carrying a pack behind the saddle. Some squaws with children hanging behind their skirts were standing at the door of Hosteen Doetin's hogan. Shefford glanced in to see Glen Naspa, pale, quiet, almost sullen. Willetts stood with his hands spread. The old Navajo's seamed face worked convulsively as he tried to lift his bent form to some semblance of dignity, and his voice rolled out, sonorously: "Me no savvy Jesus Christ! Me hungry! . . . Me no eat Jesus Christ!"

Shefford drew back as if he had received a blow. That had been Hosteen Doetin's reply to the importunities of the missionary. The old Navajo could work no longer. His sons were gone. His squaw was worn out. He had no one save Glen Naspa to help him. She was young, strong. He was hungry. What was the white man's religion to him?

With long, swift stride Shefford entered the hogan. Willetts, seeing him, did not look so mild as Shefford had him pictured in memory, nor did he appear surprised. Shefford touched Hosteen Doetin's shoulder and said, "Tell me."

The aged Navajo lifted a shaking hand.

"Me no savvy Jesus Christ! Me hungry! . . . Me no eat Jesus Christ!"

Shefford then made signs that indicated the missionary's intention to take the girl away.

"Him come—big talk—Jesus—all Jesus. . . . Me no want Glen Naspa go," replied the Indian.

Shefford turned to the missionary.

"Willetts, is he a relative of the girl?"

"There's some blood tie, I don't know what. But it's not close," replied Willetts.

"Then don't you think you'd better wait till Nas Ta Bega returns? He's her brother."

"What for?" demanded Willetts. "That Indian may be gone a week. She's willing to go."

Shefford looked at the girl.

"Glen Naspa, do you want to go?"

She was shy, ashamed, and silent, but manifestly willing to accompany the missionary. Shefford pondered a moment. How he hoped Nas Ta Bega would come back! It was thought of the Indian that made Shefford stubborn. What his stand ought to be was hard to define, unless he answered to impulse; and here in the wilds he had become imbued with the idea that his impulses and instincts were no longer false.

"Willetts, what do you want with the girl?" queried Shefford, coolly, and at the question he seemed to find himself. He peered deliberately and searchingly into the other's face. The missionary's gaze shifted and a tinge of red crept up from under his collar.

"Absurd thing to ask a missionary!" he burst out, impatiently.

"Do you care for Glen Naspa?"

"I care as God's disciple—who cares to save the soul of heathen," he replied, with the lofty tone of prayer.

"Has Glen Naspa no—no other interest in you—except to be taught religion?"

The missionary's face flamed, and his violent tremor showed that under his exterior there was a different man.

"What right have you to question me?" he demanded. "You're an adventurer—an outcast. I've my duty here. I'm a missionary with Church and state and government behind me."

"Yes, I'm an outcast," replied Shefford, bitterly. "And you may be all you say. But we're alone now out here on the desert. And this girl's brother is absent. You haven't answered me yet. . . . Is there anything between you and Glen Naspa except religion?"

"No, you insulting beggar!"

Shefford had forced the reply that he had expected and which damned the missionary beyond any consideration.

"Willetts, you are a liar!" said Shefford, steadily.

"And what are you?" cried Willetts, in shrill fury. "I've heard all about you. Heretic! Atheist! Driven from your Church! Hated and scorned for your blasphemy!"

Then he gave way to ungovernable rage, and cursed Shefford as a religious fanatic might have cursed the most debased of sinners. Shefford heard with the blood beating, strangling the pulse in his ears. Somehow this missionary had learned his secret—most likely from the Mormons in Stone Bridge. And the terms of disgrace were coals of fire upon Shefford's head. Strangely, however, he did not bow to them, as had been his humble act in the past, when his calumniators had arraigned and flayed him. Passion burned in him now, and hate, for the first time in his life, made a tiger of him. And these raw emotions, new to him, were difficult to control.

"You can't take the girl," he replied, when the other had ceased. "Not without her brother's consent."

"I will take her!"

Shefford threw him out of the hogan and strode after him. Willetts had stumbled. When he straightened up he was white and shaken. He groped for the bridle of his horse while keeping his eyes upon Shefford, and when he found it he whirled quickly, mounted, and rode off. Shefford saw him halt a moment under the cedars to speak with the three strange Indians, and then he galloped away. It came to Shefford then that he had been unconscious of the last strained moment of that encounter. He seemed all cold, tight, locked, and was amazed to find his hand on his gun. Verily the wild environment had liberated strange instincts and impulses, which he had answered. That he had no regrets proved how he had changed.

Shefford heard the old woman scolding. Peering into the hogan, he saw Glen Naspa flounce sullenly down, for all the world like any other thwarted girl. Hosteen Doetin came out and pointed down the slope at the departing missionary.

"Heap talk Jesus—all talk—all Jesus!" he exclaimed, contemptuously. Then he gave Shefford a hard rap on the chest. "Small talk—heap man!"

The matter appeared to be adjusted for the present. But Shefford felt that he had made a bitter enemy, and perhaps a powerful one.

He prepared and ate his supper alone that evening, for Joe Lake and Nas Ta Bega did not put in an appearance. He observed that the three strange Indians, whom he took for Piutes, kept to themselves, and, so far as he knew, had no intercourse with any one at the camp. This would not have seemed unusual, considering the taciturn habit of Indians, had he not remembered seeing Willetts speak to the trio. What had he to do with them? Shefford was considering the situation with vague doubts when, to his relief, the three strangers rode off into the twilight. Then he went to bed.

He was awakened by violence. It was the gray hour before dawn. Dark forms knelt over him. A cloth pressed down hard over his mouth. Strong hands bound it while other strong hands held him. He could not cry out. He could not struggle. A heavy weight, evidently a man, held down his feet. Then he was rolled over, securely bound, and carried, to be thrown like a sack over the back of a horse.

All this happened so swiftly as to be bewildering. He was too astounded to be frightened. As he hung head downward he saw the legs of a horse and a dim trail. A stirrup swung to and fro, hitting him in the face. He began to feel exceedingly uncomfortable, with a rush of blood to his head, and cramps in his arms and legs. This kept on and grew worse for what seemed a long time. Then the horse was stopped and a rude hand tumbled him to the ground. Again he was rolled over on his face. Strong fingers plucked at his clothes, and he believed he was being searched. His captors were as silent as if they had been dumb. He felt when they took his pocketbook and his knife and all that he had. Then they cut, tore, and stripped off all his clothing. He was lifted, carried a few steps, and dropped upon what seemed a soft, low mound, and left lying there, still tied and naked. Shefford heard the rustle of sage and the dull thud of hoofs as his assailants went away.

His first sensation was one of immeasurable relief. He had not been murdered. Robbery was nothing. And though roughly handled, he had not been hurt. He associated the assault with the three strange visitors of the preceding day. Still, he had no proof of that. Not the slightest clue remained to help him ascertain who had attacked him.

It might have been a short while or a long one, his mind was so filled with growing conjectures, but a time came when he felt cold. As he lay face down, only his back felt cold at first. He was grateful that he had not been thrown upon the rocks. The ground under him appeared soft, spongy, and gave somewhat as he breathed. He had really sunk down a little in this pile of soft earth. The day was not far off, as he could tell by the brightening of the gray. He began to suffer with the cold, and then slowly he seemed to freeze and grow numb. In an effort to roll over upon his back he discovered that his position, or his being bound, or the numbness of his muscles was responsible for the fact that he could not move. Here was a predicament. It began to look serious. What would a few hours of the powerful sun do to his uncovered skin? Somebody would trail and find him; still, he might not be found soon.

He saw the sky lighten, turn rosy and then gold. The sun shone upon him, but some time elapsed before he felt its warmth. All of a sudden a pain, like a sting, shot through his shoulder. He could not see what caused it; probably a bee. Then he felt another upon his leg, and about simultaneously with it a tiny, fiery stab in his side. A sickening sensation pervaded his body, slowly moving, as if poison had entered the blood of his veins. Then a puncture, as from a hot wire, entered the skin of his breast. Unmistakably it was a bite. By dint of great effort he twisted his head to see a big red ant on his breast. Then he heard a faint sound, so exceedingly faint that he could not tell what it was like. But presently his strained ears detected a low, swift, rustling, creeping sound, like the slipping rattle of an infinite number of tiny bits of moving gravel. Then it was a sound like the seeping of wind-blown sand. Several hot bites occurred at once. And then with his head twisted he saw a red stream of ants pour out of the mound and spill over his quivering flesh.

In an instant he realized his position. He had been dropped intentionally upon an ant-heap, which had sunk with his weight, wedging him between the crusts. At the mercy of those terrible desert ants! A frantic effort to roll out proved futile, as did another and another. His violent muscular contractions infuriated the ants, and in an instant he was writhing in pain so horrible and so unendurable that he nearly fainted. But he was too strong to faint suddenly. A bath of vitriol, a stripping of his skin and red embers of fire thrown upon raw flesh, could not have equaled this. There was fury in the bites and poison in the fangs of these ants. Was this an Indian's brutal trick or was it the missionary's revenge? Shefford realized that it would kill him soon. He sweat what seemed blood, although perhaps the blood came from the bites. A strange, hollow, buzzing roar filled his ears, and it must have been the pouring of the angry ants from their mound.

Then followed a time that was hell—worse than fire, for fire would have given merciful death—agony under which his physical being began spasmodically to jerk and retch—and his eyeballs turned and his breast caved in.

A cry rang through the roar in his ears. "Bi Nai! Bi Nai!"

His fading sight seemed to shade round the dark face of Nas Ta Bega.

Then powerful hands dragged him from the mound, through the grass and sage, rolled him over and over, and brushed his burning skin with strong, swift sweep.

CHAPTER 9

IN THE DESERT CRUCIBLE

That hard experience was but the beginning of many cruel trials for John Shefford.

He never knew who his assailants were, nor their motive other than robbery; and they had gotten little, for they had not found the large sum of money sewed in the lining of his coat. Joe Lake declared it was Shadd's work, and the Mormon showed the stern nature that lay hidden under his habitual mild manner. Nas Ta Bega shook his head and would not tell what he thought. But a somber fire burned in his eyes.

The three started with a heavily laden pack-train and went down the mountain slope into West Cañon. The second day they were shot at from the rim walls. Lake was wounded, hindering the swift flight necessary to escape deeper into the cañon. Here they hid for days, while the Mormon recovered and the Indian took stealthy trips to try to locate the enemy. Lack of water and grass for the burros drove them on. They climbed out of a side cañon, losing several burros on a rough trail, and had proceeded to within half a day's journey of Red Lake when they were attacked while making camp in a cedar grove. Shefford sustained an exceedingly painful injury to his leg, but, fortunately, the bullet went through without breaking a bone. With that burning pain there came to

Shefford the meaning of fight, and his rifle grew hot in his hands. Night alone saved the trio from certain fatality. Under the cover of darkness the Indian helped Shefford to escape. Joe Lake looked out for himself. The pack-train was lost, and the mustangs, except Nack-yal.

Shefford learned what it meant to lie out at night, listening for pursuit, cold to his marrow, sick with dread, and enduring frightful pain from a ragged bullet-hole. Next day the Indian led him down into the red basin, where the sun shone hot and the sand reflected the heat. They had no water. A wind arose and the valley became a place of flying sand. Through a heavy, stifling pall Nas Ta Bega somehow got Shefford to the trading-post at Red Lake. Presbrey attended to Shefford's injury and made him comfortable. Next day Joe Lake limped in, surly and somber, with the news that Shadd and eight or ten of his outlaw gang had gotten away with the pack-train.

In short time Shefford was able to ride, and with his companions went over the pass to Kayenta. Withers already knew of his loss, and all he said was that he hoped to meet Shadd some day.

Shefford showed a reluctance to go again to the hidden village in the silent cañon with the rounded walls. The trader appeared surprised, but did not press the point. And Shefford meant sooner or later to tell him, yet never quite reached the point. The early summer brought more work for the little post, and Shefford toiled with the others. He liked the outdoor tasks, and at night was grateful that he was too tired to think. Then followed trips to Durango and Bluff and Monticello. He rode fifty miles a day for many days. He knew how a man fares who packs light and rides far and fast. When the Indian was with him he got along well, but Nas Ta Bega would not go near the towns. Thus many mishaps were Shefford's fortune.

Many and many a mile he trailed his mustang, for Nack-yal never forgot the Sagi, and always headed for it when he broke his hobbles. Shefford accompanied an Indian teamster in to Durango with a wagon and four wild mustangs. Upon the return, with a heavy load of supplies, accident put Shefford in charge of the outfit. In despair he had to face the hardest task that could have been given him—to take care of a crippled Indian, catch, water, feed, harness, and drive four wild mustangs that did not know him and tried to kill him at every turn, and to get that precious load of supplies home to Kayenta. That he accomplished it proved to him the possibilities of a man, for both endurance and patience. From that time he never gave up in the front of any duty.

In the absence of an available Indian he rode to Durango and back in record time. Upon one occasion he was lost in a cañon for days, with no food and little water. Upon another he went through a sand-storm in the open desert, facing it for forty miles and keeping to the trail. When he rode in to Kayenta that night the trader, in grim praise, said there was no worse to endure. At Monticello Shefford stood off a band of desperadoes, and this time Shefford experienced a strange, sickening shock in the wounding of a man. Later he had other fights, but in none of them did he know whether or not he had shed blood.

The heat of midsummer came, when the blistering sun shone, and a hot blast blew across the sand, and the furious storms made floods in the washes. Day and night Shefford was always in the open, and any one who had ever known him in the past would have failed to recognize him now.

In the early fall, with Nas Ta Bega as companion, he set out to the south of Kayenta upon long-neglected business of the trader. They visited Red Lake, Blue Cañon, Keams Cañon, Oribi, the Moki villages, Tuba, Moencopie, and Moen Ave. This trip took many weeks and gave Shefford all the opportunity he wanted to study the Indians, and the conditions nearer to the border of civilization. He learned the truth about the Indians and the missionaries.

Upon the return trip he rode over the trail he had followed alone to Red Lake and thence on to the Sagi, and it seemed that years had passed since he first entered this wild region which had come to be home, years that had molded him in the stern and fiery crucible of the desert.

CHAPTER 10

STONEBRIDGE

In October Shefford arranged for a hunt in the Cresaw Mountains with Joe Lake and Nas Ta Bega. The Indian had gone home for a short visit, and upon his return the party expected to start. But Nas Ta Bega did not come back. Then the arrival of a Piute with news that excited Withers and greatly perturbed Lake convinced Shefford that something was wrong.

The little trading-post seldom saw such disorder; certainly Shefford had never known the trader to neglect work. Joe Lake threw a saddle on a mustang he would have scorned to notice in an ordinary moment, and without a word of explanation or farewell rode hard to the north on the Stone Bridge trail.

Shefford had long since acquired patience. He was curious, but he did not care particularly what was in the wind. However, when Withers came out and sent an Indian to drive up the horses Shefford could not refrain from a query.

"I hate to tell you," replied the trader.

"Go on," added Shefford, quickly.

"Did I tell you about the government sending a Supreme Court judge out to Utah to prosecute the polygamists?"

"No," replied Shefford.

"I forgot to, I reckon. You've been away a lot. Well, there's been hell up in Utah for six months. Lately this judge and his men have worked down into southern Utah. He visited Bluff and Monticello a few weeks ago. . . . Now what do you think?"

"Withers! Is he coming to Stone Bridge?"

"He's there now. Some one betrayed the whereabouts of the hidden village over in the cañon. All the women have been arrested and taken to Stone Bridge. The trial begins to-day."

"Arrested!" echoed Shefford, blankly. "Those poor, lonely, good women? What on earth for?"

"Sealed wives!" exclaimed Withers, tersely. "This judge is after the polygamists. They say he's absolutely relentless."

"But—women can't be polygamists. Their husbands are the ones wanted."

"Sure. But the prosecutors have got to find the sealed wives—the second wives—to find the law-breaking husbands. That'll be a job, or I don't know Mormons. . . . Are you going to ride over to Stone Bridge with me?"

Shefford shrank at the idea. Months of toil and pain and travail had not been enough to make him forget the strange girl he had loved. But he had remembered only at poignant intervals, and the lapse of time had made thought of her a dream like that sad dream which had lured him into the desert. With the query of the trader came a bitter-sweet regret.

"Better come with me," said Withers. "Have you forgotten the Sago Lily? She'll be put on trial. . . . That girl—that child! . . . Shefford, you know she hasn't any friends. And now no Mormon man dare protect her, for fear of prosecution."

"I'll go," replied Shefford, shortly.

The Indian brought up the horses. Nack-yal was thin from his long travel during the hot summer, but he was as hard as iron, and the way he pointed his keen nose toward the Sagi showed how he wanted to make for the upland country, with its clear springs and valleys of grass. Withers mounted his bay and with a hurried farewell to his wife spurred the mustang into the trail. Shefford took time to get his weapons and the light pack he always carried, and then rode out after the trader.

The pace Withers set was the long, steady lope to which these Indian mustangs had been trained all their lives. In an hour they reached the mouth of the Sagi, and at sight of it it seemed to Shefford that the hard half-year of suffering since he had been there had disappeared. Withers, to Shefford's regret, did not enter the Sagi. He turned off to the north and took a wild trail into a split of the red wall, and wound in and out, and climbed a crack so narrow that the light was obscured and the cliffs could be reached from both sides of a horse.

Once up on the wild plateau, Shefford felt again in a different world from the barren desert he had lately known. The desert had crucified him and had left him to die or survive, according to his spirit and his strength. If he had loved the glare, the endless level, the deceiving distance, the shifting sand, it had certainly not been as he loved this softer, wilder, more intimate upland. With the red peaks shining up into the blue, and the fragrance of cedar and piñon, and the purple sage and flowers and grass and splash of clear water over stones—with these there came back to him something that he had lost and which had haunted him.

It seemed he had returned to this wild upland of color and cañons and lofty crags and green valleys and silent places with a spirit gained from victory over himself in the harsher and sterner desert below. And, strange to him, he found his old self, the dreamer, the artist, the lover of beauty, the searcher for he knew not what, come to meet him on the fragrant wind.

He felt this, saw the old wildness with glad eyes, yet the greater part of his mind was given over to the thought of the unfortunate women he expected to see in Stone Bridge.

Withers was harder to follow, to keep up with, than an Indian. For one thing he was a steady and tireless rider, and for another there were times when he had no mercy on a horse. Then an Indian always found easier steps in a trail and shorter cuts. Withers put his mount to some bad slopes, and Shefford had no choice but to follow. But they crossed the great broken bench of upland without mishap, and came out upon a promontory of a plateau from which Shefford saw a wide valley and the dark-green alfalfa fields of Stone Bridge.

Stone Bridge lay in the center of a fertile valley surrounded by pink cliffs. It must have been a very old town, certainly far older than Bluff or Monticello, though smaller, and evidently it had been built to last. There was one main street, very wide, that divided the town and was crossed at right angles by a stream spanned by a small natural Stone Bridge. A line of poplar-trees shaded each foot-path. The little log cabins and stone houses and cottages were half hidden in foliage now tinted with autumn colors. Toward the center of the town the houses and stores and shops fronted upon the street and along one side of a green square, or plaza. Here were situated several edifices, the most prominent of which was a church built of wood, white-washed, and remarkable, according to Withers, for the fact that not a nail had been used in its construction. Beyond the church was a large, low structure of stone, with a split-shingle roof, and evidently this was the town hall.

Shefford saw, before he reached the square, that this day in Stone Bridge was one of singular action and excitement for a Mormon village. The town was full of people and, judging from the horses hitched everywhere and the big canvas-covered wagons, many of the people were visitors. A crowd surrounded the hall—a dusty, booted, spurred, shirt-sleeved and sombreroed assemblage that did not wear the hall-mark Shefford had come to associate with Mormons. They were riders, cowboys, horse-wranglers, and some of them Shefford had seen in Durango. Navajos and Piutes were present, also, but they loitered in the background.

Withers drew Shefford off to the side where, under a tree, they hitched their horses.

"Never saw Stone Bridge full of a riffraff gang like this to-day," said Withers. "I'll bet the Mormons are wild. There's a tough outfit from Durango. If they can get anything to drink—or if they've got it— Stone Bridge will see smoke to-day! . . . Come on. I'll get in that hall."

But before Withers reached the hall he started violently and pulled up short, then, with apparent unconcern, turned to lay a hand upon Shefford. The trader's face had blanched and his eyes grew hard and shiny, like flint. He gripped Shefford's arm.

"Look! Over to your left!" he whispered. "See that gang of Indians there—by the big wagon. See the short Indian with the chaps. He's got a face big as a ham, dark, fierce. That's Shadd! . . . You ought to know him.

Shadd and his outfit here! How's that for nerve! But he pulls a rein with the Mormons."

Shefford's keen eye took in a lounging group of ten or twelve Indians and several white men. They did not present any great contrast to the other groups except that they were isolated, appeared quiet and watchful, and were all armed. A bunch of lean, racy mustangs, restive and spirited, stood near by in charge of an Indian. Shefford had to take a second and closer glance to distinguish the half-breed. At once he recognized in Shadd the broad-faced squat Indian who had paid him a threatening visit that night long ago in the mouth of the Sagi. A fire ran along Shefford's veins and seemed to concentrate in his breast. Shadd's dark, piercing eyes alighted upon Shefford and rested there. Then the half-breed spoke to one of his white outlaws and pointed at Shefford. His action attracted the attention of others in the gang, and for a moment Shefford and Withers were treated to a keen-eyed stare.

The trader cursed low. "Maybe I wouldn't like to mix it with that damned breed," he said. "But what chance have we with that gang? Besides, we're here on other and more important business. All the same, before I forget, let me remind you that Shadd has had you spotted ever since you came out here. A friendly Piute told me only lately. Shefford, did any Indian between here and Flagstaff ever see that bunch of money you persist in carrying?"

"Why, yes, I suppose so—'way back in Tuba, when I first came out," replied Shefford.

"Huh! Well, Shadd's after that. . . . Come on now, let's get inside the hall."

The crowd opened for the trader, who appeared to be known to everybody. A huge man with a bushy beard blocked the way to a shut door.

"Hello, Meade!" said Withers. "Let us in."

The man opened the door, permitted Withers and Shefford to enter, and then closed it.

Shefford, coming out of the bright glare of sun into the hall, could not see distinctly at first. His eyes blurred. He heard a subdued murmur of many voices. Withers appeared to be affected with the same kind of blindness, for he stood bewildered a moment. But he recovered sooner than Shefford. Gradually the darkness shrouding many obscure forms lifted. Withers drew him through a crowd of men and women to one side of the hall, and squeezed along a wall to a railing where progress was stopped. Then Shefford raised his head to look with bated breath and strange curiosity.

The hall was large and had many windows. Men were in consultation upon a platform. Women to the number of twenty sat close together upon benches. Back of them stood another crowd. But the women on the benches held Shefford's gaze. They were the prisoners. They made a somber group. Some were hooded, some veiled, all clad in dark garments except one on the front bench, and she was dressed in white. She wore a long hood that concealed her face. Shefford recognized the hood and then the slender shape. She was Mary—she whom her jealous neighbors had named the Sago Lily. At sight of her a sharp pain pierced Shefford's breast. His eyes were blurred when he forced them away from her, and it took a moment for him to see clearly.

Withers was whispering to him or to some one near at hand, but Shefford did not catch the meaning of what was said. He paid more attention; however, Withers ceased speaking. Shefford gazed upon the crowd back of him. The women were hooded and it was not possible to see what they looked like. There were many stalwart, clean-cut, young Mormons of Joe Lake's type, and these men appeared troubled, even distressed and at a loss. There was little about them resembling the stern, quiet, somber austerity of the more matured men, and nothing at all of the strange, aloof, serene impassiveness of the gray-bearded old patriarchs. These venerable men were the Mormons of the old school, the sons of the pioneers, the ruthless fanatics. Instinctively Shefford felt that it was in them that polygamy was embodied; they were the husbands of the sealed wives. He conceived an absorbing curiosity to learn if his instinct was correct; and hard upon that followed a hot, hateful eagerness to see which one was the husband of Mary.

"There's Bishop Kane," whispered Withers, nudging Shefford. "And there's Waggoner with him."

Shefford saw the bishop, and then beside him a man of striking presence.

"Who's Waggoner?" asked Shefford, as he looked.

"He owns more than any Mormon in southern Utah," replied the trader. "He's the biggest man in Stone Bridge, that's sure. But I don't know his relation to the Church. They don't call him elder or bishop. But I'll bet he's some pumpkins. He never had any use for me or any Gentile. A close-fisted, tight-lipped Mormon—a skinflint if I ever saw one! Just look him over."

Shefford had been looking, and considered it unlikely that he would ever forget this individual called Waggoner. He seemed old, sixty at least, yet at that only in the prime of a wonderful physical life. Unlike most of the others, he wore his grizzled beard close-cropped, so close that it showed the lean, wolfish line of his jaw. All his features were of striking sharpness. His eyes, of a singularly brilliant blue, were yet cold and pale. The brow had a serious, thoughtful cast; long furrows sloped down the cheeks. It was a strange, secretive face, full of a power that Shefford had not seen in another man's, full of intelligence and thought that had not been used as Shefford had known them used among men. The face mystified him. It had so much more than the strange aloofness so characteristic of his fellows.

"Waggoner had five wives and fifty-five children before the law went into effect," whispered Withers. "Nobody knows and nobody will ever know how many he's got now. That's my private opinion."

Somehow, after Withers told that, Shefford seemed to understand the strange power in Waggoner's face. Absolutely it was not the force, the strength given to a man from his years of control of men. Shefford, long schooled now in his fair-mindedness, fought down the feelings of other years, and waited with patience. Who was he to judge Waggoner or any other Mormon? But whenever his glance strayed back to the quiet, slender form in white, when he realized again and again the appalling nature of this court, his heart beat heavy and labored within his breast.

Then a bustle among the men upon the platform appeared to indicate that proceedings were about to begin. Some men left the platform; several sat down at a table upon which were books and papers, and others remained standing. These last were all roughly garbed, in riding-boots and spurs, and Shefford's keen eye detected the bulge of hidden weapons. They looked like deputy-marshals upon duty.

Somebody whispered that the judge's name was Stone. The name fitted him. He was not young, and looked a man suited to the prosecution of these secret Mormons. He had a ponderous brow, a deep, cavernous eye that emitted gleams but betrayed no color or expression. His mouth was the saving human feature of his stony face.

Shefford took the man upon the judge's right hand to be a lawyer, and the one on his left an officer of court, perhaps a prosecuting attorney. Presently this fellow pounded upon the table and stood up as if to address a courtroom. Certainly he silenced that hallful of people. Then he perfunctorily and briefly stated that certain women had been arrested upon suspicion of being sealed wives of Mormon polygamists, and were to be herewith tried by a judge of the United States Court. Shefford felt how the impressive words affected that silent hall of listeners, but he gathered from the brief preliminaries that the trial could not be otherwise than a crude, rapid investigation, and perhaps for that the more sinister.

The first woman on the foremost bench was led forward by a deputy to a vacant chair on the platform just in front of the judge's table. She was told to sit down, and showed no sign that she had heard. Then the judge courteously asked her to take the chair. She refused. And Stone nodded his head as if he had experienced that sort of thing before. He stroked his chin wearily, and Shefford conceived an idea that he was a kind man, if he was a relentless judge.

"Please remove your veil," requested the prosecutor.

The woman did so, and proved to be young and handsome. Shefford had a thrill as he recognized her. She was Ruth, who had been one of his best-known acquaintances in the hidden village. She was pale, angry, almost sullen, and her breast heaved. She had no shame, but she seemed to be outraged. Her dark eyes, scornful and blazing, passed over the judge and his assistants, and on to the crowd behind the railing. Shefford, keen as a blade, with all his faculties absorbed, fancied he saw Ruth stiffen and change slightly as her glance encountered some one in that crowd. Then the prosecutor in deliberate and chosen words enjoined her to kiss the Bible handed to her and swear to tell the truth. How strange for Shefford to see her kiss the book which he had studied for so many years! Stranger still to hear the low murmur from the listening audience as she took the oath!

"What is your name?" asked Judge Stone, leaning back and fixing the cavernous eyes upon her.

"Ruth Jones," was the cool reply.

"How old are you?"

"Twenty."

"Where were you born?" went on the judge. He allowed time for the clerk to record her answers.

"Panguitch, Utah."

"Were your parents Mormons?"

"Yes."

"Are you a Mormon?"

"Yes."

"Are you a married woman?"

"No."

The answer was instant, cold, final. It seemed to be the truth. Almost Shefford believed she spoke truth. The judge stroked his chin and waited a moment, and then hesitatingly he went on.

"Have you—any children?"

"No." And the blazing eyes met the cavernous ones.

That about the children was true enough, Shefford thought, and he could have testified to it.

"You live in the hidden village near this town?"

"Yes."

"What is the name of this village?"

"It has none."

"Did you ever hear of Fre-donia, another village far west of here?"

"Yes."

"It is in Arizona, near the Utah line. There are few men there. Is it the same kind of village as this one in which you live?"

"Yes."

"What does Fre-donia mean? The name—has it any meaning?"

"It means free women."

The judge maintained silence for a moment, turned to whisper to his assistants, and presently, without glancing up, said to the woman:

"That will do."

Ruth was led back to the bench, and the woman next to her brought forward. This was a heavier person, with the figure and step of a matured woman. Upon removing her bonnet she showed the plain face of a woman of forty, and it was striking only in that strange, stony aloofness noted in the older men. Here, Shefford thought, was the real Mormon, different in a way he could not define from Ruth. This woman seated herself in the chair and calmly faced her prosecutors. She manifested no emotion whatever. Shefford remembered her and could not see any change in her deportment. This trial appeared to be of little moment to her and she took the oath as if doing so had been a habit all her life.

"What is your name?" asked Judge Stone, glancing up from a paper he held.

"Mary Danton."

"Family or married name?"

"My husband's name was Danton."

"Was. Is he living?"

"No."

"Where did you live when you were married to him?"

"In St. George, and later here in Stone Bridge."

"You were both Mormons?"

"Yes."

"Did you have any children by him?"

"Yes."

"How many?"

"Two."

"Are they living?"

"One of them is living."

Judge Stone bent over his paper and then slowly raised his eyes to her face.

"Are you married now?"

"No."

Again the judge consulted his notes, and held a whispered colloquy with the two men at his table.

"Mrs. Danton, when you were arrested there were five children found in your home. To whom do they belong?"

"Me."

"Are you their mother?"

"Yes."

"Your husband Danton is the father of only one, the eldest, according to your former statement. Is that correct?"

"Yes."

"Who, then, is the father—or who are the fathers, of your other children?"

"I do not know."

She said it with the most stony-faced calmness, with utter disregard of what significance her words had. A strong, mystic wall of cold flint insulated her. Strangely it came to Shefford how impossible either to doubt or believe her. Yet he did both! Judge Stone showed a little heat.

"You don't know the father of one or all of these children?" he queried, with sharp rising inflection of voice.

"I do not."

"Madam, I beg to remind you that you are under oath."

The woman did not reply.

"These children are nameless, then—illegitimate?"

"They are."

"You swear you are not the sealed wife of some Mormon?"

"I swear."

"How do you live—maintain yourself?"

"I work."

"What at?"

"I weave, sew, bake, and work in my garden."

"My men made note of your large and comfortable cabin, even luxurious, considering this country. How is that?"

"My husband left me comfortable."

Judge Stone shook a warning finger at the defendant.

"Suppose I were to sentence you to jail for perjury? For a year? Far from your home and children! Would you speak—tell the truth?"

"I am telling the truth. I can't speak what I don't know. . . . Send me to jail."

Baffled, with despairing, angry impatience, Judge Stone waved the woman away.

"That will do for her. Fetch the next one," he said.

One after another he examined three more women, and arrived, by various questions and answers different in tone and temper, at precisely the same point as had been made in the case of Mrs. Danton. Thereupon the proceedings rested a few moments while the judge consulted with his assistants.

Shefford was grateful for this respite. He had been worked up to an unusual degree of interest, and now, as the next Mormon woman to be examined was she whom he had loved and loved still, he felt arise in him emotion that threatened to make him conspicuous unless it could be hidden. The answers of these Mormon women had been not altogether unexpected by him, but once spoken in cold blood under oath, how tragic, how appallingly significant of the shadow, the mystery, the yoke that bound them! He was amazed, saddened. He felt bewildered. He needed to think out the meaning of the falsehoods of women he knew to be good and noble. Surely religion, instead of fear and loyalty, was the foundation and the strength of this disgrace, this sacrifice. Absolutely, shame was not in these women, though they swore to shameful facts. They had been coached to give these baffling answers, every one of which seemed to brand them, not the brazen mothers of illegitimate offspring, but faithful, unfortunate sealed wives. To Shefford the truth was not in their words, but it sat upon their somber brows.

Was it only his heightened imagination, or did the silence and the suspense grow more intense when a deputy led that dark-hooded, white-clad, slender woman to the defendant's chair? She did not walk with the poise that had been manifest in the other women, and she sank into the chair as if she could no longer stand.

"Please remove your hood," requested the prosecutor.

How well Shefford remembered the strong, shapely hands! He saw them tremble at the knot of ribbon, and that tremor was communicated to him in a sympathy which made his pulses beat. He held his breath while she removed the hood. And then there was revealed, he thought, the loveliest and the most tragic face that ever was seen in a courtroom.

A low, whispering murmur that swelled like a wave ran through the hall. And by it Shefford divined, as clearly as if the fact had been blazoned on the walls, that Mary's face had been unknown to these villagers. But the name Sago Lily had not been unknown; Shefford heard it whispered on all sides.

The murmuring subsided. The judge and his assistants stared at Mary. As for Shefford, there was no need of his personal feeling to make the situation dramatic. Not improbably Judge Stone had tried many Mormon women. But manifestly this one was different. Unhooded, Mary appeared to be only a young girl, and a court, confronted suddenly with her youth and the suspicion attached to her, could not but have been shocked. Then her beauty made her seem, in that somber company, indeed the white flower for which she had been named. But, more likely, it was her agony that bound the court into silence which grew painful. Perhaps the thought that flashed into Shefford's mind was telepathic; it seemed to him that every watcher there realized that in this defendant the judge had a girl of softer mold, of different spirit, and from her the bitter truth could be wrung.

Mary faced the court and the crowd on that side of the platform. Unlike the other women, she did not look at or seem to see any one behind the railing. Shefford was absolutely sure there was not a man or a woman who caught her glance. She gazed afar, with eyes strained, humid, fearful.

When the prosecutor swore her to the oath her lips were seen to move, but no one heard her speak.

"What is your name?" asked the judge.

"Mary." Her voice was low, with a slight tremor.

"What's your other name?"

"I won't tell."

Her singular reply, the tones of her voice, her manner before the judge, marked her with strange simplicity. It was evident that she was not accustomed to questions.

"What were your parents' names?"

"I won't tell," she replied, very low.

Judge Stone did not press the point. Perhaps he wanted to make the examination as easy as possible for her or to wait till she showed more composure.

"Were your parents Mormons?" he went on.

"No, sir." She added the sir with a quaint respect, contrasting markedly with the short replies of the women before her.

"Then you were not born a Mormon?"

"No, sir."

"How old are you?"

"Seventeen or eighteen. I'm not sure."

"You don't know your exact age?"

"No."

"Where were you born?"

"I won't tell."

"Was it in Utah?"

"Yes, sir."

"How long have you lived in this state?"

"Always—except last year."

"And that's been over in the hidden village where you were arrested?"

"Yes."

"But you often visited here—this town Stone Bridge?"

"I never was here—till yesterday."

Judge Stone regarded her as if his interest as a man was running counter to his duty as an officer. Suddenly he leaned forward.

"Are you a Mormon *now*?" he queried, forcibly.

"No, sir," she replied, and here her voice rose a little clearer.

It was an unexpected reply. Judge Stone stared at her. The low buzz ran through the listening crowd. And as for Shefford, he was astounded. When his wits flashed back and he weighed her words and saw in her face truth as clear as light, he had the strangest sensation of joy. Almost it flooded away the gloom and pain that attended this ordeal.

The judge bent his head to his assistants as if for counsel. All of them were eager where formerly they had been weary. Shefford glanced around at the dark and somber faces, and a slow wrath grew within him. Then he caught a glimpse of Waggoner. The steel-blue, piercing intensity of the Mormon's gaze impressed him at a moment when all that older generation of Mormons looked as hard and immutable as iron. Either Shefford was over-excited and mistaken or the hour had become fraught with greater suspense. The secret, the mystery, the power, the hate, the religion of a strange people were thick and tangible in that hall. For Shefford the feeling of the presence of Withers on his left was entirely different from that of the Mormon on his other side. If there was not a shadow there, then the sun did not shine so brightly as it had shone when he entered. The air seemed clogged with nameless passion.

"I gather that you've lived mostly in the country—away from people?" the judge began.

"Yes, sir," replied the girl.

"Do you know anything about the government of the United States?"

"No, sir."

He pondered again, evidently weighing his queries, leading up to the fatal and inevitable question. Still, his interest in this particular defendant had become visible.

"Have you any idea of the consequences of perjury?"

"No, sir."

"Do you understand what perjury is?"

"It's to lie."

"Do you tell lies?"

"No, sir."

"Have you ever told a single lie?"

"Not—yet," she replied, almost whispering.

It was the answer of a child and affected the judge. He fussed with his papers. Perhaps his task was not easy; certainly it was not pleasant. Then he leaned forward again and fixed those deep, cavernous eyes upon the sad face.

"Do you understand what a sealed wife is?"

"I've never been told."

"But you know there *are* sealed wives in Utah?"

"Yes, sir; I've been told that."

Judge Stone halted there, watching her. The hall was silent except for faint rustlings and here and there deep breaths drawn guardedly. The vital question hung like a sword over the white-faced girl. Perhaps she divined its impending stroke, for she sat like a stone with dilating, appealing eyes upon her executioner.

"Are you a sealed wife?" he flung at her.

She could not answer at once. She made effort, but the words would not come. He flung the question again, sternly.

"No!" she cried.

And then there was silence. That poignant word quivered in Shefford's heart. He believed it was a lie. It seemed he would have known it if this hour was the first in which he had ever seen the girl. He heard, he felt, he sensed the fatal thing. The beautiful voice had lacked some quality before present. And the thing wanting was something subtle, an essence, a beautiful ring—the truth. What a hellish thing to make that pure girl a liar—a perjurer! The heat deep within Shefford kindled to fire.

"You are not married?" went on Judge Stone.

"No, sir," she answered, faintly.

"Have you ever been married?"

"No, sir."

"Do you expect ever to be married?"

"Oh! No, sir."

She was ashen pale now, quivering all over, with her strong hands clasping the black hood, and she could no longer meet the judge's glance.

"Have you—any—any children?" the judge asked, haltingly. It was a hard question to get out.

"No."

Judge Stone leaned far over the table, and that his face was purple showed Shefford he was a man. His big fist clenched.

"Girl, you're not going to swear you, too, were visited—over there by men . . . You're not going to swear that?"

"Oh—no, sir!"

Judge Stone settled back in his chair, and while he wiped his moist face that same foreboding murmur, almost a menace, moaned through the hall.

Shefford was sick in his soul and afraid of himself. He did not know this spirit that flamed up in him. His helplessness was a most hateful fact.

"Come—confess you are a sealed wife," called her interrogator.

She maintained silence, but shook her head.

Suddenly he seemed to leap forward.

"Unfortunate child! Confess."

That forced her to lift her head and face him, yet still she did not speak. It was the strength of despair. She could not endure much more.

"Who is your husband?" he thundered at her.

She rose wildly, terror-stricken. It was terror that dominated her, not of the stern judge, for she took a faltering step toward him, lifting a shaking hand, but of some one or of some thing far more terrible than any punishment she could have received in the sentence of a court. Still she was not proof against the judge's will. She had weakened, and the terror must have been because of that weakening.

"Who is the Mormon who visits you?" he thundered, relentlessly.

"I—never—knew—his—name."

"But you'd know his face. I'll arrest every Mormon in this country and bring him before you. You'd know his face?"

"Oh, I wouldn't. I *couldn't* tell! . . . *I—never—saw his face—in the light!*"

The tragic beauty of her, the certainty of some monstrous crime to youth and innocence, the presence of an agony and terror that unfathomably seemed not to be for herself—these transfixed the court and the audience, and held them silenced, till she reached out blindly and then sank in a heap to the floor.

CHAPTER 11

AFTER THE TRIAL

Shefford might have leaped over the railing but for Withers's restraining hand, and when there appeared to be some sign of kindness in those other women for the unconscious girl Shefford squeezed through the crowd and got out of the hall.

The gang outside that had been denied admittance pressed upon Shefford, with jest and curious query, and a good nature that jarred upon him. He was far from gentle as he jostled off the first importuning fellows; the others, gaping at him, opened a lane for him to pass through.

Then there was a hand laid on his shoulder that he did not shake off. Nas Ta Bega loomed dark and tall beside him. Neither the trader nor Joe Lake nor any white man Shefford had met influenced him as this Navajo.

"Nas Ta Bega! You here, too. I guess the whole country is here. We waited at Kayenta. What kept you so long?"

The Indian, always slow to answer, did not open his lips till he drew Shefford apart from the noisy crowd.

"Bi Nai, there is sorrow in the hogan of Hosteen Doetin," he said.

"Glen Naspa!" exclaimed Shefford.

"My sister is gone from the home of her brother. She went away alone in the summer."

"Blue Cañon! She went to the missionary. Nas Ta Bega, I thought I saw her there. But I wasn't sure. I didn't want to make sure. I was afraid it might be true."

"A brave who loved my sister trailed her there."

"Nas Ta Bega, will you—will we go find her, take her home?"

"No. She will come home some day."

What bitter sadness and wisdom in his words!

"But, my friend, that damned missionary—" began Shefford, passionately. The Indian had met him at a bad hour.

"Willetts is here. I saw him go in there," interrupted Nas Ta Bega, and he pointed to the hall.

"Here! He gets around a good deal," declared Shefford. "Nas Ta Bega, what are you going to do to him?"

The Indian held his peace and there was no telling from his inscrutable face what might be in his mind. He was dark, impassive. He seemed a wise and bitter Indian, beyond any savagery of his tribe, and the suffering Shefford divined was deep.

"He'd better keep out of my sight," muttered Shefford, more to himself than to his companion.

"The half-breed is here," said Nas Ta Bega.

"Shadd? Yes, we saw him. There! He's still with his gang. Nas Ta Bega, what are they up to?"

"They will steal what they can."

"Withers says Shadd is friendly with the Mormons."

"Yes, and with the missionary, too."

"With Willetts?"

"I saw them talk together—strong talk."

"Strange. But maybe it's not so strange. Shadd is known well in Monticello and Bluff. He spends money there. They are afraid of him, but he's welcome just the same. Perhaps everybody knows him. It'd be like him to ride into Kayenta. But, Nas Ta Bega, I've got to look out for him, because Withers says he's after me."

"Bi Nai wears a scar that is proof," said the Indian.

"Then it must be he found out long ago I had a little money."

"It might be. But, Bi Nai, the half-breed has a strange step on your trail."

"What do you mean?" demanded Shefford.

"Nas Ta Bega cannot tell what he does not know," replied the Navajo. "Let that be. We shall know some day. Bi Nai, there is sorrow to tell that is not the Indian's. . . . Sorrow for my brother!"

Shefford lifted his eyes to the Indian's, and if he did not see sadness there he was much deceived.

"Bi Nai, long ago you told a story to the trader. Nas Ta Bega sat before the fire that night. You did not know he could understand your language. He listened. And he learned what brought you to the country of the Indian. That night he made you his brother. . . . All his lonely rides into the cañons have been to find the little golden-haired child, the lost girl—Fay Larkin. . . . Bi Nai, I have found the girl you wanted for your sweetheart."

Shefford was bereft of speech. He could not see steadily, and the last solemn words of the Indian seemed far away.

"Bi Nai, I have found Fay Larkin," repeated Nas Ta Bega.

"Fay Larkin!" gasped Shefford, shaking his head. "But—she's dead."

"It would be less sorrow for Bi Nai if she were dead."

Shefford clutched at the Indian. There was something terrible to be revealed. Like an aspen-leaf in the wind he shook all over. He divined the revelation—divined the coming blow—but that was as far as his mind got.

"She's in there," said the Indian, pointing toward the hall.

"Fay Larkin?" whispered Shefford.

"Yes, Bi Nai."

"My God! *How* do you know? Oh, I could have seen. I've been blind. . . . Tell me, Indian. Which one?"

"Fay Larkin is the Sago Lily."

Shefford strode away into a secluded corner of the square, where in the shade and quiet of the trees he suffered a storm of heart and mind. During that short or long time—he had no idea how long—the Indian remained with him. He never lost the feeling of Nas Ta Bega close beside him. When the period of acute pain left him and some order began to replace the tumult in his mind he felt in Nas Ta Bega the same quality—silence or strength or help—that he had learned to feel in the deep cañons and the lofty crags. He realized then that the Indian was indeed a brother. And Shefford needed him. What he had to fight was more fatal than suffering and love—it was hate rising out of the unsuspected dark gulf of his heart—the instinct to kill—the murder in his soul. Only now did he come to understand Jane Withersteen's tragic story and the passion of Venters and what had made Lassiter a gunman.

The desert had transformed Shefford. The elements had entered into his muscle and bone, into the very fiber of his heart. Sun, wind, sand, cold, storm, space, stone, the poison cactus, the racking toil, the terrible loneliness—the iron of the desert man, the cruelty of the desert savage, the wildness of the mustang, the ferocity of hawk and wolf, the bitter struggle of every surviving thing—these were as if they had been melted and merged together and now made a dark and passionate stream that was his throbbing blood. He realized what he had become and gloried in it, yet there, looking on with grave and earnest eyes, was his old self, the man of reason, of intellect, of culture, who had been a good man despite the failure and shame of his life. And he gave heed to the voice of warning, of conscience. Not by revengefully seeking the Mormon who had ruined Fay Larkin and blindly dealing a wild justice could he help this unfortunate girl. This fierce, newborn strength and passion must be tempered by reason, lest he become merely elemental, a man answering wholly to primitive impulses. In the darkness of that hour he mined deep into his heart, understood himself, trembled at the thing he faced, and won his victory. He would go forth from that hour a man. He might fight, and perhaps there was death in the balance, but hate would never overthrow him.

Then when he looked at future action he felt a strange, unalterable purpose to save Fay Larkin. She was very young—seventeen or eighteen, she had said—and there could be, there must be some happiness before her. It had been his dream to chase a rainbow—it had been his determination to find her in the lost Surprise Valley. Well, he had found her. It never occurred to him to ask Nas Ta Bega how he had discovered that the Sago Lily was Fay Larkin. The wonder was, Shefford thought, that he had so long been blind himself. How simply everything worked out now! Every thought, every recollection of her was proof. Her strange beauty like that of the sweet and rare lily, her low voice that showed the habit of silence, her shapely hands with the clasp strong as a man's, her lithe form, her swift step, her wonderful agility upon the smooth, steep walls, and the wildness of her upon the heights, and the haunting, brooding shadow of her eyes when she gazed across the cañons—all these fitted so harmoniously the conception of a child lost in a beautiful Surprise Valley and growing up in its wildness and silence, tutored by the sad love of broken Jane and Lassiter. Yes, to save her had been Shefford's dream, and he had loved that dream. He had loved the dream and he had loved the child. The secret of her hiding place as revealed by the story told him and his slow growth from dream to action—these had strangely given Fay Larkin to him. Then had come the bitter knowledge that she was dead. In the light of this subsequent revelation how easy to account for his loving Mary, too. Never would she be Mary again to him! Fay Larkin and the Sago Lily were one and the same. She was here, near him, and he was powerless for the present to help her or to reveal himself. She was held back there in that gloomy hall among those somber Mormons, alien to the women, bound in some fatal way to one of the men, and now, by reason of her weakness in the trial, surely to be hated. Thinking of her past and her present, of the future, and that secret Mormon whose face she had never seen, Shefford felt a sinking of his heart, a terrible cold pang in his breast, a fainting of his spirit. She had sworn she was no sealed wife. But had she not lied? So, then, how utterly powerless he was!

But here to save him, to uplift him, came that strange mystic insight which had been the gift of the desert to him. She was not dead. He had found her. What mattered obstacles, even that implacable creed to which she had been sacrificed, in the face of this blessed and overwhelming truth? It was as mighty as the love suddenly dawning upon him. A strong and terrible deathly sweet wind seemed to fill his soul with the love of her. It was her fate that had drawn him; and now it was her agony, her innocence, her beauty, that bound him for all time. Patience and cunning and toil, passion and blood, the unquenchable spirit of a man to save—these were nothing to give—life itself were little, could he but free her.

Patience and cunning! His sharpening mind cut these out as his greatest assets for the present. And his thoughts flashed like light through his brain. . . . Judge Stone and his court would fail to convict any Mormon in Stone Bridge, just the same as they had failed in the northern towns. They would go away, and Stone Bridge would fall to the slow, sleepy tenor of its former way. The hidden village must become known to all men, honest and outlawed, in that country, but this fact would hardly make any quick change in the plans of the Mormons. They did not soon change. They would send the sealed wives back to the cañon and, after the excitement had died down, visit them as usual. Nothing, perhaps, would ever change these old Mormons but death.

Shefford resolved to remain in Stone Bridge and ingratiate himself deeper into the regard of the Mormons. He would find work there, if the sealed wives were not returned to the hidden village. In case the women went back to the valley Shefford meant to resume his old duty of driving Withers's pack-trains. Wanting that opportunity, he would find some other work, some excuse to take him there.

In due time he would reveal to Fay Larkin that he knew her. How the thought thrilled him! She might deny, might persist in her fear, might fight to keep her secret. But he would learn it—hear her story—hear what had become of Jane Withersteen and Lassiter—and if they were alive, which now he believed he would find them—and he would take them and Fay out of the country.

The duty, the great task, held a grim fascination for him. He had a foreboding of the cost; he had a dark realization of the force he meant to oppose. There were duty here and pity and unselfish love, but these alone did not actuate Shefford. Mystically fate seemed again to come like a gleam and bid him follow.

When Shefford and Nas Ta Bega returned to the town hall the trial had been ended, the hall was closed, and only a few Indians and cowboys remained in the square, and they were about to depart. On the street, however, and the paths and in the doorways of stores were knots of people, talking earnestly. Shefford walked up and down, hoping to meet Withers or Joe Lake. Nas Ta Bega said he would take the horses to water and feed arid then return.

There were indications that Stone Bridge might experience some of the excitement and perhaps violence common to towns like Monticello and Durango. There was only one saloon in Stone Bridge, and it was full of roystering cowboys and horse-wranglers. Shefford saw the bunch of mustangs, in charge of the same Indian, that belonged to Shadd and his gang. The men were inside, drinking. Next door was a tavern called Hopewell House, a stone structure of some pretensions. There were Indians lounging outside. Shefford entered through a wide door and found himself in a large bare room, boarded like a loft, with no ceiling except the roof. The place was full of men and noise. Here he encountered Joe Lake talking to Bishop Kane and other Mormons. Shefford got a friendly greeting from the bishop, and then was well received by the strangers, to whom Joe introduced him.

"Have you seen Withers?" asked Shefford.

"Reckon he's around somewhere," replied Joe. "Better hang up here, for he'll drop in sooner or later."

"When are you going back to Kayenta?" went on Shefford.

"Hard to say. We'll have to call off our hunt. Nas Ta Bega is here, too."

"Yes, I've been with him."

The older Mormons drew aside, and then Joe mentioned the fact that he was half starved. Shefford went with him into another clapboard room, which was evidently a dining-room. There were half a dozen men at the long table. The seat at the end was a box, and scarcely large enough or safe enough for Joe and Shefford, but they risked it.

"Saw you in the hall," said Joe. "Hell—wasn't it?"

"Joe, I never knew how much I dared say to you, so I don't talk much. But, it *was* hell," replied Shefford.

"You needn't be so scared of me," spoke up Joe, testily.

That was the first time Shefford had heard the Mormon speak that way.

"I'm not scared, Joe. But I like you—respect you. I can't say so much of—of your people."

"Did you stick out the whole mix?" asked Joe.

"No. I had enough when—when they got through with Mary." Shefford spoke low and dropped his head. He heard the Mormon grind his teeth. There was silence for a little space while neither man looked at the other.

"Reckon the judge was pretty decent," presently said Joe.

"Yes, I thought so. He might have—" But Shefford did not finish that sentence. "How'd the thing end?"

"It ended all right."

"Was there no conviction—no sentence?" Shefford felt a curious eagerness.

"Naw," he snorted. "That court might have saved its breath."

"I suppose. Well, Joe, between you and me, as old friends now, that trial established one fact, even if it couldn't be proved. . . . Those women *are* sealed wives."

Joe had no reply for that. He looked gloomy, and there was a stern line in his lips. To-day he seemed more like a Mormon.

"Judge Stone knew that as well as I knew," went on Shefford. "Any man of penetration could have seen it. What an ordeal that was for good women to go through! I know they're good. And there they were swearing to—"

"Didn't it make me sick?" interrupted Joe in a kind of growl. "Reckon it made Judge Stone sick, too. After Mary went under he conducted that trial like a man cuttin' out steers at a round-up. He wanted to get it over. He never forced any question. . . . Bad job to ride down Stone Bridge way! It's out of creation. There's only six men in the party, with a poor lot of horses. Really, government officers or not, they're not safe. And they've taken a hunch."

"Have they left already?" inquired Shefford.

"Were packed an hour ago. I didn't see them go, but somebody said they went. Took the trail for Bluff, which sure is the only trail they could take, unless they wanted to go to Colorado by way of Kayenta. That might have been the safest trail."

"Joe, what might happen to them?" asked Shefford, quietly, with eyes on the Mormon.

"Aw, you know that rough trail. Bad on horses. Weathered slopes—slipping ledges—a rock might fall on you any time. Then Shadd's here with his gang. And bad Piutes."

"What became of the women?" Shefford asked, presently.

"They're around among friends."

"Where are their children?"

"Left over there with the old women. Couldn't be fetched over. But there are some pretty young babies in that bunch—need their mothers."

"I should—think so," replied Shefford, constrainedly. "When will their mothers get back to them?"

"To-night, maybe, if this mob of cow-punchers and wranglers get out of town. . . . It's a bad mix, Shefford, here's a hunch on that. These fellows will get full of whisky. And trouble might come if they—approach the women."

"You mean they might get drunk enough to take the oaths of those poor women—take the meaning literally—pretend to believe the women what they swore they were?"

"Reckon you've got the hunch," replied Joe, gloomily.

"My God! man, that would be horrible!" exclaimed Shefford.

"Horrible or not, it's liable to happen. The women can be kept here yet awhile. Reckon there won't be any trouble here. It'll be over there in the valley. Shefford, getting the women over there safe is a job that's been put to me. I've got a bunch of fellows already. Can I count on you? I'm glad to say you're well thought of. Bishop Kane liked you, and what he says goes."

"Yes, Joe, you can count on me," replied Shefford.

They finished their meal then and repaired to the big office-room of the house. Several groups of men were there and loud talk was going on outside. Shefford saw Withers talking to Bishop Kane and two other Mormons, both strangers to Shefford. The trader appeared to be speaking with unwonted force, emphasizing his words with energetic movements of his hands.

"Reckon something's up," whispered Joe, hoarsely. "It's been in the air all day."

Withers must have been watching for Shefford.

"Here's Shefford now," he said to the trio of Mormons, as Joe and Shefford reached the group. "I want you to hear him speak for himself."

"What's the matter?" asked Shefford.

"Give me a hunch and I'll put in my say-so," said Joe Lake.

"Shefford, it's the matter of a good name more than a job," replied the trader. "A little while back I told the bishop I meant to put you on the pack job over to the valley—same as when you first came to me. Well, the bishop was pleased and said he might put something in your way. Just now I ran in here to find you—not wanted. When I kicked I got the straight hunch. Willetts has said things about you. One of them—the one that sticks in my craw—was that you'd do anything, even pretend to be inclined toward Mormonism, just to be among those Mormon women over there. Willetts is your enemy. And he's worse than I thought. Now I want you to tell Bishop Kane *why* this missionary is bitter toward you."

"Gentlemen, I knocked him down," replied Shefford, simply.

"What for?" inquired the bishop, in surprise and curiosity.

Shefford related the incident which had occurred at Red Lake and that now seemed again to come forward fatefully.

"You insinuate he had evil intent toward the Indian girl?" queried Kane.

"I insinuate nothing. I merely state what led to my acting as I did."

"Principles of religion, sir?"

"No. A man's principles."

Withers interposed in his blunt way, "Bishop, did you ever see Glen Naspa?"

"No."

"She's the prettiest Navajo in the country. Willetts was after her, that's all."

"My dear man, I can't believe that of a Christian missionary. We've known Willetts for years. He's a man of influence. He has money back of him. He's doing a good work. You hint of a love relation."

"No, I don't hint," replied Withers, impatiently. "I know. It's not the first time I've known a missionary to do this sort of thing. Nor is it the first time for Willetts. Bishop Kane, I live among the Indians. I see a lot I never speak of. My work is to trade with the Indians, that's all. But I'll not have Willetts or any other damned hypocrite run down my friend here. John Shefford is the finest young man that ever came to me in the desert. And he's got to be put right before you all or I'll not set foot in Stone Bridge again. . . . Willetts was after Glen Naspa. Shefford punched him. And later threw him out of the old Indian's hogan up on the mountain. That explains Willetts's enmity. He was after the girl."

"What's more, gentlemen, he *got* her," added Shefford. "Glen Naspa has not been home for six months. I saw her at Blue Cañon. . . . I would like to face this Willetts before you all."

"Easy enough," replied Withers, with a grim chuckle. "He's just outside."

The trader went out; Joe Lake followed at his heels and the three Mormons were next; Shefford brought up the rear and lingered in the door while his eye swept the crowd of men and Indians. His feeling was in direct contrast to his movements. He felt the throbbing of fierce anger. But it seemed a face came between him and his passion—a sweet and tragic face that would have had power to check him in a vastly more critical moment than this. And in an instant he had himself in hand, and, strangely, suddenly felt the strength that had come to him.

Willetts stood in earnest colloquy with a short, squat Indian—the half-breed Shadd. They leaned against a hitching-rail. Other Indians were there, and outlaws. It was a mixed group, rough and hard-looking.

"Hey, Willetts!" called the trader, and his loud, ringing voice, not pleasant, stilled the movement and sound.

When Willetts turned, Shefford was halfway across the wide walk. The missionary not only saw him, but also Nas Ta Bega, who was striding forward. Joe Lake was ahead of the trader, the Mormons followed with decision, and they all confronted Willetts. He turned pale. Shadd had cautiously moved along the rail, nearer to his gang, and then they, with the others of the curious crowd, drew closer.

"Willetts, here's Shefford. Now say it to his face!" declared the trader. He was angry and evidently wanted the fact known, as well as the situation.

Willetts had paled, but he showed boldness. For an instant Shefford studied the smooth face, with its sloping lines, the dark, wine-colored eyes.

"Willetts, I understand you've maligned me to Bishop Kane and others," began Shefford, curtly.

"I called you an atheist," returned the missionary, harshly.

"Yes, and more than that. And I told these men *why* you vented your spite on me."

Willetts uttered a half-laugh, an uneasy, contemptuous expression of scorn and repudiation.

"The charges of such a man as you are can't hurt me," he said.

The man did not show fear so much as disgust at the meeting. He seemed to be absorbed in thought, yet no serious consideration of the situation made itself manifest. Shefford felt puzzled. Perhaps there was no fire to strike from this man. The desert had certainly not made him flint. He had not toiled or suffered or fought.

"But *I* can hurt you," thundered Shefford, with startling suddenness. "Here! Look at this Indian! Do you know him? Glen Naspa's brother. Look at him. Let us see you face him while I accuse you. . . . You made love to Glen Naspa—took her from her home!"

"Harping infidel!" replied Willetts, hoarsely. "So that's your game. Well, Glen Naspa came to my school of her own accord and she will say so."

"Why will she? Because you blinded the simple Indian girl. . . . Willetts, I'll waste little more time on you."

And swift and light as a panther Shefford leaped upon the man and, fastening powerful hands round the thick neck, bore him to his knees and bent back his head over the rail. There was a convulsive struggle, a hard flinging of arms, a straining wrestle, and then Willetts was in a dreadful position. Shefford held him in iron grasp.

"You damned, white-livered hypocrite—I'm liable to kill you!" cried Shefford. "I watched you and Glen Naspa that day up on the mountain. I saw you embrace her. I saw that she loved you. Tell *that*, you liar! That'll be enough."

The face of the missionary turned purple as Shefford forced his head back over the rail.

"I'll *kill* you, man," repeated Shefford, piercingly. "Do you want to go to your God unprepared? Say you made love to Glen Naspa—tell that you persuaded her to leave her home. Quick!"

Willetts raised a shaking hand and then Shefford relaxed the paralyzing grip and let his head come forward. The half-strangled man gasped out a few incoherent words that his livid, guilty face made unnecessary.

Shefford gave him a shove and he fell into the dust at the feet of the Navajo.

"Gentlemen, I leave him to Nas Ta Bega," said Shefford, with a strange change from passion to calmness.

* * *

L ate that night, when the roystering visitors had gone or were deep in
drunken slumber, a melancholy and strange procession filed out of
Stone Bridge. Joe Lake and his armed comrades were escorting the Mormon women back to the hidden valley. They were mounted on burros and
mustangs, and in all that dark and somber line there was only one figure
which shone white under the pale moon.

At the starting, until that white-clad figure had appeared, Shefford's
heart had seemed to be in his throat; and thereafter its beat was muffled
and painful in his breast. Yet there was some sad sweetness in the knowledge that he could see her now, be near her, watch over her.

By and by the overcast clouds drifted and the moon shone bright.
The night was still; the great dark mountain loomed to the stars; the
numberless waves of rounded rock that must be crossed and circled lay
deep in the shadow. There was only a steady pattering of light hoofs.

Shefford's place was near the end of the line, and he kept well back,
riding close to one woman and then another. No word was spoken. These
sealed wives rode where their mounts were led or driven, as blind in their
hoods as veiled Arab women in palanquins. And their heads drooped
wearily and their shoulders bent, as if under a burden. It took an hour of
steady riding to reach the ascent to the plateau, and here, with the beginning of rough and smooth and shadowed trail, the work of the escort
began. The line lengthened out and each man kept to the several women
assigned to him. Shefford had three, and one of them was the girl he
loved. She rode as if the world and time and life were naught to her. As
soon as he dared trust his voice and his control he meant to let her know
the man whom perhaps she had not forgotten was there with her, a
friend. Six months! It had been a lifetime to him. Surely eternity to her!
Had she forgotten? He felt like a coward who had basely deserted her.
Oh—had he only known!

She rode a burro that was slow, continually blocking the passage for
those behind, and eventually it became lame. Thus the other women forged
ahead. Shefford dismounted and stopped her burro. It was a moment before
she noted the halt, and twice in that time Shefford tried to speak and
failed. What poignant pain, regret, love made his utterance fail!

"Ride my horse," he finally said, and his voice was not like his own.

Obediently and wearily she dismounted from the burro and got up on Nack-yal. The stirrups were long for her and he had to change them. His fingers were all thumbs as he fumbled with the buckles.

Suddenly he became aware that there had been a subtle change in her. He knew it without looking up and he seemed to be unable to go on with his task. If his life had depended upon keeping his head lowered he could not have done it. The listlessness of her drooping form was no longer manifest. The peak of the dark hood pointed toward him. He knew then that she was gazing at him.

Never so long as he lived would that moment be forgotten! They were alone. The others had gotten so far ahead that no sound came back. The stillness was so deep it could be felt. The moon shone with white, cold radiance and the shining slopes of smooth stone waved away, crossed by shadows of piñons.

Then she leaned a little toward him. One swift hand flew up to tear the black hood back so that she could see. In its place flashed her white face. And her eyes were like the night.

"*You!*" she whispered.

His blood came leaping to sting neck and cheek and temple. What dared he interpret from that single word? Could any other word have meant so much?

"No—one—else," he replied, unsteadily.

Her white hand flashed again to him, and he met it with his own. He felt himself standing cold and motionless in the moonlight. He saw her, wonderful, with the deep, shadowy eyes, and a silver sheen on her hair. And as he looked she released her hand and lifted it, with the other, to her hood. He saw the shiny hair darken and disappear—and then the lovely face with its sad eyes and tragic lips.

He drew Nack-yal's bridle forward, and led him up the moonlit trail.

CHAPTER 12

THE REVELATION

The following afternoon cowboys and horse-wranglers, keen-eyed as Indians for tracks and trails, began to arrive in the quiet valley to which the Mormon women had been returned.

Under every cedar clump there were hobbled horses, packs, and rolled bedding in tarpaulins. Shefford and Joe Lake had pitched camp in the old site near the spring. The other men of Joe's escort went to the homes of the women; and that afternoon, as the curious visitors began to arrive, these homes became barred and dark and quiet, as if they had been closed and deserted for the winter. Not a woman showed herself.

Shefford and Joe, by reason of the location of their camp and their alertness, met all the newcomers. The ride from Stone Bridge was a long and hard one, calculated to wear off the effects of the whisky imbibed by the adventure-seekers. This fact alone saved the situation. Nevertheless, Joe expected trouble. Most of the visitors were decent, good-natured fellows, merely curious, and simple enough to believe that this really was what the Mormons had claimed—a village of free women. But there were those among them who were coarse, evil-minded, and dangerous.

By supper-time there were two dozen or more of these men in the valley, camped along the west wall. Fires were lighted, smoke curled up over the cedars, gay songs disturbed the usual serenity of the place. Later in the early twilight the curious visitors, by twos and threes, walked about the village, peering at the dark cabins and jesting among themselves. Joe had informed Shefford that all the women had been put in a limited number of cabins, so that they could be protected. So far as Shefford saw or heard there was no unpleasant incident in the village; however, as the sauntering visitors returned toward their camps they loitered at the spring, and here developments threatened.

In spite of the fact that the majority of these cowboys and their comrades were decent-minded and beginning to see the real relation of things, they were not disposed to be civil to Shefford. They were certainly not Mormons. And his position, apparently as a Gentile, among these Mormons was one open to criticism. They might have been jealous, too; at any rate, remarks were passed in his hearing, meant for his ears, that made it exceedingly trying for him not to resent. Moreover, Joe Lake's increasing impatience rendered the situation more difficult. Shefford welcomed the arrival of Nas Ta Bega. The Indian listened to the loud talk of several loungers round the campfire; and thereafter he was like Shefford's shadow, silent, somber, watchful.

Nevertheless, it did not happen to be one of the friendly and sarcastic cowboys that precipitated the crisis. A horse-wrangler named Hurley, a man of bad repute, as much outlaw as anything, took up the bantering.

"Say, Shefford, what in the hell's your job here, anyway?" he queried as he kicked a cedar branch into the campfire. The brightening blaze showed him swarthy, unshaven, a large-featured, ugly man.

"I've been doing odd jobs for Withers," replied Shefford. "Expect to drive pack-trains in here for a while."

"You must stand strong with these Mormons. Must be a Mormon yerself?"

"No," replied Shefford, briefly.

"Wal, I'm stuck on your job. Do you need a packer? I can throw a diamond-hitch better 'n any feller in this country."

"I don't need help."

"Mebbe you'll take me over to see the ladies," he went on, with a coarse laugh.

Shefford did not show that he had heard. Hurley waited, leering as he looked from the keen listeners to Shefford.

"Want to have them all yerself, eh?" he jeered. Shefford struck him—sent him tumbling heavily, like a log. Hurley, cursing as he half rose, jerked his gun out. Nas Ta Bega, swift as light, kicked the gun out of his hand. And Joe Lake picked it up.

Deliberately the Mormon cocked the weapon and stood over Hurley.

"Get up!" he ordered, and Shefford heard the ruthless Mormon in him then.

Hurley rose slowly. Then Joe prodded him in the middle with the cocked gun. Shefford, startled, expected the gun to go off. So did the others, especially Hurley, who shrank in panic from the dark Mormon.

"Rustle!" said Joe, and gave the man a harder prod. Assuredly the gun did not have a hair-trigger.

"Joe, mebbe it's loaded!" protested one of the cowboys.

Hurley shrank back, and turned to hurry away, with Joe close after him. They disappeared in the darkness. A constrained silence was maintained around the campfire for a while. Presently some of the men walked off and others began to converse. Everybody heard the sound of hoofs passing down the trail. The patter ceased, and in a few moments Lake returned. He still carried Hurley's gun.

The crowd dispersed then. There was no indication of further trouble. However, Shefford and Joe and Nas Ta Bega divided the night in watches, so that some one would be wide awake.

Early next morning there was an exodus from the village of the better element among the visitors. "No fun hangin' round hyar," one of them expressed it, and as good-naturedly as they had come they rode away. Six or seven of the desperado class remained behind, bent on mischief; and they were reinforced by more arrivals from Stone Bridge. They avoided the camp by the spring, and when Shefford and Lake attempted to go to them they gave them a wide berth. This caused Joe to assert that they were up to some dirty work. All morning they lounged around under the cedars, keeping out of sight, and evidently the reinforcement from Stone Bridge had brought liquor. When they gathered together at their camp, half drunk, all noisy, some wanting to swagger off into the village and others trying to hold them back, Joe Lake said, grimly, that somebody was going to get shot. Indeed, Shefford saw that there was every likelihood of bloodshed.

"Reckon we'd better take to one of the cabins," said Joe.

Thereupon the three repaired to the nearest cabin, and, entering, kept watch from the windows. During a couple of hours, however, they did not see or hear anything of the ruffians. Then came a shot from over in the village, a single yell, and after that, a scattering volley. The silence and suspense which followed were finally broken by hoofbeats. Nas Ta Bega called Joe and Shefford to the window he had been stationed at. From here they saw the unwelcome visitors ride down the trail, to disappear in the cedars toward the outlet of the valley. Joe, who had numbered them, said that all but one of them had gone.

"Reckon he got it," added Joe.

So indeed it turned out; one of the men, a well-known rustler named Harker, had been killed, by whom no one seemed to know. He had brazenly tried to force his way into one of the houses, and the act had cost him his life. Naturally Shefford, never free from his civilized habit of thought, remarked apprehensively that he hoped this affair would not cause the poor women to be arrested again and haled before some rude court.

"Law!" grunted Joe. "There ain't any. The nearest sheriff is in Durango. That's Colorado. And he'd give us a medal for killing Harker. It was a good job, for it'll teach these rowdies a lesson."

The Mormons, notwithstanding their indifference to the killing of the desperado, gave him decent burial and prayed for his soul.

Next day the old order of life was resumed in the village. And the arrival of a heavily laden pack-train, under the guidance of Withers, attested to the fact that the Mormons meant not only to continue to live in the valley, but also to build and plant and enlarge. This was good news to Shefford. At least the village could be made less lonely. And there was plenty of work to give him excuse for staying there. Furthermore, Withers brought a message from Bishop Kane to the effect that the young man was offered a place as teacher in the school, in cooperation with the Mormon teachers. Shefford experienced no twinge of conscience when he accepted.

It was the fourth evening after the never-to-be-forgotten moonlight ride to the valley that Shefford passed under the dark piñon-trees on his way to Fay Larkin's cottage. He paused in the gloom and memory beset him. The six months were annihilated, and it was the night he had fled. But now all was silent. He seemed to be trying to drag himself back. A beginning must be made. Only how to meet her—what to say—what to conceal!

He tapped on the door and she came out. After all, it was a meeting vastly different from what his feeling made him imagine it might have been. She was nervous, frightened, as were all the other women, for that matter. She was alone in the cottage. He made haste to reassure her about the improbability of any further trouble such as had befallen the last week. As he had always done on those former visits to her, he talked rapidly, using all his wit, and here his emotion made him eloquent; he avoided personalities, except to tell about his prospects of work in the village, and he sought above all to lead her mind from thought of herself and her condition. Before he left her he had the gladness of knowing he had succeeded.

When he said good night he felt the strange falsity of his position. He did not expect to be able to keep up the deception for long. That roused him, and half the night he lay awake, thinking. Next day he was the life of the work and study and play in that village. Kindness and good-will did not need inspiration, but it was keen, deep passion that made him a plotter for influence and friendship. Was there a woman in the village whom he might trust, in case he needed one? And his instinct guided him to her whom he had liked well—Ruth. Ruth Jones she had called herself at the trial, and when Shefford used the name she laughed mockingly. Ruth was not very religious, and sometimes she was bitter and hard. She wanted life, and here she was a prisoner in a lonely valley. She welcomed Shefford's visits. He imagined that she had slightly changed, and whether it was the added six months with its trouble and pain or a growing revolt he could not tell. After a time he divined that the inevitable retrogression had set in: she had not enough faith to uphold the burden she had accepted, nor the courage to cast it off. She was ready to love him. That did not frighten Shefford, and if she did love him he was not so sure it would not be an anchor for her. He saw her danger, and then he became what he had never really been in all the days of his ministry—the real helper. Unselfishly, for her sake, he found power to influence her; and selfishly, for the sake of Fay Larkin, he began slowly to win her to a possible need.

The days passed swiftly. Mormons came and went, though in the open day, as laborers; new cabins went up, and a store, and other improvements. Some part of every evening Shefford spent with Fay, and these visits were no longer unknown to the village. Women gossiped, in a friendly way about Shefford, but with jealous tongues about the girl. Joe Lake told Shefford the run of the village talk. Anything concerning the Sago Lily the droll Mormon took to heart. He had been hard hit, and admitted it. Sometimes he went with Shefford to call upon her, but he talked little and never remained long. Shefford had anticipated antagonism on the part of Joe; however, he did not find it.

Shefford really lived through the busy day for that hour with Fay in the twilight. And every evening seemed the same. He would find her in the dark, alone, silent, brooding, hopeless. Her mood did not puzzle him, but how to keep from plunging her deeper into despair baffled him. He exhausted all his powers trying to do for her what he had been able to do for Ruth. Yet he failed. Something had blunted her. The shadow of that baneful trial hovered over her, and he came to sense a strange terror in her. It was mostly always present. Was she thinking of Jane Withersteen and Lassiter, left dead or imprisoned in the valley from which she had been brought so mysteriously? Shefford wearied his brain revolving these questions. The fate of her friends, and the cross she bore—of these was tragedy born, but the terror—that Shefford divined came of waiting for the visit of the Mormon whose face she had never seen. Shefford prayed that he might never meet this man. Finally he grew desperate. When he first arrived at the girl's home she would speak, she showed gladness, relief, and then straightway she dropped back into the shadow of her gloom. When he got up to go then there was a wistfulness, an unspoken need, an unconscious reliance, in her reluctant good night.

Then the hour came when he reached his limit. He must begin his revelation.

"You never ask me anything—let alone about myself," he said.

"I'd like to hear," she replied, timidly.

"Do I strike you as an unhappy man?"

"No, indeed."

"Well, how *do* I strike you?"

This was an entirely new tack he had veered to.

"Very good and kind to us women," she said.

"I don't know about that. If I am so, it doesn't bring me happiness. . . . Do you remember what I told you once, about my being a preacher—disgrace, ruin, and all that—and my rainbow-chasing dream out here after a—a lost girl?"

"I—remembered all—you said," she replied, very low.

"Listen." His voice was a little husky, but behind it there seemed a tide of resistless utterance. "Loss of faith and name did not send me to this wilderness. But I had love—love for that lost girl, Fay Larkin. I dreamed about her till I loved her. I dreamed that I would find her—my treasure—at the foot of a rainbow. Dreams! . . . When you told me she was dead I accepted that. There was truth in your voice. I respected your reticence. But something died in me then. I lost myself, the best of me, the good that might have uplifted me. I went away, down upon the barren desert, and there I rode and slept and grew into another and a harder man. Yet, strange to say, I never forgot her, though my dreams were done. As I toiled and suffered and changed I loved her—if not her, the thought of her—more and more. Now I have come back to these walled valleys—to the smell of the piñon, to the flowers in the nooks, to the wind on the heights, to the silence and loneliness and beauty. And here the dreams come back and *she* is *with* me always. Her spirit is all that keeps me kind and good, as you say I am. But I suffer, I long for her alive. If I love her dead, how could I love her living! Always I torture myself with the vain dream that—that she *might* not be dead. I have never been anything but a dreamer. And here I go about my work by day and lie awake at night with that lost girl in my mind. . . . I love her. Does that seem strange to you? But it would not if you understood. Think. I had lost faith, hope. I set myself a great work—to find Fay Larkin. And by the fire and the iron and the blood that I felt it would cost to save her some faith must come to me again. . . . My work is undone—I've never saved her. But listen, how strange it is to feel—now—as I let myself go—that just the loving her and the living here in the wildness that holds her somewhere have brought me hope again. Some faith must come, too. It was through her that I met this Indian, Nas Ta Bega. He has saved my life—taught me much. What would I ever have learned of the naked and vast earth, of the sublimity of the wild uplands, of the storm and night and sun, if I had not followed a gleam she inspired? In my hunt for a lost girl perhaps I wandered into a place where I shall find a God and my salvation. Do you marvel that I love Fay Larkin—that she is not dead to me? Do you marvel that I love her, when I *know*, were she alive, chained in a cañon, or bound, or lost in any way, my destiny would lead me to her, and she should be saved?"

Shefford ended, overcome with emotion. In the dusk he could not see the girl's face, but the white form that had drooped so listlessly seemed now charged by some vitalizing current. He knew he had spoken irrationally; still he held it no dishonor to have told her he loved her as one dead. If she took that love to the secret heart of living Fay Larkin, then perhaps a spirit might light in her darkened soul. He had no thought yet that Fay Larkin might ever belong to him. He divined a crime—he had seen her agony. And this avowal of his was only one step toward her deliverance.

Softly she rose, retreating into the shadow.

"Forgive me if I—I disturb you, distress you," he said. "I wanted to tell you. She was—somehow known to you. I am not happy. And are *you* happy? . . . Let her memory be a bond between us. . . . Good night."

"Good night."

Faintly as the faintest whisper breathed her reply, and, though it came from a child forced into womanhood, it whispered of girlhood not dead, of sweet incredulity, of amazed tumult, of a wondering, frantic desire to run and hide, of the bewilderment incident to a first hint of love.

Shefford walked away into the darkness. The whisper filled his soul. Had a word of love ever been spoken to that girl? Never—not the love which had been on his lips. Fay Larkin's lonely life spoke clearly in her whisper.

Next morning as the sun gilded the looming peaks and shafts of gold slanted into the valley she came swiftly down the path to the spring. Shefford paused in his task of chopping wood. Joe Lake, on his knees, with his big hands in a pan of dough, lifted his head to stare. She had left off the somber black hood, and, although that made a vast difference in her, still it was not enough to account for what struck both men.

"Good morning," she called, brightly.

They both answered, but not spontaneously. She stopped at the spring and with one sweep of her strong arm filled the bucket and lifted it. Then she started back down the path and, pausing opposite the camp, set the bucket down.

"Joe, do you still pride yourself on your sour dough?" she asked.

"Reckon I do," replied Joe, with a grin.

"I've heard your boasts, but never tasted your bread," she went on.

"I'll ask you to eat with us some day."

"Don't forget," she replied.

And then shyly she looked at Shefford. She was like the fresh dawn, and the gold of the sun shone on her head.

"Have you chopped all that wood—so early?" she asked.

"Sure," replied Shefford, laughing. "I have to get up early to keep Joe from doing all the camp chores."

She smiled, and then to Shefford she seemed to gleam, to be radiant.

"It'd be a lovely morning to climb—'way high."

"Why—yes—it would," replied Shefford, awkwardly. "I wish I didn't have my work."

"Joe, will *you* climb with me some day?"

"I should smile I will," declared Joe.

"But I can run right up the walls."

"I reckon. Mary, it wouldn't surprise me to see you fly."

"Do you mean I'm like a cañon swallow or an angel?"

Then, as Joe stared speechlessly, she said good-by and, taking up the bucket, went on with her swift, graceful step.

"She's perked up," said the Mormon, staring after her. "Never heard her say more'n yes or no till now."

"She did seem—bright," replied Shefford.

He was stunned. What had happened to her? To-day this girl had not been Mary, the sealed wife, or the Sago Lily, alien among Mormon women. Then it flashed upon him—she was Fay Larkin. She who had regarded herself as dead had come back to life. In one short night what had transformed her—what had taken place in her heart? Shefford dared not accept, nor allow lodgment in his mind, a thrilling idea that he had made her forget her misery.

"Shefford, did you ever see her like that?" asked Joe.

"Never."

"Haven't you—something to do with it?"

"Maybe I have. I—I hope so."

"Reckon you've seen how she's faded—since the trial?"

"No," replied Shefford, swiftly. "But I've not seen her face in daylight since then."

"Well, take my hunch," said Joe, soberly. "She's begun to fade like the cañon lily when it's broken. And she's going to die unless—"

"Why man!" ejaculated Shefford. "Didn't you see—"

"Sure I see," interrupted the Mormon. "I see a lot you don't. She's so white you can look through her. She's grown thin, all in a week. She doesn't eat. Oh, I know, because I've made it my business to find out. It's no news to the women. But they'd like to see her die. And she will die unless—"

"My God!" exclaimed Shefford, huskily. "I never noticed—I never thought. . . . Joe, hasn't she any friends?"

"Sure. You and Ruth—and me. Maybe Nas Ta Bega, too. He watches her a good deal."

"We can do so little, when she needs so much."

"Nobody can help her, unless it's you," went on the Mormon. "That's plain talk. She seemed different this morning. Why, she was alive—she talked—she smiled. . . . Shefford, if you cheer her up I'll go to hell for you!"

The big Mormon, on his knees, with his hands in a pan of dough, and his shirt all covered with flour, presented an incongruous figure of a man actuated by pathos and passion. Yet the contrast made his emotion all the simpler and stronger. Shefford grew closer to Joe in that moment.

"Why do you think *I* can cheer her, help her?" queried Shefford.

"I don't know. But she's different with you. It's not that you're a Gentile, though, for all the women are crazy about you. You talk to her. You have power over her, Shefford. I feel that. She's only a kid."

"Who is she, Joe? Where did she come from?" asked Shefford, very low, with his eyes cast down.

"I don't know. I can't find out. Nobody knows. It's a mystery—to all the younger Mormons, anyway."

Shefford burned to ask questions about the Mormon whose sealed wife the girl was, but he respected Joe too much to take advantage of him in a poignant moment like this. Besides, it was only jealousy that made him burn to know the Mormon's identity, and jealousy had become a creeping, insidious, growing fire. He would be wise not to add fuel to it. He rejected many things before he thought of one that he could voice to his friend.

"Joe, it's only her body that belongs to—to . . . Her soul is lost to—"

"John Shefford, let that go. My mind's tired. I've been taught so and so, and I'm not bright. . . . But, after all, men are much alike. The thing with you and me is this—we don't want to see *her* grave!"

Love spoke there. The Mormon had seized upon the single elemental point that concerned him and his friend in their relation to this unfortunate girl. His simple, powerful statement united them; it gave the lie to his hint of denseness; it stripped the truth naked. It was such a wonderful thought-provoking statement that Shefford needed time to ponder how deep the Mormon was. To what limit would he go? Did he mean that here, between two men who loved the same girl, class, duty, honor, creed were nothing if they stood in the way of her deliverance and her life?

"Joe Lake, you Mormons are impossible," said Shefford, deliberately. "You don't want to see her grave. So long as she lives—remains on the earth—white and gold like the flower you call her, that's enough for you. It's her body you think of. And that's the great and horrible error in your religion. . . . But death of the soul is infinitely worse than death of the body. I have been thinking of her soul. . . . So here we stand, you and I. You to save her life—I to save her soul! What will you do?"

"Why, John, I'd turn Gentile," he said, with terrible softness. It was a softness that scorned Shefford for asking, and likewise it flung defiance at his creed and into the face of hell.

Shefford felt the sting and the exaltation.

"And I'd be a Mormon," he said.

"All right. We understand each other. Reckon there won't be any call for such extremes. I haven't an idea what you mean—what can be done. But I say, go slow, so we won't all find graves. First cheer her up somehow. Make her want to live. But go slow, John. *And don't be with her late!*"

That night Shefford found her waiting for him in the moonlight— a girl who was as transparent as crystal-clear water, who had left off the somber gloom with the black hood, who tremulously embraced happiness without knowing it, who was one moment timid and wild like a half-frightened fawn, and the next, exquisitely half-conscious of what it meant to be thought dead, but to be alive, to be awakening, wondering, palpitating, and to be loved.

Shefford lived the hour as a dream and went back to the quiet darkness under the cedars to lie wide-eyed, trying to recall all that she had said. For she had talked as if utterance had long been dammed behind a barrier of silence.

There followed other hours like that one, indescribable hours, so sweet they stung, and in which, keeping pace with his love, was the nobler stride of a spirit that more every day lightened her burden.

The thing he had to do, sooner or later, was to tell her he knew she was Fay Larkin, not dead, but alive, and that, not love nor religion, but sacrifice, nailed her down to her martyrdom. Many and many a time he had tried to force himself to tell her, only to fail. He hated to risk ending this sweet, strange, thoughtless, girlish mood of hers. It might not be soon won back—perhaps never. How could he tell what chains bound her? And so as he vacillated between Joe's cautious advice to go slow and his own pity the days and weeks slipped by.

One haunting fear kept him sleepless half the nights and sick even in his dreams, and it was that the Mormon whose sealed wife she was might come, surely would come, some night. Shefford could bear it. But what would that visit do to Fay Larkin? Shefford instinctively feared the awakening in the girl of womanhood, of deeper insight, of a spiritual realization of what she was, of a physical dawn.

He might have spared himself needless torture. One day Joe Lake eyed him with penetrating glance.

"Reckon you don't have to sleep right on that Stone Bridge trail," said the Mormon, significantly.

Shefford felt the blood burn his neck and face. He had pulled his tarpaulin closer to the trail, and his motive was an open page to the keen Mormon.

"Why?" asked Shefford.

"There won't be any Mormons riding in here soon—by night—to visit the women," replied Joe, bluntly. "Haven't you figured there might be government spies watching the trails?"

"No, I haven't."

"Well, take a hunch, then," added the Mormon, gruffly, and Shefford divined, as well as if he had been told, that warning word had gone to Stone Bridge. Gone despite the fact that Nas Ta Bega had reported every trail free of watchers! There was no sign of any spies, cowboys, outlaws, or Indians in the vicinity of the valley. A passionate gratitude to the Mormon overcame Shefford; and the unreasonableness of it, the nature of it, perturbed him greatly. But, something hammered into his brain, if he loved one of these sealed wives, how could he help being jealous?

The result of Joe's hint was that Shefford put off the hour of revelation, lived in his dream, helped the girl grow farther and farther away from her trouble, until that inevitable hour arrived when he was driven by accumulated emotion as much as the exigency of the case.

He had not often walked with her beyond the dark shade of the piñons round the cottage, but this night, when he knew he must tell her, he led her away down the path, through the cedar grove to the west end of the valley where it was wild and lonely and sad and silent.

The moon was full and the great peaks were crowned as with snow. A coyote uttered his cutting cry. There were a few melancholy notes from a night bird of the stone walls. The air was clear and cold, with a tang of frost in it. Shefford gazed about him at the vast, uplifted, insulating walls, and that feeling of his which was more than a sense told him how walls like these and the silence and shadow and mystery had been nearly all of Fay Larkin's life. He felt them all in her.

He stopped out in the open, near the line where dark shadow of the wall met the silver moonlight on the grass, and here, by a huge flat stone where he had come often alone and sometimes with Ruth, he faced Fay Larkin in the spirit to tell her gently that he knew her, and sternly to force her secret from her.

"Am I your friend?" he began.

"Ah!—my only friend," she said.

"Do you trust me, believe I mean well by you, want to help you?"

"Yes, indeed."

"Well, then, let me speak of you. You know one topic we've never touched upon. You!"

She was silent, and looked wonderingly, a little fearfully at him, as if vague, disturbing thoughts were entering the fringe of her mind.

"Our friendship is a strange one, is it not?" he went on.

"How do I know? I never had any other friendship. What do you mean by strange?"

"Well, I'm a young man. You're a—a married woman. We are together a good deal—and like to be."

"Why is that strange?" she asked.

Suddenly Shefford realized that there was nothing strange in what was natural. A remnant of sophistication clung to him and that had spoken. He needed to speak to her in a way which in her simplicity she would understand.

"Never mind strange. Say that I am interested in you, and, as you're not happy, I want to help you. And say that your neighbors are curious and oppose my idea. Why do they?"

"They're jealous and want you themselves," she replied, with sweet directness. "They've said things I don't understand. But I felt they—they hated in me what would be all right in themselves."

Here to simplicity she added truth and wisdom, as an Indian might have expressed them. But shame was unknown to her, and she had as yet only vague perceptions of love and passion. Shefford began to realize the quickness of her mind, that she was indeed awakening.

"They are jealous—were jealous before I ever came here. That's only human nature. I was trying to get to a point. Your neighbors are curious. They oppose me. They hate you. It's all bound up in the—the fact of your difference from them, your youth, beauty, that you're not a Mormon, that you nearly betrayed their secret at the trial in Stone Bridge."

"Please—please don't—speak of that!" she faltered.

"But I must," he replied, swiftly. "That trial was a torture to you. It revealed so much to me. . . . I know you are a sealed wife. I know there has been a crime. I know you've sacrificed yourself. I know that love and religion have nothing to do with—what you are. . . . Now, is not all that true?"

"I must not tell," she whispered.

"But I shall *make* you tell," he replied, and his voice rang.

"Oh no, you cannot," she said.

"I can—with just one word!"

Her eyes were great, starry, shadowy gulfs, dark in the white beauty of her face. She was calm now. She had strength. She invited him to speak the word, and the wistful, tremulous quiver of her lips was for his earnest thought of her.

"Wait—a—little," said Shefford, unsteadily. "I'll come to that presently. Tell me this—have you ever thought of being free?"

"Free!" she echoed, and there was singular depth and richness in her voice. That was the first spark of fire he had struck from her. "Long ago, the minute I was unwatched, I'd have leaped from a wall had I dared. Oh, I wasn't afraid. I'd love to die that way. But I never dared."

"Why?" queried Shefford, piercingly.

She was silent then.

"Suppose I offered to give you freedom that meant life?"

"I—couldn't—take it."

"Why?"

"Oh, my friend, don't ask me any more."

"I know, I can see—you want to tell me—you need to tell."

"But I daren't."

"Won't you trust me?"

"I do—I do."

"Then tell me."

"No—no—oh no!"

The moment had come. How sad, tragic, yet glorious for him! It would be like a magic touch upon this lovely, cold, white ghost of Fay Larkin, transforming her into a living, breathing girl. He held his love as a thing aloof, and, as such, intangible because of the living death she believed she lived, it had no warmth and intimacy for them. What might it not become with a lightning flash of revelation? He dreaded, yet he was driven to speak. He waited, swallowing hard, fighting the tumultuous storm of emotion, and his eyes dimmed.

"What did I come to this country for?" he asked, suddenly, in ringing, powerful voice.

"To find a girl," she whispered.

"I've found her!"

She began to shake. He saw a white hand go to her breast.

"Where is Surprise Valley? . . . How were you taken from Jane Withersteen and Lassiter? . . . I know they're alive. But where?"

She seemed to turn to stone.

"Fay!—*Fay Larkin!* . . . I KNOW YOU!" he cried, brokenly.

She slipped off the stone to her knees, swayed forward blindly with her hands reaching out, her head falling back to let the moon fall full upon the beautiful, snow-white, tragically convulsed face.

CHAPTER 13

THE STORY OF
SURPRISE VALLEY

". . . Oh, I remember so well! Even now I dream of it sometimes. I hear the roll and crash of falling rock—like thunder. . . . We rode and rode. Then the horses fell. Uncle Jim took me in his arms and started up the cliff. Mother Jane climbed close after us. They kept looking back. Down there in the gray valley came the Mormons. I see the first one now. He rode a white horse. That was Tull. Oh, I remember so well! And I was five or six years old.

"We climbed up and up and into dark cañons and wound in and out. Then there was the narrow white trail, straight up, with the little cut steps and the great, red, ruined walls. I looked down over Uncle Jim's shoulder. I saw Mother Jane dragging herself up. Uncle Jim's blood spotted the trail. He reached a flat place at the top and fell with me. Mother Jane crawled up to us.

"Then she cried out and pointed. Tull was 'way below, climbing the trail. His men came behind him. Uncle Jim went to a great, tall rock and leaned against it. There was a bloody hole in his hand. He pushed the rock. It rolled down, banging the loose walls. They crashed and crashed—then all was terrible thunder and red smoke. I couldn't hear—I couldn't see.

"Uncle Jim carried me down and down out of the dark and dust into a beautiful valley all red and gold, with a wonderful arch of stone over the entrance.

"I don't remember well what happened then for what seemed a long, long time. I can feel how the place looked, but not so clear as it is now in my dreams. I seem to see myself with the dogs, and with Mother Jane, learning my letters, marking with red stone on the walls.

"But I remember now how I felt when I first understood we were shut in for ever. Shut in Surprise Valley where Venters had lived so long. I was glad. The Mormons would never get me. I was seven or eight years old then. From that time all is clear in my mind.

"Venters had left supplies and tools and grain and cattle and burros, so we had a good start to begin life there. He had killed off the wildcats and kept the coyotes out, so the rabbits and quail multiplied till there were thousands of them. We raised corn and fruit, and stored what we didn't use. Mother Jane taught me to read and write with the soft red stone that marked well on the walls.

"The years passed. We kept track of time pretty well. Uncle Jim's hair turned white and Mother Jane grew gray. Every day was like the one before. Mother Jane cried sometimes and Uncle Jim was sad because they could never be able to get me out of the valley. It was long before they stopped looking and listening for some one. Venters would come back, Uncle Jim always said. But Mother Jane did not think so.

"I loved Surprise Valley. I wanted to stay there always. I remembered Cottonwoods, how the children there hated me, and I didn't want to go back. The only unhappy times I ever had in the valley were when Ring and Whitie, my dogs, grew old and died. I roamed the valley. I climbed to every nook upon the mossy ledges. I learned to run up the steep cliffs. I could almost stick on the straight walls. Mother Jane called me a wild girl. We had put away the clothes we wore when we got there, to save them, and we made clothes of skins. I always laughed when I thought of my little dress—how I grew out of it. I think Uncle Jim and Mother Jane talked less as the years went by. And after I'd learned all she could teach me we didn't talk much. I used to scream into the caves just to hear my voice, and the echoes would frighten me.

"The older I grew the more I was alone. I was always running round the valley. I would climb to a high place and sit there for hours, doing nothing. I just watched and listened. I used to stay in the cliff-dwellers' caves and wonder about them. I loved to be out in the wind. And my happiest time was in the summer storms with the thunder echoes under the walls. At evening it was such a quiet place—after the night bird's cry, no sound. The quiet made me sad, but I loved it. I loved to watch the stars as I lay awake.

"So it was beautiful and happy for me there till—till . . .

"Two years or more ago there was a bad storm, and one of the great walls caved. The walls were always weathering, slipping. Many and many a time have I heard the rumble of an avalanche, but most of them were in other cañons. This slide in the valley made it possible, Uncle Jim said, for men to get down into the valley. But we could not climb out unless helped from above. Uncle Jim never rested well after that. But it never worried me.

"One day, over a year ago, while I was across the valley, I heard strange shouts, and then screams. I ran to our camp. I came upon men with ropes and guns. Uncle Jim was tied, and a rope was round his neck. Mother Jane was lying on the ground. I thought she was dead until I heard her moan. I was not afraid. I screamed and flew at Uncle Jim to tear the ropes off him. The men held me back. They called me a pretty cat. Then they talked together, and some were for hanging Lassiter— that was the first time I ever knew any name for him but Uncle Jim—and some were for leaving him in the valley. Finally they decided to hang him. But Mother Jane pleaded so and I screamed and fought so that they left off. Then they went away and we saw them climb out of the valley.

"Uncle Jim said they were Mormons, and some among them had been born in Cottonwoods. I was not told why they had such a terrible hate for him. He said they would come back and kill him. Uncle Jim had no guns to fight with.

"We watched and watched. In five days they did come back, with more men, and some of them wore black masks. They came to our cave with ropes and guns. One was tall. He had a cruel voice. The others ran to obey him. I could see white hair and sharp eyes behind the mask. The men caught me and brought me before him.

"He said Lassiter had killed many Mormons. He said Lassiter had killed his father and should be hanged. But Lassiter would be let live and Mother Jane could stay with him, both prisoners there in the valley, if I would marry the Mormon. I must marry him, accept the Mormon faith, and bring up my children as Mormons. If I refused they would hang Lassiter, leave the heretic Jane Withersteen alone in the valley, and take me and break me to their rule.

"I agreed. But Mother Jane absolutely forbade me to marry him. Then the Mormons took me away. It nearly killed me to leave Uncle Jim and Mother Jane. I was carried and lifted out of the valley, and rode a long way on a horse. They brought me here, to the cabin where I live, and I have never been away except that—that time—to—Stone Bridge. Only little by little did I learn my position. Bishop Kane was kind, but stern, because I could not be quick to learn the faith.

"I am not a sealed wife. But they're trying to make me one. The master Mormon—he visited me often—at night—till lately. He threatened me. He never told me a name—except Saint George. I don't—know him—except his voice. I never—saw his face—in the light!"

Fay Larkin ended her story. Toward its close Shefford had grown involuntarily restless, and when her last tragic whisper ceased all his body seemed shaken with a terrible violence of his joy. He strode to and fro in the dark shadow of the stone. The receding blood left him cold, with a pricking, sickening sensation over his body, but there seemed to be an overwhelming tide accumulating deep in his breast—a tide of passion and pain. He dominated the passion, but the ache remained. And he returned to the quiet figure on the stone.

"Fay Larkin!" he exclaimed, with a deep breath of relief that the secret was disclosed. "So you're not a wife! . . . You're free! Thank Heaven! But I felt it was sacrifice. I knew there had been a crime. For crime it is. You child! You can't understand what crime. Oh, almost I wish you and Jane and Lassiter had never been found. But that's wrong of me. One year of agony—that shall not ruin your life. Fay, I will take you away."

"Where?" she whispered.

"Away from this Mormon country—to the East," he replied, and he spoke of what he had known, of travel, of cities, of people, of happiness possible for a young girl who had spent all her life hidden between the narrow walls of a silent, lonely valley—he spoke swiftly and eloquently till he lost his breath.

There was an instant of flashing wonder and joy on her white face, and then the radiance paled, the glow died. Her soul was the darker for that one strange, leaping glimpse of a glory not for such as she.

"I must stay here," she said, shudderingly.

"Fay!—How strange to *say* Fay aloud to *you*!—Fay, do you know the way to Surprise Valley?"

"I don't know where it is, but I could go straight to it," she replied.

"Take me there. Show me your beautiful valley. Let me see where you ran and climbed and spent so many lonely years."

"Ah, how I'd love to! But I dare not. And why should you want me to take you? We can run and climb here."

"I want to—I mean to save Jane Withersteen and Lassiter," he declared.

She uttered a little cry of pain. "Save them?"

"Yes, save them. Get them out of the valley, take them out of the country, far away where they and *you*—"

"But I can't go," she wailed. "I'm afraid. I'm bound. It *can't* be broken. If I dared—if I tried to go they would catch me. They would hang Uncle Jim and leave Mother Jane alone there to starve."

"Fay, Lassiter and Jane both will starve—at least they will die there if we do not save them. You have been terribly wronged. You're a slave. You're not a wife."

"They—said I'll be burned in hell if I don't marry him. . . . Mother Jane never taught me about God. I don't know. But *he*—he said God was there. I dare not break it."

"Fay, you have been deceived by old men. Let them have their creed. But *you* mustn't accept it."

"John, what is God to you?"

"Dear child, I—I am not sure of that myself," he replied, huskily. "When all this trouble is behind us, surely I can help you to understand and you can help me. The fact that you are alive—that Lassiter and Jane are alive—that I shall save you all—that lifts me up. I tell you—Fay Larkin will be my salvation."

"Your words trouble me. Oh, I shall be torn one way and another. . . . But, John, I daren't run away. I will not tell you where to find Lassiter and Mother Jane."

"I shall find them. I have the Indian. He found you for me. Nas Ta Bega will find Surprise Valley."

"Nas Ta Bega! . . . Oh, I remember. There was an Indian with the Mormons who found us. But he was a Piute."

"Nas Ta Bega never told me how he learned about you. That he learned was enough. And, Fay, he will find Surprise Valley. He will save Uncle Jim and Mother Jane."

Fay's hands clasped Shefford's in strong, trembling pressure; the tears streamed down her white cheeks; a tragic and eloquent joy convulsed her face.

"Oh, my friend, save them! But I can't go. . . . Let them keep me! Let him kill me!"

"Him! Fay—he shall not harm you," replied Shefford in passionate earnestness.

She caught the hand he had struck out with.

"You talk—you look like Uncle Jim when he spoke of the Mormons," she said. "Then I used to be afraid of him. He was so different. John, you must not do anything about me. Let me be. It's too late. He—and his men—they would hang you. And I couldn't bear that. I've enough to bear without losing my friend. Say you won't watch and wait—for—for him."

Shefford had to promise her. Like an Indian she gave expression to primitive feeling, for it certainly never occurred to her that, whatever Shefford might do, he was not the kind of man to wait in hiding for an enemy. Fay had faltered through her last speech and was now weak and nervous and frightened. Shefford took her back to the cabin.

"Fay, don't be distressed," he said. "I won't do anything right away. You can trust me. I won't be rash. I'll consult you before I make a move. I haven't any idea what I could do, anyway. . . . You must bear up. Why, it looks as if you're sorry I found you."

"Oh! I'm glad!" she whispered.

"Then if you're glad you mustn't break down this way again. Suppose some of the women happened to run into us."

"I won't again. It's only you—you surprised me so. I used to think how I'd like you to know—I wasn't really dead. But now—it's different. It hurts me here. Yet I'm glad—if my being alive makes you—a little happier."

Shefford felt that he had to go then. He could not trust himself any further.

"Good night, Fay," he said.

"Good night, John," she whispered. "I promise—to be good to-morrow."

She was crying softly when he left her. Twice he turned to see the dim, white, slender form against the gloom of the cabin. Then he went on under the piñons, blindly down the path, with his heart as heavy as lead. That night as he rolled in his blanket and stretched wearily he felt that he would never be able to sleep. The wind in the cedars made him shiver. The great stars seemed relentless, passionless, white eyes, mocking his little destiny and his pain. The huge shadow of the mountain resembled the shadow of the insurmountable barrier between Fay and him.

Her pitiful, childish promise to be good was in his mind when he went to her home on the next night. He wondered how she would be, and he realized a desperate need of self-control.

But that night Fay Larkin was a different girl. In the dark, before she spoke, he felt a difference that afforded him surprise and relief. He greeted her as usual. And then it seemed, though not at all clearly, that he was listening to a girl, strangely and unconsciously glad to see him, who spoke with deeper note in her voice, who talked where always she had listened, whose sadness was there under an eagerness, a subdued gaiety as new to her, as sweet as it was bewildering. And he responded with emotion, so that the hour passed swiftly, and he found himself back in camp; in a kind of dream, unable to remember much of what she had said, sure only of this strange sweetness suddenly come to her.

Upon the following night, however, he discovered what had wrought this singular change in Fay Larkin. She loved him and she did not know it. How passionately sweet and sad and painful was that realization for Shefford! The hour spent with her then was only a moment.

He walked under the stars that night and they shed a glorious light upon him. He tried to think, to plan, but the sweetness of remembered word or look made mental effort almost impossible. He got as far as the thought that he would do well to drift, to wait till she learned she loved him, and then, perhaps, she could be persuaded to let him take her and Lassiter and Jane away together.

And from that night he went at his work and the part he played in the village with a zeal and a cunning that left him free to seek Fay when he chose.

Sometimes in the afternoon, always for a while in the evening, he was with her. They climbed the walls, and sat upon a lonely height to look afar; they walked under the stars, and the cedars, and the shadows of the great cliffs. She had a beautiful mind. Listening to her, he imagined he saw down into beautiful Surprise Valley with all its weird shadows, its colored walls and painted caves, its golden shafts of morning light and the red haze at sunset; and he felt the silence that must have been there, and the singing of the wind in the cliffs, and the sweetness and fragrance of the flowers, and the wildness of it all. Love had worked a marvelous transformation in this girl who had lived her life in a cañon. The burden upon her did not weigh heavily. She could not have an unhappy thought. She spoke of the village, of her Mormon companions, of daily happenings, of Stone Bridge, of many things in a matter-of-fact way that showed how little they occupied her mind. She even spoke of sealed wives in a kind of dreamy abstraction. Something had possession of her, something as strong as the nature which had developed her, and in its power she, in her simplicity, was utterly unconscious, a watching and feeling girl. A strange, witching, radiant beauty lurked in her smile. And Shefford heard her laugh in his dreams.

The weeks slipped by. The black mountain took on a white cap of snow; in the early mornings there was ice in the crevices on the heights and frost in the valley. In the sheltered cañons where sunshine seemed to linger it was warm and pleasant, so that winter did not kill the flowers.

Shefford waited so long for Fay's awakening that he believed it would never come, and, believing, had not the heart to force it upon her. Then there was a growing fear with him. What would Fay Larkin do when she awakened to the truth? Fay was indeed like that white and fragile lily which bloomed in the silent, lonely cañons, but the same nature that had created it had created her. Would she droop as the lily would in a furnace blast? More than that, he feared a sudden flashing into life of strength, power, passion, hate. She did not hate yet because she did not yet realize love. She was utterly innocent of any wrong having been done her. More and more he began to fear, and a foreboding grew upon him. He made up his mind to broach the subject of Surprise Valley and of escaping with Lassiter and Jane; still, every time he was with Fay the girl and her beauty and her love were so wonderful that he put off the ordeal till the next night. As time flew by he excused his vacillation on the score that winter was not a good time to try to cross the desert. There was no grass for the mustangs, except in well-known valleys, and these he must shun. Spring would soon come. So the days passed, and he loved Fay more all the time, desperately living out to its limit the sweetness of every moment with her, and paying for his bliss in the increasing trouble that beset him when once away from her charm.

One starry night, about ten o'clock, he went, as was his custom, to drink at the spring. Upon his return to the cedars Nas Ta Bega, who slept under the same tree with him, had arisen, with his blanket hanging half off his shoulder.

"Listen," said the Indian.

Shefford took one glance at the dark, somber face, with its inscrutable eyes, now so strange and piercing, and then, with a kind of cold excitement, he faced the way the Indian looked, and listened. But he heard only the soft moan of the night wind in the cedars.

Nas Ta Bega kept the rigidity of his position for a moment, and then he relaxed, and stood at ease. Shefford knew the Indian had made a certainty of what must have been a doubtful sound. And Shefford leaned his ear to the wind and strained his hearing.

Then the soft night breeze brought a faint patter—the slow trot of horses on a hard trail. Some one was coming into the village at a late hour. Shefford thought of Joe Lake. But Joe lay right behind him, asleep in his blankets. It could not be Withers, for the trader was in Durango at that time. Shefford thought of Willetts and Shadd.

"Who's coming?" he asked low of the Indian.

Nas Ta Bega pointed down the trail without speaking.

Shefford peered through the white dim haze of starlight and presently he made out moving figures. Horses, with riders—a string of them—one—two—three—four—five—and he counted up to eleven. Eleven horsemen riding into the village! He was amazed, and suddenly keenly anxious. This visit might be one of Shadd's raids.

"Shadd's gang!" he whispered.

"No, Bi Nai," replied Nas Ta Bega, and he drew Shefford farther into the shade of the cedars. His voice, his action, the way he kept a hand on Shefford's shoulder, all this told much to the young man.

Mormons come on a night visit! Shefford realized it with a slight shock. Then swift as a lightning flash he was rent by another shock—one that brought cold moisture to his brow and to his heart a flame of hell.

He was shaking when he sank down to find the support of a log. Like a shadow the Indian silently moved away. Shefford watched the eleven horses pass the camp, go down the road, to disappear in the village. They vanished, and the soft clip-clops of hoofs died away. There was nothing left to prove he had not dreamed.

Nothing to prove it except this sudden terrible demoralization of his physical and spiritual being! While he peered out into the valley, toward the black patch of cedars and piñons that hid the cabins, moments and moments passed, and in them he was gripped with cold and fire.

Was the Mormon who had abducted Fay—the man with the cruel voice—was he among those eleven horsemen? He might not have been. What a torturing hope! But vain—vain, for inevitably he must be among them. He was there in the cabin already. He had dismounted, tied his horse, had knocked on her door. Did he need to knock? No, he would go in, he would call her in that cruel voice, and then . . .

Shefford pulled a blanket from his bed and covered his cold and trembling body. He had sunk down off the log, was leaning back upon it. The stars were pale, far off, and the valley seemed unreal. He found himself listening—listening with sick and terrible earnestness, trying to hear against the thrum and beat of his heart, straining to catch a sound in all that cold, star-blanched, silent valley. But he could hear no sound. It was as if death held the valley in its perfect silence. How he hated that silence! There ought to have been a million horrible, bellowing demons making the night hideous. Did the stars serenely look down upon the lonely cabins of these exiles? Was there no thunderbolt to drop down from that dark and looming mountain upon the silent cabin where tragedy had entered? In all the world, under the sea, in the abysmal caves, in the vast spaces of the air, there was no such terrible silence as this. A scream, a long cry, a moan—these were natural to a woman, and why did not one of these sealed wives, why did not Fay Larkin, damn this everlasting acquiescent silence? Perhaps she would fly out of her cabin, come running along the path. Shefford peered into the bright patches of starlight and into the shadows of the cedars. But he saw no moving form in the open, no dim white shape against the gloom. And he heard no sound—not even a whisper of wind in the branches overhead.

Nas Ta Bega returned to the shade of the cedars and, lying down on his blankets, covered himself and went to sleep. The fact seemed to bring bitter reality to Shefford. Nothing was going to happen. The valley was to be the same this night as any other night. Shefford accepted the truth. He experienced a kind of self-pity. The night he had thought so much about, prepared for, and had forgotten had now arrived. Then he threw another blanket round him, and, cold, dark, grim, he faced that lonely vigil, meaning to sit there, wide-eyed, to endure and to wait.

Jealousy and pain, following his frenzy, abided with him long hours, and when they passed he divined that selfishness passed with them. What he suffered then was for Fay Larkin and for her sisters in misfortune. He grew big enough to pity these fanatics. The fiery, racing tide of blood that had made of him only an animal had cooled with thought of others. Still he feared that stultifying thing which must have been hate. What a tempest had raged within him! This blood of his, that had received a stronger strain from his desert life, might in a single moment flood out reason and intellect and make him a vengeful man. So in those starlit hours that dragged interminably he looked deep into his heart and tried to fortify himself against a dark and evil moment to come.

Midnight—and the valley seemed a tomb! Did he alone keep wakeful? The sky was a darker blue, the stars burned a whiter fire, the peaks stood looming and vast, tranquil sentinels of that valley, and the wind rose to sigh, to breathe, to mourn through the cedars. It was a sad music.

The Indian lay prone, dark face to the stars. Joe Lake lay prone, sleeping as quietly, with his dark face exposed to the starlight. The gentle movement of the cedar branches changed the shape of the bright patches on the grass where shadow and light met. The walls of the valley waved upward, dark below and growing paler, to shine faintly at the rounded rims. And there was a tiny, silvery tinkle of running water over stones.

Here was a little nook of the vast world. Here were tranquillity, beauty, music, loneliness, life. Shefford wondered—did he alone keep watchful? Did he feel that he could see dark, wide eyes peering into the gloom? And it came to him after a time that he was not alone in his vigil, nor was Fay Larkin alone in her agony. There was some one else in the valley, a great and breathing and watchful spirit. It entered into Shefford's soul and he trembled. What had come to him? And he answered— only added pain and new love, and a strange strength from the firmament and the peaks and the silence and the shadows.

The bright belt with its three radiant stars sank behind the western wall and there was a paler gloom upon the valley.

Then a few lights twinkled in the darkness that enveloped the cabins; a woman's laugh strangely broke the silence, profaning it, giving the lie to that somber yoke which seemed to consist of the very shadows; the voices of men were heard, and then the slow clip-clop of trotting horses on the hard trail.

Shefford saw the Mormons file out into the paling starlight, ride down the valley, and vanish in the gray gloom. He was aware that the Indian sat up to watch the procession ride by, and that Joe turned over, as if disturbed.

One by one the stars went out. The valley became a place of gray shadows. In the east a light glowed. Shefford sat there, haggard and worn, watching the coming of the dawn, the kindling of the light; and had the power been his the dawn would never have broken and the rose and gold never have tipped the lofty peaks.

Shefford attended to his camp chores as usual. Several times he was aware of Joe's close scrutiny, and finally, without looking at him, Shefford told of the visit of the Mormons. A violent expulsion of breath was

Joe's answer and it might have been a curse. Straightway Joe ceased his cheery whistling and became as somber as the Indian. The camp was silent; the men did not look at one another. While they sat at breakfast Shefford's back was turned toward the village; he had not looked in that direction since dawn.

"Ugh!" suddenly exclaimed Nas Ta Bega.

Joe Lake muttered low and deep, and this time there was no mistake about the nature of his speech. Shefford did not have the courage to turn to see what had caused these exclamations. He knew since today had dawned that there was calamity in the air.

"Shefford, I reckon if I know women there's a little hell coming to you," said the Mormon, significantly.

Shefford wheeled as if a powerful force had turned him on a pivot. He saw Fay Larkin. She seemed to be almost running. She was unhooded and her bright hair streamed down. Her swift, lithe action was without its usual grace. She looked wild, and she almost fell crossing the stepping-stones of the brook.

Joe hurried to meet her, took hold of her arm and spoke, but she did not seem to hear him. She drew him along with her, up the little bench under the cedars straight toward Shefford. Her face held a white, mute agony, as if in the hour of strife it had hardened into marble. But her eyes were dark-purple fire—windows of an extraordinarily intense and vital life. In one night the girl had become a woman. But the blight Shefford had dreaded to see—the withering of the exquisite soul and spirit and purity he had considered inevitable, just as inevitable as the death of something familiar in the flower she resembled, when it was broken and defiled—nothing of this was manifest in her. Straight and swiftly she came to him back in the shade of the cedars and took hold of his hands.

"Last night—*he came!*" she said.

"Yes—Fay—I—I know," replied Shefford, haltingly.

He was tremblingly conscious of amaze at her—of something wonderful in her. She did not heed Joe, who stepped aside a little; she did not see Nas Ta Bega, who sat motionless on a log, apparently oblivious to her presence.

"You knew he came?"

"Yes, Fay. I was awake when—they rode in. I watched them. I sat up all night. I saw them ride away."

"If you knew when he came why didn't you run to me—to get to me before he did?"

Her question was unanswerable. It had the force of a blow. It stunned him. Its sharp, frank directness sprang from a simplicity and a strength that had not been nurtured in the life he had lived. So far men had wandered from truth and nature!

"I came to you as soon as I was able," she went on. "I must have fainted. I just had to drag myself around. . . . And now I can tell you."

He was powerless to reply, as if she had put another unanswerable question. What did she mean to tell him? What might she not tell him? She loosed her hands from his and lifted them to his shoulders, and that was the first conscious action of feeling, of intimacy, which she had ever shown. It quite robbed Shefford of strength, and in spite of his sorrow there was an indefinable thrill in her touch. He looked at her, saw the white-and-gold beauty that was hers yesterday and seemed changed today, and he recognized Fay Larkin in a woman he did not know.

"Listen! He came—"

"Fay, don't—tell me," interrupted Shefford.

"I *will* tell you," she said.

Did the instinct of love teach her how to mitigate his pain? Shefford felt that, as he felt the new-born strength in her.

"Listen," she went on. "He came when I was undressing for bed. I heard the horse. He knocked on the door. Something terrible happened to me then. I felt sick and my head wasn't clear. I remember next—his being in the room—the lamp was out—I couldn't see very well. He thought I was sick and he gave me a drink and let the air blow in on me through the window. I remember I lay back in the chair and I thought. And I listened. When would you come? I didn't feel that you could leave me there alone with him. For his coming was different this time. That pain like a blade in my side! . . . When it came I was not the same. I loved you. I understood then. I belonged to you. I couldn't let him touch me. I had never been his wife. When I realized this—that he was there, that you might suffer for it—I cried right out.

"He thought I was sick. He worked over me. He gave me medicine.

And then he prayed. I saw him, in the dark, on his knees, praying for me. That seemed strange. Yet he was kind, so kind that I begged him to let me go. I was not a Mormon. I couldn't marry him. I begged him to let me go.

"Then he thought I had been deceiving him. He fell into a fury. He talked for a long time. He called upon God to visit my sins upon me. He tried to make me pray. But I wouldn't. And then—I fought him. I'd have screamed for you had he not smothered me. I got weak. . . . And you never came. I know I thought you would come. But you didn't. Then I—I gave out. And after—some time—I must have fainted."

"Fay! For Heaven's sake, how could I come to you?" burst out Shefford, hoarse and white with remorse, passion, pain.

"If I'm any man's wife I'm yours. It's a thing you *feel*, isn't it? I know that now. . . . But I want to know what to do?"

"Fay!" he cried, huskily.

"I'm sick of it all. If it weren't for you I'd climb the wall and throw myself off. That would be easy for me. I'd love to die that way. All my life I've been high up on the walls. To fall would be nothing!"

"Oh, you mustn't talk like that!"

"Do you love me?" she asked, with a low and deathless sweetness.

"Love you? With all my heart! Nothing can change that!"

"Do you want me—as you used to want the Fay Larkin lost in Surprise Valley? Do you love me that way? I understand things better than before, but still—not all. I *am* Fay Larkin. I think I must have dreamed of you all my life. I was glad when you came here. I've been happy lately. I forgot—till last night. Maybe it needed that to make me see I've loved you all the time. . . . And I fought him like a wildcat! . . . Tell me the truth. I *feel* I'm yours. Is that true? If I'm not—I'll not live another hour. Something holds me up. I am the same. . . . Do you want me?"

"Yes, Fay Larkin, I want you," replied Shefford, steadily, with his grip on her arms.

"Then take me away. I don't want to live here another hour."

"Fay, I'll take you. But it can't be done at once. We must plan. I need help. There are Lassiter and Jane to get out of Surprise Valley. Give me time, dear—give me time. It'll be a hard job. And we must plan so we can positively get away. Give me time, Fay."

"Suppose *he* comes back?" she queried, with a singular depth of voice.

"We'll have to risk that," replied Shefford, miserably. "But—he won't come soon."

"He said he would," she flashed.

Shefford seemed to freeze inwardly with her words. Love had made her a woman and now the woman in her was speaking. She saw the truth as he could not see it. And the truth was nature. She had been hidden all her life from the world, from knowledge as he had it, yet when love betrayed her womanhood to her she acquired all its subtlety.

"If I wait and he *does* come will you keep me from him?" she asked.

"How can I? I'm staking all on the chance of his not coming soon. . . . But, Fay, if he does come and I don't give up our secret—how on earth can I keep you from him?" demanded Shefford.

"If you love me you will do it," she said, as simply as if she were fate.

"But how?" cried Shefford, almost beside himself.

"You are a man. Any man would save the woman who loves him from—from— Oh, from a beast! . . . How would Lassiter do it?"

"Lassiter!"

"You can kill him!"

It was there, deep and full in her voice, the strength of the elemental forces that had surrounded her, primitive passion and hate and love, as they were in woman in the beginning.

"My God!" Shefford cried aloud with his spirit when all that was red in him sprang again into a flame of hell. That was what had been wrong with him last night. He could kill this stealthy night-rider and now, face to face with Fay, who had never been so beautiful and wonderful as in this hour when she made love the only and the sacred thing of life, now he had it in him to kill. Yet, murder—even to kill a brute—that was not for John Shefford, not the way for him to save a woman. Reason and wisdom still fought the passion in him. If he could but cling to them—have them with him in the dark and contending hour!

She leaned against him now, exhausted, her soul in her eyes, and they saw only him. Shefford was all but powerless to resist the longing to take her into his arms, to hold her to his heart, to let himself go. Did not her love give her to him? Shefford gazed helplessly at the stricken Joe Lake, at the somber Indian, as if from them he expected help.

"I know him now," said Fay, breaking the silence with startling suddenness.

"What!"

"I've seen him in the light. I flashed a candle in his face. I saw it. I know him now. He was there at Stone Bridge with us, and I never knew him. But I know him now. His name is—"

"For God's sake don't tell me who he is!" implored Shefford.

Ignorance was Shefford's safeguard against himself. To make a name of this heretofore intangible man, to give him an identity apart from the crowd, to be able to recognize him—that for Shefford would be fatal.

"Fay—tell me—no more," he said, brokenly. "I love you and I will give you my life. Trust me. I swear I'll save you."

"Will you take me away soon?"

"Yes."

She appeared satisfied with that and dropped her hands and moved back from him. A light flitted over her white face, and her eyes drew dark and humid, losing their fire in changing, shadowing thought of submission, of trust, of hope.

"I can lead you to Surprise Valley," she said. "I feel the way. It's there!" And she pointed to the west.

"Fay, we'll go—soon. I must plan. I'll see you tonight. Then we'll talk. Run home now, before some of the women see you here."

She said good-by and started away under the cedars, out into the open where her hair shone like gold in the sunlight, and she took the stepping-stones with her old free grace, and strode down the path swift and lithe as an Indian. Once she turned to wave a hand.

Shefford watched her with a torture of pride, love, hope, and fear contending within him.

CHAPTER 14

THE NAVAJO

That morning a Piute rode into the valley. Shefford recognized him as the brave who had been in love with Glen Naspa. The moment Nas Ta Bega saw this visitor he made a singular motion with his hands—a motion that somehow to Shefford suggested despair—and then he waited, somber and statuesque, for the messenger to come to him. It was the Piute who did all the talking, and that was brief. Then the Navajo stood motionless, with his hands crossed over his breast. Shefford drew near and waited.

"Bi Nai," said the Navajo, "Nas Ta Bega said his sister would come home some day. . . . Glen Naspa is in the hogan of her grandfather."

He spoke in his usual slow, guttural voice, and he might have been bronze for all the emotion he expressed; yet Shefford instinctively felt the despair that had been hinted to him, and he put his hand on the Indian's shoulder.

"If I am the Navajo's brother, then I am brother to Glen Naspa," he said. "I will go with you to the hogan of Hosteen Doetin."

Nas Ta Bega went away into the valley for the horses. Shefford hurried to the village, made his excuses at the school, and then called to explain to Fay that trouble of some kind had come to the Indian.

Soon afterward he was riding Nack-yal on the rough and winding trail up through the broken country of cliffs and cañons to the great league-long sage and cedarslope of the mountain. It was weeks since he had ridden the mustang. Nack-yal was fat and lazy. He loved his master, but he did not like the climb, and so fell far behind the lean and wiry pony that carried Nas Ta Bega. The sage levels were as purple as the haze of the distance, and there was a bittersweet tang on the strong, cool wind. The sun was gold behind the dark line of fringe on the mountain-top. A flock of sheep swept down one of the safe levels, looking like a narrow stream of white and black and brown. It was always amazing for Shefford to see how swiftly these Navajo sheep grazed along. Wild mustangs plunged out of the cedar clumps and stood upon the ridges, whistling defiance or curiosity, and their manes and tails waved in the wind.

Shefford mounted slowly to the cedar bench in the midst of which were hidden the few hogans. And he halted at the edge to dismount and take a look at that downward-sweeping world of color, of wide space, at the wild desert upland which from there unrolled its magnificent panorama.

Then he passed on into the cedars. How strange to hear the lambs bleating again! Lambing-time had come early, but still spring was there in the new green of grass, in the bright upland flower. He led his mustang out of the cedars into the cleared circle. It was full of colts and lambs, and there were the shepherd-dogs and a few old rams and ewes. But the circle was a quiet place this day. There were no Indians in sight. Shefford loosened the saddle-girths on Nack-yal and, leaving him to graze, went toward the hogan of Hosteen Doetin. A blanket was hung across the door. Shefford heard a low chanting. He waited beside the door till the covering was pulled in, then he entered.

Hosteen Doetin met him, clasped his hand. The old Navajo could not speak; his fine face was working in grief; tears streamed from his dim old eyes and rolled down his wrinkled cheeks. His sorrow was no different from a white man's sorrow. Beyond him Shefford saw Nas Ta Bega standing with folded arms, somehow terrible in his somber impassiveness. At his feet crouched the old woman, Hosteen Doetin's wife, and beside her, prone and quiet, half covered with a blanket, lay Glen Naspa.

She was dead. To Shefford she seemed older than when he had last seen her. And she was beautiful. Calm, cold, dark, with only bitter lips to give the lie to peace! There was a story in those lips.

At her side, half hidden under the fold of blanket, lay a tiny bundle. Its human shape startled Shefford. Then he did not need to be told the tragedy. When he looked again at Glen Naspa's face he seemed to understand all that had made her older, to feel the pain that had lined and set her lips.

She was dead, and she was the last of Nas Ta Bega's family. In the old grandfather's agony, in the wild chant of the stricken grandmother, in the brother's stern and terrible calmness Shefford felt more than the death of a loved one. The shadow of ruin, of doom, of death hovered over the girl and her family and her tribe and her race. There was no consolation to offer these relatives of Glen Naspa. Shefford took one more fascinated gaze at her dark, eloquent, prophetic face, at the tragic tiny shape by her side, and then with bowed head he left the hogan.

Outside he paced to and fro, with an aching heart for Nas Ta Bega, with something of the white man's burden of crime toward the Indian weighing upon his soul.

Old Hosteen Doetin came to him with shaking hands and words memorable of the time Glen Naspa left his hogan.

"Me no savvy Jesus Christ. Me hungry. Me no eat Jesus Christ!"

That seemed to be all of his trouble that he could express to Shefford. He could not understand the religion of the missionary, this Jesus Christ who had called his granddaughter away. And the great fear of an old Indian was not death, but hunger. Shefford remembered a custom of the Navajos, a thing barbarous looked at with a white man's mind. If an old Indian failed on a long march he was inclosed by a wall of stones, given plenty to eat and drink, and left there to die in the desert. Not death did he fear, but hunger! Old Hosteen Doetin expected to starve, now that the young and strong squaw of his family was gone.

Shefford spoke in his halting Navajo and assured the old Indian that Nas Ta Bega would never let him starve.

At sunset Shefford stood with Nas Ta Bega facing the west. The Indian was magnificent in repose. He watched the sun go down upon the day that had seen the burial of the last of his family. He resembled an impassive destiny, upon which no shocks fell. He had the light of that flaring golden sky in his face, the majesty of the mountain in his mien, the silence of the great gulf below on his lips. This educated Navajo, who had reverted to the life of his ancestors, found in the wildness and loneliness of his environment a strength no white teaching could ever have given him. Shefford sensed in him a measureless grief, an impenetrable gloom, a tragic acceptance of the meaning of Glen Naspa's ruin and death—the vanishing of his race from the earth. Death had written the law of such bitter truth round Glen Naspa's lips, and the same truth was here in the grandeur and gloom of the Navajo.

"Bi Nai," he said, with the beautiful sonorous roll in his voice, "Glen Naspa is in her grave and there are no paths to the place of her sleep. Glen Naspa is gone."

"Gone! Where? Nas Ta Bega, remember I lost my own faith, and I have not yet learned yours."

"The Navajo has one mother—the earth. Her body has gone to the earth and it will become dust. But her spirit is in the air. It shall whisper to me from the wind. I shall hear it on running waters. It will hide in the morning music of a mocking-bird and in the lonely night cry of the cañon hawk. Her blood will go to make the red of the Indian flowers and her soul will rest at midnight in the lily that opens only to the moon. She will wait in the shadow for me, and live in the great mountain that is my home, and for ever step behind me on the trail."

"You will kill Willetts?" demanded Shefford.

"The Navajo will not seek the missionary."

"But if you meet him you'll kill him?"

"Bi Nai, would Nas Ta Bega kill after it is too late? What good could come? The Navajo is above revenge."

"If he crosses my trail I think I couldn't help but kill him," muttered Shefford in a passion that wrung the threat from him.

The Indian put his arm round the white man's shoulders.

"Bi Nai, long ago I made you my brother. And now you make me your brother. Is it not so? Glen Naspa's spirit calls for wisdom, not revenge. Willetts must be a bad man. But we'll let him live. Life will punish him. Who knows if he was all to blame? Glen Naspa was only one pretty Indian girl. There are many white men in the desert. She loved a white man when she was a baby. The thing was a curse. . . . Listen, Bi Nai, and the Navajo will talk.

"Many years ago the Spanish padres, the first white men, came into the land of the Indian. Their search was for gold. But they were not wicked men. They did not steal and kill. They taught the Indian many useful things. They brought him horses. But when they went away they left him unsatisfied with his life and his god.

"Then came the pioneers. They crossed the great river and took the pasture-lands and the hunting-grounds of the Indian. They drove him backward, and the Indian grew sullen. He began to fight. The white man's government made treaties with the Indian, and these were broken. Then war came—fierce and bloody war. The Indian was driven to the waste places. The stream of pioneers, like a march of ants, spread on into the desert. Every valley where grass grew, every river, became a place for farms and towns. Cattle choked the water holes where the buffalo and deer had once gone to drink. The forests in the hills were cut and the springs dried up. And the pioneers followed to the edge of the desert.

"Then came the prospectors, mad, like the padres, for the gleam of gold. The day was not long enough for them to dig in the creeks and the cañons; they worked in the night. And they brought weapons and rum to the Indian, to buy from him the secret of the places where the shining gold lay hidden.

"Then came the traders. And they traded with the Indian. They gave him little for much, and that little changed his life. He learned a taste for the sweet foods of the white man. Because he could trade for a sack of flour he worked less in the field. And the very fiber of his bones softened.

"Then came the missionaries. They were proselytizers for converts to their religion. The missionaries are good men. There may be a bad missionary, like Willetts, the same as there are bad men in other call-ings, or bad Indians. They say Shadd is a half-breed. But the Piutes can tell you he is a full-blood, and he, like me, was sent to a white man's school. In the beginning the missionaries did well for the Indian. They taught him cleaner ways of living, better farming, useful work with tools—many good things. But the wrong to the Indian was the under-mining of his faith. It was not humanity that sent the missionary to the Indian. Humanity would have helped the Indian in his ignorance of sickness and work, and left him his god. For to trouble the Indian about his god worked at the roots of his nature.

"The beauty of the Indian's life is in his love of the open, of all that is nature, of silence, freedom, wildness. It is a beauty of mind and soul. The Indian would have been content to watch and feel. To a white man he might be dirty and lazy—content to dream life away without trouble or what the white man calls evolution. The Indian might seem cruel be-cause he leaves his old father out in the desert to die. But the old man wants to die that way, alone with his spirits and the sunset. And the white man's medicine keeps his old father alive days and days after he ought to be dead. Which is more cruel? The Navajos used to fight with other tribes, and then they were stronger men than they are to-day.

"But leaving religion, greed, and war out of the question, contact with the white man would alone have ruined the Indian. The Indian and the white man cannot mix. The Indian brave learns the habits of the white man, acquires his diseases, and has not the mind or body to with-stand them. The Indian girl learns to love the white man—and that is death of her Indian soul, if not of life.

"So the red man is passing. Tribes once powerful have died in the life of Nas Ta Bega. The curse of the white man is already heavy upon my race in the south. Here in the north, in the wildest corner of the desert, chased here by the great soldier, Carson, the Navajo has made his last stand.

"Bi Nai, you have seen the shadow in the hogan of Hosteen Doetin. Glen Naspa has gone to her grave, and no sisters, no children, will make paths to the place of her sleep. Nas Ta Bega will never have a wife—a child. He sees the end. It is the sunset of the Navajo. . . . Bi Nai, the Na-vajo is dying—dying—dying!"

CHAPTER 15

WILD JUSTICE

A crescent moon hung above the lofty peak over the valley and a train of white stars ran along the bold rim of the western wall. A few young frogs peeped plaintively. The night was cool, yet had a touch of balmy spring, and a sweeter fragrance, as if the cedars and piñons had freshened in the warm sun of that day.

Shefford and Fay were walking in the aisles of moonlight and the patches of shade, and Nas Ta Bega, more than ever a shadow of his white brother, followed them silently.

"Fay, it's growing late. Feel the dew?" said Shefford. "Come, I must take you back."

"But the time's so short. I have said nothing that I wanted to say," she replied.

"Say it quickly, then, as we go."

"After all, it's only—will you take me away soon?"

"Yes, very soon. The Indian and I have talked. But we've made no plan yet. There are only three ways to get out of this country. By Stone Bridge, by Kayenta and Durango, and by Red Lake. We must choose one. All are dangerous. We must lose time finding Surprise Valley. I hoped the Indian could find it. Then we'd bring Lassiter and Jane here and hide them near till dark, then take you and go. That would give us a night's start. But you must help us to Surprise Valley."

"I can go right to it, blindfolded, or in the dark. . . . Oh, John, hurry! I dread the wait. *He* might come again."

"Joe says—they won't come very soon."

"Is it far—where we're going—out of the country?"

"Ten days' hard riding."

"Oh! That night ride to and from Stone Bridge nearly killed me. But I could walk very far, and climb for ever."

"Fay, we'll get out of the country if I have to carry you."

When they arrived at the cabin Fay turned on the porch step and, with her face nearer a level with his, white and sweet in the moonlight, with her eyes shining and unfathomable, she was more than beautiful.

"You've never been inside my house," she said. "Come in. I've something for you."

"But it's late," he remonstrated. "I suppose you've got me a cake or pie—something to eat. You women all think Joe and I have to be fed."

"No. You'd never guess. Come in," she said, and the rare smile on her face was something Shefford would have gone far to see.

"Well, then, for a minute."

He crossed the porch, the threshold, and entered her home. Her dim, white shape moved in the darkness. And he followed into a room where the moon shone through the open window, giving soft, mellow, shadowy light. He discerned objects, but not clearly, for his senses seemed absorbed in the strange warmth and intimacy of being for the first time with her in her home.

"No, it's not good to eat," she said, and her laugh was happy. "Here—"

Suddenly she abruptly ceased speaking. Shefford saw her plainly, and the slender form had stiffened, alert and strained. She was listening.

"What was that?" she whispered.

"I didn't hear anything," he whispered back.

He stepped softly nearer the open window and listened.

Clip-clop! clip-clop! clip-clop! Hard hoofs on the hard path outside!

A strong and rippling thrill went over Shefford. In the soft light her eyes seemed unnaturally large and black and fearful.

Clip-clop! clip-clop!

The horse stopped outside. Then followed a metallic clink of spur against stirrup—thud of boots on hard ground—heavy footsteps upon the porch.

A swift, cold contraction of throat, of breast, convulsed Shefford. His only thought was that he could not think.

"Ho—Mary!"

A voice liberated both Shefford's muscle and mind—a voice of strange, vibrant power. Authority of religion and cruelty of will—these Mormon attributes constituted that power. And Shefford suffered a transformation which must have been ordered by demons. That sudden flame seemed to curl and twine and shoot along his veins with blasting force. A rancorous and terrible cry leaped to his lips.

"Ho—Mary!" Then came a heavy tread across the threshold of the outer room.

Shefford dared not look at Fay. Yet, dimly, from the corner of his eye, he saw her, a pale shadow, turned to stone, with her arms out. If he looked, if he made sure of that, he was lost. When had he drawn his gun? It was there, a dark and glinting thing in his hand. He must fly—not through cowardice and fear, but because in one more moment he would kill a man. Swift as the thought he dove through the open window. And, leaping up, he ran under the dark piñons toward camp.

Joe Lake had been out late himself. He sat by the fire, smoking his pipe. He must have seen or heard Shefford coming, for he rose with unwonted alacrity, and he kicked the smoldering logs into a flickering blaze.

Shefford, realizing his deliverance, came panting, staggering into the light. The Mormon uttered an exclamation. Then he spoke, anxiously, but what he said was not clear in Shefford's thick and throbbing ears. He dropped his pipe, a sign of perturbation, and he stared.

But Shefford, without a word, lunged swiftly away into the shadow of the cedars. He found relief in action. He began a steep ascent of the east wall, a dangerous slant he had never dared even in daylight, and he climbed it without a slip. Danger, steep walls, perilous heights, night, and black cañon the same—these he never thought of. But something drove him to desperate effort, that the hours might seem short.

*   *   *

The red sun was tipping the eastern wall when he returned to camp, and he was neither calm nor sure of himself nor ready for sleep or food. Only he had put the night behind him.

The Indian showed no surprise. But Joe Lake's jaw dropped and his eyes rolled. Moreover, Joe bore a singular aspect, the exact nature of which did not at once dawn upon Shefford.

"By God! you've got nerve—or you're crazy!" he ejaculated, hoarsely.

Then it was Shefford's turn to stare. The Mormon was haggard, grieved, frightened, and utterly amazed. He appeared to be trying to make certain of Shefford's being there in the flesh and then to find reason for it.

"I've no nerve and I am crazy," replied Shefford. "But, Joe—what do you mean? Why do you look at me like that?"

"I reckon if I get your horse that'll square us. Did you come back for him? You'd better hit the trail quick."

"It's you now who're crazy," burst out Shefford.

"Wish to God I was," replied Joe.

It was then Shefford realized catastrophe, and cold fear gnawed at his vitals, so that he was sick.

"Joe, what has happened?" he asked, with the blood thick in his heart.

"Hadn't you better tell me?" demanded the Mormon, and a red wave blotted out the haggard shade of his face.

"You talk like a fool," said Shefford, sharply, and he strode right up to Joe.

"See here, Shefford, we've been pards. You're making it hard for me. Reckon you ain't square."

Shefford shot out a long arm and his hand clutched the Mormon's burly shoulder.

"Why am I not square? What do you mean?"

Joe swallowed hard and gave himself a shake. Then he eyed his comrade steadily.

"I was afraid you'd kill him. I reckon I can't blame you. I'll help you get away. . . . And I'm a Mormon! Do you take the hunch? . . . But don't deny you killed him!"

"Killed whom?" gasped Shefford.

"Her husband!"

Shefford seemed stricken by a slow, paralyzing horror. The Mormon's changing face grew huge and indistinct and awful in his sight. He was clutched and shaken in Joe's rude hands, yet scarcely felt them. Joe seemed to be bellowing at him, but the voice was far off. Then Shefford began to see, to hear through some cold and terrible deadness that had come between him and everything.

"Say *you* killed him!" hoarsely supplicated the Mormon.

Shefford had not yet control of speech. Something in his gaze appeared to drive Joe frantic.

"Damn you! Tell me quick. Say *you* killed him! . . . If you want to know my stand, why, I'm glad! . . . Shefford, don't look so stony! . . . For *her* sake, say you killed him!"

Shefford stood with a face as gray and still as stone. With a groan the Mormon drew away from him and sank upon a log. He bowed his head; his broad shoulders heaved; husky sounds came from him. Then with a violent wrench he plunged to his feet and shook himself like a huge, savage dog.

"Reckon it's no time to weaken," he said, huskily, and with the words a dark, hard, somber bitterness came to his face.

"Where—is—she?" whispered Shefford.

"Shut up in the school-house," he replied.

"Did she—did she—"

"She neither denied nor confessed."

"Have you—seen her?"

"Yes."

"How did—she look?"

"Cool and quiet as the Indian there. . . . Game as hell! She always had stuff in her."

"Oh, Joe! . . . It's unbelievable!" cried Shefford. "That lovely, innocent girl! She couldn't—she couldn't."

"She's fixed him. Don't think of that. It's too late. We ought to have saved her."

"God! . . . She begged me to hurry—to take her away."

"Think what we can do *now* to save her," cut in the Mormon.

Shefford sustained a vivifying shock. "To save her?" he echoed.

"Think, man!"

"Joe, I can hit the trail and let you tell them I killed him," burst out Shefford in panting excitement.

"Reckon I can."

"So help me God I'll do it!"

The Mormon turned a dark and austere glance upon Shefford.

"You mustn't leave her. She killed him for your sake. . . . You must fight for her now—save her—take her away."

"But the law!"

"Law!" scoffed Joe. "In these wilds men get killed and there's no law. But if she's taken back to Stone Bridge those iron-jawed old Mormons will make law enough to—to . . . Shefford, the thing is—get her away. Once out of the country, she's safe. Mormons keep their secrets."

"I'll take her. Joe, will you help me?"

Shefford, even in his agitation, felt the Mormon's silence to be a consent that need not have been asked. And Shefford had a passionate gratefulness toward his comrade. That stultifying and blinding prejudice which had always seemed to remove a Mormon outside the pale of certain virtue suffered final eclipse; and Joe Lake stood out a man, strange and crude, but with a heart and a soul.

"Joe, tell me what to do," said Shefford, with a simplicity that meant he needed only to be directed.

"Pull yourself together. Get your nerve back," replied Joe. "Reckon you'd better show yourself over there. No one saw you come in this morning—your absence from camp isn't known. It's better you seem curious and shocked like the rest of us. Come on. We'll go over. And afterward we'll get the Indian, and plan."

They left camp and, crossing the brook, took the shaded path toward the village. Hope of saving Fay, the need of all his strength and nerve and cunning to effect that end, gave Shefford the supreme courage to overcome his horror and fear. On that short walk under the piñons to Fay's cabin he had suffered many changes of emotion, but never anything like this change which made him fierce and strong to fight, deep and crafty to plan, hard as iron to endure.

The village appeared very quiet, though groups of women stood at the doors of cabins. If they talked, it was very low. Henninger and Smith, two of the three Mormon men living in the village, were standing before the closed door of the school-house. A tigerish feeling thrilled Shefford when he saw them on guard there. Shefford purposely avoided looking at Fay's cabin as long as he could keep from it. When he had to look he saw several hooded, whispering women in the yard, and Beal, the other Mormon man, standing in the cabin door. Upon the porch lay the long shape of a man, covered with blankets.

Shefford experienced a horrible curiosity.

"Say, Beal, I've fetched Shefford over," said Lake. "He's pretty much cut up."

Beal wagged a solemn head, but said nothing. His mind seemed absent or steeped in gloom, and he looked up as one silently praying.

Joe Lake strode upon the little porch and, reaching down, he stripped the blanket from the shrouded form.

Shefford saw a sharp, cold, ghastly face. *"Waggoner!"* he whispered.

"Yes," replied Lake.

Waggoner! Shefford remembered the strange power in his face, and, now that life had gone, that power was stripped of all disguise. Death, in Shefford's years of ministry, had lain under his gaze many times and in a multiplicity of aspects, but never before had he seen it stamped so strangely. Shefford did not need to be told that here was a man who believed he had conversed with God on earth, who believed he had a divine right to rule women, who had a will that would not yield itself to death utterly. Waggoner, then, was the devil who had come masked to Surprise Valley, had forced a martyrdom upon Fay Larkin. And this was the Mormon who had made Fay Larkin a murderess. Shefford had hated him living, and now he hated him dead. Death here was robbed of all nobility, of pathos, of majesty. It was only retribution. Wild justice! But alas! that it had to be meted out by a white-souled girl whose innocence was as great as the unconscious savagery which she had assimilated from her lonely and wild environment. Shefford laid a despairing curse upon his own head, and a terrible remorse knocked at his heart. He had left her alone, this girl in whom love had made the great change—like a coward he had left her alone. That curse he visited upon himself because he had been the spirit and the motive of this wild justice, and his should have been the deed.

Joe Lake touched Shefford's arm and pointed at the haft of a knife protruding from Waggoner's breast. It was a wooden haft. Shefford had seen it before somewhere.

Then he was struck with what perhaps Joe meant him to see—the singular impression the haft gave of one sweeping, accurate, powerful stroke. A strong arm had driven that blade home. The haft was sunk deep; there was a little depression in the cloth; no blood showed; and the weapon looked as if it could not be pulled out. Shefford's thought went fatally and irresistibly to Fay Larkin's strong arm. He saw her flash that white arm and lift the heavy bucket from the spring with an ease he wondered at. He felt the strong clasp of her hand as she had given it to him in a flying leap across a crevice upon the walls. Yes, her fine hand and the round, strong arm possessed the strength to have given that blade its singular directness and force. The marvel was not in the physical action. It hid inscrutably in the mystery of deadly passion rising out of a gentle and sad heart.

Joe Lake drew up the blanket and shut from Shefford's fascinated gaze that spare form, that accusing knife, that face of strange, cruel power.

"Anybody been sent for?" asked Lake of Beal.

"Yes. An Indian boy went for the Piute. We'll send him to Stone Bridge," replied the Mormon.

"How soon do you expect any one here from Stone Bridge?"

"To-morrow, mebbe by noon."

"Meantime what's to be done with—this?"

"Elder Smith thinks the body should stay right here where it fell till they come from Stone Bridge."

"Waggoner was found here, then?"

"Right here."

"Who found him?"

"Mother Smith. She came over early. An' the sight made her scream. The women all came runnin'. Mother Smith had to be put to bed."

"Who found—Mary?"

"See here, Joe, I told you all I knowed once before," replied the Mormon, testily.

"I've forgotten. Was sort of bewildered. Tell me again. . . . Who found—her?"

"The womenfolks. She laid right inside the door, in a dead faint. She hadn't undressed. There was blood on her hands an' a cut or scratch. The women fetched her to. But she wouldn't talk. Then Elder Smith come an' took her. They've got her locked up."

Then Joe led Shefford away from the cabin farther on into the village. When they were halted by the somber, grieving women it was Joe who did the talking. They passed the school-house, and here Shefford quickened his step. He could scarcely bear the feeling that rushed over him. And the Mormon gripped his arm as if he understood.

"Shefford, which one of these younger women do you reckon your best friend? Ruth?" asked Lake, earnestly.

"Ruth, by all means. Just lately I haven't seen her often. But we've been close friends. I think she'd do much for me."

"Maybe there'll be a chance to find out. Maybe we'll need Ruth. Let's have a word with her. I haven't seen her out among the women."

They stopped at the door of Ruth's cabin. It was closed. When Joe knocked there came a sound of footsteps inside, a hand drew aside the window-blind, and presently the door opened. Ruth stood there, dressed in somber hue. She was a pretty, slender, blue-eyed, brown-haired young woman. Shefford imagined from her pallor and the set look of shock upon her face that the tragedy had affected her more powerfully than it had the other women. When he remembered that she had been more friendly with Fay Larkin than any other neighbor, he made sure he was right in his conjecture.

"Come in," was Ruth's greeting.

"No. We just wanted to say a word. I noticed you've not been out. Do you know—all about it?"

She gave them a strange glance.

"Any of the womenfolks been in?" added Joe.

"Hester ran over. She told me through the window. Then I barred my door to keep the other women out."

"What for?" asked Joe, curiously.

"Please come in," she said, in reply.

They entered, and she closed the door after them. The change that came over her then was the loosing of restraint.

"Joe—what will they do with Mary?" she queried, tensely.

The Mormon studied her with dark, speculative eyes. "Hang her!" he rejoined in brutal harshness.

"O Mother of Saints!" she cried, and her hands went up.

"You're sorry for Mary, then?" asked Joe, bluntly.

"My heart is breaking for her."

"Well, so's Shefford's," said the Mormon, huskily. "And mine's kind of damn shaky."

Ruth glided to Shefford with a woman's swift softness.

"You've been my good—my best friend. You were hers, too. Oh, I know! . . . Can't you do something for her?"

"I hope to God I can," replied Shefford.

Then the three stood looking from one to the other, in a strong and subtly realizing moment, drawn together.

"Ruth," whispered Joe, hoarsely, and then he glanced fearfully around, at the window and door, as if listeners were there. It was certain that his dark face had paled. He tried to whisper more, only to fail. Shefford divined the weight of Mormonism that burdened Joe Lake then. Joe was faithful to a love for Fay Larkin, noble in friendship to Shefford, desperate in a bitter strait with his own manliness, but the power of that creed by which he had been raised struck his lips mute. For to speak on meant to be false to that creed. Already in his heart he had decided, yet he could not voice the thing.

"Ruth"—Shefford took up the Mormon's unfinished whisper—"if we plan to save her—if we need you—will you help?"

Ruth turned white, but an instant and splendid fire shone in her eyes.

"Try me," she whispered back. "I'll change places with her—so you can get her away. They can't do much to me."

Shefford wrung her hands. Joe licked his lips and found his voice: "We'll come back later." Then he led the way out and Shefford followed. They were silent all the way back to camp.

Nas Ta Bega sat in repose where they had left him, a thoughtful, somber figure. Shefford went directly to the Indian, and Joe tarried at the campfire, where he raked out some red embers and put one upon the bowl of his pipe. He puffed clouds of white smoke, then found a seat beside the others.

"Shefford, go ahead. Talk. It'll take a deal of talk. I'll listen. Then I'll talk. It'll be Nas Ta Bega who makes the plan out of it all."

Shefford launched himself so swiftly that he scarcely talked coherently. But he made clear the points that he must save Fay, get her away from the village, let her lead him to Surprise Valley, rescue Lassiter and Jane Withersteen, and take them all out of the country.

Joe Lake dubiously shook his head. Manifestly the Surprise Valley part of the situation presented a new and serious obstacle. It changed the whole thing. To try to take the three out by way of Kayenta and Durango was not to be thought of, for reasons he briefly stated. The Red Lake trail was the only one left, and if that were taken the chances were against Shefford. It was five days over sand to Red Lake—impossible to hide a trail—and even with a day's start Shefford could not escape the hard-riding men who would come from Stone Bridge. Besides, after reaching Red Lake, there were days and days of desert-travel needful to avoid places like Blue Cañon, Tuba, Moencopie, and the Indian villages.

"We'll have to risk all that," declared Shefford, desperately.

"It's a fool risk," retorted Joe. "Listen. By to-morrow noon all of Stone Bridge, more or less, will be riding in here. You've got to get away to-night with the girl—or never! And to-morrow you've got to find that Lassiter and the woman in Surprise Valley. This valley must be back, deep in the cañon country. Well, you've got to come out this way again. No trail through here would be safe. Why, you'd put all your heads in a rope! . . . You mustn't come through this way. It'll have to be tried across country, off the trails, and that means hell—day-and-night travel, no camp, no feed for horses—maybe no water. Then you'll have the best trackers in Utah like hounds on your trail."

When the Mormon ceased his forceful speech there was a silence fraught with hopeless meaning. He bowed his head in gloom. Shefford, growing sick again to his marrow, fought a cold, hateful sense of despair.

"Bi Nai!" In his extremity he called to the Indian.

"The Navajo has heard," replied Nas Ta Bega, strangely speaking in his own language.

With a long, slow heave of breast Shefford felt his despair leave him. In the Indian lay his salvation. He knew it. Joe Lake caught the subtle spirit of the moment and looked up eagerly.

Nas Ta Bega stretched an arm toward the east, and spoke in Navajo. But Shefford, owing to the hurry and excitement of his mind, could not translate. Joe Lake listened, gave a violent start, leaped up with all his big frame quivering, and then fired question after question at the Indian. When the Navajo had replied to all, Joe drew himself up as if facing an irrevocable decision which would wring his very soul. What did he cast off in that moment? What did he grapple with? Shefford had no means to tell, except by the instinct which baffled him. But whether the Mormon's trial was one of spiritual rending or the natural physical fear of a perilous, virtually impossible venture, the fact was he was magnificent in his acceptance of it. He turned to Shefford, white, cold, yet glowing.

"Nas Ta Bega believes he can take you down a cañon to the big river—the Colorado. He knows the head of this cañon. Nonnezoshe Boco it's called—cañon of the rainbow bridge. He has never been down it. Only two or three living Indians have ever seen the great Stone Bridge. But all have heard of it. They worship it as a god. There's water runs down this cañon and water runs to the river. Nas Ta Bega thinks he can take you down to the river."

"Go on," cried Shefford, breathlessly, as Joe paused.

"The Indian plans this way. God, it's great! . . . If only I can do my end! . . . He plans to take mustangs to-day and wait with them for you to-night or to-morrow till you come with the girl. You'll go get Lassiter and the woman out of Surprise Valley. Then you'll strike east for Non-nezoshe Boco. If possible, you must take a pack of grub. You may be days going down—and waiting for me at the mouth of the cañon, at the river."

"Joe! Where will you be?"

"I'll ride like hell for Kayenta, get another horse there, and ride like hell for the San Juan River. There's a big flatboat at the Durango crossing. I'll go down the San Juan in that—into the big river. I'll drift down by day, tie up by night, and watch for you at the mouth of every cañon till I come to Nonnezoshe Boco."

Shefford could not believe the evidence of his ears. He knew the treacherous San Juan River. He had heard of the great, sweeping, terrible red Colorado and its roaring rapids.

"Oh, it seems impossible!" he gasped. "You'll just lose your life for nothing."

"The Indian will turn the trick, I tell you. Take my hunch. It's nothing for me to drift down a swift river. I worked a ferry-boat once."

Shefford, to whom flying straws would have seemed stable, caught the inflection of defiance and daring and hope of the Mormon's spirit.

"What then—after you meet us at the mouth of Nonnezoshe Boco?" he queried.

"We'll all drift down to Lee's Ferry. That's at the head of Marble Cañon. We'll get out on the south side of the river, thus avoiding any Mormons at the ferry. Nas Ta Bega knows the country. It's open desert—on the other side of these plateaus. He can get horses from Navajos. Then you'll strike south for Willow Springs."

"Willow Springs? That's Presbrey's trading-post," said Shefford.

"Never met him. But he'll see you safe out of the Painted Desert. . . . The thing that worries me most is how not to miss you all at the mouth of Nonnezoshe. You must have sharp eyes. But I forget the Indian. A bird couldn't pass him. . . . And suppose Nonnezoshe Boco has a steep-walled, narrow mouth opening into a rapids! . . . Whew! Well, the Indian will figure that, too. Now, let's put our heads together and plan how to turn this end of the trick here. Getting the girl!"

After a short colloquy it was arranged that Shefford would go to Ruth and talk to her of the aid she had promised. Joe averred that this aid could be best given by Ruth going in her somber gown and hood to the school-house, and there, while Joe and Shefford engaged the guards outside, she would change apparel and places with Fay and let her come forth.

"What'll they do to Ruth?" demanded Shefford. "We can't accept her sacrifice if she's to suffer—or be punished."

"Reckon Ruth has a strong hunch that she can get away with it. Did you notice how strange she said that? Well, they can't do much to her. The bishop may damn her soul. But—Ruth—"

Here Lake hesitated and broke off. Not improbably he had meant to say that of all the Mormon women in the valley Ruth was the least likely to suffer from punishment inflicted upon her soul.

"Anyway, it's our only chance," went on Joe, "unless we kill a couple of men. Ruth will gladly take what comes to help you."

"All right; I consent," replied Shefford, with emotion. "And now after she comes out—the supposed Ruth—what then?"

"You can be natural-like. Go with her back to Ruth's cabin. Then stroll off into the cedars. Then climb the west wall. Meanwhile Nas Ta Bega will ride off with a pack of grub and Nack-yal and several other mustangs. He'll wait for you or you'll wait for him, as the case may be, at some appointed place. When you're gone I'll jump my horse and hit the trail for Kayenta and the San Juan."

"Very well; that's settled," said Shefford, soberly. "I'll go at once to see Ruth. You and Nas Ta Bega decide on where I'm to meet him."

"Reckon you'd do just as well to walk round and come up to Ruth's from the other side—instead of going through the village," suggested Joe.

Shefford approached Ruth's cabin in a round-about way; nevertheless, she saw him coming before he got there and, opening the door, stood pale, composed, and quietly bade him enter. Briefly, in low and earnest voice, Shefford acquainted her with the plan.

"You love her so much," she said, wistfully, wonderingly.

"Indeed I do. Is it too much to ask of you to do this thing?" he asked.

"Do it?" she queried, with a flash of spirit. "Of course I'll do it."

"Ruth, I can't thank you. I can't. I've only a faint idea what you're risking. That distresses me. I'm afraid of what may happen to you."

She gave him another of the strange glances. "I don't risk so much as you think," she said, significantly.

"Why?"

She came close to him, and her hands clasped his arms and she looked up at him, her eyes darkening and her face growing paler. "Will you swear to keep my secret?" she asked, very low.

"Yes, I swear."

"I was one of Waggoner's sealed wives!"

"God Almighty!" broke out Shefford, utterly overwhelmed.

"Yes. That's why I say I don't risk so much. I will make up a story to tell the bishop and everybody. I'll tell that Waggoner was jealous, that he was brutal to Mary, that I believed she was goaded to her mad deed, that I thought she ought to be free. They'll be terrible. But what can they do to me? My husband is dead . . . and if I have to go to hell to keep from marrying another married Mormon, I'll go!"

In that low, passionate utterance Shefford read the death-blow to the old Mormon polygamous creed. In the uplift of his spirit, in the joy at this revelation, he almost forgot the stern matter at hand. Ruth and Joe Lake belonged to a younger generation of Mormons. Their nobility in this instance was in part a revolt at the conditions of their lives. Doubt was knocking at Joe Lake's heart, and conviction had come to this young sealed wife, bitter and hopeless while she had been fettered, strong and mounting now that she was free. In a flash of inspiration Shefford saw the old order changing. The Mormon creed might survive, but that part of it which was an affront to nature, a horrible yoke on women's necks, was doomed. It could not live. It could never have survived more than a generation or two of religious fanatics. Shefford had marked a different force and religious fervor in the younger Mormons, and now he understood them.

"Ruth, you talk wildly," he said. "But I understand. I see. You are free and you're going to stay free. . . . It stuns me to think of that man of many wives. What did you feel when you were told he was dead?"

"I dare not think of that. It makes me wicked. And he was good to me. . . . Listen. Last night about midnight he came to my window and woke me. I got up and let him in. He was in a terrible state. I thought he was crazy. He walked the floor and called on his saints and prayed. When I wanted to light a lamp he wouldn't let me. He was afraid I'd see his face. But I saw well enough in the moonlight. And I knew something had happened. So I soothed and coaxed him. He had been a man as close-mouthed as a stone. Yet then I got him to talk. . . . He had gone to Mary's, and upon entering, thought he heard some one with her. She didn't answer him at first. When he found her in her bedroom she was like a ghost. He accused her. Her silence made him furious. Then he berated her, brought down the wrath of God upon her, threatened her with damnation. All of which she never seemed to hear. But when he tried to touch her she flew at him like a she-panther. That's what he called her. She said she'd kill him! And she drove him out of her house. . . . He was all weak and unstrung, and I believe scared, too, when he came to me. She must have been a fury. Those quiet, gentle women are furies when they're once roused. Well, I was hours up with him and finally he got over it. He didn't pray any more. He paced the room. It was just daybreak when he said the wrath of God had come to him. I tried to keep him from going back to

Mary. But he went. . . . An hour later the women ran to tell me he had been found dead at Mary's door."

"Ruth—she was mad—driven—she didn't know what she—was doing," said Shefford, brokenly.

"She was always a strange girl, more like an Indian than any one I ever knew. We called her the Sago Lily. I gave her the name. She was so sweet, lovely, white and gold, like those flowers. . . . And to think! Oh, it's horrible for her! You must save her. If you get her away there never will be anything come of it. The Mormons will hush it up."

"Ruth, time is flying," rejoined Shefford, hurriedly. "I must go back to Joe. You be ready for us when we come. Wear something loose, easily thrown off, and don't forget the long hood."

"I'll be ready and watching," she said. "The sooner the better, I'd say."

He left her and returned toward camp in the same circling route by which he had come. The Indian had disappeared and so had his mustang. This significant fact augmented Shefford's hurried, thrilling excitement. But one glance at Joe's face changed all that to a sudden numbness, a sinking of his heart.

"What is it?" he queried.

"Look there!" exclaimed the Mormon.

Shefford's quick eye caught sight of horses and men down the valley. He saw several Indians and three or four white men. They were making camp.

"Who are they?" demanded Shefford.

"Shadd and some of his gang. Reckon that Piute told the news. By to-morrow the valley will be full as a horse-wrangler's corral. . . . Lucky Nas Ta Bega got away before that gang rode in. Now things won't look as queer as they might have looked. The Indian took a pack of grub, six mustangs, and my guns. Then there was your rifle in your saddle-sheath. So you'll be well heeled in case you come to close quarters. Reckon you can look for a running fight. For now, as soon as your flight is discovered, Shadd will hit your trail. He's in with the Mormons. You know him—what you'll have to deal with. But the advantage will all be yours. You can ambush the trail."

"We're in for it. And the sooner we're off the better," replied Shefford, grimly.

"Reckon that's gospel. Well—come on!"

The Mormon strode off, and Shefford, catching up with him, kept at his side. Shefford's mind was full, but Joe's dark and gloomy face did not invite communication. They entered the piñon grove and passed the cabin where the tragedy had been enacted. A tarpaulin had been stretched across the front porch. Beal was not in sight, nor were any of the women.

"I forgot," said Shefford, suddenly. "Where am I to meet the Indian?"

"Climb the west wall, back of camp," replied Joe. "Nas Ta Bega took the Stone Bridge trail. But he'll leave that, climb the rocks, then hide the outfit and come back to watch for you. Reckon he'll see you when you top the wall."

They passed on into the heart of the village. Joe tarried at the window of a cabin, and passed a few remarks to a woman there, and then he inquired for Mother Smith at her house. When they left here the Mormon gave Shefford a nudge. Then they separated, Joe going toward the schoolhouse, while Shefford bent his steps in the direction of Ruth's home.

Her door opened before he had a chance to knock. He entered. Ruth, white and resolute, greeted him with a wistful smile.

"All ready?" she asked.

"Yes. Are you?" he replied, low-voiced.

"I've only to put on my hood. I think luck favors you. Hester was here and she said Elder Smith told some one that Mary hadn't been offered anything to eat yet. So I'm taking her a little. It'll be a good excuse for me to get in the school-house to see her. I can throw off this dress and she can put it on in a minute. Then the hood. I mustn't forget to hide her golden hair. You know how it flies. But this is a big hood. . . . Well, I'm ready now. And—this's our last time together."

"Ruth, what can I say—how can I thank you?"

"I don't want any thanks. It'll be something to think of always—to make me happy. . . . Only I'd like to feel you—you cared a little."

The wistful smile was there, a tremor on the sad lips, and a shadow of soul-hunger in her eyes. Shefford did not misunderstand her. She did not mean love, although it was a yearning for real love that she mutely expressed.

"Care! I shall care all my life," he said, with strong feeling. "I shall never forget you."

"It's not likely I'll forget you. . . . Good-by, John!"

Shefford took her in his arms and held her close. "Ruth—good-by!" he said, huskily.

Then he released her. She adjusted the hood and, taking up a little tray which held food covered with a napkin, she turned to the door. He opened it and they went out.

They did not speak another word.

It was not a long walk from Ruth's home to the school-house, yet if it were to be measured by Shefford's emotion the distance would have been unending. The sacrifice offered by Ruth and Joe would have been noble under any circumstances had they been Gentiles or persons with no particular religion, but, considering that they were Mormons, that Ruth had been a sealed wife, that Joe had been brought up under the strange, secret, and binding creed, their action was no less than tremendous in its import. Shefford took it to mean vastly more than loyalty to him and pity for Fay Larkin. As Ruth and Joe had arisen to this height, so perhaps would other young Mormons have arisen. It needed only the situation, the climax, to focus these long-insulated, slow-developing and inquiring minds upon the truth—that one wife, one mother of children, for one man at one time was a law of nature, love, and righteousness. Shefford felt as if he were marching with the whole younger generation of Mormons, as if somehow he had been a humble instrument in the working out of their destiny, in the awakening that was to eliminate from their religion the only thing which kept it from being as good for man, and perhaps as true, as any other religion.

And then suddenly he turned the corner of the school-house to encounter Joe talking with the Mormon Henninger. Elder Smith was not present.

"Why, hello, Ruth!" greeted Joe. "You've fetched Mary some dinner. Now that's good of you."

"May I go in?" asked Ruth.

"Reckon so," replied Henninger, scratching his head. He appeared to be tractable, and probably was good-natured under pleasant conditions. "She ought to have somethin' to eat. An' nobody 'pears to have remembered thet—we're so set up."

He unbarred the huge, clumsy door and allowed Ruth to pass in.

"Joe, you can go in if you want," he said. "But hurry out before Elder Smith comes back from his dinner."

Joe mumbled something, gave a husky cough, and then went in.

Shefford experienced great difficulty in presenting to this mild Mormon a natural and unagitated front. When all his internal structure seemed to be in a state of turmoil he did not see how it was possible to keep the fact from showing in his face. So he turned away and took aimless steps here and there.

"'Pears like we'd hev rain," observed Henninger. "It's right warm an' them clouds are unseasonable."

"Yes," replied Shefford. "Hope so. A little rain would be good for the grass."

"Joe tells me Shadd rode in, an' some of his fellers."

"So I see. About eight in the party."

Shefford was gritting his teeth and preparing to endure the ordeal of controlling his mind and expression when the door opened and Joe stalked out. He had his sombrero pulled down so that it hid the upper half of his face. His lips were a shade off healthy color. He stood there with his back to the door.

"Say, what Mary needs is quiet—to be left alone," he said. "Ruth says if she rests, sleeps a little, she won't get fever. . . . Henninger, don't let anybody disturb her till night."

"All right, Joe," replied the Mormon. "An' I take it good of Ruth an' you to concern yourselves."

A slight tap on the inside of the door sent Shefford's pulses to throbbing. Joe opened it with a strong and vigorous sweep that meant more than the mere action.

"Ruth—reckon you didn't stay long," he said, and his voice rang clear. "Sure you feel sick and weak. Why, seeing her flustered even me!"

A slender, dark-garbed woman wearing a long black hood stepped uncertainly out. She appeared to be Ruth. Shefford's heart stood still because she looked so like Ruth. But she did not step steadily, she seemed dazed, she did not raise the hooded head.

"Go home," said Joe, and his voice rang a little louder. "Take her home, Shefford. Or, better, walk her round some. She's faintish. . . . And see here, Henninger—"

Shefford led the girl away with a hand in apparent carelessness on her arm. After a few rods she walked with a freer step and then a swifter. He found it necessary to make that hold on her arm a real one, so as to keep her from walking too fast.

No one, however, appeared to observe her. When they passed Ruth's house then Shefford began to lose his fear that this was not Fay Larkin. He was far from being calm or clear-sighted. He thought he recognized that free step; nevertheless, he could not make sure. When they passed under the trees, crossed the brook, and turned down along the west wall, then doubt ceased in Shefford's mind. He knew this was not Ruth. Still, so strange was his agitation, so keen his suspense, that he needed confirmation of ear, of eye. He wanted to hear her voice, to see her face. Yet just as strangely there was a twist of feeling, a reluctance, a sadness that kept off the moment.

They reached the low, slow-swelling slant of wall and started to ascend. How impossible not to recognize Fay Larkin now in that swift grace and skill on the steep wall! Still, though he knew her, he perversely clung to the unreality of the moment. But when a long braid of dead-gold hair tumbled from under the hood, then his heart leaped. That identified Fay Larkin. He had freed her. He was taking her away. Then a sadness embittered his joy.

As always before, she distanced him in the ascent to the top. She went on without looking back. But Shefford had an irresistible desire to look again and the last time at this valley where he had suffered and loved so much.

CHAPTER 16

SURPRISE VALLEY

From the summit of the wall the plateau waved away in red and yellow ridges, with here and there little valleys green with cedar and piñon.

Upon one of these ridges, silhouetted against the sky, appeared the stalking figure of the Indian. He had espied the fugitives. He disappeared in a niche, and presently came again into view round a corner of cliff. Here he waited, and soon Shefford and Fay joined him.

"Bi Nai, it is well," he said.

Shefford eagerly asked for the horses, and Nas Ta Bega silently pointed down the niche, which was evidently an opening into one of the shallow cañons. Then he led the way, walking swiftly. It was Shefford, and not Fay, who had difficulty in keeping close to him. This speed caused Shefford to become more alive to the business, instead of the feeling, of the flight. The Indian entered a crack between low cliffs—a very narrow cañon full of rocks and clumps of cedars—and in a half-hour or less he came to where the mustangs were halted among some cedars. Three of the mustangs, including Nack-yal, were saddled; one bore a small pack, and the remaining two had blankets strapped on their backs.

"Fay, can you ride in that long skirt?" asked Shefford. How strange it seemed that his first words to her were practical when all his impassioned thought had been only mute! But the instant he spoke he experienced a relief, a relaxation.

"I'll take it off," replied Fay, just as practically. And in a twinkling she slipped out of both waist and skirt. She had worn them over the short white-flannel dress with which Shefford had grown familiar.

As Nack-yal appeared to be the safest mustang for her to ride, Shefford helped her upon him and then attended to the stirrups. When he had adjusted them to the proper length he drew the bridle over Nack-yal's head and, upon handing it to her, found himself suddenly looking into her face. She had taken off the hood, too. The instant their eyes met he realized that she was strangely afraid to meet his glance, as he was to meet hers. That seemed natural. But her face was flushed and there were unmistakable signs upon it of growing excitement, of mounting happiness. Save for that fugitive glance she would have been the Fay Larkin of yesterday. How he had expected her to look he did not know, but it was not like this. And never had he felt her strange quality of simplicity so powerfully.

"Have you ever been here—through this little cañon?" he asked.

"Oh yes, lots of times."

"You'll be able to lead us to Surprise Valley, you think?"

"I know it. I shall see Uncle Jim and Mother Jane before sunset!"

"I hope—you do," he replied, a little shakily. "Perhaps we'd better not tell them of the—the—about what happened last night."

Her beautiful, grave, and troubled glance returned to meet his, and he received a shock that he considered was amaze. And after more swift consideration he believed he was amazed because that look, instead of betraying fear or gloom or any haunting shadow of darkness, betrayed apprehension for him—grave, sweet, troubled love for him. She was not thinking of herself at all—of what he might think of her, a possible gulf between them, of a vast and terrible change in the relation of soul to soul. He experienced a profound gladness. Though he could not understand her, he was happy that the horror of Waggoner's death had escaped her. He loved her, he meant to give his life to her, and right then and there he accepted the burden of her deed and meant to bear it without ever letting her know of the shadow between them.

"Fay, we'll forget—what's behind us," he said. "Now to find Surprise

Valley. Lead on. Nack-yal is gentle. Pull him the way you want to go. We'll follow."

Shefford mounted the other saddled mustang, and they set off, Fay in advance. Presently they rode out of this cañon up to level cedar-patched, solid rock, and here Fay turned straight west. Evidently she had been over the ground before. The heights to which he had climbed with her were up to the left, great slopes and looming promontories. And the course she chose was as level and easy as any he could have picked out in that direction.

When a mile or more of this up-and-down travel had been traversed Fay halted and appeared to be at fault. The plateau was losing its rounded, smooth, wavy characteristics, and to the west grew bolder, more rugged, more cut up into low crags and buttes. After a long, sweeping glance Fay headed straight for this rougher country. Thereafter from time to time she repeated this action.

"Fay, how do you know you're going in the right direction?" asked Shefford, anxiously.

"I never forget any ground I've been over. I keep my eyes close ahead. All that seems strange to me is the wrong way. What I've seen before must be the right way, because I saw it when they brought me from Surprise Valley."

Shefford had to acknowledge that she was following an Indian's instinct for ground he had once covered.

Still Shefford began to worry, and finally dropped back to question Nas Ta Bega.

"Bi Nai, she has the eye of a Navajo," replied the Indian. "Look! Iron-shod horses have passed here. See the marks in the stone?"

Shefford indeed made out faint cut tracks that would have escaped his own sight. They had been made long ago, but they were unmistakable.

"She's following the trail by memory—she must remember the stones, trees, sage, cactus," said Shefford in surprise

"Pictures in her mind," replied the Indian.

Thereafter the farther she progressed the less at fault she appeared and the faster she traveled. She made several miles an hour, and about the middle of the afternoon entered upon the more broken region of the plateau. View became restricted. Low walls, and ruined cliffs of red rock with cedars at their base, and gullies growing into cañons and cañons opening into larger ones—these were passed and crossed and climbed and rimmed in travel that grew more difficult as the going became wilder. Then there was a steady ascent, up and up all the time, though not steep, until another level, green with cedar and piñon, was reached.

It reminded Shefford of the forest near the mouth of the Sagi. It was so dense he could not see far ahead of Fay, and often he lost sight of her entirely. Presently he rode out of the forest into a strip of purple sage. It ended abruptly, and above that abrupt line, seemingly far away, rose a long, red wall. Instantly he recognized that to be the opposite wall of a cañon which as yet he could not see.

Fay was acting strangely and he hurried forward. She slipped off Nack-yal and fell, sprang up and ran wildly, to stand upon a promontory, her arms uplifted, her hair a mass of moving gold in the wind, her attitude one of wild and eloquent significance.

Shefford ran, too, and as he ran the red wall in his eager sight seemed to enlarge downward, deeper and deeper, and then it merged into a strip of green.

Suddenly beneath him yawned a red-walled gulf, a deceiving gulf seen through transparent haze, a softly shining green-and-white valley, strange, wild, beautiful, like a picture in his memory.

"Surprise Valley!" he cried, in wondering recognition.

Fay Larkin waved her arms as if they were wings to carry her swiftly downward, and her plaintive cry fitted the wildness of her manner and the lonely height where she leaned.

Shefford drew her back from the rim.

"Fay, we are here," he said. "I recognize the valley. I miss only one thing—the arch of stone."

His words seemed to recall her to reality.

"The arch? That fell when the wall slipped, in the great avalanche. See! There is the place. We can get down there. Oh, let us hurry!"

The Indian reached the rim and his falcon gaze swept the valley. "Ugh!" he exclaimed. He, too, recognized the valley that he had vainly sought for half a year.

"Bring the lassos," said Shefford.

With Fay leading, they followed the rim toward the head of the valley. Here the wall had caved in, and there was a slope of jumbled rock a thousand feet wide and more than that in depth. It was easy to descend because there were so many rocks waist-high that afforded a handhold. Shefford marked, however, that Fay never took advantage of these. More than once he paused to watch her. Swiftly she went down; she stepped from rock to rock; lightly she crossed cracks and pits; she ran along the sharp and broken edge of a long ledge; she poised on a pointed stone and, sure-footed as a mountain-sheep, she sprang to another that had scarce surface for a foothold; her moccasins flashed, seemed to hold wondrously on any angle; and when a rock tipped or slipped with her she leaped to a surer stand. Shefford watched her performance, so swift, agile, so perfectly balanced, showing such wonderful accord between eye and foot; and then when he swept his gaze down upon that wild valley where she had roamed alone for twelve years he marveled no more.

The farther down he got the greater became the size of rocks, until he found himself amid huge pieces of cliff as large as houses. He lost sight of Fay entirely, and he anxiously threaded a narrow, winding, descending way between the broken masses. Finally he came out upon flat rock again. Fay stood on another rim, looking down. He saw that the slide had moved far out into the valley, and the lower part of it consisted of great sections of wall. In fact, the base of the great wall had just moved out with the avalanche, and this much of it held its vertical position. Looking upward, Shefford was astounded and thrilled to see how far he had descended, how the walls leaned like a great, wide, curving, continuous rim of mountain.

"Here! Here!" called Fay. "Here's where they got down—where they brought me up. Here are the sticks they used. They stuck them in this crack, down to that ledge."

Shefford ran to her side and looked down. There was a narrow split in this section of wall and it was perhaps sixty feet in depth. The floor of rock below led out in a ledge, with a sheer drop to the valley level.

As Shefford gazed, pondering on a way to descend lower, the Indian reached his side. He had no sooner looked than he proceeded to act. Selecting one of the sticks, which were strong pieces of cedar, well hewn and trimmed, he jammed it between the walls of the crack till it stuck fast. Then sitting astride this one he jammed in another some three feet below. When he got down upon that one it was necessary for Shefford to drop him a third stick. In a comparatively short time the Indian reached the ledge below. Then he called for the lassos. Shefford threw them down. His next move was an attempt to assist Fay, but she slipped out of his grasp and descended the ladder with a swiftness that made him hold his breath. Still, when his turn came, her spirit so governed him that he went down as swiftly, and even leaped sheer the last ten feet.

Nas Ta Bega and Fay were leaning over the ledge.

"Here's the place," she said, excitedly. "Let me down on the rope."

It took two thirty-foot lassos tied together to reach the floor of the valley. Shefford folded his vest, put it round Fay, and slipped a loop of the lasso under her arms. Then he and Nas Ta Bega lowered her to the grass below. Fay, throwing off the loop, bounded away like a wild creature, uttering the strangest cries he had ever heard, and she disappeared along the wall.

"I'll go down," said Shefford to the Indian. "You stay here to help pull us up."

Hand over hand Shefford descended, and when his feet touched the grass he experienced a shock of the most singular exultation.

"In Surprise Valley!" he breathed, softly. The dream that had come to him with his friend's story, the years of waiting, wondering, and then the long, fruitless, hopeless search in the desert uplands—these were in his mind as he turned along the wall where Fay had disappeared. He faced a wide terrace, green with grass and moss and starry with strange white flowers, and dark-foliaged, spear-pointed spruce-trees. Below the terrace sloped a bench covered with thick copse, and this merged into a forest of dwarf oaks, and beyond that was a beautiful strip of white aspens, their leaves quivering in the stillness. The air was close, sweet, warm, fragrant, and remarkably dry. It reminded him of the air he had smelled in dry caves under cliffs. He reached a point from where he saw a meadow dotted with red-and-white-spotted cattle and little black burros. There were many of them. And he remembered with a start the agony of toil and peril Venters had endured bringing the progenitors of this stock into the valley. What a strange, wild, beautiful story it all was! But a story connected with this valley could not have been otherwise.

Beyond the meadow, on the other side of the valley, extended the forest, and that ended in the rising bench of thicket, which gave place to green slope and mossy terrace of sharp-tipped spruces—and all this led the eye irresistibly up to the red wall where a vast, dark, wonderful cavern yawned, with its rust-colored streaks of stain on the wall, and the queer little houses of the cliff-dwellers, with their black, vacant, silent windows speaking so weirdly of the unknown past.

Shefford passed a place where the ground had been cultivated, but not as recently as the last six months. There was a scant shock of corn and many meager standing stalks. He became aware of a low, whining hum and a fragrance overpowering in its sweetness. And there round another corner of wall he came upon an orchard all pink and white in blossom and melodious with the buzz and hum of innumerable bees.

He crossed a little stream that had been dammed, went along a pond, down beside an irrigation-ditch that furnished water to orchard and vineyard, and from there he strode into a beautiful cove between two jutting corners of red wall. It was level and green and the spruces stood gracefully everywhere. Beyond their dark trunks he saw caves in the wall.

Suddenly the fragrance of blossom was overwhelmed by the stronger fragrance of smoke from a wood fire. Swiftly he strode under the spruces. Quail fluttered before him as tame as chickens. Big gray rabbits scarcely moved out of his way. The branches above him were full of mocking-birds. And then—there before him stood three figures.

Fay Larkin was held close to the side of a magnificent woman, barbarously clad in garments made of skins and pieces of blanket. Her face worked in noble emotion. Shefford seemed to see the ghost of that fair beauty Venters had said was Jane Withersteen's. Her hair was gray. Near her stood a lean, stoop-shouldered man whose long hair was perfectly white. His gaunt face was bare of beard. It had strange, sloping, sad lines. And he was staring with mild, surprised eyes.

The moment held Shefford mute till sight of Fay Larkin's tear-wet face broke the spell. He leaped forward and his strong hands reached for the woman and the man.

"Jane Withersteen! . . . Lassiter! I have found you!"

"Oh, sir, who are you?" she cried, with rich and deep and quivering voice. "This child came running—screaming. She could not speak. We thought she had gone mad—and escaped to come back to us."

"I am John Shefford," he replied, swiftly. "I am a friend of Bern Venters—of his wife Bess. I learned your story. I came west. I've searched a year. I found Fay. And we've come to take you away."

"You found Fay? But that masked Mormon who forced her to sacrifice herself to save us! . . . What of him? It's not been so many long years—I remember what my father was—and Dyer and Tull—all those cruel churchmen."

"Waggoner is dead," replied Shefford.

"Dead? She is free! Oh, what—how did he die?"

"He was killed."

"Who did it?"

"That's no matter," replied Shefford, stonily, and he met her gaze with steady eyes. "He's out of the way. Fay was never his wife. Fay's free. We've come to take you out of the country. We must hurry. We'll be tracked—pursued. But we've horses and an Indian guide. We'll get away. . . . I think it better to leave here at once. There's no telling how soon we'll be hunted. Get what things you want to take with you."

"Oh—yes—Mother Jane, let us hurry!" cried Fay. "I'm so full—I can't talk—my heart hurts so!"

Jane Withersteen's face shone with an exceedingly radiant light, and a glory blended with a terrible fear in her eyes.

"Fay! my little Fay!"

Lassiter had stood there with his mild, clear blue eyes upon Shefford.

"I shore am glad to see you-all," he drawled, and extended his hand as if the meeting were casual. "What 'd you say your name was?"

Shefford repeated it as he met the proffered hand.

"How's Bern an' Bess?" Lassiter inquired.

"They were well, prosperous, happy when last I saw them. . . . They had a baby."

"Now ain't thet fine? . . . Jane, did you hear? Bess has a baby. An', Jane, didn't I always say Bern would come back to get us out? Shore it's just the same."

How cool, easy, slow, and mild this Lassiter seemed! Had the man grown old, Shefford wondered? The past to him manifestly was only yesterday, and the danger of the present was as nothing. Looking in Lassiter's face, Shefford was baffled. If he had not remembered the greatness of this old gunman he might have believed that the lonely years in the valley had unbalanced his mind. In an hour like this coolness seemed inexplicable—assuredly would have been impossible in an ordinary man. Yet what hid behind that drawling coolness? What was the meaning of those long, sloping, shadowy lines of the face? What spirit lay in the deep, mild, clear eyes? Shefford experienced a sudden check to what had been his first growing impression of a drifting, broken old man.

"Lassiter, pack what little you can carry—mustn't be much—and we'll get out of here," said Shefford.

"I shore will. Reckon I ain't a-goin' to need a pack-train. We saved the clothes we wore in here. Jane never thought it no use. But I figgered we might need them some day. They won't be stylish, but I reckon they'll do better 'n these skins. An' there's an old coat thet was Venters's."

The mild, dreamy look became intensified in Lassiter's eyes.

"Did Venters have any hosses when you knowed him?" he asked.

"He had a farm full of horses," replied Shefford, with a smile. "And there were two blacks—the grandest horses I ever saw. Black Star and Night! You remember, Lassiter?"

"Shore. I was wonderin' if he got the blacks out. They must be growin' old by now. . . . Grand hosses, they was. But Jane had another hoss, a big devil of a sorrel. His name was Wrangle. Did Venters ever tell you about him—an' thet race with Jerry Card?"

"A hundred times!" replied Shefford.

"Wrangle run the blacks off their legs. But Jane never would believe thet. An' I couldn't change her all these years. . . . Reckon mebbe we'll get to see them blacks?"

"Indeed, I hope—I believe you will," replied Shefford, feelingly.

"Shore won't thet be fine. Jane, did you hear? Black Star an' Night are livin' an' we'll get to see them."

But Jane Withersteen only clasped Fay in her arms, and looked at Lassiter with wet and glistening eyes.

Shefford told them to hurry and come to the cliff where the ascent from the valley was to be made. He thought best to leave them alone to make their preparations and bid farewell to the cavern home they had known for so long.

Then he strolled back along the wall, loitering here to gaze into a cave, and there to study crude red paintings in the nooks. And some-times he halted thoughtfully and did not see anything. At length he rounded a corner of cliff to espy Nas Ta Bega sitting upon the ledge, re-poseful and watchful as usual. Shefford told the Indian they would be climbing out soon, and then he sat down to wait and let his gaze rove over the valley.

He might have sat there a long while, so sad and reflective and won-dering was his thought, but it seemed a very short time till Fay came in sight with her free, swift grace, and Lassiter and Jane some distance be-hind. Jane carried a small bundle and Lassiter had a sack over his shoul-der that appeared no inconsiderable burden.

"Them beans shore is heavy," he drawled, as he deposited the sack upon the ground.

Shefford curiously took hold of the sack and was amazed to find that a second and hard muscular effort was required to lift it.

"Beans?" he queried.

"Shore," replied Lassiter.

"That's the heaviest sack of beans I ever saw. Why—it's not possible it can be. . . . Lassiter, we've a long, rough trail. We've got to pack light."

"Wal, I ain't a-goin' to leave this here sack behind. Reckon I've been all of twelve years in fillin' it," he declared, mildly.

Shefford could only stare at him.

"Fay may need them beans," went on Lassiter.

"Why?"

"Because they're gold."

"Gold!" exclaimed Shefford.

"Shore. An' they represent some work. Twelve years of diggin' an' washin'!"

Shefford laughed constrainedly. "Well, Lassiter, that alters the case considerably. A sack of gold nuggets or grains, or beans, as you call them, certainly must not be left behind. . . . Come, now, we'll tackle this climb-ing job."

He called up to the Indian and, grasping the rope, began to walk up the first slant, and then by dint of hand-over-hand effort and climbing with knees and feet he succeeded, with Nas Ta Bega's help, in making the ledge. Then he let down the rope to haul up the sack and bundle.

That done, he directed Fay to fasten the noose round her as he had fixed it before. When she had complied he called to her to hold herself out from the wall while he and Nas Ta Bega hauled her up.

"Hold the rope tight," replied Fay. "I'll walk up."

And to Shefford's amaze and admiration, she virtually walked up that almost perpendicular wall by slipping her hands along the rope and stepping as she pulled herself up. There, if never before, he saw the fruit of her years of experience on steep slopes. Only such experience could have made the feat possible.

Jane had to be hauled up, and the task was a painful one for her. Lassiter's turn came then, and he showed more strength and agility than Shefford had supposed him capable of. From the ledge they turned their attention to the narrow crack with its ladder of sticks. Fay had already ascended and now hung over the rim, her white face and golden hair framed vividly in the narrow stream of blue sky above.

"Mother Jane! Uncle Jim! You are so slow," she called.

"Wal, Fay, we haven't been second cousins to a cañon squirrel all these years," replied Lassiter.

This upper half of the climb bid fair to be as difficult for Jane, if not so painful, as the lower. It was necessary for the Indian to go up and drop the rope, which was looped around her, and then, with him pulling from above and Shefford assisting Jane as she climbed, she was finally gotten up without mishap. When Lassiter reached the level they rested a little while and then faced the great slide of jumbled rocks. Fay led the way, light, supple, tireless, and Shefford never ceased looking at her. At last they surmounted the long slope and, winding along the rim, reached the point where Fay had led out of the cedars.

Nas Ta Bega, then, was the one to whom Shefford looked for every decision or action of the immediate future. The Indian said he had seen a pool of water in a rocky hole, that the day was spent, that here was a little grass for the mustangs, and it would be well to camp right there. So while Nas Ta Bega attended to the mustangs Shefford set about such preparations for camp and supper as their light pack afforded. The question of beds was easily answered for the mats of soft needles under piñon and cedar would be comfortable places to sleep.

When Shefford felt free again the sun was setting. Lassiter and Jane were walking under the trees. The Indian had returned to camp. But Fay was missing. Shefford imagined he knew where to find her, and upon going to the edge of the forest he saw her sitting on the promontory. He approached her, drawn in spite of a feeling that perhaps he ought to stay away.

"Fay, would you rather be alone?" he asked.

His voice startled her.

"I want you," she replied, and held out her hand.

Taking it in his own, he sat beside her.

The red sun was at their backs. Surprise Valley lay hazy, dusky, shadowy beneath them. The opposite wall seemed fired by crimson flame, save far down at its base, which the sun no longer touched. And the dark line of red slowly rose, encroaching upon the bright crimson. Changing, transparent, yet dusky veils seemed to float between the walls; long, red rays, where the sun shone through notch or crack in the rim, split the darker spaces; deep down at the floor the forest darkened, the strip of aspen paled, the meadow turned gray; and all under the shelves and in the great caverns a purple gloom deepened. Then the sun set. And swiftly twilight was there below while day lingered above. On the opposite wall the fire died and the stone grew cold.

A cañon night-hawk voiced his lonely, weird, and melancholy cry, and it seemed to pierce and mark the silence.

A pale star, peering out of a sky that had begun to turn blue, marked the end of twilight. And all the purple shadows moved and hovered and changed till, softly and mysteriously, they embraced black night.

Beautiful, wild, strange, silent Surprise Valley! Shefford saw it before and beneath him, a dark abyss now, the abode of loneliness. He imagined faintly what was in Fay Larkin's heart. For the last time she had seen the sun set there and night come with its dead silence and sweet mystery and phantom shadows, its velvet blue sky and white trains of stars.

He, who had dreamed and longed and searched, found that the hour had been incalculable for him in its import.

CHAPTER 17

THE TRAIL
TO NONNEZOSHE

When Shefford awoke next morning and sat up on his bed of piñon boughs the dawn had broken cold with a ruddy gold brightness under the trees. Nas Ta Bega and Lassiter were busy around a campfire; the mustangs were haltered near by; Jane Withersteen combed out her long, tangled tresses with a crude wooden comb; and Fay Larkin was not in sight. As she had been missing from the group at sunset, so she was now at sunrise. Shefford went out to take his last look at Surprise Valley.

On the evening before, the valley had been a place of dusky red veils and purple shadows, and now it was pink-walled, clear and rosy and green and white, with wonderful shafts of gold slanting down from the notched eastern rim. Fay stood on the promontory, and Shefford did not break the spell of her silent farewell to her wild home. A strange emotion abided with him and he knew he would always, all his life, regret leaving Surprise Valley.

Then the Indian called.

"Come, Fay," said Shefford, gently.

And she turned away with dark, haunted eyes and a white, still face.

The somber Indian gave a silent gesture for Shefford to make haste. While they had breakfast the mustangs were saddled and packed. And soon all was in readiness for the flight. Fay was given Nack-yal, Jane the saddled horse Shefford had ridden, and Lassiter the Indian's roan. Shefford and Nas Ta Bega were to ride the blanketed mustangs, and the sixth and last one bore the pack. Nas Ta Bega set off, leading this horse; the others of the party lined in behind, with Shefford at the rear.

Nas Ta Bega led at a brisk trot, and sometimes, on level stretches of ground, at an easy canter; and Shefford had a grim realization of what this flight was going to be for these three fugitives, now so unaccustomed to riding. Jane and Lassiter, however, needed no watching, and showed they had never forgotten how to manage a horse. The Indian back-trailed yesterday's path for an hour, then headed west to the left, and entered a low pass. All parts of this plateau country looked alike, and Shefford was at some pains to tell the difference of this strange ground from that which he had been over. In another hour they got out of the rugged, broken rock to the wind-worn and smooth, shallow cañons. Shefford calculated that they were coming to the end of the plateau. The low walls slanted lower; the cañon made a turn; Nas Ta Bega disappeared; and then the others of the party. When Shefford turned the corner of wall he saw a short strip of bare, rocky ground with only sky beyond. The Indian and his followers had halted in a group. Shefford rode to them, halted himself, and in one sweeping glance realized the meaning of their silent gaze. But immediately Nas Ta Bega started down, and the mustangs, without word or touch, followed him. Shefford, however, lingered on the promontory.

His gaze seemed impelled and held by things afar—the great yellow-and-purple corrugated world of distance, now on a level with his eyes. He was drawn by the beauty and the grandeur of that scene and transfixed by the realization that he had dared to venture to find a way through this vast, wild, and upflung fastness. He kept looking afar, sweeping the three-quartered circle of horizon till his judgment of distance was confounded and his sense of proportion dwarfed one moment and magnified the next. Then he withdrew his fascinated gaze to adopt the Indian's method of studying unlimited spaces in the desert—to look with slow, contracted eyes from near to far.

His companions had begun to zigzag down a long slope, bare of rock, with yellow gravel patches showing between the scant strips of green, and here and there a scrub-cedar. Half a mile down, the slope merged into green level. But close, keen gaze made out this level to be a rolling plain, growing darker green, with blue lines of ravines, and thin, undefined spaces that might be mirage. Miles and miles it swept and rolled and heaved to lose its waves in apparent darker level. A round, red rock stood isolated, marking the end of the barren plain, and farther on were other round rocks, all isolated, all of different shape. They resembled huge grazing cattle. But as Shefford gazed, and his sight gained strength from steadily holding it to separate features, these rocks were strangely magnified. They grew and grew into mounds, castles, domes, crags—great, red, wind-carved buttes. One by one they drew his gaze to the wall of upflung rock. He seemed to see a thousand domes of a thousand shapes and colors, and among them a thousand blue clefts, each one a little mark in his sight, yet which he knew was a cañon.

So far he gained some idea of what he saw. But beyond this wide area of curved lines rose another wall, dwarfing the lower, dark red, horizon-long, magnificent in frowning boldness, and because of its limitless deceiving surfaces, breaks, and lines, incomprehensible to the sight of man. Away to the eastward began a winding, ragged, blue line, looping back upon itself, and then winding away again, growing wider and bluer. This line was the San Juan Cañon. Where was Joe Lake at that moment? Had he embarked yet on the river—did that blue line, so faint, so deceiving, hold him and the boat? Almost it was impossible to believe. Shefford followed the blue line all its length, a hundred miles, he fancied, down toward the west where it joined a dark, purple, shadowy cleft. And this was the Grand Cañon of the Colorado. Shefford's eye swept along with that winding mark, farther and farther to the west, round to the left, until the cleft, growing larger and coming closer, losing its deception, was seen to be a wild and winding cañon. Still farther to the left, as he swung in fascinated gaze, it split the wonderful wall—a vast plateau now with great red peaks and yellow mesas. The cañon was full of purple smoke. It turned, it closed, it gaped, it lost itself and showed again in that chaos of a million cliffs. And then farther on it became again a cleft, a purple line, at last to fail entirely in deceiving distance.

Shefford imagined there was no scene in all the world to equal that. The tranquillity of lesser spaces was not here manifest. Sound, movement, life, seemed to have no fitness here. Ruin was there and desolation and decay. The meaning of the ages was flung at him, and a man became nothing. When he had gazed at the San Juan Cañon he had been appalled at the nature of Joe Lake's Herculean task. He had lost hope, faith. The thing was not possible. But when Shefford gazed at that sublime and majestic wilderness, in which the Grand Cañon was only a dim line, he strangely lost his terror and something else came to him from across the shining spaces. If Nas Ta Bega led them safely down to the river, if Joe Lake met them at the mouth of Nonnezoshe Boco, if they survived the rapids of that terrible gorge, then Shefford would have to face his soul and the meaning of this spirit that breathed on the wind.

He urged his mustang to the descent of the slope, and as he went down, slowly drawing nearer to the other fugitives, his mind alternated between this strange intimation of faith, this subtle uplift of his spirit, and the growing gloom and shadow in his love for Fay Larkin. Not that he loved her less, but more! A possible God hovering near him, like the Indian's spirit-step on the trail, made his soul the darker for Fay's crime, and he saw with clearer sight, with deeper sadness, with sterner truth.

More than once the Indian turned on his mustang to look up the slope and the light flashed from his dark, somber face. Shefford instinctively looked back himself, and then realized the unconscious motive of the action. Deep within him there had been a premonition of certain pursuit, and the Indian's reiterated backward glance had at length brought the feeling upward. Thereafter, as they descended, Shefford gradually added to his already wrought emotions a mounting anxiety.

No sign of a trail showed where the base of the slope rolled out to meet the green plain. The earth was gravelly, with dark patches of heavy silt, almost like cinders; and round, black rocks, flinty and glassy, cracked away from the hoofs of the mustangs. There was a level bench a mile wide, then a ravine, and then an ascent, and after that, rounded ridge and ravine, one after the other, like huge swells of a monstrous sea. Indian paint-brush vied in its scarlet hue with the deep magenta of cactus. There was no sage. Soapweed and meager grass and a bunch of cactus here and there lent the green to that barren; and it was green only at a distance.

Nas Ta Bega kept on a steady, even trot. The sun climbed. The wind rose and whipped dust from under the mustangs.

Shefford looked back often, and the farther out in the plain he reached the higher loomed the plateau they had descended; and as he faced ahead again the lower sank the red-domed and castled horizon to the fore. The ravines became deeper, with dry rock bottoms, and the ridge-tops sharper, with outcroppings of yellow, crumbling ledges. Once across the central depression of that wide plain a gradual ascent became evident, and the red, round rocks grew clearer in sight, began to rise and shine and grow. And thereafter every slope brought them nearer.

The sun was straight overhead and hot when Nas Ta Bega halted the party under the first lonely scrub-cedar. They all dismounted to stretch their limbs and rest the horses. It was not a talkative group. Lassiter's comments on the never-ending green plain elicited no response. Jane Withersteen looked afar with the past in her eyes. Shefford felt Fay's wistful glance and could not meet it; indeed, he seemed to want to hide something from her. The Indian bent a falcon gaze on the distant slope, and Shefford did not like that intent, searching, steadfast watchfulness. Suddenly Nas Ta Bega stiffened and whipped the halter he held.

"Ugh!" he exclaimed.

All eyes followed the direction of his dark hand. Puffs of dust rose from the base of the long slope they had descended; tiny dark specks moved with the pace of a snail.

"Shadd!" added the Indian.

"I expected it," said Shefford, darkly, as he rose.

"An' who's Shadd?" drawled Lassiter in his cool, slow speech.

Briefly Shefford explained, and then, looking at Nas Ta Bega, he added:

"The hardest-riding outfit in the country! We can't get away from them."

Jane Withersteen was silent, but Fay uttered a low cry. Shefford did not look at either of them. The Indian began swiftly to tighten the saddle-cinches of his roan, and Shefford did likewise for Nack-yal. Then Shefford drew his rifle out of the saddle-sheath and Joe Lake's big guns from the saddle-bag.

"Here, Lassiter, maybe you haven't forgotten how to use these," he said.

The old gunman started as if he had seen ghosts. His hands grew clawlike as he reached for the guns. He threw open the cylinders, spilled out the shells, snapped back the cylinders. Then he went through motions too swift for Shefford to follow. But Shefford heard the hammers falling so swiftly they blended their clicks almost in one sound. Lassiter reloaded the guns with a speed comparable with the other actions. A remarkable transformation had come over him. He did not seem the same man. The mild eyes had changed; the long, shadowy, sloping lines were tense cords; and there was a cold, ashy shade on his face.

"Twelve years!" he muttered to himself. "I dropped them old guns back there where I rolled the rock. . . . Twelve years!"

Shefford realized the twelve years were as if they had never been. And he would rather have had this old gunman with him than a dozen ordinary men.

The Indian spoke rapidly in Navajo, saying that once in the rocks they were safe. Then, after another look at the distant dust-puffs, he wheeled his mustang.

It was doubtful if the party could have kept near him had they been responsible for the gait of their mounts. The fact was that the way the Indian called to his mustang or some leadership in the one he rode drew the others to a like trot or climb or canter. For a long time Shefford did not turn round; he knew what to expect. And when he did turn he was startled at the gain made by the pursuers. But he was encouraged as well by the looming, red, rounded peaks seemingly now so close. He could see the dark splits between the sloping curved walls, the piñon patches in the amphitheater under the circled walls. That was a wild place they were approaching, and, once in there, he believed pursuit would be useless. However, there were miles to go still, and those hard-riding devils behind made alarming decrease in the intervening distance. Shefford could see the horses plainly now. How they made the dust fly! He counted up to six—and then the dust and moving line caused the others to be indistinguishable.

At last only a long, gently rising slope separated the fugitives from that labyrinthine network of wildly carved rock. But it was the clear air that made the distance seem short. Mile after mile the mustangs climbed, and when they were perhaps halfway across that last slope to the rocks the first horse of the pursuers mounted to the level behind. In a few moments the whole band was strung out in sight. Nas Ta Bega kept his mustang at a steady walk, in spite of the gaining pursuers. There came a point, however, when the Indian, reaching comparatively level ground, put his mount to a swinging canter. The other mustangs broke into the same gait.

It became a race then, with the couple of miles between fugitives and pursuers only imperceptibly lessened. Nas Ta Bega had saved his mustangs and Shadd had ridden his to the limit. Shefford kept looking back, gripping his rifle, hoping it would not come to a fight, yet slowly losing that reluctance.

Sage began to show on the slope, and other kinds of brush and cedars straggled everywhere. The great rocks loomed closer, and red color mixed with yellow, and the slopes lengthening out, not so steep, yet infinitely longer than they had seemed at a distance.

Shefford ceased to feel the dry wind in his face. They were already in the lee of the wall. He could see the rock-squirrels scampering to their holes. The mustangs valiantly held to the gait, and at last the Indian disappeared between two rounded corners of cliff. The others were close behind. Shefford wheeled once more. Shadd and his gang were a mile in the rear, but coming fast, despite winded horses.

Shefford rode around the wall into a widening space thick with cedars. It ended in a bare slope of smooth rock. Here the Indian dismounted. When the others came up with him he told them to lead their horses and follow. Then he began the ascent of the rock.

It was smooth and hard, though not slippery. There was not a crack. Shefford did not see a broken piece of stone. Nas Ta Bega climbed straight up for a while, and then wound around a swell, to turn this way and that, always going up. Shefford began to see similar mounds of rock all around him, of every shape that could be called a curve. There were yellow domes far above, and small red domes far below. Ridges ran from one hill of rock to another. There were no abrupt breaks, but holes and pits and caves were everywhere, and occasionally, deep down, an amphitheater green with cedar and piñon. The Indian appeared to have a clear idea of where he wanted to go, though there was no vestige of a trail on those bare slopes. At length Shefford was high enough to see back upon the plain, but the pursuers were no longer in sight.

Nas Ta Bega led to the top of that wall, only to disclose to his followers another and a higher wall beyond, with a ridged, bare, wild, and scalloped depression between. Here footing began to be precarious for both man and beast. When the ascent of the second wall began it was necessary to zigzag up, slowly and carefully, taking advantage of every level bulge or depression. They must have consumed half an hour mounting this slope to the summit. Once there, Shefford drew a sharp breath with both backward and forward glances. Shadd and his gang, in single file, showed dark upon the bare stone ridge behind. And to the fore there twisted and dropped and curved the most dangerous slopes Shefford had ever seen. The fugitives had reached the height of stone wall, of the divide, and many of the drops upon this side were perpendicular and too steep to see the bottom.

Nas Ta Bega led along the ridge-top and then started down, following the waves in the rock. He came out upon a round promontory from which there could not have been any turning of a horse. The long slant leading down was at an angle Shefford declared impossible for the animals. Yet the Indian started down. His mustang needed urging, but at last edged upon the steep descent. Shefford and the others had to hold back and wait. It was thrilling to see the intelligent mustang. He did not step. He slid his fore hoofs a few inches at a time and kept directly behind the Indian. If he fell he would knock Nas Ta Bega off his feet and they would both roll down together. There was no doubt in Shefford's mind that the mustang knew this as well as the Indian. Foot by foot they worked down to a swelling bulge, and here Nas Ta Bega left his mustang and came back for the pack-horse. It was even more difficult to get this beast down. Then the Indian called for Lassiter and Jane and Fay to come down. Shefford began to keep a sharp lookout behind and above, and did not see how the three fared on the slope, but evidently there was no mishap. Nas Ta Bega mounted the slope again, and at the moment sight of Shadd's dark bays silhouetted against the sky caused Shefford to call out:

"We've got to hurry!"

The Indian led one mustang and called to the others. Shefford stepped close behind. They went down in single file, inch by inch, foot by foot, and safely reached the comparative level below.

"Shadd's gang are riding their horses up and down these walls!" exclaimed Shefford.

"Shore," replied Lassiter.

Both the women were silent.

Nas Ta Bega led the way swiftly to the right. He rounded a huge dome, climbed a low, rolling ridge, descended and ascended, and came out upon the rim of a steep-walled amphitheater. Along the rim was a yard-wide level, with the chasm to the left and steep slope to the right. There was no time to flinch at the danger, when an even greater danger menaced from the rear. Nas Ta Bega led, and his mustang kept at his heels. One misstep would have plunged the animal to his death. But he was surefooted and his confidence helped the others. At the apex of the curve the only course led away from the rim, and here there was no level. Four of the mustangs slipped and slid down the smooth rock until they stopped in a shallow depression. It cost time to get them out, to straighten pack and saddles. Shefford thought he heard a yell in the rear, but he could not see anything of the gang.

They rounded this precipice only to face a worse one. Shefford's nerve was sorely tried when he saw steep slants everywhere, all apparently leading down into chasms, and no place a man, let alone a horse, could put a foot with safety. Nevertheless the imperturbable Indian never slacked his pace. Always he appeared to find a way, and he never had to turn back. His winding course, however, did not now cover much distance in a straight line, and herein lay the greatest peril. Any moment Shadd and his men might come within range.

Upon a particularly tedious and dangerous side of rocky hill the fugitives lost so much time that Shefford grew exceedingly alarmed. Still, they accomplished it without accident, and their pursuers did not heave in sight. Perhaps they were having trouble in a bad place.

The afternoon was waning. The red sun hung low above the yellow mesa to the left, and there was a perceptible shading of light.

At last Nas Ta Bega came to a place that halted him. It did not look so bad as places they had successfully passed. Yet upon closer study Shefford did not see how they were to get around the neck of the gully at their feet. Presently the Indian put the bridle over the head of his mustang and left him free. He did likewise for two more mustangs, while Lassiter and Shefford rendered a like service to theirs. Then the Indian started down, with his mustang following him. The pack-animal came next, then Fay and Nack-yal, then Lassiter and his mount, with Jane and hers next, and Shefford last. They followed the Indian, picking their steps swiftly, looking nowhere except at the stone under their feet. The right side of the chasm was rimmed, the curve at the head crossed, and then the real peril of this trap had to be faced. It was a narrow slant of ledge, doubling back parallel with the course already traversed.

A sharp warning cry from Nas Ta Bega scarcely prepared Shefford for hoarse yells, and then a rattling rifle-volley from the top of the slope opposite. Bullets thudded on the cliff, whipped up red dust, and spanged and droned away.

Fay Larkin screamed and staggered back against the wall. Nack-yal was hit, and with frightened snort he reared, pawed the air, and came down, pounding the stone. The mustang behind him went to his knees, sank with his head over the rim, and, slipping off, plunged into the depths. In an instant a dull crash came up.

For a moment there was imminent peril for the horses, more in the yawning hole than in the spanging of badly aimed bullets. Lassiter drew Jane up a little slope out of the way of the frightened mustangs, and Shefford, risking his neck, rushed to Fay. She was holding her arm, which was bleeding. Unheeding the rain of bullets, he half carried, half dragged her along the slope of the low bluff, where he hid behind a corner till the Indian drove the mustangs round it. Shefford's swift fingers were wet and red with the blood from Fay's arm when he had bound the wound with his scarf. Lassiter had gotten around with Jane and was calling Shefford to hurry.

It had been Shefford's idea to halt there and fight. But he did not want to send Fay on alone, so he hurried ahead with her. The Indian had the horses going fast on a long level, overhung by bulging wall. Lassiter and Jane were looking back. Shefford, becoming aware of a steep slope to his left, looked down to see a narrow chasm and great crevices in the cliffs, with bunches of cedars here and there.

Presently Nas Ta Bega disappeared with the mustangs. He had evidently turned off to go down behind the split cliffs. Shefford and Fay caught up with Lassiter and Jane, and, panting, hurrying, looking backward and then forward, they kept on, as best they could, in the Indian's course. Shefford made sure they had lost him, when he appeared down to the left. Then they all ran to catch up with him. They went around the chasm, and then through one of the narrow cracks to come out upon the rim, among cedars. Here the Indian waited for them. He pointed down another long swell of naked stone to a narrow green split which was evidently different from all these curved pits and holes and abysses, for this one had straight walls and wound away out of sight. It was the head of a cañon.

"Nonnezoshe Boco!" said the Indian.

"Nas Ta Bega, go on!" replied Shefford. "When Shadd comes out on that slope above he can't see you—where you go down. Hurry on with the horses and women. Lassiter, you go with them. And if Shadd passes me and comes up with you—do your best. . . . I'm going to ambush that Piute and his gang!"

"Shore you've picked out a good place," replied Lassiter.

In another moment Shefford was alone. He heard the light, soft pat and slide of the hoofs of the mustangs as they went down. Presently that sound ceased.

He looked at the red stain on his hands—from the blood of the girl he loved. And he had to stifle a terrible wrath that shook his frame. In regard to Shadd's pursuit, it had not been blood that he had feared, but capture for Fay. He and Nas Ta Bega might have expected a shot if they resisted, but to wound that unfortunate girl—it made a tiger out of him. When he had stilled the emotions that weakened and shook him and reached cold and implacable control of himself, he crawled under the cedars to the rim and, well hidden, he watched and waited.

Shadd appeared to be slow for the first time since he had been sighted. With keen eyes Shefford watched the corner where he and the others had escaped from that murderous volley. But Shadd did not come.

The sun had lost its warmth and was tipping the lofty mesa to his right. Soon twilight would make travel on those walls more perilous and darkness would make it impossible. Shadd must hurry or abandon the pursuit for that day. Shefford found himself grimly hopeful.

Suddenly he heard the click of hoofs. It came, faint yet clear, on the still air. He glued his sight upon that corner where he expected the pursuers to appear. More cracks of hoofs pierced his ear, clearer and sharper this time. Presently he gathered that they could not possibly come from beyond the corner he was watching. So he looked far to the left of that place, seeing no one, then far to the right. Out over a bulge of stone he caught sight of the bobbing head of a horse—then another—and still another.

He was astounded. Shadd had gone below that place where the attack had been made and he had come up this steep slope. More horses appeared—to the number of eight. Shefford easily recognized a low, broad, squat rider to be Shadd. Assuredly the Piute did not know this country. Possibly, however, he had feared an ambush. But Shefford grew convinced that Shadd had not expected an ambush, or at least did not fear it, and had mistaken the Indian's course. Moreover, if he led his gang a few rods farther up that slope he would do worse than make a mistake—he would be facing a double peril.

What fearless horsemen these Indians were! Shadd was mounted, as were three others of his gang. Evidently the white men, the outlaws, were the ones on foot. Shefford thrilled and his veins stung when he saw these pursuers come passing what he considered the danger mark. But manifestly they could not see their danger. Assuredly they were aware of the chasm; however, the level upon which they were advancing narrowed gradually, and they could not tell that very soon they could not go any farther nor could they turn back. The alternative was to climb the slope, and that was a desperate chance.

They came up, now about on a level with Shefford, and perhaps three hundred yards distant. He gripped his rifle with a fatal assurance that he could kill one of them now. Still he waited. Curiosity consumed him because every foot they advanced heightened their peril. Shefford wondered if Shadd would have chosen that course if he had not supposed the Navajo had chosen it first. It was plain that one of the walking Piutes stooped now and then to examine the rock. He was looking for some faint sign of a horse track.

Shadd halted within two hundred yards of where Shefford lay hidden. His keen eye had caught the significance of the narrowing level before he had reached the end. He pointed and spoke. Shefford heard his voice. The others replied. They all looked up at the steep slope, down into the chasm right below them, and across into the cedars. The Piute in the rear succeeded in turning his horse, went back, and began to circle up the slope. The others entered into an argument and they became more closely grouped upon the narrow bench. Their mustangs were lean, wiry, wild, vicious, and Shefford calculated grimly upon what a stampede might mean in that position.

Then Shadd turned his mustang up the slope. Like a goat he climbed. Another Indian in the rear succeeded in pivoting his steed and started back, apparently to circle round and up. The others of the gang appeared uncertain. They yelled hoarsely at Shadd, who halted on the steep slant some twenty paces above them. He spoke and made motions that evidently meant the climb was easy enough. It looked easy for him. His dark face flashed red in the rays of the sun.

At this critical moment Shefford decided to fire. He meant to kill Shadd, hoping if the leader was gone the others would abandon the pursuit. The rifle wavered a little as he aimed, then grew still. He fired. Shadd never flinched. But the fiery mustang, perhaps wounded, certainly terrified, plunged down with piercing, horrid scream. Shadd fell under him. Shrill yells rent the air. Like a thunderbolt the sliding horse was upon men and animals below.

A heavy shock, wild snorts, upflinging heads and hoofs, a terrible tramping, thudding, shrieking mêlée, then a brown, twisting, tangled mass shot down the slant over the rim!

Shefford dazedly thought he saw men running. He did see plunging horses. One slipped, fell, rolled, and went into the chasm.

Then up from the depths came a crash, a long, slipping roar. In another instant there was a lighter crash and a lighter sliding roar.

Two horses, shaking, paralyzed with fear, were left upon the narrow level. Beyond them a couple of men were crawling along the stone. Up on the level stood the two Indians, holding down frightened horses, and staring at the fatal slope.

And Shefford lay there under the cedar, in the ghastly grip of the moment, hardly comprehending that his ill-aimed shot had been a thunderbolt.

He did not think of shooting at the Piutes; they, however, recovering from their shock, evidently feared the ambush, for they swiftly drew up the slope and passed out of sight. The frightened horses below whistled and tramped along the lower level, finally vanishing. There was nothing left on the bare wall to prove to Shefford that it had been the scene of swift and tragic death. He leaned from his covert and peered over the rim. Hundreds of feet below he saw dark growths of piñons. There was no sign of a pile of horses and men, and then he realized that he could not tell the number that had perished. The swift finale had been as stunning to him as if lightning had struck near him.

Suddenly it flashed over him what state of suspense and torture Fay and Jane must be in at that very moment. And, leaping up, he ran out of the cedars to the slope behind and hurried down at risk of limb. The sun had set by this time. He hoped he could catch up with the party before dark. He went straight down, and the end of the slope was a smooth, low wall. The Indian must have descended with the horses at some other point. The cañon was about fifty yards wide and it headed under the great slope of Navajo Mountain. These smooth, rounded walls appeared to end at its low rim.

Shefford slid down upon a grassy bank, and finding the tracks of the horses, he followed them. They led along the wall. As soon as he had assured himself that Nas Ta Bega had gone down the cañon he abandoned the tracks and pushed ahead swiftly. He heard the soft rush of running water. In the center of the cañon wound heavy lines of bright-green foliage, bordering a rocky brook. The air was close, warm, and sweet with perfume of flowers. The walls were low, and shelving, and soon lost that rounded appearance peculiar to the wind-worn slopes above. Shefford came to where the horses had plowed down a gravelly bank into the clear, swift water of the brook. The little pools of water were still muddy. Shefford drank, finding the water cold and sweet, without the bitter bite of alkali. He crossed and pushed on, running on the grassy levels. Flowers were everywhere, but he did not notice them particularly. The cañon made many leisurely turns, and its size, if it enlarged at all, was not perceptible to him yet. The rims above him were perhaps fifty feet high. Cottonwood-trees began to appear along the brook, and blossoming buck-brush in the corners of wall.

He had traveled perhaps a mile when Nas Ta Bega, appearing to come out of the thicket, confronted him.

"Hello!" called Shefford. "Where're Fay—and the others?"

The Indian made a gesture that signified the rest of the party were beyond a little way. Shefford took Nas Ta Bega's arm, and as they walked, and he panted for breath, he told what had happened back on the slopes.

The Indian made one of his singular speaking sweeps of hand, and he scrutinized Shefford's face, but he received the news in silence. They turned a corner of wall, crossed a wide, shallow, boulder-strewn place in the brook, and mounted the bank to a thicket. Beyond this, from a clump of cottonwoods, Lassiter strode out with a gun in each hand. He had been hiding.

"Shore I'm glad to see you," he said, and the eyes that piercingly fixed on Shefford were now as keen as formerly they had been mild.

"Gone! Lassiter—they're gone," broke out Shefford. "Where's Fay—and Jane?"

Lassiter called, and presently the women came out of the thick brake, and Fay bounded forward with her swift stride, while Jane followed with eager steps and anxious face. Then they all surrounded Shefford.

"It was Shadd—and his gang," panted Shefford. "Eight in all. Three or four Piutes—the others outlaws. They lost track of us. Went below the place—where they shot at us. And they came up—on a bad slope."

Shefford described the slope and the deep chasm and how Shadd led up to the point where he saw his mistake and then how the catastrophe fell.

"I shot—and missed," repeated Shefford, with the sweat in beads on his pale face. "I missed Shadd. Maybe I hit the horse. He plunged—reared—fell back—a terrible fall—right upon that bunch of horses and men below. . . . In a horrible, wrestling, screaming tangle they slid over the rim! I don't know how many. I saw some men running along. I saw three other horses plunging. One slipped and went over. . . . I have no idea how many, but Shadd and some of his gang went to destruction."

"Shore thet's fine!" said Lassiter. "But mebbe I won't get to use them guns, after all."

"Hardly on that gang," laughed Shefford. "The two Piutes and what others escaped turned back. Maybe they'll meet a posse of Mormons—for of course the Mormons will track us, too—and come back to where Shadd lost his life. That's an awful place. Even the Piute got lost—couldn't follow Nas Ta Bega. It would take any pursuers some time to find how we got in here. I believe we need not fear further pursuit. Certainly not to-night or to-morrow. Then we'll be far down the cañon."

When Shefford concluded his earnest remarks the faces of Fay and Jane had lost the signs of suppressed dread.

"Nas Ta Bega, make camp here," said Shefford. "Water—wood—grass—why, this's something like. . . . Fay, how's your arm?"

"It hurts," she replied, simply.

"Come with me down to the brook and let me wash and bind it properly."

They went, and she sat upon a stone while he knelt beside her and untied his scarf from her arm. As the blood had hardened, it was necessary to slit her sleeve to the shoulder. Using his scarf, he washed the blood from the wound, and found it to be merely a cut, a groove, on the surface.

"That's nothing," Shefford said, lightly. "It'll heal in a day. But there'll always be a scar. And when we—we get back to civilization, and you wear a pretty gown without sleeves, people will wonder what made this mark on your beautiful arm."

Fay looked at him with wonderful eyes. "Do women wear gowns without sleeves?" she asked.

"They do."

"Have I a—beautiful arm?"

She stretched it out, white, blue-veined, the skin fine as satin, the lines graceful and flowing, a round, firm, strong arm.

"The most beautiful I ever saw," he replied.

But the pleasure his compliment gave her was not communicated to him. His last impression of that right arm had been of its strength, and his mind flashed with lightning swiftness to a picture that haunted him—Waggoner lying dead on the porch with that powerfully driven knife in his breast. Shefford shuddered through all his being. Would this phantom come often to him like that? Hurriedly he bound up her arm with the scarf and did not look at her, and was conscious that she felt a subtle change in him.

The short twilight ended with the fugitives comfortable in a camp that for natural features could not have been improved upon. Darkness found Fay and Jane asleep on a soft mossy bed, a blanket tucked around them, and their faces still and beautiful in the flickering campfire light. Lassiter did not linger long awake. Nas Ta Bega, seeing Shefford's excessive fatigue, urged him to sleep. Shefford demurred, insisting that he share the night-watch. But Nas Ta Bega, by agreeing that Shefford might have the following night's duty, prevailed upon him.

Shefford seemed to shut his eyes upon darkness and to open them immediately to the light. The stream of blue sky above, the gold tints on the western rim, the rosy, brightening colors down in the cañon, were proofs of the sunrise. This morning Nas Ta Bega proceeded leisurely, and his manner was comforting. When all was in readiness for a start he gave the mustang he had ridden to Shefford, and walked, leading the pack-animal.

The mode of travel here was a selection of the best levels, the best places to cross the brook, the best banks to climb, and it was a process of continual repetition. As the Indian picked out the course and the mustangs followed his lead there was nothing for Shefford to do but take his choice between reflection that seemed predisposed toward gloom and an absorption in the beauty, color, wildness, and changing character of Nonnezoshe Boco.

Assuredly his experience in the desert did not count in it a trip down into a strange, beautiful, lost cañon such as this. It did not widen, though the walls grew higher. They began to lean and bulge, and the narrow strip of sky above resembled a flowing blue river. Huge caverns had been hollowed out by some work of nature, what, he could not tell, though he was sure it could not have been wind. And when the brook ran close under one of these overhanging places the running water made a singular, indescribable sound. A crack from a hoof on a stone rang like a hollow bell and echoed from wall to wall. And the croak of a frog—the only living creature he had so far noted in the cañon—was a weird and melancholy thing.

Fay rode close to him, and his heart seemed to rejoice when she spoke, when she showed how she wanted to be near him, yet, try as he might, he could not respond. His speech to her—what little there was—did not come spontaneously. And he suffered a remorse that he could not be honestly natural to her. Then he would drive away the encroaching gloom, trusting that a little time would dispel it.

"We are deeper down than Surprise Valley," said Fay.

"How do you know?" he asked.

"Here are the pink and yellow sago-lilies. You remember we went once to find the white ones? I have found white lilies in Surprise Valley, but never any pink or yellow."

Shefford had seen flowers all along the green banks, but he had not marked the lilies. Here he dismounted and gathered several. They were larger than the white ones of higher altitudes, of the same exquisite beauty and fragility, of such rare pink and yellow hues as he had never seen. He gave the flowers to Fay.

"They bloom only where it's always summer," she said.

That expressed their nature. They were the orchids of the summer cañons. They stood up everywhere starlike out of the green. It was impossible to prevent the mustangs treading them under hoof. And as the cañon deepened, and many little springs added their tiny volume to the brook, every grassy bench was dotted with lilies, like a green sky starspangled. And this increasing luxuriance manifested itself in the banks of purple moss and clumps of lavender daisies and great clusters of yellow violets. The brook was lined by blossoming buck-brush; the rocky corners showed the crimson and magenta of cactus; ledges were green with shining moss that sparkled with little white flowers. The hum of bees filled the air.

But by and by this green and colorful and verdant beauty, the almost level floor of the cañon, the banks of soft earth, the thickets and the clumps of cottonwoods, the shelving caverns and the bulging walls—these features gradually were lost, and Nonnezoshe Boco began to deepen in bare red and white stone steps, the walls sheered away from one another, breaking into sections and ledges, and rising higher and higher, and there began to be manifested a dark and solemn concordance with the nature that had created this rent in the earth.

There was a stretch of miles where steep steps in hard red rock alternated with long levels of round boulders. Here one by one the mustangs went lame. And the fugitives, dismounting to spare the faithful beasts, slipped and stumbled over these loose and treacherous stones. Fay was the only one who did not show distress. She was glad to be on foot again and the rolling boulders were as stable as solid rock for her.

The hours passed; the toil increased; the progress diminished; one of the mustangs failed entirely and was left; and all the while the dimensions of Nonnezoshe Boco magnified and its character changed. It became a thousand-foot walled cañon, leaning, broken, threatening, with great yellow sides blocking passage, with huge sections split off from the main wall, with immense dark and gloomy caverns. Strangely, it had no intersecting cañons. It jealously guarded its secret. Its unusual formations of cavern and pillar and half-arch led the mind to expect any monstrous stone-shape left by an avalanche or cataclysm.

Down and down the fugitives toiled. And now the streambed was bare of boulders, and the banks of earth. The floods that had rolled down that cañon had here borne away every loose thing. All the floor was bare red and white stone, polished, glistening, slippery, affording treacherous foothold. And the time came when Nas Ta Bega abandoned the streambed to take to the rock-strewn and cactus-covered ledges above.

Jane gave out and had to be assisted upon the weary mustang. Fay was persuaded to mount Nack-yal again. Lassiter plodded along. The Indian bent tired steps far in front. And Shefford traveled on after him, footsore and hot.

The cañon widened ahead into a great, ragged, iron-hued amphitheater, and from there apparently turned abruptly at right angles. Sunset rimmed the walls. Shefford wondered dully when the Indian would halt to camp. And he dragged himself onward with eyes down on the rough ground.

When he raised them again the Indian stood on a point of slope with folded arms, gazing down where the cañon veered. Something in Nas Ta Bega's pose quickened Shefford's pulse and then his steps. He reached the Indian and the point where he, too, could see beyond that vast jutting wall that had obstructed his view.

A mile beyond all was bright with the colors of sunset, and spanning the cañon in the graceful shape and beautiful hues of a rainbow was a magnificent Stone Bridge.

"Nonnezoshe!" exclaimed the Navajo, with a deep and sonorous roll in his voice.

CHAPTER 18

AT THE FOOT
OF THE RAINBOW

The rainbow bridge was the one great natural phenomenon, the one grand spectacle, which Shefford had ever seen that did not at first give vague disappointment, a confounding of reality, a disenchantment of contrast with what the mind had conceived.

But this thing was glorious. It silenced him, yet did not awe or stun. His body and brain, weary and dull from the toil of travel, received a singular and revivifying freshness. He had a strange, mystic perception of this rosy-hued stupendous arch of stone, as if in a former life it had been a goal he could not reach. This wonder of nature, though all-satisfying, all-fulfilling to his artist's soul, could not be a resting-place for him, a destination where something awaited him, a height he must scale to find peace, the end of his strife. But it seemed all these. He could not understand his perception or his emotion. Still, here at last, apparently, was the rainbow of his boyish dreams and of his manhood—a rainbow magnified even beyond those dreams, no longer transparent and ethereal, but solidified, a thing of ages, sweeping up majestically from the red walls, its iris-hued arch against the blue sky.

Nas Ta Bega led on down the ledge and Shefford plodded thoughtfully after him. The others followed. A jutting corner of wall again hid the cañon. The Indian was working round to circle the huge amphitheater. It was slow, irritating, strenuous toil, for the way was on a steep slant, rough and loose and dragging. The rocks were as hard and jagged as lava. And the cactus further hindered progress. When at last the long half-circle had been accomplished the golden and rosy lights had faded.

Again the cañon opened to view. All the walls were pale and steely and the Stone Bridge loomed dark. Nas Ta Bega said camp would be made at the bridge, which was now close. Just before they reached it the Navajo halted with one of his singular actions. Then he stood motionless. Shefford realized that Nas Ta Bega was saying his prayer to this great stone god. Presently the Indian motioned for Shefford to lead the others and the horses on under the bridge. Shefford did so, and, upon turning, was amazed to see the Indian climbing the steep and difficult slope on the other side. All the party watched him until he disappeared behind the huge base of cliff that supported the arch. Shefford selected a level place for camp, some few rods away, and here, with Lassiter, unsaddled and unpacked the lame, drooping mustangs. When this was done twilight had fallen. Nas Ta Bega appeared, coming down the steep slope on this side of the bridge. Then Shefford divined why the Navajo had made that arduous climb. He would not go under the bridge. Nonnezoshe was a Navajo god. And Nas Ta Bega, though educated as a white man, was true to the superstition of his ancestors.

Nas Ta Bega turned the mustangs loose to fare for what scant grass grew on bench and slope. Fire-wood was even harder to find than grass. When the camp duties had been performed and the simple meal eaten there was gloom gathering in the cañon and the stars had begun to blink in the pale strip of blue above the lofty walls. The place was oppressive and the fugitives mostly silent. Shefford spread a bed of blankets for the women, and Jane at once lay wearily down. Fay stood beside the flickering fire, and Shefford felt her watching him. He was conscious of a desire to get away from her haunting gaze. To the gentle good-night he bade her she made no response.

Shefford moved away into a strange dark shadow cast by the bridge against the pale starlight. It was a weird, black belt, where he imagined he was invisible, but out of which he could see. There was a slab of rock near the foot of the bridge, and here Shefford composed himself to watch, to feel, to think the unknown thing that seemed to be inevitably coming to him.

A slight stiffening of his neck made him aware that he had been continually looking up at the looming arch. And he found that insensibly it had changed and grown. It had never seemed the same any two moments, but that was not what he meant. Near at hand it was too vast a thing for immediate comprehension. He wanted to ponder on what had formed it—to reflect upon its meaning as to age and force of nature, yet all he could do at each moment was to see. White stars hung along the dark curved line. The rim of the arch seemed to shine. The moon must be up there somewhere. The far side of the cañon was now a blank, black wall. Over its towering rim showed a pale glow. It brightened. The shades in the cañon lightened, then a white disk of moon peered over the dark line. The bridge turned to silver, and the gloomy, shadowy belt it had cast blanched and vanished.

Shefford became aware of the presence of Nas Ta Bega. Dark, silent, statuesque, with inscrutable eyes uplifted, with all that was spiritual of the Indian suggested by a somber and tranquil knowledge of his place there, he represented the same to Shefford as a solitary figure of human life brought out the greatness of a great picture. Nonnezoshe Boco needed life, wild life, life of its millions of years—and here stood the dark and silent Indian.

There was a surge in Shefford's heart and in his mind a perception of a moment of incalculable change to his soul. And at that moment Fay Larkin stole like a phantom to his side and stood there with her uncovered head shining and her white face lovely in the moonlight.

"May I stay with you—a little?" she asked, wistfully. "I can't sleep."

"Surely you may," he replied. "Does your arm hurt too badly, or are you too tired to sleep?"

"No—it's this place. I—I—can't tell you how I feel."

But the feeling was there in her eyes for Shefford to read. Had he too great an emotion—did he read too much—did he add from his soul? For him the wild, starry, haunted eyes mirrored all that he had seen and felt under Nonnezoshe. And for herself they shone eloquently of courage and love.

"I need to talk—and I don't know how," she said.

He was silent, but he took her hands and drew her closer.

"Why are you so—so different?" she asked, bravely.

"Different?" he echoed.

"Yes. You are kind—you speak the same to me as you used to. But since we started you've been different, somehow."

"Fay, think how hard and dangerous the trip's been! I've been worried—and sick with dread—with—Oh, you can't imagine the strain I'm under! How could I be my old self?"

"It isn't worry I mean."

He was too miserable to try to find out what she did mean; besides, he believed, if he let himself think about it, he would know what troubled her.

"I—I am almost happy," she said, softly.

"Fay! . . . Aren't you at all afraid?"

"No. You'll take care of me. . . . Do—do you love me—like you did before?"

"Why, child! Of course—I love you," he replied, brokenly, and he drew her closer. He had never embraced her, never kissed her. But there was a whiteness about her then—a wraith—a something from her soul, and he could only gaze at her.

"I love you," she whispered. "I thought I knew it that—that night. But I'm only finding it out now . . . And somehow I had to tell you here."

"Fay, I haven't said much to you," he said, hurriedly, huskily. "I haven't had a chance. I love you. I—I ask you—will you be my wife?"

"Of course," she said, simply, but the white, moon-blanched face colored with a dark and leaping blush.

"We'll be married as soon as we get out of the desert," he went on. "And we'll forget—all—all that's happened. You're so young. You'll forget."

"I'd forgotten already, till this difference came in you. And pretty soon—when I can say something more to you—I'll forget all except Surprise Valley—and my evenings in the starlight with you."

"Say it then—quick!"

She was leaning against him, holding his hands in her strong clasp, soulful, tender, almost passionate.

"You couldn't help it. . . . I'm to blame. . . . I remember what I said."

"What?" he queried in amaze.

"*'You can kill him!'* . . . I said that. I made you kill him."

"Kill—whom?" cried Shefford.

"Waggoner. I'm to blame. . . . That must be what's made you different. And, oh, I've wanted you to know it's all my fault. . . . But I wouldn't be sorry if you weren't. . . . I'm glad he's dead."

"*You—think—I—*" Shefford's gasping whisper failed in the shock of the revelation that Fay believed he had killed Waggoner. Then with the inference came the staggering truth—her guiltlessness; and a paralyzing joy held him stricken.

A powerful hand fell upon Shefford's shoulder, startling him. Nas Ta Bega stood there, looking down upon him and Fay. Never had the Indian seemed so dark, inscrutable of face. But in his magnificent bearing, in the spirit that Shefford sensed in him, there were nobility and power and a strange pride.

The Indian kept one hand on Shefford's shoulder, and with the other he struck himself on the breast. The action was that of an Indian, impressive and stern, significant of an Indian's prowess.

"My God!" breathed Shefford, very low.

"Oh, what does he mean?" cried Fay.

Shefford held her with shaking hands, trying to speak, to fight a way out of these stultifying emotions.

"Nas Ta Bega—you heard. She thinks—I killed Waggoner!"

All about the Navajo then was dark and solemn disproof of her belief. He did not need to speak. His repetition of that savage, almost boastful blow on his breast added only to the dignity, and not to the denial, of a warrior.

"Fay, he means he killed the Mormon," said Shefford. "He must have, for *I* did not!"

"Ah!" murmured Fay, and she leaned to him with passionate, quivering gladness. It was the woman—the human—the soul born in her that came uppermost then; now, when there was no direct call to the wild and elemental in her nature, she showed a heart above revenge, the instinct of a saving right, of truth as Shefford knew them. He took her into his arms and never had he loved her so well.

"Nas Ta Bega, you killed the Mormon," declared Shefford, with a voice that had gained strength. No silent Indian suggestion of a deed would suffice in that moment. Shefford needed to hear the Navajo speak—to have Fay hear him speak. "Nas Ta Bega, I know—I understand. But tell her. Speak so she will know. Tell it as a white man would!"

"I heard her cry out," replied the Indian, in his slow English. "I waited. When he came I killed him."

A poignant why was wrenched from Shefford. Nas Ta Bega stood silent.

"*Bi Nai!*" And when that sonorous Indian name rolled in dignity from his lips he silently stalked away into the gloom. That was his answer to the white man.

Shefford bent over Fay, and as the strain on him broke he held her closer and closer and his tears streamed down and his voice broke in exclamations of tenderness and thanksgiving. It did not matter what she had thought, but she must never know what he had thought. He clasped her as something precious he had lost and regained. He was shaken with a passion of remorse. How could he have believed Fay Larkin guilty of murder? Women less wild and less justified than she had been driven to such a deed, yet how could he have believed it of her, when for two days he had been with her, had seen her face, and deep into her eyes? There was a mystery in his very blindness. He cast the whole thought from him for ever. There was no shadow between Fay and him. He had found her. He had saved her. She was free. She was innocent. And suddenly, as he seemed delivered from contending tumults within, he became aware that it was no unresponsive creature he had folded to his breast.

He became suddenly alive to the warm, throbbing contact of her bosom, to her strong arms clinging round his neck, to her closed eyes, to the rapt whiteness of her face. And he bent to cold lips that seemed to receive his first kisses as new and strange; but tremulously changed, at last to meet his own, and then to burn with sweet and thrilling fire.

"My darling, my dream's come true," he said. "You are my treasure. I found you here at the foot of the rainbow! . . . What if it is a stone rainbow—if all is not as I had dreamed? I followed a gleam. And it's led me to love and faith!"

* * *

Hours afterward Shefford walked alone to and fro under the bridge. His trouble had given place to serenity. But this night of nights he must live out wide-eyed to its end.

The moon had long since crossed the streak of star-fired blue above and the cañon was black in shadow. At times a current of wind, with all the strangeness of that strange country in its hollow moan, rushed through the great stone arch. At other times there was silence such as Shefford imagined dwelt deep under this rocky world. At still other times an owl hooted, and the sound was nameless. But it had a mocking echo that never ended. An echo of night, silence, gloom, melancholy death, age, eternity!

The Indian lay asleep with his dark face upturned, and the other sleepers lay calm and white in the starlight.

Shefford saw in them the meaning of life and the past—the illimitable train of faces that had shone under the stars. There was a spirit in the cañon, and whether or not it was what the Navajo embodied in the great Nonnezoshe, or the life of the present, or the death of the ages, or the nature so magnificently manifested in those silent, dreaming, waiting walls—the truth for Shefford was that this spirit was God.

Life was eternal. Man's immortality lay in himself. Love of a woman was hope—happiness. Brotherhood—that mystic and grand "Bi Nai!" of the Navajo—that was religion.

CHAPTER 19

THE GRAND CAÑON
OF THE COLORADO

The night passed, the gloom turned gray, the dawn stole cool and pale into the cañon. When Nas Ta Bega drove the mustangs into camp the lofty ramparts of the walls were rimmed with gold and the dark arch of Nonnezoshe began to lose its steely gray.

The women had rested well and were in better condition to travel. Jane was cheerful and Fay radiant one moment and in a dream the next. She was beginning to live in that wonderful future. They talked more than usual at breakfast, and Lassiter made droll remarks. Shefford, with his great and haunting trouble ended for ever, with now only danger to face ahead, was a different man, but thoughtful and quiet.

This morning the Indian leisurely made preparations for the start. For all the concern he showed he might have known every foot of the cañon below Nonnezoshe. But, for Shefford, with the dawn had returned anxiety, a restless feeling of the need of hurry. What obstacles, what impassable gorges, might lie between this bridge and the river! The Indian's inscrutable serenity and Fay's trust, her radiance, the exquisite glow upon her face, sustained Shefford and gave him patience to endure and conceal his dread.

At length the flight was resumed, with Nas Ta Bega leading on foot, and Shefford walking in the rear. A quarter of a mile below camp the Indian led down a declivity into the bottom of the narrow gorge, where the stream ran. He did not gaze backward for a last glance at Nonnezoshe; nor did Jane or Lassiter. Fay, however, checked Nack-yal at the rim of the descent and turned to look behind. Shefford contrasted her tremulous smile, her half-happy good-by to this place, with the white stillness of her face when she had bade farewell to Surprise Valley. Then she rode Nack-yal down into the gorge.

Shefford knew that this would be his last look at the rainbow bridge. As he gazed the tip of the great arch lost its cold, dark stone color and began to shine. The sun had just arisen high enough over some low break in the wall to reach the bridge. Shefford watched. Slowly, in wondrous transformation, the gold and blue and rose and pink and purple blended their hues, softly, mistily, cloudily, until once again the arch was a rainbow.

Ages before life had evolved upon the earth it had spread its grand arch from wall to wall, black and mystic at night, transparent and rosy in the sunrise, at sunset a flaming curve limned against the heavens. When the race of man had passed it would, perhaps, stand there still. It was not for many eyes to see. Only by toil, sweat, endurance, blood, could any man ever look at Nonnezoshe. So it would always be alone, grand, silent, beautiful, unintelligible.

Shefford bade Nonnezoshe a mute, reverent farewell. Then plunging down the weathered slope of the gorge to the stream below, he hurried forward to join the others. They had progressed much farther than he imagined they would have, and this was owing to the fact that the floor of the gorge afforded easy travel. It was gravel on rock bottom, tortuous, but open, with infrequent and shallow downward steps. The stream did not now rush and boil along and tumble over rock-encumbered ledges. In corners the water collected in round, green, eddying pools. There were patches of grass and willows and mounds of moss. Shefford's surprise equaled his relief, for he believed that the violent descent of Nonnezoshe Boco had been passed. Any turn now, he imagined, might bring the party out upon the river. When he caught up with them he imparted this conviction, which was received with cheer. The hopes of all, except the Indian, seemed mounting; and if he ever hoped or despaired it was never manifest.

Shefford's anticipation, however, was not soon realized. The fugitives traveled miles farther down Nonnezoshe Boco, and the only changes were that the walls of the lower gorge heightened and merged into those above and that these upper ones towered ever loftier. Shefford had to throw his head straight back to look up at the rims, and the narrow strip of sky was now indeed a flowing stream of blue.

Difficult steps were met, too, yet nothing compared to those of the upper cañon. Shefford calculated that this day's travel had advanced several hours; and more than ever now he was anticipating the mouth of Nonnezoshe Boco. Still another hour went by. And then came striking changes. The cañon narrowed till the walls were scarcely twenty paces apart; the color of stone grew dark red above and black down low; the light of day became shadowed, and the floor was a level, gravelly, winding lane, with the stream meandering slowly and silently.

Suddenly the Indian halted. He turned his ear down the cañon lane. He had heard something. The others grouped round him, but did not hear a sound except the soft flow of water and the heave of the mustangs. Then the Indian went on. Presently he halted again. And again he listened. This time he threw up his head and upon his dark face shone a light which might have been pride.

"Tse ko-n-tsa-igi," he said.

The others could not understand, but they were impressed.

"Shore he means somethin' big," drawled Lassiter.

"Oh, what did he say?" queried Fay in eagerness.

"Nas Ta Bega, tell us," said Shefford. "We are full of hope."

"Grand Cañon," replied the Indian.

"How do you know?" asked Shefford.

"I hear the roar of the river."

But Shefford, listen as he might, could not hear it. They traveled on, winding down the wonderful lane. Every once in a while Shefford lagged behind, let the others pass out of hearing, and then he listened. At last he was rewarded. Low and deep, dull and strange, with some quality to incite dread, came a roar. Thereafter, at intervals, usually at turns in the cañon, and when a faint stir of warm air fanned his cheeks, he heard the sound, growing clearer and louder.

He rounded an abrupt corner to have the roar suddenly fill his ears, to see the lane extend straight to a ragged vent, and beyond that, at some distance, a dark, ragged, bulging wall, like iron. As he hurried forward he was surprised to find that the noise did not increase. Here it kept a strange uniformity of tone and volume. The others of the party passed out of the mouth of Nonnezoshe Boco in advance of Shefford, and when he reached it they were grouped upon a bank of sand. A dark-red cañon yawned before them, and through it slid the strangest river Shefford had ever seen. At first glance he imagined the strangeness consisted of the dark-red color of the water, but at the second he was not so sure. All the others, except Nas Ta Bega, eyed the river blankly, as if they did not know what to think. The roar came from round a huge bulging wall downstream. Up the cañon, half a mile, at another turn, there was a leaping rapid of dirty red-white waves, and the sound of this, probably, was drowned in the unseen but nearer rapid.

"This is the Grand Cañon of the Colorado," said Shefford. "We've come out at the mouth of Nonnezoshe Boco. . . . And now to wait for Joe Lake!"

They made camp on a dry, level sand-bar under a shelving wall. Nas Ta Bega collected a pile of driftwood to be used for fire, and then he took the mustangs back up the side cañon to find grass for them. Lassiter appeared unusually quiet, and soon passed from weary rest on the sand to deep slumber. Fay and Jane succumbed to an exhaustion that manifested itself the moment relaxation set in, and they, too, fell asleep. Shefford patrolled the long strip of sand under the wall, and watched up the river for Joe Lake. The Indian returned and went along the river, climbed over the jutting, sharp slopes that reached into the water, and passed out of sight up-stream toward the rapid.

Shefford had a sense that the river and the cañon were too magnificent to be compared with others. Still, all his emotions and sensations had been so wrought upon, he seemed not to have any left by which he might judge of what constituted the difference. He would wait. He had a grim conviction that before he was safely out of this earth-riven crack he would know. One thing, however, struck him, and it was that up the cañon, high over the lower walls, hazy and blue, stood other walls, and beyond and above them, dim in purple distance, upreared still other walls. The haze and the blue and the purple meant great distance, and, likewise, the height seemed incomparable.

The red river attracted him most. Since this was the medium by which he must escape with his party, it was natural that it absorbed him, to the neglect of the gigantic cliffs. And the more he watched the river, studied it, listened to it, imagined its nature, its power, its relentlessness, the more he dreaded it. As the hours of the afternoon wore away, and he strolled along and rested on the banks, his first impressions, and what he realized might be his truest ones, were gradually lost. He could not bring them back. The river was changing, deceitful. It worked upon his mind. The low, hollow roar filled his ears and seemed to mock him. Then he endeavored to stop thinking about it, to confine his attention to the gap up-stream where sooner or later he prayed that Joe Lake and his boat would appear. But, though he controlled his gaze, he could not his thought, and his strange, impondering dread of the river augmented.

The afternoon waned. Nas Ta Bega came back to camp and said any likelihood of Joe's arrival was past for that day. Shefford could not get over an impression of strangeness—of the impossibility of the reality presented to his naked eyes. These lonely fugitives in the huge-walled cañon waiting for a boatman to come down that river! Strange and wild— those were the words which, inadequately at best, suited this country and the situations it produced.

After supper he and Fay walked along the bars of smooth, red sand. There were a few moments when the distant peaks and domes and turrets were glorified in changing sunset hues. But the beauty was fleeting. Fay still showed lassitude. She was quiet, yet cheerful, and the sweetness of her smile, her absolute trust in him, stirred and strengthened anew his spirit. Yet he suffered torture when he thought of trusting Fay's life, her soul, and her beauty to this strange red river.

Night brought him relief. He could not see the river; only the low roar made its presence known out there in the shadows. And, there being no need to stay awake, he dropped at once into heavy slumber. He was roused by hands dragging at him. Nas Ta Bega bent over him. It was broad daylight. The yellow wall high above was glistening. A fire was crackling and pleasant odors were wafted to him. Fay and Jane and Lassiter sat around the tarpaulin at breakfast. After the meal suspense and strain were manifested in all the fugitives, even the imperturbable Indian being more than usually watchful. His eyes scarcely ever left the black gap where the river slid round the turn above. Soon, as on the preceding day, he disappeared up the ragged, iron-bound shore. There was scarcely an attempt at conversation. A controlling thought bound that group into silence—if Joe Lake was ever going to come he would come today.

Shefford asked himself a hundred times if it were possible, and his answer seemed to be in the low, sullen, muffled roar of the river. And as the morning wore on toward noon his dread deepened until all chance appeared hopeless. Already he had begun to have vague and unformed and disquieting ideas of the only avenue of escape left—to return up Nonnezoshe Boco—and that would be to enter a trap.

Suddenly a piercing cry pealed down the cañon. It was followed by echoes, weird and strange, that clapped from wall to wall in mocking concatenation. Nas Ta Bega appeared high on the ragged slope. The cry had been the Indian's. He swept an arm out, pointing up-stream, and stood like a statue on the iron rocks.

Shefford's keen gaze sighted a moving something in the bend of the river. It was long, low, dark, and flat, with a lighter object upright in the middle. A boat and a man!

"Joe! It's Joe!" yelled Shefford, madly. "There! . . . Look!"

Jane and Fay were on their knees in the sand, clasping each other, pale faces toward that bend in the river.

Shefford ran up the shore toward the Indian. He climbed the jutting slant of rock. The boat was now full in the turn—it moved faster—it was nearing the smooth incline above the rapid. There! it glided down—heaved darkly up—settled back—and disappeared in the frothy, muddy roughness of water. Shefford held his breath and watched. A dark, bobbing object showed, vanished, showed again to enlarge—to take the shape of a big flatboat—and then it rode the swift, choppy current out of the lower end of the rapid.

Nas Ta Bega began to make violent motions, and Shefford, taking his cue, frantically waved his red scarf. There was a five-mile-an-hour current right before them, and Joe must needs see them so that he might steer the huge and clumsy craft into the shore before it drifted too far down.

Presently Joe did see them. He appeared to be half-naked; he raised aloft both arms, and bellowed down the cañon. The echoes boomed from wall to wall, every one stronger with the deep, hoarse triumph in the Mormon's voice, till they passed on, growing weaker, to die away in the roar of the river below. Then Joe bent to a long oar that appeared to be fastened to the stern of the boat, and the craft drifted out of the swifter current toward the shore. It reached a point opposite to where Shefford and the Indian waited, and, though Joe made prodigious efforts, it slid on. Still, it also drifted shoreward, and halfway down to the mouth of Nonnezoshe Boco Joe threw the end of a rope to the Indian.

"Ho! Ho!" yelled the Mormon, again setting into motion the fiendish echoes. He was naked to the waist; he had lost flesh; he was haggard, worn, dirty, wet. While he pulled on a shirt Nas Ta Bega made the rope fast to a snag of a log of driftwood embedded in the sand, and the boat swung to shore. It was perhaps thirty feet long by half as many wide, crudely built of rough-hewn boards. The steering gear was a long pole with a plank nailed to the end. The craft was empty save for another pole and plank, Joe's coat, and a broken-handled shovel. There were water and sand on the flooring.

Joe stepped ashore and he was gripped first by Shefford and then by the Indian. He was an unkempt and gaunt giant, yet how steadfast and reliable, how grimly strong to inspire hope!

"Reckon most of me's here," he said in reply to greetings. "I've had water aplenty. My God! I've had *water*!" He rolled out a grim laugh. "But no grub for three days. . . . Forgot to fetch some!"

How practical he was! He told Fay she looked good for sore eyes, but he needed a biscuit most of all. There was just a second of singular hesitation when he faced Lassiter, and then the big, strong hand of the young Mormon went out to meet the old gunman's. While they fed him and he ate like a starved man Shefford told of the flight from the village, the rescuing of Jane and Lassiter from Surprise Valley, the descent from the plateau, the catastrophe to Shadd's gang—and, concluding, Shefford, without any explanation, told that Nas Ta Bega had killed the Mormon Waggoner.

"Reckon I had that figured," replied Joe. "First off I didn't think so. . . . So Shadd went over the cliff. That's good riddance. It beats me, though. Never knew that Piute's like with a horse. And he had some grand horses in his outfit. Pity about them."

Later when Joe had a moment alone with Shefford he explained that during his ride to Kayenta he had realized Fay's innocence and who had been responsible for the tragedy. He took Withers, the trader, into his confidence, and they planned a story, which Withers was to carry to Stone Bridge, that would exculpate Fay and Shefford of anything more serious than flight. If Shefford got Fay safely out of the country at once that would end the matter for all concerned.

"Reckon I'm some ferry-boatman, too—a *fairy* boatman. Haw! Haw!" he added. "And we're going through. . . . Now I want you to help me rig this tarpaulin up over the bow of the boat. If we can fix it up strong it'll keep the waves from curling over. They filled her four times for me."

They folded the tarpaulin three times, and with stout pieces of split plank and horseshoe nails from Shefford's saddle-bags and pieces of rope they rigged up a screen around bow and front corners.

Nas Ta Bega put the saddles in the boat. The mustangs were far up Nonnezoshe Boco and would work their way back to green and luxuriant cañons. The Indian said they would soon become wild and would never be found. Shefford regretted Nack-yal, but was glad the faithful little mustang would be free in one of those beautiful cañons.

"Reckon we'd better be off," called Joe. "All aboard!" He placed Fay and Jane in a corner of the bow, where they would be spared sight of the rapids. Shefford loosed the rope and sprang aboard. "Pard," said Joe, "it's one hell of a river! And now with the snow melting up in the mountains it's twenty feet above normal and rising fast. But that's well for us. It covers the stones in the rapids. If it hadn't been in flood Joe would be an angel now!"

The boat cleared the sand, lazily wheeled in the eddying water, and suddenly seemed caught by some powerful gliding force. When it swept out beyond the jutting wall Shefford saw a quarter of a mile of sliding water that appeared to end abruptly. Beyond lengthened out the gigantic gap between the black and frowning cliffs.

"Wow!" exclaimed Joe. "Drops out of sight there. But that one ain't much. I can tell by the roar. When you see my hair stand up straight—then watch out! . . . Lassiter, you look after the women. Shefford, you stand ready to bail out with the shovel, for we'll sure ship water. Nas Ta Bega, you help here with the oar."

The roar became a heavy, continuous rumble; the current quickened; little streaks and ridges seemed to race along the boat; strange gurglings rose from under the bow. Shefford stood on tiptoe to see the break in the river below. Swiftly it came into sight—a wonderful, long, smooth, red slant of water, a swelling mound, a huge back-curling wave, another and another, a sea of frothy, uplifting crests, leaping and tumbling and diminishing down to the narrowing apex of the rapid. It was a frightful sight, yet it thrilled Shefford. Joe worked the steering-oar back and forth and headed the boat straight for the middle of the incline. The boat reached the round rim, gracefully dipped with a heavy sop, and went shooting down. The wind blew wet in Shefford's face. He stood erect, thrilling, fascinated, frightened. Then he seemed to feel himself lifted; the curling wave leaped at the boat; there was a shock that laid him flat; and when he rose to his knees all about him was roar and spray and leaping, muddy waves. Shock after shock jarred the boat. Splashes of water stung his face. And then the jar and the motion, the confusion and roar, gradually lessened until presently Shefford rose to see smooth water ahead and the long, trembling rapid behind.

"Get busy, bailer," yelled Joe. "Pretty soon you'll be glad you have to bail—so you *can't* see!"

There were several inches of water in the bottom of the boat and Shefford learned for the first time the expediency of a shovel in the art of bailing.

"That tarpaulin worked powerful good," went on Joe. "And it saves the women. Now if it just don't bust on a big wave! That one back there was little."

When Shefford had scooped out all the water he went forward to see how Fay and Jane and Lassiter had fared. The women were pale, but composed. They had covered their heads.

"But the dreadful roar!" exclaimed Fay.

Lassiter looked shaken for once.

"Shore I'd rather taken a chance meetin' them Mormons on the way out," he said.

Shefford spoke with an encouraging assurance which he did not himself feel. Almost at the moment he marked a silence that had fallen into the cañon; then it broke to a low, dull, strange roar.

"Aha! Hear that?" The Mormon shook his shaggy head. "Reckon we're in Cataract Cañon. We'll be standing on end from now on. Hang on to her, boys!"

Danger of this unusual kind had brought out a peculiar levity in the somber Mormon—a kind of wild, gay excitement. His eyes rolled as he watched the river ahead and he puffed out his cheek with his tongue.

The rugged, overhanging walls of the cañon grew sinister in Shefford's sight. They were jaws. And the river—that made him shudder to look down into it. The little whirling pits were eyes peering into his, and they raced on with the boat, disappeared, and came again, always with the little, hollow gurgles.

The craft drifted swiftly and the roar increased. Another rapid seemed to move up into view. It came at a bend in the cañon. When the breeze struck Shefford's cheeks he did not this time experience exhilaration. The current accelerated its sliding motion and bore the flatboat straight for the middle of the curve. Shefford saw the bend, a long, dark, narrow, gloomy cañon, and a stretch of contending waters, then, crouching low, he waited for the dip, the race, the shock. They came— the last stopping the boat—throwing it aloft—letting it drop—and crests of angry waves curled over the side. Shefford, kneeling, felt the water slap around him, and in his ears was a deafening roar. There were endless moments of strife and hell and flying darkness of spray all about him, and under him the rocking boat. When they lessened— ceased in violence—he stood ankle-deep in water, and then madly he began to bail.

Another roar deadened his ears, but he did not look up from his toil. And when he had to get down to avoid the pitch he closed his eyes. That rapid passed and with more water to bail, he resumed his share in the manning of the crude craft. It was more than a share—a tremendous responsibility to which he bent with all his might. He heard Joe yell—and again—and again. He heard the increasing roars one after another till they seemed one continuous bellow. He felt the shock, the pitch, the beating waves, and then the lessening power of sound and current. That set him to his task. Always in these long intervals of toil he seemed to see, without looking up, the growing proportions of the cañon. And the river had become a living, terrible thing. The intervals of his tireless effort when he scooped the water overboard were fleeting, and the rides through rapid after rapid were endless periods of waiting terror. His spirit and his hope were overwhelmed by the rush and roar and fury.

Then, as he worked, there came a change—a rest to deafened ears—a stretch of river that seemed quiet after chaos—and here for the first time he bailed the boat clear of water.

Jane and Fay were huddled in a corner, with the flapping tarpaulin now half fallen over them. They were wet and muddy. Lassiter crouched like a man dazed by a bad dream, and his white hair hung, stained and bedraggled, over his face. The Indian and the Mormon, grim, hard, worn, stood silent at the oar.

The afternoon was far advanced and the sun had already descended below the western ramparts. A cool breeze blew up the cañon, laden with a sound that was the same, yet not the same, as those low, dull roars which Shefford dreaded more and more.

Joe Lake turned his ear to the breeze. A stronger puff brought a heavy, quivering rumble. This time he did not vent his wild defiance to the river. He bent lower—listened. Then as the rumble became a strange, deep, reverberating roll, as if the monstrous river were rolling huge stones down a subterranean cañon, Shefford saw with dilating eyes that the Mormon's hair was rising stiff upon his head.

"Hear that!" said Joe, turning an ashen face to Shefford. "We'll drop off the earth now. Hang on to the girl, so if we go you can go together. . . . And, pard, if you've a God—*pray!*"

Nas Ta Bega faced the bend from whence that rumble came, and he was the same dark, inscrutable, impassive Indian as of old. What was death to him?

Shefford felt the strong, rushing love of life surge in him, and it was not for himself he thought, but for Fay and the happiness she merited. He went to her, patted the covered head, and tried with words choking in his throat to give hope. And he leaned with hands gripping the gunwale, with eyes wide open, ready for the unknown.

The river made a quick turn and from round the bend rumbled a terrible uproar. The current racing that way was divided or uncertain, and it gave strange motion to the boat. Joe and Nas Ta Bega shoved desperately upon the oar, all to no purpose. The currents had their will. The bow of the boat took the place of the stern. Then swift at the head of a curved incline it shot beyond the bulging wall.

And Shefford saw an awful place before them. The cañon had narrowed to half its width, and turned almost at right angles. The huge clamor of appalling sound came from under the cliff where the swollen river had to pass and where there was not space. The rapid rushed in gigantic swells right upon the wall, boomed against it, climbed and spread and fell away, to recede and gather new impetus, to leap madly on down the cañon.

Shefford went to his knees, clasped Fay, and Jane, too. But facing this appalling thing he had to look. Courage and despair came to him at the last. This must be the end. With long, buoyant swing the boat sailed down, shot over the first waves, was caught and lifted upon the great swell and impelled straight toward the cliff. Huge whirlpools raced alongside, and from them came a horrible, engulfing roar. Monstrous bulges rose on the other side. All the stupendous power of that mighty river of downward-rushing silt swung the boat aloft, up and up, as the swell climbed the wall. Shefford, with transfixed eyes and harrowed soul, watched the wet black wall. It loomed down upon him. The stern of the boat went high. Then when the crash that meant doom seemed imminent the swell spread and fell back from the wall and the boat never struck at all. By some miraculous chance it had been favored by a strange and momentary receding of the huge spent swell. Then it slid back, was caught and whirled by the current into a red, frothy, up-flung rapids below. Shefford bowed his head over Fay and saw no more, nor felt nor heard. What seemed a long time after that the broken voice of the Mormon recalled him to his labors.

The boat was half full of water. Nas Ta Bega scooped out great sheets of it with his hands. Shefford sprang to aid him, found the shovel, and plunged into the task. Slowly but surely they emptied the boat. And then

Shefford saw that twilight had fallen. Joe was working the craft toward a narrow bank of sand, to which, presently, they came, and the Indian sprang out to moor to a rock.

The fugitives went ashore and, weary and silent and drenched, they dropped in the warm sand.

But Shefford could not sleep. The river kept him awake. In the distance it rumbled, low, deep, reverberating, and near at hand it was a thing of mutable mood. It moaned, whined, mocked, and laughed. It had the soul of a devil. It was a river that had cut its way to the bowels of the earth, and its nature was destructive. It harbored no life. Fighting its way through those dead walls, cutting and tearing and wearing, its heavy burden of silt was death, destruction, and decay. A silent river, a murmuring, strange, fierce, terrible, thundering river of the desert! Even in the dark it seemed to wear the hue of blood.

All night long Shefford heard it, and toward the dark hours before dawn, when a restless, broken sleep came to him, his dreams were dreams of a river of sounds.

All the beautiful sounds he knew and loved he heard—the sigh of the wind in the pines, the mourn of the wolf, the cry of the laughing-gull, the murmur of running brooks, the song of a child, the whisper of a woman. And there were the boom of the surf, the roar of the north wind in the forest, the roll of thunder. And there were the sounds not of earth—a river of the universe rolling the planets, engulfing the stars, pouring the sea of blue into infinite space.

Night with its fitful dreams passed. Dawn lifted the ebony gloom out of the cañon and sunlight far up on the ramparts renewed Shefford's spirit. He rose and awoke the others. Fay's wistful smile still held its faith. They ate of the gritty, water-soaked food. Then they embarked. The current carried them swiftly down and out of hearing of the last rapid. The character of the river and the cañon changed. The current lessened to a slow, smooth, silent, eddying flow. The walls grew straight, sheer, gloomy, and vast. Shefford noted these features, but he was listening so hard for the roar of the next rapid that he scarcely appreciated them. All the fugitives were listening. Every bend in the cañon—and now the turns were numerous—might hold a rapid. Shefford strained his ears. He imagined the low, dull, strange rumble. He had it in his ears, yet there was the growing sensation of silence.

"Shore this's a dead place," muttered Lassiter.

"She's only slowed up for a bigger plunge," replied Joe. "Listen! Hear that?"

But there was no true sound. Joe only imagined what he expected and hated and dreaded to hear.

Mile after mile they drifted through the silent gloom between those vast and magnificent walls. After the speed, the turmoil, the whirling, shrieking, thundering, the never-ceasing sound and change and motion of the rapids above, this slow, quiet drifting, this utter, absolute silence, these eddying stretches of still water below, worked strangely upon Shefford's mind and he feared he was going mad.

There was no change to the silence, no help for the slow drift, no lessening of the strain. And the hours of the day passed as moments, the sun crossed the blue gap above, the golden lights hung on the upper walls, the gloom returned, and still there was only the dead, vast, insupportable silence.

There came bends where the current quickened, ripples widened, long lanes of little waves roughened the surface, but they made no sound.

And then the fugitives turned through a V-shaped vent in the cañon. The ponderous walls sheered away from the river. There was space and sunshine, and far beyond this league-wide open rose vermilion-colored cliffs. A mile below the river disappeared in a dark, boxlike passage from which came a rumble that made Shefford's flesh creep.

The Mormon flung high his arms and let out the stentorian yell that had rolled down to the fugitives as they waited at the mouth of Nonnezoshe Boco. But now it had a wilder, more exultant note. Strange how he shifted his gaze to Fay Larkin!

"Girl! Get up and look!" he called. "The Ferry! The Ferry!"

Then he bent his brawny back over the steering-oar, and the clumsy craft slowly turned toward the left-hand shore, where a long, low bank of green willows and cottonwoods gave welcome relief to the eyes. Upon the opposite side of the river Shefford saw a boat, similar to the one he was in, moored to the bank.

"Shore, if I ain't losin' my eyes, I seen an Injun with a red blanket," said Lassiter.

"Yes, Lassiter," cried Shefford. "Look, Fay! Look, Jane! See! Indians—hogans—mustangs—there above the green bank!"

The boat glided slowly shoreward. And the deep, hungry, terrible rumble of the remorseless river became something no more to dread.

CHAPTER 20

WILLOW SPRINGS

Two days' travel from the river, along the saw-toothed range of Echo Cliffs, stood Presbrey's trading-post, a little red-stone square house in a green and pretty valley called Willow Springs.

It was nearing the time of sunset—that gorgeous hour of color in the Painted Desert—when Shefford and his party rode down upon the post.

The scene lacked the wildness characteristic of Kayenta or Red Lake. There were wagons and teams, white men and Indians, burros, sheep, lambs, mustangs saddled and unsaddled, dogs, and chickens. A young, sweet-faced woman stood in the door of the post and she it was who first sighted the fugitives. Presbrey was weighing bags of wool on a scale, and when she called he lazily turned, as if to wonder at her eagerness.

Then he flung up his head, with its shock of heavy hair, in a start of surprise, and his florid face lost its lazy indolence to become wreathed in a huge smile.

"Haven't seen a white person in six months!" was his extraordinary greeting.

An hour later Shefford, clean-shaven, comfortably clothed once more, found himself a different man; and when he saw Fay in white again, with a new and indefinable light shining through that old, haunting shadow in her eyes, then the world changed and he embraced perfect happiness.

There was a dinner such as Shefford had not seen for many a day, and such as Fay had never seen, and that brought to Jane Withersteen's eyes the dreamy memory of the bountiful feasts which, long years ago, had been her pride. And there was a story told to the curious trader and his kind wife—a story with its beginning back in those past years, of riders of the purple sage, of Fay Larkin as a child and then as a wild girl in Surprise Valley, of the flight down Nonnezoshe Boco and the cañon, of a great Mormon and a noble Indian.

Presbrey stared with his deep-set eyes and wagged his tousled head and stared again; then with the quick perception of the practical desert man he said:

"I'm sending teamsters in to Flagstaff to-morrow. Wife and I will go along with you. We've light wagons. Three days, maybe—or four—and we'll be there. . . . Shefford, I'm going to see you marry Fay Larkin!"

Fay and Jane and Lassiter showed strangely against this background of approaching civilization. And Shefford realized more than ever the loneliness and isolation and wildness of so many years for them.

When the women had retired Shefford and the men talked awhile. Then Joe Lake rose to stretch his big frame.

"Friends, reckon I'm all in," he said. "Good night." In passing he laid a heavy hand on Shefford's shoulder. "Well, you got out. I've only a strange notion how. But *Some One* besides an Indian and a Mormon guided you out! . . . Be good to the girl. . . . Good-by, pard!"

Shefford grasped the big hand and in the emotion of the moment did not catch the significance of Joe's last words.

Later Shefford stepped outside into the starlight for a few moments' quiet walk and thought before he went to bed. It was a white night. The coyotes were yelping. The stars shone steadfast, bright, cold. Nas Ta Bega stalked out of the shadow of the house and joined Shefford. They walked in silence. Shefford's heart was too full for utterance and the Indian seldom spoke at any time. When Shefford was ready to go in Nas Ta Bega extended his hand.

"Good-by—Bi Nai!" he said, strangely, using English and Navajo in what Shefford supposed to be merely good night. The starlight shone full upon the dark, inscrutable face of the Indian. Shefford bade him good night and then watched him stride away in the silver gloom.

But next morning Shefford understood. Nas Ta Bega and Joe Lake were gone. It was a shock to Shefford. Yet what could he have said to either? Joe had shirked saying good-by to him and Fay. And the Indian had gone out of Shefford's life as he had come into it.

What these two men represented in Shefford's uplift was too great for the present to define, but they and the desert that had developed them had taught him the meaning of life. He might fail often, since failure was the lot of his kind, but could he ever fail again in faith in man or God while he had mind to remember the Indian and the Mormon?

Still, though he placed them on a noble height and loved them well, there would always abide with him a sorrow for the Mormon and a sleepless and eternal regret for that Indian on his lonely cedarslope with the spirits of his vanishing race calling him.

Willow Springs appeared to be a lively place that morning. Presbrey and his sweet-faced wife were excited. The teamsters were a jolly, whistling lot. And the lean mustangs kicked and bit at one another. The trader had brought out two light wagons for the trip, and, after the manner of desert men, desired to start at sunrise.

Far across the Painted Desert towered the San Francisco peaks, black-timbered, blue-cañoned, purple-hazed, with white snow, like the clouds, around their summits.

Jane Withersteen looked at the radiant Fay and lived again in her happiness. And at last excitement had been communicated to the old gunman.

"Shore we're goin' to live with Fay an' John, an' be near Venters an' Bess, an' see the blacks again, Jane. . . . An' Venters will tell you, as he did me, how Wrangle run Black Star off his legs!"

All connected with that early start was sweet, sad, hopeful.

And so they rode away from Willow Springs, through the green fields of alfalfa and cottonwood, down the valley with its smoking hogans and whistling mustangs and scarlet-blanketed Indians, and out upon the bare, ridgy, colorful desert toward the rosy sunrise.

EPILOGUE

On the outskirts of a little town in Illinois there was a farm of rolling pasture-land. And here a beautiful meadow, green and red in clover, merged upon an orchard in the midst of which a brown-tiled roof showed above the trees.

One afternoon in May a group of people, strangely agitated, walked down a shady lane toward the meadow.

"Wal, Jane, I always knew we'd get a look at them hosses again—I shore knew," Lassiter was saying in the same old, cool, careless drawl. But his clawlike hands shook a little.

"Oh! will they know me?" asked Jane Withersteen, turning to a stalwart man—no other than the dark-faced Venters, her rider of other days.

"Know you? I'll bet they will," replied Venters. "What do you say, Bess?"

The shadow brightened in Bess's somber blue eyes, as if his words had recalled her from a sad and memorable past.

"Black Star will know her, surely," replied Bess. "Sometimes he points his nose toward the west and watches as if he saw the purple slopes and smelt the sage of Utah! He has never forgotten. But Night has grown deaf and partly blind of late. I doubt if he'll remember."

Shefford and Fay walked arm in arm in the background.

Out in the meadow two horses were grazing. They were sleek, shiny, long-maned, long-tailed, black as coal, and, though old, still splendid in every line.

"Do you remember them?" whispered Shefford.

"Oh, I only needed to see Black Star," murmured Fay, her voice quivering. "I can remember being lifted on his back. . . . How strange! It seems so long ago. . . . Look! Mother Jane is going out to them."

Jane Withersteen advanced alone through the clover, and it was with unsteady steps. Presently she halted. What glorious and bitter memories were expressed in her strange, poignant call!

Black Star started and swept up' his noble head and looked. But Night went on calmly grazing. Then Jane called again—the same strange call, only louder, and this time broken. Black Star raised his head higher and he whistled a piercing blast. He saw Jane; he knew her as he had remembered the call; and he came pounding toward her. She met him, encircled his neck with her arms, and buried her face in his mane.

"Shore I reckon I'd better never say any more about Wrangle runnin' the blacks off their legs thet time," muttered Lassiter, as if to himself.

"Lassiter, you only dreamed that race," replied Venters, with a smile.

"Oh, Bern, isn't it good that Black Star remembered her—that she'll have him—something left of her old home?" asked Bess, wistfully.

"Indeed it is good. But, Bess, Jane Withersteen will find a new spirit and new happiness here."

Jane came toward them, leading both horses. "Dear friends, I am happy. To-day I bury all regrets. Of the past I shall remember only—my riders of the purple sage."

Venters smiled his gladness. "And you—Lassiter—what shall you remember?" he queried.

The old gunman looked at Jane and then at his clawlike hands and then at Fay. His eyes lost their shadow and began to twinkle.

"Wal, I rolled a stone once, but I reckon now thet time Wrangle—"

"Lassiter, I said you dreamed that race. Wrangle never beat the blacks," interrupted Venters. . . . "And you, Fay, what shall you remember?"

"Surprise Valley," replied Fay, dreamily.

"And you—Shefford?"

Shefford shook his head. For him there could never be one memory only. In his heart there would never change or die memories of the wild uplands, of the great towers and walls, of the golden sunsets on the cañon ramparts, of the silent, fragrant valleys where the cedars and the sago-lilies grew, of those starlit nights when his love and faith awoke, of grand and lonely Nonnezoshe, of that red, sullen, thundering, mysterious Colorado River, of a wonderful Indian and a noble Mormon—of all that was embodied for him in the meaning of the rainbow trail.

DESERT GOLD

A face haunted Cameron—a woman's face. It was there in the white heart of the dying campfire; it hung in the shadows that hovered over the flickering light; it drifted in the darkness beyond.

This hour, when the day had closed and the lonely desert night set in with its dead silence, was one in which Cameron's mind was thronged with memories of a time long past—of a home back in Peoria, of a women he had wronged and lost, and loved too late. He was a prospector for gold, a hunter of solitude, a lover of the drear, rock-ribbed infinitude, because he wanted to be alone to remember.

A sound disturbed Cameron's reflections. He bent his head, listening. A soft wind fanned the paling embers, blew sparks and white ashes and thin smoke away into the enshrouding circle of blackness. His burro did not appear to be moving about. The quiet split to the cry of a coyote. It rose strange, wild, mournful—not the howl of a prowling upland beast baying the campfire or barking at a lonely prospector, but the wail of a wolf, full-voiced, crying out the meaning of the desert and the night. Hunger throbbed in it—hunger for a mate, for offspring, for life. When it ceased, the terrible desert silence smote Cameron, and the cry echoed in his soul. He and that wandering wolf were brothers.

Then a sharp clink of metal on stone and soft pads of hoofs in sand prompted Cameron to reach for his gun, and to move out of the light of the waning campfire. He was somewhere along the wild borderline between Sonora and Arizona; and the prospector who dared the heat and barrenness of that region risked other dangers sometimes as menacing.

Figures darker than the gloom approached and took shape, and in the light turned out to be those of a white man and a heavily packed burro.

"Hello there," the man called, as he came to a halt and gazed about him. "I saw your fire. May I make camp here?"

Cameron came forth out of the shadow and greeted his visitor, whom he took for a prospector like himself. Cameron resented the breaking of his lonely campfire vigil, but he respected the law of the desert.

The stranger thanked him, and then slipped the pack from his burro. Then he rolled out his pack and began preparations for a meal. His movements were slow and methodical.

Cameron watched him, still with resentment, yet with a curious and growing interest. The campfire burst into a bright blaze, and by its light Cameron saw a man whose gray hair somehow did not seem to make him old, and whose stooped shoulders did not detract from an impression of rugged strength.

"Find any mineral?" asked Cameron, presently.

His visitor looked up quickly, as if startled by the sound of a human voice. He replied, and then the two men talked a little. But the stranger evidently preferred silence. Cameron understood that. He laughed grimly and bent a keener gaze upon the furrowed, shadowy face. Another of those strange desert prospectors in whom there was some relentless driving power besides the lust for gold! Cameron felt that between this man and himself there was a subtle affinity, vague and undefined, perhaps born of the divination that here was a desert wanderer like himself, perhaps born of a deeper, an unintelligible relation having its roots back in the past. A long-forgotten sensation stirred in Cameron's breast, one so long forgotten that he could not recognize it. But it was akin to pain.

II

When he awakened he found, to his surprise, that his companion had departed. A trail in the sand led off to the north. There was no water in that direction. Cameron shrugged his shoulders; it was not his affair; he had his own problems. And straightway he forgot his strange visitor.

Cameron began his day, grateful for the solitude that was now unbroken, for the cañon-furrowed and cactus-spired scene that now showed no sign of life. He traveled southwest, never straying far from the dry streambed; and in a desultory way, without eagerness, he hunted for signs of gold.

The work was toilsome, yet the periods of rest in which he indulged were not taken because of fatigue. He rested to look, to listen, to feel. What the vast silent world meant to him had always been a mystical thing, which he felt in all its incalculable power, but never understood.

That day, while it was yet light, and he was digging in a moist white-bordered wash for water, he was brought sharply up by hearing the crack of hard hoofs on stone. There down the cañon came a man and a burro. Cameron recognized them.

"Hello, friend," called the man, halting. "Our trails crossed again. That's good."

"Hello," replied Cameron, slowly. "Any mineral sign today?"

"No."

They made camp together, ate their frugal meal, smoked a pipe, and rolled in their blankets without exchanging many words. In the morning the same reticence, the same aloofness characterized the manner of both. But Cameron's companion, when he had packed his burro and was ready to start, faced about and said: "We might stay together, if it's all right with you."

"I never take a partner," replied Cameron.

"You're alone; I'm alone," said the other, mildly. "It's a big place. If we find gold there'll be enough for two."

"I don't go down into the desert for gold alone," rejoined Cameron, with a chill note in his swift reply.

His companion's deep-set, luminous eyes emitted a singular flash. It moved Cameron to say that in the years of his wandering he had met no man who could endure equally with him the blasting heat, the blinding dust storms, the wilderness of sand and rock and lava and cactus, the terrible silence and desolation of the desert. Cameron waved a hand toward the wide, shimmering, shadowy descent of plain and range. "I may strike through the Sonora Desert. I may head for Pinacate or north for the Colorado Basin. You are an old man."

"I don't know the country, but to me one place is the same as another," replied his companion. For moments he seemed to forget himself, and swept his far-reaching gaze out over the colored gulf of stone and sand. Then with gentle slaps he drove his burro in behind Cameron. "Yes, I'm old. I'm lonely, too. It's come to me just lately. But, friend, I can still travel, and for a few days my company won't hurt you."

"Have it your way," said Cameron.

They began a slow march down into the desert. At sunset they camped under the lee of a low mesa. Cameron was glad his comrade had the Indian habit of silence. Another day's travel found the prospectors deep in the wilderness. Then there came a breaking of reserve, noticeable in the elder man, almost imperceptibly gradual in Cameron. Besides the meager mesquite campfire this gray-faced, thoughtful old prospector would remove his black pipe from his mouth to talk a little, and Cameron would listen, and sometimes unlock his lips to speak a word. And so, as Cameron began to respond to the influence of a desert less lonely than habitual, he began to take keener note of his comrade, and found him different from any other he had ever encountered in the wilderness. This man never grumbled at the heat, the glare, the driving sand, the sour water, the scant fare. During the daylight hours he was seldom idle. At night he sat dreaming before the fire or paced to and fro in the gloom. He slept but little, and that long after Cameron had had his own rest. He was tireless, patient, brooding.

Cameron's awakened interest brought home to him the realization that for years he had shunned companionship. In those years only three men had wandered into the desert with him, and these had left their bones to bleach in the shifting sands. Cameron had not cared to know their secrets. But the more he studied this latest comrade the more he began to suspect that he might have missed something in the others. In his own driving passion to take his secret into the limitless abode of silence and desolation, where he could be alone with it, he had forgotten that life dealt shocks to other men. Somehow this silent comrade reminded him.

One afternoon late, after they had toiled up a white, winding wash of sand and gravel, they came upon a dry water hole. Cameron dug deep into the sand, but without avail. He was turning to retrace weary steps back to the last water when his comrade asked him to wait. Cameron watched him search in his pack and bring forth what appeared to be a small, forked branch of a peach tree. He grasped the prongs of the fork and held them before him with the end standing straight out, and then he began to walk along the streambed. Cameron, at first amused, then amazed, then pitying and at last curious, kept pace with the prospector. He saw a strong tension of his comrade's wrists, as if he was holding hard against a considerable force. The end of the peach branch began to quiver and turn. Cameron reached out a hand to touch it, and was astounded at feeling a powerful vibrant force pulling the branch downward. He felt it as a magnetic shock. The branch kept turning, and at length pointed to the ground.

"Dig here," said the prospector.

"What!" ejaculated Cameron. Had the man lost his mind?

Then Cameron stood by while his comrade dug in the sand. Three feet he dug—four—five, and the sand grew dark, then moist. At six feet water began to seep through.

"Get the little basket in my pack," he said.

Cameron complied, and saw his comrade drop the basket into the deep hole, where it kept the sides from caving in and allowed the water to seep through. While Cameron watched, the basket filled. Of all the strange incidents of his desert career this was the strangest. Curiously he picked up the peach branch and held it as he had seen it held. The thing, however, was dead in his hands.

"I see you haven't got it," remarked his comrade. "Few men have."

"Got what?" demanded Cameron.

"A power to find water that way. Back in Illinois an old German used to do that to locate wells. He showed me I had the same power. I can't explain. But you needn't look so dumbfounded. There's nothing supernatural about it."

"You mean it's a simple fact—that some men have a magnetism, a force or power to find water as you did?"

"Yes. It's not unusual on the farms back in Illinois, Ohio, Pennsylvania. The old German I spoke of made money traveling round with his peach fork."

"What a gift for a man in the desert!"

Cameron's comrade smiled—the second time in all those days.

They entered a region where mineral abounded, and their march became slower. Generally they took the course of a wash, one on each side, and let the burros travel leisurely along nipping at the bleached blades of scant grass, or at sage or cactus, while they searched in the cañons and under the ledges for signs of gold. When they found any rock that hinted of gold they picked off a piece and gave it a chemical test. The search was fascinating. They interspersed the work with long, restful moments when they looked afar down the vast reaches and smoky shingles to the line of dim mountains. Some impelling desire, not all the lure of gold, took them to the top of mesas and escarpments; and here, when they had dug and picked, they rested and gazed out at the wide prospect. Then, as the sun lost its heat and sank lowering to dent its red disk behind far-distant spurs, they halted in a shady cañon or likely spot in a dry wash and tried for water. When they found it they unpacked, gave drink to the tired burros, and turned them loose. Dead mesquite served for the campfire. While the strange twilight deepened into weird night they sat propped against stones, with eyes on the dying embers of the fire, and soon they lay on the sand with the light of white stars on their dark faces.

Each succeeding day and night Cameron felt himself more and more drawn to this strange man. He found that after hours of burning toil he had insensibly grown nearer to his comrade. He reflected that after a few weeks in the desert he had always become a different man. In civilization, in the rough mining camps, he had been a prey to unrest and gloom. But once down on the great billowing sweep of this lonely world, he could look into his unquiet soul without bitterness. Did not the desert magnify men? Cameron believed that wild men in wild places, fighting cold, heat, starvation, thirst, barrenness, facing the elements in all their ferocity, usually retrograded, descended to the savage, lost all heart and soul and became mere brutes. Likewise he believed that men wandering or lost in the wilderness often reversed that brutal order of life and became noble, wonderful, superhuman. So now he did not marvel at a slow stir stealing warmer along his veins, and at the premonition that perhaps he and this man, alone on the desert, driven there by life's mysterious and remorseless motive, were to see each other through God's eyes.

His companion was one who thought of himself last. It humiliated Cameron that in spite of growing keenness he could not hinder him from doing more than an equal share of the day's work. The man was mild, gentle, quiet, mostly silent, yet under all his softness he seemed to be made of the fiber of steel. Cameron could not thwart him. Moreover, he appeared to want to find gold for Cameron, not for himself. Cameron's hands always trembled at the turning of rock that promised gold; he had enough of the prospector's passion for fortune to thrill at the chance of a strike. But the other never showed the least trace of excitement.

One night they were encamped at the head of a cañon. The day had been exceedingly hot, and long after sundown the radiation of heat from the rocks persisted. A desert bird whistled a wild, melancholy note from a dark cliff, and a distant coyote wailed mournfully. The stars shone white until the huge moon rose to burn out all their whiteness. And on this night Cameron watched his comrade, and yielded to interest he had not heretofore voiced.

"Pardner, what drives you into the desert?"

"Do I seem to be a driven man?"

"No. But I feel it. Do you come to forget?"

"Yes."

"Ah!" softly exclaimed Cameron. Always he seemed to have known that. He said no more. He watched the old man rise and begin his nightly pace to and fro, up and down. With slow, soft tread, forward and back, tirelessly and ceaselessly, he paced that beat. He did not look up at the stars or follow the radiant track of the moon along the cañon ramparts. He hung his head. He was lost in another world. It was a world which the lonely desert made real. He looked a dark, sad, plodding figure, and somehow impressed Cameron with the helplessness of men.

Cameron grew acutely conscious of the pang in his own breast, of the fire in his heart, the strife and torment of his passion-driven soul. He had come into the desert to remember a woman. She appeared to him then as she had looked when first she entered his life—a golden-haired girl, blue-eyed, white-skinned, red-lipped, tall and slender and beautiful. He had never forgotten, and an old, sickening remorse knocked at his heart. He rose and climbed out of the cañon and to the top of a mesa, where he paced to and fro and looked down into the weird and mystic shadows, like the darkness of his passion, and farther on down the moon track and the glittering stretches that vanished in the cold, blue horizon. The moon soared radiant and calm, the white stars shone serene. The vault of heaven seemed illimitable and divine. The desert surrounded him, silver-streaked and black-mantled, a chaos of rock and sand, silent, austere, ancient, always waiting. It spoke to Cameron. It was a naked corpse, but it had a soul. In that wild solitude the white stars looked down upon him pitilessly and pityingly. They had shone upon a desert that might once have been alive and was now dead, and might again throb with life, only to die. It was a terrible ordeal for him to stand there alone and realize that he was only a man facing eternity. But that was what gave him strength to endure. Somehow he was a part of it all, some atom in that vastness, somehow necessary to an inscrutable purpose, something indestructible in that desolate world of ruin and death and decay, something perishable and changeable and growing under all the fixity of heaven. In that endless, silent hall of desert there was a spirit; and Cameron felt hovering near him what he imagined to be phantoms of peace.

He returned to camp and sought his comrade.

"I reckon we're two of a kind," he said. "It was a woman who drove me into the desert. But I come to remember. The desert's the only place I can do that."

"Was she your wife?" asked the elder man.

"No."

A long silence ensued. A cool wind blew up the cañon sifting the sand through the dry sage, driving away the last of the lingering heat. The campfire wore down to a ruddy ashen heap.

"I had a daughter," said Cameron's comrade. "She lost her mother at birth. And I—I didn't know how to bring up a girl. She was pretty and gay. It was the—the old story."

His words were peculiarly significant to Cameron. They distressed him. He had been wrapped up in his remorse. If ever in the past he had thought of any one connected with the girl he had wronged he had long forgotten. But the consequences of such wrong were far-reaching. They struck at the roots of a home. Here in the desert he was confronted by the spectacle of a splendid man, a father, wasting his life because he could not forget—because there was nothing left to live for. Cameron understood better now why his comrade was drawn by the desert.

"Well, tell me more?" asked Cameron, earnestly.

"It was the old, old story. My girl was pretty and free. The young bucks ran after her. I guess she did not run away from them. And I was away a good deal—working in another town. She was in love with a wild fellow. I knew nothing of it till too late. He was engaged to marry her. But he didn't come back. And when the disgrace became plain to all, my girl left home. She went west. After a while I heard from her. She was well—working—living for her baby. A long time passed. I had no ties. I drifted west. Her lover had also gone west. In those days everybody went west. I trailed him, intending to kill him. But I lost his trail. Neither could I find any trace of her. She had moved on, driven, no doubt, by the hound of her past. Since then I have taken to the wilds, hunting gold on the desert."

"Yes, it's the old, old story, only sadder, I think," said Cameron; and his voice was strained and unnatural. "Pardner, what Illinois town was it you hailed from?"

"Peoria."

"And your—your name?" went on Cameron, huskily.

"Warren—Jonas Warren."

That name might as well have been a bullet. Cameron stood erect, motionless, as men sometimes stand momentarily when shot straight through the heart. In an instant, when thoughts resurged like blinding flashes of lightning through his mind, he was a swaying, quivering, terror-stricken man. He mumbled something hoarsely and backed into the shadow. But he needed not have feared discovery, however surely his agitation might have betrayed him. Warren sat brooding over the campfire, oblivious of his comrade, absorbed in the past.

Cameron swiftly walked away in the gloom, with the blood thrumming thick in his ears, whispering over and over:

"Merciful God! Nell was *his* daughter!"

III

As thought and feeling multiplied, Cameron was overwhelmed. Beyond belief, indeed, was it that out of the millions of men in the world two who had never seen each other could have been driven into the desert by memory of the same woman. It brought the past so close. It showed Cameron how inevitably all his spiritual life was governed by what had happened long ago. That which made life significant to him was a wandering in silent places where no eye could see him with his secret. Some fateful chance had thrown him with the father of the girl he had wrecked. It was incomprehensible; it was terrible. It was the one thing of all possible happenings in the world of chance that both father and lover would have found unendurable.

Cameron's pain reached to despair when he felt this relation between Warren and himself. Something within him cried out to him to reveal his identity. Warren would kill him; but it was not fear of death that put Cameron on the rack. He had faced death too often to be afraid. It was the thought of adding torture to this long-suffering man. All at once Cameron swore that he would not augment Warren's trouble, or let him stain his hands with blood. He would tell the truth of Nell's sad story and his own, and make what amends he could.

Then Cameron's thought shifted from father to daughter. She was somewhere beyond the dim horizon line. In those past lonely hours by the campfire his fancy had tortured him with pictures of Nell. But his remorseful and cruel fancy had lied to him. Nell had struggled upward out of menacing depths. She had reconstructed a broken life. And now she was fighting for the name and happiness of her child. Little Nell! Cameron experienced a shuddering ripple in all his being—the physical rack of an emotion born of a new and strange consciousness.

As Cameron gazed out over the bloodred, darkening desert suddenly the strife in his soul ceased. The moment was one of incalculable change, in which his eyes seemed to pierce the vastness of cloud and range, and mystery of gloom and shadow—to see with strong vision the illimitable space before him. He felt the grandeur of the desert, its simplicity, its truth. He had learned at last the lesson it taught. No longer strange was his meeting and wandering with Warren. Each had marched in the steps of destiny; and as the lines of their fates had been inextricably tangled in the years that were gone, so now their steps had crossed and turned them toward one common goal. For years they had been two men marching alone, answering to an inward driving search, and the desert had brought them together. For years they had wandered alone in silence and solitude, where the sun burned white all day and the stars burned white all night, blindly following the whisper of a spirit. But now Cameron knew that he was no longer blind, and in this flash of revelation he felt that it had been given him to help Warren with his burden.

He returned to camp trying to evolve a plan. As always at that long hour when the afterglow of sunset lingered in the west, Warren plodded to and fro in the gloom. All night Cameron lay awake thinking.

In the morning, when Warren brought the burros to camp and began preparations for the usual packing, Cameron broke silence.

"Pardner, your story last night made me think. I want to tell you something about myself. It's hard enough to be driven by sorrow for someone you've loved, as you've been driven; but to suffer sleepless and eternal remorse for the *ruin* of one you've loved as I have suffered—that is hell. . . . Listen. In my younger days—it seems long now, yet it's not so many years—I was wild. I wronged the sweetest and loveliest girl I ever knew. I went away not dreaming that any disgrace might come to her. Along about that time I fell into terrible moods—I changed—I learned I really loved her. Then came a letter I should have gotten months before. It told of her trouble—importuned me to hurry to save her. Half frantic with shame and fear, I got a marriage certificate and rushed back to her town. She was gone—had been gone for weeks, and her disgrace was known. Friends warned me to keep out of reach of her father. I trailed her—found her. I married her. But too late! . . . She would not live with me. She left me—I followed her west, but never found her."

Warren leaned forward a little and looked into Cameron's eyes, as if searching there for the repentance that might make him less deserving of a man's scorn.

Cameron met the gaze unflinchingly, and again began to speak:

"You know, of course, how men out here somehow lose old names, old identities. It won't surprise you much to learn my name really isn't Cameron, as I once told you."

Warren stiffened upright. It seemed that there might have been a blank, a suspension, between his grave interest and some strange mood to come.

Cameron felt his heart bulge and contract in his breast; all his body grew cold; and it took tremendous effort for him to make his lips form words.

"Warren, I'm the man you're hunting. I'm Burton. I was Nell's lover!"

The old man rose and towered over Cameron, and then plunged down upon him, and clutched at his throat with terrible stifling hands. The harsh contact, the pain awakened Cameron to his peril before it was too late. Desperate fighting saved him from being hurled to the ground and stamped and crushed. Warren seemed a maddened giant. There was a reeling, swaying, wrestling struggle before the elder man began to weaken. Then Cameron, buffeted, bloody, half-stunned, panted for speech.

"Warren—hold on! Give me—a minute. I married Nell. Didn't you know that? . . . I saved the child!"

Cameron felt the shock that vibrated through Warren. He repeated the words again and again. As if compelled by some resistless power, Warren released Cameron, and, staggering back, stood with uplifted, shaking hands. In his face was a horrible darkness.

"Warren! Wait—listen!" panted Cameron. "I've got that marriage certificate—I've had it by me all these years. I kept it—to prove to myself I did right."

The old man uttered a broken cry.

Cameron stole off among the rocks. How long he absented himself or what he did he had no idea. When he returned Warren was sitting before the campfire, and once more he appeared composed. He spoke, and his voice had a deeper note; but otherwise he seemed as usual.

They packed the burros and faced the north together.

Cameron experienced a singular exaltation. He had lightened his comrade's burden. Wonderfully it came to him that he had also lightened his own. From that hour it was not torment to think of Nell. Walking with his comrade through the silent places, lying beside him under the serene luminous light of the stars, Cameron began to feel the haunting presence of invisible things that were real to him—phantoms whispering peace. In the moan of the cool wind, in the silken seep of sifting sand, in the distant rumble of a slipping ledge, in the faint rush of a shooting star he heard these phantoms of peace coming with whispers of the long pain of men at the last made endurable. Even in the white noonday, under the burning sun, these phantoms came to be real to him. In the dead silence of the midnight hours he heard them breathing nearer on the desert wind— nature's voices of motherhood, whispers of God, peace in the solitude.

IV

There came a morning when the sun shone angry and red through a dull, smoky haze.

"We're in for sandstorms," said Cameron.

They had scarcely covered a mile when a desert-wide, moaning, yellow wall of flying sand swooped down upon them. Seeking shelter in the lee of a rock, they waited, hoping the storm was only a squall, such as frequently whipped across the open places. The moan increased to a roar, and the dull red slowly dimmed, to disappear in the yellow pall, and the air grew thick and dark. Warren slipped the packs from the burros. Cameron feared the sandstorms had arrived some weeks ahead of their usual season.

The men covered their heads and patiently waited. The long hours dragged, and the storm increased in fury. Cameron and Warren wet scarfs with water from their canteens, and bound them round their faces, and then covered their heads. The steady, hollow bellow of flying sand went on. It flew so thickly that enough sifted down under the shelving rock to weight the blankets and almost bury the men. They were frequently compelled to shake off the sand to keep from being borne to the ground. And it was necessary to keep digging out the packs. The floor of their shelter gradually rose higher and higher. They tried to eat, and seemed to be grinding only sand between their teeth. They lost the count of time. They dared not sleep, for that would have meant being buried alive. They could only crouch close to the leaning rock, shake off the sand, blindly dig out their packs, and every moment gasp and cough and choke to fight suffocation.

The storm finally blew itself out. It left the prospectors heavy and stupid for want of sleep. Their burros had wandered away, or had been buried in the sand. Far as eye could reach the desert had marvelously changed; it was now a rippling sea of sand dunes. Away to the north rose the peak that was their only guiding mark. They headed toward it, carrying a shovel and part of their packs.

At noon the peak vanished in the shimmering glare of the desert. The prospectors pushed on, guided by the sun. In every wash they tried for water. With the forked peach branch in his hands Warren always succeeded in locating water. They dug, but it lay too deep. At length, spent and sore, they fell and slept through that night and part of the next day. Then they succeeded in getting water, and quenched their thirst, and filled the canteens, and cooked a meal.

The burning day found them in an interminably wide plain, where there was no shelter from the fierce sun. The men were exceedingly careful with their water, though there was absolute necessity of drinking a little every hour. Late in the afternoon they came to a cañon that they believed was the lower end of the one in which they had last found water. For hours they traveled toward its head, and, long after night had set, found what they sought. Yielding to exhaustion, they slept, and next day were loath to leave the water hole. Cool night spurred them on with canteens full and renewed strength.

Morning told Cameron that they had turned back miles into the desert, and it was desert new to him. The red sun, the increasing heat, and especially the variety and large size of the cactus plants warned Cameron that he had descended to a lower level. Mountain peaks loomed on all sides, some near, others distant; and one, a blue spur, splitting the glaring sky far to the north, Cameron thought he recognized as a landmark. The ascent toward it was heartbreaking, not in steepness, but in its league-and-league-long monotonous rise. Cameron knew there was only one hope—to make the water hold out and never stop to rest. Warren began to weaken. Often he had to halt. The burning white day passed, and likewise the night, with its white stars shining so pitilessly cold and bright.

Cameron measured the water in his canteen by its weight. Evaporation by heat consumed as much as he drank. During one of the rests, when he had wetted his parched mouth and throat, he found opportunity to pour a little water from his canteen into Warren's.

At first Cameron had curbed his restless activity to accommodate the pace of his elder comrade. But now he felt that he was losing something of his instinctive and passionate zeal to get out of the desert. The thought of water came to occupy his mind. He began to imagine that his last little store of water did not appreciably diminish. He knew he was not quite right in his mind regarding water; nevertheless, he felt this to be more of fact than fancy, and he began to ponder.

When next they rested he pretended to be in a kind of stupor; but he covertly watched Warren. The man appeared far gone, yet he had cunning. He cautiously took up Cameron's canteen and poured water into it from his own.

This troubled Cameron. The old irritation at not being able to thwart Warren returned to him. Cameron reflected, and concluded that he had been unwise not to expect this very thing. Then, as his comrade dropped into weary rest, he lifted both canteens. If there were any water in Warren's, it was only very little. Both men had been enduring the terrible desert thirst, concealing it, each giving his water to the other, and the sacrifice had been useless.

Instead of ministering to the parched throats of one or both, the water had evaporated. When Cameron made sure of this, he took one more drink, the last, and poured the little water left into Warren's canteen. He threw his own away.

Soon afterward Warren discovered the loss.

"Where's your canteen?" he asked.

"The heat was getting my water, so I drank what was left."

"My son!" said Warren.

The day opened for them in a red and green hell of rock and cactus. Like a flame the sun scorched and peeled their faces. Warren went blind from the glare, and Cameron had to lead him. At last Warren plunged down, exhausted, in the shade of a ledge.

Cameron rested and waited, hopeless, with hot, weary eyes gazing down from the height where he sat. The ledge was the top step of a ragged gigantic stairway. Below stretched a sad, austere, and lonely valley. A dim, wide streak, lighter than the bordering gray, wound down the valley floor. Once a river had flowed there, leaving only a forlorn trace down the winding floor of this forlorn valley.

Movement on the part of Warren attracted Cameron's attention. Evidently the old prospector had recovered his sight and some of his strength. For he had arisen, and now began to walk along the arroyo bed with his forked peach branch held before him. He had clung to that precious bit of wood. Cameron considered the prospect for water hopeless, because he saw that the arroyo had once been a cañon, and had been filled with sands by desert winds. Warren, however, stopped in a deep pit, and, cutting his canteen in half, began to use one side of it as a scoop. He scooped out a wide hollow, so wide that Cameron was certain he had gone crazy. Cameron gently urged him to stop, and then forcibly tried to make him. But these efforts were futile. Warren worked with slow, ceaseless, methodical movement. He toiled for what seemed hours. Cameron, seeing the darkening, dampening sand, realized a wonderful possibility of water, and he plunged into the pit with the other half of the canteen. Then both men toiled, round and round the wide hole, down deeper and deeper. The sand grew moist, then wet. At the bottom of the deep pit the sand coarsened, gave place to gravel. Finally water welled in, a stronger volume than Cameron ever remembered finding on the desert. It would soon fill the hole and run over. He marveled at the circumstance. The time was near the end of the dry season. Perhaps an underground stream flowed from the range behind down to the valley floor, and at this point came near to the surface. Cameron had heard of such desert miracles.

The finding of water revived Cameron's flagging hopes. But they were short-lived. Warren had spent himself utterly.

"I'm done. Don't linger," he whispered. "My son, go—go!"

Then he fell. Cameron dragged him out of the sand pit to a sheltered place under the ledge. While sitting beside the failing man Cameron discovered painted images on the wall. Often in the desert he had found these evidences of a prehistoric people. Then, from long habit, he picked up a piece of rock and examined it. Its weight made him closely scrutinize it. The color was a peculiar black. He scraped through the black rust to find a piece of gold. Around him lay scattered heaps of black pebbles and bits of black, weathered rock and pieces of broken ledge, and they showed gold.

"Warren! Look! See it! Feel it! Gold!"

But Warren had never cared, and now he was too blind to see.

"Go—go!" he whispered.

Cameron gazed down the gray reaches of that forlorn valley, and something within him that was neither intelligence nor emotion—something inscrutably strange—impelled him to promise.

Then Cameron built up stone monuments to mark his gold strike. That done, he tarried beside the unconscious Warren. Moments passed—grew into hours. Cameron still had strength left to make an effort to get out of the desert. But that same inscrutable something which had ordered his strange involuntary promise to Warren held him beside his fallen comrade. He watched the white sun turn to gold, and then to red, and sink behind mountains in the west. Twilight stole into the arroyo. It lingered, slowly turning to gloom. The vault of blue-black lightened to the blinking of stars. Then fell the serene, silent, luminous desert night.

Cameron kept his vigil. As the long hours wore on he felt creep over him the comforting sense that he need not forever fight sleep. A wan glow flared behind the dark, uneven horizon, and a melancholy misshapen moon rose to make the white night one of shadows. Absolute silence claimed the desert. It was mute. Then that inscrutable something breathed to him, telling him when he was alone. He need not have looked at the dark, still face beside him.

Another face haunted Cameron's—a woman's face. It was there in the white moonlit shadows; it drifted in the darkness beyond; it softened, changed to that of a young girl, sweet, with the same dark, haunting eyes of her mother. Cameron prayed to that nameless thing within him, the spirit of something deep and mystical as life. He prayed to that nameless thing outside, of which the rocks and the sand, the spiked cactus and the ragged lava, the endless waste, with its vast star-fired mantle, were but atoms. He prayed for mercy to a woman—for happiness to her child. Both mother and daughter were close to him then. Time and distance were annihilated. He had faith—he saw into the future. The fateful threads of the past, so inextricably woven with his error, wound out their tragic length here in this forlorn desert.

Cameron then took a little tin box from his pocket, and, opening it, removed a folded certificate. He had kept a pen, and now he wrote something upon the paper, and in lieu of ink he wrote with blood. The moon afforded him enough light to see; and, having replaced the paper, he laid the little box upon a shelf of rock. It would remain there unaffected by dust, moisture, heat, time. How long had those painted images been there clear and sharp on the dry stone walls? There were no trails in that desert, and always there were incalculable changes. Cameron saw this mutable mood of nature—the sands would fly and seep and carve and bury; the floods would dig and cut; the ledges would weather in the heat and rain; the avalanches would slide; the cactus seeds would roll in the wind to catch in a niche and split the soil with thirsty roots. Years would pass. Cameron seemed to see them, too; and likewise destiny leading a child down into this forlorn waste, where she would find love and fortune, and the grave of her father.

Cameron covered the dark, still face of his comrade from the light of the waning moon.

That action was the severing of his hold on realities. They fell away from him in final separation. Vaguely, dreamily he seemed to behold his soul. Night merged into gray day; and night came again, weird and dark. Then up out of the vast void of the desert, from the silence and illimitableness, trooped his phantoms of peace. Majestically they formed around him, marshaling and mustering in ceremonious state, and moved to lay upon him their passionless serenity.

CHAPTER 1

OLD FRIENDS

Richard Gale reflected that his sojourn in the West had been what his disgusted father had predicted—idling here and dreaming there, with no objective point or purpose.

It was reflection such as this, only more serious and perhaps somewhat desperate, that had brought Gale down to the border. For some time the newspapers had been printing news of Mexican revolution, guerrilla warfare, United States cavalry patrolling the international line, American cowboys fighting with the rebels, and wild stories of bold raiders and bandits. Regarding these rumors Gale was skeptical. But as opportunity, and adventure, too, had apparently given him a wide berth in Montana, Wyoming, Colorado, he had struck southwest for the Arizona border, where he hoped to see some stirring life. He did not care very much what happened. Months of futile wandering in the hope of finding a place where he fitted had inclined Richard to his father's opinion.

It was after dark one evening in early October when Richard arrived in Casita. He was surprised to find that it was evidently a town of importance. There was a jostling, jabbering, sombreroed crowd of Mexicans around the railroad station. He felt as if he were in a foreign country. After a while he saw several men of his nationality, one of whom he engaged to carry his luggage to a hotel. They walked up a wide well-lighted street lined with buildings in which were bright windows. Of the many people encountered by Gale most were Mexicans. His guide explained that the smaller half of Casita lay in Arizona, the other half in Mexico, and of several thousand inhabitants the majority belonged on the southern side of the street, which was the boundary line. He also said that rebels had entered the town that day, causing a good deal of excitement.

Gale was almost at the end of his financial resources, which fact occasioned him to turn away from a pretentious hotel and ask his guide for a cheaper lodging house. When this was found, a sight of the loungers in the office, and also a desire for comfort, persuaded Gale to change his traveling clothes for rough outing garb and boots.

"Well, I'm almost broke," he soliloquized, thoughtfully. "The governor said I wouldn't make any money. He's right—so far. And he said I'd be coming home beaten. There he's wrong. I've got a hunch that something'll happen to me in this Greaser town."

He went out into a wide, whitewashed, high-ceiled corridor, and from that into an immense room which, but for pool tables, bar, and benches, would have been like a courtyard. The floor was cobblestoned, the walls were of adobe, and the large windows opened like doors. A blue cloud of smoke filled the place. Gale heard the click of pool balls and the clink of glasses along the crowded bar. Bare-legged, sandal-footed Mexicans in white rubbed shoulders with Mexicans mantled in black and red. There were others in tight-fitting blue uniforms with gold fringe or tassels at the shoulders. These men wore belts with heavy, bone-handled guns, and evidently were the rurales, or native policemen. There were black-bearded, coarse-visaged Americans, some gambling round the little tables, others drinking. The pool tables were the center of a noisy crowd of younger men, several of whom were unsteady on their feet. There were khaki-clad cavalrymen strutting in and out.

At one end of the room, somewhat apart from the general melee, was a group of six men round a little table, four of whom were seated, the other two standing. These last two drew a second glance from Gale. The sharp-featured, bronzed faces and piercing eyes, the tall, slender, loosely jointed bodies, the quiet, easy, reckless air that seemed to be a part of the men—these things would plainly have stamped them as cowboys without the buckled sombreros, the colored scarfs, the high-topped, high-heeled boots with great silver-roweled spurs. Gale did not fail to note, also, that these cowboys wore guns, and this fact was rather a shock to his idea of the modern West. It caused him to give some credence to the rumors of fighting along the border, and he felt a thrill.

He satisfied his hunger in a restaurant adjoining, and as he stepped back into the saloon a man wearing a military cape jostled him. Apologies from both were instant. Gale was moving on when the other stopped short as if startled, and, leaning forward, exclaimed:

"Dick Gale?"

"You've got me," replied Gale, in surprise. "But I don't know you."

He could not see the stranger's face, because it was wholly shaded by a wide-brimmed hat pulled well down.

"By Jove! It's Dick! If this isn't great! Don't you know me?"

"I've heard your voice somewhere," replied Gale. "Maybe I'll recognize you if you come out from under that bonnet."

For answer the man, suddenly manifesting thought of himself, hurriedly drew Gale into the restaurant, where he thrust back his hat to disclose a handsome, sunburned face.

"George Thorne! So help me—"

"'S-s-ssh. You needn't yell," interrupted the other, as he met Gale's outstretched hand. There was a close, hard, straining grip. "I must not be recognized here. There are reasons. I'll explain in a minute. Say, but it's fine to see you! Five years, Dick, five years since I saw you run down University Field and spread-eagle the whole Wisconsin football team."

"Don't recollect that," replied Dick, laughing. "George, I'll bet you I'm gladder to see you than you are to see me. It seems so long. You went into the army, didn't you?"

"I did. I'm here now with the Ninth Cavalry. But—never mind me. What're you doing way down here? Say, I just noticed your togs. Dick, you can't be going in for mining or ranching, not in this God-forsaken desert?"

"On the square, George, I don't know any more why I'm here than—than you know."

"Well, that beats me!" ejaculated Thorne, sitting back in his chair, amaze and concern in his expression. "What the devil's wrong? Your old man's got too much money for you ever to be up against it. Dick, you couldn't have gone to the bad?"

A tide of emotion surged over Gale. How good it was to meet a friend—someone to whom to talk! He had never appreciated his loneliness until that moment.

"George, how I ever drifted down here I don't know. I didn't exactly quarrel with the governor. But—damn it, Dad hurt me—shamed me, and I dug out for the West. It was this way. After leaving college I tried to please him by tackling one thing after another that he set me to do. On the square, I had no head for business. I made a mess of everything. The governor got sore. He kept ramming the harpoon into me till I just couldn't stand it. What little ability I possessed deserted me when I got my back up, and there you are. Dad and I had a rather uncomfortable half hour. When I quit—when I told him straight out that I was going West to fare for myself, why, it wouldn't have been so tough if he hadn't laughed at me. He called me a rich man's son—an idle, easygoing, spineless swell. He said I didn't even have character enough to be out-and-out bad. He said I didn't have sense enough to marry one of the nice girls in my sister's crowd. He said I couldn't earn a dollar—that I'd starve out West, and couldn't get back home unless I sent to him for money. He said he didn't believe I could fight—could really make a fight for anything under the sun. Oh—he—he shot it into me, all right."

Dick dropped his head upon his hands, somewhat ashamed of the smarting dimness in his eyes. He had not meant to say so much. Yet what a relief to let out that long-congested burden!

"Fight!" cried Thorne, hotly. "What's ailing him? Didn't they call you Biff Gale in college? Dick, you were one of the best men Stagg ever developed. I heard him say so—that you were the fastest one-hundred-and-seventy-five-pound man he'd ever trained, the hardest to stop."

"The governor didn't count football," said Dick. "He didn't mean that kind of a fight. When I left home I don't think I had an idea what was wrong with me. But George, I think I know now. I was a rich man's son—spoiled, dependent, absolutely ignorant of the value of money. I haven't yet discovered any earning capacity in me. I seem to be unable to do anything with my hands. That's the trouble. But I'm at the end of my tether now. And I'm going to punch cattle or be a miner, or do some real stunt—like joining the rebels."

"Aha! I thought you'd spring that last one on me," declared Thorne, wagging his head. "Well, you just forget it. Say, old boy, there's something doing in Mexico. The United States in general doesn't realize it. But across that line there are crazy revolutionists, ill-paid soldiers, guerrilla leaders, raiders, robbers, outlaws, bandits galore, starving peons by the thousand, girls and women in terror. Mexico is like some of her volcanoes—ready to erupt fire and hell! Don't make the awful mistake of joining the rebel forces. Americans are hated by Mexicans of the lower class—the fighting class, both rebel and federal. Half the time these crazy Greasers are on one side, then on the other. If you didn't starve or get shot in ambush, or die of thirst, some Greaser would knife you in the back for your belt buckle or boots. There are a good many Americans with the rebels eastward toward Agua Prieta and Juarez. Orozco is operating in Chihuahua, and I guess he has some idea of warfare. But this is Sonora, a mountainous desert, the home of the slave and the Yaqui. There's unorganized revolt everywhere. The American miners and ranchers, those who could get away, have fled across into the States, leaving property. Those who couldn't or wouldn't come must fight for their lives, are fighting now."

"That's bad," said Gale. "It's news to me. Why doesn't the government take action, do something?"

"Afraid of international complications. Don't want to offend the Maderists, or be criticized by jealous foreign nations. It's a delicate situation, Dick. The Washington officials know the gravity of it, you can bet. But the United States in general is in the dark, and the army—well, you ought to hear the inside talk back at San Antonio. We're patrolling the boundary line. We're making a grand bluff. I could tell you of a dozen instances where cavalry should have pursued raiders on the other side of the line. But we won't do it. The officers are a grouchy lot these days. You see, of course, what significance would attach to United States cavalry going into Mexican territory. There would simply be hell. My own colonel is the sorest man on the job. We're all sore. It's like sitting on a powder magazine. We can't keep the rebels and raiders from crossing the line. Yet we don't fight. My commission expires soon. I'll be discharged in three months. You can bet I'm glad for more reasons than I've mentioned."

Thorne was evidently laboring under strong, suppressed excitement. His face showed pale under the tan, and his eyes gleamed with a dark fire. Occasionally his delight at meeting, talking with Gale, dominated the other emotions, but not for long. He had seated himself at a table near one of the door-like windows leading into the street, and every little while he would glance sharply out. Also he kept consulting his watch.

These details gradually grew upon Gale as Thorne talked.

"George, it strikes me that you're upset," said Dick presently. "I seem to remember you as a coolheaded fellow whom nothing could disturb. Has the army changed you?"

Thorne laughed. It was a laugh with a strange, high note. It was reckless—it hinted of exaltation. He rose abruptly; he gave the waiter money to go for drinks; he looked into the saloon, and then into the street. On this side of the house there was a porch opening on a plaza with trees and shrubbery and branches. Thorne peered out one window, then another. His actions were rapid. Returning to the table, he put his hands upon it and leaned over to look closely into Gale's face.

"I'm away from camp without leave," he said.

"Isn't that a serious offense?" asked Dick.

"Serious? For me, if I'm discovered, it means ruin. There are rebels in town. Any moment we might have trouble. I ought to be ready for duty—within call. If I'm discovered it means arrest. That means delay—the failure of my plans—ruin."

Gale was silenced by his friend's intensity. Thorne bent over closer with his dark eyes searchingly bright.

"We were old pals—once?"

"Surely," replied Dick.

"What would you say, Dick Gale, if I told you that you're the one man I'd rather have had come along than any other at this crisis of my life?"

The earnest gaze, the passionate voice with its deep tremor drew Dick upright, thrilling and eager, conscious of strange, unfamiliar impetuosity.

"Thorne, I should say I was glad to be the fellow," replied Dick.

Their hands locked for a moment, and they sat down again with heads close over the table.

"Listen," began Thorne, in low, swift whisper, "a few days, a week ago—it seems like a year!—I was of some assistance to refugees fleeing from Mexico into the States. They were all women, and one of them was dressed as a nun. Quite by accident I saw her face. It was that of a beautiful girl. I observed she kept aloof from the others. I suspected a disguise, and, when opportunity afforded, spoke to her, offered my services. She replied to my poor efforts at Spanish in fluent English. She had fled in terror from her home, someplace down in Sinaloa. Rebels are active there. Her father was captured and held for ransom. When the ransom was paid the rebels killed him. The leader of these rebels was a bandit named Rojas. Long before the revolution began he had been feared by people of class—loved by the peons. Bandits are worshiped by the peons. All of the famous bandits have robbed the rich and given to the poor. Rojas saw the daughter, made off with her. But she contrived to bribe her guards, and escaped almost immediately before any harm befell her. She hid among friends. Rojas nearly tore down the town in his efforts to find her. Then she disguised herself, and traveled by horseback, stage, and train to Casita.

"Her story fascinated me, and that one fleeting glimpse I had of her face I couldn't forget. She had no friends here, no money. She knew Rojas was trailing her. This talk I had with her was at the railroad station, where all was bustle and confusion. No one noticed us, so I thought. I advised her to remove the disguise of a nun before she left the waiting-room. And I got a boy to guide her. But he fetched her to this house. I had promised to come in the evening to talk over the situation with her.

"I found her, Dick, and when I saw her—I went stark, staring, raving mad over her. She is the most beautiful, wonderful girl I ever saw. Her name is Mercedes Castañeda, and she belongs to one of the old wealthy Spanish families. She has lived abroad and in Havana. She speaks French as well as English. She is—but I must be brief.

"Dick, think, think! With Mercedes also it was love at first sight. My plan is to marry her and get her farther to the interior, away from the border. It may not be easy. She's watched. So am I. It was impossible to see her without the women of this house knowing. At first, perhaps, they had only curiosity—an itch to gossip. But the last two days there has been a change. Since last night there's some powerful influence at work. Oh, these Mexicans are subtle, mysterious! After all, they are Spaniards. They work in secret, in the dark. They are dominated first by religion, then by gold, then by passion for a woman. Rojas must have got word to his friends here; yesterday his gang of cutthroat rebels arrived, and today he came. When I learned that, I took my chance and left camp; I hunted up a priest. He promised to come here. It's time he's due. But I'm afraid he'll be stopped."

"Thorne, why don't you take the girl and get married without waiting, without running these risks?" said Dick.

"I fear it's too late now. I should have done that last night. You see, we're over the line—"

"Are we in Mexican territory now?" queried Gale, sharply.

"I guess yes, old boy. That's what complicates it. Rojas and his rebels have Casita in their hands. But Rojas without his rebels would be able to stop me, get the girl, and make for his mountain haunts. If Mercedes is really watched—if her identity is known, which I am sure is the case—we couldn't get far from this house before I'd be knifed and she seized."

"Good Heavens! Thorne, can that sort of thing happen less than a stone's throw from the United States line?" asked Gale, incredulously.

"It *can* happen, and don't you forget it. You don't seem to realize the power these guerrilla leaders, these rebel captains, and particularly these bandits, exercise over the mass of Mexicans. A bandit is a man of honor in Mexico. He is feared, envied, loved. In the hearts of the people he stands next to the national idol—the bullfighter, the matador. The race has a wild, barbarian, bloody strain. Take Quinteros, for instance. He was a peon, a slave. He became a famous bandit. At the outbreak of the revolution he proclaimed himself a leader, and with a band of followers he devastated whole counties. The opposition to federal forces was only a blind to rob and riot and carry off women. The motto of this man and his followers was: 'Let us enjoy ourselves while we may!'

"There are other bandits besides Quinteros, not so famous or such great leaders, but just as bloodthirsty. I've seen Rojas. He's a handsome, bold, sneering devil, vainer than any peacock. He decks himself in gold lace and silver trappings, in all the finery he can steal. He was one of the rebels who helped sack Sinaloa and carry off half a million in money and valuables. Rojas spends gold like he spills blood. But he is chiefly famous for abducting women. The peon girls consider it an honor to be ridden off with. Rojas has shown a penchant for girls of the better class."

Thorne wiped the perspiration from his pale face and bent a dark gaze out of the window before he resumed his talk.

"Consider what the position of Mercedes really is. I can't get any help from our side of the line. If so, I don't know where. The population on that side is mostly Mexican, absolutely in sympathy with whatever actuates those on this side. The whole caboodle of Greasers on both sides belong to the class in sympathy with the rebels, the class that secretly respects men like Rojas and hates an aristocrat like Mercedes. They would conspire to throw her into his power. Rojas can turn all the hidden underground influences to his ends. Unless I thwart him he'll get Mercedes as easily as he can light a cigarette. But I'll kill him or some of his gang or her before I let him get her. . . . This is the situation, old friend. I've little time to spare. I face arrest for desertion. Rojas is in town. I think I was followed to this hotel. The priest has betrayed me or has been stopped. Mercedes is here alone, waiting, absolutely dependent upon me to save her from—from . . . She's the sweetest, loveliest girl! . . . In a few moments—sooner or later there'll be hell here! Dick, are you with me?"

Dick Gale drew a long, deep breath. A coldness, a lethargy, an indifference that had weighed upon him for months had passed out of his being. On the instant he could not speak, but his hand closed powerfully upon his friend's. Thorne's face changed wonderfully, the distress, the fear, the appeal all vanishing in a smile of passionate gratefulness.

Then Dick's gaze, attracted by some slight sound, shot over his friend's shoulder to see a face at the window—a handsome, bold, sneering face, with glittering dark eyes that flashed in sinister intentness.

Dick stiffened in his seat. Thorne, with sudden clenching of hands, wheeled toward the window.

"Rojas!" he whispered.

CHAPTER 2

MERCEDES CASTAÑEDA

The dark face vanished. Dick Gale heard footsteps and the tinkle of spurs. He strode to the window, and was in time to see a Mexican swagger into the front door of the saloon. Dick had only a glimpse; but in that he saw a huge black sombrero with a gaudy band, the back of a short, tight-fitting jacket, a heavy pearl-handled gun swinging with a fringe of sash, and close-fitting trousers spreading wide at the bottom. There were men passing in the street, also several Mexicans lounging against the hitching-rail at the curb.

"Did you see him? Where did he go?" whispered Thorne, as he joined Gale. "Those Greasers out there with the cartridge belts crossed over their breasts—they are rebels."

"I think he went into the saloon," replied Dick. "He had a gun, but for all I can see the Greasers out there are unarmed."

"Never believe it! There! Look, Dick! That fellow's a guard, though he seems so unconcerned. See, he has a short carbine, almost concealed. . . . There's another Greaser farther down the path. I'm afraid Rojas has the house spotted."

"If we could only be sure."

"I'm sure, Dick. Let's cross the hall; I want to see how it looks from the other side of the house."

Gale followed Thorne out of the restaurant into the high-ceiled corridor which evidently divided the hotel, opening into the street and running back to a patio. A few dim yellow lamps flickered. A Mexican with a blanket round his shoulders stood in the front entrance. Back toward the patio there were sounds of boots on the stone floor. Shadows flitted across that end of the corridor. Thorne entered a huge chamber which was even more poorly lighted than the hall. It contained a table littered with papers, a few high-backed chairs, a couple of couches, and was evidently a parlor.

"Mercedes has been meeting me here," said Thorne. "At this hour she comes every moment or so to the head of the stairs there, and if I am here she comes down. Mostly there are people in this room a little later. We go out into the plaza. It faces the dark side of the house, and that's the place I must slip out with her if there's any chance at all to get away."

They peered out of the open window. The plaza was gloomy, and at first glance apparently deserted. In a moment, however, Gale made out a slow-pacing dark form on the path. Farther down there was another. No particular keenness was required to see in these forms a sentinel-like stealthiness.

Gripping Gale's arm, Thorne pulled back from the window.

"You saw them," he whispered. "It's just as I feared. Rojas has the place surrounded. I should have taken Mercedes away. But I had no time—no chance! I'm bound! . . . . There's Mercedes now! My God! . . . . Dick, think—think if there's a way to get her out of this trap!"

Gale turned as his friend went down the room. In the dim light at the head of the stairs stood the slim, muffled figure of a woman. When she saw Thorne she flew noiselessly down the stairway to him. He caught her in his arms. Then she spoke softly, brokenly, in a low, swift voice. It was a mingling of incoherent Spanish and English; but to Gale it was mellow, deep, unutterably tender, a voice full of joy, fear, passion, hope, and love. Upon Gale it had an unaccountable effect. He found himself thrilling, wondering.

Thorne led the girl to the center of the room, under the light where

Gale stood. She had raised a white hand, holding a black-lace mantilla half aside. Dick saw a small, dark head proudly held, an oval face half hidden, white as a flower, and magnificent black eyes.

Then Thorne spoke.

"Mercedes—Dick Gale, an old friend—the best friend I ever had."

She swept the mantilla back over her head, disclosing a lovely face, strange and striking to Gale in its pride and fire, its intensity.

"Señor Gale—ah! I cannot speak my happiness. His friend!"

"Yes, Mercedes; my friend and yours," said Thorne, speaking rapidly. "We'll have need of him. Dear, there's bad news and no time to break it gently. The priest did not come. He must have been detained. And listen—be brave, dear Mercedes—Rojas is here!"

She uttered an inarticulate cry, the poignant terror of which shook Gale's nerve, and swayed as if she would faint. Thorne caught her, and in husky voice importuned her to bear up.

"My darling! For God's sake don't faint—don't go to pieces! We'd be lost! We've got a chance. We'll think of something. Be strong! Fight!"

It was plain to Gale that Thorne was distracted. He scarcely knew what he was saying. Pale and shaking, he clasped Mercedes to him. Her terror had struck him helpless. It was so intense—it was so full of horrible certainty of what fate awaited her.

She cried out in Spanish, beseeching him; and as he shook his head, she changed to English:

"Señor, my lover, I will be strong—I will fight—I will obey. But swear by my Virgin, if need be to save me from Rojas—you will kill me!"

"Mercedes! Yes, I'll swear," he replied, hoarsely. "I know—I'd rather have you dead than—But don't give up. Rojas can't be sure of you, or he wouldn't wait. He's in there. He's got his men there—all round us. But he hesitates. A beast like Rojas doesn't stand idle for nothing. I tell you we've a chance. Dick, here, will think of something. We'll slip away. Then he'll take you somewhere. Only—speak to him—show him you won't weaken. Mercedes, this is more than love and happiness for us. It's life or death."

She became quiet, and slowly recovered control of herself.

Suddenly she wheeled to face Gale with proud dark eyes, tragic sweetness of appeal, an exquisite grace.

"Señor, you are an American. You cannot know the Spanish blood—
the peon bandit's hate and cruelty. I wish to die before Rojas's hand
touches me. If he takes me alive, then the hour, the little day that my life
lasts afterward will be torture—torture of hell. If I live two days his brutal men will have me. If I live three, the dogs of his camp. . . . Señor, have
you a sister whom you love? Help Señor Thorne to save me. He is a soldier. He is bound. He must not betray his honor, his duty, for me. . . .
Ah, you two splendid Americans—so big, so strong, so fierce! What is
that little black half-breed slave Rojas to such men? Rojas is a coward.
Now, let me waste no more precious time. I am ready. I will be brave."

She came close to Gale, holding out her white hands, a woman all
fire and soul and passion. To Gale she was wonderful. His heart leaped.
As he bent over her hands and kissed them he seemed to feel himself renewed, remade.

"Señorita," he said, "I am happy to be your servant. I can conceive of
no greater pleasure than giving the service you require."

"And what is that?" inquired Thorne, hurriedly.

"That of incapacitating Señor Rojas for tonight, and perhaps several
nights to come," repined Gale.

"Dick, what will you do?" asked Thorne, now in alarm.

"I'll make a row in that saloon," returned Dick, bluntly. "I'll start
something. I'll rush Rojas and his crowd. I'll—"

"Lord, no; you mustn't, Dick—you'll be knifed!" cried Thorne. He
was in distress, yet his eyes were shining.

"I'll take a chance. Maybe I can surprise that slow Greaser bunch
and get away before they know what's happened. . . . You be ready watching at the window. When the row starts those fellows out there in the
plaza will run into the saloon. Then you slip out, go straight through
the plaza down the street. It's a dark street, I remember. I'll catch up with
you before you get far."

Thorne gasped, but did not say a word. Mercedes leaned against
him, her white hands now at her breast, her great eyes watching Gale as
he went out.

In the corridor Gale stopped long enough to pull on a pair of heavy
gloves, to muss his hair, and disarrange his collar. Then he stepped into
the restaurant, went through, and halted in the door leading into the

ɔon. His five feet eleven inches and one hundred and eighty pounds ɛre more noticeable there, and it was part of his plan to attract attention ɔ himself. No one, however, appeared to notice him. The pool-players were noisily intent on their game, the same crowd of motley-robed Mexicans hung over the reeking bar. Gale's roving glance soon fixed upon the man he took to be Rojas. He recognized the huge, high-peaked, black sombrero with its ornamented band. The Mexican's face was turned aside. He was in earnest, excited colloquy with a dozen or more comrades, most of whom were sitting round a table. They were listening, talking, drinking. The fact that they wore cartridge belts crossed over their breasts satisfied Gale that these were the rebels. He had noted the belts of the Mexicans outside, who were apparently guards. A waiter brought more drinks to this group at the table, and this caused the leader to turn so Gale could see his face. It was indeed the sinister, sneering face of the bandit Rojas. Gale gazed at the man with curiosity. He was under medium height, and striking in appearance only because of his dandified dress and evil visage. He wore a lace scarf, a tight, bright-buttoned jacket, a buckskin vest embroidered in red, a sash and belt joined by an enormous silver clasp. Gale saw again the pearl-handled gun swinging at the bandit's hip. Jewels flashed in his scarf. There were gold rings in his ears and diamonds on his fingers.

Gale became conscious of an inward fire that threatened to overrun his coolness. Other emotions harried his self-control. It seemed as if sight of the man liberated or created a devil in Gale. And at the bottom of his feelings there seemed to be a wonder at himself, a strange satisfaction for the something that had come to him.

He stepped out of the doorway, down the couple of steps to the floor of the saloon, and he staggered a little, simulating drunkenness. He fell over the pool tables, jostled Mexicans at the bar, laughed like a maudlin fool, and, with his hat slouched down, crowded here and there. Presently his eye caught sight of the group of cowboys whom he had before noticed with such interest.

They were still in a corner somewhat isolated. With fertile mind working, Gale lurched over to them. He remembered his many unsuccessful attempts to get acquainted with cowboys. If he were to get any help from these silent aloof rangers it must be by striking fire from them in one swift stroke. Planting himself squarely before the two tall cowboys who were standing, he looked straight into their lean, bronzed faces. He spared a full moment for that keen, cool gaze before he spoke.

"I'm not drunk. I'm throwing a bluff, and I mean to start a rough house. I'm going to rush that damned bandit Rojas. It's to save a girl—to give her lover, who is my friend, a chance to escape with her. She's in the house. Rojas is here to get her. When I start a row my friend will try to slip out with her. Every door and window is watched. I've got to raise hell to draw the guards in. . . . Well, you're my countrymen. We're in Mexico. A beautiful girl's honor and life are at stake. Now, gentlemen, watch me!"

One cowboy's eyes narrowed, blinking a little, and his lean jaw dropped; the other's hard face rippled with a fleeting smile.

Gale backed away, and his pulse leaped when he saw the two cowboys, as if with one purpose, slowly stride after him. Then Gale swerved, staggering along, brushed against the tables, kicked over the empty chairs. He passed Rojas and his gang, and out of the tail of his eye saw that the bandit was watching him, waving his hands and talking fiercely. The hum of the many voices grew louder, and when Dick lurched against a table, overturning it and spilling glasses into the laps of several Mexicans, there arose a shrill cry. He had succeeded in attracting attention; almost every face turned his way. One of the insulted men, a little tawny fellow, leaped up to confront Gale, and in a frenzy screamed a volley of Spanish, of which Gale distinguished "Gringo!" The Mexican stamped and made a threatening move with his right hand. Dick swung his leg and with a swift side kick knocked the fellow's feet from under him, whirling him down with a thud.

The action was performed so suddenly, so adroitly, it made the Mexican such a weakling, so like a tumbled tenpin, that the shrill jabbering hushed. Gale knew this to be the significant moment.

Wheeling, he rushed at Rojas. It was his old line-breaking plunge. Neither Rojas nor his men had time to move. The black-skinned bandit's face turned a dirty white; his jaw dropped; he would have shrieked if Gale had not hit him. The blow swept him backward against his men. Then Gale's heavy body, swiftly following with the momentum of that rush, struck the little group of rebels. They went down with table and chairs in a sliding crash.

Gale, carried by his plunge, went with them. Like a cat he landed on top. As he rose his powerful hands fastened on Rojas. He jerked the little bandit off the tangled pile of struggling, yelling men, and, swinging him with terrific force, let go his hold. Rojas slid along the floor, knocking over tables and chairs. Gale bounded back, dragged Rojas up, handling him as if he were a limp sack.

A shot rang out above the yells. Gale heard the jingle of breaking glass. The room darkened perceptibly. He flashed a glance backward. The two cowboys were between him and the crowd of frantic rebels. One cowboy held two guns low down, level in front of him. The other had his gun raised and aimed. On the instant it spouted red and white. With the crack came the crashing of glass, another darkening shade over the room. With a cry Gale slung the bleeding Rojas from him. The bandit struck a table, toppled over it, fell, and lay prone.

Another shot made the room full of moving shadows, with light only back of the bar. A white-clad figure rushed at Gale. He tripped the man, but had to kick hard to disengage himself from grasping hands. Another figure closed in on Gale. This one was dark, swift. A blade glinted— described a circle aloft. Simultaneously with a close, red flash the knife wavered; the man wielding it stumbled backward. In the din Gale did not hear a report, but the Mexican's fall was significant. Then pandemonium broke loose. The din became a roar. Gale heard shots that sounded like dull spats in the distance. The big lamp behind the bar seemingly split, then sputtered and went out, leaving the room in darkness.

Gale leaped toward the restaurant door, which was outlined faintly by the yellow light within. Right and left he pushed the groping men who jostled with him. He vaulted a pool table, sent tables and chairs flying, and gained the door, to be the first of a wedging mob to squeeze through. One sweep of his arm knocked the restaurant lamp from its stand; and he ran out, leaving darkness behind him. A few bounds took him into the parlor. It was deserted. Thorne had gotten away with Mercedes!

It was then Gale slowed up. For the space of perhaps sixty seconds he had been moving with startling velocity. He peered cautiously out into the plaza. The paths, the benches, the shady places under the trees contained no skulking men. He ran out, keeping to the shade, and did not go into the path till he was halfway through the plaza. Under a street lamp at the far end of the path he thought he saw two dark figures. He ran faster, and soon reached the street. The uproar back in the hotel began to diminish, or else he was getting out of hearing. The few people he saw close at hand were all coming his way, and only the foremost showed any excitement. Gale walked swiftly, peering ahead for two figures. Presently he saw them—one tall, wearing a cape; the other slight, mantled. Gale drew a sharp breath of relief. Thorne and Mercedes were not far ahead.

From time to time Thorne looked back. He strode swiftly, almost carrying Mercedes, who clung closely to him. She, too, looked back. Once Gale saw her white face flash in the light of a street lamp. He began to overhaul them; and soon when the last lamp had been passed and the street was dark, he ventured a whistle. Thorne heard it, for he turned, whistled a low reply, and went on. Not for some distance beyond, where the street ended in open country, did they halt to wait. The desert began here. Gale felt the soft sand under his feet and saw the grotesque forms of cactus. Then he came up with the fugitives.

"Dick! Are you—all right?" panted Thorne, grasping Gale.

"I'm—out of breath—but—OK," replied Gale.

"Good! Good!" choked Thorne. "I was scared—helpless. . . . Dick, it worked splendidly. We had no trouble. What on earth did you do?"

"I made the row, all right," said Dick.

"Good Heavens! It was like a row I once heard made by a mob. But the shots, Dick—were they at you? They paralyzed me. Then the yells. What happened? Those guards of Rojas ran round in front at the first shot. Tell me what happened."

"While I was rushing Rojas a couple of cowboys shot out the lamp-lights. A Mexican who pulled a knife on me got hurt, I guess. Then I think there was some shooting from the rebels after the room was dark."

"Rushing Rojas?" queried Thorne, leaning close to Dick. His voice was thrilling, exultant, deep with a joy that yet needed confirmation. "What did you do to him?"

"I handed him one off side, tackled, then tried a forward pass," replied Dick, lightly speaking the football vernacular so familiar to Thorne.

Thorne leaned closer, his fine face showing fierce and corded in the starlight. "Tell me straight," he demanded, in thick voice.

Gale then divined something of the suffering Thorne had undergone—something of the hot, wild, vengeful passion of a lover who must have brutal truth.

It stilled Dick's lighter mood, and he was about to reply when Mercedes pressed close to him, touched his hands, and looked up into his face with wonderful eyes. He thought he would not soon forget their beauty—the shadow of pain that had been, the hope dawning so fugitively.

"Dear lady," said Gale, with voice not wholly steady. "Rojas himself will hound you no more tonight, nor for many nights."

She seemed to shake, to thrill, to rise with the intelligence. She pressed his hand close over her heaving breast. Gale felt the quick throb of her heart.

"Señor! Señor Dick!" she cried. Then her voice failed. But her hands flew up; quick as a flash she raised her face—kissed him. Then she turned and with a sob fell into Thorne's arms.

There ensued a silence broken only by Mercedes's sobbing. Gale walked some paces away. If he were not stunned, he certainly was agitated. The strange, sweet fire of that girl's lips remained with him. On the spur of the moment he imagined he had a jealousy of Thorne. But presently this passed. It was only that he had been deeply moved—stirred to the depths during the last hour—had become conscious of the awakening of a spirit. What remained with him now was the splendid glow of gladness that he had been of service to Thorne. And by the intensity of Mercedes's abandon of relief and gratitude he measured her agony of terror and the fate he had spared her.

"Dick, Dick, come here!" called Thorne, softly. "Let's pull ourselves together now. We've got a problem yet. What to do? Where to go? How to get anyplace? We don't dare risk the station—the corrals where Mexicans hire out horses. We're on good old U.S. ground this minute, but we're not out of danger."

As he paused, evidently hoping for a suggestion from Gale, the silence was broken by the clear, ringing peal of a bugle. Thorne gave a violent start. Then he bent over, listening. The beautiful notes of the bugle floated out of the darkness, clearer, sharper, faster.

"It's a call, Dick! It's a call!" he cried.

Gale had no answer to make. Mercedes stood as if stricken. The bugle call ended. From a distance another faintly pealed. There were other sounds too remote to recognize. Then scattering shots rattled out.

"Dick, the rebels are fighting somebody," burst out Thorne, excitedly. "The little federal garrison still holds its stand. Perhaps it is attacked again. Anyway, there's something doing over the line. Maybe the crazy Greasers are firing on our camp. We've feared it—in the dark. . . . And here I am, away without leave—practically a deserter!"

"Go back! Go back, before you're too late!" cried Mercedes.

"Better make tracks, Thorne," added Gale. "It can't help our predicament for you to be arrested. I'll take care of Mercedes."

"No, no, no," replied Thorne. "I can get away—avoid arrest."

"That'd be all right for the immediate present. But it's not best for the future. George, a deserter is a deserter! . . . Better hurry. Leave the girl to me till to-morrow."

Mercedes embraced her lover, begged him to go. Thorne wavered.

"Dick, I'm up against it," he said. "You're right. If only I can run back in time. But, oh, I hate to leave her! Old fellow, you've saved her! I already owe you everlasting gratitude. Keep out of Casita, Dick. The U.S. side might be safe, but I'm afraid to trust it at night. Go out in the desert, up in the mountains, in some safe place. Then come to me in camp. We'll plan. I'll have to confide in Colonel Weede. Maybe he'll help us. Hide her from the rebels—that's all."

He wrung Dick's hand, clasped Mercedes tightly in his arms, kissed her, and murmured low over her, then released her to rush off into the darkness. He disappeared in the gloom. The sound of his dull footfalls gradually died away.

For a moment the desert silence oppressed Gale. He was unaccustomed to such strange stillness. There was a low stir of sand, a rustle of stiff leaves in the wind. How white the stars burned! Then a coyote barked, to be bayed by a dog. Gale realized that he was between the edge of an unknown desert and the edge of a hostile town. He had to choose the desert, because, though he had no doubt that in Casita there were many Americans who might befriend him, he could not chance the risks of seeking them at night.

He felt a slight touch on his arm, felt it move down, felt Mercedes slip a trembling cold little hand into his. Dick looked at her. She seemed a white-faced girl now, with staring, frightened black eyes that flashed up at him. If the loneliness, the silence, the desert, the unknown dangers of the night affected him, what must they be to this hunted, driven girl? Gale's heart swelled. He was alone with her. He had no weapon, no money, no food, no drink, no covering, nothing except his two hands. He had absolutely no knowledge of the desert, of the direction or where-abouts of the boundary line between the republics; he did not know where to find the railroad, or any road or trail, or whether or not there were towns near or far. It was a critical, desperate situation. He thought first of the girl, and groaned in spirit, prayed that it would be given him to save her. When he remembered himself it was with the stunning con-sciousness that he could conceive of no situation which he would have exchanged for this one—where fortune had set him a perilous task of loyalty to a friend, to a helpless girl.

"Señor, señor!" suddenly whispered Mercedes, clinging to him. "Listen! I hear horses coming!"

CHAPTER 3

A FLIGHT INTO
THE DESERT

Uneasy and startled, Gale listened and, hearing nothing, wondered if Mercedes's fears had not worked upon her imagination. He felt a trembling seize her, and he held her hands tightly.

"You were mistaken, I guess," he whispered.

"No, no, señor."

Dick turned his ear to the soft wind. Presently he heard, or imagined he heard, low beats. Like the first faint, far-off beats of a drumming grouse, they recalled to him the Illinois forests of his boyhood. In a moment he was certain the sounds were the padlike steps of hoofs in yielding sand. The regular tramp was not that of grazing horses.

On the instant, made cautious and stealthy by alarm, Gale drew Mercedes deeper into the gloom of the shrubbery. Sharp pricks from thorns warned him that he was pressing into a cactus growth, and he protected Mercedes as best he could. She was shaking as one with a severe chill. She breathed with little hurried pants and leaned upon him almost in collapse. Gale ground his teeth in helpless rage at the girl's fate. If she had not been beautiful she might still have been free and happy in her home. What a strange world to live in—how unfair was fate!

The sounds of hoofbeats grew louder. Gale made out a dark moving mass against a background of dull gray. There was a line of horses. He could not discern whether or not all the horses carried riders. The murmur of a voice struck his ear—then a low laugh. It made him tingle, for it sounded American. Eagerly he listened. There was an interval when only the hoofbeats could be heard.

"It shore was, Laddy, it shore was," came a voice out of the darkness. "Rough house! Laddy, since wire fences drove us out of Texas we ain't seen the like of that. An' we never had such a call."

"Call? It was a burnin' roast," replied another voice. "I felt low down. He vamoosed some sudden, an' I hope he an' his friends shook the dust of Casita. That's a rotten town, Jim."

Gale jumped up in joy. What luck! The speakers were none other than the two cowboys whom he had accosted in the Mexican hotel.

"Hold on, fellows," he called out, and strode into the road.

The horses snorted and stamped. Then followed swift rustling sounds—a clinking of spurs, then silence. The figures loomed clearer in the gloom. Gale saw five or six horses, two with riders, and one other, at least, carrying a pack. When Gale got within fifteen feet of the group the foremost horseman said:

"I reckon that's close enough, stranger."

Something in the cowboy's hand glinted darkly bright in the starlight.

"You'd recognize me, if it wasn't so dark," replied Gale, halting. "I spoke to you a little while ago—in the saloon back there."

"Come over an' let's see you," said the cowboy, curtly.

Gale advanced till he was close to the horse. The cowboy leaned over the saddle and peered into Gale's face. Then, without a word, he sheathed the gun and held out his hand. Gale met a grip of steel that warmed his blood. The other cowboy got off his nervous, spirited horse and threw the bridle. He, too, peered closely into Gale's face.

"My name's Ladd," he said. "Reckon I'm some glad to meet you again."

Gale felt another grip as hard and strong as the other had been. He realized he had found friends who belonged to a class of men whom he had despaired of ever knowing.

"Gale—Dick Gale is my name," he began, swiftly. "I dropped into Casita tonight hardly knowing where I was. A boy took me to that hotel.

There I met an old friend whom I had not seen for years. He belongs to the cavalry stationed here. He had befriended a Spanish girl—fallen in love with her. Rojas had killed this girl's father—tried to abduct her . . . You know what took place at the hotel. Gentlemen, if it's ever possible, I'll show you how I appreciate what you did for me there. I got away, found my friend with the girl. We hurried out here beyond the edge of the town. Then Thorne had to make a break for camp. We heard bugle calls, shots, and he was away without leave. That left the girl with me. I don't know what to do. Thorne swears Casita is no place for Mercedes at night."

"The girl ain't no peon, no common Greaser?" interrupted Ladd.

"No. Her name is Castañeda. She belongs to an old Spanish family, once rich and influential."

"Reckoned as much," replied the cowboy. "There's more than Rojas's wantin' to kidnap a pretty girl. Shore he does that every day or so. Must be somethin' political or feelin' against class. Well, Casita ain't no place for your friend's girl at night or day, or any time. Shore, there's Americans who'd take her in an' fight for her, if necessary. But it ain't wise to risk that. Lash, what do you say?"

"It's been gettin' hotter round this Greaser corral for some weeks," replied the other cowboy. "If that two-bit of a garrison surrenders, there's no tellin' what'll happen. Orozco is headin' west from Agua Prieta with his guerrillas. Campo is burnin' bridges an' tearin' up the railroad south of Nogales. Then there's all these bandits callin' themselves revolutionists just for an excuse to steal, burn, kill, an' ride off with women. It's plain facts, Laddy, an' bein' across the U.S. line a few inches or so don't make no hell of a difference. My advice is, don't let Miss Castañeda ever set foot in Casita again."

"Looks like you've shore spoke sense," said Ladd. "I reckon, Gale, you an' the girl ought to come with us. Casita shore would be a little warm for us to-morrow. We didn't kill anybody, but I shot a Greaser's arm off, an' Lash strained friendly relations by destroyin' property. We know people who'll take care of the señorita till your friend can come for her."

Dick warmly spoke his gratefulness, and, inexpressibly relieved and happy for Mercedes, he went toward the clump of cactus where he had left her. She stood erect, waiting, and, dark as it was, he could tell she had lost the terror that had so shaken her.

"Señor Gale, you are my good angel," she said, tremulously.

"I've been lucky to fall in with these men, and I'm glad with all my heart," he replied. "Come."

He led her into the road up to the cowboys, who now stood bareheaded in the starlight. They seemed shy, and Lash was silent while Ladd made embarrassed, unintelligible reply to Mercedes's thanks.

There were five horses—two saddled, two packed and the remaining one carried only a blanket. Ladd shortened the stirrups on his mount, and helped Mercedes up into the saddle. From the way she settled herself and took the few restive prances of the mettlesome horse Gale judged that she could ride. Lash urged Gale to take his horse. But this Gale refused to do.

"I'll walk," he said. "I'm used to walking. I know cowboys are not."

They tried again to persuade him, without avail. Then Ladd started off, riding bareback. Mercedes fell in behind, with Gale walking beside her. The two pack animals came next, and Lash brought up the rear.

Once started with protection assured for the girl and a real objective point in view, Gale relaxed from the tense strain he had been laboring under. How glad he would have been to acquaint Thorne with their good fortune! Later, of course, there would be some way to get word to the cavalryman. But till then what torments his friend would suffer!

It seemed to Dick that a very long time had elapsed since he stepped off the train; and one by one he went over every detail of incident which had occurred between that arrival and the present moment. Strange as the facts were, he had no doubts. He realized that before that night he had never known the deeps of wrath undisturbed in him; had never conceived even a passing idea that it was possible for him to try to kill a man. His right hand was swollen stiff, so sore that he could scarcely close it. His knuckles were bruised and bleeding, and ached with a sharp pain. Considering the thickness of his heavy glove, Gale was of the opinion that so to bruise his hand he must have struck Rojas a powerful blow. He remembered that for him to give or take a blow had been nothing. This blow to Rojas, however, had been a different matter. The hot wrath which had been his motive was not puzzling; but the effect on him after he had cooled off, a subtle difference, something puzzled and eluded him. The more it baffled him the more he pondered. All those wandering months of his had been filled with dissatisfaction, yet he had been too apathetic to understand himself. So he had not been much of a person to try. Perhaps it had not been the blow to Rojas any more than other things that had wrought some change in him.

His meeting with Thorne; the wonderful black eyes of a Spanish girl; her appeal to him; the hate inspired by Rojas, and the rush, the blow, the action; sight of Thorne and Mercedes hurrying safely away; the girl's hands pressing his to her heaving breast; the sweet fire of her kiss; the fact of her being alone with him, dependent upon him—all these things Gale turned over and over in his mind, only to fail of any definite conclusion as to which had affected him so remarkably, or to tell what had really happened to him.

Had he fallen in love with Thorne's sweetheart? The idea came in a flash. Was he, all in an instant, and by one of those incomprehensible reversals of character, jealous of his friend? Dick was almost afraid to look up at Mercedes. Still he forced himself to do so, and as it chanced Mercedes was looking down at him. Somehow the light was better, and he clearly saw her white face, her black and starry eyes, her perfect mouth. With a quick, graceful impulsiveness she put her hand upon his shoulder. Like her appearance, the action was new, strange, striking to Gale; but it brought home suddenly to him the nature of gratitude and affection in a girl of her blood. It was sweet and sisterly. He knew then that he had not fallen in love with her. The feeling that was akin to jealousy seemed to be of the beautiful something for which Mercedes stood in Thorne's life. Gale then grasped the bewildering possibilities, the infinite wonder of what a girl could mean to a man.

The other haunting intimations of change seemed to be elusively blended with sensations—the heat and thrill of action, the sense of something done and more to do, the utter vanishing of an old weary hunt for he knew not what. Maybe it had been a hunt for work, for energy, for spirit, for love, for his real self. Whatever it might be, there appeared to be now some hope of finding it.

The desert began to lighten. Gray openings in the border of shrubby growths changed to paler hue. The road could be seen some rods ahead, and it had become a stony descent down, steadily down. Dark, ridged backs of mountains bounded the horizon, and all seemed near at hand, hemming in the plain. In the east a white glow grew brighter and brighter, reaching up to a line of cloud, defined sharply below by a rugged notched range. Presently a silver circle rose behind the black mountain, and the gloom of the desert underwent a transformation. From a gray mantle it changed to a transparent haze. The moon was rising.

"Señor, I am cold," said Mercedes.

Dick had been carrying his coat upon his arm. He had felt warm, even hot, and had imagined that the steady walk had occasioned it. But his skin was cool. The heat came from an inward burning. He stopped the horse and raised the coat up, and helped Mercedes put it on.

"I should have thought of you," he said. "But I seemed to feel warm. . . . The coat's a little large; we might wrap it around you twice."

Mercedes smiled and lightly thanked him in Spanish. The flash of mood was in direct contrast to the appealing, passionate, and tragic states in which he had successively viewed her; and it gave him a vivid impression of what vivacity and charm she might possess under happy conditions. He was about to start when he observed that Ladd had halted and was peering ahead in evident caution. Mercedes's horse began to stamp impatiently, raised his ears and head, and acted as if he was about to neigh.

A warning "hist" from Ladd bade Dick put a quieting hand on the horse. Lash came noiselessly forward to join his companion. The two then listened and watched.

An uneasy yet thrilling stir ran through Gale's veins. This scene was not fancy. These men of the ranges had heard or seen or scented danger. It was all real, as tangible and sure as the touch of Mercedes's hand upon his arm. Probably for her the night had terrors beyond Gale's power to comprehend. He looked down into the desert, and would have felt no surprise at anything hidden away among the bristling cactus, the dark, winding arroyos, the shadowed rocks with their moonlit tips, the ragged plain leading to the black bold mountains. The wind appeared to blow softly, with an almost imperceptible moan, over the desert. That was a new sound to Gale. But he heard nothing more.

Presently Lash went to the rear and Ladd started ahead. The progress now, however, was considerably slower, not owing to a bad road—for that became better—but probably owing to caution exercised by the cowboy guide. At the end of a half hour this marked deliberation changed, and the horses followed Ladd's at a gait that put Gale to his best walking-paces.

Meanwhile the moon soared high above the black corrugated peaks. The gray, the gloom, the shadow whitened. The clearing of the dark foreground appeared to lift a distant veil and show endless aisles of desert reaching down between dim horizon-bounding ranges.

Gale gazed abroad, knowing that as this night was the first time for him to awake to consciousness of a vague, wonderful other self, so it was one wherein he began to be aware of an encroaching presence of physical things—the immensity of the star-studded sky, the soaring moon, the bleak, mysterious mountains, and limitless slope, and plain, and ridge, and valley. These things in all their magnificence had not been unnoticed by him before; only now they spoke a different meaning. A voice that he had never heard called him to see, to feel the vast hard externals of heaven and earth, all that represented the open, the free, silence and solitude and space.

Once more his thoughts, like his steps, were halted by Ladd's actions. The cowboy reined in his horse, listened a moment, then swung down out of the saddle. He raised a cautioning hand to the others, then slipped into the gloom and disappeared. Gale marked that the halt had been made in a ridged and cut-up pass between low mesas. He could see the columns of cactus standing out black against the moon-white sky. The horses were evidently tiring, for they showed no impatience. Gale heard their panting breaths, and also the bark of some animal—a dog or a coyote. It sounded like a dog, and this led Gale to wonder if there was any house near at hand. To the right, up under the ledges some distance away, stood two square black objects, too uniform, he thought, to be rocks. While he was peering at them, uncertain what to think, the shrill whistle of a horse pealed out, to be followed by the rattling of hoofs on hard stone. Then a dog barked. At the same moment that Ladd hurriedly appeared in the road a light shone out and danced before one of the square black objects.

"Keep close an' don't make no noise," he whispered, and led his horse at right angles off the road.

Gale followed, leading Mercedes's horse. As he turned he observed that Lash also had dismounted.

To keep closely at Ladd's heels without brushing the cactus or stumbling over rocks and depressions was a task Gale found impossible. After he had been stabbed several times by the bayonetlike spikes, which seemed invisible, the matter of caution became equally one of self-preservation. Both the cowboys, Dick had observed, wore leather chaps. It was no easy matter to lead a spirited horse through the dark, winding lanes walled by thorns. Mercedes's horse often balked and had to be coaxed and carefully guided. Dick concluded that Ladd was making a wide detour. The position of certain stars grown familiar during the march veered round from one side to another. Dick saw that the travel was fast, but by no means noiseless. The pack animals at times crashed and ripped through the narrow places. It seemed to Gale that any one within a mile could have heard these sounds. From the tops of knolls or ridges he looked back, trying to locate the mesas where the light had danced and the dog had barked alarm. He could not distinguish these two rocky eminences from among many rising in the background.

Presently Ladd led out into a wider lane that appeared to run straight. The cowboy mounted his horse, and this fact convinced Gale that they had circled back to the road. The march proceeded then once more at a good, steady, silent walk. When Dick consulted his watch he was amazed to see the hour was still early. How much had happened in little time! He now began to be aware that the night was growing colder; and, strange to him, he felt something damp that in a country he knew he would have recognized as dew. He had not been aware there was dew on the desert. The wind blew stronger, the stars shone whiter, the sky grew darker, and the moon climbed toward the zenith. The road stretched level for miles, then crossed arroyos and ridges, wound between mounds of broken ruined rock, found a level again, and then began a long ascent. Dick asked Mercedes if she was cold, and she answered that she was, speaking especially of her feet, which were growing numb. Then she asked to be helped down to walk awhile. At first she was cold and lame, and accepted the helping hand Dick proffered. After a little, however, she recovered and went on without assistance. Dick could scarcely believe his eyes, as from time to time he stole a sidelong glance at this silent girl, who walked with lithe and rapid stride. She was wrapped in his long coat, yet it did not hide her slender grace. He could not see her face, which was concealed by the black mantle.

A low-spoken word from Ladd recalled Gale to the question of surroundings and of possible dangers. Ladd had halted a few yards ahead. They had reached the summit of what was evidently a high ridge which sloped with much greater steepness on the far side. It was only after a few more forward steps, however, that Dick could see down the slope. Then full in view flashed a bright campfire around which clustered a group of dark figures. They were encamped in a wide arroyo, where horses could be seen grazing in black patches of grass between clusters of trees. A second look at the campers told Gale they were Mexicans. At this moment Lash came forward to join Ladd, and the two spent a long, uninterrupted moment studying the arroyo. A hoarse laugh, faint yet distinct, floated up on the cool wind.

"Well, Laddy, what 'r you makin' of that outfit?" inquired Lash, speaking softly.

"Same as any of them raider outfits," replied Ladd. "They're across the line for beef. But they'll run off any good stock. As hoss thieves these rebels have got 'em all beat. That outfit is waitin' till it's late. There's a ranch up the arroyo."

Gale heard the first speaker curse under his breath.

"Sure, I feel the same," said Ladd. "But we've got a girl an' the young man to look after, not to mention our pack outfit. An' we're huntin' for a job, not a fight, old hoss. Keep on your chaps!"

"Nothin' to it but head south for the Rio Forlorn."

"You're talkin' sense now, Jim. I wish we'd headed that way long ago. But it ain't strange I'd want to travel away from the border, thinkin' of the girl. Jim, we can't go round this Greaser outfit an' strike the road again. Too rough. So we'll have to give up gettin' to San Felipe."

"Perhaps it's just as well, Laddy. Rio Forlorn is on the borderline, but it's country where these rebels ain't been yet."

"Wait till they learn of the oasis an' Beldin's hosses!" exclaimed

Laddy. "I'm not anticipatin' peace anywhere along the border, Jim. But we can't go ahead; we can't go back."

"What'll we do, Laddy? It's a hike to Beldin's ranch. An' if we get there in daylight some Greaser will see the girl before Beldin' can hide her. It'll get talked about. The news'll travel to Casita like sage balls before the wind."

"Shore we won't ride into Rio Forlorn in the daytime. Let's slip the packs, Jim. We can hide them off in the cactus an' come back after them. With the young man ridin' we—"

The whispering was interrupted by a loud ringing neigh that whistled up from the arroyo. One of the horses had scented the travelers on the ridge-top. The indifference of the Mexicans changed to attention.

Ladd and Lash turned back and led the horses into the first opening on the south side of the road. There was nothing more said at the moment, and manifestly the cowboys were in a hurry. Gale had to run in the open places to keep up. When they did stop it was welcome to Gale, for he had begun to fall behind.

The packs were slipped, securely tied and hidden in a mesquite clump. Ladd strapped a blanket around one of the horses. His next move was to take off his chaps.

"Gale, you're wearin' boots, an' by liftin' your feet you can beat the cactus," he whispered. "But the—the—Miss Castañeda, she'll be torn all to pieces unless she puts these on. Please tell her—an' hurry."

Dick took the chaps, and, going up to Mercedes, he explained the situation. She laughed, evidently at his embarrassed earnestness, and slipped out of the saddle.

"Señor, chapparejos and I are not strangers," she said.

Deftly and promptly she equipped herself, and then Gale helped her into the saddle, called to her horse, and started off. Lash directed Gale to mount the other saddled horse and go next.

Dick had not ridden a hundred yards behind the trotting leaders before he had sundry painful encounters with reaching cactus arms. The horse missed these by a narrow margin. Dick's knees appeared to be in line, and it became necessary for him to lift them high and let his boots take the onslaught of the spikes. He was at home in the saddle, and the accomplishment was about the only one he possessed that had been of any advantage during his sojourn in the West.

Ladd pursued a zigzag course southward across the desert, trotting down the aisles, cantering in wide, bare patches, walking through the clumps of cacti. The desert seemed all of a sameness to Dick—a wilderness of rocks and jagged growths hemmed in by lowering ranges, always looking close, yet never growing any nearer. The moon slanted back toward the west, losing its white radiance, and the gloom of the earlier evening began to creep into the washes and to darken under the mesas. By and by Ladd entered an arroyo, and here the travelers turned and twisted with the meanderings of a dry streambed. At the head of the cañon they had to take once more to the rougher ground. Always it led down, always it grew rougher, more rolling, with wider bare spaces, always the black ranges loomed close.

Gale became chilled to the bone, and his clothes were damp and cold. His knees smarted from the wounds of the poisoned thorns, and his right hand was either swollen stiff or too numb to move. Moreover, he was tiring. The excitement, the long walk, the miles on miles of jolting trot—these had wearied him. Mercedes must be made of steel, he thought, to stand all that she had been subjected to and yet, when the stars were paling and dawn perhaps not far away, stay in the saddle.

So Dick Gale rode on, drowsier for each mile, and more and more giving the horse a choice of ground. Sometimes a prod from a murderous spine roused Dick. A grayness had blotted out the waning moon in the west and the clear, dark, starry sky overhead. Once when Gale, thinking to fight his weariness, raised his head, he saw that one of the horses in the lead was riderless. Ladd was carrying Mercedes. Dick marveled that her collapse had not come sooner. Another time, rousing himself again, he imagined they were now on a good hard road.

It seemed that hours passed, though he knew only little time had elapsed, when once more he threw off the spell of weariness. He heard a dog bark. Tall trees lined the open lane down which he was riding. Presently in the gray gloom he saw low, square houses with flat roofs. Ladd turned off to the left down another lane, gloomy between trees. Every few rods there was one of the squat houses. This lane opened into wider, lighter space. The cold air bore a sweet perfume—whether of flowers or fruit Dick could not tell. Ladd rode on for perhaps a quarter of a mile, though it seemed interminably long to Dick. A grove of trees loomed dark in the gray of morning. Ladd entered it and was lost in the shade. Dick rode on among trees. Presently he heard voices, and soon another house, low and flat like the others, but so long he could not see the farther end, stood up blacker than the trees. As he dismounted, cramped and sore, he could scarcely stand. Lash came alongside. He spoke, and someone with a big, hearty voice replied to him. Then it seemed to Dick that he was led into blackness like pitch, where, presently, he felt blankets thrown on him, and then his drowsy faculties faded.

CHAPTER 4

FORLORN RIVER

When Dick opened his eyes a flood of golden sunshine streamed in at the open window under which he lay. His first thought was one of blank wonder as to where in the world he happened to be. The room was large, square, adobe-walled. It was littered with saddles, harness, blankets. Upon the floor was a bed spread out upon a tarpaulin. Probably this was where someone had slept. The sight of huge dusty spurs, a gun belt with sheath and gun, and a pair of leather chaps bristling with broken cactus thorns recalled to Dick the cowboys, the ride, Mercedes, and the whole strange adventure that had brought him there.

He did not recollect having removed his boots; indeed, upon second thought, he knew he had not done so. But there they stood upon the floor. Ladd and Lash must have taken them off when he was so exhausted and sleepy that he could not tell what was happening. He felt a dead weight of complete lassitude, and he did not want to move. A sudden pain in his hand caused him to hold it up. It was black and blue, swollen to almost twice its normal size, and stiff as a board. The knuckles were skinned and crusted with dry blood. Dick soliloquized that it was the worst-looking hand he had seen since football days, and that it would inconvenience him for some time.

A warm, dry, fragrant breeze came through the window. Dick caught again the sweet smell of flowers or fruit. He heard the fluttering of leaves, the murmur of running water, the twittering of birds, then the sound of approaching footsteps and voices. The door at the far end of the room was open. Through it he saw poles of peeled wood upholding a porch roof, a bench, rosebushes in bloom, grass, and beyond these bright-green foliage of trees.

"He shore was sleepin' when I looked in an hour ago," said a voice that Dick recognized as Ladd's.

"Let him sleep," came the reply in deep, good-natured tones. "Mrs. B. says the girl's never moved. Must have been a tough ride for them both. Forty miles through cactus!"

"Young Gale hoofed darn near half the way," replied Ladd. "We tried to make him ride one of our hosses. If we had, we'd never got here. A walk like that'd killed me an' Jim."

"Well, Laddy, I'm right down glad to see you boys, and I'll do all I can for the young couple," said the other. "But I'm doing some worry here; don't mistake me."

"About your stock?"

"I've got only a few head of cattle at the oasis now. I'm worrying some, mostly about my horses. The U.S. is doing some worrying, too, don't mistake me. The rebels have worked west and north as far as Casita. There are no cavalrymen along the line beyond Casita, and there can't be. It's practically waterless desert. But these rebels are desert men. They could cross the line beyond the Rio Forlorn and smuggle arms into Mexico. Of course, my job is to keep tab on Chinese and Japs trying to get into the U.S. from Magdalena Bay. But I'm supposed to patrol the borderline. I'm going to hire some rangers. Now, I'm not so afraid of being shot up, though out in this lonely place there's danger of it; what I'm afraid of most is losing that bunch of horses. If any rebels come this far, or if they ever hear of my horses, they're going to raid me. You know what those guerrilla Mexicans will do for horses. They're crazy on horseflesh. They know fine horses. They breed the finest in the world. So I don't sleep nights any more."

"Reckon me an' Jim might as well tie up with you for a spell, Beldin'.

We've been ridin' up an' down Arizona tryin' to keep out of sight of wire fences."

"Laddy, it's open enough around Forlorn River to satisfy even an old-time cowpuncher like you," laughed Belding. "I'd take your staying on as some favor, don't mistake me. Perhaps I can persuade the young man Gale to take a job with me."

"That's shore likely. He said he had no money, no friends. An' if a scrapper's all you're lookin' for he'll do," replied Ladd, with a dry chuckle.

"Mrs. B. will throw some broncho capers round this ranch when she hears I'm going to hire a stranger."

"Why?"

"Well, there's Nell—And you said this Gale was a young American. My wife will be scared to death for fear Nell will fall in love with him."

Laddy choked off a laugh, then evidently slapped his knee or Belding's, for there was a resounding smack.

"He's a fine-spoken, good-looking chap, you said?" went on Belding.

"Shore he is," said Laddy, warmly. "What do you say, Jim?"

By this time Dick Gale's ears began to burn and he was trying to make himself deaf when he wanted to hear every little word.

"Husky young fellow, nice voice, steady, clear eyes, kinda proud, I thought, an' some handsome, he was," replied Jim Lash.

"Maybe I ought to think twice before taking a stranger into my family," said Belding, seriously. "Well, I guess he's all right, Laddy, being the cavalryman's friend. No bum or lunger? He must be all right?"

"Bum? Lunger? Say, didn't I tell you I shook hands with this boy an' was plumb glad to meet him?" demanded Laddy, with considerable heat. Manifestly he had been affronted. "Tom Beldin', he's a gentleman, an' he could lick you in—in half a second. How about that, Jim?"

"Less time," replied Lash. "Tom, here's my stand. Young Gale can have my hoss, my gun, anythin' of mine."

"Aw, I didn't mean to insult you, boys, don't mistake me," said Belding. "Course he's all right."

The object of this conversation lay quiet upon his bed, thrilling and amazed at being so championed by the cowboys, delighted with Belding's idea of employing him, and much amused with the quaint seriousness of the three.

"How's the young man?" called a woman's voice. It was kind and mellow and earnest.

Gale heard footsteps on flagstones.

"He's asleep yet, wife," replied Belding. "Guess he was pretty much knocked out. . . . I'll close the door there so we won't wake him."

There were slow, soft steps, then the door softly closed. But the fact scarcely made a perceptible difference in the sound of the voices outside.

"Laddy and Jim are going to stay," went on Belding. "It'll be like the old Panhandle days a little. I'm powerful glad to have the boys, Nellie. You know I meant to send to Casita to ask them. We'll see some trouble before the revolution is ended. I think I'll make this young man Gale an offer."

"He isn't a cowboy?" asked Mrs. Belding, quickly.

"No."

"Shore he'd make a darn good one," put in Laddy.

"What is he? Who is he? Where did he come from? Surely you must be—"

"Laddy swears he's all right," interrupted the husband. "That's enough reference for me. Isn't it enough for you?"

"Humph! Laddy knows a lot about young men, now doesn't he, especially strangers from the East? . . . Tom, you must be careful!"

"Wife, I'm only too glad to have a nervy young chap come along. What sense is there in your objection, if Jim and Laddy stick up for him?"

"But, Tom—he'll fall in love with Nell!" protested Mrs. Belding.

"Well, wouldn't that be regular? Doesn't every man who comes along fall in love with Nell? Hasn't it always happened? When she was a school-girl in Kansas didn't it happen? Didn't she have a hundred moon-eyed ninnies after her in Texas? I've had some peace out here in the desert, except when a Greaser or a prospector or a Yaqui would come along. Then same old story—in love with Nell!"

"But, Tom, Nell might fall in love with this young man!" exclaimed the wife, in distress.

"Laddy, Jim, didn't I tell you?" cried Belding. "I knew she'd say that. . . . My dear wife, I would be simply overcome with joy if Nell did fall in love once. Real good and hard! She's wilder than any antelope out there on the desert. Nell's nearly twenty now, and so far as we know she's never cared a rap for any fellow. And she's just as gay and full of the devil as she was at fourteen. Nell's as good and lovable as she is pretty, but I'm afraid she'll never grow into a woman while we live out in this lonely land. And you've always hated towns where there was a chance for the girl—just because you were afraid she'd fall in love. You've always been strange, even silly, about that. I've done my best for Nell—loved her as if she were my own daughter. I've changed many business plans to suit your whims. There are rough times ahead, maybe. I need men. I'll hire this chap Gale if he'll stay. Let Nell take her chance with him, just as she'll have to take chances with men when we get out of the desert. She'll be all the better for it."

"I hope Laddy's not mistaken in his opinion of this newcomer," replied Mrs. Belding, with a sigh of resignation.

"Shore I never made a mistake in my life figger'n' people," said Laddy, stoutly.

"Yes, you have, Laddy," replied Mrs. Belding. "You're wrong about Tom. . . . Well, supper is to be got. That young man and the girl will be starved. I'll go in now. If Nell happens around don't—don't flatter her, Laddy, like you did at dinner. Don't make her think of her looks."

Dick heard Mrs. Belding walk away.

"Shore she's powerful particular about that girl," observed Laddy. "Say, Tom, Nell knows she's pretty, doesn't she?"

"She's liable to find it out unless you shut up, Laddy. When you visited us out here some weeks ago, you kept paying cowboy compliments to her."

"An' it's your idee that cowboy compliments are plumb bad for girls?"

"Downright bad, Laddy, so my wife says."

"I'll be darned if I believe any girl can be hurt by a little sweet talk. It pleases 'em. . . . But say, Beldin', speaking of looks, have you got a peek yet at the Spanish girl?"

"Not in the light."

"Well, neither have I in daytime. I had enough by moonlight. Nell is some on looks, but I'm regretful passin' the ribbon to the lady from Mex. Jim, where are you?"

"My money's on Nell," replied Lash. "Gimme a girl with flesh an' color, an' blue eyes a-laughin'. Miss Castañeda is some peach, I'll not gainsay. But her face seemed too white. An' when she flashed those eyes on me, I thought I was shot! When she stood up there at first, thankin' us, I felt as if a—a princess was round somewhere. Now, Nell is kiddish an' sweet an'—"

"Chop it," interrupted Belding. "Here comes Nell now."

Dick's tingling ears took in the pattering of light footsteps, the rush of some one running.

"Here you are," cried a sweet, happy voice. "Dad, the Señorita is perfectly lovely. I've been peeping at her. She sleeps like—like death. She's so white. Oh, I hope she won't be ill."

"Shore she's only played out," said Laddy. "But she had spunk while it lasted. . . . I was just arguin' with Jim an' Tom about Miss Castañeda."

"Gracious! Why, she's beautiful. I never saw any one so beautiful. . . . How strange and sad, that about her! Tell me more, Laddy. You promised. I'm dying to know. I never hear anything in this awful place. Didn't you say the Señorita had a sweetheart?"

"Shore I did."

"And he's a cavalryman?"

"Yes."

"Is he the young man who came with you?"

"Nope. That fellow's the one who saved the girl from Rojas."

"Ah! Where is he, Laddy?"

"He's in there asleep."

"Is he hurt?"

"I reckon not. He walked about fifteen miles."

"Is he—nice, Laddy?"

"Shore."

"What is he like?"

"Well, I'm not long acquainted, never saw him by day, but I was some tolerable took with him. An' Jim here, Jim says the young man can have his gun an' his hoss."

"Wonderful! Laddy, what on earth did this stranger do to win you cowboys in just one night?"

"I'll shore have to tell you. Me an' Jim was watchin' a game of cards in the Del Sol saloon in Casita. That's across the line. We had acquaintances—four fellows from the Cross Bar outfit, where we worked a while back. This Del Sol is a billiard hall, saloon, restaurant, an' the like. An' it was full of Greasers. Some of Campo's rebels were there drinkin' an' playin' games. Then pretty soon in come Rojas with some of his outfit. They were packin' guns an' kept to themselves off to one side. I didn't give them a second look till Jim said he reckoned there was somethin' in the wind. Then, carelesslike, I began to peek at Rojas. They call Rojas the 'dandy rebel,' an' he shore looked the part. It made me sick to see him in all that lace an' glitter, knowin' him to be the cutthroat robber he is. It's no oncommon sight to see excited Greasers. They're all crazy. But this bandit was shore some agitated. He kept his men in a tight bunch round a table. He talked an' waved his hands. He was actually shakin'. His eyes had a wild glare. Now I figgered that trouble was brewin', most likely for the little Casita garrison. People seemed to think Campo an' Rojas would join forces to oust the federals. Jim thought Rojas's excitement was at the hatchin' of some plot. Anyway, we didn't join no card games, an' without pretendin' to, we was some watchful.

"A little while afterward I seen a fellow standin' in the restaurant door. He was a young American dressed in corduroys an' boots, like a prospector. You know it's no onusual fact to see prospectors in these parts. What made me think twice about this one was how big he seemed, how he filled up that door. He looked round the saloon, an' when he spotted Rojas he sorta jerked up. Then he pulled his slouch hat lopsided an' began to stagger down, down the steps. First off I made shore he was drunk. But I remembered he didn't seem drunk before. It was some queer. So I watched that young man.

"He reeled around the room like a fellow who was drunker'n a lord. Nobody but me seemed to notice him. Then he began to stumble over pool-players an' get his feet tangled up in chairs an' bump against tables. He got some pretty hard looks. He came round our way, an' all of a sudden he seen us cowboys. He gave another start, like the one when he first seen Rojas, then he made for us. I tipped Jim off that some-thin' was doin'.

"When he got close he straightened up, put back his slouch hat, an' looked at us. Then I saw his face. It sorta electrified yours truly. It was white, with veins standin' out an' eyes flamin'—a face of fury. I was plumb amazed, didn't know what to think. Then this queer young man shot some cool, polite words at me an' Jim.

"He was only bluffin' at bein' drunk—he meant to rush Rojas, to start a rough house. The bandit was after a girl. This girl was in the hotel, an' she was the sweetheart of a soldier, the young fellow's friend. The hotel was watched by Rojas's guards, an' the plan was to make a fuss an' get the girl away in the excitement. Well, Jim an' me got a hint of our bein' Americans—that cowboys generally had a name for loyalty to women. Then this amazin' chap—you can't imagine how scornful—said for me an' Jim to watch him.

"Before I could catch my breath an' figger out what he meant by 'rush' an' 'rough house' he had knocked over a table an' crowded some Greaser half off the map. One little funny man leaped up like a wild monkey an' began to screech. An' in another second he was in the air upside down. When he lit, he laid there. Then, quicker'n I can tell you, the young man dove at Rojas. Like a mad steer on the rampage he charged Rojas an' his men. The whole outfit went down—smash! I figgered then what 'rush' meant. The young fellow came up out of the pile with Rojas, an' just like I'd sling an empty sack along the floor he sent the bandit. But swift as that went he was on top of Rojas before the chairs an' tables had stopped rollin'.

"I woke up then, an' made for the center of the room, Jim with me. I began to shoot out the lamps. Jim throwed his guns on the crazy rebels, an' I was afraid there'd be blood spilled before I could get the room dark. Bein' shore busy, I lost sight of the young fellow for a second or so, an' when I got an eye free for him I seen a Greaser about to knife him. Think I was some considerate of the Greaser by only shootin' his arm off. Then I cracked the last lamp, an' in the hullabaloo me an' Jim vamoosed.

"We made tracks for our hosses an' packs, an' was hittin' the San Felipe road when we run right plumb into the young man. Well, he said his name was Gale—Dick Gale. The girl was with him safe an' well; but her sweetheart, the soldier bein' away without leave, had to go back sudden. There shore was some trouble, for Jim an' me heard shootin'. Gale said he had no money, no friends, was a stranger in a desert country; an' he was distracted to know how to help the girl. So me an' Jim started off with them for San Felipe, got switched, an' then we headed for the Rio Forlorn."

"Oh, I think he was perfectly splendid!" exclaimed the girl.

"Shore he was. Only, Nell, you can't lay no claim to bein' the original discoverer of that fact."

"But, Laddy, you haven't told me what he looks like."

At this juncture Dick Gale felt it absolutely impossible for him to play the eavesdropper any longer. Quietly he rolled out of bed. The voices still sounded close outside, and it was only by effort that he kept from further listening. Belding's kindly interest, Laddy's blunt and sincere cowboy eulogy, the girl's sweet eagerness and praise—these warmed Gale's heart. He had fallen among simple people, into whose lives the advent of an unknown man was welcome. He found himself in a singularly agitated mood. The excitement, the thrill, the difference felt in himself, experienced the preceding night, had extended on into his present. And the possibilities suggested by the conversation he had unwittingly overheard added sufficiently to the other feelings to put him into a peculiarly receptive state of mind. He was wild to be one of Belding's rangers. The idea of riding a horse in the open desert, with a dangerous duty to perform, seemed to strike him with an appealing force. Something within him went out to the cowboys, to this blunt and kind Belding. He was afraid to meet the girl. If every man who came along fell in love with this sweet-voiced Nell, then what hope had he to escape—now, when his whole inner awakening betokened a change of spirit, hope, a finding of real worth, real good, real power in himself? He did not understand wholly; yet he felt ready to ride, to fight, to love the desert, to love these outdoor men, to love a woman. That beautiful Spanish girl had spoken to something dead in him, and it had quickened to life. The sweet voice of an audacious, unseen girl warned him that presently a still more wonderful thing would happen to him.

Gale imagined he made noise enough as he clumsily pulled on his boots; yet the voices, split by a merry laugh, kept on murmuring outside the door. It was awkward for him, having only one hand available to lace up his boots. He looked out of the window. Evidently this was at the end of the house. There was a flagstone walk, beside which ran a ditch full of swift, muddy water. It made a pleasant sound. There were trees strange of form and color to him. He heard bees, birds, chickens, saw the red of roses and green of grass. Then he saw, close to the wall, a tub full of water, and a bench upon which lay basin, soap, towel, comb, and brush. The window was also a door, for under it there was a step.

Gale hesitated a moment, then went out. He stepped naturally, hoping and expecting that the cowboys would hear him. But nobody came. Awkwardly, with his left hand, he washed his face. Upon a nail in the wall hung a little mirror, by the aid of which Dick combed and brushed his hair. He imagined he looked a most haggard wretch. With that he faced forward, meaning to go round the corner of the house to greet the cowboys and these newfound friends.

Dick had taken but one step when he was halted by laughter and the patter of light feet.

From close around the corner pealed out that sweet voice. "Dad, you'll have your wish, and Mama will be wild!"

Dick saw a little foot sweep into view, a white dress, then the swiftly moving form of a girl. She was looking backward.

"Dad, I shall fall in love with your new ranger. I will—I have—"

Then she plumped squarely into Dick's arms.

She started back violently.

Dick saw a fair face and dark-blue, audaciously flashing eyes. Swift as lightning their expression changed to surprise, fear, wonder. For an instant they were level with Dick's grave questioning. Suddenly, sweetly, she blushed.

"Oh-h!" she faltered.

Then the blush turned to a scarlet fire. She whirled past him, and like a white gleam was gone.

Dick became conscious of the quickened beating of his heart. He experienced a singular exhilaration. That moment had been the one for which he had been ripe, the event upon which strange circumstances had been rushing him.

With a couple of strides he turned the corner. Laddy and Lash were there talking to a man of burly form. Seen by day, both cowboys were gray-haired, red-skinned, and weather-beaten, with lean, sharp features, and gray eyes so much alike that they might have been brothers.

"Hello, there's the young fellow," spoke up the burly man. "Mr. Gale, I'm glad to meet you. My name's Belding."

His greeting was as warm as his handclasp was long and hard. Gale saw a heavy man of medium height. His head was large and covered with grizzled locks. He wore a short-cropped mustache and chin beard. His skin was brown, and his dark eyes beamed with a genial light.

The cowboys were as cordial as if Dick had been their friend for years.

"Young man, did you run into anything as you came out?" asked Belding, with twinkling eyes.

"Why, yes; I met something white and swift flying by," replied Dick.

"Did she see you?" asked Laddy.

"I think so; but she didn't wait for me to introduce myself."

"That was Nell Burton, my girl—stepdaughter, I should say," said Belding. "She's sure some whirlwind, as Laddy calls her. Come, let's go in and meet the wife."

The house was long, like a barracks, with porch extending all the way, and doors every dozen paces. When Dick was ushered into a sitting-room, he was amazed at the light and comfort. This room had two big windows and a door opening into a patio, where there were luxuriant grass, roses in bloom, and flowering trees. He heard a slow splashing of water.

In Mrs. Belding, Gale found a woman of noble proportions and striking appearance. Her hair was white. She had a strong, serious, well-lined face that bore haunting evidences of past beauty. The gaze she bent upon him was almost piercing in its intensity. Her greeting, which seemed to Dick rather slow in coming, was kind though not cordial. Gale's first thought, after he had thanked these good people for their hospitality, was to inquire about Mercedes. He was informed that the Spanish girl had awakened with a considerable fever and nervousness. When, however, her anxiety had been allayed and her thirst relieved, she had fallen asleep again. Mrs. Belding said the girl had suffered no great hardship, other than mental, and would very soon be rested and well.

"Now, Gale," said Belding, when his wife had excused herself to get supper, "the boys, Jim and Laddy, told me about you and the mix-up at Casita. I'll be glad to take care of the girl till it's safe for your soldier friend to get her out of the country. That won't be very soon, don't mistake me. . . . I don't want to seem overcurious about you—Laddy has interested me in you—and straight out I'd like to know what you propose to do now."

"I haven't any plans," replied Dick; and, taking the moment as propitious, he decided to speak frankly concerning himself. "I just drifted down here. My home is in Chicago. When I left school some years ago—I'm twenty-five now—I went to work for my father. He's—he has business interests there. I tried all kinds of inside jobs. I couldn't please my father. I guess I put no real heart in my work. The fact was I didn't know how to work. The governor and I didn't exactly quarrel; but he hurt my feelings, and I quit. Six months or more ago I came West, and have knocked about from Wyoming southwest to the border. I tried to find congenial work, but nothing came my way. To tell you frankly, Mr. Belding, I suppose I didn't much care. I believe, though, that all the time I didn't know what I wanted. I've learned—well, just lately—"

"What do you want to do?" interposed Belding.

"I want a man's job. I want to do things with my hands. I want action. I want to be outdoors."

Belding nodded his head as if he understood that, and he began to speak again, cut something short, then went on, hesitatingly:

"Gale—you could go home again—to the old man—it'd be all right?"

"Mr. Belding, there's nothing shady in my past. The governor would be glad to have me home. That's the only consolation I've got. But I'm not going. I'm broke. I won't be a tramp. And it's up to me to do something."

"How'd you like to be a border ranger?" asked Belding, laying a hand on Dick's knee. "Part of my job here is United States Inspector of Immigration. I've got that boundary line to patrol—to keep out Chinks and Japs. This revolution has added complications, and I'm looking for smugglers and raiders here any day. You'll not be hired by the U.S. You'll simply be my ranger, same as Laddy and Jim, who have promised to work for me. I'll pay you well, give you a room here, furnish everything down to guns, and the finest horse you ever saw in your life. Your job won't be safe and healthy, sometimes, but it'll be a man's job—don't mistake me! You can gamble on having things to do outdoors. Now, what do you say?"

"I accept, and I thank you—I can't say how much," replied Gale, earnestly.

"Good! That's settled. Let's go out and tell Laddy and Jim."

Both boys expressed satisfaction at the turn of affairs, and then with Belding they set out to take Gale around the ranch. The house and several outbuildings were constructed of adobe, which, according to Belding, retained the summer heat on into winter, and the winter cold on into summer. These gray-red mud habitations were hideous to look at, and this fact, perhaps, made their really comfortable interiors more vividly a contrast. The wide grounds were covered with luxuriant grass and flowers and different kinds of trees. Gale's interest led him to ask about fig trees and pomegranates, and especially about a beautiful specimen that Belding called *palo verde*.

Belding explained that the luxuriance of this desert place was owing to a few springs and the dammed-up waters of the Rio Forlorn. Before he had come to the oasis it had been inhabited by a Papago Indian tribe and a few peon families. The oasis lay in an arroyo a mile wide, and sloped southwest for some ten miles or more. The river went dry most of the year; but enough water was stored in flood season to irrigate the gardens and alfalfa fields.

"I've got one never-failing spring on my place," said Belding. "Fine, sweet water! You know what that means in the desert. I like this oasis. The longer I live here the better I like it. There's not a spot in southern Arizona that'll compare with this valley for water or grass or wood. It's beautiful and healthy. Forlorn and lonely, yes, especially for women like my wife and Nell; but I like it. . . . And between you and me, boys, I've got something up my sleeve. There's gold dust in the arroyos, and there's mineral up in the mountains. If we only had water! This hamlet has steadily grown since I took up a station here. Why, Casita is no place beside Forlorn River. Pretty soon the Southern Pacific will shoot a railroad branch out here. There are possibilities, and I want you boys to stay with me and get in on the ground floor. I wish this rebel war was over. . . . Well, here are the corrals and the fields. Gale, take a look at that bunch of horses!"

Belding's last remark was made as he led his companions out of shady gardens into the open. Gale saw an adobe shed and a huge pen fenced by strangely twisted and contorted branches or trunks of mesquite, and, beyond these, wide, flat fields, green—a dark, rich green—and dotted with beautiful horses. There were whites and blacks, and bays and grays. In his admiration Gale searched his memory to see if he could remember the like of these magnificent animals, and had to admit that the only ones he could compare with them were the Arabian steeds.

"Every rancher loves his horses," said Belding. "When I was in the Panhandle I had some fine stock. But these are Mexican. They came from Durango, where they were bred. Mexican horses are the finest in the world, bar none."

"Shore I reckon I savvy why you don't sleep nights," drawled Laddy. "I see a Greaser out there—no, it's an Indian."

"That's my Papago herdsman. I keep watch over the horses now day and night. Lord, how I'd hate to have Rojas or Salazar any of those bandit rebels—find my horses! . . . Gale, can you ride?"

Dick modestly replied that he could, according to the Eastern idea of horsemanship.

"You don't need to be half horse to ride one of that bunch. But over there in the other field I've iron-jawed bronchos I wouldn't want you to tackle—except to see the fun. I've an outlaw I'll gamble even Laddy can't ride."

"So. How much'll you gamble?" asked Laddy, instantly.

The ringing of a bell, which Belding said was a call to supper, turned the men back toward the house. Facing that way, Gale saw dark, beetling ridges rising from the oasis and leading up to bare, black mountains. He had heard Belding call them No Name Mountains, and somehow the appellation suited those lofty, mysterious, frowning peaks.

It was not until they reached the house and were about to go in that Belding chanced to discover Gale's crippled hand.

"What an awful hand!" he exclaimed. "Where the devil did you get that?"

"I stove in my knuckles on Rojas," replied Dick.

"You did that in one punch? Say, I'm glad it wasn't me you hit! Why didn't you tell me? That's a bad hand. Those cuts are full of dirt and sand. Inflammation's setting in. It's got to be dressed. Nell!" he called.

There was no answer. He called again, louder.

"Mother, where's the girl?"

"She's there in the dining room," replied Mrs. Belding.

"Did she hear me?" he inquired, impatiently.

"Of course."

"*Nell!*" roared Belding.

This brought results. Dick saw a glimpse of golden hair and a white dress in the door. But they were not visible longer than a second.

"Dad, what's the matter?" asked a voice that was still as sweet as formerly, but now rather small and constrained.

"Bring the antiseptics, cotton, bandages—and things out here. Hurry now."

Belding fetched a pail of water and a basin from the kitchen. His wife followed him out, and, upon seeing Dick's hand, was all solicitude. Then Dick heard light, quick footsteps, but he did not look up.

"Nell, this is Mr. Gale—Dick Gale, who came with the boys last night," said Belding. "He's got an awful hand. Got it punching that greaser Rojas. I want you to dress it. . . . Gale, this is my stepdaughter, Nell Burton, of whom I spoke. She's some good when there's somebody sick or hurt. Shove out your fist, my boy, and let her get at it. Supper's nearly ready."

Dick felt that same strange, quickening heart throb, yet he had never been cooler in his life. More than anything else in the world he wanted to look at Nell Burton; however, divining that the situation might be embarrassing to her, he refrained from looking up. She began to bathe his injured knuckles. He noted the softness, the deftness of her touch, and then it seemed her fingers were not quite as steady as they might have been. Still, in a moment they appeared to become surer in their work. She had beautiful hands, not too large, though certainly not small, and they were strong, brown, supple. He observed next, with stealthy, upward-stealing glance, that she had rolled up her sleeves, exposing fine, round arms graceful in line. Her skin was brown—no, it was more gold than brown. It had a wonderful clear tint. Dick stoically lowered his eyes then, putting off as long as possible the alluring moment when he was to look into her face. That would be a fateful moment. He played with a certain strange joy of anticipation. When, however, she sat down beside him and rested his injured hand in her lap as she cut bandages, she was so thrillingly near that he yielded to an irrepressible desire to look up. She had a sweet, fair face warmly tinted with that same healthy golden-brown sunburn. Her hair was light gold and abundant, a waving mass. Her eyes were shaded by long, downcast lashes, yet through them he caught a gleam of blue.

Despite the stir within him, Gale, seeing she was now absorbed in her task, critically studied her with a second closer gaze. She was a sweet, wholesome, joyous, pretty girl.

"Shore it musta hurt?" inquired Laddy, who sat an interested spectator.

"Yes, I confess it did," replied Dick, slowly, with his eyes on Nell's face. "But I didn't mind."

The girl's lashes swept up swiftly in surprise. She had taken his words literally. But the dark-blue eyes met his for only a fleeting second. Then the warm tint in her cheeks turned as red as her lips. Hurriedly she finished tying the bandage and rose to her feet.

"I thank you," said Gale, also rising.

With that Belding appeared in the doorway, and, finding the operation concluded, called them in to supper. Dick had the use of only one arm, and he certainly was keenly aware of the shy, silent girl across the table; but in spite of these considerable handicaps he eclipsed both hungry cowboys in the assault upon Mrs. Belding's bounteous supper. Belding talked, the cowboys talked more or less, Mrs. Belding put in a word now and then, and Dick managed to find brief intervals when it was possible for him to say yes or no. He observed gratefully that no one round the table seemed to be aware of his enormous appetite.

After supper, having a favorable opportunity when for a moment no one was at hand, Dick went out through the yard, past the gardens and fields, and climbed the first knoll. From that vantage point he looked out over the little hamlet, somewhat to his right, and was surprised at its extent, its considerable number of adobe houses. The overhanging mountains, ragged and darkened, a great heave of splintered, sundered rock, rather chilled and affronted him.

Westward the setting sun gilded a spiked, frost-colored, limitless expanse of desert. It awed Gale. Everywhere rose blunt, broken ranges or isolated groups of mountains. Yet the desert stretched away down between and beyond them. When the sun set and Gale could not see so far, he felt a relief.

That grand and austere attraction of distance gone, he saw the desert nearer at hand—the valley at his feet. What a strange, gray, somber place! There was a lighter strip of gray winding down between darker hues. This he realized presently was the riverbed, and he saw how the pools of water narrowed and diminished in size till they lost themselves in gray sand. This was the rainy season near its end, and here a little river struggled hopelessly, forlornly to live in the desert. He received a potent impression of the nature of that blasted age-worn waste which he had divined was to give him strength and work and love.

CHAPTER 5

A DESERT ROSE

Belding assigned Dick to a little room which had no windows but two doors, one opening into the patio, the other into the yard on the west side of the house. It contained only the barest necessities for comfort. Dick mentioned the baggage he had left in the hotel at Casita, and it was Belding's opinion that to try to recover this property would be rather risky; at the moment Richard Gale was probably not popular with the Mexicans at Casita. So Dick bade good-by to fine suits of clothes and linen with a feeling that, as he had said farewell to an idle and useless past, it was just as well not to have any old luxuries as reminders. As he possessed, however, not a thing save the clothes on his back, and not even a handkerchief, he expressed regret that he had come to Forlorn River a beggar.

"Beggar hell!" exploded Belding, with his eyes snapping in the lamp-light. "Money's the last thing we think of out here. All the same, Gale, if you stick you'll be rich."

"It wouldn't surprise me," replied Dick, thoughtfully. But he was not thinking of material wealth. Then, as he viewed his stained and torn shirt, he laughed and said: "Belding, while I'm getting rich I'd like to have some respectable clothes."

"We've a little Mex store in town, and what you can't get there the womenfolks will make for you."

When Dick lay down he was dully conscious of pain and headache, that he did not feel well. Despite this, and a mind thronging with memories and anticipations, he succumbed to weariness and soon fell asleep.

It was light when he awoke, but a strange brightness seen through what seemed blurred eyes. A moment passed before his mind worked clearly, and then he had to make an effort to think. He was dizzy. When he essayed to lift his right arm, an excruciating pain made him desist. Then he discovered that his arm was badly swollen, and the hand had burst its bandages. The injured member was red, angry, inflamed, and twice its normal size. He felt hot all over, and a raging headache consumed him.

Belding came stamping into the room.

"Hello, Dick. Do you know it's late? How's the busted fist this morning?"

Dick tried to sit up, but his effort was a failure. He got about half up, then felt himself weakly sliding back.

"I guess—I'm pretty sick," he said.

He saw Belding lean over him, feel his face, and speak, and then everything seemed to drift, not into darkness, but into some region where he had dim perceptions of gray moving things, and of voices that were remote. Then there came an interval when all was blank. He knew not whether it was one of minutes or hours, but after it he had a clearer mind. He slept, awakened during nighttime, and slept again. When he again unclosed his eyes the room was sunny, and cool with a fragrant breeze that blew through the open door. Dick felt better; but he had no particular desire to move or talk or eat. He had, however, a burning thirst. Mrs. Belding visited him often; her husband came in several times, and once Nell slipped in noiselessly. Even this last event aroused no interest in Dick.

On the next day he was very much improved.

"We've been afraid of blood poisoning," said Belding. "But my wife thinks the danger's past. You'll have to rest that arm for a while."

Ladd and Jim came peeping in at the door.

"Come in, boys. He can have company—the more the better—if it'll keep him content. He mustn't move, that's all."

The cowboys entered, slow, easy, cool, kind-voiced.

"Shore it's tough," said Ladd, after he had greeted Dick. "You look used up."

Jim Lash wagged his half-bald, sunburned head. "Musta been more'n tough for Rojas."

"Gale, Laddy tells me one of our neighbors, fellow named Carter, is going to Casita," put in Belding. "Here's a chance to get word to your friend the soldier."

"Oh, that will be fine!" exclaimed Dick. "I declare I'd forgotten Thorne. . . . How is Miss Castañeda? I hope—"

"She's all right, Gale. Been up and around the patio for two days. Like all the Spanish—the real thing—she's made of Damascus steel. We've been getting acquainted. She and Nell made friends at once. I'll call them in."

He closed the door leading out into the yard, explaining that he did not want to take chances of Mercedes's presence becoming known to neighbors. Then he went to the patio and called.

Both girls came in, Mercedes leading. Like Nell, she wore white, and she had a red rose in her hand. Dick would scarcely have recognized anything about her except her eyes and the way she carried her little head, and her beauty burst upon him strange and anew. She was swift, impulsive in her movements to reach his side.

"Señor, I am so sorry you were ill—so happy you are better."

Dick greeted her, offering his left hand, gravely apologizing for the fact that, owing to a late infirmity, he could not offer the right. Her smile exquisitely combined sympathy, gratitude, admiration. Then Dick spoke to Nell, likewise offering his hand, which she took shyly. Her reply was a murmured, unintelligible one; but her eyes were glad, and the tint in her cheeks threatened to rival the hue of the rose she carried.

Everybody chatted then, except Nell, who had apparently lost her voice. Presently Dick remembered to speak of the matter of getting news to Thorne.

"Señor, may I write to him? Will someone take a letter? . . . I shall hear from him!" she said; and her white hands emphasized her words.

"Assuredly. I guess poor Thorne is almost crazy. I'll write to him. . . . No, I can't with this crippled hand."

"That'll be all right, Gale," said Belding. "Nell will write for you. She writes all my letters."

So Belding arranged it, and Mercedes flew away to her room to write, while Nell fetched pen and paper and seated herself beside Gale's bed to take his dictation.

What with watching Nell and trying to catch her glance, and listening to Belding's talk with the cowboys, Dick was hard put to it to dictate any kind of a creditable letter. Nell met his gaze once, then no more. The color came and went in her cheeks, and sometimes when he told her to write so and so, there was a demure smile on her lips. She was laughing at him. And Belding was talking over the risks involved in a trip to Casita.

"Shore I'll ride in with the letters," Ladd said.

"No you won't," replied Belding. "That bandit outfit will be laying for you."

"Well, I reckon if they was I wouldn't be oncommon grieved."

"I'll tell you, boys, I'll ride in myself with Carter. There's business I can see to, and I'm curious to know what the rebels are doing. Laddy, keep one eye open while I'm gone. See the horses are locked up. . . . Gale, I'm going to Casita myself. Ought to get back to-morrow sometime. I'll be ready to start in an hour. Have your letter ready. And say—if you want to write home it's a chance. Sometimes we don't go to the P.O. in a month."

He tramped out, followed by the tall cowboys, and then Dick was enabled to bring his letter to a close. Mercedes came back, and her eyes were shining. Dick imagined a letter received from her would be something of an event for a fellow. Then, remembering Belding's suggestion, he decided to profit by it.

"May I trouble you to write another for me?" asked Dick, as he received the letter from Nell.

"It's no trouble, I'm sure—I'd be pleased," she replied.

That was altogether a wonderful speech of hers, Dick thought, because the words were the first coherent ones she had spoken to him.

"May I stay?" asked Mercedes, smiling.

"By all means," he answered, and then he settled back and began.

Presently Gale paused, partly because of genuine emotion, and stole a look from under his hand at Nell. She wrote swiftly, and her downcast face seemed to be softer in its expression of sweetness. If she had in the very least been drawn to him—But that was absurd—impossible!

When Dick finished dictating, his eyes were upon Mercedes, who sat smilingly curious and sympathetic. How responsive she was! He heard the hasty scratch of Nell's pen. He looked at Nell. Presently she rose, holding out his letter. He was just in time to see a wave of red recede from her face. She gave him one swift gaze, unconscious, searching, then averted it and turned away. She left the room with Mercedes before he could express his thanks.

But that strange, speaking flash of eyes remained to haunt and torment Gale. It was indescribably sweet, and provocative of thoughts that he believed were wild without warrant. Something within him danced for very joy, and the next instant he was conscious of wistful doubt, a gravity that he could not understand. It dawned upon him that for the brief instant when Nell had met his gaze she had lost her shyness. It was a woman's questioning eyes that had pierced through him.

During the rest of the day Gale was content to lie still on his bed thinking and dreaming, dozing at intervals, and watching the lights change upon the mountain peaks, feeling the warm, fragrant desert wind that blew in upon him. He seemed to have lost the faculty of estimating time. A long while, strong in its effect upon him, appeared to have passed since he had met Thorne. He accepted things as he felt them, and repudiated his intelligence. His old inquisitive habit of mind returned. Did he love Nell? Was he only attracted for the moment? What was the use of worrying about her or himself? He refused to answer, and deliberately gave himself up to dreams of her sweet face and of that last dark-blue glance.

Next day he believed he was well enough to leave his room; but Mrs. Belding would not permit him to do so. She was kind, soft-handed, motherly, and she was always coming in to minister to his comfort. This attention was sincere, not in the least forced; yet Gale felt that the friendliness so manifest in the others of the household did not extend to her. He was conscious of something that a little thought persuaded him was antagonism. It surprised and hurt him. He had never been much of a success with girls and young married women, but their mothers and old people had generally been fond of him. Still, though Mrs. Belding's hair was snow-white, she did not impress him as being old. He reflected that there might come a time when it would be desirable, far beyond any ground of everyday friendly kindliness, to have Mrs. Belding be well disposed toward him. So he thought about her, and pondered how to make her like him. It did not take very long for Dick to discover that he liked her. Her face, except when she smiled, was thoughtful and sad. But it seemed too strong, too intense, too nobly lined. It was a face to make one serious. Like a haunting shadow, like a phantom of happier years, the sweetness of Nell's face was there, and infinitely more of beauty than had been transmitted to the daughter. Dick believed Mrs. Belding's friendship and motherly love were worth much striving to win, entirely aside from any more selfish motive. He decided both would be hard to get. Often he felt her deep, penetrating gaze upon him; and, though this in no wise embarrassed him—for he had no shameful secrets of past or present—it showed him how useless it would be to try to conceal anything from her. Naturally, on first impulse, he wanted to hide his interest in the daughter; but he resolved to be absolutely frank and true, and through that win or lose. Moreover, if Mrs. Belding asked him any questions about his home, his family, his connections, he would not avoid direct and truthful answers.

Toward evening Gale heard the tramp of horses and Belding's hearty voice. Presently the rancher strode in upon Gale, shaking the gray dust from his broad shoulders and waving a letter.

"Hello, Dick! Good news and bad!" he said, putting the letter in Dick's hand. "Had no trouble finding your friend Thorne. Looked like he'd been drunk for a week! Say, he nearly threw a fit. I never saw a fellow so wild with joy. He made sure you and Mercedes were lost in the desert. He wrote two letters which I brought. Don't mistake me, boy, it was some fun with Mercedes just now. I teased her, wouldn't give her the letter. You ought to have seen her eyes. If ever you see a black-and-white desert hawk swoop down upon a quail, then you'll know how Mercedes pounced upon her letter. . . . Well, Casita is one hell of a place these days. I tried to get your baggage, and think I made a mistake. We're going to see travel toward Forlorn River. The federal garrison got reinforcements from somewhere, and is holding out. There's been fighting for three days. The rebels have a string of flat railroad cars, all iron, and they ran this up within range of the barricades. They've got some machine guns, and they're going to lick the federals sure. There are dead soldiers in the ditches, Mexican noncombatants lying dead in the streets—and buzzards everywhere! It's reported that Campo, the rebel leader, is on the way up from Sinaloa, and Huerta, a federal general, is coming to relieve the garrison. I don't take much stock in reports. But there's hell in Casita, all right."

"Do you think we'll have trouble out here?" asked Dick, excitedly.

"Sure. Some kind of trouble sooner or later," replied Belding, gloomily. "Why, you can stand on my ranch and step over into Mexico. Laddy says we'll lose horses and other stock in night raids. Jim Lash doesn't look for any worse. But Jim isn't as well acquainted with Greasers as I am. Anyway, my boy, as soon as you can hold a bridle and a gun you'll be on the job, don't mistake me."

"With Laddy and Jim?" asked Dick, trying to be cool.

"Sure. With them and me, and by yourself."

Dick drew a deep breath, and even after Belding had departed he forgot for a moment about the letter in his hand. Then he unfolded the paper and read:

Dear Dick,

You've more than saved my life. To the end of my days you'll be the one man to whom I owe everything. Words fail to express my feelings.

This must be a brief note. Belding is waiting, and I used up most of the time writing to Mercedes. I like Belding. He was not unknown to me, though I never met or saw him before. You'll be interested to learn that he's the unadulterated article, the real Western goods. I've heard of some of his stunts, and they made my hair curl. Dick, your luck is staggering. The way Belding spoke of you was great. But you deserve it, old man.

I'm leaving Mercedes in your charge, subject, of course, to advice from Belding. Take care of her, Dick, for my life is wrapped up in her. By all means keep her from being seen by Mexicans. We are sitting tight here—nothing doing. If some action doesn't come soon it'll be darned strange. Things are centering this way. There's scrapping right along, and people have begun to move. We're still patrolling the line eastward of Casita. It'll be impossible to keep any tab on the line west of Casita, for it's too rough. That cactus desert is awful. Cowboys or rangers with desert-bred horses might keep raiders and smugglers from crossing. But if cavalrymen could stand that waterless wilderness, which I doubt much, their horses would drop under them.

If things do quiet down before my commission expires, I'll get leave of absence, run out to Forlorn River, marry my beautiful Spanish princess, and take her to a civilized country, where, I opine, every son of a gun who sees her will lose his head, and drive me mad. It's my great luck, old pal, that you are a fellow who never seemed to care about pretty girls. So you won't give me the double cross and run off with Mercedes—carry her off, like the villain in the play, I mean.

That reminds me of Rojas. Oh, Dick, it was glorious! You didn't do anything to the Dandy Rebel! Not at all! You merely caressed him—gently moved him to one side. Dick, harken to these glad words: Rojas is in the hospital. I was interested to inquire. He had a smashed finger, a dislocated collarbone, three broken ribs, and a fearful gash on his face. He'll be in the hospital for a month. Dick, when I meet that pig-headed dad of yours I'm going to give him the surprise of his life.

Send me a line whenever any one comes in from F.R., and inclose Mercedes's letter in yours. Take care of her, Dick, and may the future hold in store for you some of the sweetness I know now!

Faithfully yours,
Thorne.

Dick reread the letter, then folded it and placed it under his pillow.

"Never cared for pretty girls, huh?" he soliloquized. "George, I never saw any till I struck Southern Arizona! Guess I'd better make up for lost time."

While he was eating his supper, with appetite rapidly returning to normal, Ladd and Jim came in, bowing their tall heads to enter the door. Their friendly advances were singularly welcome to Gale, but he was still backward. He allowed himself to show that he was glad to see them, and he listened. Jim Lash had heard from Belding the result of the mauling given to Rojas by Dick. And Jim talked about what a grand thing that was. Ladd had a good deal to say about Belding's horses. It took no keen judge of human nature to see that horses constituted Ladd's ruling passion.

"I've had wimmen go back on me, but never no hoss!" declared Ladd, and manifestly that was a controlling truth with him.

"Shore it's a cinch Beldin' is agoin' to lose some of them hosses," he said. "You can search me if I don't think there'll be more doin' on the border here than along the Rio Grande. We're just the same as on Greaser soil. Mebbe we don't stand no such chance of bein' shot up as we would across the line. But who's goin' to give up his hosses without a fight? Half the time when Beldin's stock is out of the alfalfa it's grazin' over the line. He thinks he's careful about them hosses, but he ain't."

"Look a-here, Laddy; you cain't believe all you hear," replied Jim, seriously. "I reckon we mightn't have any trouble."

"Back up, Jim. Shore you're standin' on your bridle. I ain't goin' much on reports. Remember that American we met in Casita, the prospector who'd just gotten out of Sonora? He had some story, he had. Swore he'd killed seventeen Greasers breakin' through the rebel line round the mine where he an' other Americans were corralled. The next day when I met him again, he was drunk, an' then he told me he'd shot thirty Greasers. The chances are he did kill some. But reports are exaggerated. There are miners fightin' for life down in Sonora, you can gamble on that. An' the truth is bad enough. Take Rojas's harryin' of the Señorita, for instance. Can you beat that? Shore, Jim, there's more doin' than the raidin' of a few hosses. An' Forlorn River is goin' to get hers!"

Another dawn found Gale so much recovered that he arose and looked after himself, not, however, without considerable difficulty and rather disheartening twinges of pain.

Some time during the morning he heard the girls in the patio and called to ask if he might join them. He received one response, a mellow, "Sí, señor." It was not as much as he wanted, but considering that it was enough, he went out. He had not as yet visited the patio, and surprise and delight were in store for him. He found himself lost in a labyrinth of green and rose-bordered walks. He strolled around, discovering that the patio was a courtyard, open at an end; but he failed to discover the young ladies. So he called again. The answer came from the center of the square. After stooping to get under shrubs and wading through bushes he entered an open sandy circle, full of magnificent and murderous cactus plants, strange to him. On the other side, in the shade of a beautiful tree, he found the girls, Mercedes sitting in a hammock, Nell upon a blanket.

"What a beautiful tree!" he exclaimed. "I never saw one like that. What is it?"

"*Palo verde*," replied Nell.

"Señor, *palo verde* means 'green tree,'" added Mercedes.

This desert tree, which had struck Dick as so new and strange and beautiful, was not striking on account of size, for it was small, scarcely reaching higher than the roof; but rather because of its exquisite color of green, trunk and branch alike, and owing to the odd fact that it seemed not to possess leaves. All the tree from ground to tiny flat twigs was a soft polished green. It bore no thorns.

Right then and there began Dick's education in desert growths; and he felt that even if he had not had such charming teachers he would still have been absorbed. For the patio was full of desert wonders. A twisting-bunked tree with full foliage of small gray leaves Nell called a mesquite. Then Dick remembered the name, and now he saw where the desert got its pale-gray color. A huge, lofty, fluted column of green was a *saguaro*, or giant cactus. Another odd-shaped cactus, resembling the legs of an inverted devil-fish, bore the name *ocatillo*. Each branch rose high and symmetrical, furnished with sharp blades that seemed to be at once leaves and thorns. Yet another cactus interested Gale, and it looked like a huge, low barrel covered with green-ribbed cloth and long thorns. This was the *bisnaga*, or barrel cactus. According to Nell and Mercedes, this plant was a happy exception to its desert neighbors, for it secreted water which had many times saved the lives of men. Last of the cacti to attract Gale, and the one to make him shiver, was a low plant, consisting of stem and many rounded protuberances of a frosty, steely white, and covered with long, murderous spikes. From this plant the desert got its frosty glitter. It was as stiff, as unyielding as steel, and bore the name *cholla*.

Dick's enthusiasm was contagious, and his earnest desire to learn was flattering to his teachers. When it came to assimilating Spanish, however, he did not appear to be so apt a pupil. He managed, after many trials, to acquire *"buenos días"* and *"buenos tardes,"* and *"señorita"* and *"gracias,"* and a few other short terms. Dick was indeed eager to get a little smattering of Spanish, and perhaps he was not really quite so stupid as he pretended to be. It was delightful to be taught by a beautiful Spaniard who was so gracious and intense and magnetic of personality, and by a sweet American girl who moment by moment forgot her shyness. Gale wished to prolong the lessons.

So that was the beginning of many afternoons in which he learned desert lore and Spanish verbs, and something else that he dared not name.

Nell Burton had never shown to Gale that daring side of her character which had been so suggestively defined in Belding's terse description and Ladd's encomiums, and in her own audacious speech and merry laugh and flashing eye of that never-to-be-forgotten first meeting. She might have been an entirely different girl. But Gale remembered; and when the ice had been somewhat broken between them, he was always trying to surprise her into her real self. There were moments that fairly made him tingle with expectation. Yet he saw little more than a ghost of her vivacity, and never a gleam of that individuality which Belding had called a devil. On the few occasions that Dick had been left alone with her in the patio Nell had grown suddenly unresponsive and restrained, or she had left him on some transparent pretext. On the last occasion Mercedes returned to find Dick staring disconsolately at the rose-bordered path, where Nell had evidently vanished. The Spanish girl was wonderful in her divination.

"Señor Dick!" she cried.

Dick looked at her, soberly nodded his head, and then he laughed. Mercedes had seen through him in one swift glance. Her white hand touched his in wordless sympathy and thrilled him. This Spanish girl was all fire and passion and love. She understood him, she was his friend, she pledged him what he felt would be the most subtle and powerful influence.

Little by little he learned details of Nell's varied life. She had lived in many places. As a child she remembered moving from town to town, of going to school among schoolmates whom she never had time to know. Lawrence, Kansas, where she studied for several years, was the later exception to this changeful nature of her schooling. Then she moved to Stillwater, Oklahoma, from there to Austin, Texas, and on to Waco, where her mother met and married Belding. They lived in New Mexico awhile, in

Tucson, Arizona, in Douglas, and finally had come to lonely Forlorn River.

"Mother could never live in one place any length of time," said Nell. "And since we've been in the Southwest she has never ceased trying to find some trace of her father. He was last heard of in Nogales fourteen years ago. She thinks Grandfather was lost in the Sonora Desert. . . . And every place we go is worse. Oh, I love the desert. But I'd like to go back to Lawrence—or to see Chicago or New York—some of the places Mr. Gale speaks of . . . I remember the college at Lawrence, though I was only twelve. I saw races—and once real football. Since then I've read magazines and papers about big football games, and I was always fascinated. . . . Mr. Gale, of course, you've seen games?"

"Yes, a few," replied Dick; and he laughed a little. It was on his lips then to tell her about some of the famous games in which he had participated. But he refrained from exploiting himself. There was little, however, of the color and sound and cheer, of the violent action and rush and battle incidental to a big college football game that he did not succeed in making Mercedes and Nell feel just as if they had been there. They hung breathless and wide-eyed upon his words.

Someone else was present at the latter part of Dick's narrative. The moment he became aware of Mrs. Belding's presence he remembered fancying he had heard her call, and now he was certain she had done so. Mercedes and Nell, however, had been and still were oblivious to everything except Dick's recital. He saw Mrs. Belding cast a strange, intent glance upon Nell, then turn and go silently through the patio. Dick concluded his talk, but the brilliant beginning was not sustained.

Dick was haunted by the strange expression he had caught on Mrs. Belding's face, especially the look in her eyes. It had been one of repressed pain liberated in a flash of certainty. The mother had seen just as quickly as Mercedes how far he had gone on the road of love. Perhaps she had seen more—even more than he dared hope. The incident roused Gale. He could not understand Mrs. Belding, nor why that look of hers, that seeming baffled, hopeless look of a woman who saw the inevitable forces of life and could not thwart them, should cause him perplexity and distress. He wanted to go to her and tell her how he felt about Nell, but fear of absolute destruction of his hopes held him back. He would wait. Nevertheless, an instinct that was perhaps akin to self-preservation prompted him to want to let Nell know the state of his mind. Words crowded his brain seeking utterance. Who and what he was, how he loved her, the work he expected to take up soon, his longings, hopes, and plans—there was all this and more. But something checked him. And the repression made him so thoughtful and quiet, even melancholy, that he went outdoors to try to throw off the mood. The sun was yet high, and a dazzling white light enveloped valleys and peaks. He felt that the wonderful sunshine was the dominant feature of that arid region. It was like white gold. It had burned its color in a face he knew. It was going to warm his blood and brown his skin. A hot, languid breeze, so dry that he felt his lips shrink with its contact, came from the desert; and it seemed to smell of wide-open, untainted places where sand blew and strange, pungent plants gave a bittersweet tang to the air.

When he returned to the house, some hours later, his room had been put in order. In the middle of the white coverlet on his table lay a fresh red rose. Nell had dropped it there. Dick picked it up, feeling a throb in his breast. It was a bud just beginning to open, to show between its petals a dark-red, unfolding heart. How fragrant it was, how exquisitely delicate, how beautiful its inner hue of red, deep and dark, the crimson of lifeblood!

Had Nell left it there by accident or by intent? Was it merely kindness or a girl's subtlety? Was it a message couched elusively, a symbol, a hope in a half-blown desert rose?

CHAPTER 6

THE YAQUI

Toward evening of a lowering December day, some fifty miles west of Forlorn River, a horseman rode along an old, dimly defined trail. From time to time he halted to study the lay of the land ahead. It was bare, somber, ridgy desert, covered with dun-colored greasewood and stunted prickly pear. Distant mountains hemmed in the valley, raising black spurs above the round lomas and the square-walled mesas.

This lonely horseman bestrode a steed of magnificent build, perfectly white except for a dark bar of color running down the noble head from ears to nose. Sweat-caked dust stained the long flanks. The horse had been running. His mane and tail were laced and knotted to keep their length out of reach of grasping cactus and brush. Clumsy homemade leather shields covered the front of his forelegs and ran up well to his wide breast. What otherwise would have been muscular symmetry of limb was marred by many a scar and many a lump. He was lean, gaunt, worn, a huge machine of muscle and bone, beautiful only in head and mane, a weight-carrier, a horse strong and fierce like the desert that had bred him.

The rider fitted the horse as he fitted the saddle. He was a young man of exceedingly powerful physique, wide-shouldered, long-armed, big-legged. His lean face, where it was not red, blistered, and peeling, was the hue of bronze. He had a dark eye, a falcon gaze, roving and keen. His jaw was prominent and set, mastiff-like; his lips were stern. It was youth with its softness not yet quite burned and hardened away that kept the whole cast of his face from being ruthless.

This young man was Dick Gale, but not the listless traveler, nor the lounging wanderer who, two months before, had by chance dropped into Casita. Friendship, chivalry, love—the deep-seated, unplumbed emotions that had been stirred into being with all their incalculable power for spiritual change, had rendered different the meaning of life. In the moment almost of their realization the desert had claimed Gale, and had drawn him into its crucible. The desert had multiplied weeks into years. Heat, thirst, hunger, loneliness, toil, fear, ferocity, pain—he knew them all. He had felt them all—the white sun, with its glazed, coalescing, lurid fire; the caked split lips and rasping, dry-puffed tongue; the sickening ache in the pit of his stomach; the insupportable silence, the empty space, the utter desolation, the contempt of life; the weary ride, the long climb, the plod in sand, the search, search, search for water; the sleepless night alone, the watch and wait, the dread of ambush, the swift flight; the fierce pursuit of men wild as Bedouins and as fleet, the willingness to deal sudden death, the pain of poison thorn, the stinging tear of lead through flesh; and that strange paradox of the burning desert, the cold at night, the piercing icy wind, the dew that penetrated to the marrow, the numbing desert cold of the dawn.

Beyond any dream of adventure he had ever had, beyond any wild story he had ever read, had been his experience with those hard-riding rangers, Ladd and Lash. Then he had traveled alone the hundred miles of desert between Forlorn River and the Sonoyta Oasis. Ladd's prophecy of trouble on the border had been mild compared to what had become the actuality. With rebel occupancy of the garrison at Casita, outlaws, bandits, raiders in rioting bands had spread westward. Like troops of Arabs, magnificently mounted, they were here, there, everywhere along the line; and if murder and worse were confined to the Mexican side, pillage and raiding were perpetrated across the border. Many a dark-skinned raider bestrode one of Belding's fast horses; and, indeed, all except his selected white thoroughbreds had been stolen. So the job of the rangers had become more than a patrolling of the boundary line to keep Japanese and Chinese from being smuggled into the United States. Belding kept close at home to protect his family and to hold his property. But the three rangers, in fulfilling their duty, had incurred risks on their own side of the line, had been outraged, robbed, pursued, and injured on the other. Some of the few water holes that had to be reached lay far across the border in Mexican territory. Horses had to drink, men had to drink; and Ladd and Lash were not of the stripe that forsook a task because of danger. Slow to wrath at first, as became men who had long lived peaceful lives, they had at length revolted; and desert vultures could have told a gruesome story. Made a comrade and ally of these bordermen, Dick Gale had leaped at the desert action and strife with an intensity of heart and a rare physical ability which accounted for the remarkable fact that he had not yet fallen by the way.

On this December afternoon the three rangers, as often were separated. Lash was far to the westward of Sonoyta, somewhere along Camino del Diablo, that terrible Devil's Road, where many desert wayfarers had perished. Ladd had long been overdue in a prearranged meeting with Gale. The fact that Ladd had not shown up miles west of the Papago Well was significant.

The sun had hidden behind clouds all the latter part of that day, an unusual occurrence for that region even in winter. And now, as the light waned suddenly, telling of the hidden sunset, a cold, dry, penetrating wind sprang up and blew in Gale's face. Not at first, but by imperceptible degrees it chilled him. He untied his coat from the back of the saddle and put it on. A few cold drops of rain touched his cheek.

He halted upon the edge of a low escarpment. Below him the narrowing valley showed bare, black ribs of rock, long, winding gray lines leading down to a central floor where mesquite and cactus dotted the barren landscape. Moving objects, diminutive in size, gray and white in color, arrested Gale's roving sight. They bobbed away for a while, then stopped. They were antelope, and they had seen his horse. When he rode on they started once more, keeping to the lowest level. These wary animals were often desert watchdogs for the ranger; they would betray the proximity of horse or man. With them trotting forward, he made better time for some miles across the valley. When he lost them, caution once more slowed his advance.

The valley sloped up and narrowed, to head into an arroyo where grass began to show gray between the clumps of mesquite. Shadows formed ahead in the hollows, along the walls of the arroyo, under the trees, and they seemed to creep, to rise, to float into a veil cast by the background of bold mountains, at last to claim the skyline. Night was not close at hand; but it was there in the east, lifting upward, drooping downward, encroaching upon the west.

Gale dismounted to lead his horse, to go forward more slowly. He had ridden sixty miles since morning, and he was tired, and a not entirely healed wound in his hip made one leg drag a little. A mile up the arroyo, near its head, lay the Papago Well. The need of water for his horse entailed a risk that otherwise he could have avoided. The well was on Mexican soil. Gale distinguished a faint light flickering through the thin, sharp foliage. Campers were at the well, and, whoever they were, no doubt they had prevented Ladd from meeting Gale. Ladd had gone back to the next water-hole, or maybe he was hiding in an arroyo to the eastward, awaiting developments.

Gale turned his horse, not without urge of iron arm and persuasive speech, for the desert steed scented water, and plodded back to the edge of the arroyo, where in a secluded circle of mesquite he halted. The horse snorted his relief at the removal of the heavy, burdened saddle and accoutrements, and sagging, bent his knees, lowered himself with slow heave, and plunged down to roll in the sand. Gale poured the contents of his larger canteen into his hat and held it to the horse's nose.

"Drink, Sol," he said.

It was but a drop for a thirsty horse. However, Blanco Sol rubbed a wet muzzle against Gale's hand in appreciation. Gale loved the horse, and was loved in return. They had saved each other's lives, and had spent long days and nights of desert solitude together. Sol had known other masters, though none so kind as this new one; but it was certain that Gale had never before known a horse.

The spot of secluded ground was covered with bunches of galleta grass upon which Sol began to graze. Gale made a long halter of his lariat to keep the horse from wandering in search of water. Next Gale kicked off the cumbersome chapparejos, with their flapping, tripping folds of leather over his feet, and drawing a long rifle from its saddle-sheath, he slipped away into the shadows.

The coyotes were howling, not here and there, but in concerted volume at the head of the arroyo. To Dick this was no more reassuring than had been the flickering light of the campfire. The wild desert dogs, with their characteristic insolent curiosity, were baying men round a campfire. Gale proceeded slowly, halting every few steps, careful not to brush against the stiff greasewood. In the soft sand his steps made no sound. The twinkling light vanished occasionally, like a Jack-o'-lantern, and when it did show it seemed still a long way off. Gale was not seeking trouble or inviting danger. Water was the thing that drove him. He must see who these campers were, and then decide how to give Blanco Sol a drink.

A rabbit rustled out of brush at Gale's feet and thumped away over the sand. The wind pattered among dry, broken stalks of dead *ocatilla*. Every little sound brought Gale to a listening pause. The gloom was thickening fast into darkness. It would be a night without starlight. He moved forward up the pale, zigzag aisles between the mesquite. He lost the light for a while, but the coyotes' chorus told him he was approaching the campfire. Presently the light danced through the black branches, and soon grew into a flame. Stooping low, with bushy mesquites between him and the fire, Gale advanced. The coyotes were in full cry. Gale heard the tramping, stamping thumps of many hoofs. The sound worried him. Foot by foot he advanced, and finally began to crawl. The wind favored his position, so that neither coyotes nor horses could scent him. The nearer he approached the head of the arroyo, where the well was located, the thicker grew the desert vegetation. At length a dead *palo verde*, with huge, black clumps of its parasite mistletoe thick in the branches, marked a distance from the well that Gale considered close enough. Noiselessly he crawled here and there until he secured a favorable position, and then rose to peep from behind his covert.

He saw a bright fire, not a cooking fire, for that would have been low and red, but a crackling blaze of mesquite. Three men were in sight, all close to the burning sticks. They were Mexicans and of the coarse type of raiders, rebels, bandits that Gale had expected to see. One stood up, his back to the fire; another sat with shoulders enveloped in a blanket, and the third lounged in the sand, his feet almost in the blaze. They had cast off belts and weapons. A glint of steel caught Gale's eye. Three short, shiny carbines leaned against a rock. A little to the left, within the circle of light, stood a square house made of adobe bricks. Several untrimmed poles upheld a roof of brush, which was partly fallen in. This house was a Papago Indian habitation, and a month before had been occupied by a family that had been murdered or driven off by a roving band of outlaws. A rude corral showed dimly in the edge of firelight, and from a black mass within came the snort and stamp and whinny of horses.

Gale took in the scene in one quick glance, then sank down at the foot of the mesquite. He had naturally expected to see more men. But the situation was by no means new. This was one, or part of one, of the raider bands harrying the border. They were stealing horses, or driving a herd already stolen. These bands were more numerous than the water holes of northern Sonora; they never camped long at one place; like Arabs, they roamed over the desert all the way from Nogales to Casita. If Gale had gone peaceably up to this campfire there were a hundred chances that the raiders would kill and rob him to one chance that they might not. If they recognized him as a ranger comrade of Ladd and Lash, if they got a glimpse of Blanco Sol, then Gale would have no chance.

These Mexicans had evidently been at the well some time. Their horses being in the corral meant that grazing had been done by day. Gale revolved questions in his mind. Had this trio of outlaws run across Ladd? It was not likely, for in that event they might not have been so comfortable and carefree in camp. Were they waiting for more members of their gang? That was very probable. With Gale, however, the most important consideration was how to get his horse to water. Sol must have a drink if it cost a fight. There was stern reason for Gale to hurry eastward along the trail. He thought it best to go back to where he had left his horse and not make any decisive move until daylight.

With the same noiseless care he had exercised in the advance, Gale retreated until it was safe for him to rise and walk on down the arroyo. He found Blanco Sol contentedly grazing. A heavy dew was falling, and, as the grass was abundant, the horse did not show the usual restlessness and distress after a dry and exhausting day. Gale carried his saddle, blankets, and bags into the lee of a little greasewood-covered mound, from around which the wind had cut the soil; and here, in a wash, he risked building a small fire. By this time the wind was piercingly cold. Gale's hands were numb, and he moved them to and fro in the little blaze. Then he made coffee in a cup, cooked some slices of bacon on the end of a stick, and took a couple of hard biscuits from a saddle-bag. Of these his meal consisted. After that he removed the halter from Blanco Sol, intending to leave him free to graze for a while.

Then Gale returned to his little fire, replenished it with short sticks of dead greasewood and mesquite, and, wrapping his blanket round his shoulders, he sat down to warm himself and to wait till it was time to bring in the horse and tie him up.

The fire was inadequate, and Gale was cold and wet with dew. Hunger and thirst were with him. His bones ached, and there was a dull, deep-seated pain throbbing in his unhealed wound. For days unshaven, his beard seemed like a million pricking needles in his blistered skin. He was so tired that, once having settled himself, he did not move hand or foot. The night was dark, dismal, cloudy, windy, growing colder. A moan of wind in the mesquites was occasionally pierced by the high-keyed yelp of a coyote. There were lulls in which the silence seemed to be a thing of stifling, encroaching substance—a thing that enveloped, buried the desert.

Judged by the great average of ideals and conventional standards of life, Dick Gale was a starved, lonely, suffering, miserable wretch. But in his case the judgment would have hit only externals, would have missed the vital inner truth. For Gale was happy with a kind of strange, wild glory in the privations, the pains, the perils, and the silence and solitude to be endured on this desert land. In the past he had not been of any use to himself or others; and he had never known what it meant to be hungry, cold, tired, lonely. He had never worked for anything. The needs of the day had been provided, and to-morrow and the future looked the same. Danger, peril, toil—these had been words read in books and papers.

In the present he used his hands, his senses, and his wits. He had a duty to a man who relied on his services. He was a comrade, a friend, a valuable ally to riding, fighting rangers. He had spent endless days, weeks that seemed years, alone with a horse, trailing over, climbing over, hunting

over a desert that was harsh and hostile by nature, and made more perilous by the invasion of savage men. That horse had become human to
Gale. And with him Gale had learned to know the simple needs of existence. Like dead scales the superficialities, the falsities, the habits that
had once meant all of life dropped off, useless things in this stern waste
of rock and sand.

Gale's happiness, as far as it concerned the toil and strife, was perhaps a grim and stoical one. But love abided with him, and it had engendered and fostered other undeveloped traits—romance and a feeling for
beauty, and a keen observation of nature. He felt pain, but he was never
miserable. He felt the solitude, but he was never lonely.

As he rode across the desert, even though keen eyes searched for the
moving black dots, the rising puffs of white dust that were warnings, he
saw Nell's face in every cloud. The clean-cut mesas took on the shape of
her straight profile, with its strong chin and lips, its fine nose and forehead. There was always a glint of gold or touch of red or graceful line or
gleam of blue to remind him of her. Then at night her face shone warm
and glowing, flushing and paling, in the campfire.

Tonight, as usual, with a keen ear to the wind, Gale listened as one
on guard; yet he watched the changing phantom of a sweet face in the
embers, and as he watched he thought. The desert developed and multiplied thought. A thousand sweet faces glowed in the pink and white ashes
of his campfire, the faces of other sweethearts or wives that had gleamed
for other men. Gale was happy in his thought of Nell, for something,
when he was alone this way in the wilderness, told him she was near him,
she thought of him, she loved him. But there were many men alone on
that vast southwestern plateau, and when they saw dream faces, surely
for some it was a fleeting flash, a gleam soon gone, like the hope and the
name and the happiness that had been and was now no more. Often Gale
thought of those hundreds of desert travelers, prospectors, wanderers who
had ventured down the Camino del Diablo, never to be heard of again.
Belding had told him of that most terrible of all desert trails—a trail of
shifting sands. Lash had traversed it, and brought back stories of buried
water holes, of bones bleaching white in the sun, of gold mines as lost as
were the prospectors who had sought them, of the merciless Yaqui and
his hatred for the Mexican. Gale thought of this trail and the men who

had camped along it. For many there had been one night, one campfire that had been the last. This idea seemed to creep in out of the darkness, the loneliness, the silence, and to find a place in Gale's mind, so that it had strange fascination for him. He knew now as he had never dreamed before how men drifted into the desert, leaving behind graves, wrecked homes, ruined lives, lost wives and sweethearts. And for every wanderer every campfire had a phantom face. Gale measured the agony of these men at their last campfire by the joy and promise he traced in the ruddy heart of his own.

By and by Gale remembered what he was waiting for; and, getting up, he took the halter and went out to find Blanco Sol. It was pitch-dark now, and Gale could not see a rod ahead. He felt his way, and presently as he rounded a mesquite he saw Sol's white shape outlined against the blackness. The horse jumped and wheeled, ready to run. It was doubtful if any one unknown to Sol could ever have caught him. Gale's low call reassured him, and he went on grazing. Gale haltered him in the likeliest patch of grass and returned to his camp. There he lifted his saddle into a protected spot under a low wall of the mound, and, laying one blanket on the sand, he covered himself with the other and stretched himself for the night.

Here he was out of reach of the wind; but he heard its melancholy moan in the mesquite. There was no other sound. The coyotes had ceased their hungry cries. Gale dropped to sleep, and slept soundly during the first half of the night; and after that he seemed always to be partially awake, aware of increasing cold and damp. The dark mantle turned gray, and then daylight came quickly. The morning was clear and nipping cold. He threw off the wet blanket and got up cramped and half frozen. A little brisk action was all that was necessary to warm his blood and loosen his muscles, and then he was fresh, tingling, eager. The sun rose in a golden blaze, and the descending valley took on wondrous changing hues. Then he fetched up Blanco Sol, saddled him, and tied him to the thickest clump of mesquite.

"Sol, we'll have a drink pretty soon," he said, patting the splendid neck.

Gale meant it. He would not eat till he had watered his horse. Sol had gone nearly forty-eight hours without a sufficient drink, and that was long enough, even for a desert-bred beast. No three raiders could keep Gale away from that well. Taking his rifle in hand, he faced up the arroyo. Rabbits were frisking in the short willows, and some were so tame he could have kicked them. Gale walked swiftly for a goodly part of the distance, and then, when he saw blue smoke curling up above the trees, he proceeded slowly, with alert eye and ear. From the lay of the land and position of trees seen by daylight, he found an easier and safer course than the one he had taken in the dark. And by careful work he was enabled to get closer to the well, and somewhat above it.

The Mexicans were leisurely cooking their morning meal. They had two fires, one for warmth, the other to cook over. Gale had an idea these raiders were familiar to him. It seemed all these border hawks resembled one another—being mostly small of build, wiry, angular, swarthy-faced, and blackhaired, and they wore the oddly styled Mexican clothes and sombreros. A slow wrath stirred in Gale as he watched the trio. They showed not the slightest indication of breaking camp. One fellow, evidently the leader, packed a gun at his hip, the only weapon in sight. Gale noted this with speculative eyes. The raiders had slept inside the little adobe house, and had not yet brought out the carbines. Next Gale swept his gaze to the corral, in which he saw more than a dozen horses, some of them fine animals. They were stamping and whistling, fighting one another, and pawing the dirt. This was entirely natural behavior for desert horses penned in when they wanted to get at water and grass.

But suddenly one of the blacks, a big, shaggy fellow, shot up his ears and pointed his nose over the top of the fence. He whistled. Other horses looked in the same direction, and their ears went up, and they, too, whistled. Gale knew that other horses or men, very likely both, were approaching. But the Mexicans did not hear the alarm, or show any interest if they did. These mescal-drinking raiders were not scouts. It was notorious how easily they could be surprised or ambushed. Mostly they were ignorant, thick-skulled peons. They were wonderful horsemen, and could go long without food or water; but they had no other accomplishments or attributes calculated to help them in desert warfare. They had poor sight, poor hearing, poor judgment, and when excited they resembled crazed ants running wild.

Gale saw two Indians on burros come riding up the other side of the knoll upon which the adobe house stood; and apparently they were not aware of the presence of the Mexicans, for they came on up the path. One Indian was a Papago. The other, striking in appearance for other reasons than that he seemed to be about to fall from the burro, Gale took to be a Yaqui. These travelers had absolutely nothing for an outfit except a blanket and a half-empty bag. They came over the knoll and down the path toward the well, turned a corner of the house, and completely surprised the raiders.

Gale heard a short, shrill cry, strangely high and wild, and this came from one of the Indians. It was answered by hoarse shouts. Then the leader of the trio, the Mexican who packed a gun, pulled it and fired point-blank. He missed once—and again. At the third shot the Papago shrieked and tumbled off his burro to fall in a heap. The other Indian swayed, as if the taking away of the support lent by his comrade had brought collapse, and with the fourth shot he, too, slipped to the ground.

The reports had frightened the horses in the corral; and the vicious black, crowding the rickety bars, broke them down. He came plunging out. Two of the Mexicans ran for him, catching him by nose and mane, and the third ran to block the gateway.

Then, with a splendid vaulting mount, the Mexican with the gun leaped to the back of the horse. He yelled and waved his gun, and urged the black forward. The manner of all three was savagely jocose. They were having sport. The two on the ground began to dance and jabber. The mounted leader shot again, and then stuck like a leech upon the bare back of the rearing black. It was a vain show of horsemanship. Then this Mexican, by some strange grip, brought the horse down, plunging almost upon the body of the Indian that had fallen last.

Gale stood aghast with his rifle clutched tight. He could not divine the intention of the raider, but suspected something strikingly brutal. The horse answered to that cruel, guiding hand, yet he swerved and bucked. He reared aloft, pawing the air, wildly snorting, then he plunged down upon the prostrate Indian. Even in the act the intelligent animal tried to keep from striking the body with his hoofs. But that was not possible. A yell, hideous in its passion, signaled this feat of horsemanship.

The Mexican made no move to trample the body of the Papago. He turned the black to ride again over the other Indian. That brought into

Gale's mind what he had heard of a Mexican's hate for a Yaqui. It recalled the barbarism of these savage peons, and the war of extermination being waged upon the Yaquis.

Suddenly Gale was horrified to see the Yaqui writhe and raise a feeble hand. The action brought renewed and more savage cries from the Mexicans. The horse snorted in terror.

Gale could bear no more. He took a quick shot at the rider. He missed the moving figure, but hit the horse. There was a bound, a horrid scream, a mighty plunge, then the horse went down, giving the Mexican a stunning fall. Both beast and man lay still.

Gale rushed from his cover to intercept the other raiders before they could reach the house and their weapons. One fellow yelled and ran wildly in the opposite direction; the other stood stricken in his tracks. Gale ran in close and picked up the gun that had dropped from the raider leader's hand. This fellow had begun to stir, to come out of his stunned condition. Then the frightened horses burst the corral bars, and in a thundering, dust-mantled stream fled up the arroyo.

The fallen raider sat up, mumbling to his saints in one breath, cursing in his next. The other Mexican kept his stand, intimidated by the threatening rifle.

"Go, Greasers! Run!" yelled Gale. Then he yelled it in Spanish. At the point of his rifle he drove the two raiders out of the camp. His next move was to run into the house and fetch out the carbines. With a heavy stone he dismantled each weapon. That done, he set out on a run for his horse. He took the shortest cut down the arroyo, with no concern as to whether or not he would encounter the raiders. Probably such a meeting would be all the worse for them, and they knew it. Blanco Sol heard him coming and whistled a welcome, and when Gale ran up the horse was snorting war. Mounting, Gale rode rapidly back to the scene of the action, and his first thought, when he arrived at the well, was to give Sol a drink and to fill his canteens.

Then Gale led his horse up out of the water hole, and decided before remounting to have a look at the Indians. The Papago had been shot through the heart, but the Yaqui was still alive. Moreover, he was conscious and staring up at Gale with great, strange, somber eyes, black as volcanic slag.

"Gringo good—no kill," he said, in husky whisper.

His speech was not affirmative so much as questioning.

"Yaqui, you're done for," said Gale, and his words were positive. He was simply speaking aloud his mind.

"Yaqui—no hurt—much," replied the Indian, and then he spoke a strange word—repeated it again and again.

An instinct of Gale's, or perhaps some suggestion in the husky, thick whisper or dark face, told Gale to reach for his canteen. He lifted the Indian and gave him a drink, and if ever in all his life he saw gratitude in human eyes he saw it then. Then he examined the injured Yaqui, not forgetting for an instant to send wary, fugitive glances on all sides. Gale was not to be surprised. The Indian had three wounds—a bullet-hole in his shoulder, a crushed arm, and a badly lacerated leg. What had been the matter with him before being set upon by the raider Gale could not be certain.

The ranger thought rapidly. This Yaqui would live unless left there to die or be murdered by the Mexicans when they found courage to sneak back to the well. It never occurred to Gale to abandon the poor fellow. That was where his old training, the higher order of human feeling, made impossible the following of any elemental instinct of self-preservation. All the same, Gale knew he multiplied his perils a hundredfold by burdening himself with a crippled Indian. Swiftly he set to work, and with rifle ever under his hand, and shifting glance spared from his task, he bound up the Yaqui's wounds. At the same time he kept keen watch.

The Indians' burros and the horses of the raiders were all out of sight. Time was too valuable for Gale to use any in what might be vain search. Therefore, he lifted the Yaqui upon Sol's broad shoulders and climbed into the saddle. At a word Sol dropped his head and started eastward up the trail, walking swiftly, without resentment for his double burden.

Far ahead, between two huge mesas where the trail mounted over a pass, a long line of dust clouds marked the position of the horses that had escaped from the corral. Those that had been stolen would travel straight and true for home, and perhaps would lead the others with them. The raiders were left on the desert without guns or mounts.

Blanco Sol walked or jog-trotted six miles to the hour. At that gait fifty miles would not have wet or turned a hair of his dazzling white coat.

Gale, bearing in mind the ever-present possibility of encountering more raiders and of being pursued, saved the strength of the horse. Once out of sight of Papago Well, Gale dismounted and walked beside the horse, steadying with one firm hand the helpless, dangling Yaqui.

The sun cleared the eastern ramparts, and the coolness of morning fled as if before a magic foe. The whole desert changed. The grays wore bright; the mesquites glistened; the cactus took the silver hue of frost, and the rocks gleamed gold and red. Then, as the heat increased, a wind rushed up out of the valley behind Gale, and the hotter the sun blazed down the swifter rushed the wind. The wonderful transparent haze of distance lost its bluish hue for one with a tinge of yellow. Flying sand made the peaks dimly outlined.

Gale kept pace with his horse. He bore the twinge of pain that darted through his injured hip at every stride. His eye roved over the wide, smoky prospect seeking the landmarks he knew. When the wild and bold spurs of No Name Mountains loomed through a rent in flying clouds of sand he felt nearer home. Another hour brought him abreast of a dark, straight shaft rising clear from a beetling escarpment. This was a monument marking the international boundary line. When he had passed it he had his own country underfoot. In the heat of midday he halted in the shade of a rock, and, lifting the Yaqui down, gave him a drink. Then, after a long, sweeping survey of the surrounding desert, he removed Sol's saddle and let him roll, and took for himself a welcome rest and a bite to eat.

The Yaqui was tenacious of life. He was still holding his own. For the first time Gale really looked at the Indian to study him. He had a large head nobly cast, and a face that resembled a shrunken mask. It seemed chiseled in the dark-red, volcanic lava of his Sonora wilderness. The Indians' eyes were always black and mystic, but this Yaqui's encompassed all the tragic desolation of the desert. They were fixed on Gale, moved only when he moved. The Indian was short and broad, and his body showed unusual muscular development, although he seemed greatly emaciated from starvation or illness.

Gale resumed his homeward journey. When he got through the pass he faced a great depression, as rough as if millions of gigantic spikes had been driven by the hammer of Thor into a seamed and cracked floor. This was Altar Valley. It was a chaos of arroyos, cañons, rocks, and ridges all mantled with cactus, and at its eastern end it claimed the dry bed of Forlorn River and water when there was any.

With a wounded, helpless man across the saddle, this stretch of thorny and contorted desert was practically impassable. Yet Gale headed into it unflinchingly. He would carry the Yaqui as far as possible, or until death made the burden no longer a duty. Blanco Sol plodded on over the dragging sand, up and down the steep, loose banks of washes, out on the rocks, and through the rows of white-toothed *chollas*.

The sun sloped westward, bending fiercer heat in vengeful, parting reluctance. The wind slackened. The dust settled. And the bold, forbidding front of No Name Mountains changed to red and gold. Gale held grimly by the side of the tireless, implacable horse, holding the Yaqui on the saddle, taking the brunt of the merciless thorns. In the end it became heartrending toil. His heavy chaps dragged him down; but he dared not go on without them, for, thick and stiff as they were, the terrible, steel-bayoneted spikes of the *chollas* pierced through to sting his legs.

To the last mile Gale held to Blanco Sol's gait and kept ever-watchful gaze ahead on the trail. Then, with the low, flat houses of Forlorn River shining red in the sunset, Gale flagged and rapidly weakened. The Yaqui slipped out of the saddle and dropped limp in the sand. Gale could not mount his horse. He clutched Sol's long tail and twisted his hand in it and staggered on.

Blanco Sol whistled a piercing blast. He scented cool water and sweet alfalfa hay. Twinkling lights ahead meant rest. The melancholy desert twilight rapidly succeeded the sunset. It accentuated the forlorn loneliness of the gray, winding river of sand and its grayer shores. Night shadows trooped down from the black and looming mountains.

CHAPTER 7

WHITE HORSES

A crippled Yaqui! Why the hell did you saddle yourself with him?" roared Belding, as he laid Gale upon the bed.

Belding had grown hard these late, violent weeks.

"Because I chose," whispered Gale, in reply. "Go after him—he dropped in the trail—across the river—near the first big *saguaro*."

Belding began to swear as he fumbled with matches and the lamp; but as the light flared up he stopped short in the middle of a word.

"You said you weren't hurt?" he demanded, in sharp anxiety, as he bent over Gale.

"I'm only—all in. . . . Will you go—or send someone—for the Yaqui?"

"Sure, Dick, sure," Belding replied, in softer tones. Then he stalked out; his heels rang on the flagstones; he opened a door and called: "Mother—girls, here's Dick back. He's done up. . . . Now—no, no, he's not hurt or in bad shape. You women! . . . Do what you can to make him comfortable. I've got a little job on hand."

There were quick replies that Gale's dulling ears did not distinguish. Then it seemed Mrs. Belding was beside his bed, her very presence so cool and soothing and helpful; and Mercedes and Nell, wide-eyed and white-faced, were fluttering around him. He drank thirstily, but refused food. He wanted rest. And with their faces drifting away in a kind of haze, with the feeling of gentle hands about him, he lost consciousness.

He slept twenty hours. Then he arose, thirsty, hungry, lame, over-worn, and presently went in search of Belding and the business of the day.

"Your Yaqui was near dead, but guess we'll pull him through," said Belding. "Dick, the other day that Indian came here by rail and foot and Lord only knows how else, all the way from New Orleans! He spoke English better than most Indians, and I know a little Yaqui. I got some of his story and guessed the rest. The Mexican government is trying to root out the Yaquis. A year ago his tribe was taken in chains to a Mexican port on the Gulf. The fathers, mothers, children, were separated and put in ships bound for Yucatán. There they were made slaves on the great henequen plantations. They were driven, beaten, starved. Each slave had for a day's rations a hunk of sourdough, no more. Yucatán is low, marshy, damp, hot. The Yaquis were bred on the high, dry Sonoran plateau, where the air is like a knife. They dropped dead in the henequen fields, and their places were taken by more. You see, the Mexicans won't kill outright in their war of extermination of the Yaquis. They get use out of them. It's a horrible thing. . . . Well, this Yaqui you brought in escaped from his cap-tors, got aboard ship, and eventually reached New Orleans. Somehow he traveled way out here. I gave him a bag of food, and he went off with a Papago Indian. He was a sick man then. And he must have fallen foul of some Greasers."

Gale told of his experience at Papago Well.

"That raider who tried to grind the Yaqui under a horse's hoofs—he was a hyena!" concluded Gale, shuddering. "I've seen some blood spilled and some hard sights, but that inhuman devil took my nerve. Why, as I told you, Belding, I missed a shot at him—not twenty paces!"

"Dick, in cases like that the sooner you clean up the bunch the better," said Belding, grimly. "As for hard sights—wait till you've seen a Yaqui do up a Mexican. Bar none, that is the limit! It's bloodlust, a racial hate, deep as life, and terrible. The Spaniards crushed the Aztecs four or five hundred years ago. That hate has had time to grow as deep as a cactus root. The Yaquis are mountain Aztecs. Personally, I think they are noble and intelligent, and if let alone would be peaceable and industrious. I like the few I've known. But they are a doomed race. Have you any idea what ailed this Yaqui before the raider got in his work?"

"No, I haven't. I noticed the Indian seemed in bad shape; but I couldn't tell what was the matter with him."

"Well, my idea is another personal one. Maybe it's off color. I think that Yaqui was, or is, for that matter, dying of a broken heart. All he wanted was to get back to his mountains and die. There are no Yaquis left in that part of Sonora he was bound for."

"He had a strange look in his eyes," said Gale, thoughtfully.

"Yes, I noticed that. But all Yaquis have a wild look. Dick, if I'm not mistaken, this fellow was a chief. It was a waste of strength, a needless risk for you to save him, pack him back here. But, damn the whole Greaser outfit generally, I'm glad you did!"

Gale remembered then to speak of his concern for Ladd.

"Laddy didn't go out to meet you," replied Belding. "I knew you were due in any day, and, as there's been trouble between here and Casita, I sent him that way. Since you've been out our friend Carter lost a bunch of horses and a few steers. Did you get a good look at the horses those raiders had at Papago Well?"

Dick had learned, since he had become a ranger, to see everything with keen, sure, photographic eye; and, being put to the test so often required of him, he described the horses as a dark-colored drove, mostly bays and blacks, with one spotted sorrel.

"Some of Carter's—sure as you're born!" exclaimed Belding. "His bunch has been split up, divided among several bands of raiders. He has a grass ranch up here in Three Mile Arroyo. It's a good long ride in U.S. territory from the border."

"Those horses I saw will go home, don't you think?" asked Dick.

"Sure. They can't be caught or stopped."

"Well, what shall I do now?"

"Stay here and rest," bluntly replied Belding. "You need it. Let the women fuss over you—doctor you a little. When Jim gets back from Sonoyta I'll know more about what we ought to do. By Lord! it seems our job now isn't keeping Japs and Chinks out of the U.S. It's keeping our property from going into Mexico."

"Are there any letters for me?" asked Gale.

"Letters! Say, my boy, it'd take something pretty important to get me or any man here back Casita way. If the town is safe these days the road isn't. It's a month now since any one went to Casita."

Gale had received several letters from his sister Elsie, the last of which he had not answered. There had not been much opportunity for writing on his infrequent returns to Forlorn River; and, besides, Elsie had written that her father had stormed over what he considered Dick's falling into wild and evil ways.

"Time flies," said Dick. "George Thorne will be free before long, and he'll be coming out. I wonder if he'll stay here or try to take Mercedes away?"

"Well, he'll stay right here in Forlorn River, if I have any say," replied Belding. "I'd like to know how he'd ever get that Spanish girl out of the country now, with all the trails overrun by rebels and raiders. It'd be hard to disguise her. Say, Dick, maybe we can get Thorne to stay here. You know, since you've discovered the possibility of a big water supply, I've had dreams of a future for Forlorn River. . . . If only this war was over! Dick, that's what it is—war—scattered war along the northern border of Mexico from gulf to gulf. What if it isn't our war? We're on the fringe. No, we can't develop Forlorn River until there's peace."

The discovery that Belding alluded to was one that might very well lead to the making of a wonderful and agricultural district of Altar Valley. While in college Dick Gale had studied engineering, but he had not set the scientific world afire with his brilliance. Nor after leaving college had he been able to satisfy his father that he could hold a job. Nevertheless, his smattering of engineering skill bore fruit in the last place on earth where anything might have been expected of it—in the desert. Gale had always wondered about the source of Forlorn River. No white man or Mexican, or, so far as known, no Indian, had climbed those mighty broken steps of rock called No Name Mountains, from which Forlorn River was supposed to come. Gale had discovered a long, narrow, rock-bottomed and rock-walled gulch that could be dammed at the lower end by the dynamiting of leaning cliffs above. An inexhaustible supply of water could be stored there. Furthermore, he had worked out an irrigation plan to bring the water down for mining uses, and to make a paradise out of that part of

Altar Valley which lay in the United States. Belding claimed there was gold in the arroyos, gold in the gulches, not in quantities to make a prospector rejoice, but enough to work for. And the soil on the higher levels of Altar Valley needed only water to make it grow anything the year round. Gale, too, had come to have dreams of a future for Forlorn River.

On the afternoon of the following day Ladd unexpectedly appeared leading a lame and lathered horse into the yard. Belding and Gale, who were at work at the forge, looked up and were surprised out of speech. The legs of the horse were raw and red, and he seemed about to drop. Ladd's sombrero was missing; he wore a bloody scarf round his head; sweat and blood and dust had formed a crust on his face; little streams of powdery dust slid from him; and the lower half of his scarred chaps were full of broken white thorns.

"Howdy, boys," he drawled. "I shore am glad to see you all."

"Where'n hell's your hat?" demanded Belding, furiously. It was a ridiculous greeting. But Belding's words signified little. The dark shade of worry and solicitude crossing his face told more than his blank amaze.

The ranger stopped unbuckling the saddle girths, and, looking at Belding, broke into his slow, cool laugh.

"Tom, you recollect that whopper of a *saguaro* up here where Carter's trail branches off the main trail to Casita? Well, I climbed it an' left my hat on top for a woodpecker's nest."

"You've been running—fighting?" queried Belding, as if Ladd had not spoken at all.

"I reckon it'll dawn on you after a while," replied Ladd, slipping the saddle.

"Laddy, go in the house to the women," said Belding. "I'll tend to your horse."

"Shore, Tom, in a minute. I've been down the road. An' I found hoss tracks an' steer tracks goin' across the line. But I seen no sign of raiders till this mornin'. Slept at Carter's last night. That raid the other day cleaned him out. He's shootin' mad. Well, this mornin' I rode plumb into a bunch of Carter's hosses, runnin' wild for home. Some Greasers were tryin' to head them round an' chase them back across the line. I rode in between an' made matters embarrassin'. Carter's hosses got away. Then me an' the Greasers had a little game of hide-an'-seek in the cactus. I was on the wrong side, an' had to break through their line to head toward home. We run some. But I had a closer call than I'm stuck on havin'."

"Laddy, you wouldn't have any such close calls if you'd ride one of my horses," expostulated Belding. "This broncho of yours can run, and Lord knows he's game. But you want a big, strong horse, Mexican bred, with cactus in his blood. Take one of the bunch—Bull, White Woman, Blanco José."

"I had a big, fast horse a while back, but I lost him," said Ladd. "This bronch ain't so bad. Shore Bull an' that white devil with his Greaser name— they could run down my bronch, kill him in a mile of cactus. But, some-how, Tom, I can't make up my mind to take one of them grand white hosses. Shore I reckon I'm kinda soft. An' mebbe I'd better take one be-fore the raiders clean up Forlorn River."

Belding cursed low and deep in his throat, and the sound resembled muttering thunder. The shade of anxiety on his face changed to one of dark gloom and passion. Next to his wife and daughter there was nothing so dear to him as those white horses. His father and his grandfather—all his progenitors of whom he had trace—had been lovers of horses. It was in Belding's blood.

"Laddy, before it's too late can't I get the whites away from the border?"

"Mebbe it ain't too late; but where can we take them?"

"To San Felipe?"

"No. We've more chance to hold them here."

"To Casita and the railroad?"

"Afraid to risk gettin' there. An' the town's full of rebels who need hosses."

"Then straight north?"

"Shore man, you're crazy. There's no water, no grass for a hundred miles. I'll tell you, Tom, the safest plan would be to take the white bunch south into Sonora, into some wild mountain valley. Keep them there till the raiders have traveled on back east. Pretty soon there won't be any rich pickin' left for these Greasers. An' then they'll ride on to new ranges."

"Laddy, I don't know the trails into Sonora. An' I can't trust a Mexi-can or a Papago. Between you and me, I'm afraid of this Indian who herds for me."

"I reckon we'd better stick here, Tom. . . . Dick, it's some good to see you again. But you seem kinda quiet. Shore you get quieter all the time. Did you see any sign of Jim out Sonoyta way?"

Then Belding led the lame horse toward the watering-trough while the two rangers went toward the house. Dick was telling Ladd about the affair at Papago Well when they turned the corner under the porch. Nell was sitting in the door. She rose with a little scream and came flying toward them.

"Now I'll get it," whispered Ladd. "The women'll make a baby of me. An' shore I can't help myself."

"Oh, Laddy, you've been hurt!" cried Nell, as with white cheeks and dilating eyes she ran to him and caught his arm.

"Nell, I only run a thorn in my ear."

"Oh, Laddy, don't lie! You've lied before. I know you're hurt. Come in to mother."

"Shore, Nell, it's only a scratch. My bronch throwed me."

"Laddy, no horse ever threw you." The girl's words and accusing eyes only hurried the ranger on to further duplicity.

"Mebbe I got it when I was ridin' hard under a mesquite, an' a sharp snag—"

"You've been shot! . . . Mamma, here's Laddy, and he's been shot! . . . . Oh, these dreadful days we're having! I can't bear them! Forlorn River used to be so safe and quiet. Nothing happened. But now! Jim comes home with a bloody hole in him—then Dick—then Laddy! . . . Oh, I'm afraid someday they'll *never* come home."

The morning was bright, still, and clear as crystal. The heat waves had not yet begun to rise from the desert. A soft gray, white, and green tint perfectly blended lay like a mantle over mesquite and sand and cactus. The cañons of distant mountain showed deep and full of lilac haze.

Nell sat perched high upon the topmost bar of the corral gate. Dick leaned beside her, now with his eyes on her face, now gazing out into the alfalfa field where Belding's thoroughbreds grazed and pranced and romped and whistled. Nell watched the horses. She loved them, never tired of watching them. But her gaze was too consciously averted from the yearning eyes that tried to meet hers to be altogether natural.

A great fenced field of velvety green alfalfa furnished a rich background for the drove of about twenty white horses. Even without the horses the field would have presented a striking contrast to the surrounding hot, glaring blaze of rock and sand. Belding had bred a hundred or more horses from the original stock he had brought up from Durango. His particular interest was in the almost unblemished white, and these he had given especial care. He made a good deal of money selling this strain to friends among the ranchers back in Texas. No mercenary consideration, however, could have made him part with the great, rangy white horses he had gotten from the Durango breeder. They were named Blanco Diablo (White Devil), Blanco Sol (White Sun), Blanca Reina (White Queen), Blanca Mujer (White Woman), and El Grande Blanco Torres (The Big White Bull). Belding had been laughed at by ranchers for preserving the sentimental Durango names, and he had been unmercifully ridiculed by cowboys. But the names had never been changed.

Blanco Diablo was the only horse in the field that was not free to roam and graze where he listed. A stake and a halter held him to one corner, where he was severely let alone by the other horses. He did not like this isolation. Blanco Diablo was not happy unless he was running, or fighting a rival. Of the two he would rather fight. If anything white could resemble a devil, this horse surely did. He had nothing beautiful about him, yet he drew the gaze and held it. The look of him suggested discontent, anger, revolt, viciousness. When he was not grazing or prancing, he held his long, lean head level, pointing his nose and showing his teeth. Belding's favorite was almost all the world to him, and he swore Diablo could stand more heat and thirst and cactus than any other horse he owned, and could run down and kill any horse in the Southwest. The fact that Ladd did not agree with Belding on these salient points was a great disappointment, and also a perpetual source for argument. Ladd and Lash both hated Diablo; and Dick Gale, after one or two narrow escapes from being brained, had inclined to the cowboys' side of the question.

El Grande Blanco Torres upheld his name. He was a huge, massive, thick-flanked stallion, a kingly mate for his full-bodied, glossy consort, Blanca Reina. The other mare, Blanca Mujer, was dazzling white, without a spot, perfectly pointed, racy, graceful, elegant, yet carrying weight and brawn and range that suggested her relation to her forebears.

The cowboys admitted some of Belding's claims for Diablo, but they gave loyal and unshakable allegiance to Blanco Sol. As for Dick, he had to fight himself to keep out of arguments, for he sometimes imagined he was unreasonable about the horse. Though he could not understand himself, he knew he loved Sol as a man loved a friend, a brother. Free of heavy saddle and the clumsy leg shields, Blanco Sol was somehow all-satisfying to the eyes of the rangers. As long and big as Diablo was, Sol was longer and bigger. Also, he was higher, more powerful. He looked more a thing for action—speedier. At a distance the honorable scars and lumps that marred his muscular legs were not visible. He grazed aloof from the others, and did not cavort nor prance; but when he lifted his head to whistle, how wild he appeared, and proud and splendid! The dazzling whiteness of the desert sun shone from his coat; he had the fire and spirit of the desert in his noble head, its strength and power in his gigantic frame.

"Belding swears Sol never beat Diablo," Dick was saying.

"He believes it," replied Nell. "Dad is queer about that horse."

"But Laddy rode Sol once—made him beat Diablo. Jim saw the race."

Nell laughed. "I saw it, too. For that matter, even I have made Sol put his nose before Dad's favorite."

"I'd like to have seen that. Nell, aren't you ever going to ride with me?"

"Someday—when it's safe."

"Safe!"

"I—I mean when the raiders have left the border."

"Oh, I'm glad you mean that," said Dick, laughing. "Well, I've often wondered how Belding ever came to give Blanco Sol to me."

"He was jealous. I think he wanted to get rid of Sol."

"No? Why, Nell, he'd give Laddy or Jim one of the whites any day."

"Would he? Not Devil or Queen or White Woman. Never in this world! But Dad has lots of fast horses the boys could pick from. Dick, I tell you Dad wants Blanco Sol to run himself out—lose his speed on the desert. Dad is just jealous for Diablo."

"Maybe. He surely has strange passion for horses. I think I understand better than I used to. I owned a couple of racers once. They were just animals to me, I guess. But Blanco Sol!"

"Do you love him?" asked Nell; and now a warm, blue flash of eyes swept his face.

"Do I? Well, rather."

"I'm glad. Sol has been finer, a better horse since you owned him. He loves you, Dick. He's always watching for you. See him raise his head. That's for you. I know as much about horses as Dad or Laddy any day. Sol always hated Diablo, and never had much use for Dad."

Dick looked up at her.

"It'll be—be pretty hard to leave Sol—when I go away."

Nell sat perfectly still.

"Go away?" she asked, presently, with just the faintest tremor in her voice.

"Yes. Sometimes when I get blue—as I am today—I think I'll go. But, in sober truth, Nell, it's not likely that I'll spend all my life here."

There was no answer to this. Dick put his hand softly over hers; and, despite her halfhearted struggle to free it, he held on.

"Nell!"

Her color fled. He saw her lips part. Then a heavy step on the gravel, a cheerful, complaining voice interrupted him, and made him release Nell and draw back. Belding strode into view round the adobe shed.

"Hey, Dick, that darned Yaqui Indian can't be driven or hired or coaxed to leave Forlorn River. He's well enough to travel. I offered him horse, gun, blanket, grub. But no go."

"That's funny," replied Gale, with a smile. "Let him stay—put him to work."

"It doesn't strike me funny. But I'll tell you what I think. That poor, homeless, heartbroken Indian has taken a liking to you, Dick. These desert Yaquis are strange folk. I've heard strange stories about them. I'd believe 'most anything. And that's how I figure his case. You saved his life. That sort of thing counts big with any Indian, even with an Apache. With a Yaqui maybe it's of deep significance. I've heard a Yaqui say that with his tribe no debt to friend or foe ever went unpaid. Perhaps that's what ails this fellow."

"Dick, don't laugh," said Nell. "I've noticed the Yaqui. It's pathetic the way his great gloomy eyes follow you."

"You've made a friend," continued Belding. "A Yaqui could be a real friend on this desert. If he gets his strength back he'll be of service to you, don't mistake me. He's welcome here. But you're responsible for him, and you'll have trouble keeping him from massacring all the Greasers in Forlorn River."

The probability of a visit from the raiders, and a dash bolder than usual on the outskirts of a ranch, led Belding to build a new corral. It was not sightly to the eye, but it was high and exceedingly strong. The gate was a massive affair, swinging on huge hinges and fastening with heavy chains and padlocks. On the outside it had been completely covered with barbed wire, which would make it a troublesome thing to work on in the dark.

At night Belding locked his white horses in this corral. The Papago herdsman slept in the adobe shed adjoining. Belding did not imagine that any wooden fence, however substantially built, could keep determined raiders from breaking it down. They would have to take time, however, and make considerable noise; and Belding relied on these facts. Belding did not believe a band of night raiders would hold out against a hot rifle fire. So he began to make up some of the sleep he had lost. It was noteworthy, however, that Ladd did not share Belding's sanguine hopes.

Jim Lash rode in, reporting that all was well out along the line toward the Sonoyta Oasis. Days passed, and Belding kept his rangers home. Nothing was heard of raiders at hand. Many of the newcomers, both American and Mexican, who came with wagons and pack trains from Casita stated that property and life were cheap back in that rebel-infested town.

One January morning Dick Gale was awakened by a shrill, menacing cry. He leaped up bewildered and frightened. He heard Belding's booming voice answering shouts, and rapid steps on flagstones. But these had not awakened him. Heavy breaths, almost sobs, seemed at his very door. In the cold and gray dawn Dick saw something white. Gun in hand, he bounded across the room. Just outside his door stood Blanco Sol.

It was not unusual for Sol to come poking his head in at Dick's door during daylight. But now in the early dawn, when he had been locked in the corral, it meant raiders—no less. Dick called softly to the snorting horse; and, hurriedly getting into clothes and boots, he went out with a gun in each hand. Sol was quivering in every muscle. Like a dog he followed Dick around the house. Hearing shouts in the direction of the corrals, Gale bent swift steps that way.

He caught up with Jim Lash, who was also leading a white horse.

"Hello, Jim! Guess it's all over but the fireworks," said Dick.

"I cain't say just what has come off," replied Lash. "I've got the Bull. Found him runnin' in the yard."

They reached the corral to find Belding shaking, roaring like a madman. The gate was open, the corral was empty. Ladd stooped over the ground, evidently trying to find tracks.

"I reckon we might jest as well cool off an' wait for daylight," suggested Jim.

"Shore. They've flown the coop, you can gamble on that. Tom, where's the Papago?" said Ladd.

"He's gone, Laddy—gone!"

"Double-crossed us, eh? I see here's a crowbar lyin' by the gatepost. That Indian fetched it from the forge. It was used to pry out the bolts an' steeples. Tom, I reckon there wasn't much time lost forcin' that gate."

Belding, in shirtsleeves and barefooted, roared with rage. He said he had heard the horses running as he leaped out of bed.

"What woke you?" asked Laddy.

"Sol. He came whistling for Dick. Didn't you hear him before I called you?"

"Hear him! He came thunderin' right under my window. I jumped up in bed, an' when he let out that blast Jim lit square in the middle of the floor, an' I was scared stiff. Dick, seein' it was your room he blew into, what did you think?"

"I couldn't think. I'm shaking yet, Laddy."

"Boys, I'll bet Sol spilled a few raiders if any got hands on him," said Jim. "Now, let's sit down an' wait for daylight. It's my idea we'll find some of the hosses runnin' loose. Tom, you go an' get some clothes on. It's freezin' cold. An' don't forget to tell the womenfolks we're all right."

Daylight made clear some details of the raid. The cowboys found tracks of eight raiders coming up from the riverbed where their horses had been left. Evidently the Papago had been false to his trust. His few personal belongings were gone. Lash was correct in his idea of finding more horses loose in the fields. The men soon rounded up eleven of the whites, all more or less frightened, and among the number were Queen and Blanca Mujer. The raiders had been unable to handle more than one horse for each man. It was bitter irony of fate that Belding should lose his favorite, the one horse more dear to him than all the others. Somewhere out on the trail a raider was fighting the iron-jawed savage Blanco Diablo.

"I reckon we're some lucky," observed Jim Lash.

"Lucky ain't enough word," replied Ladd. "You see, it was this way. Some of the raiders piled over the fence while the others worked on the gate. Mebbe the Papago went inside to pick out the best hosses. But it didn't work except with Diablo, an' how they ever got him I don't know. I'd have gambled it'd take all of eight men to steal him. But Greasers have got us skinned on handlin' hosses."

Belding was unconsolable. He cursed and railed, and finally declared he was going to trail the raiders.

"Tom, you just ain't agoin' to do nothin' of the kind," said Laddy, coolly.

Belding groaned and bowed his head.

"Laddy, you're right," he replied, presently. "I've got to stand it. I can't leave the women and my property. But it's sure tough. I'm sore way down deep, and nothin' but blood would ever satisfy me."

"Leave that to me an' Jim," said Ladd.

"What do you mean to do?" demanded Belding, starting up.

"Shore I don't know yet. . . . Give me a light for my pipe. An' Dick, go fetch out your Yaqui."

CHAPTER 8

THE RUNNING OF
BLANCO SOL

The Yaqui's strange dark glance roved over the corral, the swinging gate with its broken fastenings, the tracks in the road, and then rested upon Belding.

"Malo," he said, and his Spanish was clear.

"Shore Yaqui, about eight bad men, an' a traitor Indian," said Ladd.

"I think he means my herder," added Belding. "If he does, that settles any doubt it might be decent to have—Yaqui—malo Papago—*Sí?*"

The Yaqui spread wide his hands. Then he bent over the tracks in the road. They led everywhither, but gradually he worked out of the thick net to take the trail that the cowboys had followed down to the river. Belding and the rangers kept close at his heels. Occasionally Dick lent a helping hand to the still feeble Indian. He found a trampled spot where the raiders had left their horses. From this point a deeply defined narrow trail led across the dry riverbed.

Belding asked the Yaqui where the raiders would head for in the Sonora Desert. For answer the Indian followed the trail across the stream of sand, through willows and mesquite, up to the level of rock and cactus. At this point he halted. A sand-filled, almost obliterated trail led off to the left, and evidently went round to the east of No Name Mountains.

To the right stretched the road toward Papago Well and the Sonoyta Oasis. The trail of the raiders took a southeasterly course over untrodden desert. The Yaqui spoke in his own tongue, then in Spanish.

"Think he means slow march," said Belding. "Laddy, from the looks of that trail the Greasers are having trouble with the horses."

"Tom, shore a boy could see that," replied Laddy. "Ask Yaqui to tell us where the raiders are headin', an' if there's water."

It was wonderful to see the Yaqui point. His dark hand stretched; he sighted over his stretched finger at a low white escarpment in the distance. Then with a stick he traced a line in the sand, and then at the end of that another line at right angles. He made crosses and marks and holes, and as he drew the rude map he talked in Yaqui, in Spanish; with a word here and there in English. Belding translated as best he could. The raiders were heading southeast toward the railroad that ran from Nogales down into Sonora. It was four days' travel, bad trail, good sure water hole one day out; then water not sure for two days. Raiders traveling slow; bothered by too many horses, not looking for pursuit; were never pursued, could be headed and ambushed that night at the first water hole, a natural trap in a valley.

The men returned to the ranch. The rangers ate and drank while making hurried preparations for travel. Blanco Sol and the cowboys' horses were fed, watered, and saddled. Ladd again refused to ride one of Belding's whites. He was quick and cold.

"Get me a long-range rifle an' lots of shells. Rustle now," he said.

"Laddy, you don't want to be weighted down?" protested Belding.

"Shore I want a gun that'll outshoot the dinky little carbines an' muskets used by the rebels. Trot one out an' be quick."

"I've got a .405, a long-barreled heavy rifle that'll shoot a mile. I use it for mountain sheep. But Laddy, it'll break that bronch's back."

"His back won't break so easy. . . . Dick, take plenty of shells for your Remington. An' don't forget your field glass."

In less than an hour after the time of the raid the three rangers, heavily armed and superbly mounted on fresh horses, rode out on the trail. As Gale turned to look back from the far bank of Forlorn River, he saw Nell waving a white scarf. He stood high in his stirrups and waved his sombrero. Then the mesquite hid the girl's slight figure, and Gale wheeled grim-faced to follow the rangers.

They rode in single file with Ladd in the lead. He did not keep to the trail of the raiders all the time. He made short cuts. The raiders were traveling leisurely, and they evinced a liking for the most level and least cactus-covered stretches of ground. But the cowboy took a beeline course for the white escarpment pointed out by the Yaqui; and nothing save deep washes and impassable patches of cactus or rocks made him swerve from it. He kept the broncho at a steady walk over the rougher places and at a swinging Indian canter over the hard and level ground. The sun grew hot and the wind began to blow. Dust clouds rolled along the blue horizon. Whirling columns of sand, like water spouts at sea, circled up out of white arid basins, and swept away and spread aloft before the wind. The escarpment began to rise, to change color, to show breaks upon its rocky face.

Whenever the rangers rode out on the brow of a knoll or ridge or an eminence, before starting to descend, Ladd required of Gale a long, careful, sweeping survey of the desert ahead through the field glass. There were streams of white dust to be seen, streaks of yellow dust, trailing low clouds of sand over the glistening dunes, but no steadily rising, uniformly shaped puffs that would tell a tale of moving horses on the desert.

At noon the rangers got out of the thick cactus. Moreover, the gravel-bottomed washes, the low weathering, rotting ledges of yellow rock gave place to hard sandy rolls and bare clay knolls. The desert resembled a rounded hummocky sea of color. All light shades of blue and pink and yellow and mauve were there dominated by the glaring white sun. Mirages glistened, wavered, faded in the shimmering waves of heat. Dust as fine as powder whiffed from under the tireless hoofs.

The rangers rode on and the escarpment began to loom. The desert floor inclined perceptibly upward. When Gale got an unobstructed view of the slope of the escarpment he located the raiders and horses. In another hour's travel the rangers could see with naked eyes a long, faint moving streak of black and white dots.

"They're headin' for that yellow pass," said Ladd, pointing to a break in the eastern end of the escarpment. "When they get out of sight we'll rustle. I'm thinkin' that water hole the Yaqui spoke of lays in the pass."

The rangers traveled swiftly over the remaining miles of level desert leading to the ascent of the escarpment. When they achieved the gateway of the pass the sun was low in the west. Dwarfed mesquite and greasewood appeared among the rocks. Ladd gave the word to tie up horses and go forward on foot.

The narrow neck of the pass opened and descended into a valley half a mile wide, perhaps twice that in length. It had apparently unscalable slopes of weathered rock leading up to beetling walls. With floor bare and hard and white, except for a patch of green mesquite near the far end, it was a lurid and desolate spot, the barren bottom of a desert bowl.

"Keep down, boys," said Ladd. "There's the water hole, an' hosses have sharp eyes. Shore the Yaqui figgered this place. I never seen its like for a trap."

Both white and black horses showed against the green, and a thin curling column of blue smoke rose lazily from amid the mesquites.

"I reckon we'd better wait till dark, or mebby daylight," said Jim Lash.

"Let me figger some. Dick, what do you make of the outlet to this hole? Looks rough to me."

With his glass Gale studied the narrow construction of walls and roughened rising floor.

"Laddy, it's harder to get out at that end than here," he replied.

"Shore that's hard enough. Let me have a look. . . . Well, boys, it don't take no figgerin' for this job. Jim, I'll want you at the other end blockin' the pass when we're ready to start."

"When'll that be?" inquired Jim.

"Soon as it's light enough in the mornin'. That Greaser outfit will hang till to-morrow. There's no sure water ahead for two days, you remember."

"I reckon I can slip through to the other end after dark," said Lash, thoughtfully. "It might get me in bad to go round."

The rangers stole back from the vantage point and returned to their horses, which they untied and left farther round among broken sections of cliff. For the horses it was a dry, hungry camp, but the rangers built a fire and had their short though strengthening meal.

The location was high, and through a break in the jumble of rocks the great colored void of desert could be seen rolling away endlessly to the west. The sun set, and after it had gone down the golden tips of mountains dulled, their lower shadows creeping upward.

Jim Lash rolled in his saddle blanket, his feet near the fire, and went to sleep. Ladd told Gale to do likewise while he kept the fire up and waited until it was late enough for Jim to undertake circling round the raiders. When Gale awakened the night was dark, cold, windy. The stars shone with white brilliance. Jim was up saddling his horse, and Ladd was talking low. When Gale rose to accompany them both rangers said he need not go. But Gale wanted to go, because that was the thing Ladd or Jim would have done.

With Ladd leading, they moved away into the gloom. Advance was exceedingly slow, careful, silent. Under the walls the blackness seemed impenetrable. The horse was as cautious as his master. Ladd did not lose his way, nevertheless he wound between blocks of stone and clumps of mesquite, and often tried a passage to abandon it. Finally the trail showed pale in the gloom, and eastern stars twinkled between the lofty ramparts of the pass.

The advance here was still as stealthily made as before, but not so difficult or slow. When the dense gloom of the pass lightened, and there was a wide space of sky and stars overhead, Ladd halted and stood silent a moment.

"Luck again!" he whispered. "The wind's in your face, Jim. The horses won't scent you. Go slow. Don't crack a stone. Keep close under the wall. Try to get up as high as this at the other end. Wait till daylight before riskin' a loose slope. I'll be ridin' the job early. That's all."

Ladd's cool, easy speech was scarcely significant of the perilous undertaking. Lash moved very slowly away, leading his horse. The soft pads of hoofs ceased to sound about the time the gray shape merged into the black shadows. Then Ladd touched Dick's arm, and turned back up the trail.

But Dick tarried a moment. He wanted a fuller sense of that ebony-bottomed abyss, with its pale encircling walls reaching up to the dusky blue sky and the brilliant stars. There was absolutely no sound.

He retraced his steps down, soon coming up with Ladd; and together they picked a way back through the winding recesses of cliff. The camp-fire was smoldering. Ladd replenished it and lay down to get a few hours' sleep, while Gale kept watch. The after part of the night wore on till the paling of stars, the thickening of gloom indicated the dark hour before dawn. The spot was secluded from wind, but the air grew cold as ice. Gale spent the time stripping wood from a dead mesquite, in pacing to and fro, in listening. Blanco Sol stamped occasionally, which sound was all that broke the stillness. Ladd awoke before the faintest gray appeared. The rangers ate and drank. When the black did lighten to gray they saddled the horses and led them out to the pass and down to the point where they had parted with Lash. Here they awaited daylight.

To Gale it seemed long in coming. Such a delay always aggravated the slow fire within him. He had nothing of Ladd's patience. He wanted action. The gray shadow below thinned out, and the patch of mesquite made a blot upon the pale valley. Then day dawned.

Still Ladd waited. He grew more silent, grimmer as the time of action approached. Gale wondered what the plan of attack would be. Yet he did not ask. He waited ready for orders.

The valley grew clear of gray shadow except under leaning walls on the eastern side. Then a straight column of smoke rose from among the mesquites. Manifestly this was what Ladd had been awaiting. He took the long .405 from its sheath and tried the lever. Then he lifted a cartridge belt from the pommel of his saddle. Every ring held a shell and these shells were four inches long. He buckled the belt round him.

"Come on, Dick."

Ladd led the way down the slope until he reached a position that commanded the rising of the trail from a level. It was the only place a man or horse could leave the valley for the pass.

"Dick, here's your stand. If any raider rides in range take a crack at him. . . . Now I want the lend of your hoss."

"Blanco Sol!" exclaimed Gale, more in amaze that Ladd should ask for the horse than in reluctance to lend him.

"Will you let me have him?" Ladd repeated, almost curtly.

"Certainly, Laddy."

A smile momentarily chased the dark cold gloom that had set upon the ranger's lean face.

"Shore I appreciate it, Dick. I know how you care for that hoss. I guess mebbe Charlie Ladd has loved a hoss! An' one not so good as Sol. I was only tryin' your nerve, Dick, askin' you without tellin' my plan. Sol won't get a scratch, you can gamble on that! I'll ride him down into the valley an' pull the Greasers out in the open. They've got short-ranged carbines. They can't keep out of range of the .405, an' I'll be takin' the dust of their lead. Sabe, señor?"

"Laddy! You'll run Sol away from the raiders when they chase you? Run him after them when they try to get away?"

"Shore. I'll run all the time. They can't gain on Sol, an' he'll run them down when I want. Can you beat it?"

"No. It's great! . . . But suppose a raider comes out on Blanco Diablo?"

"I reckon that's the one weak place in my plan. I'm figgerin' they'll never think of that till it's too late. But if they do, well, Sol can outrun Diablo. An' I can always kill the white devil!"

Ladd's strange hate of the horse showed in the passion of his last words, in his hardening jaw and grim set lips.

Gale's hand went swiftly to the ranger's shoulder.

"Laddy. Don't kill Diablo unless it's to save your life."

"All right. But, by God, if I get a chance I'll make Blanco Sol run him off his legs!"

He spoke no more and set about changing the length of Sol's stirrups. When he had them adjusted to suit he mounted and rode down the trail and out upon the level. He rode leisurely as if merely going to water his horse. The long black rifle lying across his saddle, however, was ominous.

Gale securely tied the other horse to a mesquite at hand, and took a position behind a low rock over which he could easily see and shoot when necessary. He imagined Jim Lash in a similar position at the far end of the valley blocking the outlet. Gale had grown accustomed to danger and the hard and fierce feelings peculiar to it. But the coming drama was so peculiarly different in promise from all he had experienced, that he awaited the moment of action with thrilling intensity. In him stirred long, brooding wrath at these border raiders—affection for Belding, and keen desire to avenge the outrages he had suffered—warm admiration for the cold, implacable Ladd and his absolute fearlessness, and a curious throbbing interest in the old, much-discussed and never-decided argument as to whether Blanco Sol was a fleeter, stronger horse than Blanco Diablo. Gale felt that he was to see a race between these great rivals—the kind of race that made men and horses terrible.

Ladd rode a quarter of a mile out upon the flat before anything happened. Then a whistle rent the still, cold air. A horse had seen or scented Blanco Sol. The whistle was prolonged, faint, but clear. It made the blood thrum in Gale's ears. Sol halted. His head shot up with the old, wild, spirited sweep. Gale leveled his glass at the patch of mesquites. He saw the raiders running to an open place, pointing, gesticulating. The glass brought them so close that he saw dark faces. Suddenly they broke and fled back among the trees. Then he got only white and dark gleams of moving bodies. Evidently that moment was one of boots, guns, and saddles for the raiders.

Lowering the glass, Gale saw that Blanco Sol had started forward again. His gait was now a canter, and he had covered another quarter of a mile before horses and raiders appeared upon the outskirts of the mesquites. Then Blanco Sol stopped. His shrill, ringing whistle came distinctly to Gale's ears. The raiders were mounted on dark horses, and they stood abreast in a motionless line. Gale chuckled as he appreciated what a puzzle the situation presented for them. A lone horseman in the middle of the valley did not perhaps seem so menacing himself as the possibilities his presence suggested.

Then Gale saw a raider gallop swiftly from the group toward the farther outlet of the valley. This might have been owing to characteristic cowardice; but it was more likely a move of the raiders to make sure of retreat. Undoubtedly Ladd saw this galloping horseman. A few waiting moments ensued. The galloping horseman reached the slope, began to climb. With naked eyes Gale saw a puff of white smoke spring out of the rocks. Then the raider wheeled his plunging horse back to the level, and went racing wildly down the valley.

The compact bunch of bays and blacks seemed to break apart and spread rapidly from the edge of the mesquites. Puffs of white smoke indicated firing, and showed the nature of the raiders' excitement. They were far out of ordinary range; but they spurred toward Ladd, shooting as they rode. Ladd held his ground; the big white horse stood like a rock in his tracks. Gale saw little spouts of dust rise in front of Blanco Sol and spread swift as sight to his rear. The raiders' bullets, striking low, were skipping along the hard, bare floor of the valley. Then Ladd raised the long rifle. There was no smoke, but three high, spanging reports rang out. A gap opened in the dark line of advancing horsemen; then a riderless steed sheered off to the right. Blanco Sol seemed to turn as on a pivot and charged back toward the lower end of the valley. He circled over to Gale's right and stretched out into his run. There were now five raiders in pursuit, and they came sweeping down, yelling and shooting, evidently sure of their quarry. Ladd reserved his fire. He kept turning from back to front in his saddle.

Gale saw how the space widened between pursuers and pursued, saw distinctly when Ladd eased up Sol's running. Manifestly Ladd intended to try to lead the raiders round in front of Gale's position, and, presently, Gale saw he was going to succeed. The raiders, riding like vaqueros, swept on in a curve, cutting off what distance they could. One fellow, a small, wiry rider, high on his mount's neck like a jockey, led his companions by many yards. He seemed to be getting the range of Ladd, or else he shot high, for his bullets did not strike up the dust behind Sol. Gale was ready to shoot. Blanco Sol pounded by, his rapid, rhythmic hoofbeats plainly to be heard. He was running easily.

Gale tried to still the jump of heart and pulse, and turned his eye again on the nearest pursuer. This raider was crossing in, his carbine held muzzle up in his right hand, and he was coming swiftly. It was a long shot, upward of five hundred yards. Gale had not time to adjust the sights of the Remington, but he knew the gun and, holding coarsely upon the swiftly moving blot, he began to shoot. The first bullet sent up a great splash of dust beneath the horse's nose, making him leap as if to hurdle a fence. The rifle was automatic; Gale needed only to pull the trigger. He saw now that the raiders behind were in line. Swiftly he worked the trigger. Suddenly the leading horse leaped convulsively, not up nor aside, but straight ahead, and then he crashed to the ground, throwing his rider like a catapult, and then slid and rolled. He half got up, fell back, and kicked; but his rider never moved.

The other rangers sawed the reins of plunging steeds and whirled to escape the unseen battery. Gale slipped a fresh clip into the magazine of his rifle. He restrained himself from useless firing and gave eager eye to the duel below. Ladd began to shoot while Sol was running. The .405 rang out sharply—then again. The heavy bullets streaked the dust all the way across the valley. Ladd aimed deliberately and pulled slowly, unmindful of the kicking dust-puffs behind Sol, and to the side. The raiders spurred madly in pursuit, loading and firing. They shot ten times while Ladd shot once, and all in vain; and on Ladd's sixth shot a raider toppled backward, threw his carbine, and fell with his foot catching in a stirrup. The frightened horse plunged away, dragging him in a path of dust.

Gale had set himself to miss nothing of that fighting race, yet the action passed too swiftly for clear sight of all. Ladd had emptied a magazine, and now Blanco Sol quickened and lengthened his running stride. He ran away from his pursuers. Then it was that the ranger's ruse was divined by the raiders. They hauled sharply up and seemed to be conferring. But that was a fatal mistake. Blanco Sol was seen to break his gait and slow down in several jumps, then square away and stand stock-still. Ladd fired at the closely grouped raiders. An instant passed. Then Gale heard the spat of a bullet out in front, saw a puff of dust, then heard the lead strike the rocks and go whining away. And it was after this that one of the raiders fell prone from his saddle. The steel-jacketed .405 had gone through him on its uninterrupted way to hum past Gale's position.

The remaining two raiders frantically spurred their horses and fled up the valley. Ladd sent Sol after them. It seemed to Gale, even though he realized his excitement, that Blanco Sol made those horses seem like snails. The raiders split, one making for the eastern outlet, the other circling back of the mesquites. Ladd kept on after the latter. Then puffs of white smoke and rifle shots faintly crackling told of Jim Lash's hand in the game. However, he succeeded only in driving the raider back into the valley. But Ladd had turned the other horseman, and now it appeared the two raiders were between Lash above on the stony slope and Ladd below on the level. There was desperate riding on part of the raiders to keep from being hemmed in closer. Only one of them got away, and he came riding for life down under the eastern wall. Blanco Sol settled into his graceful, beautiful swing. He gained steadily, though he was far from extending himself. By Gale's actual count the raider fired eight times in that race down the valley, and all his bullets went low and wide. He pitched the carbine away and lost all control in headlong flight.

Some few hundred rods to the left of Gale the raider put his horse to the weathered slope. He began to climb. The horse was superb, infinitely more courageous than his rider. Zigzag they went up and up, and when Ladd reached the edge of the slope they were high along the cracked and guttered rampart. Once—twice Ladd raised the long rifle, but each time he lowered it. Gale divined that the ranger's restraint was not on account of the Mexican, but for that valiant and faithful horse. Up and up he went, and the yellow dust clouds rose, and an avalanche rolled rattling and cracking down the slope. It was beyond belief that a horse, burdened or unburdened, could find footing and hold it upon that wall of narrow ledges and inverted, slanting gullies. But he climbed on, sure-footed as a mountain goat, and, surmounting the last rough steps, he stood a moment silhouetted against the white sky. Then he disappeared. Ladd sat astride Blanco Sol gazing upward. How the cowboy must have honored that raider's brave steed!

Gale, who had been too dumb to shout the admiration he felt, suddenly leaped up, and his voice came with a shriek:

"LOOK OUT, LADDY!"

A big horse, like a white streak, was bearing down to the right of the ranger. Blanco Diablo! A matchless rider swung with the horse's motion. Gale was stunned. Then he remembered the first raider, the one Lash had shot at and driven away from the outlet. This fellow had made for the mesquite and had put a saddle on Belding's favorite. In the heat of the excitement, while Ladd had been intent upon the climbing horse, this last raider had come down with the speed of the wind straight for the western outlet. Perhaps, very probably, he did not know Gale was there to block it; and certainly he hoped to pass Ladd and Blanco Sol.

A touch of the spur made Sol lunge forward to head off the raider. Diablo was in his stride, but the distance and angle favored Sol. The raider had no carbine. He held aloft a gun ready to level it and fire. He sat the saddle as if it were a stationary seat. Gale saw Ladd lean down and drop the .405 in the sand. He would take no chances of wounding Belding's best-loved horse.

Then Gale sat transfixed with suspended breath watching the horses thundering toward him. Blanco Diablo was speeding low, fleet as an antelope, fierce and terrible in his devilish action, a horse for war and blood and death. He seemed unbeatable. Yet to see the magnificently running Blanco Sol was but to court a doubt. Gale stood spellbound. He might have shot the raider; but he never thought of such a thing. The distance swiftly lessened. Plain it was the raider could not make the opening ahead of Ladd. He saw it and swerved to the left, emptying his six-shooter as he turned. His dark face gleamed as he flashed by Gale.

Blanco Sol thundered across. Then the race became straight away up the valley. Diablo was cold and Sol was hot: therein lay the only handicap and vantage. It was a fleet, beautiful, magnificent race. Gale thrilled and exulted and yelled as his horse settled into a steadily swifter run and began to gain. The dust rolled in a funnel-shaped cloud from the flying hoofs. The raider wheeled with gun puffing white and Ladd ducked low over the neck of his horse.

The gap between Diablo and Sol narrowed yard by yard. At first it had been a wide one. The raider beat his mount and spurred, beat and spurred, wheeled round to shoot, then bent forward again. In his circle at the upper end of the valley he turned far short of the jumble of rocks.

All the devil that was in Blanco Diablo had its running on the downward stretch. The strange, cruel urge of bit and spur, the crazed rider who stuck like a burr upon him, the shots and smoke added terror to his natural violent temper. He ran himself off his feet. But he could not elude that relentless horse behind him. The running of Blanco Sol was that of a sure, remorseless driving power—steadier—stronger—swifter with every long and wonderful stride.

The raider tried to sheer Diablo off closer under the wall, to make the slope where his companion had escaped. But Diablo was uncontrollable. He was running wild, with breaking gait. Closer and closer crept that white, smoothly gliding, beautiful machine of speed.

Then, like one white flash following another, the two horses gleamed down the bank of a wash and disappeared in clouds of dust.

Gale watched with strained and smarting eyes. The thick throb in his ears was pierced by faint sounds of gunshots. Then he waited in almost unendurable suspense.

Suddenly something whiter than the background of dust appeared above the low roll of valley floor. Gale leveled his glass. In the clear circle shone Blanco Sol's noble head with its long black bar from ears to nose. Sol's head was drooping now. Another second showed Ladd still in the saddle.

The ranger was leading Blanco Diablo—spent—broken—dragging—riderless.

CHAPTER 9

AN INTERRUPTED SIESTA

No man ever had a more eloquent and beautiful pleader for his cause than had Dick Gale in Mercedes Castañeda. He peeped through the green, shining twigs of the *palo verde* that shaded his door. The hour was high noon, and the patio was sultry. The only sounds were the hum of bees in the flowers and the low murmur of the Spanish girl's melodious voice. Nell lay in the hammock, her hands behind her head, with rosy cheeks and arch eyes. Indeed she looked rebellious. Certain it was, Dick reflected, that the young lady had fully recovered the willful personality which had lain dormant for a while. Equally certain it seemed that Mercedes's earnestness was not apparently having the effect it should have had.

Dick was inclined to be rebellious himself. Belding had kept the rangers in off the line, and therefore Dick had been idle most of the time, and, though he tried hard, he had been unable to stay far from Nell's vicinity. He believed she cared for him; but he could not catch her alone long enough to verily his tormenting hope. When alone she was as elusive as a shadow, as quick as a flash, as mysterious as a Yaqui. When he tried to catch her in the garden or fields, or corner her in the patio, she eluded him, and left behind a memory of dark-blue, haunting eyes. It was that look in her eyes which lent him hope. At other times, when it might have been possible for Dick to speak, Nell clung closely to Mercedes. He had long before enlisted the loyal Mercedes in his cause; but in spite of this Nell had been more than a match for them both.

Gale pondered over an idea he had long revolved in his mind, and which now suddenly gave place to a decision that made his heart swell and his cheek burn. He peeped again through the green branches to see Nell laughing at the fiery Mercedes.

"*Quién sabe,*" he called, mockingly, and was delighted with Nell's quick, amazed start.

Then he went in search of Mrs. Belding, and found her busy in the kitchen.

The relation between Gale and Mrs. Belding had subtly and incomprehensively changed. He understood her less than when at first he divined an antagonism in her. If such a thing were possible she had retained the antagonism while seeming to yield to some influence that must have been fondness for him. Gale was in no wise sure of her affection, and he had long imagined she was afraid of him, or of something that he represented. He had gone on, openly and fairly, though discreetly, with his rather one-sided love affair; and as time passed he had grown less conscious of what had seemed her unspoken opposition. Gale had come to care greatly for Nell's mother. Not only was she the comfort and strength of her home, but also of the inhabitants of Forlorn River. Indian, Mexican, American were all the same to her in trouble or illness; and then she was nurse, doctor, peacemaker, helper. She was good and noble, and there was not a child or grownup in Forlorn River who did not love and bless her. But Mrs. Belding did not seem happy. She was brooding, intense, deep, strong, eager for the happiness and welfare of others; and she was dominated by a worship of her daughter that was as strange as it was pathetic. Mrs. Belding seldom smiled, and never hugged. There was always a soft, sad, hurt look in her eyes. Gale often wondered if there had been other tragedy in her life than the supposed loss of her father in the desert. Perhaps it was the very unsolved nature of that loss which made it haunting.

Mrs. Belding heard Dick's step as he entered the kitchen and, looking up, greeted him.

"Mother," began Dick, earnestly. Belding called her that, and so did

Ladd and Lash, but it was the first time for Dick. "Mother—I want to speak to you."

The only indication Mrs. Belding gave of being startled was in her eyes, which darkened, shadowed with multiplying thought.

"I love Nell," went on Dick, simply, "and I want you to let me ask her to be my wife."

Mrs. Belding's face blanched to a deathly white. Gale, thinking with surprise and concern that she was going to faint, moved quickly toward her, took her arm.

"Forgive me. I was blunt. . . . But I thought you knew."

"I've known for a long time," replied Mrs. Belding. Her voice was steady, and there was no evidence of agitation except in her pallor. "Then you—you haven't spoken to Nell?"

Dick laughed. "I've been trying to get a chance to tell her. I haven't had it yet. But she knows. There are other ways besides speech. And Mercedes has told her. I hope, I almost believe Nell cares a little for me."

"I've known that, too, for a long time," said Mrs. Belding, low almost as a whisper.

"You know!" cried Dick, with a glow and rush of feeling.

"Dick, you must be very blind not to see what has been plain to all of us. . . . I guess—it couldn't have been helped. You're a splendid fellow. No wonder she loves you."

"Mother! You'll give her to me?"

She drew him to the light and looked with strange, piercing intentness into his face. Gale had never dreamed a woman's eyes could hold such a world of thought and feeling. It seemed all the sweetness of life was there, and all the pain.

"Do you love her?" she asked.

"With all my heart."

"You want to marry her?"

"Ah, I want to! As much as I want to live and work for her."

"*When* would you marry her?"

"Why! . . . Just as soon as she will do it. To-morrow!" Dick gave a wild, exultant little laugh.

"Dick Gale, you want my Nell? You love her just as she is—her sweetness—her goodness? Just herself, body and soul? . . . There's nothing could change you—nothing?"

"Dear Mrs. Belding, I love Nell for herself. If she loves me I'll be the happiest of men. There's absolutely nothing that could make any difference in me."

"But your people? Oh, Dick, you come of a proud family. I can tell. I—I once knew a young man like you. A few months can't change pride—blood. Years can't change them. You've become a ranger. You love the adventure—the wild life. That won't last. Perhaps you'll settle down to ranching. I know you love the West. But, Dick, there's your family—"

"If you want to know anything about my family, I'll tell you," interrupted Dick, with strong feeling. "I've no secrets about them or myself. My future and happiness are Nell's to make. No one else shall count with me."

"Then, Dick—you may have her. God—bless—you—both."

Mrs. Belding's strained face underwent a swift and mobile relaxation, and suddenly she was weeping in strangely mingled happiness and bitterness.

"Why, Mother!" Gale could say no more. He did not comprehend a mood seemingly so utterly at variance with Mrs. Belding's habitual temperament. But he put his arm around her. In another moment she had gained command over herself, and, kissing him, she pushed him out of the door.

"There! Go tell her, Dick. . . . And have some spunk about it!"

Gale went thoughtfully back to his room. He vowed that he would answer for Nell's happiness, if he had the wonderful good fortune to win her. Then remembering the hope Mrs. Belding had given him, Dick lost his gravity in a flash, and something began to dance and ring within him. He simply could not keep his steps turned from the patio. Every path led there. His blood was throbbing, his hopes mounting, his spirit soaring. He knew he had never before entered the patio with that inspirited presence.

"Now for some spunk!" he said, under his breath.

Plainly he meant his merry whistle and his buoyant step to interrupt this first languorous stage of the siesta which the girls always took during the hot hours. Nell had acquired the habit long before Mercedes came to show how fixed a thing it was in the life of the tropics. But neither girl heard him. Mercedes lay under the *palo verde*, her beautiful head dark and still upon a cushion. Nell was asleep in the hammock. There was an abandonment in her deep repose, and a faint smile upon her face. Her sweet, red lips, with the soft, perfect curve, had always fascinated Dick, and now drew him irresistibly. He had always been consumed with a desire to kiss her, and now he was overwhelmed with his opportunity. It would be a terrible thing to do, but if she did not awaken at once— No, he would fight the temptation. That would be more than spunk. It would— Suddenly an ugly green fly sailed low over Nell, appeared about to alight on her. Noiselessly Dick stepped close to the hammock bent under the tree, and with a sweep of his hand chased the intruding fly away. But he found himself powerless to straighten up. He was close to her—bending over her face—near the sweet lips. The insolent, dreaming smile just parted them. Then he thought he was lost. But she stirred—he feared she would awaken.

He had stepped back erect when she opened her eyes. They were sleepy, yet surprised until she saw him. Then she was wide awake in a second, bewildered, uncertain.

"Why—you here?" she asked, slowly.

"Large as life!" replied Dick, with unusual gayety.

"How long have you been here?"

"Just got here this fraction of a second," he replied, lying shamelessly.

It was evident that she did not know whether or not to believe him, and as she studied him a slow blush dyed her cheek.

"You are absolutely truthful when you say you just stepped there?"

"Why, of course," answered Dick, right glad he did not have to lie about that.

"I thought—I was—dreaming," she said, and evidently the sound of her voice reassured her.

"Yes, you looked as if you were having pleasant dreams," replied Dick. "So sorry to wake you. I can't see how I came to do it, I was so quiet. Mercedes didn't wake. Well, I'll go and let you have your siesta and dreams."

But he did not move to go. Nell regarded him with curious, speculative eyes.

"Isn't it a lovely day?" queried Dick.

"I think it's hot."

"Only ninety in the shade. And you've told me the mercury goes to one hundred and thirty in midsummer. This is just a glorious golden day."

"Yesterday was finer, but you didn't notice it."

"Oh, yesterday was somewhere back in the past—the inconsequential past."

Nell's sleepy blue eyes opened a little wider. She did not know what to make of this changed young man. Dick felt gleeful and tried hard to keep the fact from becoming manifest.

"What's the inconsequential past? You seem remarkably happy today."

"I certainly am happy. *Adiós*. Pleasant dreams."

Dick turned away then and left the patio by the opening into the yard. Nell was really sleepy, and when she had fallen asleep again he would return. He walked around for a while. Belding and the rangers were shoeing a broncho. Yaqui was in the field with the horses. Blanco Sol grazed contentedly, and now and then lifted his head to watch. His long ears went up at sight of his master, and he whistled. Presently Dick, as if magnet-drawn, retraced his steps to the patio and entered noiselessly.

Nell was now deep in her siesta. She was inert, relaxed, untroubled by dreams. Her hair was damp on her brow.

Again Nell stirred, and gradually awakened. Her eyes unclosed, humid, shadowy, unconscious. They rested upon Dick for a moment before they became clear and comprehensive. He stood back fully ten feet from her, and to all outside appearances regarded her calmly.

"I've interrupted your siesta again," he said. "Please forgive me. I'll take myself off."

He wandered away, and when it became impossible for him to stay away any longer he returned to the patio.

The instant his glance rested upon Nell's face he divined she was feigning sleep. The faint rose-blush had paled. The warm, rich, golden tint of her skin had fled. Dick dropped upon his knees and bent over her. Though his blood was churning in his veins, his breast laboring, his mind whirling with the wonder of that moment and its promise, he made himself deliberate. He wanted more than anything he had ever wanted in his life to see if she would keep up that pretense of sleep and let him kiss her. She must have felt his breath, for her hair waved off her brow. Her cheeks were now white. Her breast swelled and sank. He bent down closer—closer. But he must have been maddeningly slow, for as he bent still closer Nell's eyes opened, and he caught a swift purple gaze of eyes as she whirled her head. Then, with a little cry, she rose and fled.

CHAPTER 10

ROJAS

No word from George Thorne had come to Forlorn River in weeks. Gale grew concerned over the fact, and began to wonder if anything serious could have happened to him. Mercedes showed a slow, wearing strain.

Thorne's commission expired the end of January, and if he could not get his discharge immediately, he surely could obtain leave of absence. Therefore, Gale waited, not without growing anxiety, and did his best to cheer Mercedes. The first of February came bringing news of rebel activities and bandit operations in and around Casita, but not a word from the cavalryman.

Mercedes became silent, mournful. Her eyes were great black windows of tragedy. Nell devoted herself entirely to the unfortunate girl; Dick exerted himself to persuade her that all would yet come well; in fact, the whole household could not have been kinder to a sister or a daughter. But their united efforts were unavailing. Mercedes seemed to accept with fatalistic hopelessness a last and crowning misfortune.

A dozen times Gale declared he would ride in to Casita and find out why they did not hear from Thorne; however, older and wiser heads prevailed over his impetuosity. Belding was not sanguine over the safety of the Casita trail. Refugees from there arrived every day in Forlorn River, and if the tales they told were true, real war would have been preferable to what was going on along the border. Belding and the rangers and the Yaqui held a consultation. Not only had the Indian become a faithful servant to Gale, but he was also of value to Belding. Yaqui had all the craft of his class, and superior intelligence. His knowledge of Mexicans was second only to his hate of them. And Yaqui, who had been scouting on all the trails, gave information that made Belding decide to wait some days before sending any one to Casita. He required promises from his rangers, particularly Gale, not to leave without his consent.

It was upon Gale's coming from this conference that he encountered Nell. Since the interrupted siesta episode she had been more than ordinarily elusive, and about all he had received from her was a tantalizing smile from a distance. He got the impression now, however, that she had awaited him. When he drew close to her he was certain of it, and he experienced more than surprise.

"Dick," she began, hurriedly. "Dad's not going to send any one to see about Thorne?"

"No, not yet. He thinks it best not to. We all think so. I'm sorry. Poor Mercedes!"

"I knew it. I tried to coax him to send Laddy or even Yaqui. He wouldn't listen to me. Dick, Mercedes is dying by inches. Can't you see what ails her? It's more than love or fear. It's uncertainty—suspense. Oh, can't we find out for her?"

"Nell, I feel as badly as you about her. I wanted to ride in to Casita. Belding shut me up quick, the last time."

Nell came close to Gale, clasped his arm. There was no color in her face. Her eyes held a dark, eager excitement.

"Dick, will you skip off without Dad's consent? Risk it! Go to Casita and find out what's happened to Thorne—at least if he ever started for Forlorn River?"

"No, Nell, I won't do that."

She drew away from him with passionate suddenness.

"Are you afraid?"

This certainly was not the Nell Burton that Gale knew.

"No, I'm not afraid," Gale replied, a little nettled.

"Will you go—for my sake?" Like lightning her mood changed and she was close to him again, hands on his, her face white, her whole presence sweetly alluring.

"Nell, I won't disobey Belding," protested Gale. "I won't break my word."

"Dick, it'll not be so bad as that. But—what if it is? . . . Go, Dick, if not for poor Mercedes's sake, then for mine—to please me. I'll—I'll. . . . you won't lose anything by going. I think I know how Mercedes feels. Just a word from Thorne or about him would save her. Take Blanco Sol and go, Dick. What rebel outfit could ever ride you down on that horse? Why, Dick, if I was up on Sol I wouldn't be afraid of the whole rebel army."

"My dear girl, it's not a question of being afraid. It's my word—my duty to Belding."

"You said you loved me. If you do love me you will go. . . . You don't love me!"

Gale could only stare at this transformed girl.

"Dick, listen! . . . If you go—if you fetch some word of Thorne to comfort Mercedes, you—well, you will have your reward."

"*Nell!*"

Her dangerous sweetness was as amazing as this newly revealed character.

"Dick, will you go?"

"No—no!" cried Gale, in violence, struggling with himself. "Nell Burton, I'll tell you this. To have the reward I want would mean pretty near heaven for me. But not even for that will I break my word to your father."

She seemed the incarnation of girlish scorn and willful passion.

"*Gracias*, señor," she replied, mockingly. "*Adiós*." Then she flashed out of his sight.

Gale went to his room at once, disturbed and thrilling, and did not soon recover from that encounter.

The following morning at the breakfast table Nell was not present. Mrs. Belding evidently considered the fact somewhat unusual, for she called out into the patio and then into the yard. Then she went to Mercedes's room. But Nell was not there, either.

"She's in one of her tantrums lately," said Belding. "Wouldn't speak to me this morning. Let her alone, Mother. She's spoiled enough, without running after her. She's always hungry. She'll be on hand presently, don't mistake me."

Notwithstanding Belding's conviction, which Gale shared, Nell did not appear at all during the hour. When Belding and the rangers went outside, Yaqui was eating his meal on the bench where he always sat.

"Yaqui—*Lluvia d'oro, sí?*" asked Belding, waving his hand toward the corrals. The Indian's beautiful name for Nell meant "shower of gold," and Belding used it in asking Yaqui if he had seen her. He received a negative reply.

Perhaps half an hour afterward, as Gale was leaving his room, he saw the Yaqui running up the path from the fields. It was markedly out of the ordinary to see the Indian run. Gale wondered what was the matter. Yaqui ran straight to Belding, who was at work at his bench under the wagon shed. In less than a moment Belding was bellowing for his rangers. Gale got to him first, but Ladd and Lash were not far behind.

"Blanco Sol gone!" yelled Belding, in a rage.

"Gone? In broad daylight, with the Indian a-watchin'?" queried Ladd.

"It happened while Yaqui was at breakfast. That's sure. He'd just watered Sol."

"Raiders!" exclaimed Jim Lash.

"Lord only knows. Yaqui says it wasn't raiders."

"Mebbe Sol's just walked off somewheres."

"He was haltered in the corral."

"Send Yaqui to find the hoss's trail, an' let's figger," said Ladd. "Shore this's no raider job."

In the swift search that ensued Gale did not have anything to say; but his mind was forming a conclusion. When he found his old saddle and bridle missing from the peg in the barn his conclusion became a positive conviction, and it made him, for the moment, cold and sick and speechless.

"Hey, Dick, don't take it so much to heart," said Belding. "We'll likely find Sol, and if we don't, there's other good horses."

"I'm not thinking of Sol," replied Gale.

Ladd cast a sharp glance at Gale, snapped his fingers, and said:

"Damn me if I ain't guessed it, too!"

"What's wrong with you locoed gents?" bluntly demanded Belding.

"Nell has slipped away on Sol," answered Dick.

There was a blank pause, which presently Belding broke.

"Well, that's all right, if Nell's on him. I was afraid we'd lost the horse."

"Belding, you're trackin' bad," said Ladd, wagging his head.

"Nell has started for Casita," burst out Gale. "She has gone to fetch Mercedes some word about Thorne. Oh, Belding, you needn't shake your head. I know she's gone. She tried to persuade me to go, and was furious when I wouldn't."

"I don't believe it," replied Belding, hoarsely. "Nell may have her temper. She's a little devil at times, but she always had good sense."

"Tom, you can gamble she's gone," said Ladd.

"Aw, hell, no! Jim, what do you think?" implored Belding.

"I reckon Sol's white head is pointed level an' straight down the Casita trail. An' Nell can ride. We're losin' time."

That roused Belding to action.

"I say you're all wrong," he yelled, starting for the corrals. "She's only taking a little ride, same as she's done often. But rustle now. Find out. Dick, you ride cross the valley. Jim, you hunt up and down the river. I'll head up San Felipe way. And you, Laddy, take Diablo and hit the Casita trail. If she really has gone after Thorne you can catch her in an hour or so."

"Shore I'll go," replied Ladd. "But, Beldin', if you're not plumb crazy you're close to it. That big white devil can't catch Sol. Not in an hour or a day or a week! What's more, at the end of any runnin' time, with an even start, Sol will be farther in the lead. An' now Sol's got an hour's start."

"Laddy, you mean to say Sol is a faster horse than Diablo?" thundered Belding, his face purple.

"Shore. I mean to tell you just that there," replied the ranger.

"I'll—I'll bet a—"

"We're wastin' time," curtly interrupted Ladd. "You can gamble on this if you want to. I'll ride your Blanco Devil as he never was rid before, 'cept once when a damn sight better hossman than I am couldn't make him outrun Sol."

Without more words the men saddled and were off, not waiting for the Yaqui to come in with possible information as to what trail Blanco Sol had taken. It certainly did not show in the clear sand of the level valley where Gale rode to and fro. When Gale returned to the house he found Belding and Lash awaiting him. They did not mention their own search, but stated that Yaqui had found Blanco Sol's tracks in the Casita trail. After some consultation Belding decided to send Lash along after Ladd.

The interminable time that followed contained for Gale about as much suspense as he could well bear. What astonished him and helped him greatly to fight off actual distress was the endurance of Nell's mother.

Early on the morning of the second day, Gale, who had acquired an unbreakable habit of watching, saw three white horses and a bay come wearily stepping down the road. He heard Blanco Sol's familiar whistle, and he leaped up wild with joy. The horse was riderless. Gale's sudden joy received a violent check, then resurged when he saw a limp white form in Jim Lash's arms. Ladd was supporting a horseman who wore a military uniform.

Gale shouted with joy and ran into the house to tell the good news. It was the ever-thoughtful Mrs. Belding who prevented him from rushing in to tell Mercedes. Then he hurried out into the yard, closely followed by the Beldings.

Lash handed down a ragged, travel-stained, wan girl into Belding's arms.

"Dad! Mama!"

It was indeed a repentant Nell, but there was spirit yet in the tired blue eyes. Then she caught sight of Gale and gave him a faint smile.

"Hello—Dick."

"Nell!" Gale reached for her hand, held it tightly, and found speech difficult.

"You needn't worry—about your old horse," she said, as Belding carried her toward the door. "Oh, Dick! Blanco Sol is—glorious!"

Gale turned to greet his friend. Indeed, it was but a haggard ghost of the cavalryman. Thorne looked ill or wounded. Gale's greeting was also a question full of fear.

Thorne's answer was a faint smile. He seemed ready to drop from the saddle. Gale helped Ladd hold Thorne upon the horse until they reached the house. Belding came out again. His welcome was checked as he saw the condition of the cavalryman. Thorne reeled into Dick's arms. But he was able to stand and walk.

"I'm not—hurt. Only weak—starved," he said. "Is Mercedes— Take me to her."

"She'll be well the minute she sees him," averred Belding, as he and Gale led the cavalryman to Mercedes's room. There they left him; and Gale, at least, felt his ears ringing with the girl's broken cry of joy.

When Belding and Gale hurried forth again the rangers were tending the tired horses. Upon returning to the house Jim Lash calmly lit his pipe, and Ladd declared that, hungry as he was, he had to tell his story.

"Shore, Beldin'," began Ladd, "that was funny about Diablo catchin' Blanco Sol. Funny ain't the word. I nearly laughed myself to death. Well, I rode in Sol's tracks all the way to Casita. Never seen a rebel or a raider till I got to town. Figgered Nell made the trip in five hours. I went straight to the camp of the cavalrymen, an' found them just coolin' off an' dressin' down their hosses after what looked to me like a big ride. I got there too late for the fireworks.

"Some soldier took me to an officer's tent. Nell was there, some white an' all in. She just said, 'Laddy!' Thorne was there, too, an' he was bein' worked over by the camp doctor. I didn't ask no questions, because I seen quiet was needed round that tent. After satisfying myself that Nell was all right, an' Thorne in no danger, I went out.

"Shore there was so darn many fellers who wanted to an' tried to tell me what'd come off, I thought I'd never find out. But I got the story piece by piece. An' here's what happened.

"Nell rode Blanco Sol a-tearin' into camp, an' had a crowd round her in a jiffy. She told who she was, where she'd come from, an' what she wanted. Well, it seemed a day or so before Nell got there the cavalrymen had heard word of Thorne. You see, Thorne had left camp on leave of absence some time before. He was shore mysterious, they said, an' told nobody where he was goin'. A week or so after he left camp some Greaser give it away that Rojas had a prisoner in a dobe shack near his camp. Nobody paid much attention to what the Greaser said. He wanted money for mescal. An' it was usual for Rojas to have prisoners. But in a few more days it turned out pretty sure that for some reason Rojas was holdin' Thorne.

"Now it happened when this news came Colonel Weede was in Nogales with his staff, an' the officer left in charge didn't know how to proceed. Rojas's camp was across the line in Mexico, an' ridin' over there was serious business. It meant a whole lot more than just scatterin' one Greaser camp. It was what had been botherin' more'n one colonel along the line. Thorne's feller soldiers was anxious to get him out of a bad fix, but they had to wait for orders.

"When Nell found out Thorne was bein' starved an' beat in a dobe shack no more'n two mile across the line, she shore stirred up that cavalry camp. Shore! She told them soldiers Rojas was holdin' Thorne—torturin' him to make him tell where Mercedes was. She told about Mercedes—how sweet an' beautiful she was—how her father had been murdered by Rojas—how she had been hounded by the bandit—how ill an' miserable she was, waitin' for her lover. An' she begged the cavalrymen to rescue Thorne.

"From the way it was told to me I reckon them cavalrymen went up in the air. Fine fiery lot of youngbloods, I thought, achin' for a scrap. But the officer in charge, bein' in a ticklish place, still held out for higher orders.

"Then Nell broke loose. You-all know Nell's tongue is sometimes like a *cholla* thorn. I'd have give somethin' to see her work up that soldier outfit. Nell's never so pretty as when she's mad. An' this last stunt of hers was no girly tantrum, as Beldin' calls it. She musta been ragin' with all the hell there's in a woman. . . . Can't you fellers see her on Blanco Sol with her eyes turnin' black?"

Ladd mopped his sweaty face with his dusty scarf. He was beaming. He was growing excited, hurried in his narrative.

"Right out then Nell *swore* she'd go after Thorne. If them cavalrymen couldn't ride with a Western girl to save a brother American—let them hang back! One feller, under orders, tried to stop Blanco Sol. An' that feller invited himself to the hospital. Then the cavalrymen went flyin' for their hosses. Mebbe Nell's move was just foxy—woman's cunnin'. But I'm thinkin' as she felt then she'd have sent Blanco Sol straight into Rojas's camp, which, I'd forgot to say, was in plain sight.

"It didn't take long for every cavalryman in that camp to get wind of what was comin' off. Shore they musta been wild. They strung out after Nell in a thunderin' troop.

"Say, I wish you fellers could see the lane that bunch of hosses left in the greasewood an' cactus. Looks like there'd been a cattle stampede on the desert. . . . Blanco Sol stayed out in front, you can gamble on that. Right into Rojas's camp! *Sabe*, you señors? Gawd Almighty! I never had a grief that'd hold a candle to this one of bein' too late to see Nell an' Sol in their one best race.

"Rojas an' his men vamoosed without a shot. That ain't surprisin'. There wasn't a shot fired by anybody. The cavalrymen soon found Thorne an' hurried with him back on Uncle Sam's land. Thorne was half naked, black an' blue all over, thin as a rail. He looked mighty sick when I seen him first. That was a little after midday. He was given food an' drink. Shore he seemed a starved man. But he picked up wonderful, an' by the time Jim came along he was wantin' to start for Forlorn River. So was Nell. By main strength as much as persuasion we kept the two of them quiet till next evenin' at dark.

"Well, we made as sneaky a start in the dark as Jim an' me could manage, an' never hit the trail till we was miles from town. Thorne's nerve held him up for a while. Then all at once he tumbled out of his saddle. We got him back, an' Lash held him on. Nell didn't give out till daybreak."

As Ladd paused in his story Belding began to stutter, and finally he exploded. His mighty utterances were incoherent. But plainly the wrath he had felt toward the wilful girl was forgotten. Gale remained gripped by silence.

"I reckon you'll all be some surprised when you see Casita," went on Ladd. "It's half burned an' half tore down. An' the rebels are livin' fat. There was rumors of another federal force on the road from Case Grandes. I seen a good many Americans from interior Mexico, an' the stories they told would make your hair stand up. They all packed guns, was fightin' mad at Greasers, an' sore on the good old U.S. But shore glad to get over the line! Some were waitin' for trains, which don't run reg'lar no more, an' others were ready to hit the trails north."

"Laddy, what knocks me is Rojas holding Thorne prisoner, trying to make him tell where Mercedes had been hidden," said Belding.

"Shore. It 'd knock anybody."

"The bandit's crazy over her. That's the Spanish of it," replied Belding, his voice rolling. "Rojas is a peon. He's been a slave to the proud Castilian. He loves Mercedes as he hates her. When I was down in Durango I saw something of these peons' insane passions. Rojas wants this girl only to have her, then kill her. It's damn strange, boys, and even with Thorne here our troubles have just begun."

"Tom, you spoke correct," said Jim Ladd, in his cool drawl.

"Shore I'm not sayin' what I think," added Ladd. But the look of him was not indicative of a tranquil optimism.

Thorne was put to bed in Gale's room. He was very weak, yet he would keep Mercedes's hand and gaze at her with unbelieving eyes. Mercedes's failing hold on hope and strength seemed to have been a fantasy; she was again vivid, magnetic, beautiful, shot through and through with intense and throbbing life. She induced him to take food and drink. Then, fighting sleep with what little strength he had left, at last he succumbed.

For all Dick could ascertain his friend never stirred an eyelash nor a finger for twenty-seven hours. When he awoke he was pale, weak, but the old Thorne.

"Hello, Dick, I didn't dream it then," he said. "There you are, and my darling with the proud, dark eyes—she's here?"

"Why, yes, you locoed cavalryman."

"Say, what's happened to you? It can't be those clothes and a little bronze on your face. . . . Dick, you're older—you've changed. You're not so thickly built. By Gad, if you don't look fine!"

"Thanks. I'm sorry I can't return the compliment. You're about the seediest, hungriest-looking fellow I ever saw. . . . Say, old man, you must have had a tough time."

A dark and somber fire burned out the happiness in Thorne's eyes.

"Dick, don't make me—don't let me think of that fiend Rojas! . . . I'm here now. I'll be well in a day or two. Then! . . ."

Mercedes came in, radiant and soft-voiced. She fell upon her knees beside Thorne's bed, and neither of them appeared to see Nell enter with a tray. Then Gale and Nell made a good deal of unnecessary bustle in moving a small table close to the bed. Mercedes had forgotten for the moment that her lover had been a starving man. If Thorne remembered it he did not care. They held hands and looked at each other without speaking.

"Nell, I thought I had it bad," whispered Dick. "But I'm not—"

"Hush. It's beautiful," replied Nell, softly; and she tried to coax Dick from the room.

Dick, however, thought he ought to remain at least long enough to tell Thorne that a man in his condition could not exist solely upon love.

Mercedes sprang up blushing with pretty, penitent manner and moving white hands eloquent of her condition.

"Oh, Mercedes—don't go!" cried Thorne, as she stepped to the door.

"Señor Dick will stay. He is not *mucha malo* for you—as I am."

Then she smiled and went out.

"Good Lord!" exclaimed Thorne. "How I love her! Dick, isn't she the most beautiful, the loveliest, the finest—"

"George, I share your enthusiasm," said Dick, dryly, "but Mercedes isn't the only girl on earth."

Manifestly this was a startling piece of information, and struck Thorne in more than one way.

"George," went on Dick, "did you happen to observe the girl who saved your life—who incidentally just fetched in your breakfast?"

"Nell Burton! Why, of course. She's brave, a wonderful girl, and really nice-looking."

"You long, lean, hungry beggar! That was the young lady who might answer the raving eulogy you just got out of your system. . . . I—well, you haven't cornered the love market!"

Thorne uttered some kind of a sound that his weakened condition would not allow to be a whoop.

"Dick! Do you mean it?"

"I shore do, as Laddy says."

"I'm glad, Dick, with all my heart. I wondered at the changed look you wear. Why, boy, you've got a different front. . . . Call the lady in, and you bet I'll look her over right. I can see better now."

"Eat your breakfast. There's plenty of time to dazzle you afterward."

Thorne fell to upon his breakfast and made it vanish with magic speed. Meanwhile Dick told him something of a ranger's life along the border.

"You needn't waste your breath," said Thorne. "I guess I can see.

Belding and those rangers have made you the real thing—the real Western goods. . . . What I want to know is all about the girl."

"Well, Laddy swears she's got your girl roped in the corral for looks."

"That's not possible. I'll have to talk to Laddy. . . . But she must be a wonder, or Dick Gale would never have fallen for her. . . . Isn't it great, Dick? I'm here! Mercedes is well—safe! You've got a girl! Oh! . . . But say, I haven't a dollar to my name. I had a lot of money, Dick, and those robbers stole it, my watch—everything. Damn that little black Greaser! He got Mercedes's letters. I wish you could have seen him trying to read them. He's simply nutty over her, Dick. I could have borne the loss of money and valuables—but those beautiful, wonderful letters—they're gone!"

"Cheer up. You have the girl. Belding will make you a proposition presently. The future smiles, old friend. If this rebel business was only ended!"

"Dick, you're going to be my savior twice over. . . . Well, now, listen to me." His gay excitement changed to earnest gravity. "I want to marry Mercedes at once. Is there a padre here?"

"Yes. But are you wise in letting any Mexican, even a priest, know Mercedes is hidden in Forlorn River?"

"It couldn't be kept much longer."

Gale was compelled to acknowledge the truth of this statement.

"I'll marry her first, then I'll face my problem. Fetch the padre, Dick. And ask our kind friends to be witnesses at the ceremony."

Much to Gale's surprise neither Belding nor Ladd objected to the idea of bringing a padre into the household, and thereby making known to at least one Mexican the whereabouts of Mercedes Castañeda. Belding's caution was wearing out in wrath at the persistent unsettled condition of the border, and Ladd grew only the cooler and more silent as possibilities of trouble multiplied.

Gale fetched the padre, a little, wizened, timid man who was old and without interest or penetration. Apparently he married Mercedes and Thorne as he told his beads or mumbled a prayer. It was Mrs. Belding who kept the occasion from being a merry one, and she insisted on not exciting Thorne. Gale marked her unusual pallor and the singular depth and sweetness of her voice.

"Mother, what's the use of making a funeral out of a marriage?"

protested Belding. "A chance for some fun doesn't often come to Forlorn River. You're a fine doctor. Can't you see the girl is what Thorne needed? He'll be well to-morrow, don't mistake me."

"George, when you're all right again we'll add something to present congratulations," said Gale.

"We shore will," put in Ladd.

So with parting jests and smiles they left the couple to themselves.

Belding enjoyed a laugh at his good wife's expense, for Thorne could not be kept in bed, and all in a day, it seemed, he grew so well and so hungry that his friends were delighted, and Mercedes was radiant. In a few days his weakness disappeared and he was going the round of the fields and looking over the ground marked out in Gale's plan of water development. Thorne was highly enthusiastic, and at once staked out his claim for one hundred and sixty acres of land adjoining that of Belding and the rangers. These five tracts took in all the ground necessary for their operations, but in case of the success of the irrigation project the idea was to increase their squatter holding by purchase of more land down the valley. A hundred families had lately moved to Forlorn River; more were coming all the time; and Belding vowed he could see a vision of the whole Altar Valley green with farms.

Meanwhile everybody in Belding's household, except the quiet Ladd and the watchful Yaqui, in the absence of disturbance of any kind along the border, grew freer and more unrestrained, as if anxiety was slowly fading in the peace of the present. Jim Lash made a trip to the Sonoyta Oasis, and Ladd patrolled fifty miles of the line eastward without incident or sight of raiders. Evidently all the border hawks were in at the picking of Casita.

The February nights were cold, with a dry, icy, penetrating coldness that made a warm fire most comfortable. Belding's household usually congregated in the sitting-room, where burning mesquite logs crackled in the open fireplace. Belding's one passion besides horses was the game of checkers, and he was always wanting to play. On this night he sat playing with Ladd, who never won a game and never could give up trying. Mrs. Belding worked with her needle, stopping from time to time to gaze with thoughtful eyes into the fire. Jim Lash smoked his pipe by the hearth and played with the cat on his knee. Thorne and Mercedes were at the table with pencil and paper; and he was trying his best to keep his attention from his wife's beautiful, animated face long enough to read and write a little Spanish. Gale and Nell sat in a corner watching the bright fire.

There came a low knock on the door. It may have been an ordinary knock, for it did not disturb the women; but to Belding and his rangers it had a subtle meaning.

"Who's that?" asked Belding, as he slowly pushed back his chair and looked at Ladd.

"Yaqui," replied the ranger.

"Come in," called Belding.

The door opened, and the short, square, powerfully built Indian entered. He had a magnificent head, strangely staring, somber black eyes, and very darkly bronzed face. He carried a rifle and strode with impressive dignity.

"Yaqui, what do you want?" asked Belding, and repeated his question in Spanish.

"Señor Dick," replied the Indian.

Gale jumped up, stifling an exclamation, and he went outdoors with Yaqui. He felt his arm gripped, and allowed himself to be led away without asking a question. Yaqui's presence was always one of gloom, and now his stern action boded catastrophe. Once clear of trees he pointed to the level desert across the river, where a row of campfires shone bright out of the darkness.

"Raiders!" ejaculated Gale.

Then he cautioned Yaqui to keep sharp lookout, and, hurriedly returning to the house, he called the men out and told them there were rebels or raiders camping just across the line.

Ladd did not say a word. Belding, with an oath, slammed down his cigar.

"I knew it was too good to last. . . . Dick, you and Jim stay here while Laddy and I look around."

Dick returned to the sitting-room. The women were nervous and not to be deceived. So Dick merely said Yaqui had sighted some lights off in the desert, and they probably were campfires. Belding did not soon return, and when he did he was alone, and saying he wanted to consult with the men, he sent Mrs. Belding and the girls to their rooms. His gloomy anxiety had returned.

"Laddy's gone over to scout around and try to find out who the outfit belongs to and how many are in it," said Belding.

"I reckon if they're raiders with bad intentions we wouldn't see no fires," remarked Jim, calmly.

"It'd be useless, I suppose, to send for the cavalry," said Gale. "Whatever's coming off would be over before the soldiers could be notified, let alone reach here."

"Hell, fellows! I don't look for an attack on Forlorn River," burst out Belding. "I can't believe that possible. These rebel-raiders have a little sense. They wouldn't spoil their game by pulling U.S. soldiers across the line from Yuma to El Paso. But, as Jim says, if they wanted to steal a few horses or cattle they wouldn't build fires. I'm afraid it's—"

Belding hesitated and looked with grim concern at the cavalryman.

"What?" queried Thorne.

"I'm afraid it's Rojas."

Thorne turned pale but did not lose his nerve.

"I thought of that at once. If true, it'll be terrible for Mercedes and me. But Rojas will never get his hands on my wife. If I can't kill him, I'll kill her! . . . Belding, this is tough on you—this risk we put upon your family. I regret—"

"Cut that kind of talk," replied Belding, bluntly. "Well, if it is Rojas he's acting damn strange for a raider. That's what worries me. We can't do anything but wait. With Laddy and Yaqui out there we won't be surprised. Let's take the best possible view of the situation until we know more. That'll not likely be before to-morrow."

The women of the house might have gotten some sleep that night, but it was certain the men did not get any. Morning broke cold and gray, the 19th of February. Breakfast was prepared earlier than usual, and an air of suppressed waiting excitement pervaded the place. Otherwise the ordinary details of the morning's work continued as on any other day. Ladd came in hungry and cold, and said the Mexicans were not breaking camp. He reported a good-sized force of rebels, and was taciturn as to his idea of forthcoming events.

About an hour after sunrise Yaqui ran in with the information that part of the rebels were crossing the river.

"That can't mean a fight yet," declared Belding. "But get in the house, boys, and make ready anyway. I'll meet them."

"Drive them off the place same as if you had a company of soldiers backin' you," said Ladd. "Don't give them an inch. We're in bad, and the bigger bluff we put up the more likely our chance."

"Belding, you're an officer of the United States. Mexicans are much impressed by show of authority. I've seen that often in camp," said Thorne.

"Oh, I know the white-livered Greasers better than any of you, don't mistake me," replied Belding. He was pale with rage, but kept command over himself.

The rangers, with Yaqui and Thorne, stationed themselves at the several windows of the sitting-room. Rifles and smaller arms and boxes of shells littered the tables and window seats. No small force of besiegers could overcome a resistance such as Belding and his men were capable of making.

"Here they come, boys," called Gale, from his window. "Rebel-raiders I should say, Laddy."

"Shore. An' a fine outfit for buzzards!"

"Reckon there's about a dozen in the bunch," observed the calm Lash. "Some hosses they're ridin'. Where'n the hell do they get such hosses, anyhow?"

"Shore, Jim, they work hard an' buy 'em with real silver pesos," replied Ladd, sarcastically.

"Do any of you see Rojas?" whispered Thorne.

"Nix. No dandy bandit in that outfit."

"It's too far to see," said Gale.

The horsemen halted at the corrals. They were orderly and showed no evidence of hostility. They were, however, fully armed. Belding stalked out to meet them. Apparently a leader wanted to parley with him, but Belding would hear nothing. He shook his head, waved his arms, stamped to and fro, and his loud, angry voice could be heard clear back at the house. Whereupon the detachment of rebels retired to the bank of the river, beyond the white post that marked the boundary line, and there they once more drew rein. Belding remained by the corrals watching them, evidently still in a threatening mood. Presently a single rider left the troop and trotted his horse back down the road. When he reached the corrals he was seen to halt and pass something to Belding. Then he galloped away to join his comrades.

Belding looked at whatever it was he held in his hand, shook his burly head, and started swiftly for the house. He came striding into the room holding a piece of soiled paper.

"Can't read it and don't know as I want to," he said, savagely.

"Beldin', shore we'd better read it," replied Ladd. "What we want is a line on them Greasers. Whether they're Campo's men or Salazar's, or just a wanderin' bunch of rebels—or Rojas's bandits. *Sabe*, señor?"

Not one of the men was able to translate the garbled scrawl.

"Shore Mercedes can read it," said Ladd.

Thorne opened a door and called her. She came into the room followed by Nell and Mrs. Belding. Evidently all three divined a critical situation.

"My dear, we want you to read what's written on this paper," said Thorne, as he led her to the table. "It was sent in by rebels, and—and we fear contains bad news for us."

Mercedes gave the writing one swift glance, then fainted in Thorne's arms. He carried her to a couch, and with Nell and Mrs. Belding began to work over her.

Belding looked at his rangers. It was characteristic of the man that, now when catastrophe appeared inevitable, all the gloom and care and angry agitation passed from him.

"Laddy, it's Rojas all right. How many men has he out there?"

"Mebbe twenty. Not more."

"We can lick twice that many Greasers."

"Shore."

Jim Lash removed his pipe long enough to speak.

"I reckon. But it ain't sense to start a fight when mebbe we can avoid it."

"What's your idea?"

"Let's stave the Greaser off till dark. Then Laddy an' me an' Thorne will take Mercedes an' hit the trail for Yuma."

"Camino del Diablo! That awful trail with a woman! Jim, do you forget how many *hundreds of men* have perished on the Devil's Road?"

"I reckon I ain't forgettin' nothin'," replied Jim. "The water-holes are full now. There's grass, an' we can do the job in six days."

"It's three hundred miles to Yuma."

"Beldin', Jim's idea hits me pretty reasonable," interposed Ladd. "Lord knows that's about the only chance we've got except fightin'."

"But suppose we do stave Rojas off, and you get safely away with Mercedes. Isn't Rojas going to find it out quick? Then what'll he try to do to us who're left here?"

"I reckon he'd find out by daylight," replied Jim. "But, Tom, he ain't agoin' to start a scrap then. He'd want time an' hosses an' men to chase us out on the trail. You see, I'm figgerin' on the crazy Greaser wantin' the girl. I reckon he'll try to clean up here to get her. But he's too smart to fight you for nothin'. Rojas may be nutty about women, but he's afraid of the U.S. Take my word for it he'd discover the trail in the mornin' an' light out on it. I reckon with ten hours' start we could travel comfortable."

Belding paced up and down the room. Jim and Ladd whispered together. Gale walked to the window and looked out at the distant group of bandits, and then turned his gaze to rest upon Mercedes. She was conscious now, and her eyes seemed all the larger and blacker for the whiteness of her face. Thorne held her hands, and the other women were trying to still her tremblings. No one but Gale saw the Yaqui in the background looking down upon the Spanish girl. All of Yaqui's looks were strange; but this was singularly so. Gale marked it, and felt he would never forget. Mercedes's beauty had never before struck him as being so exquisite, so alluring as now when she lay stricken. Gale wondered if the Indian was affected by her loveliness, her helplessness, or her terror. Yaqui had seen Mercedes only a few times, and upon each of these he had appeared to be fascinated. Could the strange Indian, because his hate for Mexicans was so great, be gloating over her misery? Something about Yaqui—a noble austerity of countenance—made Gale feel his suspicion unjust.

Presently Belding called his rangers to him, and then Thorne.

"Listen to this," he said, earnestly. "I'll go out and have a talk with Rojas. I'll try to reason with him; tell him to think a long time before he sheds blood on Uncle Sam's soil. That he's now after an American's wife!

I'll not commit myself, nor will I refuse outright to consider his demands, nor will I show the least fear of him. I'll play for time. If my bluff goes through . . . well and good. . . . After dark the four of you, Laddy, Jim, Dick and Thorne, will take Mercedes and my best white horses, and, with Yaqui as guide, circle round through Altar Valley to the trail, and head for Yuma. . . . Wait now, Laddy. Let me finish. I want you to take the white horses for two reasons—to save them and to save you. Savvy? If Rojas should follow on my horses he'd be likely to catch you. Also, you can pack a great deal more than on the bronchs. Also, the big horses can travel faster and farther on little grass and water. I want you to take the Indian, because in a case of this kind he'll be a godsend. If you get headed or lost or have to circle off the trail, think what it'd mean to have a Yaqui with you. He knows Sonora as no Greaser knows it. He could hide you, find water and grass, when you would absolutely believe it impossible. The Indian is loyal. He has his debt to pay, and he'll pay it, don't mistake me. When you're gone I'll hide Nell so Rojas won't see her if he searches the place. Then I think I could sit down and wait without any particular worry."

The rangers approved of Belding's plan, and Thorne choked in his effort to express his gratitude.

"All right, we'll chance it," concluded Belding. "I'll go out now and call Rojas and his outfit over. . . . Say, it might be as well for me to know just what he said in that paper."

Thorne went to the side of his wife.

"Mercedes, we've planned to outwit Rojas. Will you tell us just what he wrote?"

The girl sat up, her eyes dilating, and with her hands clasping Thorne's, she said:

"Rojas swore—by his saints and his virgin—that if I wasn't given—to him—in twenty-four hours—he would set fire to the village—kill the men—carry off the women—hang the children on cactus thorns!"

A moment's silence followed her last halting whisper.

"By his saints an' his virgin!" echoed Ladd. He laughed—a cold, cutting, deadly laugh—significant and terrible.

Then the Yaqui uttered a singular cry. Gale had heard this once before, and now he remembered it was at the Papago Well.

"Look at the Indian," whispered Belding, hoarsely. "Damn if I don't believe he understood every word Mercedes said. And, gentlemen, don't mistake me, if he ever gets near Señor Rojas there'll be some gory Aztec knife work."

Yaqui had moved close to Mercedes, and stood beside her as she leaned against her husband. She seemed impelled to meet the Indian's gaze, and evidently it was so powerful or hypnotic that it wrought irresistibly upon her. But she must have seen or divined what was beyond the others, for she offered him her trembling hand. Yaqui took it and laid it against his body in a strange motion, and bowed his head. Then he stepped back into the shadow of the room.

Belding went outdoors while the rangers took up their former position at the west window. Each had his own somber thoughts, Gale imagined, and knew his own were dark enough. A slow fire crept along his veins. He saw Belding halt at the corrals and wave his hand. Then the rebels mounted and came briskly up the road, this time to rein in abreast.

Wherever Rojas had kept himself upon the former advance was not clear; but he certainly was prominently in sight now. He made a gaudy, almost a dashing figure. Gale did not recognize the white sombrero, the crimson scarf, the velvet jacket, nor any feature of the dandy's costume; but their general effect, the whole ensemble, recalled vividly to mind his first sight of the bandit. Rojas dismounted and seemed to be listening. He betrayed none of the excitement Gale had seen in him that night at the Del Sol. Evidently this composure struck Ladd and Lash as unusual in a Mexican supposed to be laboring under stress of feeling. Belding made gestures, vehemently bobbed his big head, appeared to talk with his body as much as with his tongue. Then Rojas was seen to reply, and after that it was clear that the talk became painful and difficult. It ended finally in what appeared to be mutual understanding. Rojas mounted and rode away with his men, while Belding came tramping back to the house.

As he entered the door his eyes were shining, his big hands were clenched, and he was breathing audibly.

"You can rope me if I'm not locoed!" he burst out. "I went out to conciliate a red-handed little murderer, and damn me if I didn't meet a—a—well, I've no suitable name handy. I started my bluff and got along pretty well, but I forgot to mention that Mercedes was Thorne's wife.

And what do you think? Rojas swore he loved Mercedes—swore he'd marry her right here in Forlorn River—swore he would give up robbing and killing people, and take her away from Mexico. He has gold—jewels. He swore if he didn't get her nothing mattered. He'd die anyway without her. . . . And here's the strange thing. I believe him! He was cold as ice, and all hell inside. Never saw a Greaser like him. Well, I pretended to be greatly impressed. We got to talking friendly, I suppose, though I didn't understand half he said, and I imagine he gathered less what I said. Anyway, without my asking he said for me to think it over for a day and then we'd talk again."

"Shore we're born lucky!" ejaculated Ladd.

"I reckon Rojas'll be smart enough to string his outfit across the few trails leadin' out of Forlorn River," remarked Jim.

"That needn't worry us. All we want is dark to come," replied Belding. "Yaqui will slip through. If we thank any lucky stars let it be for the Indian. . . . Now, boys, put on your thinking caps. You'll take eight horses, the pick of my bunch. You must pack all that's needed for a possible long trip. Mind, Yaqui may lead you down into some wild Sonora valley and give Rojas the slip. You may get to Yuma in six days, and maybe in six weeks. Yet you've got to pack light—a small pack in saddles—larger ones on the two free horses. You may have a big fight. Laddy, take the .405. Dick will pack his Remington. All of you go gunned heavy. But the main thing is a pack that'll be light enough for swift travel, yet one that'll keep you from starving on the desert."

The rest of that day passed swiftly. Dick had scarcely a word with Nell, and all the time, as he chose and deliberated and worked over his little pack, there was a dull pain in his heart.

The sun set, twilight fell, then night closed down, fortunately a night slightly overcast. Gale saw the white horses pass his door like silent ghosts. Even Blanco Diablo made no sound, and that fact was indeed a tribute to the Yaqui. Gale went out to put his saddle on Blanco Sol. The horse rubbed a soft nose against his shoulder. Then Gale returned to the sitting room. There was nothing more to do but wait and say good-by. Mercedes came clad in leather chaps and coat, a slim stripling of a cowboy, her dark eyes flashing. Her beauty could not be hidden, and now hope and courage had fired her blood.

Gale drew Nell off into the shadow of the room. She was trembling, and as she leaned toward him she was very different from the coy girl who had so long held him aloof. He took her into his arms.

"Dearest, I'm going—soon. . . . And maybe I'll never—"

"Dick, do—don't say it," sobbed Nell, with her head on his breast.

"I might never come back," he went on, steadily. "I love you—I've loved you ever since the first moment I saw you. Do you care for me—a little?"

"Dear Dick—de-dear Dick, my heart is breaking," faltered Nell, as she clung to him.

"It might be breaking for Mercedes—for Laddy and Jim. I want to hear something for myself. Something to have on long marches—round lonely campfires. Something to keep my spirit alive. Oh, Nell, you can't imagine that silence out there—that terrible world of sand and stone! . . . Do you love me?"

"Yes, yes. Oh, I love you so! I never knew it till now. I love you so. Dick, I'll be safe and I'll wait—and hope and pray for your return.

"If I come back—no—*when* I come back, will you marry me?"

"I—I—oh yes!" she whispered, and returned his kiss.

Belding was in the room speaking softly.

"Nell, darling, I must go," said Dick.

"I'm a selfish little coward," cried Nell. "It's so splendid of you all. I ought to glory in it, but I can't. . . . Fight if you must, Dick. Fight for that lovely persecuted girl. I'll love you—the more. . . . Oh! Good-by! Good-by!"

With a wrench that shook him Gale let her go. He heard Belding's soft voice.

"Yaqui says the early hour's best. Trust him, Laddy. Remember what I say—Yaqui's a godsend."

Then they were all outside in the pale gloom under the trees. Yaqui mounted Blanco Diablo; Mercedes was lifted upon White Woman; Thorne climbed astride Queen; Jim Lash was already upon his horse, which was as white as the others but bore no name; Ladd mounted the stallion Blanco Torres, and gathered up the long halters of the two pack horses; Gale came last with Blanco Sol.

As he toed the stirrup, hand on mane and pommel, Gale took one more look in at the door. Nell stood in the gleam of light, her hair shining, face like ashes, her eyes dark, her lips parted, her arms outstretched. That sweet and tragic picture etched its cruel outlines into Gale's heart. He waved his hand and then fiercely leaped into the saddle.

Blanco Sol stepped out.

Before Gale stretched a line of moving horses, white against dark shadows. He could not see the head of that column; he scarcely heard a soft hoofbeat. A single star shone out of a rift in thin clouds. There was no wind. The air was cold. The dark space of desert seemed to yawn. To the left across the river flickered a few campfires. The chill night, silent and mystical, seemed to close in upon Gale; and he faced the wide, quivering, black level with keen eyes and grim intent, and an awakening of that wild rapture which came like a spell to him in the open desert.

CHAPTER 11

ACROSS CACTUS AND LAVA

Blanco Sol showed no inclination to bend his head to the alfalfa which swished softly about his legs. Gale felt the horse's sensitive, almost human alertness. Sol knew as well as his master the nature of that flight.

At the far corner of the field Yaqui halted, and slowly the line of white horses merged into a compact mass. There was a trail here leading down to the river. The campfires were so close that the bright blazes could be seen in movement, and dark forms crossed in front of them. Yaqui slipped out of his saddle. He ran his hand over Diablo's nose and spoke low, and repeated this action for each of the other horses. Gale had long ceased to question the strange Indian's behavior. There was no explaining or understanding many of his maneuvers. But the results of them were always thought provoking. Gale had never seen horses stand so silently as in this instance; no stamp—no champ of bit—no toss of head—no shake of saddle or pack—no heave or snort! It seemed they had become imbued with the spirit of the Indian.

Yaqui moved away into the shadows as noiselessly as if he were one of them. The darkness swallowed him. He had taken a direction parallel with the trail. Gale wondered if Yaqui meant to try to lead his string of horses by the rebel sentinels. Ladd had his head bent low, his ear toward the trail. Jim's long neck had the arch of a listening deer. Gale listened, too, and as the slow, silent moments went by his faculty of hearing grew more acute from strain. He heard Blanco Sol breathe; he heard the pound of his own heart; he heard the silken rustle of the alfalfa; he heard a faint, far-off sound of voice, like a lost echo. Then his ear seemed to register a movement of air, a disturbance so soft as to be nameless. Then followed long, silent moments.

Yaqui appeared as he had vanished. He might have been part of the shadows. But he was there. He started off down the trail leading Diablo. Again the white line stretched slowly out. Gale fell in behind. A bench of ground, covered with sparse greasewood, sloped gently down to the deep, wide arroyo of Forlorn River. Blanco Sol shied a few feet out of the trail. Peering low with keen eyes, Gale made out three objects—a white sombrero, a blanket, and a Mexican lying facedown. The Yaqui had stolen upon this sentinel like a silent wind of death. Just then a desert coyote wailed, and the wild cry fitted the darkness and the Yaqui's deed.

Once under the dark lee of the river bank Yaqui caused another halt, and he disappeared as before. It seemed to Gale that the Indian started to cross the pale level sandbed of the river, where stones stood out gray, and the darker line of opposite shore was visible. But he vanished, and it was impossible to tell whether he went one way or another. Moments passed. The horses held heads up, looked toward the glimmering camp-fires, and listened. Gale thrilled with the meaning of it all—the night—the silence—the flight—and the wonderful Indian stealing with the slow inevitability of doom upon another sentinel. An hour passed and Gale seemed to have become deadened to all sense of hearing. There were no more sounds in the world. The desert was as silent as it was black. Yet again came that strange change in the tensity of Gale's ear-strain, a check, a break, a vibration—and this time the sound did not go nameless. It might have been moan of wind or wail of far-distant wolf, but Gale imagined it was the strangling death-cry of another guard, or that strange, involuntary utterance of the Yaqui. Blanco Sol trembled in all his great frame, and then Gale was certain the sound was not imagination.

That certainty, once for all, fixed in Gale's mind the mood of his flight. The Yaqui dominated the horses and the rangers. Thorne and Mercedes were as persons under a spell. The Indian's strange silence, the feeling of mystery and power he seemed to create, all that was incomprehensible about him were emphasized in the light of his slow, sure, and ruthless action. If he dominated the others, surely he did more for Gale—colored his thoughts—presaged the wild and terrible future of that flight. If Rojas embodied all the hatred and passion of the peon—scourged slave for a thousand years—then Yaqui embodied all the darkness, the cruelty, the white, sun-heated blood, the ferocity, the tragedy of the desert.

Suddenly the Indian stalked out of the gloom. He mounted Diablo and headed across the river. Once more the line of moving white shadows stretched out. The soft sand gave forth no sound at all. The glimmering campfires sank behind the western bank. Yaqui led the way into the willows, and there was faint swishing of leaves; then into the mesquite, and there was faint rustling of branches. The glimmering lights appeared again, and grotesque forms of *saguaros* loomed darkly. Gale peered sharply along the trail, and, presently, on the pale sand under a cactus, there lay a blanketed form, prone, outstretched, a carbine clutched in one hand, a cigarette, still burning, in the other.

The cavalcade of white horses passed within five hundred yards of campfires, around which dark forms moved in plain sight. Soft pads in sand, faint metallic tickings of steel on thorns, low, regular breathing of horses—these were all the sounds the fugitives made, and they could not have been heard at one-fifth the distance. The lights disappeared from time to time, grew dimmer, more flickering, and at last they vanished altogether. Belding's fleet and tireless steeds were out in front; the desert opened ahead wide, dark, vast. Rojas and his rebels were behind, eating, drinking, careless. The somber shadow lifted from Gale's heart. He held now an unquenchable faith in the Yaqui. Belding would be listening back there along the river. He would know of the escape. He would tell Nell, and then hide her safely. As Gale had accepted a strange and fatalistic foreshadowing of toil, blood, and agony in this desert journey, so he believed in Mercedes's ultimate freedom and happiness, and his own return to the girl who had grown dearer than life.

A cold, gray dawn was fleeing before a rosy sun when Yaqui halted the march at Papago Well. The horses were taken to water, then led down the arroyo into the grass. Here packs were slipped, saddles removed. Mercedes was cold, lame, tired, but happy. It warmed Gale's blood to look at her. The shadow of fear still lay in her eyes, but it was passing. Hope and courage shone there, and affection for her ranger protectors and the Yaqui, and unutterable love for the cavalryman. Jim Lash remarked how cleverly they had fooled the rebels.

"Shore they'll be comin' along," replied Ladd.

They built a fire, cooked and ate. The Yaqui spoke only one word: "Sleep." Blankets were spread. Mercedes dropped into a deep slumber, her head on Thorne's shoulder. Excitement kept Thorne awake. The two rangers dozed beside the fire. Gale shared the Yaqui's watch. The sun began to climb and the icy edge of dawn to wear away. Rabbits bobbed their cotton tails under the mesquite. Gale climbed a rocky wall above the arroyo bank, and there, with command over the miles of the back-trail, he watched.

It was a sweeping, rolling, wrinkled, and streaked range of desert that he saw, ruddy in the morning sunlight, with patches of cactus and mesquite rough-etched in shimmering gloom. No Name Mountains split the eastern sky, towering high, gloomy, grand, with purple veils upon their slopes. They were forty miles away and looked five. Gale thought of the girl who was there under their shadow.

Yaqui kept the horses bunched, and he led them from one little park of galleta grass to another. At the end of three hours he took them to water. Upon his return Gale clambered down from his outlook, the rangers grew active, Mercedes was awakened; and soon the party faced westward, their long shadows moving before them. Yaqui led with Blanco Diablo in a long, easy lope. The arroyo washed itself out into flat desert, and the greens began to shade into gray, and then the gray into red. Only sparse cactus and weathered ledges dotted the great low roll of a rising escarpment. Yaqui suited the gait of his horse to the lay of the land, and his followers accepted his pace. There were canter and trot, and swift walk and slow climb, and long swing—miles up and down and forward. The sun soared hot. The heated air lifted, and incoming currents from the west swept low and hard over the barren earth. In the distance, all around the horizon, accumulations of dust seemed like ranging, mushrooming yellow clouds.

Yaqui was the only one of the fugitives who never looked back. Mercedes did it the most. Gale felt what compelled her; he could not resist it himself. But it was a vain search. For a thousand puffs of white and yellow dust rose from that backward sweep of desert, and any one of them might have been blown from under horses' hoofs. Gale had a conviction that when Yaqui gazed back toward the well and the shining plain beyond, there would be reason for it. But when the sun lost its heat and the wind died down Yaqui took long and careful surveys westward from the high points on the trail. Sunset was not far off, and there in a bare, spotted valley lay Coyote Tanks, the only water hole between Papago Well and the Sonoyta Oasis. Gale used his glass, told Yaqui there was no smoke, no sign of life; still the Indian fixed his falcon eyes on distant spots and looked long. It was as if his vision could not detect what reason or cunning, or intuition, perhaps an instinct, told him was there. Presently in a sheltered spot, where blown sand had not obliterated the trail, Yaqui found the tracks of horses. The curve of the iron shoes pointed westward. An intersecting trail from the north came in here. Gale thought the tracks either one or two days old. Ladd said they were one day. The Indian shook his head.

No farther advance was undertaken. The Yaqui headed south and traveled slowly, climbing to the brow of a bold height of weathered mesa. There he sat his horse and waited. No one questioned him. The rangers dismounted to stretch their legs, and Mercedes was lifted to a rock, where she rested. Thorne had gradually yielded to the desert's influence for silence. He spoke once or twice to Gale, and occasionally whispered to Mercedes. Gale fancied his friend would soon learn that necessary speech in desert travel meant a few greetings, a few words to make real the fact of human companionship, a few short, terse terms for the business of day or night, and perhaps a stern order or a soft call to a horse.

The sun went down, and the golden, rosy veils turned to blue and shaded darker till twilight was there in the valley. Only the spurs of mountains, spiring the near and far horizon, retained their clear outline. Darkness approached, and the clear peaks faded. The horses stamped to be on the move.

"*Malo!*" exclaimed the Yaqui.

He did not point with his arm, but his falcon head was outstretched, and his piercing eyes gazed at the blurring spot which marked the location of Coyote Tanks.

"Jim, can you see anything?" asked Ladd.

"Nope, but I reckon he can."

Darkness increased momentarily till night shaded the deepest part of the valley.

Then Ladd suddenly straightened up, turned to his horse, and muttered low under his breath.

"I reckon so," said Lash, and for once his easy, good-natured tone was not in evidence. His voice was harsh.

Gale's eyes, keen as they were, were last of the rangers to see tiny needle-points of light just faintly perceptible in the blackness.

"Laddy! Campfires?" he asked, quickly.

"Shore's you're born, my boy."

"How many?"

Ladd did not reply; but Yaqui held up his hand, his fingers wide. Five campfires! A strong force of rebels or raiders or some other desert troop was camping at Coyote Tanks.

Yaqui sat his horse for a moment, motionless as stone, his dark face immutable and impassive. Then he stretched wide his right arm in the direction of No Name Mountains, now losing their last faint traces of the afterglow, and he shook his head. He made the same impressive gesture toward the Sonoyta Oasis with the same somber negation.

Thereupon he turned Diablo's head to the south and started down the slope. His manner had been decisive, even stern. Lash did not question it, nor did Ladd. Both rangers hesitated, however, and showed a strange, almost a sullen reluctance which Gale had never seen in them before. Raiders were one thing, Rojas was another; Camino del Diablo still another; but that vast and desolate and unwatered waste of cactus and lava, the Sonora Desert, might appall the stoutest heart. Gale felt his own sink—felt himself flinch.

"Oh, where is he going?" cried Mercedes. Her poignant voice seemed to break a spell.

"Shore, lady, Yaqui's goin' home," replied Ladd gently. "An' considerin' our troubles I reckon we ought to thank God he knows the way."

They mounted and rode down the slope toward the darkening south.

Not until night travel was obstructed by a wall of cactus did the Indian halt to make a dry camp. Water and grass for the horses and fire to cook by were not to be had. Mercedes bore up surprisingly; but she fell asleep almost the instant her thirst had been allayed. Thorne laid her upon a blanket and covered her. The men ate and drank. Diablo was the only horse that showed impatience; but he was angry, and not in distress. Blanco Sol licked Gale's hand and stood patiently. Many a time had he taken his rest at night without a drink. Yaqui again bade the men sleep. Ladd said he would take the early watch; but from the way the Indian shook his head and settled himself against a stone, it appeared if Ladd remained awake he would have company. Gale lay down weary of limb and eye. He heard the soft thump of hoofs, the sough of wind in the cactus—then no more.

When he awoke there was bustle and stir about him. Day had not yet dawned, and the air was freezing cold. Yaqui had found a scant bundle of greasewood which served to warm them and to cook breakfast. Mercedes was not aroused till the last moment.

Day dawned with the fugitives in the saddle. A picketed wall of cactus hedged them in, yet the Yaqui made a tortuous path, that, zigzag as it might, in the main always headed south. It was wonderful how he slipped Diablo through the narrow aisles of thorns, saving the horse and saving himself. The others were torn and clutched and held and stung. The way was a flat, sandy pass between low mountain ranges. There were open spots and aisles and squares of sand; and hedging rows of prickly pear and the huge spider-legged *ocatillo* and hummocky masses of clustered *bisnagi*. The day grew dry and hot. A fragrant wind blew through the pass. Cactus flowers bloomed, red and yellow and magenta. The sweet, pale Ajo lily gleamed in shady corners.

Ten miles of travel covered the length of the pass. It opened wide upon a wonderful scene, an arboreal desert, dominated by its pure light green, yet lined by many merging colors. And it rose slowly to a low dim and dark-red zone of lava, spurred, peaked, domed by volcano cones, a wild and ragged region, illimitable as the horizon.

The Yaqui, if not at fault, was yet uncertain. His falcon eyes searched and roved, and became fixed at length at the southwest, and toward this he turned his horse. The great, fluted *saguaros*, fifty, sixty feet high, raised columnal forms, and their branching limbs and curving lines added a grace to the desert. It was the low-bushed cactus that made the toil and pain of travel. Yet these thorny forms were beautiful.

In the basins between the ridges, to right and left along the floor of low plains the mirage glistened, wavered, faded, vanished—lakes and trees and clouds. Inverted mountains hung suspended in the lilac air and faint tracery of white-walled cities.

At noon Yaqui halted the cavalcade. He had selected a field of *bisnagi* cactus for the place of rest. Presently his reason became obvious. With long, heavy knife he cut off the tops of these barrel-shaped plants. He scooped out soft pulp and with stone and hand then began to pound the deeper pulp into a juicy mass. When he threw this out there was a little water left, sweet, cool water which man and horse shared eagerly. Thus he made even the desert's fiercest growths minister to their needs.

But he did not halt long. Miles of gray-green spiked walls lay between him and that line of ragged, red lava which manifestly he must reach before dark. The travel became faster, straighter. And the glistening thorns clutched and clung to leather and cloth and flesh. The horses reared, snorted, balked, leaped—but they were sent on. Only Blanco Sol, the patient, the plodding, the indomitable, needed no goad or spur. Waves and scarfs and wreaths of heat smoked up from the sand. Mercedes reeled in her saddle. Thorne bade her drink, bathed her face, supported her, and then gave way to Ladd, who took the girl with him on Torres's broad back. Yaqui's unflagging purpose and iron arm were bitter and hateful to the proud and haughty spirit of Blanco Diablo. For once Belding's great white devil had met his master. He fought rider, bit, bridle, cactus, sand—and yet he went on and on, zigzagging, turning, winding, crashing through the barbed growths. The middle of the afternoon saw Thorne reeling in his saddle, and then, wherever possible, Gale's powerful arm lent him strength to hold his seat.

The giant cactus came to be only so in name. These *saguaros* were thinning out, growing stunted, and most of them were single columns. Gradually other cactus forms showed a harder struggle for existence, and the spaces of sand between were wider. But now the dreaded, glistening *cholla* began to show pale and gray and white upon the rising slope. Round-topped hills, sunset-colored above, blue-black below, intervened to hide the distant spurs and peaks. Mile and mile long tongues of red lava streamed out between the hills and wound down to stop abruptly upon the slope.

The fugitives were entering a desolate, burned-out world. It rose above them in limitless, gradual ascent and spread wide to east and west. Then the waste of sand began to yield to cinders. The horses sank to their fetlocks as they toiled on. A fine, choking dust blew back from the leaders, and men coughed and horses snorted. The huge, round hills rose smooth, symmetrical, colored as if the setting sun was shining on bare, blue-black surfaces. But the sun was now behind the hills. In between ran the streams of lava. The horsemen skirted the edge between slope of hill and perpendicular ragged wall. This red lava seemed to have flowed and hardened there only yesterday. It was broken, sharp, dull rust color, full of cracks and caves and crevices, and everywhere upon its jagged surface grew the white-thorned *cholla*.

Again twilight encompassed the travelers. But there was still light enough for Gale to see the constricted passage open into a wide, deep space where the dull color was relieved by the gray of gnarled and dwarfed mesquite. Blanco Sol, keenest of scent, whistled his welcome herald of water. The other horses answered, quickened their gait. Gale smelled it, too, sweet, cool, damp on the dry air.

Yaqui turned the corner of a pocket in the lava wall. The file of white horses rounded the corner after him. And Gale, coming last, saw the pale, glancing gleam of a pool of water beautiful in the twilight.

Next day the Yaqui's relentless driving demand on the horses was no longer in evidence. He lost no time, but he did not hasten. His course wound between low cinder dunes which limited their view of the surrounding country. These dunes finally sank down to a black floor as hard as flint with tongues of lava to the left, and to the right the slow descent into the cactus plain. Yaqui was now traveling due west. It was Gale's idea that the Indian was skirting the first sharp-toothed slope of a vast volcanic plateau which formed the western half of the Sonora Desert and extended to the Gulf of California. Travel was slow, but not exhausting for rider or beast. A little sand and meager grass gave a grayish tinge to the strip of black ground between lava and plain.

That day, as the manner rather than the purpose of the Yaqui changed, so there seemed to be subtle differences in the others of the party. Gale himself lost a certain sickening dread, which had not been for himself, but for Mercedes and Nell, and Thorne and the rangers. Jim, good-natured again, might have been patrolling the boundary line. Ladd lost his taciturnity and his gloom changed to a cool, careless air. A mood that was almost defiance began to be manifested in Thorne. It was in Mercedes, however, that Gale marked the most significant change. Her collapse the preceding day might never have been. She was lame and sore; she rode her saddle sidewise, and often she had to be rested and helped; but she had found a reserve fund of strength, and her mental condition was not the same that it had been. Her burden of fear had been lifted. Gale saw in her the difference he always felt in himself after a few days in the desert. Already Mercedes and he, and all of them, had begun to respond to the desert spirit. Moreover, Yaqui's strange influence must have been a call to the primitive.

Thirty miles of easy stages brought the fugitives to another water hole, a little round pocket under the heaved-up edge of lava. There was spare, short, bleached grass for the horses, but no wood for a fire. This night there were question and reply, conjecture, doubt, opinion, and conviction expressed by the men of the party. But the Indian, who alone could have told where they were, where they were going, what chance they had to escape, maintained his stoical silence. Gale took the early watch, Ladd the midnight one, and Lash that of the morning.

The day broke rosy, glorious, cold as ice. Action was necessary to make useful benumbed hands and feet. Mercedes was fed while yet wrapped in blankets. Then, while the packs were being put on and horses saddled, she walked up and down, slapping her hands, warming her ears. The rose color of the dawn was in her cheeks, and the wonderful clearness of desert light in her eyes. Thorne's eyes sought her constantly. The rangers watched her. The Yaqui bent his glance upon her only seldom; but when he did look it seemed that his strange, fixed, and inscrutable face was about to break into a smile. Yet that never happened. Gale himself was surprised to find how often his own glance found the slender, dark, beautiful Spaniard. Was this because of her beauty? he wondered. He thought not altogether. Mercedes was a woman. She represented something in life that men of all races for thousands of years had loved to see and own, to revere and debase, to fight and die for.

It was a significant index to the day's travel that Yaqui should keep a blanket from the pack and tear it into strips to bind the legs of the horses. It meant the dreaded *cholla* and the knife-edged lava. That Yaqui did not mount Diablo was still more significant. Mercedes must ride; but the others must walk.

The Indian led off into one of the gray notches between the tumbled streams of lava. These streams were about thirty feet high, a rotting mass of splintered lava, rougher than any other kind of roughness in the world. At the apex of the notch, where two streams met, a narrow gully wound and ascended. Gale caught sight of the dim, pale shadow of a onetime trail. Near at hand it was invisible; he had to look far ahead to catch the faint tracery. Yaqui led Diablo into it, and then began the most laborious and vexatious and painful of all slow travel.

Once up on top of that lava bed, Gale saw stretching away, breaking into millions of crests and ruts, a vast, red-black field sweeping onward and upward, with ragged, low ridges and mounds and spurs leading higher and higher to a great, split escarpment wall, above which dim peaks shone hazily blue in the distance.

He looked no more in that direction. To keep his foothold, to save his horse, cost him all energy and attention. The course was marked out for him in the tracks of the other horses. He had only to follow. But nothing could have been more difficult. The disintegrating surface of a lava bed was at once the roughest, the hardest, the meanest, the cruelest, the most deceitful kind of ground to travel.

It was rotten, yet it had corners as hard and sharp as pikes. It was rough, yet as slippery as ice. If there was a foot of level surface, that space would be one to break through under a horse's hoofs. It was seamed, lined, cracked, ridged, knotted iron. This lava bed resembled a tremendously magnified blinker. It had been a running sea of molten flint, boiling, bubbling, spouting, and it had burst its surface into a million sharp facets as it hardened. The color was dull, dark, angry red, like no other red, inflaming to the eye. The millions of minute crevices were dominated by deep fissures and holes, ragged and rough beyond all comparison.

The fugitives made slow progress. They picked a cautious, winding way to and fro in little steps here and there along the many twists of the trail, up and down the unavoidable depressions, round and round the holes. At noon, so winding back upon itself had been their course, they appeared to have come only a short distance up the lava slope.

It was rough work for them; it was terrible work for the horses. Blanco Diablo refused to answer to the power of the Yaqui. He balked, he plunged, he bit and kicked. He had to be pulled and beaten over many places. Mercedes's horse almost threw her, and she was put upon Blanco Sol. The white charger snorted a protest, then, obedient to Gale's stern call, patiently lowered his noble head and pawed the lava for a footing that would hold.

The lava caused Gale toil and worry and pain, but he hated the *chollas*. As the travel progressed this species of cactus increased in number of plants and in size. Everywhere the red lava was spotted with little round patches of glistening frosty white. And under every bunch of *cholla*, along and in the trail, were the discarded joints, like little frosty pinecones covered with spines. It was utterly impossible always to be on the lookout for these, and when Gale stepped on one, often as not the steel-like thorns pierced leather and flesh. Gale came almost to believe what he had heard claimed by desert travelers—that the *cholla* was alive and leaped at man or beast. Certain it was when Gale passed one, if he did not put all attention to avoiding it, he was hooked through his chaps and held by barbed thorns. The pain was almost unendurable. It was like no other. It burned, stung, beat—almost seemed to freeze. It made useless arm or leg. It made him bite his tongue to keep from crying out. It made the sweat roll off him. It made him sick.

Moreover, bad as the *cholla* was for man, it was infinitely worse for beast. A jagged stab from this poisoned cactus was the only thing Blanco Sol could not stand. Many times that day, before he carried Mercedes, he had wildly snorted, and then stood trembling while Gale picked broken thorns from the muscular legs. But after Mercedes had been put upon Sol Gale made sure no *cholla* touched him.

The afternoon passed like the morning, in ceaseless winding and twisting and climbing along this abandoned trail. Gale saw many water holes, mostly dry, some containing water, all of them catch-basins, full only after rainy season. Little ugly bunched bushes, that Gale scarcely recognized as mesquites, grew near these holes; also stunted greasewood and prickly pear. There was no grass, and the *cholla* alone flourished in that hard soil.

Darkness overtook the party as they unpacked beside a pool of water deep under an overhanging shelf of lava. It had been a hard day. The horses drank their fill, and then stood patiently with drooping heads. Hunger and thirst were appeased, and a warm fire cheered the weary and footsore fugitives. Yaqui said, "Sleep." And so another night passed.

U pon the following morning, ten miles or more up the slow-ascending lava slope, Gale's attention was called from his somber search for the less rough places in the trail.

"Dick, why does Yaqui look back?" asked Mercedes.

Gale was startled.

"Does he?"

"Every little while," replied Mercedes.

Gale was in the rear of all the other horses, so as to take, for Mercedes's sake, the advantage of the broken trail. Yaqui was leading Diablo, winding around a break. His head was bent as he stepped slowly and unevenly upon the lava. Gale turned to look back, the first time in several days. The mighty hollow of the desert below seemed a wide strip of red—wide strip of green—wide strip of gray—streaking to purple peaks. It was all too vast, too mighty to grasp any little details. He thought, of course, of Rojas in certain pursuit; but it seemed absurd to look for him.

Yaqui led on, and Gale often glanced up from his task to watch the Indian. Presently he saw him stop, turn, and look back. Ladd did likewise, and then Jim and Thorne. Gale found the desire irresistible. Thereafter he often rested Blanco Sol, and looked back the while. He had his field glass, but did not choose to use it.

"Rojas will follow," said Mercedes.

Gale regarded her in amaze. The tone of her voice had been indefinable. If there were fear then he failed to detect it. She was gazing back down the colored slope, and something about her, perhaps the steady, falcon gaze of her magnificent eyes, reminded him of Yaqui.

Many times during the ensuing hour the Indian faced about, and always his followers did likewise. It was high noon, with the sun beating hot and the lava radiating heat, when Yaqui halted for a rest. The place selected was a ridge of lava, almost a promontory, considering its outlook. The horses bunched here and drooped their heads. The rangers were about to slip the packs and remove saddles when Yaqui restrained them.

He fixed a changeless, gleaming gaze on the slow descent, but did not seem to look afar.

Suddenly he uttered his strange cry—the one Gale considered involuntary, or else significant of some tribal trait or feeling. It was incomprehensible, but no one could have doubted its potency. Yaqui pointed down the lava slope, pointing with finger and arm and neck and head—his whole body was instinct with direction. His whole being seemed to have been animated and then frozen. His posture could not have been misunderstood, yet his expression had not altered. Gale had never seen the Indian's face change its hard, red-bronze calm. It was the color and the flintiness and the character of the lava at his feet.

"Shore he sees somethin'," said Ladd. "But my eyes are no good."

"I reckon I ain't sure of mine," replied Jim. "I'm bothered by a dim movin' streak down there."

Thorne gazed eagerly down as he stood beside Mercedes, who sat motionless facing the slope. Gale looked and looked till he hurt his eyes. Then he took his glass out of its case on Sol's saddle.

There appeared to be nothing upon the lava but the innumerable dots of *cholla* shining in the sun. Gale swept his glass slowly forward and back. Then into a nearer field of vision crept a long white-and-black line of horses and men. Without a word he handed the glass to Ladd. The ranger used it, muttering to himself.

"They're on the lava fifteen miles down in an air line," he said, presently. "Jim, shore they're twice that an' more accordin' to the trail."

Jim had his look and replied: "I reckon we're a day an' a night in the lead."

"Is it Rojas?" burst out Thorne, with set jaw.

"Yes, Thorne. It's Rojas and a dozen men or more," replied Gale, and he looked up at Mercedes.

She was transformed. She might have been a medieval princess embodying all the Spanish power and passion of that time, breathing revenge, hate, unquenchable spirit of fire. If her beauty had been wonderful in her helpless and appealing moments, now, when she looked back white-faced and flame-eyed, it was transcendent.

Gale drew a long, deep breath. The mood which had presaged pursuit, strife, blood on this somber desert, returned to him tenfold. He saw Thorne's face corded by black veins, and his teeth exposed like those of a snarling wolf. These rangers, who had coolly risked death many times, and had dealt it often, were white as no fear or pain could have made them. Then, on the moment, Yaqui raised his hand, not clenched or doubled tight, but curled rigid like an eagle's claw; and he shook it in a strange, slow gesture which was menacing and terrible.

It was the woman that called to the depths of these men. And their passion to kill and to save was surpassed only by the wild hate which was yet love, the unfathomable emotion of a peon slave. Gale marveled at it, while he felt his whole being cold and tense, as he turned once more to follow in the tracks of his leaders. The fight predicted by Belding was at hand. What a fight that must be! Rojas was traveling light and fast. He was gaining. He had bought his men with gold, with extravagant promises, perhaps with offers of the body and blood of an aristocrat hateful to their kind. Lastly, there was the wild, desolate environment, a tortured wilderness of jagged lava and poisoned *cholla*, a lonely, fierce, and repellent world, a red stage most somberly and fittingly colored for a supreme struggle between men.

Yaqui looked back no more. Mercedes looked back no more. But the others looked, and the time came when Gale saw the creeping line of pursuers with naked eyes.

A level line above marked the rim of the plateau. Sand began to show in the little lava pits. On and upward toiled the cavalcade, still very slowly advancing. At last Yaqui reached the rim. He stood with his hand on Blanco Diablo; and both were silhouetted against the sky. That was the outlook for a Yaqui. And his great horse, dazzlingly white in the sunlight, with head wildly and proudly erect, mane and tail flying in the wind, made a magnificent picture. The others toiled on and upward, and at last Gale led Blanco Sol over the rim. Then all looked down the red slope.

But shadows were gathering there and no moving line could be seen.

Yaqui mounted and wheeled Diablo away. The others followed. Gale saw that the plateau was no more than a vast field of low, ragged circles, levels, mounds, cones, and whirls of lava. The lava was of a darker red than that down upon the slope, and it was harder than flint. In places fine sand and cinders covered the uneven floor. Strange varieties of cactus vied with the omnipresent *cholla*. Yaqui, however, found ground that his horse covered at a swift walk.

But there was only an hour, perhaps, of this comparatively easy going. Then the Yaqui led them into a zone of craters. The top of the earth seemed to have been blown out in holes from a few rods in width to large craters, some shallow, others deep, and all red as fire. Yaqui circled close to abysses which yawned sheer from a level surface, and he appeared always to be turning upon his course to avoid them.

The plateau had now a considerable dip to the west. Gale marked the slow heave and ripple of the ocean of lava to the south, where high, rounded peaks marked the center of this volcanic region. The uneven nature of the slope westward prevented any extended view, until suddenly the fugitives emerged from a rugged break to come upon a sublime and awe-inspiring spectacle.

They were upon a high point of the western slope of the plateau. It was a slope, but so many leagues long in its descent that only from a great height could any slant have been perceptible. Yaqui and his white horse stood upon the brink of a crater miles in circumference, a thousand feet deep, with its red walls patched in frost-colored spots by the silvery *cholla*. The giant tracery of lava streams waved down the slope to disappear in undulating sand dunes. And these bordered a seemingly endless arm of blue sea. This was the Gulf of California. Beyond the Gulf rose dim, bold mountains, and above them hung the setting sun, dusky red, flooding all that barren empire with a sinister light.

It was strange to Gale then, and perhaps to the others, to see their guide lead Diablo into a smooth and well-worn trail along the rim of the awful crater. Gale looked down into that red chasm. It resembled an inferno. The dark cliffs upon the opposite side were veiled in blue haze that seemed like smoke. Here Yaqui was at home. He moved and looked about him as a man coming at last into his own. Gale saw him stop and gaze out over that red-ribbed void to the Gulf.

Gale divined that somewhere along this crater of hell the Yaqui would make his final stand; and one look into his strange, inscrutable eyes made imagination picture a fitting doom for the pursuing Rojas.

CHAPTER 12

THE CRATER OF HELL

The trail led along a gigantic fissure in the side of the crater, and then down and down into a red-walled, blue-hazed labyrinth.

Presently Gale, upon turning a sharp corner, was utterly amazed to see that the split in the lava sloped out and widened into an arroyo. It was so green and soft and beautiful in all the angry, contorted red surrounding that Gale could scarcely credit his sight. Blanco Sol whistled his welcome to the scent of water. Then Gale saw a great hole, a pit in the shiny lava, a dark, cool, shady well. There was evidence of the fact that at flood seasons the water had an outlet into the arroyo. The soil appeared to be a fine sand, in which a reddish tinge predominated; and it was abundantly covered with a long grass, still partly green. Mesquites and *palo verdes* dotted the arroyo and gradually closed in thickets that obstructed the view.

"Shore it all beats me," exclaimed Ladd. "What a place to hole up in! We could have hid here for a long time. Boys, I saw mountain sheep, the real old genuine Rocky Mountain bighorn. What do you think of that?"

"I reckon it's a Yaqui hunting ground," replied Lash. "That trail we hit must be hundreds of years old. It's worn deep and smooth in the iron lava."

"Well, all I got to say is—Beldin' was shore right about the Indian. An' I can see Rojas's finish somewhere up along that awful hellhole."

Camp was made on a level spot. Yaqui took the horses to water, and then turned them loose in the arroyo. It was a tired and somber group that sat down to eat. The strain of suspense equaled the wearing effects of the long ride. Mercedes was calm, but her great dark eyes burned in her white face. Yaqui watched her. The others looked at her with unspoken pride. Presently Thorne wrapped her in his blankets, and she seemed to fall asleep at once. Twilight deepened. The campfire blazed brighter. A cool wind played with Mercedes's black hair, waving strands across her brow.

Little of Yaqui's purpose or plan could be elicited from him. But the look of him was enough to satisfy even Thorne. He leaned against a pile of wood, which he had collected, and his gloomy gaze pierced the camp-fire, and at long intervals strayed over the motionless form of the Spanish girl.

The rangers and Thorne, however, talked in low tones. It was absolutely impossible for Rojas and his men to reach the water hole before noon of the next day. And long before that time the fugitives would have decided on a plan of defense. What that defense would be, and where it would be made, were matters over which the men considered gravely. Ladd averred the Yaqui would put them into an impregnable position, that at the same time would prove a death trap for their pursuers. They exhausted every possibility, and then, tired as they were, still kept on talking.

"What stuns me is that Rojas stuck to our trail," said Thorne, his lined and haggard face expressive of dark passion. "He has followed us into this fearful desert. He'll lose men, horses, perhaps his life. He's only a bandit, and he stands to win no gold. If he ever gets out of here it'll be by herculean labor and by terrible hardship. All for a poor little helpless woman—just a woman! My God, I can't understand it."

"Shore—just a woman," replied Ladd, solemnly nodding his head.

Then there was a long silence during which the men gazed into the fire. Each, perhaps, had some vague conception of the enormity of Rojas's love or hate—some faint and amazing glimpse of the gulf of human passion. Those were cold, hard, grim faces upon which the light flickered.

"Sleep," said the Yaqui.

Thorne rolled in his blanket close beside Mercedes. Then one by one the rangers stretched out, feet to the fire. Gale found that he could not sleep. His eyes were weary, but they would not stay shut; his body ached for rest, yet he could not lie still. The night was so somber, so gloomy, and the lava-encompassed arroyo full of shadows. The dark velvet sky, fretted with white fire, seemed to be close. There was an absolute silence, as of death. Nothing moved—nothing outside of Gale's body appeared to live. The Yaqui sat like an image carved out of lava. The others lay prone and quiet. Would another night see any of them lie that way, quiet forever? Gale felt a ripple pass over him that was at once a shudder and a contraction of muscles. Used as he was to the desert and its oppression, why should he feel tonight as if the weight of its lava and the burden of its mystery were bearing him down?

He sat up after a while and again watched the fire. Nell's sweet face floated like a wraith in the pale smoke—glowed and flushed and smiled in the embers. Other faces shone there—his sister's—that of his mother. Gale shook off the tender memories. This desolate wilderness with its forbidding silence and its dark promise of hell on the morrow—this was not the place to unnerve oneself with thoughts of love and home. But the torturing paradox of the thing was that this was just the place and just the night for a man to be haunted.

By and by Gale rose and walked down a shadowy aisle between the mesquites. On his way back the Yaqui joined him. Gale was not surprised. He had become used to the Indian's strange guardianship. But now, perhaps because of Gale's poignancy of thought, the contending tides of love and regret, the deep, burning premonition of deadly strife, he was moved to keener scrutiny of the Yaqui. That, of course, was futile. The Indian was impenetrable, silent, strange. But suddenly, inexplicably, Gale felt Yaqui's human quality. It was aloof, as was everything about this Indian; but it was there. This savage walked silently beside him, without glance or touch or word. His thought was as inscrutable as if mind had never awakened in his race. Yet Gale was conscious of greatness, and, somehow, he was reminded of the Indian's story. His home had been desolated, his people carried off to slavery, his wife and children separated from him to die. What had life meant to the Yaqui? What had been in his heart? What was now in his mind? Gale could not answer these questions. But the difference between himself and Yaqui, which he had vaguely felt as that between savages and civilized men, faded out of his mind forever. Yaqui might have considered he owed Gale a debt, and, with a Yaqui's austere and noble fidelity to honor, he meant to pay it. Nevertheless, this was not the thing Gale found in the Indian's silent presence. Accepting the desert with its subtle and inconceivable influence, Gale felt that the savage and the white man had been bound in a tie which was no less brotherly because it could not be comprehended.

Toward dawn Gale managed to get some sleep. Then the morning broke with the sun hidden back of the uplift of the plateau. The horses trooped up the arroyo and snorted for water. After a hurried breakfast the packs were hidden in holes in the lava. The saddles were left where they were, and the horses allowed to graze and wander at will. Canteens were filled, a small bag of food was packed, and blankets made into a bundle. Then Yaqui faced the steep ascent of the lava slope.

The trail he followed led up on the right side of the fissure, opposite to the one he had come down. It was a steep climb, and encumbered as the men were they made but slow progress. Mercedes had to be lifted up smooth steps and across crevices. They passed places where the rims of the fissure were but a few yards apart. At length the rims widened out and the red, smoky crater yawned beneath. Yaqui left the trail and began clambering down over the rough and twisted convolutions of lava which formed the rim. Sometimes he hung sheer over the precipice. It was with extreme difficulty that the party followed him. Mercedes had to be held on narrow, foot-wide ledges. Tbe *cholla* was there to hinder passage. Finally the Indian halted upon a narrow bench of flat, smooth lava, and his followers worked with exceeding care and effort down to his position.

At the back of this bench, between bunches of *cholla*, was a niche, a shallow cave with floor lined apparently with mold. Ladd said the place was a refuge which had been inhabited by mountain sheep for many years. Yaqui spread blankets inside, left the canteen and the sack of food, and with a gesture at once humble, yet that of a chief, he invited Mercedes to enter. A few more gestures and fewer words disclosed his plan. In this inaccessible nook Mercedes was to be hidden. The men were to go around upon the opposite rim, and block the trail leading down to the water hole.

Gale marked the nature of this eyrie. It was the wildest and most rugged place he had ever stepped upon. Only a sheep could have climbed up the wall above or along the slanting shelf of lava beyond. Below glistened a whole bank of *cholla*, frosty in the sunlight, and it overhung an apparently bottomless abyss.

Ladd chose the smallest gun in the party and gave it to Mercedes.

"Shore it's best to go the limit on bein' ready," he said, simply. "The chances are you'll never need it. But if you do—"

He left off there, and his break was significant. Mercedes answered him with a fearless and indomitable flash of eyes. Thorne was the only one who showed any shaken nerve. His leave-taking of his wife was affecting and hurried. Then he and the rangers carefully stepped in the tracks of the Yaqui.

They climbed up to the level of the rim and went along the edge. When they reached the fissure and came upon its narrowest point, Yaqui showed in his actions that he meant to leap it. Ladd restrained the Indian. They then continued along the rim till they reached several bridges of lava which crossed it. The fissure was deep in some parts, choked in others. Evidently the crater had no direct outlet into the arroyo below. Its bottom, however, must have been far beneath the level of the water hole.

After the fissure was crossed the trail was soon found. Here it ran back from the rim. Yaqui waved his hand to the right, where along the corrugated slope of the crater there were holes and crevices and coverts for a hundred men. Yaqui strode on up the trail toward a higher point, where presently his dark figure stood motionless against the sky. The rangers and Thorne selected a deep depression, out of which led several ruts deep enough for cover. According to Ladd it was as good a place as any, perhaps not so hidden as others, but freer from the dreaded *cholla*. Here the men laid down rifles and guns, and, removing their heavy cartridge belts, settled down to wait.

Their location was close to the rim wall and probably five hundred yards from the opposite rim, which was now seen to be considerably below them. The glaring red cliff presented a deceitful and baffling appearance. It had a thousand ledges and holes in its surfaces, and one moment it looked perpendicular and the next there seemed to be a long slant. Thorne pointed out where he thought Mercedes was hidden; Ladd selected another place, and Lash still another. Gale searched for the bank of the *cholla* he had seen under the bench where Mercedes's retreat lay, and when he found it the others disputed his opinion. Then Gale brought his field glass into requisition, proving that he was right. Once located and fixed in sight, the white patch of *cholla*, the bench, and the sheep eyrie stood out from the other features of that rugged wall. But all the men were agreed that Yaqui had hidden Mercedes where only the eyes of a vulture could have found her.

Jim Lash crawled into a little strip of shade and bided the time tranquilly. Ladd was restless and impatient and watchful, every little while rising to look up the far-reaching slope, and then to the right, where Yaqui's dark figure stood out from a high point of the rim. Thorne grew silent, and seemed consumed by a slow, sullen rage. Gale was neither calm nor free of a gnawing suspense nor of a waiting wrath. But as best he could he put the pending action out of mind.

It came over him all of a sudden that he had not grasped the stupendous nature of this desert setting. There was the measureless red slope, its lower ridges finally sinking into white sand dunes toward the blue sea. The cold, sparkling light, the white sun, the deep azure of sky, the feeling of boundless expanse all around him—these meant high altitude. Southward the barren red simply merged into distance. The field of craters rose in high, dark wheels toward the dominating peaks. When Gale withdrew his gaze from the magnitude of these spaces and heights the crater beneath him seemed dwarfed. Yet while he gazed it spread and deepened and multiplied its ragged lines. No, he could not grasp the meaning of size or distance here. There was too much to stun the sight. But the mood in which nature had created this convulsed world of lava seized hold upon him.

Meanwhile the hours passed. As the sun climbed the clear, steely lights vanished, the blue hazes deepened, and slowly the glistening surfaces of lava turned redder. Ladd was concerned to discover that Yaqui was missing from his outlook upon the high point. Jim Lash came out of the shady crevice, and stood up to buckle on his cartridge belt. His narrow, gray glance slowly roved from the height of lava down along the slope, paused in doubt, and then swept on to resurvey the whole vast eastern dip of the plateau.

"I reckon my eyes are pore," he said. "Mebbe it's this damn red glare. Anyway, what's them creepin' spots up there?"

"Shore I seen them. Mountain sheep," replied Ladd.

"Guess again, Laddy. Dick, I reckon you'd better flash the glass up the slope."

Gale adjusted the field glass and began to search the lava, beginning close at hand and working away from him. Presently the glass became stationary.

"I see half a dozen small animals, brown in color. They look like sheep. But I couldn't distinguish mountain sheep from antelope."

"Shore they're bighorn," said Laddy.

"I reckon if you'll pull around to the east an' search under that long wall of lava—there—you'll see what I see," added Jim.

The glass climbed and circled, wavered an instant, then fixed steady as a rock. There was a breathless silence.

"Fourteen horses—two packed—some mounted—others without riders, and lame," said Gale slowly.

Yaqui appeared far up the trail, coming swiftly. Presently he saw the rangers and halted to wave his arms and point. Then he vanished as if the lava had opened beneath him.

"Lemme have that glass," suddenly said Jim Lash. "I'm seein' red, I tell you. . . . Well, pore as my eyes are they had it right. Rojas an' his outfit have left the trail."

"Jim, you ain't meanin' they've taken to that awful slope?" queried Ladd.

"I sure do. There they are—still comin', but goin' down, too."

"Mebbe Rojas is crazy, but it begins to look like he—"

"Laddy, I'll be danged if the Greaser bunch hasn't vamoosed. Gone out of sight! Right there not a half mile away, the whole caboodle—gone!"

"Shore they're behind a crust or have gone down into a rut," suggested Ladd. "They'll show again in a minute. Look sharp, boys, for I'm figgerin' Rojas'll spread his men."

Minutes passed, but nothing moved upon the slope. Each man crawled up to a vantage point along the crest of rotting lava. The watchers were careful to peer through little notches or from behind a spur, and the constricted nature of their hiding place kept them close together. Ladd's muttering grew into a growl, then lapsed into the silence that marked his companions. From time to time the rangers looked inquiringly at Gale. The field glass, however, like the naked sight, could not catch the slightest moving object out there upon the lava. A long hour of slow, mounting suspense wore on.

"Shore it's all goin' to be as queer as the Yaqui," said Ladd.

Indeed, the strange mien, the silent action, the somber character of the Indian had not been without effect upon the minds of the men. Then the weird, desolate, tragic scene added to the vague sense of mystery. And now the disappearance of Rojas's band, the long wait in the silence, the boding certainty of invisible foes crawling, circling closer and closer, lent to the situation a final touch that made it unreal.

"I'm reckonin' there's a mind behind them Greasers," replied Jim. "Or mebbe we ain't done Rojas credit. . . . If somethin' would only come off!"

That Lash, the coolest, most provokingly nonchalant of men in times of peril, should begin to show a nervous strain was all the more indicative of a subtle pervading unreality.

"Boys, look sharp!" suddenly called Lash. "Low down to the left—mebbe three hundred yards. See, along by them seams of lava—behind the *chollas*. First off I thought it was a sheep. But it's the Yaqui! . . . Crawlin' swift as a lizard! Can't you see him?"

It was a full moment before Jim's companions could locate the Indian. Flat as a snake Yaqui wound himself along with incredible rapidity. His advance was all the more remarkable for the fact that he appeared to pass directly under the dreaded *chollas*. Sometimes he paused to lift his head and look. He was directly in line with a huge whorl of lava that rose higher than any point on the slope. This spur was a quarter of a mile from the position of the rangers.

"Shore he's headin' for that high place," said Ladd. "He's going slow now. There, he's stopped behind some *chollas*. He's gettin' up—no' he's kneelin'. . . . Now what the hell!"

"Laddy, take a peek at the side of that lava ridge," sharply called Jim. "I guess mebbe somethin' ain't comin' off. See! There's Rojas an' his outfit climbin'. Don't make out no hosses. . . . Dick, use your glass an' tell us what's doin'. I'll watch Yaqui an' tell you what his move means."

Clearly and distinctly, almost as if he could have touched them, Gale had Rojas and his followers in sight. They were toiling up the rough lava on foot. They were heavily armed. Spurs, chaps, jackets, scarfs were not in evidence. Gale saw the lean, swarthy faces, the black straggly hair, the ragged, soiled garments which had once been white.

"They're almost up now," Gale was saying. "There! They halt on top. I see Rojas. He looks wild. By—! fellows, an Indian! . . . It's a Papago. Belding's old herder! . . . The Indian points—this way—then down. He's showing Rojas the lay of the trail."

"Boys, Yaqui's in range of that bunch," said Jim, swiftly. "He's raisin' his rifle slow—Lord, how slow he is! . . . He's covered someone. Which one I can't say. But I think he'll pick Rojas."

"The Yaqui can shoot. He'll pick Rojas," added Gale, grimly.

"Rojas—yes—yes!" cried Thorne, in passion of suspense.

"Not on your life!" Ladd's voice cut in with scorn. "Gentlemen, you can gamble Yaqui'll kill the Papago. That traitor Indian knows these sheep haunts. He's tellin' Rojas—"

A sharp rifle shot rang out.

"Laddy's right," called Gale. "The Papago's hit—his arm falls— There, he tumbles!"

More shots rang out. Yaqui was seen standing erect firing rapidly at the darting Mexicans. For all Gale could make out no second bullet took effect. Rojas and his men vanished behind the bulge of lava. Then Yaqui deliberately backed away from his position. He made no effort to run or hide. Evidently he watched cautiously for signs of pursuers in the ruts and behind the *choyas*. Presently he turned and came straight toward the position of the rangers, sheered off perhaps a hundred paces below it, and disappeared in a crevice. Plainly his intention was to draw pursuers within rifle shot.

"Shore, Jim, you had your wish. Somethin' come off," said Ladd. "An'

I'm sayin' thank God for the Yaqui! That Papago'd have ruined us. Even so, mebbe he's told Rojas more'n enough to make us sweat blood."

"He had a chance to kill Rojas," cried out the drawn-faced, passionate Thorne. "He didn't take it! . . . He didn't take it!"

Only Ladd appeared to be able to answer the cavalryman's poignant cry.

"Listen, son," he said, and his voice rang. "We-all know how you feel. An' if I'd had that one shot never in the world could I have picked the Papago guide. I'd have had to kill Rojas. That's the white man of it. But Yaqui was right. Only an Indian could have done it. You can gamble the Papago alive meant slim chance for us. Because he'd lead straight to where Mercedes is hidden, an' then we'd have left cover to fight it out. . . . When you come to think of the Yaqui's hate for Greasers, when you just seen him pass up a shot at one—well, I don't know how to say what I mean, but damn me, my som-brer-ro is off to the Indian!"

"I reckon so, an' I reckon the ball's opened," rejoined Lash, and now that former nervous impatience so unnatural to him was as if it had never been. He was smilingly cool, and his voice had almost a caressing note. He tapped the breach of his Winchester with a sinewy brown hand, and he did not appear to be addressing any one in particular. "Yaqui's opened the ball. Look up your pardners there, gents, an' get ready to dance."

Another wait set in then, and judging by the more direct rays of the sun and a receding of the little shadows cast by the *chollas*, Gale was of the opinion that it was a long wait. But it seemed short. The four men were lying under the bank of a half circular hole in the lava. It was notched and cracked, and its rim was fringed by *chollas*. It sloped down and opened to an unobstructed view of the crater. Gale had the upper position, farthest to the right, and therefore was best shielded from possible fire from the higher ridges of the rim, some three hundred yards distant. Jim came next, well hidden in a crack. The positions of Thorne and Ladd were most exposed. They kept sharp lookout over the uneven rampart of their hiding place.

The sun passed the zenith, began to slope westward, and to grow hotter as it sloped. The men waited and waited. Gale saw no impatience even in Thorne. The sultry air seemed to be laden with some burden or quality that was at once composed of heat, menace, color, and silence.

Even the light glancing up from the lava seemed red, and the silence had substance. Sometimes Gale felt that it was unbearable. Yet he made no effort to break it.

Suddenly this dead stillness was rent by a shot, clear and stinging, close at hand. It was from a rifle, not a carbine. With startling quickness a cry followed—a cry that pierced Gale—it was so thin, so high-keyed, so different from all other cries. It was the involuntary human shriek of death.

"Yaqui's called out another pardner," said Jim Lash, laconically.

Carbines began to crack. The reports were quick, light, like sharp spats without any ring. Gale peered from behind the edge of his covert. Above the ragged wave of lava floated faint whitish clouds, all that was visible of smokeless powder. Then Gale made out round spots, dark against the background of red, and in front of them leaped out small tongues of fire. Ladd's .405 began to "spang" with its beautiful sound of power. Thorne was firing, somewhat wildly Gale thought. Then Jim Lash pushed his Winchester over the rim under a *cholla*, and between shots Gale could hear him singing: "Turn the lady, turn—turn the lady, turn! . . . Alaman left! Swing your pardners! . . . Forward an' back! . . . Turn the lady, turn!" Gale got into the fight himself, not so sure that he hit any of the round, bobbing objects he aimed at, but growing sure of himself as action liberated something forced and congested within his breast.

Then over the position of the rangers came a hail of steel bullets. Those that struck the lava hissed away into the crater; those that came biting through the *chollas* made a sound which resembled a sharp ripping of silk. Bits of cactus stung Gale's face, and he dreaded the flying thorns more than he did the flying bullets.

"Hold on, boys," called Ladd, as he crouched down to reload his rifle. "Save your shells. The Greasers are spreadin' on us, some goin' down below Yaqui, others movin' up for that high ridge. When they get up there I'm damned if it won't be hot for us. There ain't room for all of us to hide here."

Ladd raised himself to peep over the rim. Shots were now scattering, and all appeared to come from below. Emboldened by this he rose higher. A shot from in front, a rip of bullet through the *cholla*, a spat of something hitting Ladd's face, a steel missile hissing onwards—these inseparably blended sounds were all registered by Gale's sensitive ear.

With a curse Ladd tumbled down into the hole. His face showed a great gray blotch, and starting blood. Gale felt a sickening assurance of desperate injury to the ranger. He ran to him calling: "Laddy! Laddy!"

"Shore I ain't plugged. It's a damn *cholla* burr. The bullet knocked it in my face. Pull it out!"

The oval, long-spiked cone was firmly imbedded in Ladd's cheek. Blood streamed down his face and neck. Carefully, yet with no thought of pain to himself, Gale tried to pull the cactus joint away. It was as firm as if it had been nailed there. That was the damnable feature of the barbed thorns: once set, they held on as that strange plant held to its desert life. Ladd began to writhe, and sweat mingled with the blood on his face. He cursed and raved, and his movements made it almost impossible for Gale to do anything.

"Put your knife-blade under an' tear it out!" shouted Ladd, hoarsely.

Thus ordered, Gale slipped a long blade in between the imbedded thorns, and with a powerful jerk literally tore the *cholla* out of Ladd's quivering flesh. Then, where the ranger's face was not red and raw, it certainly was white.

A volley of shots from a different angle was followed by the quick ring of steel bullets striking the lava all around Gale. His first idea, as he heard the projectiles sing and hum and whine away into the air, was that they were coming from above him. He looked up to see a number of low, white and dark knobs upon the high point of lava. They had not been there before. Then he saw little, pale, leaping tongues of fire. As he dodged down he distinctly heard a bullet strike Ladd. At the same instant he seemed to hear Thorne cry out and fall, and Lash's boots scrape rapidly away.

Ladd fell backward still holding the .405. Gale dragged him into the shelter of his own position, and dreading to look at him, took up the heavy weapon. It was with a kind of savage strength that he gripped the rifle; and it was with a cold and deadly intent that he aimed and fired. The first Greaser huddled low, let his carbine go clattering down, and then crawled behind the rim. The second and third jerked back. The fourth seemed to flop up over the crest of lava. A dark arm reached for him, clutched his leg, tried to drag him up. It was in vain. Wildly grasping at the air the bandit fell, slid down a steep shelf, rolled over the rim, to go hurtling down out of sight.

Fingering the hot rifle with close-pressed hands, Gale watched the skyline along the high point of lava. It remained unbroken. As his passion left him he feared to look back at his companions, and the cold chill returned to his breast.

"Shore—I'm damn glad—them Greasers ain't usin' soft-nose bullets," drawled a calm voice.

Swift as lightning Gale whirled.

"Laddy! I thought you were done for," cried Gale, with a break in his voice.

"I ain't a-mindin' the bullet much. But that *cholla* joint took my nerve, an' you can gamble on it. Dick, this hole's pretty high up, ain't it?"

The ranger's blouse was open at the neck, and on his right shoulder under the collarbone was a small hole just beginning to bleed.

"Sure it's high, Laddy," replied Gale, gladly. "Went clear through, clean as a whistle!"

He tore a handkerchief into two parts, made wads, and pressing them close over the wounds he bound them there with Ladd's scarf.

"Shore it's funny how a bullet can floor a man an' then not do any damage," said Ladd. "I felt a zip of wind an' somethin' like a pat on my chest an' down I went. Well, so much for the small caliber with their steel bullets. Supposin' I'd connected with a .405!"

"Laddy, I—I'm afraid Thorne's done for," whispered Gale. "He's lying over there in that crack. I can see part of him. He doesn't move."

"I was wonderin' if I'd have to tell you that. Dick, he went down hard hit, fallin', you know, limp an' soggy. It was a moral cinch one of us would get it in this fight; but God! I'm sorry Thorne had to be the man."

"Laddy, maybe he's not dead," replied Gale. He called aloud to his friend. There was no answer.

Ladd got up, and, after peering keenly at the height of lava, he strode swiftly across the space. It was only a dozen steps to the crack in the lava where Thorne had fallen in headfirst. Ladd bent over, went to his knees, so that Gale saw only his head. Then he appeared rising with arms round the cavalryman. He dragged him across the hole to the sheltered corner that alone afforded protection. He had scarcely reached it when a carbine cracked and a bullet struck the flinty lava, striking sparks, then singing away into the air.

Thorne was either dead or unconscious, and Gale, with a contracting throat and numb heart, decided for the former. Not so Ladd, who probed the bloody gash on Thorne's temple, and then felt his breast.

"He's alive an' not bad hurt. That bullet hit him glancin'. Shore them steel bullets are some lucky for us. Dick, you needn't look so glum. I tell you he ain't bad hurt. I felt his skull with my finger. There's no hole in it. Wash him off an' tie— Wow! did you get the wind of that one? An' mebbe it didn't sing off the lava! . . . Dick, look after Thorne now while I—"

The completion of his speech was the stirring ring of the .405, and then he uttered a laugh that was unpleasant.

"Shore, Greaser, there's a man's size bullet for you. No slim, sharp-point, steel-jacket nail! I'm takin' it on me to believe you're appreciatin' of the .405, seein' as you don't make no fuss."

It was indeed a joy to Gale to find that Thorne had not received a wound necessarily fatal, though it was serious enough. Gale bathed and bound it, and laid the cavalryman against the slant of the bank, his head high to lessen the probability of bleeding.

As Gale straightened up Ladd muttered low and deep, and swung the heavy rifle around to the left. Far along the slope a figure moved. Ladd began to work the lever of the Winchester and to shoot. At every shot the heavy firearm sprang up, and the recoil made Ladd's shoulder give back. Gale saw the bullets strike the lava behind, beside, before the flee-ing Mexican, sending up dull puffs of dust. On the sixth shot he plunged down out of sight, either hit or frightened into seeking cover.

"Dick, mebbe there's one or two left above; but we needn't figger much on it," said Ladd, as, loading the rifle, he jerked his fingers quickly from the hot breech. "Listen! Jim an' Yaqui are hittin' it up lively down below. I'll sneak down there. You stay here an' keep about half an eye peeled up yonder, an' keep the rest my way."

Ladd crossed the hole, climbed down into the deep crack where Thorne had fallen, and then went stooping along with only his head above the level. Presently he disappeared. Gale, having little to fear from the high ridge, directed most of his attention toward the point beyond which

Ladd had gone. The firing had become desultory, and the light carbine shots outnumbered the sharp rifle shots five to one. Gale made a note of the fact that for some little time he had not heard the unmistakable report of Jim Lash's automatic. Then ensued a long interval in which the desert silence seemed to recover its grip. The .405 ripped it asunder—*spang—spang—spang*. Gale fancied he heard yells. There were a few pattering shots still farther down the trail. Gale had an uneasy conviction that Rojas and some of his band might go straight to the water hole. It would be hard to dislodge even a few men from that retreat.

There seemed a lull in the battle. Gale ventured to stand high, and, screened behind *chollas*, he swept the three-quarter circle of lava with his glass. In the distance he saw horses, but no riders. Below him, down the slope along the crater rim and the trail, the lava was bare of all except tufts of *cholla*. Gale gathered assurance. It looked as if the day was favoring his side. Then Thorne, coming partly to consciousness, engaged Gale's care. The cavalryman stirred and moaned, called for water, and then for Mercedes. Gale held him back with a strong hand, and presently he was once more quiet.

For the first time in hours, as it seemed, Gale took note of the physical aspect of his surroundings. He began to look upon them without keen gaze strained for crouching form, or bobbing head, or spouting carbine. Either Gale's sense of color and proportion had become deranged during the fight, or the encompassing air and the desert had changed. Even the sun had changed. It seemed lowering, oval in shape, magenta in hue, and it had a surface that gleamed like oil on water. Its red rays shone through red haze. Distances that had formerly been clearly outlined were now dim, obscured. The yawning chasm was not the same. It circled wider, redder, deeper. It was a weird, ghastly mouth of hell. Gale stood fascinated, unable to tell how much he saw was real, how much the exaggeration of overwrought emotions. There was no beauty here, but an unparalleled grandeur, a sublime scene of devastation and desolation which might have had its counterpart upon the burned-out moon. The mood that gripped Gale now added to its somber portent an unshakable foreboding of calamity.

He wrestled with the spell as if it were a physical foe. Reason and intelligence had their voices in his mind; but the moment was not one wherein these things could wholly control. He felt life strong within his breast, yet there, a step away, was death, yawning, glaring, smoky, red. It was a moment—an hour for a savage, born, bred, developed in this scarred and blasted place of jagged depths and red distances and silences never meant to be broken. Since Gale was not a savage he fought that call of the red gods which sent him back down the long ages toward his primitive day. His mind combated his sense of sight and the hearing that seemed useless; and his mind did not win all the victory. Something fatal was here, hanging in the balance, as the red haze hung along the vast walls of that crater of hell.

Suddenly harsh, prolonged yells brought him to his feet, and the unrealities vanished. Far down the trails where the crater rims closed in the deep fissure he saw moving forms. They were three in number. Two of them ran nimbly across the lava bridge. The third staggered far behind. It was Ladd. He appeared hard hit. He dragged at the heavy rifle, which he seemed unable to raise. The yells came from him. He was calling the Yaqui.

Gale's heart stood still momentarily. Here, then, was the catastrophe! He hardly dared sweep that fissure with his glass. The two fleeing figures halted—turned to fire at Ladd. Gale recognized the foremost one— small, compact, gaudy—Rojas! The bandit's arm was outstretched. Puffs of white smoke rose, and shots rapped out. When Ladd went down Rojas threw his gun aside and with a wild yell bounded over the lava. His companion followed.

A tide of passion, first hot as fire, then cold as ice, rushed over Gale when he saw Rojas take the trail toward Mercedes's hiding place. The little bandit appeared to have the sure-footedness of a mountain sheep. The Mexican following was not so sure or fast. He turned back. Gale heard the trenchant bark of the .405. Ladd was kneeling. He shot again— again. The retreating bandit seemed to run full into an invisible obstacle, then fell lax, inert, lifeless. Rojas sped on unmindful of the spurts of dust about him. Yaqui, high above Ladd, was also firing at the bandit. Then both rifles were emptied. Rojas turned at a high break in the trail. He shook a defiant hand, and his exulting yell pealed faintly to Gale's ears. About him there was something desperate, magnificent. Then he clambered down the trail.

Ladd dropped the .405, and rising, gun in hand, he staggered toward the bridge of lava. Before he had crossed it Yaqui came bounding down the slope, and in one splendid leap he cleared the fissure. He ran beyond the trail and disappeared on the lava above. Rojas had not seen this sudden, darting move of the Indian.

Gale felt himself bitterly powerless to aid in that pursuit. He could only watch. He wondered, fearfully, what had become of Lash. Presently, when Rojas came out of the cracks and ruts of lava there might be a chance of disabling him by a long shot. His progress was now slow. But he was making straight for Mercedes's hiding place. What was it leading him there—an eagle eye, or hate, or instinct? Why did he go on when there could be no turning back for him on that trail? Ladd was slow, heavy, staggering on the trail; but he was relentless. Only death could stop the ranger now. Surely Rojas must have known that when he chose the trail. From time to time Gale caught glimpses of Yaqui's dark figure stealing along the higher rim of the crater. He was making for a point above the bandit.

Moments—endless moments dragged by. The lowering sun colored only the upper half of the crater walls. Far down the depths were murky blue. Again Gale felt the insupportable silence. The red haze became a transparent veil before his eyes. Sinister, evil, brooding, waiting, seemed that yawning abyss. Ladd staggered along the trail, at times he crawled. The Yaqui gained; he might have had wings; he leaped from jagged crust to jagged crust; his sure-footedness was a wonderful thing.

But for Gale the marvel of that endless period of watching was the purpose of the bandit Rojas. He had now no weapon. Gale's glass made this fact plain. There was death behind him, death below him, death before him, and though he could not have known it, death above him. He never faltered—never made a misstep upon the narrow, flinty trail. When he reached the lower end of the level ledge Gale's poignant doubt became a certainty. Rojas had seen Mercedes. It was incredible, yet Gale believed it. Then, his heart clamped as in an icy vise, Gale threw forward the Remington, and sinking on one knee, began to shoot. He emptied the magazine. Puffs of dust near Rojas did not even make him turn.

As Gale began to reload he was horror-stricken by a low cry from Thorne. The cavalryman had recovered consciousness. He was half raised, pointing with shaking hand at the opposite ledge. His distended eyes were riveted upon Rojas. He was trying to utter speech that would not come.

Gale wheeled, rigid now, steeling himself to one last forlorn hope—that Mercedes could defend herself. She had a gun. He doubted not at all that she would use it. But, remembering her terror of this savage, he feared for her.

Rojas reached the level of the ledge. He halted. He crouched. It was the act of a panther. Manifestly he saw Mercedes within the cave. Then faint shots patted the air, broke in quick echo. Rojas went down as if struck a heavy blow. He was hit. But even as Gale yelled in sheer madness the bandit leaped erect. He seemed too quick, too supple to be badly wounded. A slight, dark figure flashed out of the cave. Mercedes! She backed against the wall. Gale saw a puff of white—heard a report. But the bandit lunged at her. Mercedes ran, not to try to pass him, but straight for the precipice. Her intention was plain. But Rojas outstripped her, even as she reached the verge. Then a piercing scream pealed across the crater—a scream of despair.

Gale closed his eyes. He could not bear to see more.

Thorne echoed Mercedes's scream. Gale looked round just in time to leap and catch the cavalryman as he staggered, apparently for the steep slope. And then, as Gale dragged him back, both fell. Gale saved his friend, but he plunged into a *cholla*. He drew his hands away full of the great glistening cones of thorns.

"For God's sake, Gale, shoot! Shoot! *Kill her! Kill her!* . . . Can't—you—see—Rojas—"

Thorne fainted.

Gale, stunned for the instant, stood with uplifted hands and gazed from Thorne across the crater. Rojas had not killed Mercedes. He was overpowering her. His actions seemed slow, wearing, purposeful. Hers were violent. Like a trapped she-wolf, Mercedes was fighting. She tore, struggled, flung herself.

Rojas's intention was terribly plain.

In agony now, both mental and physical, cold and sick and weak, Gale gripped his rifle and aimed at the struggling forms on the ledge. He pulled the trigger. The bullet struck up a cloud of red dust close to the struggling couple. Again Gale fired, hoping to hit Rojas, praying to kill Mercedes. The bullet struck high. A third—fourth—fifth time the Remington spoke—in vain! The rifle fell from Gale's racked hands.

How horribly plain that fiend's intention! Gale tried to close his eyes, but could not. He prayed wildly for a sudden blindness—to faint as Thorne had fainted. But he was transfixed to the spot with eyes that pierced the red light.

Mercedes was growing weaker, seemed about to collapse.

"Oh, Jim Lash, are you dead?" cried Gale. "Oh, Laddy! . . . Oh, Yaqui!"

Suddenly a dark form literally fell down the wall behind the ledge where Rojas fought the girl. It sank in a heap, then bounded erect.

"Yaqui!" screamed Gale, and he waved his bleeding hands till the blood bespattered his face. Then he choked. Utterance became impossible.

The Indian bent over Rojas and flung him against the wall. Mercedes, sinking back, lay still. When Rojas got up the Indian stood between him and escape from the ledge. Rojas backed the other way along the narrowing shelf of lava. His manner was abject, stupefied. Slowly he stepped backward.

It was then that Gale caught the white gleam of a knife in Yaqui's hand. Rojas turned and ran. He rounded a corner of wall where the footing was precarious. Yaqui followed slowly. His figure was dark and menacing. But he was not in a hurry. When he passed off the ledge Rojas was edging farther and farther along the wall. He was clinging now to the lava, creeping inch by inch. Perhaps he had thought to work around the buttress or climb over it. Evidently he went as far as possible, and there he clung, an unscalable wall above, the abyss beneath.

The approach of the Yaqui was like a slow dark shadow of gloom. If it seemed so to the stricken Gale what must it have been to Rojas? He appeared to sink against the wall. The Yaqui stole closer and closer. He was the savage now, and for him the moment must have been glorified. Gale saw him gaze up at the great circling walls of the crater, then down into the depths. Perhaps the red haze hanging above him, or the purple haze below, or the deep caverns in the lava, held for Yaqui spirits of the desert, his gods to whom he called. Perhaps he invoked shadows of his loved ones and his race, calling them in this moment of vengeance.

Gale heard—or imagined he heard—that wild, strange Yaqui cry.

Then the Indian stepped close to Rojas and bent low, keeping out of reach. How slow were his motions! Would Yaqui never—never end it? . . . A wail drifted across the crater to Gale's ears.

Rojas fell backward and plunged sheer. The bank of white *chollas* caught him, held him upon their steel spikes. How long did the dazed Gale sit there watching Rojas wrestling and writhing in convulsive frenzy? The bandit now seemed mad to win the delayed death.

When he broke free he was a white patched object no longer human, a ball of *cholla* burrs, and he slipped off the bank to shoot down and down into the purple depths of the crater.

CHAPTER 13

CHANGES AT FORLORN RIVER

The first of March saw the federal occupation of the garrison at Casita. After a short, decisive engagement the rebels were dispersed into small bands and driven eastward along the boundary line toward Nogales.

It was the destiny of Forlorn River, however, never to return to the slow, sleepy tenor of its former existence. Belding's predictions came true. That straggling line of homeseekers was but a forerunner of the real invasion of Altar Valley. Refugees from Mexico and from Casita spread the word that water and wood and grass and land were to be had at Forlorn River; and as if by magic the white tents and red adobe houses sprang up to glisten in the sun.

Belding was happier than he had been for a long time. He believed that evil days for Forlorn River, along with the apathy and lack of enterprise, were in the past. He hired a couple of trustworthy Mexicans to ride the boundary line, and he settled down to think of ranching and irrigation and mining projects. Every morning he expected to receive some word from Sonoyta or Yuma, telling him that Yaqui had guided his party safely across the desert.

Belding was simpleminded, a man more inclined to action than reflection. When the complexities of life hemmed him in, he groped his way out, never quite understanding. His wife had always been a mystery to him. Nell was sunshine most of the time, but, like the sun-dominated desert, she was subject to strange changes, wilful, stormy, sudden. It was enough for Belding now to find his wife in a lighter, happier mood, and to see Nell dreamily turning a ring round and round the third finger of her left hand and watching the west. Every day both mother and daughter appeared further removed from the past darkly threatening days. Belding was hearty in his affections, but undemonstrative. If there was any sentiment in his makeup it had an outlet in his memory of Blanco Diablo and a longing to see him. Often Belding stopped his work to gaze out over the desert toward the west. When he thought of his rangers and Thorne and Mercedes he certainly never forgot his horse. He wondered if Diablo was running, walking, resting; if Yaqui was finding water and grass.

In March, with the short desert winter over, the days began to grow warm. The noon hours were hot, and seemed to give promise of the white summer blaze and blasting furnace wind soon to come. No word was received from the rangers. But this caused Belding no concern, and it seemed to him that his womenfolks considered no news good news.

Among the many changes coming to pass in Forlorn River were the installing of post-office service and the building of a mescal drinking-house. Belding had worked hard for the post office, but he did not like the idea of a saloon for Forlorn River. Still, that was an inevitable evil. The Mexicans would have mescal. Belding had kept the little border hamlet free of an establishment for distillation of the fiery cactus drink. A good many Americans drifted into Forlorn River—miners, cowboys, prospectors, outlaws, and others of nondescript character; and these men, of course, made the saloon, which was also an inn, their headquarters. Belding, with Carter and other old residents, saw the need of a sheriff for Forlorn River.

One morning early in this spring month, while Belding was on his way from the house to the corrals, he saw Nell running Blanco José down the road at a gait that amazed him. She did not take the turn of the road to come in by the gate. She put José at a four-foot wire fence, and came clattering into the yard.

"Nell must have another tantrum," said Belding. "She's long past due."

Blanco José, like the other white horses, was big of frame and heavy, and thunder rolled from under his great hoofs. Nell pulled him up, and as he pounded and slid to a halt in a cloud of dust she swung lightly down.

It did not take more than half an eye for Belding to see that she was furious.

"Nell, what's come off now?" asked Belding.

"I'm not going to tell you," she replied, and started away, leading José toward the corral.

Belding leisurely followed. She went into the corral, removed José's bridle, and led him to the watering trough. Belding came up and without saying anything began to unbuckle José's saddle girths. But he ventured a look at Nell. The red had gone from her face, and he was surprised to see her eyes brimming with tears. Most assuredly this was not one of Nell's tantrums. While taking off José's saddle and hanging it in the shed Belding pondered in his slow way. When he came back to the corral Nell had her face against the bars, and she was crying. He slipped a big arm around her and waited. Although it was not often expressed, there was a strong attachment between them.

"Dad, I don't want you to think me a—a baby any more," she said. "I've been insulted."

With a specific fact to make clear thought in Belding's mind he was never slow.

"I knew something unusual had come off. I guess you'd better tell me."

"Dad, I will, if you promise."

"What?"

"Not to mention it to Mother, not to pack a gun down there, and never, never tell Dick."

Belding was silent. Seldom did he make promises readily.

"Nell, sure something must have come off, for you to ask all that."

"If you don't promise I'll never tell, that's all," she declared, firmly.

Belding deliberated a little longer. He knew the girl.

"Well, I promise not to tell Mother," he said, presently; "and seeing you're here safe and well, I guess I won't go packing a gun down there, wherever that is. But I won't promise to keep anything from Dick that perhaps he ought to know."

"Dad, what would Dick do if—if he were here and I were to tell him I'd—I'd been horribly insulted?"

"I guess that'd depend. Mostly, you know, Dick does what you want. But you couldn't stop him—nobody could—if there was reason, a man's reason, to get started. Remember what he did to Rojas! . . . Nell, tell me what's happened."

Nell, regaining her composure, wiped her eyes and smoothed back her hair.

"The other day, Wednesday," she began, "I was coming home, and in front of that mescal drinking-place there was a crowd. It was a noisy crowd. I didn't want to walk out into the street or seem afraid. But I had to do both. There were several young men, and if they weren't drunk they certainly were rude. I never saw them before, but I think they must belong to the mining company that was run out of Sonora by rebels. Mrs. Carter was telling me. Anyway, these young fellows were Americans. They stretched themselves across the walk and smiled at me. I had to go out in the road. One of them, the rudest, followed me. He was a big fellow, red-faced, with prominent eyes and a bold look. He came up beside me and spoke to me. I ran home. And as I ran I heard his companions jeering.

"Well, to-day, just now, when I was riding up the valley road I came upon the same fellows. They had instruments and were surveying. Remembering Dick, and how he always wished for an instrument to help work out his plan for irrigation, I was certainly surprised to see these strangers surveying—and surveying upon Laddy's plot of land. It was a sandy road there, and José happened to be walking. So I reined in and asked these engineers what they were doing. The leader, who was that same bold fellow who had followed me, seemed much pleased at being addressed. He was swaggering—too friendly, not my idea of a gentleman at all. He said he was glad to tell me he was going to run water all over Altar Valley. Dad, you can bet that made me wild. That was Dick's plan, his discovery, and here were surveyors on Laddy's claim.

"Then I told him that he was working on private land and he'd better get off. He seemed to forget his flirty proclivities in amazement. Then he looked cunning. I read his mind. It was news to him that all the land along the valley had been taken up.

"He said something about not seeing any squatters on the land, and then he shut up tight on that score. But he began to be flirty again. He got hold of José's bridle, and before I could catch my breath he said I was a peach, that he wanted to make a date with me, that his name was Chase, that he owned a gold mine in Mexico. He said a lot more I didn't gather, but when he called me 'Dearie' I—well, I lost my temper.

"I jerked on the bridle and told him to let go. He held on and rolled his eyes at me. I dare say he imagined he was a gentleman to be infatuated with. He seemed sure of conquest. One thing was certain, he didn't know the least bit about horses. It scared me the way he got in front of José. I thanked my stars I wasn't up on Blanco Diablo. Well, Dad, I'm a little ashamed now, but I was mad. I slashed him across the face with my quirt. José jumped and knocked Mr. Chase into the sand. I didn't get the horse under control till I was out of sight of those surveyors, and then I let him run home."

"Nell, I guess you punished the fellow enough. Maybe he's only a conceited softy. But I don't like that sort of thing. It isn't Western. I guess he won't be so smart next time. Any fellow would remember being hit by Blanco José. If you'd been up on Diablo we'd have to bury Mr. Chase."

"Thank goodness I wasn't! I'm sorry now, Dad. Perhaps the fellow was hurt. But what could I do? Let's forget all about it, and I'll be careful where I ride in the future. . . . Dad, what does it mean, this surveying around Forlorn River?"

"I don't know, Nell," replied Belding, thoughtfully. "It worries me. It looks good for Forlorn River, but bad for Dick's plan to irrigate the valley. Lord, I'd hate to have someone forestall Dick on that!"

"No, no, we won't let anybody have Dick's rights," declared Nell.

"Where have I been keeping myself not to know about these surveyors?" muttered Belding. "They must have just come."

"Go see Mrs. Carter. She told me there were strangers in town, Americans, who had mining interests in Sonora, and were run out by Orozco. Find out what they're doing, Dad."

Belding discovered that he was, indeed, the last man of consequence in Forlorn River to learn of the arrival of Ben Chase and son, mine owners and operators in Sonora. They, with a force of miners, had been besieged by rebels and finally driven off their property. This property was not destroyed, but held for ransom. And the Chases, pending developments, had packed outfits and struck for the border. Casita had been their objective point, but, for some reason which Belding did not learn, they had arrived instead at Forlorn River. It had taken Ben Chase just one day to see the possibilities of Altar Valley, and in three days he had men at work.

Belding returned home without going to see the Chases and their operations. He wanted to think over the situation. Next morning he went out to the valley to see for himself. Mexicans were hastily erecting adobe houses upon Ladd's one hundred and sixty acres, upon Dick Gale's, upon Jim Lash's and Thorne's. There were men staking the valley floor and the riverbed. That was sufficient for Belding. He turned back toward town and headed for the camp of these intruders.

In fact, the surroundings of Forlorn River, except on the river side, reminded Belding of the mushroom growth of a newly discovered mining camp. Tents were everywhere; adobe shacks were in all stages of construction; rough clapboard houses were going up. The latest of this work was new and surprising to Belding, all because he was a busy man, with no chance to hear village gossip. When he was directed to the headquarters of the Chase Mining Company he went thither in slow-growing wrath.

He came to a big tent with a huge canvas fly stretched in front, under which sat several men in their shirtsleeves. They were talking and smoking.

"My name's Belding. I want to see this Mr. Chase," said Belding, gruffly.

Slow-witted as Belding was, and absorbed in his own feelings, he yet saw plainly that his advent was disturbing to these men. They looked alarmed, exchanged glances, and then quickly turned to him. One of them, a tall, rugged man with sharp face and shrewd eyes and white hair, got up and offered his hand.

"I'm Chase, senior," he said. "My son Radford Chase is here somewhere. You're Belding, the line inspector, I take it? I meant to call on you."

He seemed a rough-and-ready, loud-spoken man, withal cordial enough.

"Yes, I'm the inspector," replied Belding, ignoring the proffered hand, "and I'd like to know what in the hell you mean by taking up land claims—staked ground that belongs to my rangers?"

"Land claims?" slowly echoed Chase, studying his man. "We're taking up only unclaimed land."

"That's a lie. You couldn't miss the stakes."

"Well, Mr. Belding, as to that, I think my men did run across some staked ground. But we recognize only squatters. If your rangers think they've got property just because they drove a few stakes in the ground they're much mistaken. A squatter has to build a house and live on his land so long, according to law, before he owns it."

This argument was unanswerable, and Belding knew it.

"According to law!" exclaimed Belding. "Then you own up; you've jumped our claims."

"Mr. Belding, I'm a plain businessman. I come along. I see a good opening. Nobody seems to have tenable grants. I stake out claims, locate squatters, start to build. It seems to me your rangers have overlooked certain precautions. That's unfortunate for them. I'm prepared to hold my claim and to back all the squatters who work for me. If you don't like it you can carry the matter to Tucson. The law will uphold me."

"The law? Say, on this southwest border we haven't any law except a man's word and a gun."

"Then you'll find United States law has come along with Ben Chase," replied the other, snapping his fingers. He was still smooth, outspoken, but his mask had fallen.

"You're not a Westerner?" queried Belding.

"No, I'm from Illinois."

"I thought the West hadn't bred you. I know your kind. You'd last a long time on the Texas border; now, wouldn't you? You're one of the land and water hogs that has come to root in the West. You're like the timber sharks—take it all and leave none for those who follow. Mr. Chase, the West would fare better and last longer if men like you were driven out."

"You can't drive me out."

"I'm not so sure of that. Wait till my rangers come back. I wouldn't be in your boots. Don't mistake me. I don't suppose you could be accused of stealing another man's ideas or plan, but sure you've stolen these four claims. Maybe the law might uphold you. But the spirit, not the letter counts with us bordermen."

"See here, Belding, I think you're taking the wrong view of the matter. I'm going to develop this valley. You'd do better to get in with me.

I've a proposition to make you about that strip of land of yours facing the river."

"You can't make any deals with me. I won't have anything to do with you."

Belding abruptly left the camp and went home. Nell met him, probably intended to question him, but one look into his face confirmed her fears. She silently turned away. Belding realized he was powerless to stop Chase, and he was sick with disappointment for the ruin of Dick's hopes and his own.

CHAPTER 14

A LOST SON

Time passed. The population of Forlorn River grew apace. Belding, who had once been the head of the community, found himself a person of little consequence. Even had he desired it he would not have had any voice in the selection of postmaster, sheriff, and a few other officials. The Chases divided their labors between Forlorn River and their Mexican gold mine, which had been restored to them. The desert trips between these two places were taken in automobiles. A month's time made the motorcars almost as familiar a sight in Forlorn River as they had been in Casita before the revolution.

Belding was not so busy as he had been formerly. As he lost ambition he began to find less work to do. His wrath at the usurping Chases increased as he slowly realized his powerlessness to cope with such men. They were promoters, men of big interests and wide influence in the Southwest. The more they did for Forlorn River the less reason there seemed to be for his own grievance. He had to admit that it was personal; that he and Gale and the rangers would never have been able to develop the resources of the valley as these men were doing it.

All day long he heard the heavy booming blasts and the rumble of avalanches up in the gorge. Chase's men were dynamiting the cliffs in the narrow box cañon. They were making the dam just as Gale had planned to make it. When this work of blasting was over Belding experienced a relief. He would not now be continually reminded of his and Gale's loss. Resignation finally came to him. But he could not reconcile himself to misfortune for Gale.

Moreover, Belding had other worry and strain. April arrived with no news of the rangers. From Casita came vague reports of raiders in the Sonoyta country—reports impossible to verify until his Mexican rangers returned. When these men rode in, one of them, Gonzales, an intelligent and reliable half-breed, said he had met prospectors at the oasis. They had just come in on the Camino del Diablo, reported a terrible trip of heat and drought, and not a trace of the Yaqui's party.

"That settles it," declared Belding. "Yaqui never went to Sonoyta. He's circled round to the Devil's Road, and the rangers, Mercedes, Thorne, the horses—they—I'm afraid they have been lost in the desert. It's an old story on Camino del Diablo."

He had to tell Nell that, and it was an ordeal which left him weak.

Mrs. Belding listened to him, and was silent for a long time while she held the stricken Nell to her breast. Then she opposed his convictions with that quiet strength so characteristic of her arguments.

"Well, then," decided Belding, "Rojas headed the rangers at Papago Well or the Tanks."

"Tom, when you are down in the mouth you use poor judgment," she went on. "You know only by a miracle could Rojas or anybody have headed those white horses. Where's your old stubborn confidence? Yaqui was up on Diablo. Dick was up on Sol. And there were the other horses. They could not have been headed or caught. Miracles don't happen."

"All right, Mother, it's sure good to hear you," said Belding. She always cheered him, and now he grasped at straws. "I'm not myself these days, don't mistake that. Tell us what you think. You always say you feel things when you really don't know them."

"I can say little more than what you said yourself the night Mercedes was taken away. You told Laddy to trust Yaqui, that he was a godsend. He might go south into some wild Sonora valley. He might lead Rojas into a trap. He would find water and grass where no Mexican or American could."

"But Mother, they're gone seven weeks. Seven weeks! At the most I gave them six weeks. Seven weeks in the desert!"

"How do the Yaquis live?" she asked.

Belding could not reply to that, but hope revived in him. He had faith in his wife, though he could not in the least understand what he imagined was something mystic in her.

"Years ago when I was searching for my father I learned many things about this country," said Mrs. Belding. "You can never tell how long a man may live in the desert. The fiercest, most terrible and inaccessible places often have their hidden oasis. In his later years my father became a prospector. That was strange to me, for he never cared for gold or money. I learned that he was often gone in the desert for weeks, once for months. Then the time came when he never came back. That was years before I reached the southwest border and heard of him. Even then I did not for long give up hope of his coming back. I know now—something tells me—indeed, it seems his spirit tells me—he was lost. But I don't have that feeling for Yaqui and his party. Yaqui has given Rojas the slip or has ambushed him in some trap. Probably that took time and a long journey into Sonora. The Indian is too wise to start back now over dry trails. He'll curb the rangers; he'll wait. I seem to know this, dear Nell, so be brave, patient. Dick Gale will come back to you."

"Oh, Mother!" cried Nell. "I can't give up hope while I have you."

That talk with the strong mother worked a change in Nell and in Belding. Nell, who had done little but brood and watch the west and take violent rides, seemed to settle into a waiting patience that was sad, yet serene. She helped her mother more than ever; she was a comfort to Belding; she began to take active interest in the affairs of the growing village. Belding, who had been breaking under the strain of worry, recovered himself so that to outward appearance he was his old self. He alone knew, however, that his humor was forced, and that the slow burning wrath he felt for the Chases was flaming into hate.

Belding argued with himself that if Ben Chase and his son, Radford, had turned out to be big men in other ways than in the power to carry on great enterprises he might have become reconciled to them. But the father was greedy, grasping, hard, cold; the son added to those traits an overbearing disposition to rule, and he showed a fondness for drink and cards. These men were developing the valley, to be sure, and a horde of poor Mexicans and many Americans were benefiting from that development; nevertheless these Chases were operating in a way which proved they cared only for themselves.

Belding shook off a lethargic spell and decided he had better set about several by no means small tasks, if he wanted to get them finished before the hot months. He made a trip to the Sonoyta Oasis. He satisfied himself that matters along the line were favorable, and that there was absolutely no trace of his rangers. Upon completing this trip he went to Casita with a number of his white thoroughbreds and shipped them to ranchers and horse-breeders in Texas. Then, being near the railroad, and having time, he went up to Tucson. There he learned some interesting particulars about the Chases. They had an office in the city; influential friends in the Capitol. They were powerful men in the rapidly growing finance of the West. They had interested the Southern Pacific Railroad, and in the near future a branch line was to be constructed from San Felipe to Forlorn River. These details of the Chase development were insignificant when compared to a matter striking close home to Belding. His responsibility had been subtly attacked. A doubt had been cast upon his capability of executing the duties of immigration inspector to the best advantage of the state. Belding divined that this was only an entering wedge. The Chases were bent upon driving him out of Forlorn River; but, perhaps to serve better their own ends, they were proceeding at leisure. Belding returned home consumed by rage. But he controlled it. For the first time in his life he was afraid of himself. He had his wife and Nell to think of; and the old law of the West had gone forever.

"Dad, there's another Rojas round these diggings," was Nell's remark, after the greetings were over and the usual questions and answers passed.

Belding's exclamation was cut short by Nell's laugh. She was serious with a kind of amused contempt.

"Mr. Radford Chase!"

"Now Nell, what the—" roared Belding.

"Hush, Dad! Don't swear," interrupted Nell. "I only meant to tease you."

"Humph! Say, my girl, that name Chase makes me see red. If you must tease me hit on some other way. *Sabe*, señorita?"

"*Sí, sí*, Dad."

"Nell, you may as well tell him and have it over," said Mrs. Belding, quietly.

"You promised me once, Dad, that you'd not go packing a gun off down there, didn't you?"

"Yes, I remember," replied Belding; but he did not answer her smile.

"Will you promise again?" she asked, lightly. Here was Nell with arch eyes, yet not the old arch eyes, so full of fun and mischief. Her lips were tremulous; her cheeks seemed less round.

"Yes," rejoined Belding; and he knew why his voice was a little thick.

"Well, if you weren't such a good old blind Dad you'd have seen long ago the way Mr. Radford Chase ran round after me. At first it was only annoying, and I did not want to add to your worries. But these two weeks you've been gone I've been more than annoyed. After that time I struck Mr. Chase with my quirt he made all possible efforts to meet me. He did meet me wherever I went. He sent me letters till I got tired of sending them back.

"When you left home on your trips I don't know that he grew bolder but he had more opportunity. I couldn't stay in the house all the time. There were Mama's errands and sick people and my Sunday school, and whatnot. Mr. Chase waylaid me every time I went out. If he works any more I don't know when, unless it's when I'm asleep. He followed me until it was less embarrassing for me to let him walk with me and talk his head off. He made love to me. He begged me to marry him. I told him I was already in love and engaged to be married. He said that didn't make any difference. Then I called him a fool.

"Next time he saw me he said he must explain. He meant I was being true to a man who, everybody on the border knew, had been lost in the desert. That—that hurt. Maybe—maybe it's true. Sometimes it seems terribly true. Since then, of course, I have stayed in the house to avoid being hurt again.

"But, Dad, a little thing like a girl sticking close to her mother and her room doesn't stop Mr. Chase. I think he's crazy. Anyway, he's a most persistent fool. I want to be charitable, because the man swears he loves me, and maybe he does, but he is making me nervous. I don't sleep. I'm afraid to be in my room at night. I've gone to Mother's room. He's always hanging round. Bold! Why, that isn't the thing to call Mr. Chase. He's absolutely without a sense of decency. He bribes our servants. He comes into our patio. Think of that! He makes the most ridiculous excuses. He bothers Mother to death. I feel like a poor little rabbit holed by a hound. And I daren't peep out."

Somehow the thing struck Belding as funny, and he laughed. He had not had a laugh for so long that it made him feel good. He stopped only at sight of Nell's surprise and pain. Then he put his arms round her.

"Never mind dear. I'm an old bear. But it tickled me, I guess. I sure hope Mr. Radford Chase *has* got it bad. . . . Nell, it's only the old story. The fellows fall in love with you. It's your good looks, Nell. What a price women like you and Mercedes have to pay for beauty! I'd a d— good deal rather be ugly as a mud fence."

"So would I, Dad, if—if Dick would still love me."

"He wouldn't, you can gamble on that, as Laddy says. . . . Well, the first time I catch this locoed Romeo sneaking round here I'll—I'll—"

"Dad, you promised."

"Confound it, Nell, I promised not to pack a gun. That's all. I'll only shoot this fellow off the place, gently, mind you, gently. I'll leave the rest for Dick Gale!"

"*Oh, Dad!*" cried Nell; and she clung to him wistful, frightened, yet something more.

"Don't mistake me, Nell. You have your own way, generally. You pull the wool over Mother's eyes, and you wind me round your little finger. But you can't do either with Dick Gale. You're tenderhearted; you overlook the doings of this hound, Chase. But when Dick comes back, you just make up your mind to a little hell in the Chase camp. Oh, he'll find it out. And I sure want to be round when Dick hands Mr. Radford the same as he handed Rojas!"

Belding kept a sharp lookout for young Chase, and then, a few days later, learned that both son and father had gone off upon one of their frequent trips to Casa Grandes, near where their mines were situated.

April grew apace, and soon gave way to May. One morning Belding was called from some garden work by the whirring of an automobile and a "Holloa!" He went forward to the front yard and there saw a car he thought resembled one he had seen in Casita. It contained a familiar-looking driver, but the three figures in gray coats and veils were strange to him. By the time he had gotten to the road he decided two were women and the other a man. At the moment their faces were emerging from dusty veils. Belding saw an elderly, sallow-faced, rather frail-appearing man who was an entire stranger to him; a handsome dark-eyed woman whose hair showed white through her veil; and a superbly built girl, whose face made Belding at once think of Dick Gale.

"Is this Mr. Tom Belding, inspector of immigration?" inquired the gentleman, courteously.

"I'm Belding, and I know who you are," replied Belding in hearty amaze, as he stretched forth his big hand. "You're Dick Gale's Dad—the Governor, Dick used to say. I'm sure glad to meet you."

"Thank you. Yes, I'm Dick's governor, and here, Mr. Belding—Dick's mother and his sister Elsie."

Beaming his pleasure, Belding shook hands with the ladies, who showed their agitation clearly.

"Mr. Belding, I've come west to look up my lost son," said Mr. Gale. "His sister's letters were unanswered. We haven't heard from him in months. Is he still here with you?"

"Well, now, sure I'm awful sorry," began Belding, his slow mind at work. "Dick's away just now—been away for a considerable spell. I'm expecting him back any day. . . . Won't you come in? You're all dusty and hot and tired. Come in, and let Mother and Nell make you comfortable. Of course you'll stay. We've a big house. You must stay till Dick comes back. Maybe that'll be— Aw, I guess it won't be long. . . . Let me handle the baggage, Mr. Gale. . . . Come in. I sure am glad to meet you all."

Eager, excited, delighted, Belding went on talking as he ushered the Gales into the sitting-room, presenting them in his hearty way to the astounded Mrs. Belding and Nell. For the space of a few moments his wife and daughter were bewildered. Belding did not recollect any other occasion when a few callers had thrown them off their balance. But of course this was different. He was a little flustered himself—a circumstance that dawned upon him with surprise. When the Gales had been shown to rooms, Mrs. Belding gained the poise momentarily lost; but Nell came rushing back, wilder than a deer, in a state of excitement strange even for her.

"Oh! Dick's mother, his sister!" whispered Nell.

Belding observed the omission of the father in Nell's exclamation of mingled delight and alarm.

"His mother!" went on Nell. "Oh, I knew it! I always guessed it! Dick's people are proud, rich; they're somebody. I thought I'd faint when she looked at me. She was just curious—curious, but so cold and proud. She was wondering about me. Dick has never written her that he's—he's engaged to me. I'm wearing his ring. It was his mother's, he said. I won't—I can't take it off. And I'm scared. . . . But the sister—oh, she's lovely and sweet—proud, too. I felt warm all over when she looked at me. I—I wanted to kiss her. She looks like Dick when he first came to us. But he's changed. They'll hardly recognize him. . . . To think they've come! And I had to be looking a fright, when of all times on earth I'd want to look my best."

Nell, out of breath, ran away evidently to make herself presentable, according to her idea of the exigency of the case. Belding caught a glimpse of his wife's face as she went out, and it wore a sad, strange, anxious expression. Then Belding sat alone, pondering the contrasting emotions of his wife and daughter. It was beyond his understanding. Women were creatures of feeling. Belding saw reason to be delighted to entertain Dick's family; and for the time being no disturbing thought entered his mind.

Presently the Gales came back into the sitting-room, looking very different without the long gray cloaks and veils. Belding saw distinction and elegance. Mr. Gale seemed a grave, troubled, kindly person, ill in body and mind. Belding received the same impression of power that Ben Chase had given him, only here it was minus any harshness or hard quality. He gathered that Mr. Gale was a man of authority. Mrs. Gale rather frightened Belding, but he could not have told why. The girl was just like Dick as he used to be.

Their manner of speaking also reminded Belding of Dick. They talked of the ride from Ash Fork down to the border, of the ugly and torn-up Casita, of the heat and dust and cactus along the trail. Presently Nell came in, now cool and sweet in white, with a red rose at her breast. Belding had never been so proud of her. He saw that she meant to appear well in the eyes of Dick's people, and began to have a faint perception of what the ordeal was for her. Belding imagined the sooner the Gales were told that Dick was to marry Nell the better for all concerned, and especially for Nell. In the general conversation that ensued he sought for an opening in which to tell this important news, but he was kept so busy answering questions about his position on the border, the kind of place Forlorn River was, the reason for so many tents, etc., that he was unable to find opportunity.

"It's interesting, very interesting," said Mr. Gale. "At another time I want to learn all you'll tell me about the West. It's new to me. I'm surprised, amazed, sir, I may say. . . . But, Mr. Belding, what I want to know most is about my son. I'm broken in health. I've worried myself ill over him. I don't mind telling you, sir, that we quarreled. I laughed at his threats. He went away. And I've come to see I didn't know Richard. I was wrong to upbraid him. For a year we've known nothing of his doings, and now for almost six months we've not heard from him at all. Frankly, Mr. Belding, I weakened first, and I've come to hunt him up. My fear is that I didn't start soon enough. The boy will have a great position someday— God knows, perhaps soon! I should not have allowed him to run over this wild country for so long. But I hope, though I hardly believed, that he might find himself. Now I'm afraid he s—"

Mr. Gale paused, and the white hand he raised expressively shook a little.

Belding was not so thick-witted where men were concerned. He saw how the matter lay between Dick Gale and his father.

"Well, Mr. Gale, sure most young bucks from the East go to the bad out here," he said, bluntly.

"I've been told that," replied Mr. Gale, and a shade overspread his worn face.

"They blow their money, then go to punching cows, take to whisky."

"Yes," rejoined Mr. Gale, feebly nodding.

"Then they get to gambling, lose their jobs," went on Belding.

Mr. Gale lifted haggard eyes.

"Then it's bumming around, regular tramps, and to the bad generally."

Belding spread wide his big arms, and when one of them dropped round Nell, who sat beside him, she squeezed his hand tight. "Sure, it's the regular thing," he concluded, cheerfully.

He rather felt a little glee at Mr. Gale's distress, and Mrs. Gale's crushed I-told-you-so woe in no wise bothered him; but the look in the big, dark eyes of Dick's sister was too much for Belding.

He choked off his characteristic oath when excited and blurted out, "Say, but *Dick Gale* never went to the bad! . . . Listen!"

Belding had scarcely started Dick Gale's story when he perceived that never in his life had he such an absorbed and breathless audience. Presently they were awed, and at the conclusion of that story they sat white-faced, still, amazed beyond speech. Dick Gale's advent in Casita, his rescue of Mercedes, his life as a border ranger certainly lost no picturesque or daring or even noble detail in Belding's telling. He kept back nothing but the present doubt of Dick's safety.

Dick's sister was the first of the three to recover herself.

"Oh, Father!" she cried; and there was a glorious light in her eyes. "Deep down in my heart I knew Dick was a man!"

Mr. Gale rose unsteadily from his chair. His frailty was now painfully manifest.

"Mr. Belding, do you mean my son—Richard Gale—has done all that you told us?" he asked, incredulously.

"I sure do," replied Belding, with hearty good-will.

"Martha, do you hear?" Mr. Gale turned to question his wife. She could not answer. Her face had not yet regained its natural color.

"He faced that bandit and his gang alone—he *fought* them?" demanded Mr. Gale, his voice stronger.

"Dick mopped up the floor with the whole outfit!"

"He rescued a Spanish girl, went into the desert without food, weapons, anything but his hands? Richard Gale, whose hands were always useless?"

Belding nodded with a grin.

"He's a ranger now—riding, fighting, sleeping on the sand, preparing his own food?"

"Well, I should smile," rejoined Belding.

"He cares for his horse, with his own hands?" This query seemed to be the climax of Mr. Gale's strange hunger for truth. He had raised his head a little higher, and his eye was brighter.

Mention of a horse fired Belding's blood.

"Does Dick Gale *care* for his horse? Say, there are not many *men* as well loved as that white horse of Dick's. Blanco Sol he is, Mr. Gale. That's Mex for White Sun. Wait till you see Blanco Sol! Bar one, the whitest, biggest, strongest, fastest, grandest horse in the Southwest!"

"So he loves a horse! I shall not know my own son. . . . Mr. Belding, you say Richard works for you. May I ask, at what salary?"

"He gets forty dollars, board and outfit," replied Belding, proudly.

"Forty dollars?" echoed the father. "By the day or week?"

"The month, of course," said Belding, somewhat taken aback.

"Forty dollars a month for a young man who spent five hundred in the same time when he was at college, and who ran it into thousands when he got out!"

Mr. Gale laughed for the first time, and it was the laugh of a man who wanted to believe what he heard yet scarcely dared to do it.

"What does he do with so much money—money earned by peril, toil, sweat, and blood? Forty dollars a month!"

"He saves it," replied Belding.

Evidently this was too much for Dick Gale's father, and he gazed at his wife in sheer speechless astonishment. Dick's sister clapped her hands like a little child.

Belding saw that the moment was propitious.

"Sure he saves it. Dick's engaged to marry Nell here. My stepdaughter, Nell Burton."

"Oh-h, Dad!" faltered Nell; and she rose, white as her dress.

How strange it was to see Dick's mother and sister rise, also, and turn to Nell with dark, proud, searching eyes. Belding vaguely realized some blunder he had made. Nell's white, appealing face gave him a pang. What had he done? Surely this family of Dick's ought to know his relation to Nell. There was a silence that positively made Belding nervous.

Then Elsie Gale stepped close to Nell.

"Miss Burton, are you really Richard's betrothed?"

Nell's tremulous lips framed an affirmative, but never uttered it. She held out her hand, showing the ring Dick had given her. Miss Gale's recognition was instant, and her response was warm, sweet, gracious.

"I think I am going to be very, very glad," she said, and kissed Nell.

"Miss Burton, we are learning wonderful things about Richard," added Mr. Gale, in an earnest though shaken voice. "If you have had to do with making a man of him—and now I begin to see, to believe so—may God bless you! . . . My dear girl, I have not really looked at you. Richard's fiancée! . . . Mother, we have not found him yet, but I think we've found his secret. We believed him a lost son. But here is his sweetheart!"

It was only then that the pride and hauteur of Mrs. Gale's face broke into an expression of mingled pain and joy. She opened her arms. Nell, uttering a strange little stifled cry, flew into them.

Belding suddenly discovered an unaccountable blur in his sight. He could not see perfectly, and that was why, when Mrs. Belding entered the sitting room, he was not certain that her face was as sad and white as it seemed.

CHAPTER 15

BOUND IN THE DESERT

F ar away from Forlorn River Dick Gale sat stunned, gazing down into the purple depths where Rojas had plunged to his death. The Yaqui stood motionless upon the steep red wall of lava from which he had cut the bandit's hold. Mercedes lay quietly where she had fallen. From across the depths there came to Gale's ear the Indian's strange, wild cry.

Then silence, hollow, breathless, stony silence enveloped the great abyss and its upheaved lava walls. The sun was setting. Every instant the haze reddened and thickened.

Action on the part of the Yaqui loosened the spell which held Gale as motionless as his surroundings. The Indian was edging back toward the ledge. He did not move with his former lithe and sure freedom. He crawled, slipped, dragged himself, rested often, and went on again. He had been wounded. When at last he reached the ledge where Mercedes lay Gale jumped to his feet, strong and thrilling, spurred to meet the responsibility that now rested upon him.

Swiftly he turned to where Thorne lay. The cavalryman was just returning to consciousness. Gale ran for a canteen, bathed his face, made him drink. The look in Thorne's eyes was hard to bear.

"Thorne! Thorne! it's all right, it's all right!" cried Gale, in piercing tones. "Mercedes is safe! Yaqui saved her! Rojas is done for! Yaqui jumped down the wall and drove the bandit off the ledge. Cut him loose from the wall, foot by foot, hand by hand! We've won the fight, Thorne."

For Thorne these were marvelous strength-giving words. The dark horror left his eyes, and they began to dilate, to shine. He stood up, dizzily but unaided, and he gazed across the crater. Yaqui had reached the side of Mercedes, was bending over her. She stirred. Yaqui lifted her to her feet. She appeared weak, unable to stand alone. But she faced across the crater and waved her hand. She was unharmed. Thorne lifted both arms above his head, and from his lips issued a cry. It was neither call nor holler nor welcome nor answer. Like the Yaqui's, it could scarcely be named. But it was deep, husky, prolonged, terribly human in its intensity. It made Gale shudder and made his heart beat like a trip-hammer. Mercedes again waved a white hand. The Yaqui waved, too, and Gale saw in the action an urgent signal.

Hastily taking up canteen and rifles, Gale put a supporting arm around Thorne.

"Come, old man. Can you walk? Sure you can walk! Lean on me, and we'll soon get out of this. Don't look across. Look where you step. We've not much time before dark. Oh Thorne, I'm afraid Jim has cashed in! And the last I saw of Laddy he was badly hurt."

Gale was keyed up to a high pitch of excitement and alertness. He seemed to be able to do many things. But once off the ragged notched lava into the trail he had not such difficulty with Thorne, and could keep his keen gaze shifting everywhere for sight of enemies.

"Listen, Thorne! What's that?" asked Gale, halting as they came to a place where the trail led down through rough breaks in the lava. The silence was broken by a strange sound, almost unbelievable considering the time and place. A voice was droning: "Turn the lady, turn! Turn the lady, turn! Alaman left. All swing; turn the lady, turn!"

"Hello, Jim," called Gale, dragging Thorne round the corner of lava. "Where are you? Oh, you son of a gun! I thought you were dead. Oh, I'm glad to see you! Jim, are you hurt?"

Jim Lash stood in the trail leaning over the butt of his rifle, which evidently he was utilizing as a crutch. He was pale but smiling. His hands were bloody. A scarf had been bound tightly round his left leg just above the knee. The leg hung limp, and the foot dragged.

"I reckon I ain't injured much," replied Jim. "But my leg hurts like hell, if you want to know."

"Laddy! Oh, where's Laddy?"

"He's just across the crack there. I was trying to get to him. We had it hot and heavy down here. Laddy was pretty bad shot up before he tried to head Rojas off the trail. . . . Dick, did you see the Yaqui go after Rojas?"

"Did I!" exclaimed Gale, grimly.

"The finish was all that saved me from runnin' loco plumb over the rim. You see I was closer'n you to where Mercedes was hid. When Rojas an' his last Greaser started across, Laddy went after them, but I couldn't. Laddy did for Rojas's man, then went down himself. But he got up an' fell, got up, went on, an' fell again. Laddy kept doin' that till he dropped for good. I reckon our chances are against findin' him alive. . . . I tell you, boys, Rojas was hell-bent. An' Mercedes was game. I saw her shoot him. But mebbe bullets couldn't stop him then. If I didn't sweat blood when Mercedes was fightin' him on the cliff! Then the finish! Only a Yaqui could have done that. . . . Thorne, you didn't miss it?"

"Yes, I was down and out," replied the cavalryman.

"It's a shame. Greatest stunt I ever seen! Thorne, you're standin' up pretty fair. How about you? Dick, is he bad hurt?"

"No, he's not. A hard knock on the skull and a scalp wound," replied Dick. "Here, Jim, let me help you over this place."

Step by step Gale got the two injured men down the uneven declivity and then across the narrow lava bridge over the fissure. Here he bade them rest while he went along the trail on that side to search for Laddy. Gale found the ranger stretched out, face downward, a reddened hand clutching a gun. Gale thought he was dead. Upon examination, however, it was found that Ladd still lived, though he had many wounds. Gale lifted him and carried him back to the others.

"He's alive, but that's all," said Dick, as he laid the ranger down. "Do what you can. Stop the blood. Laddy's tough as cactus, you know. I'll hurry back for Mercedes and Yaqui."

Gale, like a fleet, sure-footed mountain sheep, ran along the trail.

When he came across the Mexican, Rojas's last ally, Gale had evidence of the terrible execution of the .405. He did not pause. On the first part of that descent he made faster time than had Rojas. But he exercised care along the hard, slippery, ragged slope leading to the ledge. Presently he came upon Mercedes and the Yaqui. She ran right into Dick's arms, and there her strength, if not her courage, broke, and she grew lax.

"Mercedes, you're safe! Thorne's safe. It's all right now."

"Rojas!" she whispered.

"Gone! To the bottom of the crater! A Yaqui vengeance, Mercedes."

He heard the girl whisper the name of the Virgin. Then he gathered her up in his arms.

"Come, Yaqui."

The Indian grunted. He had one hand pressed close over a bloody place in his shoulder. Gale looked keenly at him. Yaqui was inscrutable, as of old, yet Gale somehow knew that wound meant little to him. The Indian followed him.

Without pausing, moving slowly in some places, very carefully in others, and swiftly on the smooth part of the trail, Gale carried Mercedes up to the rim and along to the others. Jim Lash worked awkwardly over Ladd. Thorne was trying to assist. Ladd, himself, was conscious, but he was a pallid, apparently a death-stricken man. The greeting between Mercedes and Thorne was calm—strangely so, it seemed to Gale. But he was now calm himself. Ladd smiled at him, and evidently would have spoken had he the power. Yaqui then joined the group, and his piercing eyes roved from one to the other, lingering longest over Ladd.

"Dick, I'm figger'n' hard," said Jim, faintly. "In a minute it'll be up to you an' Mercedes. I've about shot my bolt. . . . Reckon you'll do—best by bringin' up blankets—water—salt—fire-wood. Laddy's got—one chance—in a hundred. Fix him up—first. Use hot salt water. If my leg's broken—set it best you can. That hole in Yaqui—only'll bother him a day. Thorne's bad hurt. . . . Now rustle—Dick, old—boy."

Lash's voice died away in a husky whisper, and he quietly lay back, stretching out all but the crippled leg. Gale examined it, assured himself the bones had not been broken, and then rose ready to go down the trail.

"Mercedes, hold Thorne's head up, in your lap—so. Now I'll go."

On the moment Yaqui appeared to have completed the binding of his wounded shoulder, and he started to follow Gale. He paid no attention to Gale's order for him to stay back. But he was slow, and gradually Gale forged ahead. The lingering brightness of the sunset lightened the trail, and the descent to the arroyo was swift and easy. Some of the white horses had come in for water. Blanco Sol spied Gale and whistled and came pounding toward him. It was twilight down in the arroyo. Yaqui appeared and began collecting a bundle of mesquite sticks. Gale hastily put together the things he needed; and, packing them all in a tarpaulin, he turned to retrace his steps up the trail.

Darkness was setting in. The trail was narrow, exceedingly steep, and in some places fronted on precipices. Gale's burden was not very heavy, but its bulk made it unwieldy, and it was always overbalancing him or knocking against the wall side of the trail. Gale found it necessary to wait for Yaqui to take the lead. The Indian's eyes must have seen as well at night as by day. Gale toiled upward, shouldering, swinging, dragging the big pack; and, though the ascent of the slope was not really long, it seemed endless. At last they reached a level, and were soon on the spot with Mercedes and the injured men.

Gale then set to work. Yaqui's part was to keep the fire blazing and the water hot, Mercedes's to help Gale in what way she could. Gale found Ladd had many wounds, yet not one of them was directly in a vital place. Evidently, the ranger had almost bled to death. He remained unconscious through Gale's operations. According to Jim Lash, Ladd had one chance in a hundred, but Gale considered it one in a thousand. Having done all that was possible for the ranger, Gale slipped blankets under and around him, and then turned his attention to Lash.

Jim came out of his stupor. A mushrooming bullet had torn a great hole in his leg. Gale, upon examination, could not be sure the bones had been missed, but there was no bad break. The application of hot salt water made Jim groan. When he had been bandaged and laid beside Ladd, Gale went on to the cavalryman. Thorne was very weak and scarcely conscious. A furrow had been plowed through his scalp down to the bone. When it had been dressed, Mercedes collapsed. Gale laid her with the three in a row and covered them with blankets and the tarpaulin.

Then Yaqui submitted to examination. A bullet had gone through the Indian's shoulder. To Gale it appeared serious. Yaqui said it was a fleabite. But he allowed Gale to bandage it, and obeyed when he was told to lie quiet in his blanket beside the fire.

Gale stood guard. He seemed still calm, and wondered at what he considered a strange absence of poignant feeling. If he had felt weariness it was now gone. He coaxed the fire with as little wood as would keep it burning; he sat beside it; he walked to and fro close by; sometimes he stood over the five sleepers, wondering if two of them, at least, would ever awaken.

Time had passed swiftly, but as the necessity for immediate action had gone by, the hours gradually assumed something of their normal length. The night wore on. The air grew colder, the stars brighter, the sky bluer, and, if such could be possible, the silence more intense. The fire burned out, and for lack of wood could not be rekindled. Gale patrolled his short beat, becoming colder and damper as dawn approached. The darkness grew so dense that he could not see the pale faces of the sleepers. He dreaded the gray dawn and the light. Slowly the heavy black belt close to the lava changed to a pale gloom, then to gray, and after that morning came quickly.

The hour had come for Dick Gale to face his great problem. It was natural that he hung back a little at first; natural that when he went forward to look at the quiet sleepers he did so with a grim and stern force urging him. Yaqui stirred, roused, yawned, got up; and, though he did not smile at Gale, a light shone swiftly across his dark face. His shoulder drooped and appeared stiff, otherwise he was himself. Mercedes lay in deep slumber. Thorne had a high fever, and was beginning to show signs of restlessness. Ladd seemed just barely alive. Jim Lash slept as if he was not much the worse for his wound.

Gale rose from his examination with a sharp breaking of his cold mood. While there was life in Thorne and Ladd there was hope for them. Then he faced his problem, and his decision was instant.

He awoke Mercedes. How wondering, wistful, beautiful was that first opening flash of her eyes! Then the dark, troubled thought came. Swiftly she sat up.

"Mercedes—come. Are you all right? Laddy is alive. Thorne's not—not so bad. But we've got a job on our hands! You must help me."

She bent over Thorne and laid her hands on his hot face. Then she rose—a woman such as he had imagined she might be in an hour of trial.

Gale took up Ladd as carefully and gently as possible.

"Mercedes, bring what you can carry and follow me," he said. Then, motioning for Yaqui to remain there, he turned down the slope with Ladd in his arms.

Neither pausing nor making a misstep nor conscious of great effort, Gale carried the wounded man down into the arroyo. Mercedes kept at his heels, light, supple, lithe as a panther. He left her with Ladd and went back. When he had started off with Thorne in his arms he felt the tax on his strength. Surely and swiftly, however, he bore the cavalryman down the trail to lay him beside Ladd. Again he started back, and when he began to mount the steep lava steps he was hot, wet, breathing hard. As he reached the scene of that night's camp a voice greeted him. Jim Lash was sitting up.

"Hello, Dick. I woke some late this mornin'. Where's Laddy? Dick, you ain't a-goin' to say—"

"Laddy's alive—that's about all," replied Dick.

"Where's Thorne an' Mercedes? Look here, man! I reckon you ain't packin' this crippled outfit down that awful trail?"

"Had to, Jim. An hour's sun—would kill—both Laddy and Thorne. Come on now."

For once Jim Lash's cool good nature and careless indifference gave precedence to amaze and concern.

"Always knew you was a husky chap. But, Dick, you're no hoss! Get me a crutch an' give me a lift on one side."

"Come on," replied Gale. "I've no time to monkey."

He lifted the ranger, called to Yaqui to follow with some of the camp outfit, and once more essayed the steep descent. Jim Lash was the heaviest man of the three, and Gale's strength was put to enormous strain to carry him on that broken trail. Nevertheless, Gale went down, down, walking swiftly and surely over the bad places; and at last he staggered into the arroyo with bursting heart and red-blinded eyes. When he had recovered he made a final trip up the slope for the camp effects which Yaqui had been unable to carry.

Then he drew Jim and Mercedes and Yaqui, also, into an earnest discussion of ways and means whereby to fight for the life of Thorne. Ladd's case Gale now considered hopeless, though he meant to fight for him, too, as long as he breathed.

In the labor of watching and nursing it seemed to Gale that two days and two nights slipped by like a few hours. During that time the Indian recovered from his injury, and became capable of performing all except heavy tasks. Then Gale succumbed to weariness. After his much-needed rest he relieved Mercedes of the care and watch over Thorne which, up to that time, she had absolutely refused to relinquish. The cavalryman had high fever, and Gale feared he had developed blood poisoning. He required constant attention. His condition slowly grew worse, and there came a day which Gale thought surely was the end. But that day passed, and the night, and the next day, and Thorne lived on, ghastly, stricken, raving. Mercedes hung over him with jealous, passionate care and did all that could have been humanly done for a man. She grew wan, absorbed, silent. But suddenly, and to Gale's amaze and thanksgiving, there came an abatement of Thorne's fever. With it some of the heat and redness of the inflamed wound disappeared. Next morning he was conscious, and Gale grasped some of the hope that Mercedes had never abandoned. He forced her to rest while he attended to Thorne. That day he saw that the crisis was past. Recovery for Thorne was now possible, and would perhaps depend entirely upon the care he received.

Jim Lash's wound healed without any aggravating symptoms. It would be only a matter of time until he had the use of his leg again. All these days, however, there was little apparent change in Ladd's condition, unless it was that he seemed to fade away as he lingered. At first his wounds remained open; they bled a little all the time outwardly, perhaps internally also; his blood did not seem to clot, and so the bullet-holes did not close. Then Yaqui asked for the care of Ladd. Gale yielded it with opposing thoughts—that Ladd would waste slowly away till life ceased, and that there never was any telling what might lie in the power of this strange Indian. Yaqui absented himself from camp for a while, and when he returned he carried the roots and leaves of desert plants unknown to Gale. From these the Indian brewed an ointment. Then he stripped the bandages from Ladd and applied the mixture to his wounds. That done, he let him lie with the wounds exposed to the air, at night covering him. Next day he again exposed the wounds to the warm, dry air. Slowly they closed, and Ladd ceased to bleed externally.

Days passed and grew into what Gale imagined must have been weeks. Yaqui recovered fully. Jim Lash began to move about on a crutch; he shared the Indian's watch over Ladd. Thorne lay a haggard, emaciated ghost of his former rugged self, but with life in the eyes that turned always toward Mercedes. Ladd lingered and lingered. The life seemingly would not leave his bullet-pierced body. He faded, withered, shrunk till he was almost a skeleton. He knew those who worked and watched over him, but he had no power of speech. His eyes and eyelids moved; the rest of him seemed stone. All those days nothing except water was given him. It was marvelous how tenaciously, however feebly, he clung to life. Gale imagined it was the Yaqui's spirit that held back death. That tireless, implacable, inscrutable savage was ever at the ranger's side. His great somber eyes burned. At length he went to Gale, and, with that strange light flitting across the hard bronzed face, he said Ladd would live.

The second day after Ladd had been given such thin nourishment as he could swallow he recovered the use of his tongue.

"Shore—this's—hell," he whispered.

That was a characteristic speech for the ranger, Gale thought; and indeed it made all who heard it smile while their eyes were wet.

From that time forward Ladd gained, but he gained so immeasurably slowly that only the eyes of hope could have seen any improvement. Jim Lash threw away his crutch, and Thorne was well, if still somewhat weak, before Ladd could lift his arm or turn his head. A kind of long, immovable gloom passed, like a shadow, from his face. His whispers grew stronger. And the day arrived when Gale, who was perhaps the least optimistic, threw doubt to the winds and knew the ranger would get well. For Gale that joyous moment of realization was one in which he seemed to return to a former self long absent. He experienced an elevation of soul. He was suddenly overwhelmed with gratefulness, humility, awe. A gloomy black terror had passed by. He wanted to thank the faithful Mercedes, and Thorne for getting well, and the cheerful Lash, and Ladd himself, and that strange and wonderful Yaqui, now such a splendid figure. He thought of home and Nell. The terrible encompassing red slopes lost something of their fearsomeness, and there was a good spirit hovering near.

B oys, come round," said Ladd, in his low voice. "An' you, Mercedes. An' call the Yaqui."

Ladd lay in the shade of the brush shelter that had been erected. His head was raised slightly on a pillow. There seemed little of him but long lean lines, and if it had not been for his keen, thoughtful, kindly eyes, his face would have resembled a death mask of a man starved.

"Shore I want to know what day is it an' what month?" asked Ladd.

Nobody could answer him. The question seemed a surprise to Gale, and evidently was so to the others.

"Look at that cactus," went on Ladd.

Near the wall of lava a stunted *saguaro* lifted its head.

A few shriveled blossoms that had once been white hung along the fluted column.

"I reckon according to that giant cactus it's somewheres along the end of March," said Jim Lash, soberly.

"Shore it's April. Look where the sun is. An' can't you feel it's gettin' hot?"

"Supposin' it is April?" queried Lash, slowly.

"Well, what I'm drivin' at is it's about time you all was hittin' the trail back to Forlorn River, before the water holes dry out."

"Laddy, I reckon we'll start soon as you're able to be put on a hoss."

"Shore that'll be too late."

A silence ensued, in which those who heard Ladd gazed fixedly at him and then at one another. Lash uneasily shifted the position of his lame leg, and Gale saw him moisten his lips with his tongue.

"Charlie Ladd, I ain't reckonin' you mean we're to ride off an' leave you here?"

"What else is there to do? The hot weather's close. Pretty soon most of the water holes will be dry. You can't travel then. . . . I'm on my back here, an' God only knows when I could be packed out. Not for weeks, mebbe. I'll never be any good again, even if I was to get out alive. . . . You see, shore this sort of case comes round sometimes in the desert. It's common enough. I've heard of several cases where men had to go an' leave a feller behind. It's reasonable. If you're fightin' the desert you can't afford to be sentimental. . . . Now, as I said, I'm all in. So what's the sense of you waitin' here, when it means the old desert story? By goin' now mebbe you'll get home. If you wait on a chance of takin' me, you'll be too late. Pretty soon this lava'll be one roastin' hell. Shore now, boys, you'll see this the right way? Jim, old pard?"

"No, Laddy, an' I can't figger how you could ever ask me."

"Shore then leave me here with Yaqui an' a couple of the hosses. We can eat sheep meat. An' if the water holds out—"

"No!" interrupted Lash, violently.

Ladd's eyes sought Gale's face.

"Son, you ain't bullheaded like Jim. You'll see the sense of it. There's Nell a-waitin' back at Forlorn River. Think what it means to her! She's a damn fine girl, Dick, an' what right have you to break her heart for an old worn-out cow-puncher? Think how she's watchin' for you with that sweet face all sad an' troubled, an' her eyes turnin' black. You'll go son, won't you?"

Dick shook his head.

The ranger turned his gaze upon Thorne, and now the keen, glistening light in his gray eyes had blurred.

"Thorne, it's different with you. Jim's a fool, an' young Gale has been punctured by *cholla* thorns. He's got the desert poison in his blood. But you now—you've no call to stick—you can find that trail out. It's easy to follow, made by so many shod hosses. Take your wife an' go. . . . Shore you'll go, Thorne?"

Deliberately and without an instant's hesitation the cavalryman replied, "No."

Ladd then directed his appeal to Mercedes. His face was now convulsed, and his voice, though it had sunk to a whisper, was clear, and beautiful with some rich quality that Gale had never before heard in it.

"Mercedes, you're a woman. You're the woman we fought for. An' some of us are shore goin' to die for you. Don't make it all for nothin'. Let us feel we saved the woman. Shore you can make Thorne go. He'll have to go if you say. They'll all have to go. Think of the years of love an' happiness in store for you. A week or so an' it'll be too late. Can you stand for me seein' you? . . . Let me tell you, Mercedes, when the summer heat hits the lava we'll all wither an' curl up like shavin's near a fire. A wind of hell will blow up this slope. Look at them mesquites. See the twist in them. That's the torture of heat an' thirst. Do you want me or all us men seein' you like that? . . . Mercedes, don't make it all for nothin'. Say you'll persuade Thorne, if not the others."

For all the effect his appeal had to move her Mercedes might have possessed a heart as hard and fixed as the surrounding lava.

"Never!"

White-faced, with great black eyes flashing, the Spanish girl spoke the word that bound her and her companions in the desert.

The subject was never mentioned again. Gale thought that he read a sinister purpose in Ladd's mind. To his astonishment, Lash came to him with the same fancy. After that they made certain there never was a gun within reach of Ladd's clutching, clawlike hands.

Gradually a somber spell lifted from the ranger's mind. When he was entirely free of it he began to gather strength daily. Then it was as if he had never known patience—he who had shown so well how to wait. He was in a frenzy to get well. His appetite could not be satisfied.

The sun climbed higher, whiter, hotter. At midday a wind from gulfward roared up the arroyo, and now only the *palo verdes* and the few *saguaros* were green. Every day the water in the lava hole sank an inch.

The Yaqui alone spent the waiting time in activity. He made trips up on the lava slope, and each time, he returned with guns or boots or sombreros, or something belonging to the bandits that had fallen. He never fetched in a saddle or bridle, and from that the rangers concluded Rojas's horses had long before taken their back trail. What speculation, what consternation those saddled horses would cause if they returned to Forlorn River!

As Ladd improved there was one story he had to hear every day. It was the one relating to what he had missed—the sight of Rojas pursued and plunged to his doom. The thing had a morbid fascination for the sick ranger. He reveled in it. He tortured Mercedes. His gentleness and consideration, heretofore so marked, were in abeyance to some sinister, ghastly joy. But to humor him Mercedes racked her soul with the sensations she had suffered when Rojas hounded her out on the ledge; when she shot him; when she sprang to throw herself over the precipice; when she fought him; when with half-blinded eyes she looked up to see the merciless Yaqui reaching for the bandit. Ladd fed his cruel longing with Thorne's poignant recollections, with the keen, clear, never-to-be-forgotten shocks to Gale's eye and ear. Jim Lash, for one at least, never tired of telling how he had seen and heard the tragedy, and every time in the telling it gathered some more tragic and gruesome detail. Jim believed in satiating the ranger. Then in the twilight, when the campfire burned, Ladd would try to get the Yaqui to tell his side of the story. But this the Indian would never do. There was only the expression of his fathomless eyes and the set passion of his massive face.

Those waiting days grew into weeks. Ladd gained very slowly. Nevertheless, at last he could walk about, and soon he averred that, strapped to a horse, he could last out the trip to Forlorn River.

There was rejoicing in camp, and plans were eagerly suggested. The Yaqui happened to be absent. When he returned the rangers told him they were now ready to undertake the journey back across lava and cactus.

Yaqui shook his head. They declared again their intention.

"No!" replied the Indian, and his deep, sonorous voice rolled out upon the quiet of the arroyo. He spoke briefly then. They had waited too long. The smaller water holes back in the trail were dry. The hot summer was upon them. There could be only death waiting down in the burning valley. Here was water and grass and wood and shade from the sun's rays and sheep to be killed on the peaks. The water would hold unless the season was that dreaded *año seco* of the Mexicans.

"Wait for rain," concluded Yaqui, and now as never before he spoke as one with authority. "If no rain—" Silently he lifted a speaking hand.

CHAPTER 16

MOUNTAIN SHEEP

What Gale might have thought an appalling situation, if considered from a safe and comfortable home away from the desert, became, now that he was shut in by the red-ribbed lava walls and great dry wastes, a matter calmly accepted as inevitable. So he imagined it was accepted by the others. Not even Mercedes uttered a regret. No word was spoken of home. If there was thought of loved ones, it was locked deep in their minds. In Mercedes there was no change in womanly quality, perhaps because all she had to love was there in the desert with her.

Gale had often pondered over this singular change in character. He had trained himself, in order to fight a paralyzing something in the desert's influence, to oppose with memory and thought an insidious primitive retrogression to what was scarcely consciousness at all, merely a savage's instinct of sight and sound. He felt the need now of redoubled effort. For there was a sheer happiness in drifting. Not only was it easy to forget, it was hard to remember. His idea was that a man laboring under a great wrong, a great crime, a great passion might find the lonely desert a fitting place for either remembrance or oblivion, according to the nature of his soul. But an ordinary, healthy, reasonably happy mortal who loved the open with its blaze of sun and sweep of wind would have a task to keep from going backward to the natural man as he was before civilization.

By tacit agreement Ladd again became the leader of the party. Ladd was a man who would have taken all the responsibility whether or not it was given him. In moments of hazard, of uncertainty, Lash and Gale, even Belding, unconsciously looked to the ranger. He had that kind of power.

The first thing Ladd asked was to have the store of food that remained spread out upon a tarpaulin. Assuredly, it was a slender enough supply. The ranger stood for long moments gazing down at it. He was groping among past experiences, calling back from his years of life on range and desert that which might be valuable for the present issue. It was impossible to read the gravity of Ladd's face, for he still looked like a dead man, but the slow shake of his head told Gale much. There was a grain of hope, however, in the significance with which he touched the bags of salt and said, "Shore it was sense packin' all that salt!"

Then he turned to face his comrades.

"That's little grub for six starvin' people corralled in the desert. But the grub end ain't worryin' me. Yaqui can get sheep up the slopes. Water! That's the beginnin' an' middle an' end of our case."

"Laddy, I reckon the water hole here never goes dry," replied Jim.

"Ask the Indian."

Upon being questioned, Yaqui repeated what he had said about the dreaded *año seco* of the Mexicans. In a dry year this water hole failed.

"Dick, take a rope an' see how much water's in the hole."

Gale could not find bottom with a thirty-foot lasso. The water was as cool, clear, sweet as if it had been kept in a shaded iron receptacle.

Ladd welcomed this information with surprise and gladness.

"Let's see. Last year was shore pretty dry. Mebbe this summer won't be. Mebbe our wonderful good luck'll hold. Ask Yaqui if he thinks it'll rain."

Mercedes questioned the Indian.

"He says no man can tell surely. But he thinks the rain will come," she replied.

"Shore it'll rain, you can gamble on that now," continued Ladd. "If there's only grass for the hosses! We can't get out of here without hosses. Dick, take the Indian an' scout down the arroyo. To-day I seen the hosses were gettin' fat. Gettin' fat in this desert! But mebbe they've about grazed up all the grass. Go an' see, Dick. An' may you come back with more good news!"

Gale, upon the few occasions when he had wandered down the arroyo, had never gone far. The Yaqui said there was grass for the horses, and until now no one had given the question more consideration. Gale found that the arroyo widened as it opened. Near the head, where it was narrow, the grass lined the course of the dry streambed. But farther down this streambed spread out. There was every indication that at flood seasons the water covered the floor of the arroyo. The farther Gale went the thicker and larger grew the gnarled mesquites and *palo verdes*, the more cactus and greasewood there were, and other desert growths. Patches of gray grass grew everywhere. Gale began to wonder where the horses were. Finally the trees and brush thinned out, and a milewide gray plain stretched down to reddish sand dunes. Over to one side were the white horses, and even as Gale saw them both Blanco Diablo and Sol lifted their heads and, with white manes tossing in the wind, whistled clarion calls. Here was grass enough for many horses; the arroyo was indeed an oasis.

Ladd and the others were awaiting Gale's report, and they received it with calmness, yet with a joy no less evident because it was restrained. Gale, in his keen observation at the moment, found that he and his comrades turned with glad eyes to the woman of the party.

"Señor Laddy, you think—you—believe—we shall—" she faltered, and her voice failed. It was the woman in her, weakening in the light of real hope, of the happiness now possible beyond that desert barrier.

"Mercedes, no white man can tell what'll come to pass out here," said Ladd, earnestly. "Shore I have hopes now I never dreamed of. I was pretty near a dead man. The Indian saved me. Queer notions have come into my head about Yaqui. I don't understand them. He seems when you look at him only a squalid, sullen, vengeful savage. But Lord! that's far from truth. Mebbe Yaqui's different from most Indians. He *looks* the same, though. Mebbe the trouble is we white folks never knew the Indian.

Anyway, Beldin' had it right. Yaqui's our godsend. Now as to the future, I'd like to know mebbe as well as you if we're ever to get home. Only bein' what I am, I say *Quién sabe?* But somethin' tells me Yaqui knows. Ask him, Mercedes. Make him tell. We'll all be the better for knowin'. We'd be stronger for havin' more'n our faith in him. He's a silent Indian, but make him tell."

Mercedes called to Yaqui. At her bidding there was always a suggestion of hurry, which otherwise was never manifest in his actions. She put a hand on his bared muscular arm and began to speak in Spanish. Her voice was low, swift, full of deep emotion, sweet as the sound of a bell. It thrilled Gale, though he understood scarcely a word she said. He did not need translation to know that here spoke the longing of a woman for life, love, home, the heritage of a woman's heart.

Gale doubted his own divining impression. It was that the Yaqui understood this woman's longing. In Gale's sight the Indian's stoicism, his inscrutability, the lavalike hardness of his face, although they did not change, seemed to give forth light, gentleness, loyalty. For an instant Gale seemed to have a vision; but it did not last, and he failed to hold some beautiful illusive thing.

"*Si!*" rolled out the Indian's reply, full of power and depth.

Mercedes drew a long breath, and her hand sought Thorne's.

"He says yes," she whispered. "He answers he'll save us; he'll take us all back—he knows!"

The Indian turned away to his tasks, and the silence that held the little group was finally broken by Ladd.

"Shore I said so. Now all we've got to do is use sense. Friends, I'm the commissary department of this outfit, an' what I say goes. You all won't eat except when I tell you. Mebbe it'll not be so hard to keep our health. Starved beggars don't get sick. But there's the heat comin', an' we can all go loco, you know. To pass the time! Lord, that's our problem. Now if you all only had a hankerin' for checkers. Shore I'll make a board an' make you play. Thorne, you're the luckiest. You've got your girl, an' this can be a honeymoon. Now with a few tools an' little material see what a grand house you can build for your wife. Dick, you're lucky, too. You like to hunt, an' up there you'll find the finest bighorn huntin' in the West. Take Yaqui and the .405. We need the meat, but while you're gettin' it have your sport. The same chance will never come again. I wish we all was able to go. But crippled men can't climb the lava. Shore you'll see some country from the peaks. There's no wilder place on earth, except the poles. An' when you're older, you an' Nell, with a couple of fine boys, think what it'll be to tell them about bein' lost in the lava, an' about huntin' sheep with a Yaqui. Shore I've hit it. You can take yours out in huntin' and thinkin'. Now if I had a girl like Nell I'd never go crazy. That's your game, Dick. Hunt, an' think of Nell, an' how you'll tell those fine boys about it all, an' about the old cowman you knowed, Laddy, who'll by then be long past the divide. Rustle now, son. Get some enthusiasm. For shore you'll need it for yourself an' us."

Gale climbed the lava slope, away round to the right of the arroyo, along an old trail that Yaqui said the Papagos had made before his own people hunted there. Partway it led through spiked, crested, upheaved lava that would have been almost impassable even without its silver coating of *cholla* cactus. There were benches and ledges and ridges bare and glistening in the sun. From the crests of these Yaqui's searching falcon gaze roved near and far for signs of sheep, and Gale used his glass on the reaches of lava that slanted steeply upward to the corrugated peaks, and down over endless heave and roll and red-waved slopes. The heat smoked up from the lava, and this, with the red color and shiny *chollas*, gave the impression of a world of smoldering fire.

Farther along the slope Yaqui halted and crawled behind projections to a point commanding a view over an extraordinary section of country. The peaks were off to the left. In the foreground were gullies, ridges, cañons, arroyos, all glistening with *chollas* and some other and more numerous white bushes, and here and there towered a green cactus. This region was only a splintered and more devastated part of the volcanic slope, but it was miles in extent. Yaqui peeped over the top of a blunt block of lava and searched the sharp-billowed wilderness. Suddenly he grasped Gale and pointed across a deep wide gully.

With the aid of his glass Gale saw five sheep. They were much larger than he had expected, dull brown in color, and two of them were rams with great curved horns. They were looking in his direction. Remembering what he had heard about the wonderful eyesight of these mountain animals, Gale could only conclude that they had seen the hunters.

Then Yaqui's movements attracted and interested him. The Indian had brought with him a red scarf and a mesquite branch. He tied the scarf on the stick, and propped this up in a crack of the lava. The scarf waved in the wind. That done, the Indian bade Gale watch.

Once again he leveled the glass at the sheep. All five now were motionless, standing like statues, heads pointed across the gully. They were more than a mile distant. When Gale looked without his glass they merged into the roughness of the lava. He was intensely interested. Did the sheep see the red scarf? It seemed incredible, but nothing else could account for that statuesque alertness. The sheep held this rigid position for perhaps fifteen minutes. Then the leading ram started to approach. The others followed. He took a few steps, then halted. Always he held his head up, nose pointed.

"By George, they're coming!" exclaimed Gale. "They see that flag. They're hunting us. They're curious. If this doesn't beat me!"

Evidently the Indian understood, for he grunted.

Gale found difficulty in curbing his impatience. The approach of the sheep was slow. The advances of the leader and the intervals of watching had a singular regularity. He worked like a machine. Gale followed him down the opposite wall, around holes, across gullies, over ridges. Then Gale shifted the glass back to find the others. They were coming also, with exactly the same pace and pause of their leader. What steppers they were! How sure-footed! What leaps they made! It was thrilling to watch them. Gale forgot he had a rifle. The Yaqui pressed a heavy hand down upon his shoulder. He was to keep well hidden and to be quiet. Gale suddenly conceived the idea that the sheep might come clear across to investigate the puzzling red thing fluttering in the breeze. Strange, indeed, would that be for the wildest creatures in the world.

The big ram led on with the same regular persistence, and in half an hour's time he was in the bottom of the great gulf, and soon he was facing up the slope. Gale knew then that the alluring scarf had fascinated him. It was no longer necessary now for Gale to use his glass. There was a short period when an intervening crest of lava hid the sheep from view. After that the two rams and their smaller followers were plainly in sight for perhaps a quarter of an hour. Then they disappeared behind another ridge. Gale kept watching, sure they would come out farther on. A tense period of waiting passed, then a sudden electrifying pressure of Yaqui's hand made Gale tremble with excitement.

Very cautiously he shifted his position. There, not fifty feet distant upon a high mound of lava, stood the leader of the sheep. His size astounded Gale. He seemed all horns. But only for a moment did the impression of horns overbalancing body remain with Gale. The sheep was graceful, sinewy, slender, powerfully built, and in poise magnificent. As Gale watched, spellbound, the second ram leaped lightly upon the mound, and presently the three others did likewise.

Then, indeed, Gale feasted his eyes with a spectacle for a hunter. It came to him suddenly that there had been something he expected to see in this Rocky Mountain bighorn, and it was lacking. They were beautiful, as wonderful as even Ladd's encomiums had led him to suppose. He thought perhaps it was the contrast these soft, sleek, short-furred, graceful animals afforded to what he imagined the barren, terrible lava mountains might develop.

The splendid leader stepped closer, his round, protruding amber eyes, which Gale could now plainly see, intent upon that fatal red flag. Like automatons the other four crowded into his tracks. A few little slow steps, then the leader halted.

At this instant Gale's absorbed attention was directed by Yaqui to the rifle, and so to the purpose of the climb. A little cold shock affronted Gale's vivid pleasure. With it dawned a realization of what he had imagined was lacking in these animals. They did not look wild! The so-called wildest of wild creatures appeared tamer than sheep he had followed on a farm. It would be little less than murder to kill them. Gale regretted the need of slaughter. Nevertheless, he could not resist the desire to show himself and see how tame they really were.

He reached for the .405, and as he threw a shell into the chamber the slight metallic click made the sheep jump. Then Gale rose quickly to his feet.

The noble ram and his band simply stared at Gale. They had never seen a man. They showed not the slightest indication of instinctive fear. Curiosity, surprise, even friendliness, seemed to mark their attitude of attention. Gale imagined that they were going to step still closer. He did not choose to wait to see if this were true. Certainly it already took a grim resolution to raise the heavy .405.

His shot killed the big leader. The others bounded away with remarkable nimbleness. Gale used up the remaining four shells to drop the second ram, and by the time he had reloaded the others were out of range.

The Yaqui's method of hunting was sure and deadly and saving in energy, but Gale never would try it again. He chose to stalk the game. This entailed a great expenditure of strength, the eyes and the lungs of a mountaineer, and, as Gale put it to Ladd, the need of seven-league boots. After being hunted a few times and shot at, the sheep became exceedingly difficult to approach. Gale learned to know that their fame as the keenest-eyed of all animals was well founded. If he worked directly toward a flock, crawling over the sharp lava, always a sentinel ram espied him before he got within range. The only method of attack that he found successful was to locate sheep with his glass, work round to windward of them, and then, getting behind a ridge or buttress, crawl like a lizard to a vantage point. He failed often. The stalk called forth all that was in him of endurance, cunning, speed. As the days grew hotter he hunted in the early morning hours and a while before the sun went down. More than one night he lay out on the lava, with the great stars close overhead and the immense void all beneath him. This pursuit he learned to love. Upon those scarred and blasted slopes the wild spirit that was in him had free rein. And like a shadow the faithful Yaqui tried ever to keep at his heels.

One morning the rising sun greeted him as he surmounted the higher cone of the volcano. He saw the vastness of the east aglow with a glazed rosy whiteness, like the changing hue of an ember. At this height there was a sweeping wind, still cool. The western slopes of lava lay dark, and all that world of sand and gulf and mountain barrier beyond was shrouded in the mystic cloud of distance. Gale had assimilated much of the loneliness and the sense of ownership and the love of lofty heights that might well belong to the great condor of the peak. Like this wide-winged bird, he had an unparalleled range of vision. The very corners whence came the winds seemed pierced by Gale's eyes.

Yaqui spied a flock of sheep far under the curved broken rim of the main crater. Then began the stalk. Gale had taught Yaqui something— that speed might win as well as patient cunning. Keeping out of sight, Gale ran over the spike-crusted lava, leaving the Indian far behind. His feet were magnets, attracting supporting holds, and he passed over them too fast to fall. The wind, the keen air of the heights, the red lava, the boundless surrounding blue, all seemed to have something to do with his wildness. Then, hiding, slipping, creeping, crawling, he closed in upon his quarry until the long rifle grew like stone in his grip, and the whipping "spang" ripped the silence, and the strange echo boomed deep in the crater, and rolled around, as if in hollow mockery at the hopelessness of escape.

Gale's exultant yell was given as much to free himself of some bursting joy of action as it was to call the slower Yaqui. Then he liked the strange echoes. It was a maddening whirl of sound that bored deeper and deeper along the whorled and caverned walls of the crater. It was as if these aged walls resented the violating of their silent sanctity. Gale felt himself a man, a thing alive, something superior to all this savage, dead, upflung world of iron, a master even of all this grandeur and sublimity because he had a soul.

He waited beside his quarry, and breathed deep, and swept the long slopes with searching eyes of habit.

When Yaqui came up they set about the hardest task of all, to pack the best of that heavy sheep down miles of steep, ragged, *cholla*-covered lava. But even in this Gale rejoiced. The heat was nothing, the millions of little pits which could hold and twist a foot were nothing; the blade-edged crusts and the deep fissures and the choked cañons and the tangled, dwarfed mesquites, all these were as nothing but obstacles to be cheerfully overcome. Only the *cholla* hindered Dick Gale.

When his heavy burden pulled him out of sure-footedness, and he plunged into a *cholla*, or when the strange, deceitful, uncanny, almost invisible frosty thorns caught and pierced him, then there was call for all of his fortitude and endurance. For this cactus had a malignant power of torture. Its pain was a stinging, blinding, burning, sickening poison in the blood. If thorns pierced his legs he felt the pain all over his body; if his hands rose from a fall full of the barbed joints, he was helpless and quivering till Yaqui tore them out.

But this one peril, dreaded more than dizzy height of precipice or sunblindness on the glistening peak, did not daunt Gale. His teacher was the Yaqui, and always before him was an example that made him despair of a white man's equality. Color, race, blood, breeding—what were these in the wilderness? Verily, Dick Gale had come to learn the use of his hands.

So in a descent of hours he toiled down the lava slope, to stalk into the arroyo like a burdened giant, wringing wet, panting, clear-eyed and dark-faced, his ragged clothes and boots white with *cholla* thorns.

The gaunt Ladd rose from his shaded seat, removed his pipe from smiling lips, and turned to nod at Jim, and then looked back again.

The torrid summer heat came imperceptibly, or it could never have been borne by white men. It changed the lives of the fugitives, making them partly nocturnal in habit. The nights had the balmy coolness of spring, and would have been delightful for sleep, but that would have made the blazing days unendurable.

The sun rose in a vast white flame. With it came the blasting, withering wind from the gulf. A red haze, like that of earlier sunsets, seemed to come sweeping on the wind, and it roared up the arroyo, and went bellowing into the crater, and rushed on in fury to lash the peaks.

During these hot, windy hours the desert-bound party slept in deep recesses in the lava; and if necessity brought them forth they could not remain out long. The sand burned through boots, and a touch of bare hand on lava raised a blister.

A short while before sundown the Yaqui went forth to build a campfire, and soon the others came out, heat-dazed, half blinded, with parching throats to allay and hunger that was never satisfied. A little action and a cooling of the air revived them, and when night set in they were comfortable round the campfire.

As Ladd had said, one of their greatest problems was the passing of time. The nights were interminably long, but they had to be passed in work or play or dream—anything except sleep. That was Ladd's most inflexible command. He gave no reason. But not improbably the ranger thought that the terrific heat of the day spent in slumber lessened a wear and strain, if not a real danger of madness.

Accordingly, at first the occupations of this little group were many and various. They worked if they had something to do, or could invent a pretext. They told and retold stories until all were wearisome. They sang songs. Mercedes taught Spanish. They played every game they knew. They invented others that were so trivial children would scarcely have been interested, and these they played seriously. In a word, with intelligence and passion, with all that was civilized and human, they fought the ever-infringing loneliness, the savage solitude of their environment.

But they had only finite minds. It was not in reason to expect a complete victory against this mighty Nature, this abounding horizon of death and desolation and decay. Gradually they fell back upon fewer and fewer occupations, until the time came when the silence was hard to break.

Gale believed himself the keenest of the party, the one who thought most, and he watched the effect of the desert upon his companions. He imagined that he saw Ladd grow old sitting around the campfire. Certain it was that the ranger's gray hair had turned white. What had been at times hard and cold and grim about him had strangely vanished in sweet temper and a vacant-mindedness that held him longer as the days passed. For hours, it seemed, Ladd would bend over his checkerboard and never make a move. It mattered not now whether or not he had a partner. He was always glad of being spoken to, as if he were called back from some vague region of mind. Jim Lash, the calmest, coolest, most nonchalant, best-humored Westerner Gale had ever met, had by slow degrees lost that cheerful character which would have been of such infinite good to his companions, and always he sat brooding, silently brooding. Jim had no ties, few memories, and the desert was claiming him.

Thorne and Mercedes, however, were living, wonderful proof that spirit, mind, and heart were free—free to soar in scorn of the colossal barrenness and silence and space of that terrible hedging prison of lava. They were young; they loved; they were together; and the oasis was almost a paradise. Gale believed he helped himself by watching them. Imagination had never pictured real happiness to him. Thorne and Mercedes had forgotten the outside world. If they had been existing on the burned-out desolate moon they could hardly have been in a harsher, grimmer, lonelier spot than this red-walled arroyo. But it might have been a statelier Eden than that of the primitive day.

Mercedes grew thinner, until she was a slender shadow of her former self. She became hard, brown as the rangers, lithe and quick as a panther. She seemed to live on water and the air—perhaps, indeed, on love. For of the scant fare, the best of which was continually urged upon her, she partook but little. She reminded Gale of a wild brown creature, free as the wind on the lava slopes. Yet, despite the great change, her beauty remained undiminished. Her eyes, seeming so much larger now in her small face, were great black, starry gulfs. She was the life of that camp. Her smiles, her rapid speech, her low laughter, her quick movements, her playful moods with the rangers, the dark and passionate glance, which rested so often on her lover, the whispers in the dusk as hand in hand they paced the campfire beat—these helped Gale to retain his loosening hold on reality, to resist the lure of a strange beckoning life where a man stood free in the golden open, where emotion was not, nor trouble, nor sickness, nor anything but the savage's rest and sleep and action and dream.

Although the Yaqui was as his shadow, Gale reached a point when he seemed to wander alone at twilight, in the night, at dawn. Far down the arroyo, in the deepening red twilight, when the heat rolled away on slow-dying wind, Blanco Sol raised his splendid head and whistled for his master. Gale reproached himself for neglect of the noble horse. Blanco Sol was always the same. He loved four things—his master, a long drink of cool water, to graze at will, and to run. Time and place, Gale thought, meant little to Sol if he could have those four things. Gale put his arm over the great arched neck and laid his cheek against the long white mane, and then even as he stood there forgot the horse. What was that dull, red-tinged, horizon-wide mantle creeping up the slope? Through it the copper sun glowed, paled, died. Was it only twilight? Was it gloom? If he thought about it he had a feeling that it was the herald of night, and the night must be a vigil, and that made him tremble.

At night he had formed a habit of climbing up the lava slope as far as the smooth trail extended, and there on a promontory he paced to and fro, and watched the stars, and sat stone-still for hours looking down at the vast void with its moving, changing shadows. From that promontory he gazed up at a velvet-blue sky, deep and dark, bright with millions of cold, distant, blinking stars, and he grasped a little of the meaning of infinitude. He gazed down into the shadows, which, black as they were and impenetrable, yet gave a conception of immeasurable space.

Then the silence! He was dumb, he was awed, he bowed his head, he trembled, he marveled at the desert silence. It was the one thing always present. Even when the wind roared there seemed to be silence. But at night, in this lava world of ashes and canker, he waited for this terrible strangeness of nature to come to him with the secret. He seemed at once a little child and a strong man, and something very old. What tortured him was the incomprehensibility that the vaster the space the greater the silence! At one moment Gale felt there was only death here, and that was the secret; at another he heard the slow beat of a mighty heart.

He came at length to realize that the desert was a teacher. He did not realize all that he had learned, but he was a different man. And when he decided upon that, he was not thinking of the slow, sure call to the primal instincts of man; he was thinking that the desert, as much as he had experienced and no more, would absolutely overturn the whole scale of a man's values, break old habits, form new ones, remake him. More of desert experience, Gale believed, would be too much for intellect. The desert did not breed civilized man, and that made Gale ponder over a strange thought: after all, was the civilized man inferior to the savage?

Yaqui was the answer to that. When Gale acknowledged this he always remembered his present strange manner of thought. The past, the old order of mind, seemed as remote as this desert world was from the haunts of civilized men. A man must know a savage as Gale knew Yaqui before he could speak authoritatively, and then something stilled his tongue. In the first stage of Gale's observation of Yaqui he had marked tenaciousness of life, stoicism, endurance, strength. These were the attributes of the desert. But what of that second stage wherein the Indian had loomed up a colossal figure of strange honor, loyalty, love? Gale doubted his convictions and scorned himself for doubting.

There in the gloom sat the silent, impassive, inscrutable Yaqui. His dark face, his dark eyes were plain in the light of the stars. Always he was near Gale, unobtrusive, shadowy, but there. Why? Gale absolutely could not doubt that the Indian had heart as well as mind. Yaqui had from the very first stood between Gale and accident, toil, peril. It was his own choosing. Gale could not change him or thwart him. He understood the Indian's idea of obligation and sacred duty. But there was more, and that baffled Gale. In the night hours, alone on the slope, Gale felt in Yaqui, as he felt the mighty throb of that desert pulse, a something that drew him irresistibly to the Indian. Sometimes he looked around to find the Indian, to dispel these strange, pressing thoughts of unreality, and it was never in vain.

Thus the nights passed, endlessly long, with Gale fighting for his old order of thought, fighting the fascination of that infinite sky, and the gloomy insulating whirl of the wide shadows, fighting for belief, hope, prayer, fighting against that terrible ever-recurring idea of being lost, lost, lost in the desert, fighting harder than any other thing the insidious, penetrating, tranquil, unfeeling self that was coming between him and his memory.

He was losing the battle, losing his hold on tangible things, losing his power to stand up under this ponderous, merciless weight of desert space and silence.

He acknowledged it in a kind of despair, and the shadows of the night seemed whirling fiends. Lost! Lost! Lost! What are you waiting for? *Rain?* . . . Lost! Lost! Lost in the desert! So the shadows seemed to scream in voiceless mockery.

At the moment he was alone on the promontory. The night was far spent. A ghastly moon haunted the black volcanic spurs. The winds blew silently. Was he alone? No, he did not seem to be alone. The Yaqui was there. Suddenly a strange, cold sensation crept over Gale. It was new. He felt a presence. Turning, he expected to see the Indian, but instead, a slight shadow, pale, almost white, stood there, not close nor yet distant. It seemed to brighten. Then he saw a woman who resembled a girl he had seemed to know long ago. She was white-faced, golden-haired, and her lips were sweet, and her eyes were turning black. *Nell!* He had forgotten her. Over him flooded a torrent of memory. There was tragic woe in this sweet face. Nell was holding out her arms—she was crying aloud to him across the sand and the cactus and the lava. She was in trouble, and he had been forgetting.

That night he climbed the lava to the topmost cone, and never slipped on a ragged crust nor touched a *cholla* thorn. A voice had called to him. He saw Nell's eyes in the stars, in the velvet blue of sky, in the blackness of the engulfing shadows. She was with him, a slender shape, a spirit, keeping step with him, and memory was strong, sweet, beating, beautiful. Far down in the west, faintly golden with light of the sinking moon, he saw a cloud that resembled her face. A cloud on the desert horizon! He gazed and gazed. Was that a spirit face like the one by his side? No—he did not dream.

In the hot, sultry morning Yaqui appeared at camp, after long hours of absence, and he pointed with a long, dark arm toward the west. A bank of clouds was rising above the mountain barrier.

"*Rain!*" he cried; and his sonorous voice rolled down the arroyo.

Those who heard him were as shipwrecked mariners at sight of a distant sail.

Dick Gale, silent, grateful to the depths of his soul, stood with his arm over Blanco Sol and watched the transforming west, where clouds of wondrous size and hue piled over one another, rushing, darkening, spreading, sweeping upward toward that white and glowing sun.

When they reached the zenith and swept round to blot out the blazing orb, the earth took on a dark, lowering aspect. The red of sand and lava changed to steely gray. Vast shadows, like ripples on water, sheeted in from the gulf with a low, strange moan. Yet the silence was like death. The desert was awaiting a strange and hated visitation—storm! If all the endless torrid days, the endless mystic nights had seemed unreal to Gale, what, then, seemed this stupendous spectacle?

"Oh! I felt a drop of rain on my face!" cried Mercedes; and, whispering the name of a saint, she kissed her husband.

The white-haired Ladd, gaunt, old, bent, looked up at the maelstrom of clouds, and he said, softly, "Shore we'll get in the hosses, an' pack light, an' hit the trail, an' make night marches!"

Then up out of the gulf of the west swept a bellowing wind and a black pall and terrible flashes of lightning and thunder like the end of the world—fury, blackness, chaos, the desert storm.

CHAPTER 17

THE WHISTLE OF A HORSE

At the ranch house at Forlorn River Belding stood alone in his darkened room. It was quiet there and quiet outside; the sickening midsummer heat, like a hot heavy blanket, lay upon the house.

He took up the gun belt from his table and with slow hands buckled it around his waist. He seemed to feel something familiar and comfortable and inspiring in the weight of the big gun against his hip. He faced the door as if to go out, but hesitated, and then began a slow, plodding walk up and down the length of the room. Presently he halted at the table, and with reluctant hands he unbuckled the gun belt and laid it down.

The action did not have an air of finality, and Belding knew it. He had seen border life in Texas in the early days; he had been a sheriff when the law in the West depended on a quickness of wrist; he had seen many a man lay down his gun for good and all. His own action was not final. Of late he had done the same thing many times, and this last time it seemed a little harder to do, a little more indicative of vacillation. There were reasons why Belding's gun held for him a gloomy fascination.

The Chases, those grasping and conscienceless agents of a new force in the development of the West, were bent upon Belding's ruin, and, so far as his fortunes at Forlorn River were concerned, had almost accomplished it. One by one he lost points for which he contended with them. He carried into the Tucson courts the matter of the staked claims, and mining claims, and water claims, and he lost all. Following that he lost his government position as inspector of immigration; and this fact, because of what he considered its injustice, had been a hard blow. He had been made to suffer a humiliation equally as great. It came about that he actually had to pay the Chases for water to irrigate his alfalfa fields. The never-failing spring upon his land answered for the needs of household and horses, but no more.

These matters were unfortunate for Belding, but not by any means wholly accountable for his worry and unhappiness and brooding hate. He believed Dick Gale and the rest of the party taken into the desert by the Yaqui had been killed or lost. Two months before a string of Mexican horses, riderless, saddled, starved for grass and wild for water, had come in to Forlorn River. They were a part of the horses belonging to Rojas and his band. Their arrival complicated the mystery and strengthened convictions of the loss of both pursuers and pursued. Belding was wont to say that he had worried himself gray over the fate of his rangers.

Belding's unhappiness could hardly be laid to material loss. He had been rich and was now poor, but change of fortune such as that could not have made him unhappy. Something more somber and mysterious and sad than the loss of Dick Gale and their friends had come into the lives of his wife and Nell. He dated the time of this change back to a certain day when Mrs. Belding recognized in the elder Chase an old schoolmate and a rejected suitor. It took time for slow-thinking Belding to discover anything wrong in his household, especially as the fact of the Gales lingering there made Mrs. Belding and Nell, for the most part, hide their real and deeper feelings. Gradually, however, Belding had forced on him the fact of some secret cause for grief other than Gale's loss. He was sure of it when his wife signified her desire to make a visit to her old home back in Peoria. She did not give many reasons, but she did show him a letter that had found its way from old friends. This letter contained news that may or may not have been authentic; but it was enough, Belding thought, to interest his wife. An old prospector had returned to Peoria, and he had told relatives of meeting Robert Burton at the Sonoyta Oasis fifteen years before, and that Burton had gone into the desert never to return. To Belding this was no surprise, for he had heard that before his marriage. There appeared to have been no doubts as to the death of his wife's first husband. The singular thing was that both Nell's father and grandfather had been lost somewhere in the Sonora Desert.

Belding did not oppose his wife's desire to visit her old home. He thought it would be a wholesome trip for her, and did all in his power to persuade Nell to accompany her. But Nell would not go.

It was after Mrs. Belding's departure that Belding discovered in Nell a condition of mind that amazed and distressed him. She had suddenly become strangely wretched, so that she could not conceal it from even the Gales, who, of all people, Belding imagined, were the ones to make Nell proud. She would tell him nothing. But after a while, when he had thought it out, he dated this further and more deplorable change in Nell back to a day on which he had met Nell with Radford Chase. This indefatigable wooer had not in the least abandoned his suit. Something about the fellow made Belding grind his teeth. But Nell grew not only solicitously, but now strangely, entreatingly earnest in her importunities to Belding not to insult or lay a hand on Chase. This had bound Belding so far; it had made him think and watch. He had never been a man to interfere with his womenfolks. They could do as they liked, and usually that pleased him. But a slow surprise gathered and grew upon him when he saw that Nell, apparently, was accepting young Chase's attentions. At least, she no longer hid from him. Belding could not account for this, because he was sure Nell cordially despised the fellow. And toward the end he divined, if he did not actually know, that these Chases possessed some strange power over Nell, and were using it. That stirred a hate in Belding—a hate he had felt at the first and had manfully striven against, which now gave him over to dark brooding thoughts.

Midsummer passed, and the storms came late. But when they arrived they made up for tardiness. Belding did not remember so terrible a storm of wind and rain as that which broke the summer's drought.

In a few days, it seemed, Altar Valley was a bright and green expanse, where dust clouds did not rise. Forlorn River ran, a slow, heavy, turgid torrent. Belding never saw the river in flood that it did not give him joy; yet now, desert man as he was, he suffered a regret when he thought of the great Chase reservoir full and overflowing. The dull thunder of the spillway was not pleasant. It was the first time in his life that the sound of falling water jarred upon him.

Belding noticed workmen once more engaged in the fields bounding his land. The Chases had extended a main irrigation ditch down to Belding's farm, skipped the width of his ground, then had gone on down through Altar Valley. They had exerted every influence to obtain right to connect these ditches by digging through his land, but Belding had remained obdurate. He refused to have any dealings with them. It was therefore with some curiosity and suspicion that he saw a gang of Mexicans once more at work upon these ditches.

At daylight next morning a tremendous blast almost threw Belding out of his bed. It cracked the adobe walls of his house and broke windows and sent pans and crockery to the floor with a crash. Belding's idea was that the store of dynamite kept by the Chases for blasting had blown up. Hurriedly getting into his clothes, he went to Nell's room to reassure her; and, telling her to have a thought for their guests, he went out to see what had happened.

The villagers were pretty badly frightened. Many of the poorly constructed adobe huts had crumbled almost into dust. A great yellow cloud, like smoke, hung over the river. This appeared to be at the upper end of Belding's plot, and close to the river. When he reached his fence the smoke and dust were so thick he could scarcely breathe, and for a little while he was unable to see what had happened. Presently he made out a huge hole in the sand just about where the irrigation ditch had stopped near his line. For some reason or other, not clear to Belding, the Mexicans had set off an extraordinarily heavy blast at that point.

Belding pondered. He did not now for a moment consider an accidental discharge of dynamite. But why had this blast been set off? The loose sandy soil had yielded readily to shovel; there were no rocks; as far as construction of a ditch was concerned such a blast would have done more harm than good.

Slowly, with reluctant feet, Belding walked toward a green hollow, where in a cluster of willows lay the never-failing spring that his horses loved so well, and, indeed, which he loved no less. He was actually afraid to part the drooping willows to enter the little cool, shady path that led to the spring. Then, suddenly seized by suspense, he ran the rest of the way.

He was just in time to see the last of the water. It seemed to sink as in quicksand. The shape of the hole had changed. The tremendous force of the blast had obstructed or diverted the underground stream of water.

Belding's never-failing spring had been ruined. What had made this little plot of ground green and sweet and fragrant was now no more. Belding's first feeling was for the pity of it. The pale Ajo lilies would bloom no more under those willows. The willows themselves would soon wither and die. He thought how many times in the middle of hot summer nights he had come down to the spring to drink. Never again!

Suddenly he thought of Blanco Diablo. How the great white thoroughbred had loved this spring! Belding straightened up and looked with tear-blurred eyes out over the waste of desert to the west. Never a day passed that he had not thought of the splendid horse; but this moment, with its significant memory, was doubly keen, and there came a dull pang in his breast.

"Diablo will never drink here again!" muttered Belding.

The loss of Blanco Diablo, though admitted and mourned by Belding, had never seemed quite real until this moment.

The pall of dust drifting over him, the din of the falling water up at the dam, diverted Belding's mind to the Chases. All at once he was in the harsh grip of a cold certainty. The blast had been set off intentionally to ruin his spring. What a hellish trick! No Westerner, no Indian or Mexican, no desert man could have been guilty of such a crime. To ruin a beautiful clear, cool, never-failing stream of water in the desert!

It was then that Belding's worry and indecision and brooding were as if they had never existed. As he strode swiftly back to the house, his head, which had long been bent thoughtfully and sadly, was held erect. He went directly to his room, and with an air that was now final he buckled on his gun belt. He looked the gun over and tried the action. He squared himself and walked a little more erect. Some long-lost individuality had returned to Belding.

"Let's see," he was saying. "I can get Carter to send the horses I've got left back to Waco to my brother. I'll make Nell take what money there is and go hunt up her mother. The Gales are ready to go—today, if I say the word. Nell can travel with them partway East. That's your game, Tom Belding, don't mistake me."

As he went out he encountered Mr. Gale coming up the walk. The long sojourn at Forlorn River, despite the fact that it had been laden with a suspense which was gradually changing to a sad certainty, had been of great benefit to Dick's father. The dry air, the heat, and the quiet had made him, if not entirely a well man, certainly stronger than he had been in many years.

"Belding, what was that terrible roar?" asked Mr. Gale. "We were badly frightened until Miss Nell came to us. We feared it was an earthquake."

"Well, I'll tell you, Mr. Gale, we've had some quakes here, but none of them could hold a candle to this jar we just had."

Then Belding explained what had caused the explosion, and why it had been set off so close to his property.

"It's an outrage, sir, an unspeakable outrage," declared Mr. Gale, hotly. "Such a thing would not be tolerated in the East. Mr. Belding, I'm amazed at your attitude in the face of all this trickery."

"You see—there was Mother and Nell," began Belding, as if apologizing. He dropped his head a little and made marks in the sand with the toe of his boot. "Mr. Gale, I've been sort of half hitched, as Laddy used to say. I'm planning to have a little more elbow room round this ranch. I'm going to send Nell East to her mother. Then I'll— See here, Mr. Gale, would you mind having Nell with you partway when you go home?"

"We'd all be delighted to have her go all the way and make us a visit," replied Mr. Gale.

"That's fine. And you'll be going soon? Don't take that as if I wanted to—" Belding paused, for the truth was that he did want to hurry them off.

"We would have been gone before this, but for you," said Mr. Gale. "Long ago we gave up hope of—of Richard ever returning. And I believe, now we're sure he was lost, that we'd do well to go home at once. You wished us to remain till the heat was broken—till the rains came to make traveling easier for us. Now I see no need for further delay. My stay here has greatly benefited my health. I shall never forget your hospitality. This Western trip would have made me a new man if—only—Richard—"

"Sure. I understand," said Belding, gruffly. "Let's go in and tell the women to pack up."

Nell was busy with the servants preparing breakfast. Belding took her into the sitting room while Mr. Gale called his wife and daughter.

"My girl, I've some news for you," began Belding. "Mr. Gale is leaving today with his family. I'm going to send you with them—partway, anyhow. You're invited to visit them. I think that'd be great for you—help you to forget. But the main thing is—you're going East to join Mother."

Nell gazed at him, white-faced, without uttering a word.

"You see, Nell, I'm about done in Forlorn River," went on Belding. "That blast this morning sank my spring. There's no water now. It was the last straw. So we'll shake the dust of Forlorn River. I'll come on a little later—that's all."

"Dad, you're packing your gun!" exclaimed Nell, suddenly pointing with a trembling finger. She ran to him, and for the first time in his life Belding put her away from him. His movements had lost the old slow gentleness.

"Why, so I am," replied Belding, coolly, as his hand moved down to the sheath swinging at his hip. "Nell, I'm that absentminded these days!"

"Dad!" she cried.

"That'll do from you," he replied, in a voice he had never used to her. "Get breakfast now, then pack to leave Forlorn River."

"Leave Forlorn River!" whispered Nell, with a thin white hand stealing up to her breast. How changed the girl was! Belding reproached himself for his hardness, but did not speak his thought aloud. Nell was fading here, just as Mercedes had faded before the coming of Thorne.

Nell turned away to the west window and looked out across the desert toward the dim blue peaks in the distance. Belding watched her; likewise the Gales; and no one spoke. There ensued a long silence. Belding felt a lump rise in his throat. Nell laid her arm against the window frame, but gradually it dropped, and she was leaning with her face against the wood. A low sob broke from her. Elsie Gale went to her, embraced her, took the drooping head on her shoulder.

"We've come to be such friends," she said. "I believe it'll be good for you to visit me in the city. Here—all day you look out across that awful lonely desert. . . . Come, Nell."

Heavy steps sounded outside on the flagstones, then the door rattled under a strong knock. Belding opened it. The Chases, father and son, stood beyond the threshold.

"Good morning, Belding," said the elder Chase. "We were routed out early by that big blast and came up to see what was wrong. All a blunder. The Greaser foreman was drunk yesterday, and his ignorant men made a mistake. Sorry if the blast bothered you."

"Chase, I reckon that's the first of your blasts I was ever glad to hear," replied Belding, in a way that made Chase look blank.

"So? Well, I'm glad you're glad," he went on, evidently puzzled. "I was a little worried—you've always been so touchy—we never could get together. I hurried over, fearing maybe you might think the blast—you see, Belding—"

"I see this, Mr. Ben Chase," interrupted Belding, in curt and ringing voice. "The blast *was* a mistake, the biggest you ever made in your life."

"What do you mean?" demanded Chase.

"You'll have to excuse me for a while, unless you're dead set on having it out right now. Mr. Gale and his family are leaving, and my daughter is going with them. I'd rather you'd wait a little."

"Nell going away!" exclaimed Radford Chase. He reminded Belding of an overgrown boy in disappointment.

"Yes. But—*Miss Burton* to you, young man—"

"Mr. Belding, I certainly would prefer a conference with you right now," interposed the elder Chase, cutting short Belding's strange speech. "There are other matters—important matters to discuss. They've got to be settled. May we step in, sir?"

"No, you may not," replied Belding, bluntly. "I'm sure particular who I invite into my house. But I'll go with you."

Belding stepped out and closed the door. "Come away from the house so the women won't hear the—the talk."

The elder Chase was purple with rage, yet seemed to be controlling it. The younger man looked black, sullen, impatient. He appeared not to have a thought of Belding. He was absolutely blind to the situation, as considered from Belding's point of view. Ben Chase found his voice about the time Belding halted under the trees out of earshot from the house.

"Sir, you've insulted me—my son. How dare you? I want you to understand that you're—"

"Chop that kind of talk with me, you——!" interrupted Belding. He had always been profane, and now he certainly did not choose his language. Chase turned livid, gasped, and seemed about to give way to fury. But something about Belding evidently exerted a powerful quieting influence. "If you talk sense I'll listen," went on Belding.

Belding was frankly curious. He did not think any argument or inducement offered by Chase could change his mind on past dealings or his purpose of the present. But he believed by listening he might get some light on what had long puzzled him. The masterly effort Chase put forth to conquer his aroused passions gave Belding another idea of the character of this promoter.

"I want to make a last effort to propitiate you," began Chase, in his quick, smooth voice. That was a singular change to Belding—the dropping instantly into an easy flow of speech. "You've had losses here, and naturally you're sore. I don't blame you. But you can't see this thing from my side of the fence. Business is business. In business the best man wins. The law upheld those transactions of mine the honesty of which you questioned. As to mining and water claims, you lost on this technical point—that you had nothing to prove you had held them for five years. Five years is the time necessary in law. A dozen men might claim the source of Forlorn River, but if they had no house or papers to prove their squatters' rights any man could go in and fight them for the water. . . . Now I want to run that main ditch along the river, through your farm. Can't we make a deal? I'm ready to be liberal—to meet you more than halfway. I'll give you an interest in the company. I think I've influence enough up at the Capitol to have you reinstated as inspector. A little reasonableness on your part will put you right again in Forlorn River, with a chance of growing rich. There's a big future here. . . . My interest, Belding, has become personal. Radford is in love with your stepdaughter. He wants to marry her. I'll admit now if I had foreseen this situation I wouldn't have pushed you so hard. But we can square the thing. Now let's get together not only in business, but in a family way. If my son's happiness depends upon having this girl, you may rest assured I'll do all

I can to get her for him. I'll absolutely make good all your losses. Now what do you say?"

"No," replied Belding. "Your money can't buy a right of way across my ranch. And Nell doesn't want your son. That settles that."

"But you could persuade her."

"I won't, that's all."

"May I ask why?" Chase's voice was losing its suave quality but it was even swifter than before.

"Sure I don't mind your asking," replied Belding, in slow deliberation. "I wouldn't do such a low-down trick. Besides, if I would, I'd want it to be a man I was persuading for. I know Greasers—I know a Yaqui I'd rather give Nell to than your son."

Radford Chase began to roar in inarticulate rage. Belding paid no attention to him; indeed, he never glanced at the young man. The elder Chase checked a violent start. He plucked at the collar of his gray flannel shirt, opened it at the neck.

"My son's offer of marriage is an honor—more an honor, sir, than you perhaps are aware of."

Belding made no reply. His steady gaze did not turn from the long lane that led down to the river. He waited coldly, sure of himself.

"Mrs. Belding's daughter has no right to the name of Burton," snapped Chase. "Did you know that?"

"I did not," replied Belding, quietly.

"Well, you know it now," added Chase, bitingly.

"Sure you can prove what you say?" queried Belding, in the same cool, unemotional tone. It struck him strangely at the moment what little knowledge this man had of the West and of Western character.

"Prove it? Why, yes, I think so, enough to make the truth plain to any reasonable man. I come from Peoria—was born and raised there. I went to school with Nell Warren. That was your wife's maiden name. She was a beautiful, gay girl. All the fellows were in love with her. I knew Bob Burton well. He was a splendid fellow, but wild. Nobody ever knew for sure, but we all supposed he was engaged to marry Nell. He left Peoria, however, and soon after that the truth about Nell came out. She ran away. It was at least a couple of months before Burton showed up in

Peoria. He did not stay long. Then for years nothing was heard of either of them. When word did come Nell was in Oklahoma, Burton was in Denver. There's a chance, of course, that Burton followed Nell and married her. That would account for Nell Warren taking the name of Burton. But it isn't likely. None of us ever heard of such a thing and wouldn't have believed it if we had. The affair seemed destined to end unfortunately. But Belding, while I'm at it, I want to say that Nell Warren was one of the sweetest, finest, truest girls in the world. If she drifted to the Southwest and kept her past a secret that was only natural. Certainly it should not be held against her. Why, she was only a child—a girl—seventeen—eighteen years old. . . . In a moment of amazement—when I recognized your wife as an old schoolmate—I blurted the thing out to Radford. You see now how little it matters to me when I ask your stepdaughter's hand in marriage for my son."

Belding stood listening. The genuine emotion in Chase's voice was as strong as the ring of truth. Belding knew truth when he heard it. The revelation did not surprise him. Belding did not soften, for he divined that Chase's emotion was due to the probing of an old wound, the recalling of a past both happy and painful. Still, human nature was so strange that perhaps kindness and sympathy might yet have a place in this Chase's heart. Belding did not believe so, but he was willing to give Chase the benefit of the doubt.

"So you told my wife you'd respect her secret—keep her dishonor from husband and daughter?" demanded Belding, his dark gaze sweeping back from the lane.

"What! I—I—" stammered Chase.

"You made your son swear to be a man and die before he'd hint the thing to Nell?" went on Belding, and his voice rang louder.

Ben Chase had no answer. The red left his face. His son slunk back against the fence.

"I say you never held this secret over the heads of my wife and her daughter?" thundered Belding.

He had his answer in the gray faces, in the lips that fear made mute. Like a flash Belding saw the whole truth of Mrs. Belding's agony, the reason for her departure; he saw what had been driving Nell; and it seemed that all the dogs of hell were loosed within his heart. He struck out blindly, instinctively in his pain, and the blow sent Ben Chase staggering into the fence corner. Then he stretched forth a long arm and whirled Radford Chase back beside his father.

"I see it all now," went on Belding, hoarsely. "You found the woman's weakness—her love for the girl. You found the girl's weakness—her pride and fear of shame. So you drove the one and hounded the other. God, what a base thing to do! To *tell* the girl was bad enough, but to *threaten* her with betrayal; there's no name for that!"

Belding's voice thickened, and he paused, breathing heavily. He stepped back a few paces; and this, an ominous action for an armed man of his kind, instead of adding to the fear of the Chases, seemed to relieve them. If there had been any pity in Belding's heart he would have felt it then.

"And now, gentlemen," continued Belding, speaking low and with difficulty, "seeing I've turned down your proposition, I suppose you think you've no more call to keep your mouths shut?"

The elder Chase appeared fascinated by something he either saw or felt in Belding, and his gray face grew grayer. He put up a shaking hand. Then Radford Chase, livid and snarling, burst out: "I'll talk till I'm black in the face. You can't stop me!"

"You'll go black in the face, but it won't be from talking," hissed Belding.

His big arm swept down, and when he threw it up the gun glittered in his hand. Simultaneously with the latter action pealed out a shrill, penetrating whistle.

The whistle of a horse! It froze Belding's arm aloft. For an instant he could not move even his eyes. The familiarity of that whistle was terrible in its power to rob him of strength. Then he heard the rapid, heavy pound of hoofs, and again the piercing whistle.

"*Blanco Diablo!*" he cried, huskily.

He turned to see a huge white horse come thundering into the yard. A wild, gaunt, terrible horse; indeed, the loved Blanco Diablo. A bronzed, long-haired Indian bestrode him. More white horses galloped into the yard, pounded to a halt, whistling home. Belding saw a slim shadow of a girl who seemed all great black eyes.

Under the trees flashed Blanco Sol, as dazzling white, as beautiful as if he had never been lost in the desert. He slid to a halt, then plunged and stamped. His rider leaped, throwing the bridle. Belding saw a powerful, spare, ragged man, with dark, gaunt face and eyes of flame.

Then Nell came running from the house, her golden hair flying, her hands outstretched, her face wonderful.

"Dick! Dick! Oh-h-h, Dick!" she cried. Her voice seemed to quiver in Belding's heart.

Belding's eyes began to blur. He was not sure he saw clearly. Whose face was this now close before him—a long thin, shrunken face, haggard, tragic in its semblance of torture, almost of death? But the eyes were keen and kind. Belding thought wildly that they proved he was not dreaming.

"I shore am glad to see you all," said a well-remembered voice in a slow, cool drawl.

CHAPTER 18

REALITY AGAINST DREAMS

Ladd, Lash, Thorne, Mercedes, they were all held tight in Belding's arms. Then he ran to Blanco Diablo. For once the great horse was gentle, quiet, glad. He remembered this kindest of masters and reached for him with warm, wet muzzle.

Dick Gale was standing bowed over Nell's slight form, almost hidden in his arms. Belding hugged them both. He was like a boy. He saw Ben Chase and his son slip away under the trees, but the circumstance meant nothing to him then.

"Dick! Dick!" he roared. "Is it you? . . . Say, who do you think's here—here, in Forlorn River?"

Gale gripped Belding with a hand as rough and hard as a file and as strong as a vise. But he did not speak a word. Belding thought Gale's eyes would haunt him forever.

It was then three more persons came upon the scene—Elsie Gale, running swiftly, her father assisting Mrs. Gale, who appeared about to faint.

"Belding! Who on earth's that?" cried Dick, hoarsely.

"*Quién sabe*, my son," replied Belding; and now his voice seemed a little shaky. "Nell, come here. Give him a chance."

Belding slipped his arm round Nell, and whispered in her ear. "This'll be great!"

Elsie Gale's face was white and agitated, a face expressing extreme joy.

"Oh, Brother! Mama saw you—Papa saw you, and never knew you! But I knew you when you jumped quick—that way—off your horse. And now I don't know you. You wild man! You giant! You splendid barbarian! . . . Mama, Papa, hurry! It *is* Dick! Look at him. Just look at him! Oh-h, thank God!"

Belding turned away and drew Nell with him. In another second she and Mercedes were clasped in each other's arms. Then followed a time of joyful greetings all round.

The Yaqui stood leaning against a tree watching the welcoming home of the lost. No one seemed to think of him, until Belding, ever mindful of the needs of horses, put a hand on Blanco Diablo and called to Yaqui to bring the others. They led the string of whites down to the barn, freed them of wet and dusty saddles and packs, and turned them loose in the alfalfa, now breast-high. Diablo found his old spirit; Blanco Sol tossed his head and whistled his satisfaction; White Woman pranced to and fro; and presently they all settled down to quiet grazing. How good it was for Belding to see those white shapes against the rich background of green! His eyes glistened. It was a sight he had never expected to see again. He lingered there many moments when he wanted to hurry back to his rangers.

At last he tore himself away from watching Blanco Diablo and returned to the house. It was only to find that he might have spared himself the hurry. Jim and Ladd were lying on the beds that had not held them for so many months. Their slumber seemed as deep and quiet as death. Curiously Belding gazed down upon them. They had removed only boots and chaps. Their clothes were in tatters. Jim appeared little more than skin and bones, a long shape, dark and hard as iron. Ladd's appearance shocked Belding. The ranger looked an old man, blasted, shriveled, starved. Yet his gaunt face, though terrible in its records of tortures, had something fine and noble, even beautiful to Belding, in its strength, its victory.

Thorne and Mercedes had disappeared. The low murmur of voices came from Mrs. Gale's room, and Belding concluded that Dick was still with his family. No doubt he, also, would soon seek rest and sleep. Belding went through the patio and called in at Nell's door. She was there sitting by her window. The flush of happiness had not left her face, but she looked stunned, and a shadow of fear lay dark in her eyes. Belding had intended to talk. He wanted someone to listen to him. The expression in Nell's eyes, however, silenced him. He had forgotten. Nell read his thought in his face, and then she lost all her color and dropped her head. Belding entered, stood beside her with a hand on hers. He tried desperately hard to think of the right thing to say, and realized so long as he tried that he could not speak at all.

"Nell—Dick's back safe and sound," he said, slowly. "That's the main thing. I wish you could have seen his eyes when he held you in his arms out there. . . . Of course, Dick's coming knocks out your trip East and changes plans generally. We haven't had the happiest time lately. But now it'll all be different. Dick's as true as a Yaqui. He'll chase that Chase fellow, don't mistake me. . . . Then Mother will be home soon. She'll straighten out this—this mystery. And Nell—however it turns out—I know Dick Gale will feel just the same as I feel. Brace up now, girl."

Belding left the patio and traced thoughtful steps back toward the corrals. He realized the need of his wife. If she had been at home he would not have come so close to killing two men. Nell would never have fallen so low in spirit. Whatever the real truth of the tragedy of his wife's life, it would not make the slightest difference to him. What hurt him was the pain mother and daughter had suffered, were suffering still. Somehow he must put an end to that pain.

He found the Yaqui curled up in a corner of the barn in as deep a sleep as that of the rangers. Looking down at him, Belding felt again the rush of curious thrilling eagerness to learn all that had happened since the dark night when Yaqui had led the white horses away into the desert. Belding curbed his impatience and set to work upon tasks he had long neglected. Presently he was interrupted by Mr. Gale, who came out, beside himself with happiness and excitement. He flung a hundred questions at Belding and never gave him time to answer one, even if that had been possible. Finally, when Mr. Gale lost his breath, Belding got a word in. "See here, Mr. Gale, you know as much as I know. Dick's back. They're all back—a hard lot, starved, burned, torn to pieces, worked out to the limit I never saw in desert travelers, but they're alive—alive and well, man! Just wait. Just gamble I won't sleep or eat till I hear that story. But *they've* got to sleep and eat."

Belding gathered with growing amusement that besides the joy, excitement, anxiety, impatience expressed by Mr. Gale there was something else which Belding took for pride. It pleased him. Looking back, he remembered some of the things Dick had confessed his father thought of him. Belding's sympathy had always been with the boy. But he had learned to like the old man, to find him kind and wise, and to think that perhaps college and business had not brought out the best in Richard Gale. The West had done that, however, as it had for many a wild youngster; and Belding resolved to have a little fun at the expense of Mr. Gale. So he began by making a few remarks that appeared to rob Dick's father of both speech and breath.

"And don't mistake me," concluded Belding, "just keep out of earshot when Laddy tells us the story of that desert trip, unless you're hankering to have your hair turn *pure* white and stand *curled* on end *and freeze* that way."

About the middle of the forenoon on the following day the rangers hobbled out of the kitchen to the porch.

"I'm a sick man, I tell you," Ladd was complaining, "an' I gotta be fed. Soup! Beef tea! That ain't so much as wind to me. I want about a barrel of bread an' butter, an' a whole platter of mashed potatoes with gravy an' green stuff—all kinds of green stuff—an' a whole big apple pie. Give me everythin' an' anythin' to eat but meat. Shore I never, never want to taste meat again, an' sight of a piece of sheep meat would jest about finish me. . . . Jim, you used to be a human bein' that stood up for Charlie Ladd."

"Laddy, I'm lined up beside you with both guns," replied Jim, plaintively. "Hungry? Say, the smell of breakfast in that kitchen made my mouth water so I near choked to death. I reckon we're gettin' most onhuman treatment."

"But I'm a sick man," protested Ladd, "an' I'm agoin' to fall over in a minute if somebody doesn't feed me. Nell, you *used* to be fond of me."

"Oh, Laddy, I am yet," replied Nell.

"Shore I don't believe it. Any girl with a tender heart just couldn't let a man starve under her eyes. . . . Look at Dick, there. I'll bet he's had something to eat, mebbe potatoes an' gravy, an' pie an'—"

"Laddy, Dick has had no more than I gave you—indeed, not nearly so much."

"Shore he's had a lot of kisses then, for he hasn't hollered onct about this treatment."

"Perhaps he has," said Nell, with a blush; "and if you think that—they would help you to be reasonable I might—I'll—"

"Well, powerful fond as I am of you, just now kisses'll have to run second to bread an' butter."

"Oh, Laddy, what a gallant speech!" laughed Nell. "I'm sorry, but I've Dad's orders."

"Laddy," interrupted Belding, "you've got to be broke in gradually to eating. Now you know that. You'd be the severest kind of a boss if you had some starved beggars on your hands."

"But I'm sick—I'm dyin'," howled Ladd.

"You were never sick in your life, and if all the bullet-holes I see in you couldn't kill you, why, you never will die."

"Can I smoke?" queried Ladd, with sudden animation. "My Gawd, I used to smoke. Shore I've forgot. Nell, if you want to be reinstated in my gallery of angels, just find me a pipe an' tobacco."

"I've hung onto my pipe," said Jim, thoughtfully. "I reckon I had it empty in my mouth for seven years or so, wasn't it, Laddy? A long time! I can see the red lava an' the red haze, an' the red twilight creepin' up. It was hot an' some lonely. Then the wind, and always that awful silence! An' always Yaqui watchin' the west, an' Laddy with his checkers, an' Mercedes burnin' up, wastin' away to nothin' but eyes! It's all there—I'll never get rid—"

"Chop that kind of talk," interrupted Belding, bluntly. "Tell us where Yaqui took you—what happened to Rojas—why you seemed lost for so long."

"I reckon Laddy can tell all that best; but when it comes to Rojas's finish I'll tell what I seen, an' so'll Dick an' Thorne. Laddy missed Rojas's finish. Bar none, that was the—"

"I'm a sick man, but I can talk," put in Ladd, "an' shore I don't want the whole story exaggerated none by Jim."

Ladd filled the pipe Nell brought, puffed ecstatically at it, and settled himself upon the bench for a long talk. Nell glanced appealingly at Dick, who tried to slip away. Mercedes did go, and was followed by Thorne. Mr. Gale brought chairs, and in subdued excitement called his wife and daughter. Belding leaned forward, rendered all the more eager by Dick's reluctance to stay, the memory of the quick tragic change in the expression of Mercedes's beautiful eyes, by the strange gloomy cast stealing over Ladd's face.

The ranger talked for two hours—talked till his voice weakened to a husky whisper. At the conclusion of his story there was an impressive silence. Then Elsie Gale stood up, and with her hand on Dick's shoulder, her eyes bright and warm as sunlight, she showed the rangers what a woman thought of them and of the Yaqui. Nell clung to Dick, weeping silently. Mrs. Gale was overcome, and Mr. Gale, very white and quiet, helped her up to her room.

"The Indian! the Indian!" burst out Belding, his voice deep and rolling. "What did I tell you? Didn't I say he'd be a godsend? Remember what I said about Yaqui and some gory Aztec knife work? So he cut Rojas loose from that awful crater wall, foot by foot, finger by finger, slow and terrible? And Rojas didn't hang long on the *cholla* thorns? Thank the Lord for that! . . . Laddy, no story of Camino del Diablo can hold a candle to yours. The flight and the fight were jobs for men. But living through this long hot summer and coming out—that's a miracle. Only the Yaqui could have done it. The Yaqui! the Yaqui!"

"Shore. Charlie Ladd looks up at an Indian these days. But Beldin', as for the comin' out, don't forget the hosses. Without grand old Sol an' Diablo, who I don't hate no more, an' the other Blancos, we'd never have got here. Yaqui *an'* the hosses, that's my story!"

Early in the afternoon of the next day Belding encountered Dick at the water barrel.

"Belding, this is river water, and muddy at that," said Dick. "Lord knows I'm not kicking. But I've dreamed some of our cool running spring, and I want a drink from it."

"Never again, son. The spring's gone, faded, sunk, dry as dust."

"Dry!" Gale slowly straightened. "We've had rains. The river's full. The spring ought to be overflowing. What's wrong? Why is it dry?"

"Dick, seeing you're interested, I may as well tell you that a big charge of nitroglycerin choked my spring."

"Nitroglycerin?" echoed Gale. Then he gave a quick start. "My mind's been on home, Nell, my family. But all the same I felt something was wrong here with the ranch, with you, with Nell. . . . Belding, that ditch there is dry. The roses are dead. The little green in that grass has come with the rains. What's happened? The ranch's run down. Now I look around I see a change."

"Some change, yes," replied Belding, bitterly. "Listen, son."

Briefly, but not the less forcibly for that, Belding related his story of the operations of the Chases.

Astonishment appeared to be Gale's first feeling. "Our water gone, our claims gone, our plans forestalled! Why, Belding, it's unbelievable. Forlorn River with promoters, business, railroad, bank, and whatnot!"

Suddenly he became fiery and suspicious. "These Chases—did they do all this on the level?"

"Barefaced robbery! Worse than a Greaser holdup," replied Belding, grimly.

"You say the law upheld them?"

"Sure. Why, Ben Chase has a pull as strong as Diablo's on a downgrade. Dick, we're jobbed, outfigured, beat, tricked, and we can't do a thing."

"Oh, I'm sorry, Belding, most of all for Laddy," said Gale, feelingly. "He's all in. He'll never ride again. He wanted to settle down here on the farm he thought he owned, grow grass and raise horses, and take it easy. Oh, but it's tough! Say, he doesn't know it yet. He was just telling me he'd like to go out and look the farm over. Who's going to tell him? What's he going to do when he finds out about this deal?

"Son, that's made me think some," replied Belding, with keen eyes fast upon the young man. "And I was kind of wondering how you'd take it."

"I? Well, I'll call on the Chases. Look here, Belding, I'd better do some forestalling myself. If Laddy gets started now there'll be blood spilled. He's not just right in his mind yet. He talks in his sleep sometimes about how Yaqui finished Rojas. If it's left to him—he'll kill these men. But if I take it up—"

"You're talking sense, Dick. Only here, I'm not so sure of you. And there's more to tell. Son, you've Nell to think of, and your mother."

Belding's ranger gave him a long and searching glance.

"You can be sure of me," he said.

"All right, then; listen," began Belding. With deep voice that had many a break and tremor he told Gale how Nell had been hounded by Radford Chase, how her mother had been driven by Ben Chase—the whole sad story.

"So that's the trouble! Poor little girl!" murmured Gale, brokenly. "I felt something was wrong. Nell wasn't natural, like her old self. And when I begged her to marry me soon, while Dad was here, she couldn't talk. She could only cry."

"It *was* hard on Nell," said Belding, simply. "But it'll be better now you're back. Dick, I know the girl. She'll refuse to marry you, and you'll have a hard job to break her down, as hard as the one you just rode in off of. I think I know you, too, or I wouldn't be saying—"

"Belding, what're you hinting at?" demanded Gale. "Do you dare insinuate that—that—if the thing were true it'd make any difference to me?"

"Aw, come now, Dick; I couldn't mean that. I'm only awkward at saying things. And I'm cut pretty deep—"

"For God's sake, you don't *believe* what Chase said?" queried Gale, in passionate haste. "It's a lie. I swear it's a lie. I know it's a lie. And I've got to tell Nell this minute. Come on in with me. I want you, Belding. Oh, why didn't you tell me sooner?"

Belding felt himself dragged by an iron arm into the sitting-room, out into the patio, and across that to where Nell sat in her door. At sight of them she gave a little cry, drooped for an instant, then raised a pale, still face, with eyes beginning to darken.

"Dearest, I know now why you are not wearing my mother's ring," said Gale, steadily and low-voiced.

"Dick, I am not worthy," she replied, and held out a trembling hand with the ring lying in the palm.

Swift as light Gale caught her hand and slipped the ring back upon the third finger.

"Nell! Look at me. It is your engagement ring. . . . Listen. I don't believe this—this that's been torturing you. I know it's a lie. I am absolutely sure your mother will prove it a lie. She must have suffered once—perhaps there was a sad error—but the thing you fear is not true. But, hear me, dearest; even if it *was* true it wouldn't make the slightest difference to me. I'd promise you on my honor I'd never think of it again. I'd love you all the more because you'd suffered. I want you all the more to be my wife—to let me make you forget—to—"

She rose swiftly with the passionate abandon of a woman stirred to her depths, and she kissed him.

"Oh, Dick, you're good—so good! You'll never know—just what those words mean to me. They've saved me—I think."

"Then, dearest, it's all right?" Dick questioned, eagerly. "You will keep your promise? You will marry me?"

The glow, the light faded out of her face, and now the blue eyes were almost black. She drooped and shook her head.

"Nell!" exclaimed Gale, sharply catching his breath.

"Don't ask me, Dick. I—I won't marry you."

"Why?"

"You know. It's true that I—"

"It's a lie," interrupted Gale, fiercely. "But even if it's true—why—why won't you marry me? Between you and me love is the thing. Love, and nothing else! Don't you love me any more?"

They had forgotten Belding, who stepped back into the shade.

"I love you with my whole heart and soul. I'd die for you," whispered Nell, with clenching hands. "But I won't disgrace you."

"Dear, you have worried over this trouble till you're morbid. It has grown out of all proportion. I tell you that I'll not only be the happiest man on earth, but the luckiest, if you marry me."

"Dick, you give not one thought to your family. Would they receive me as your wife?"

"They surely would," replied Gale, steadily.

"No! Oh no!"

"You're wrong, Nell. I'm glad you said that. You give me a chance to prove something. I'll go this minute and tell them all. I'll be back here in less than—"

"Dick, you will not tell her—your mother?" cried Nell, with her eyes streaming. "You will not? Oh, I can't bear it! She's so proud! And Dick, I love her. Don't tell her! Please, please don't! She'll be going soon. She needn't ever know—about me. I want her always to think well of me. Dick, I beg of you. Oh, the fear of her knowing has been the worst of all! Please don't go!"

"Nell, I'm sorry. I hate to hurt you. But you're wrong. You can't see things clearly. This is your happiness I'm fighting for. And it's my life. . . . Wait here, dear. I won't be long."

Gale ran across the patio and disappeared. Nell sank to the doorstep, and as she met the question in Belding's eyes she shook her head mournfully. They waited without speaking. It seemed a long while before Gale returned. Belding thrilled at sight of him. There was more boy about him than Belding had ever seen. Dick was coming swiftly, flushed, glowing, eager, erect, almost smiling.

"I told them. I swore it was a lie, but I wanted them to decide as if it were true. I didn't have to waste a minute on Elsie. She loves you, Nell. The governor is crazy about you. I didn't have to waste two minutes on him. Mother used up the time. She wanted to know all there was to tell. She is proud, yes; but, Nell, I wish you could have seen how she took the—the story about you. Why, she never thought of me at all, until she had cried over you. Nell, she loves you, too. They all love you. Oh, it's so good to tell you. I think Mother realizes the part you have had in the—what shall I call it?—the regeneration of Richard Gale. Doesn't that sound fine? Darling, Mother not only consents, she wants you to be my wife. Do you hear that? And listen—she had me in a corner and, of course, being my mother, she put on the screws. She made me promise that we'd live in the East half the year. That means Chicago, Cape May, New York—you see, I'm not exactly the lost son any more. Why, Nell, dear, you'll have to learn who Dick Gale really is. But I always want to be the ranger you helped me become, and ride Blanco Sol, and see a little of the desert. Don't let the idea of big cities frighten you. We'll always love the open places best. Now, Nell, say you'll forget this trouble. I know it'll come all right. Say you'll marry me soon. . . . Why, dearest, you're crying . . . Nell!"

"My—heart—is broken," sobbed Nell, "for—I—I can't marry you."

The boyish brightness faded out of Gale's face. Here, Belding saw, was the stern reality arrayed against his dreams.

"That devil Radford Chase—he'll tell my secret," panted Nell. "He swore if you ever came back and married me he'd follow us all over the world to tell it."

Belding saw Gale grow deathly white and suddenly stand stock-still.

"Chase threatened you, then?" asked Dick; and the forced natural-ness of his voice struck Belding.

"Threatened me? He made my life a nightmare," replied Nell, in a rush of speech. "At first I wondered how he was worrying Mother sick. But she wouldn't tell me. Then when she went away he began to hint things. I hated him all the more. But when he told me—I was frightened, shamed. Still I did not weaken. He was pretty decent when he was sober. But when he was half drunk he was a devil. He laughed at me and my pride. I didn't dare shut the door in his face. After a while he found out that your mother loved me and that I loved her. Then he began to threaten me. If I didn't give in to him he'd see she learned the truth. That made me weaken. It nearly killed me. I simply could not bear the thought of Mrs. Gale knowing. But I couldn't marry him. Besides, he got so half the time, when he was drunk, he didn't want or ask me to be his wife. I was about ready to give up and go mad when you—you came home."

She ended in a whisper, looking up wistfully and sadly at him. Beld-ing was a raging fire within, cold without. He watched Gale, and be-lieved he could foretell that young man's future conduct. Gale gathered Nell up into his arms and held her to his breast for a long moment.

"Dear Nell, I'm sure the worst of your trouble is over," he said, gen-tly. "I *will* not give you up. Now, won't you lie down, try to rest and calm yourself? Don't grieve any more. This thing isn't so bad as you make it. Trust me. I'll shut Mr. Radford Chase's mouth."

As he released her she glanced quickly up at him, then lifted appeal-ing hands.

"Dick, you won't hunt for him—go after him?"

Gale laughed, and the laugh made Belding jump.

"Dick, I beg of you. Please don't make trouble. The Chases have been hard enough on us. They are rich, powerful. Dick, say you will not make matters worse. Please promise me you'll not go to him."

"You ask me that?" he demanded.

"Yes. Oh yes!"

"But you know it's useless. What kind of a man do you want me to be?"

"It's only that I'm afraid. Oh, Dick, he'd shoot you in the back."

"No, Nell, a man of his kind wouldn't have nerve enough even for that."

"You'll go?" she cried, wildly.

Gale smiled, and the smile made Belding cold.

"Dick, I cannot keep you back?"

"No," he said.

Then the woman in her burst through instinctive fear, and with her eyes blazing black in her white face she lifted parted quivering lips and kissed him.

Gale left the patio, and Belding followed closely at his heels. They went through the sitting room. Outside upon the porch sat the rangers, Mr. Gale, and Thorne. Dick went into his room without speaking.

"Shore somethin's comin' off," said Ladd, sharply; and he sat up with his keen eyes narrowing.

Belding spoke a few words; and, remembering an impression he had wished to make upon Mr. Gale, he made them strong. But now it was with a grim humor that he spoke.

"Better stop that boy," he concluded, looking at Mr. Gale. "He'll do some mischief. He's wilder'n hell."

"Stop him? Why, assuredly," replied Mr. Gale, rising with nervous haste.

Just then Dick came out of his door. Belding eyed him keenly. The only change he could see was that Dick had put on a hat and a pair of heavy gloves.

"Richard, where are you going?" asked his father.

"I'm going over here to see a man."

"No. It is my wish that you remain. I forbid you to go," said Mr. Gale, with a hand on his son's shoulder.

Dick put Mr. Gale aside gently, respectfully, yet forcibly. The old man gasped.

"Dad, I haven't gotten over my bad habit of disobeying you. I'm sorry. Don't interfere with me now. And don't follow me. You might see something unpleasant."

"But my son! What are you going to do?"

"I'm going to beat a dog."

Mr. Gale looked helplessly from this strangely calm and cold son to the restless Belding. Then Dick strode off the porch.

"Hold on!" Ladd's voice would have stopped almost any man. "Dick, you wasn't agoin' without me?"

"Yes, I was. But I'm thoughtless just now, Laddy."

"Shore you was. Wait a minute, Dick. I'm a sick man, but at that nobody can pull any stunts round here without me."

He hobbled along the porch and went into his room. Jim Lash knocked the ashes out of his pipe, and, humming his dance tune, he followed Ladd. In a moment the rangers appeared, and both were packing guns.

Not a little of Belding's grim excitement came from observation of Mr. Gale. At sight of the rangers with their guns the old man turned white and began to tremble.

"Better stay behind," whispered Belding. "Dick's going to beat that two-legged dog, and the rangers get excited when they're packing guns."

"I will not stay behind," replied Mr. Gale, stoutly. "I'll see this affair through. Belding, I've guessed it. Richard is going to fight the Chases, those robbers who have ruined you."

"Well, I can't guarantee any fight on *their* side," returned Belding, dryly. "But maybe there'll be Greasers with a gun or two."

Belding stalked off to catch up with Dick, and Mr. Gale came trudging behind with Thorne.

"Where will we find these Chases?" asked Dick of Belding.

"They've got a place down the road adjoining the inn. They call it their club. At this hour Radford will be there sure. I don't know about the old man. But his office is now just across the way."

They passed several houses, turned a corner into the main street, and stopped at a wide, low adobe structure. A number of saddled horses stood haltered to posts. Mexicans lolled around the wide doorway.

"There's Ben Chase now over on the corner," said Belding to Dick. "See, the tall man with the white hair, and leather band on his hat. He sees us. He knows there's something up. He's got men with him. They'll come over. We're after the young buck, and sure he'll be in here."

They entered. The place was a hall, and needed only a bar to make it a saloon. There were two rickety pool tables. Evidently Chase had fitted up this amusement room for his laborers as well as for the use of his engineers and assistants, for the crowd contained both Mexicans and Americans. A large table near a window was surrounded by a noisy, smoking, drinking circle of card-players.

"Point out this Radford Chase to me," said Gale.

"There! the big fellow with the red face. His eyes stick out a little. See! He's dropped his cards and his face isn't red any more."

Dick strode across the room.

Belding grasped Mr. Gale and whispered hoarsely: "Don't miss anything. It'll be great. Watch Dick and watch Laddy! If there's any gun play, dodge behind me."

Belding smiled with a grim pleasure as he saw Mr. Gale's face turn white.

Dick halted beside the table. His heavy boot shot up, and with a crash the table split, and glasses, cards, chips flew everywhere. As they rattled down and the chairs of the dumbfounded players began to slide Dick called out: "My name is Gale. I'm looking for Mr. Radford Chase."

A tall, heavy-shouldered fellow rose, boldly enough, even swaggeringly, and glowered at Gale.

"I'm Radford Chase," he said. His voice betrayed the boldness of his action.

It was over in a few moments. The tables and chairs were tumbled into a heap; one of the pool tables had been shoved aside; a lamp lay shattered, with oil running dark upon the floor. Ladd leaned against a post with a smoking gun in his hand. A Mexican crouched close to the wall moaning over a broken arm. In the far corner upheld by comrades another wounded Mexican cried out in pain. These two had attempted to draw weapons upon Gale, and Ladd had crippled them.

In the center of the room lay Radford Chase, a limp, torn, hulking, bloody figure. He was not seriously injured. But he was helpless, a miserable beaten wretch, who knew his condition and felt the eyes upon him. He sobbed and moaned and howled. But no one offered to help him to his feet.

Backed against the door of the hall stood Ben Chase, for once stripped of all authority and confidence and courage. Gale confronted him, and now Gale's mien was in striking contrast to the coolness with which he had entered the place. Though sweat dripped from his face, it was white as chalk. Like dark flames his eyes seemed to leap and dance and burn. His lean jaw hung down and quivered with passion. He shook a huge gloved fist in Chase's face.

"Your gray hairs save you this time. But keep out of my way! And when that son of yours comes to, tell him every time I meet him I'll add some more to what he got today!"

CHAPTER 19

THE SECRET OF
FORLORN RIVER

In the early morning Gale, seeking solitude where he could brood over his trouble, wandered alone. It was not easy for him to elude the Yaqui, and just at the moment when he had cast himself down in a secluded shady corner the Indian appeared, noiseless, shadowy, mysterious as always.

"*Malo*," he said, in his deep voice.

"Yes, Yaqui, it's bad—very bad," replied Gale.

The Indian had been told of the losses sustained by Belding and his rangers.

"Go—me!" said Yaqui, with an impressive gesture toward the lofty lilac-colored steps of No Name Mountains.

He seemed the same as usual, but a glance on Gale's part, a moment's attention, made him conscious of the old strange force in the Yaqui.

"Why does my brother want me to climb the nameless mountains with him?" asked Gale.

"*Lluvia d'oro*," replied Yaqui, and he made motions that Gale found difficult of interpretation.

"Shower of Gold," translated Gale. That was the Yaqui's name for Nell. What did he mean by using it in connection with a climb into the

mountains? Were his motions intended to convey an idea of a shower of
golden blossoms from that rare and beautiful tree, or a golden rain?
Gale's listlessness vanished in a flash of thought. The Yaqui meant gold.
Gold! He meant he could retrieve the fallen fortunes of the white brother
who had saved his life that evil day at the Papago Well. Gale thrilled as
he gazed piercingly into the wonderful eyes of this Indian. Would Yaqui
never consider his debt paid?

"Go—me?" repeated the Indian, pointing with the singular directness that always made this action remarkable in him.

"Yes, Yaqui."

Gale ran to his room, put on hobnailed boots, filled a canteen, and
hurried back to the corral. Yaqui awaited him. The Indian carried a coiled
lasso and a short stout stick. Without a word he led the way down the lane,
turned up the river toward the mountains. None of Belding's household
saw their departure.

What had once been only a narrow mesquite-bordered trail was now
a well-trodden road. A deep irrigation ditch, full of flowing muddy water,
ran parallel with the road. Gale had been curious about the operations of
the Chases, but a bitterness he could not help had kept him from going
out to see the work. He was not surprised to find that the engineers who
had constructed the ditches and dam had anticipated him in every particular. The dammed-up gulch made a magnificent reservoir, and Gale
could not look upon the long narrow lake without a feeling of gladness.
The dreaded *año seco* of the Mexicans might come again and would come,
but never to the inhabitants of Forlorn River. That stonewalled, stone-
floored gulch would never leak, and already it contained water enough to
irrigate the whole of Altar Valley for two dry seasons.

Yaqui led swiftly along the lake to the upper end, where the stream
roared down over unscalable walls. This point was the farthest Gale had
ever penetrated into the rough foothills, and he had Belding's word for it
that no white man had ever climbed No Name Mountains from the west.

But a white man was not an Indian. The former might have stolen
the range and valley and mountain, even the desert, but his possessions
would ever remain mysteries. Gale had scarcely faced the great gray ponderous wall of cliff before the old strange interest in the Yaqui seized
him again. It recalled the tie that existed between them, a tie almost as

close as blood. Then he was eager and curious to see how the Indian would conquer those seemingly insurmountable steps of stone.

Yaqui left the gulch and clambered up over a jumble of weathered slides and traced a slow course along the base of the giant wall. He looked up and seemed to select a point for ascent. It was the last place in that mountainside where Gale would have thought climbing possible. Before him the wall rose, leaning over him, shutting out the light, a dark mighty mountain mass. Innumerable cracks and crevices and caves roughened the bulging sides of dark rock.

Yaqui tied one end of his lasso to the short, stout stick and, carefully disentangling the coils, he whirled the stick round and round and threw it almost over the first rim of the shelf, perhaps thirty feet up. The stick did not lodge. Yaqui tried again. This time it caught in a crack. He pulled hard. Then, holding to the lasso, he walked up the steep slant, hand over hand on the rope. When he reached the shelf he motioned for Gale to follow. Gale found that method of scaling a wall both quick and easy. Yaqui pulled up the lasso and threw the stick aloft into another crack. He climbed to another shelf, and Gale followed him. The third effort brought them to a more rugged bench a hundred feet above the slides. The Yaqui worked round to the left and turned into a dark fissure. Gale kept close at his heels. They came out presently into lighter space, yet one that restricted any extended view. Broken sections of cliff were on all sides.

Here the ascent became toil. Gale could distance Yaqui going downhill; on the climb, however, he was hard put to it to keep the Indian in sight. It was not a question of strength or lightness of foot. These Gale had beyond the share of most men. It was a matter of lung power, and the Yaqui's life had been spent scaling the desert heights. Moreover, the climbing was infinitely slow, tedious, dangerous. On the way up several times Gale imagined he heard a dull roar of falling water. The sound seemed to be under him, over him, to this side and to that. When he was certain he could locate the direction from which it came then he heard it no more until he had gone on. Gradually he forgot it in the physical sensations of the climb. He burned his hands and knees. He grew hot and wet and winded. His heart thumped so that it hurt, and there were instants when his sight was blurred. When at last he had toiled to where the Yaqui sat awaiting him upon the rim of that great wall, it was none too soon.

Gale lay back and rested for a while without note of anything except the blue sky. Then he sat up. He was amazed to find that after that wonderful climb he was only a thousand feet or so above the valley. Judged by the nature of his effort, he would have said he had climbed a mile. The village lay beneath him, with its new adobe structures and tents and buildings in bright contrast with the older habitations. He saw the green alfalfa fields, and Belding's white horses, looking very small and motionless. He pleased himself by imagining he could pick out Blanco Sol. Then his gaze swept on to the river.

Indeed, he realized now why someone had named it Forlorn River. Even at this season when it was full of water it had a forlorn aspect. It was doomed to fail out there on the desert—doomed never to mingle with the waters of the Gulf. It wound away down the valley, growing wider and shallower, encroaching more and more on the gray flats, until it disappeared on its sad journey toward Sonoyta. That vast shimmering, sun-governed waste recognized its life only at this flood season, and was already with parched tongue and insatiate fire licking and burning up its futile waters.

Yaqui put a hand on Gale's knee. It was a bronzed, scarred, powerful hand, always eloquent of meaning. The Indian was listening. His bent head, his strange dilating eyes, his rigid form, and that close-pressing hand, how these brought back to Gale the terrible lonely night hours on the lava!

"What do you hear, Yaqui?" asked Gale. He laughed a little at the mood that had come over him. But the sound of his voice did not break the spell. He did not want to speak again. He yielded to Yaqui's subtle nameless influence. He listened himself, heard nothing but the scream of an eagle. Often he wondered if the Indian could hear things that made no sound. Yaqui was beyond understanding.

Whatever the Indian had listened to or for, presently he satisfied himself, and, with a grunt that might mean anything, he rose and turned away from the rim. Gale followed, rested now and eager to go on. He saw that the great cliff they had climbed was only a stairway up to the huge looming dark bulk of the plateau above.

Suddenly he again heard the dull roar of falling water. It seemed to have cleared itself of muffled vibrations. Yaqui mounted a little ridge and halted. The next instant Gale stood above a bottomless cleft into which a white stream leaped. His astounded gaze swept backward along this narrow swift stream to its end in a dark, round, boiling pool. It was a huge spring, a bubbling well, the outcropping of an underground river coming down from the vast plateau above.

Yaqui had brought Gale to the source of Forlorn River.

Flashing thoughts in Gale's mind were no swifter than the thrills that ran over him. He would stake out a claim here and never be cheated out of it. Ditches on the benches and troughs on the steep walls would carry water down to the valley. Ben Chase had built a great dam which would be useless if Gale chose to turn Forlorn River from its natural course. The fountainhead of that mysterious desert river belonged to him.

His eagerness, his mounting passion, was checked by Yaqui's unusual action. The Indian showed wonder, hesitation, even reluctance. His strange eyes surveyed this boiling well as if they could not believe the sight they saw. Gale divined instantly that Yaqui had never before seen the source of Forlorn River. If he had ever ascended to this plateau, probably it had been to some other part, for the water was new to him. He stood gazing aloft at peaks, at lower ramparts of the mountain, and at nearer landmarks of prominence. Yaqui seemed at fault. He was not sure of his location.

Then he strode past the swirling pool of dark water and began to ascend a little slope that led up to a shelving cliff. Another object halted the Indian. It was a pile of stones, weathered, crumbled, fallen into ruin, but still retaining shape enough to prove it had been built there by the hands of men. Round and round this the Yaqui stalked, and his curiosity attested a further uncertainty. It was as if he had come upon something surprising. Gale wondered about the pile of stones. Had it once been a prospector's claim?

"Ugh!" grunted the Indian; and, though his exclamation expressed no satisfaction, it surely put an end to doubt. He pointed up to the roof of the sloping yellow shelf of stone. Faintly outlined there in red were the imprints of many human hands with fingers spread wide. Gale had often seen such paintings on the walls of the desert caverns. Manifestly these told Yaqui he had come to the spot for which he had aimed.

Then his actions became swift—and Yaqui seldom moved swiftly. The fact impressed Gale. The Indian searched the level floor under the shelf. He gathered up handfuls of small black stones, and he thrust them at Gale. Their weight made Gale start, and then he trembled. The Indi-